TOR:
The City
of Patarshp

WRITA BHATTACHARJEE

INDIA • SINGAPORE • MALAYSIA

Notion Press

Old No. 38, New No. 6
McNichols Road, Chetpet
Chennai - 600 031

First Published by Notion Press 2018
Copyright © Writa Bhattacharjee 2018
All Rights Reserved.

ISBN 978-1-64546-447-1

This book is dedicated to

Dr. Anamika Ray
(30 December 1979 to 19 July 2015)
Mother, Wife, Teacher, Friend
The world is poorer for losing you. As am I.
And to
Puneet Setpal (1988-2014)
Nilesh Harish Ruparel (1988-2015)
Ketan Bankar (1988-2015)
You were too young to be taken from those who loved you.

"One short sleep past, we wake eternally,
And death shall be no more; Death, thou shalt die."

—John Donne

CONTENTS

APPENDICES

I need to thank some people for their contribution to this volume of Tornain. My heartfelt gratitude to:

My husband, Mr. Arindam Pal, whose indefatigable support, encouragement and guidance are the pillars on which this series rests.

My father, Mr. Nirmalya Bhattacharyya, for embracing this adventure of mine with wholehearted enthusiasm.

Ms. Gargi Chakrabarti, for her continued friendship and feedback as well as one of the most unexpected characters in this book that I have had the pleasure of writing about.

Dr. Ankuran Dutta, for his longstanding friendship and constant efforts at promoting Tornain.

Ms. Isha Karandikar, for her hard work in helping me sort out tons of background information.

Ms. Lea Ramaswamy, for the brilliant portrayal of my vision for the cover of this book.

The team at Notion Press for their wonderful handling of my book and for accommodating my requests and needs pertaining to its publication.

And last, but not the least, my babies—Frodo, Sam, Merry, Pippin and Eva—who are following in the proud footsteps of all those felines who have loved, inspired and helped many, many authors who inspire me.

Map of Yennthem

AVEYAN SEA

VALIARD

ROMINOMA

OLFENSOR

SAVARIL

HAMISARL

BAY OF GHIYXU

A

N O I U V

ARNAVOSSEA

ASNPER

BAY OF ME

BALIGNOR

STRAITS OF SOFYUM

STRAITS OF LOFISOPEN

SAYNON SEA

MISCERNA

GINGIBAR

B O R T U

DOVAAR SEA

TUSKIN

BORISUL

VONIDELOS

BAY OF PARAFET

K h o P E

I S h

MUERD

LEGEND

- 〰 → MOUNTAIN
- ⛰ → PLATEAU
- ⬭ → DESERT
- 🌲 → FOREST
- ⬯ → LAKE
- 〰 → RIVER
- ⋈ → BRIDGE
- ◉ → CAPITAL CITY
- • → CITY
- ○ → TOWN
- × → VILLAGE

50 150
100 200 300 400   600   800 MILES

A Tale Old Yet New

From far across the seven seas,
Where the mind shakes off cares with ease:
A king who seeks to fight a curse.
Seers speak in riddling verse.
Children who never grow older.
Ice is cold but hearts are colder.
Friendships stronger than brotherhood.
Trees of bone, people of wood.
Noble rogues and roguish nobles.
Trials, torments, tortures, troubles.
A pen that writes only the truth.
Fountains of eternal youth.
Fire horses, talking cats.
Soldiers dying in fierce combats.
Light is dark and dark is light;
What is wrong and what is right?
A tale as old as hill and glen,
Yet, in telling, new again.

THE STORY SO FAR

Then...

Astoreth and Zavak. Twin brothers turned mortal enemies. The two most powerful beings in Pretvain, capable even of defeating the Guardians in combat. Both reputed to be immortal. They meet in battle to decide the fate of Yennthem, one fighting to bring it under his dominance, the other to prevent such a disaster. Zavak has the strength of Vynobhem behind him while Astoreth leads the forces of mortals aided by Yodiri's soldiers of obsidian. When they face each other, the entire battlefield comes to a halt to watch them fight. Suddenly, something entirely unexpected happens. The two run each other through, falling to their deaths while the ground around them dissolves away. Unseen by any, their essence merges into nature, leaving behind their mortal belongings. Kawiti, the Guardian of Immortality, makes a prophecy about their return, but with time, the prophecy is forgotten and Astoreth and Zavak pass into myth.

5000 anni later...

In the kereighe kingdom of Lyisl, Lord Sanfion is accused of treason and sentenced to death by King Rannzen. His pregnant wife, Rosa, escapes with the help of his cousin Lord Carahan but is attacked on the way and takes shelter with three witches. Conversant in dark magic, they take her in and train her as an acolyte, providing her with the resources for revenge but at the terrible cost of her innocence, youth, beauty and sanity. In the neighbouring seleighe country of Samion, King Arlem dies of a mysterious illness at a young age. His queen, Melicie, evades her enemies with the help of Prince Arlem, the late king's brother, even as the reins of the kingdom are usurped by Prime Minister Holexar.

On the last day of the annus 5000 A.E., a volcano dormant for five thousand anni erupts, laying waste to the village of Idhaghloz nestled at its feet. The next day, the day of prophecy, four children are born. First are Avita, daughter of Lord Sanfion and Rosa, and Temeron, younger son of King Rannzen and Queen Iramina. Rosa arrives just as Temeron is born and, with the help of powerful dark magic, swaps him for Avita, carrying away the newborn prince to wreak her vengeance. Second is Arizumel, son of the exiled queen of Samion. Pursued by her enemies, she is forced to battle them to save her life and that of her unborn child. During this struggle, she goes into labour and faints. When she wakes, she finds herself and her son being looked after by the landlady of an inn to which she was brought by a mysterious 'husband' who never reappears. Last to be born is Prince

Amishar, son of King Amiroth, ruler of Balignor, the most powerful of the human kingdoms. When a difficult labour threatens the lives of both Queen Lamella and the unborn child, King Amiroth finds help from a powerful wandering maga who saves the queen and delivers a stillborn baby. But her miracles do not end there; she brings the child back to life.

In the meantime, the sumagi, immortal beings with the power to control matter and minds, search for the prophecy and the reincarnations of Astoreth and Zavak. However, only one child born on the fateful day is known to them, and things become more complicated when their leader, Mesmen, vanishes and cannot be found despite a vigorous search in all five hems. She reappears briefly, only to order them to cease the search for her. Baffled by this, the sumagi reorganise themselves with Nishtar as their leader to continue the search for the prophecy. But their search is nearly impossible as no knowledge about the prophecy or about Astoreth and Zavak can be found. The discovery of an old copy of the prophecy leads to more confusion as the elements mentioned in it are almost as mythical as its subjects—Astoreth and Zavak. While the sumagi do make some headway in beginning to locate these elements, in the end, their conflicts with each other become too powerful, and they part ways.

Queen Melicie continues to live the life of a fugitive, roaming from place to place with her son. Realising that she can find no refuge in any of the eighe countries, she moves to the human kingdoms in disguise, hoping that her enemies will be baulked at such an unexpected move. She finds shelter in the penurious village of Bolsana under the alias of Misa. Under her guidance and the leadership of its chief, Leormane, Bolsana begins to grow in prosperity. Mizu—as Arizumel is now known—is beloved of all, especially of Chief Leormane. But the young boy shows a strange propensity to figure out things hidden from normal folks, a quality that leaves his mother anxious. When the village is threatened by vynobnie, Misa saves the villagers but not before she has to save her friend's son by killing her friend's obetulfer-possessed husband.

Prince Amishar is the apple of his father's eye, which causes King Amiroth to often neglect his duties as a king. His cousin, Lord Aminor, helps him to come to his senses and averts disaster and civil war. As the young prince grows older, he shows an avid curiosity and an inborn talent at both his education and martial training. However, his precociousness is countered by his increasing tendency towards wilfulness, and both Queen Lamella and Lord Aminor worry that the king is spoiling his son. A tour of the neighbouring human kingdom of Cordemim leads to a prophecy by the Sorceress regarding Prince Amishar: a prophecy that speaks of death and sacrifice.

Rosa's revenge is foiled when King Rannzen is overthrown and executed in a coup. Frustrated, she turns to torture to fulfil her desire for vengeance.

When maternal feelings get in the way, she magically cuts them out of her, becoming a cold, mad, evil witch who constantly torments young Temeron. Then, in an inspired burst of sheer evil, she turns Temeron human so that he is abused and hurt by all kereighes, for the kereighes consider humans worthy of nothing better. In a strange twist of fate, Temeron manages to escape one day, only to encounter Avita, whose touch renders him unconscious. When he awakes, he realises that his life is a little better now because, despite the witch's constant torment, he feels comforted through some strange link with Avita.

Avita, oblivious of the mystery of her birth, is in exile with her brother Avator and their sole guardian Forsith after the dethronement of King Rannzen and the death of their parents and loyalists. At first, they take shelter with their uncle, who exploits their dependency to rob them of their limited wealth. Avator stands up to him and manages to secure a relatively better life for all of them. He becomes the apprentice of Miehaf, a master-smith, and soon demonstrates skill at metalworking. However, their uncle's conspiracy to hand them over to their enemies forces them to flee and settle in a small town in the kingdom of Emense. Disaster strikes again when Avita encounters Temeron. She is thereafter plagued by a strange ailment because of which she screams in her sleep and wakes up severely wounded. Avita's seemingly incurable malaise forces them to depart and live a nomadic life. A chance encounter with a throng leads them to the Witch of Temtema, who declares that Avita's problems are the result of a spiritual bond with Temeron.

Beyond the dreaded Lyudzbradh Mountain Range that separates the east of the Elthrusian continent from the west, lie the Shadow Lands. Here, Haalzona is the last of the kingdoms that have not yet fallen to the dark forces of the vynobnie. However, King Eamarilus cannot keep the forces of evil at bay, especially when the rot is within his own household in the form of his first wife, Lilluana, a kocovusa in human disguise. When the attack comes, King Eamarilus becomes a slave to Lilluana's magic, and Prince Eamilus, who is half human and half kocovus, turns on his younger brother in the madness of bloodlust. When he comes to his senses, Eamilus tries to kill himself, but the monster within keeps him alive. He flees his home and is found and nursed back to health by Nishtar, who also trains him to control his unique abilities.

In the dharvhish kingdom of Ghrangghirm, Rauz Augurk is faced with the greatest personal challenge of his life: getting his daughter wed to a suitable groom without sparking off a war. Dharvh marriages are long, elaborate and complex affairs; the slightest insult—real or perceived—can lead to war between the fourteen veradhen of the dharvhs. With the help of his brother, Angbruk, his wife, Rauzina Marizha, and other members of his family, Rauz Augurk succeeds beyond his wildest dreams when Rauzoon Valhazar wins the Hravisht-envar as well as

Meizha's heart. Son of the rauz of Khwaznon, the only other dharvh kingdom, Valhazar is an extremely unusual young dharvh with as much promise of success as of trouble. Just as Rauz Augurk is basking in this success, he receives a message from Nishtar that alters his life overnight. For, the message is an order to locate the mythical City of Patarshp.

And now, moving on…

ASTORETH AND ZAVAK
(4 A.N.)

Astoreth watched in awe as the two women embraced. They were not real women, he knew; they were not even mortals. They had merely taken their Yennthian forms for his benefit. They were, in truth, embodiments of two of the greatest forces in the Universe: Vyidie was the Guardian of Birth, and Yodiri was the Guardian of Destruction. But for now, both appeared as tall, strong women. Astoreth had always wondered why the Guardians' Yennthian forms were human rather than eighe or, for that matter, any other race. But who could tell why the kaitsyas did what they did?

In her current form, Vyidie wore the clothes of a hunter. She carried a longbow of horn and a quiver on her back and a pair of long, curved knives in her boots. A horn hung at her belt. She was fair in colouring and had eyes as green as a tiger's. In contrast, Yodiri had flaming red hair and azure eyes. She was dressed for battle in gleaming armour. On her person, she carried an arsenal of weapons including swords, daggers, spears, axes, a bow and arrows, many other sharp and blunt weapons and a massive shield.

Given their seemingly contradictory purposes in the universe, their friendship had seemed unexpected to Astoreth. After he was introduced to Yodiri by Vyidie, he mentioned it without thinking. Their mortal forms had lulled him into a false sense of familiarity, he realised as soon as the words had escaped his lips.

'I thought you said that this mortal was wise,' Yodiri said to Vyidie. Both kaitsyas were much taller than Astoreth even in their human forms, and he felt a little uncomfortable.

'He is,' Vyidie said with a smile. 'He is probably a little awestruck by you right now and has lost his wits!'

'A jest!' remarked Yodiri. 'I thought that was Niwuik's prerogative.'

Vyidie shrugged. 'The Guardian of Time is not the only one with a sense of humour,' she said.

Yodiri admonished her. 'You are too fond of these mortals. You have lived too long among them; their qualities appear to be rubbing off on you.'

'It isn't as if I have a choice, is it?' Vyidie responded. 'I cannot return to Kaitshem even if I wish to.'

'And do you wish to?' Yodiri asked pointedly. Vyidie shrugged again. Yodiri shook her head sadly. She would never understand what Vyidie saw in the mortals. Kiel, the Kaitsya of Death, was so much more powerful than even the most powerful yennt; why anyone would prefer a mortal like Astoreth—any mortal, in fact—over Kiel was a matter of bafflement to her. Sachi, the Guardian of Emotions, would have had some complicated explanation but Yodiri was not going to ask her; Samar, the Guardian of Knowledge, would have a more sensible explanation but would not tell even if asked. Yodiri almost sighed with exasperation. It always bothered her when kaitsyas behaved like yennts. And it bothered her that she was having to meet a yennt and, that too, on Yennthem. If anyone but Vyidie had asked her, she would have unhesitatingly refused. But she and Vyidie shared a connection that was as old and as strong as the roots of Creation.

Astoreth, meanwhile, had decided to leave the talking to Vyidie. He could sense that Yodiri was unhappy to be there and would leave on the slightest pretext. She would never listen to him. There was a slim chance that she might listen to Vyidie.

'Why have you called me here?' Yodiri asked Vyidie, turning her back to Astoreth. Vyidie glanced at Astoreth with a hint of embarrassment on her face, but he shook his head behind Yodiri's back to indicate that she should continue with the conversation. What they had to ask of Yodiri was far more important than the kaitsya's insult to him. The kaitsya's insult! It was almost laughable. Insult and honour existed between equals, and to imagine that a Guardian and a mortal could be equals was not merely sacrilegious but ludicrous as well. Yet, Astoreth knew, Vyidie considered him her equal. And he was her equal, he reminded himself. He had become her equal through countless sacrifices and extraordinary trials.

'You are aware of the army of vynobnie that Zavak has raised. There are mortals, too, who wait to join his war against Yennthem. We need your support to defeat him. If you don't help us, he will succeed in his intent to destroy all life as we know it,' Vyidie said to Yodiri.

'Then, perhaps, I should help him!' Yodiri said with a hint of dry irony in her voice.

'This is not a matter of levity, Yodiri!' Vyidie said with passion. 'The Creation itself is at stake. You are the warrior Guardian. If you do not help us, how can we hope to win?'

'Do you think that I care for the Creation?' Yodiri declared. 'Destruction is a natural part of life. What is born must die. What is created must be destroyed. Even the entire Creation must one day come to an end. Even we must one day cease to exist. You cannot deny Destruction, just as you cannot deny Creation. One is meaningless without the other. If Zavak brings destruction, it will lead to the creation of something new.'

'Something new and evil,' retorted Vyidie.

'You were never so mortal-like,' Yodiri commented with distaste. 'Since when have we, kaitsyas, been concerned with questions of morality, like the yennts? What is good? What is evil? It is not for us to say. Once you too would not have cared about what happened between the denizens of the lesser hems, but now you plead on their behalf like a puny mortal.'

'Yes, I do care,' said Vyidie and her eyes went unbidden to the quiet figure standing behind Yodiri, his face calm despite the turbulence in his world and in his heart.

Yodiri snorted with disgust. 'I have no desire to help the mortal with whatever he wishes, but because you plead on his behalf, I agree.'

Then, turning towards Astoreth, she said, 'I can provide you with a force so powerful and so lethal that no army in all of Pretvain can stand before it. I can provide you with an army the likes of which the world has never seen: an army of soldiers made of stone. Soldiers who need neither sustenance nor rest, who know neither good nor evil, who feel neither pain nor mercy. However, I cannot just give them to you. There are conditions that must be fulfilled first. Having arrived in Yennthem, they will remain here forever. They will remain asleep as long as they are not needed. But need alone will not suffice to harness them, for they will not be awoken or controlled by just anybody. Only those who know the secret of waking the soldiers and bending them to their will can do it. Even so, it will require unfathomable inner strength to manage the task. I will tell you the secret of rousing and leading these soldiers; if what I have heard of you is true, you should be able to command them. Yet, you may not be the only one who can. Others may come after you who will use this army for their own purposes. Those purposes may be far less noble than yours. Are you willing to take that risk? Even if you are, there is no place in Yennthem that is strong enough to contain them while they remain dormant. Before I give you these soldiers, you must find a place where they can sleep as long as they need to. For, without such a place, their power will destroy Yennthem even before your brother has the opportunity to do so.'

Having delivered this long speech, Yodiri did not wait for a reply. She vanished into thin air, leaving behind a gloomy Guardian and a sombre mortal hero.

'I must apologise for her brusqueness,' Vyidie said. She shrank until she was as tall as Astoreth.

'There is no need to apologise,' Astoreth declared. 'That she has condescended to aid me is more than I could have ever imagined. She is right, you know. A kaitsya being friends with a mortal is unnatural and unheard of.'

Vyidie smiled. 'It is unheard of, I agree,' she said. 'But had it been unnatural, would it have occurred? Who knows what is natural and what is not? All the mysteries of the Creation are not known even to us kaitsyas.'

'I do not know how I can ever thank you for your kindness, your graciousness or your generosity!' Astoreth said with feeling.

'You do know how, Astoreth, son of Barhusa, king of Effine,' Vyidie said playfully.

Astoreth's face darkened. 'I must beseech you, my lady, not to ask of me that which I cannot give without tarnishing my honour for eternity.'

'Do not worry, Astoreth of Yennthem,' Vyidie said kindly. 'The friendship of Vyidie is not so self-seeking that it would require you to relinquish the path of honour. Now let us not talk about these matters any longer. Yodiri has left us with a nice situation. Her aid is indispensable, but how do we convince her to help us?'

'By doing what she asked us to do,' replied Astoreth with determination. 'She has asked us to find a place where her soldiers can sleep forever if need be, and we must provide her with such a place. She cannot then refuse to aid us.'

'But there is no such place in Yennthem!' Vyidie said. 'That is why she asked you to find it.'

'No, there is not,' Astoreth agreed smugly, 'but there is one who can build such a place here.'

Vyidie laughed. 'You do have some impertinence! First you ask for help from Yodiri, and then you want to ask Patarshp to build you a shelter for Yodiri's soldiers!'

'I don't have much choice, do I? Who else can create a place that can contain the power of Yodiri's soldiers?'

Patarshp was in high spirits when he came to meet Astoreth and Vyidie. Unlike Yodiri, he wasn't disdainful of mortals. They were, after all, capable of creating extraordinary beauty through their art, poetry, architecture, sculptures, gardens, dance and music. Being the Guardian of Creation, Patarshp admired the ability to create. Which was why he was far less supportive of Zavak than his partner, Yodiri, was.

'I agree with Yodiri that kaitsyas should not get involved in the matters of mortals,' he said after hearing what Vyidie had to say. 'But I have heard that Zavak has become powerful enough to threaten even us. I fear we can no longer remain aloof even if we want to.'

'Will you help us?' Astoreth asked the Guardian whose Yennthian form of a human sculptor was characterised by unkempt hair, a salt and pepper stubble and a look of absent-minded benevolence.

'I am not sure what I can do but I am willing to aid you,' the Guardian replied.

'Yodiri has promised to provide us with an invincible army if we can find a place on Yennthem where her soldiers can be stationed while not needed in war. There is currently no place on Yennthem that can contain the power of that army. But, perhaps, such a place can be built,' Astoreth suggested.

Patarshp understood what Astoreth wanted of him. 'Perhaps it can,' he said. 'But not by mortals.'

'No, not by mortals,' Astoreth agreed. 'So, will you build such a place for us?'

Patarshp thought about what he was being asked to do as he surveyed the mortal who was standing in front of him. Astoreth was tall and broad-shouldered, with fair hair and blue eyes that looked cold and hard as steel. His face was noble and elegant, his features sharp and majestic. There was strength there, and courage, but also wisdom and compassion. Patarshp knew about Vyidie's fascination with the king of Effine and could see why any mortal would have been awed by him. But a Guardian? It was hard to understand; no wonder Kiel had felt humiliated and had cursed Vyidie. What was surprising was that he had not cursed the mortal. Perhaps Kiel had felt Astoreth too beneath him to merit even that. Kiel had underestimated Astoreth, Patarshp thought.

'All right, I will build you a place in Yennthem where Yodiri's soldiers can be contained, but there is something that you must do before I commence my work.'

'What?' asked Astoreth unhesitatingly.

'Find a place which is virtually impossible to find. From a distance, it must be visible from no more than one single spot in the entire hem. From nowhere else—land or sea or air—must it be visible unless one is standing right in its vicinity. It must also be in a place where no one will willingly set foot. Essentially, the place must be undiscoverable by any who does not already know where it is and has a genuine need to reach it. If you can find such a place, then I will build you a shelter worthy of Yodiri's soldiers there. Can you do that?'

Astoreth hesitated before answering, 'I do not know whether such a place exists upon the face of Yennthem. I will make no promises to you, but I will do my best to find it if it does exist. Is there no other way that I can convince you to help me?'

Patarshp smiled and replied, 'No, there isn't. But I wouldn't worry about it if I were you. I believe that you started out in life as a dirsfer, a descrier, and a pretty good one at that? If half the stories I have heard about you are correct, you should be able to find such a place. And yes, it does *exist.'*

'Then I will find it!' declared Astoreth confidently.

When next they met, Patarshp could not help but praise Astoreth.

'I must say that you live up to your reputation. This is indeed the perfect location for the structure that I have in mind. It is visible only from this spot upon this mountain and that too only at sunrise. In this, you have surpassed my expectations. It is in the middle of deadly wilderness where no one will come willingly, and it is large enough for what I have in mind. Since you have fulfilled your part of the bargain, I will build here a city the likes of which has never been seen before and will never be seen again. And in that city, the soldiers of Yodiri can sleep until they are called upon to serve.'

'Thank you,' Astoreth said gratefully. It had taken every bit of his ability as a dirsfer to locate the spot hidden in one of the valleys of the Lyudzbradh. 'I cannot express in words how grateful I am.'

'There is no need for that. I made a promise, and it behoves me to keep it. But you must ensure that this city is well-guarded, or it might fall into the wrong hands.'

'I will do what I can to safeguard it and its secret,' promised Astoreth.

'Good. Then I can get to work immediately,' declared the Guardian of Creation enthusiastically. To create the city that he had in mind would be a great challenge, and he loved the idea.

For nine days and nine nights, Patarshp toiled in the concealed valley. On the morning of the tenth day, the city of stone stood glimmering in the light of the rising sun as Astoreth, Vyidie, Patarshp and Yodiri stood watching it upon the only mountaintop from where it could be seen.

'It is quite well hidden,' Patarshp acknowledged. 'The chances of anyone discovering it by accident are very, very slim.'

Yodiri said nothing. She looked at the city of stone grimly. It was, of course, ideal for housing her soldiers. It also meant that she would have to keep her promise to Astoreth. She had not been all that willing to do so, but Patarshp had made it impossible for her to refuse.

'And what shall we name this fateful city?' she asked all those gathered there.

'I suggest we name it after its esteemed creator,' suggested Astoreth. 'I like the name Patrisha.'

'I agree,' said Vyidie. 'I, too, like the name Patrisha.'

'You do, do you?' mocked Yodiri. 'But, yes, it is a good name.'

Patarshp took a bow in acknowledgement of the tribute. He could not help feeling a little proud of himself and beamed. Then he vanished. By then, the sun had risen higher and Patrisha was no longer visible to the watchers on the mountain.

Yodiri addressed her companions and spoke without mincing words, 'Since you have fulfilled the condition set by me, I have no choice but to keep my word to you. Even we kaitsyas are bound by our promises. And so I will give you an army that is unequalled by any other in existence.'

Yodiri unexpectedly drew her sword Demosnart. Vyidie grasped her bow but Astoreth did not flinch. He remained standing, looking at Yodiri's dark eyes, unafraid. Suddenly the ferocious Guardian smiled. She extended the sword towards Astoreth and said, 'Take this. This is the key to awakening the power of my soldiers. The sword that you already possess will let you control them.'

Yodiri then told Astoreth all that he needed to know in order to command the undefeatable soldiers that the Guardian had grudgingly provided to him. The more he heard, the more he wished that he could have defeated the forces of Zavak without needing those soldiers. But he did need them. The vynobnie were too powerful. Without those soldiers, there was no way to defeat Zavak. He hated what he was bringing to Yennthem, but he had no choice, as he had told Vyidie earlier. All he could do was ensure that no one would ever be able to awaken those soldiers again once the battle with Zavak's forces was over, and Zavak had been defeated.

Yodiri finished instructing him and said, 'I think that you will be able to control my soldiers. But remember my warning—power can be a two-edged sword. Be careful that you do not sow the seeds of destruction in the very act of trying to prevent it! Of course, if you do, no one will be happier than I.' Then she vanished.

Vyidie and Astoreth remained standing on the mountaintop for a while longer, staring into the distant horizon where nothing but green wilderness was now visible.

'I wish I could be certain that no one will discover this place by accident,' Astoreth sighed.

'It is practically undiscoverable already,' Vyidie encouraged him. 'As for chance, well, it is in no one's hands. Not even the kaitsyas'.'

'Still, if only mortals could be prevented or discouraged from coming up this mountain, the chances of Patrisha's discovery would be even more remote. But I don't know how I can ensure that.'

'Perhaps I can be of service there,' Vyidie suggested.

'How, my lady?' Astoreth asked.

'A guardian who will protect this mountain and its adjoining forest and, thereby, Patrisha as well. A guardian who will prevent anyone from coming close enough to discover Patrisha. A guardian who will hand the responsibility down through generations without ever feeling the desire to take advantage of his position.'

'And where will we find such a guardian?'

'I will create such a guardian for you. A guardian who is a reflection of you,' she added, stroking his cheek. 'Not you as you are now, but you as you were when first I met you. Brave as a tiger, more stubborn than a mountain, magnificent as a forest, and wiser than any mortal.'

Astoreth blushed. Such words of praise still embarrassed him. He removed Vyidie's hand from his face gently and asked her, 'How how will you create such a guardian? I know that you are the Kaitsya of Birth; but can you create such an individual?'

'You forget, Astoreth, that I am also the patron kaitsya of all animals. And that should be enough for our purpose.'

Astoreth still did not understand what Vyidie meant to do, and nothing would make Vyidie reveal her plans. She smiled mischievously while he persisted in wheedling her to no avail. Finally, he gave up and changed the subject.

'It truly is a beautiful forest,' he said.

'Yes, it is,' Vyidie agreed. 'Almost as beautiful as the one I left behind in Kaitshem.'

'I am sorry that you are trapped in Yennthem because of me,' Astoreth said sorrowfully.

'Do not fret because of what has happened to me. It was not your doing. And Yennthem has many beautiful forests. Like this one. Does it have a name, my hero?'

'Yes, it does,' Astoreth replied.

'What is its name?' Vyidie asked.

'Vyidiegh loifar,' Astoreth answered.

For a momon, Vyidie stared at him in startlement. Then she laughed. 'Vyidie's dream! You made that up right now, did you not?'

Astoreth did not deny the playful accusation. He smiled at his patron, his friend, his mentor. He had meant the name as a token of gratitude. What would he be without her? Everything that he was, was because of her dreams for him. She deserved more than an eternity of heartache and a curse keeping her away from her home. But he could not make Kiel take back his curse. And he could not…as he had told her, his troth was pledged to another. And he would not ruin his honour. Or hers.

'It is a good name, is it not?' he asked her. 'Mere mortal that I am, this is the only gift that I can give you. A forest that you find beautiful named after you for eternity. I wish it were enough.'

Vyidie smiled, and there were tears in her eyes. The other Guardians would have been disgusted to see those tears, she was sure. But she did not care. 'You are no mere mortal, Lord of Effine,' she said to Astoreth with passion. 'And it is enough.'

PART ONE

Chapter 1

PRINCE OF ASHPERTH

The Ufharn Hills were one of the oldest inhabited areas of Ashperth. One of the most ancient sections of the geography of Elthrusia, the hills lined almost the entire northern coast of Ashperth, cradling the Bay of Seluvinia. Ashperth was shaped like a crab's claw and the Bay of Seluvinia was the space between the pincers of the claw. Despite the age of their culture, the tribes inhabiting these regions still lived as their ancestors had done hundreds of anni ago. They controlled the Bay of Seluvinia through their geographic advantage, yet showed no interest in either ships or seafaring. Nor did they allow the entry of others into this strategically significant area that they considered their ancestral right.

Historically, the tribes had always minded their own business. But they had repeatedly become the target of would-be conquerors because of their location and control of the Bay. Since days of old, many had tried to subdue the tribes of the Ufharn Hills, but none had succeeded. The tribes had their own leaders and bowed to no king. Ego had prompted some monarchs of Ashperth to attack them, only to be humbled by crushing defeat. Even when King Graniphor's rivals had managed to bring almost the entire kingdom of Ashperth under their control, the tribes of the Ufharn Hills had remained independent. They had refused to support the claims of either party in the power struggle that had shaken the whole kingdom and had followed their own path just as they had for aeons past.

In Madal of the annus 5006 A.E., Prince Feyanor of Ashperth declared to his father, King Graniphor, that he wanted to launch an expedition to bring the tribes of the Ufharn Hills under their dominion.

'Why on Yennthem?' asked his father with astonishment. 'The tribes don't bother us. They mind their own business.'

'That's precisely what bothers me. I don't know what their business is. They live the way their ancestors did while the rest of Ashperth has moved on. There might be things that we can teach them, help them with. There might even be things they can teach us. They need to be better integrated with the rest of the country.'

'Is that your only concern?' King Graniphor asked shrewdly.

'Well, no,' confessed his son. 'The Hills have a strategically important location. Everyone knows that. That also makes the tribesmen vulnerable. You know how volatile the situation in the north of the mainland is. What happens if an eighe country decides to build an empire by enslaving humans, starting with Ashperth? The Bay of Seluvinia will be their obvious target. If they can conquer the Ufharn Hills, we'll be in no position to stop them. If we can't defeat the tribesmen who fight with primitive weapons, how will we take the Hills from an extremely well-armed eighe army?'

'No one has ever taken the Bay or defeated the tribes before,' King Graniphor reminded his son.

'No one human,' Prince Feyanor corrected his father. 'The tribesmen might have defeated every fleet that sailed up the Bay due to their geographical advantage, but will they be able to stand up to an armada of eighe ships? Will their primitive weapons suffice then? I know how they have defeated every fleet until now. They surround the ships all along the hillside and shoot at them in concert. The ships are trapped and cannot escape without sustaining heavy losses. This will not work with the eighes. If I know of this strategy, so will they. They will prepare for it.'

'Have you heard anything to indicate an impending attack?' King Graniphor asked. He still wasn't keen on launching an attack on the tribesmen.

'No, I haven't,' Feyanor conceded. 'That does not mean anything. We cannot take peace or security for granted in the current situation. We need control of those hills.'

'They may not display my standards, but they are still my men. I don't want unnecessary bloodshed in the name of security or expediency or ego,' the king said sternly.

Prince Feyanor blushed. 'I assure you that my intention has nothing to do with my ego,' he said.

'Maybe you are bored,' his father suggested sharply. 'It has been a while since you had any battles to fight. You used to love fighting.'

'Only in your service,' Feyanor said with as much dignity as he could muster. 'I would not launch a military expedition for so selfish a reason as boredom.'

King Graniphor scrutinised his son's expression carefully. Feyanor appeared to be telling the truth, not that he had ever really suspected his son of such base motives. He knew that Feyanor was right. Yet he was averse to unnecessary bloodshed, as he had told his son categorically.

Finally, he gave in. 'All right, start planning. Come and talk to me before you do anything,' he said. 'I am giving provisional permission with grave reservations.

Draw up plans that will let you take the Hills with minimal bloodshed. If I have any doubts about your plans, I will withdraw permission. Is that clear?'

'Yes, Your Majesty,' said Feyanor with a bow.

But when he sat down to plan for the actual mission, he was forced to wonder if he would have to eat humble pie and withdraw. A marine attack was out of the question for the very reason he had explained to his father. An out-and-out invasion by land was equally bound to end in failure. The tribesmen were large in number, were masters of guerrilla warfare and knew the forests and terrain like the backs of their hands, which meant that they could attack out of thin air and disappear into the landscape in an instant. They could travel quickly and safely across the terrain even on a new moon night and not be found despite thorough searches. Rumour had even started endowing them with supernatural powers. No army could stand before them in a straightforward invasion. Nor had any.

He then considered a combined strategy. He could draw the bulk of the tribes' warriors away to the waterfront by sending in a fleet and then attack their rear with a landbound army. He rejected the plan even before discussing it with his generals. He knew his father would never agree to it. The sailors acting as a decoy would be slaughtered. Because he would have to split his forces, the landbound army would be stretched too thin as well and would be at greater risk. If King Graniphor wasn't willing to shed the blood of the tribesmen any more than necessary, he was definitely not going to sanction such a bloodbath. No, Feyanor had to find another way.

The problem was that most regular strategies would not work. He needed to think differently. To do that, he needed information. He called a meeting of his generals and asked them to compile all the information they had on the tribes and to separate the information into two parts—confirmed and rumoured. Both could be useful in planning a strategy. When the document finally came together, Prince Feyanor began to see his target much more clearly. They had an advantage of territory, unity and mobility. Each of the tribes lived on and controlled between one to three hills, passing on their knowledge and communal ownership of those hills through generations. Every tribe was self-sufficient and, therefore, their supply lines could not be cut to weaken them. They had no cities to which siege could be laid. And they would have greater motivation because they would be fighting for their homes.

Their only weakness, he found, lay in the lack of singularity of command. Though all the tribes worked closely, each had its own leader, and the loyalties of the tribesmen lay primarily with their own leader. This weakness, he realised, could be used to overturn some of the strengths. For instance, their self-sufficiency could prove to be a curse rather than a blessing if a tribe could be forced to run low on supplies. They would not have ready lines of accessing resources from others, especially if they were completely cut-off. The biggest problem still was gaining an upper hand on them in that terrain. For that, Feyanor concluded, he would have to walk in the enemy's shoes. When he finally revealed his plan to King Graniphor, the king had to agree that it might just be possible to take the hills without a bloodbath.

Feyanor's men trained long and hard for what they had to do once they infiltrated the Ufharn Hills. They ran drills and manoeuvres until they could have performed the actions blindfolded. They spent horas getting to know their teammates so that they could work seamlessly together. They practised the dialects spoken by the tribes until they were as fluent as the native speakers. Finally, on the first of Lokrin, Feyanor and his men stealthily took to the easternmost hills of the range, moving in small, camouflaged groups that could blend in easily and go unnoticed. Once within the cover of the forests, they gathered at the designated place and began their campaign.

Groups of soldiers launched swift, sudden attacks on the villages of the tribesmen, disappearing before the tribesmen could retaliate. Some groups marched long distances every day and attacked villages far from each other, which gave them the appearance of being in many places at once. When they weren't marching, they were carefully exploring the terrain in their teams until they knew the secret paths and routes as well as the tribesmen did. They found or made secret hiding places that could not be detected even by the natives.

Their mission was to harass the tribes living on a particular hill until the locals were compelled to leave their territories and move to the adjoining hills. By Feyanor's orders, the leaders were to be captured before the migration could happen. He wanted leaderless masses to seek refuge with other tribes, causing a greater burden on the free tribes for their limited resources and creating chaos in the combined population until their unity fractured under the stress. It was emphasised in no uncertain terms that the soldiers were to arrest the tribal warriors instead of killing them. Anyone found to cause wanton bloodshed or destruction met with speedy and severe punishment. Those who led successful sorties with minimal or no loss of life received generous rewards.

Feyanor's men took one hill after another, moving steadily westwards, always leaving behind enough soldiers to ensure that the tribes could not return to retake their homes once they had been driven from there. They endured the rains, the heat and moisture and the cold as the seasons passed in the forest. They toiled through mud and grass and undergrowth, facing snakes and mosquitoes and predators, never giving up. Their strategy and determination finally paid off after nine mondans when, in the first tempora of Yodirin, tired of the burgeoning pressure on their resources and hassled beyond endurance, the tribes split into two factions. One group decided to face the enemy in frontal battle; the other decided to surrender.

Prince Feyanor stood upon a rock in a clearing in Demilor Forest, appraising his captives.

Those who agreed to surrender were stationed in camps and enlisted to help. They received assurances of leniency but were clearly made to understand that betrayal would be met with harsh retribution, even death. Those who joined Feyanor's armies were treated as equals of the other soldiers. The supreme commander of those armies, the prince of Ashperth, allowed no discrimination. These new soldiers were, however, forbidden from returning to their homes until all the tribes had capitulated. This would prevent them from betraying Feyanor's army and attacking from the rear. As a result, many of the new recruits were eager to help Feyanor in his war against the remaining tribes so that the war could be over soon and they could return home.

With the help of his new allies, and with his army already having made a considerable impact on the strength and morale of the enemy, it was not long before Feyanor either conquered or forced the capitulation of the remaining tribes. By the twentieth of Yodirin, not one of the tribes was in a position to fight back. Some rebel groups still continued to engage his soldiers in skirmishes, but all the leaders had either been captured or killed. The next day, the surviving leaders were brought before Feyanor for judgement.

Prince Feyanor stood upon a rock in a clearing in Demilor Forest, appraising his captives. In front of him stood several men in ragged, dirty clothes, their hands bound behind them. They were short and wiry, with unusual coppery skin that was several shades darker than any race's this side of the Lyudzbradh. Their eyes were dark too, as was their long curly hair that they wore coiled at the base of their neck. They wore close-fitting leather and woollen clothes in shades of brown and green that helped them blend in with their environs. On their feet were soft leather boots that made no sound when they stalked their prey. They wore earrings of bone or horn, and some of them had rings tied around their necks with leather thongs. But there was no evidence of metal ornaments on any of them. No one knew where they had come from, or when. Ever since men could remember, the Ufharn Hills had been their domain. Until that day.

The men lined up before of Feyanor ranged in age from under twenty to over sixty, but to a man they wore a look of anger and hatred. The man standing in front of them was their enemy, and they were willing to sell their souls to see him dead. He, however, cared neither for their hatred nor for their anger. He stood calmly, surveying the scene. The chieftains of all the tribes now stood before him, prisoners. It had been a long, difficult and tricky war, but he had won where none had even come close before, and he had won without breaking his word to his father. Fewer than five hundred men had died. Only a quarter of those were soldiers, and a large number of those casualties had been due to accidents or illness rather than at the hands of the tribals. Among the tribes, the greatest losses had occurred only at the final battle.

To ensure the prince's security, the gathering had been arranged in Demilor Forest. There Prince Feyanor stood observing his enemies, surrounded by a detachment of armed soldiers standing in a tight circle ten feet wide. At the centre of this circle stood the captives. At Feyanor's feet were piles of weapons that had been surrendered by the defeated tribal warriors in a ceremony that had lasted horas. After the ceremony, the warriors had been taken away and their leaders had been fetched. In front of the defeated leaders, Feyanor ordered his men to carry the weapons away; the massive piles had already had their effect if the thunderous faces of the leaders were anything to go by. As he looked from one prisoner to another, Feyanor wondered how he could achieve his ultimate aim—to convince the tribes to be vassals of King Graniphor. He knew that if any man refused, he would have to be executed. Dissent could not be allowed to go unpunished. Imprisonment would not work as it would turn the imprisoned leader into a mascot of rebellion. Death was the only option for any who refused his terms. He also knew that the death of a leader would only solidify the tribes' resolve to resist submission, making the situation worse than it had ever been. He needed the tribes to be on his side, not dead. He had to walk the razor's edge. He hoped that none of them would refuse to accept King Graniphor's suzerainty but was not too sanguine. From what he had seen of his enemies, they were proud, stubborn and fiercely independent men. He decided to play to those qualities in them.

Feyanor asked his soldiers to set aside their own weapons, taking off his sword belt as a precedent. Next, he asked that the leaders of the tribes be released from their bonds. Finally, he sent for chairs for the captured leaders and requested them to sit. The captives were as surprised by these orders as the soldiers were. Their surprise, however, was mingled with suspicion. The soldiers obeyed Feyanor without a murmur of protest.

'You are not my enemies,' Feyanor declared, addressing the prisoners, 'but subjects of my father. I have no desire to harm you. Nor am I afraid of you. If you are unarmed, so will I be, and so will be my men. I respect you enough to treat you the way you deserve to be treated. And I trust my men enough to know that you cannot escape from here even if you are released from your bonds.'

This announcement was met with a loud cheer by the gathered soldiers and by bemused looks from the seated tribal leaders. In truth, Feyanor had issued the orders to throw the captives off balance. He had had their bonds removed to show them that he was willing to respect their authority, knowing that it would help him to convince them of his honourable motives. He had asked his men to remove their weapons for a completely different reason; he did not want the leaders of the tribes to surprise them and snatch their weapons. He had left only as many of his soldiers armed as would be needed to stop the leaders from escaping while the rest rearmed. These armed soldiers remained concealed among the rest, unseen and unknown save by their commanders with whom

Feyanor had discussed his plans beforehand. Having the tribal leaders sitting down while he stood also gave him the advantage of being able to look down at them without actually demeaning them.

He stepped off the stone and strolled past the seated men. Each man looked up as he passed, and Feyanor held his gaze; none could stare up into his eyes for long. One by one, they lowered their gazes. The only one who did not back down was Maldufa, a man in his sixties who was still straight as a ramrod, tough as nails and fierce as a mountain lion. He was highly respected and looked up to by the others. He had been one of the hardest to beat, and Feyanor had almost lost to him. Only bad weather had allowed Feyanor to win. Feyanor nodded to Maldufa and moved on.

He addressed the gathered leaders, 'King Graniphor is the undisputed and rightful ruler of Ashperth. There are many who have questioned his sovereignty, but where are they now? Their bones are rotting under the earth, their souls are wailing in Kiel's kingdom, and their names are not whispered even by their children and grandchildren. I have sworn that that shall be the fate of all who challenge my king's rightful reign. You have refused to accept him as your overlord. And so you have made me your enemy. You have brought destruction upon your men and mine, all subjects of my king. For that, I should have you beheaded. But King Graniphor is merciful. He does not wish to destroy the tribes, or he would have already done it. All he wants is for you to accept his rule and to live as loyal vassals. What do you say to that?'

The leaders of the tribes looked at one another, none willing to be the first to speak. Finally, Maldufa spoke. 'What are you offering us as terms of surrender?' he asked.

Feyanor smiled. He did not need to offer anything since the men were his prisoners. However, he answered, 'I offer you your lives, your homes, the right to bear arms and the freedom to live as you choose. In return, I ask that you accept King Graniphor as your lord and master and you swear your loyalty to him by your strongest oath. You will pay him a tithe every annus, as do the lords of all the strongholds, manors, holdings, villages, towns and cities in Ashperth. Like all other young men of this country, every lad who turns twenty from this day forth shall give the next five anni of his life to the kingdom's standing army in whatever capacity his talents allow him to. Following this, the choice to stay on, to return or to join the reserves will be his. Additionally, since you have never sent soldiers to King Graniphor's army, all your men between the ages of twenty and thirty-five will serve in the army of Ashperth for five anni, with the same option at the end of that period. This is the same choice that every male citizen of Ashperth is offered. You will openly avow your fealty to King Graniphor and support him against his enemies. You will allow unhindered passage to all citizens of Ashperth who wish to travel among the Hills either in peace or upon the king's purpose. You will nominate a representative to be present at the court, who will receive the same honours and privileges as any other member of the king's ministry and who will be held responsible for the actions of all the tribes. Any attempt to violate the terms will be met with swift and suitable retaliation. Remember, I have defeated you once, and I can do it again. King Graniphor has offered you very generous terms. If you accept, you get back your lives, your livelihoods and your homes—everything that you have been fighting for.'

'And if we refuse?' Maldufa asked with a sardonic smile.

Feyanor replied calmly, 'I shall have no choice but to execute you.' Maldufa was about to say something when Feyanor raised his hand to stop him and added, 'If I do that, however, the others in your tribe would rise up against me. Isn't that what you were about to say, Maldufa? I am aware of that. Therefore, to prevent that, I will have to destroy your entire tribe. Believe me when I say that I will not hesitate to do so in the interests of my country and my king! If need be, I will destroy every man, woman and child of every single tribe of these hills until there is none left even to remember that you ever existed. And if you deny my king, I will not blink once as I put you all to the sword.' Feyanor's voice was cold as he said these words, while his eyes blazed menacingly. Those who saw and heard him were left in no doubt that he meant every word. Complete silence reigned in the clearing for a few momons as each man thought his own thoughts.

Again, Feyanor walked past the line of defeated warriors, holding each man's gaze until he lowered his eyes. Again, Maldufa was the only one who did not look away. Finally, the youngest of the leaders, a youth of seventeen anni, declared, 'On behalf of my tribe and the tribe of my brother-in-law, who was killed in battle, I accept King Graniphor's terms and his authority.' This began a cascade of acceptances until only Maldufa was left. He waited until the others had finished. Then, in a steady voice, he said, 'If I surrender, I betray my men to dishonour; if I don't, I condemn them to destruction.'

Feyanor nodded and said, 'I understand.' He looked at the older man with respect. He was sorry for what he was about to do. He wished that Maldufa had surrendered. He could have done with men like Maldufa among his loyals. 'Who do you wish to nominate as your successor?' he asked Maldufa.

'My nephew Ronean,' Maldufa answered.

Feyanor ordered Ronean to be fetched. As the others watched curiously, wondering what was happening, a proud young man in his twenties was led into the clearing, bound hand and foot. His straight bearing and unafraid gaze highlighted his resemblance to Maldufa. Feyanor had Ronean's bonds removed and provided him with a seat opposite Maldufa. The two men sat and talked in urgent whispers, Maldufa clearly trying to convince the younger man of something that the latter was not happy to accept. Ronean repeatedly shook his head, and Maldufa continued to persuade him until, finally, Ronean gave in to his uncle. His shoulders slouching, he nodded in agreement. When he rose, he looked sad and defeated. Feyanor asked him to be returned to his makeshift prison, but he wanted to stay. Only when Maldufa intervened and asked him to leave did he concede. He bowed to Feyanor and to his uncle before leaving with his guards, not turning back even once.

Feyanor ordered his men to clear the area. They moved back, taking the surrendered leaders with them. The prince then asked for a sword to be brought for Maldufa. He added whispered instructions that were immediately passed down the ranks. Armed soldiers took position around the surrendered tribal leaders, alert to their movements and oblivious of everything else that was going on in the clearing while the prince refastened his sword belt. A sword was given into Maldufa's hands. Feyanor drew his own sword.

'This is a good sword,' Maldufa said, checking the weapon he had been given.

'I wish this could have been avoided,' Feyanor said, facing his opponent.

Maldufa smiled and said, 'Thank you. Someday you will make a great king. Now that I understand that, I no longer hate you for conquering us. I can now die in peace.'

Feyanor acknowledged the older man's comment with a tiny nod. The duel began immediately. Both were good swordsmen, but the man of the Ufharn Hills was no match for the prince of Ashperth. He fought well but fell in the end, Feyanor's sword passing through his heart and ending his life cleanly and instantly. Feyanor ordered a state funeral for him and declared his nephew Ronean as his successor. As he returned his sword to its scabbard, he turned to address all those staring at him in awe.

'The war is over. Long live King Graniphor! Long live Ashperth!'

The cry was taken up by everyone present, including the prisoners. Casting one last, melancholy look at the body of Maldufa, Prince Feyanor of Ashperth turned to leave. He was tired to the bone and wanted nothing more at that moment than to return home. He was relieved beyond measure that finally all of Ashperth was under the banner of King Graniphor. All his enemies had been beaten; all rebellions had been suppressed; all opposition to his rule had been ground to dust. Prince Feyanor felt strangely dissatisfied. He wondered what he would do now. He was thirty-eight anni old, and he had achieved everything that he had wanted to. For one brief moment, he wished that he could travel to other lands, conquering them as his illustrious ancestors had, thousands of anni ago. The moment passed, and he joined in the jubilation of his generals as they rode back towards Ontar.

Chapter 2

A WISECRACKING HORSE

On the evening of the eleventh of Supprom, Avator, Avita and Forsith found themselves in a village named Xylliot. It was their seventh stop since leaving the village where they had hoped to settle down. After their visit to the witch of Temtema had revealed the futility of wandering in search of a cure for Avita, they had decided that a settled life in a remote place was their best option. That hope had been dashed after three temporas when Avita's condition had given rise to whispered rumours once again.

They had been to Xylliot before during their travels but had not stayed long enough to be remembered. They never stayed anywhere long. Typically, they spent two to four days at each village or town on their route before moving on, before anyone became too interested in them. Despite that, they did not wish to stay at the village inn, partly due to a paucity of funds and partly due to the chance of being recognised. After some searching, they found refuge with a farmer who agreed to provide them with food and shelter for a couple of nights in exchange for assistance with repairs to his thatching. Forsith and Avator readily agreed.

The farmer's house wasn't big enough to accommodate his large family as well as these three. So he arranged for the travellers to stay in a small barn next to his house. Though the weather was chilly and their provisions were not exactly luxurious, Forsith, Avator and Avita were comfortable in the barn. Hardly anything was stored in it, it was clean and it smelled pleasant. They had no objection to spending the night there. They thanked the farmer for his hospitality and settled in, carrying over the blankets and sheets that their host had provided.

Late at night, Avator awoke. He did not know what had disturbed his sleep. He sat peering into the darkness towards Avita; he usually woke when she had one of her fits. Her mysterious illness had driven them to live a nomadic life. At first, they had hoped to cure her, taking whatever work they could find, managing with whatever they earned, moving from place to place to find a cure. Their search had led them to the witch of Temtema. She had told them that there was no cure; Avita's condition was the result of a spiritual bond that she had formed with the human boy whom she had accidentally encountered in Kinqur. She had given the girl a charm to help heal her injuries and calm her quickly when she had an incident.

Tonight, though, she was sleeping peacefully, her aura cocooning her in a cosy halo. An eighe child her age did not usually have an aura, but her unusual rate of maturity had endowed her with one. Auras were unique to all eighes—a physical manifestation of their spiritual force that surrounded them at all times. Seleighes had light-coloured auras, and kereighes had dark ones; however, each aura was as different in hue and density as eighes were in personality and temperament. Avita's was a shade of purple similar to her eyes. The state of an eighe's aura was usually a good indication of his or her emotions. Avita's, just then, was placid and softly aglow. She was sleeping peacefully, her dark, velvet-soft curls falling across her pretty, heart-shaped face.

Avator surmised that he must have had a nightmare and lay back down. He had just closed his eyes when he heard voices.

'It's really cold tonight, too cold for outomy,' someone said. The speaker's voice was slightly whiny, like someone complaining.

'The vernurt is going to be bad too. If the villagers don't take care, we will suffer badly,' another replied. This voice was female.

'Shut up and sleep,' a third voice ordered. This voice was deep and carried authority. The other two grumbled a little about the tyranny of the third and then fell quiet.

Avator got up again and looked out of the door to see who was talking. If there were eighes walking about late at night, they might mean harm to their host. On the other hand, if these were poor or homeless eighes and had no better place to sleep than the farmer's yard, it would be right to share their resting place with the less fortunate. He saw no one. The grounds attached to the farmer's house were not large. Even at night, Avator could clearly see that no one was around. The houses next door were too far away for voices to carry. However, there were some stables behind the farmer's house. Perhaps, the boy thought, some of the grooms were staying over. He had never heard of female grooms, though. Perhaps the eighee whom he had heard was a relation of one of the grooms. He tried to forget the conversation and went back to sleep. No other sounds disturbed him that night.

The next morning, he awoke to hugs and kisses from Avita. It was his birthday! He was thirteen[1] anni old though he looked older. And it was not just because he was tall for his age. The hardships that he had endured at such a young age had forced him to grow up before his time. He was lean, though not as thin as he had been a few anni ago. Working with the master-smith Miehaf as an apprentice had developed his strength and physique. He had long, straight, black hair that fell to

---

1   At thirteen, Avator was the equivalent of an eight/nine-annus-old human. For more details about the correlations in age between the different races, see Appendix 4 of Tornain: The Prophecy of Kawiti

his shoulders and framed his unusually pale face. His eyes were as black as his hair and far too intense for one so young. His sharp features would have looked delicate had not the strength of his soul shown in the lines of his features. His aura was quite dark though marbled through with odd lines of golden.

Forsith gifted Avator a new pair of shoes; Avita gave him a handkerchief. It was one of his old handkerchiefs, but she had written his name in a corner of it. She was just learning her letters, and her writing was still shaky; nonetheless, this gift was most precious to the receiver.

Soon after freshening up, Forsith and Avator set to work repairing the farmer's roof. It had not been fixed in anni, and the thatching had thinned or was missing in several places. They had a long day's work ahead, and it was tedious to work in silence. Since the farmer himself worked alongside them, they did not feel comfortable chatting. There were many repairs to be made, and they went about their work diligently. Soon it was time for lunch. Avator and Forsith were asked by the farmer's wife to share their food, and they gratefully accepted. Avita was being looked after along with the other children of the household. As usual, she had managed to endear herself to everyone. She was a sweet child and had a smile that could melt hearts of stone. All who met her loved her. Until they encountered one of her episodes.

After lunch, the farmer went to the fields while Forsith and Avator returned to complete the work on the roof. While they worked, they talked. They deliberately avoided talking about how different Avator's thirteenth birthday would have been had misfortune not befallen them. Both were thinking about it, though. Sensing this, Avator began to tell Forsith about the conversation that he had heard the night before, hoping to distract him.

'Yes, I know you woke up,' Forsith said when Avator had finished. 'I was wondering where you were going when you opened the door of the barn. Then you closed it and returned to bed, so I gave it no more thought,' Forsith said.

'I was just checking if anyone was around,' Avator said.

'And there was no one around, you say?' Forsith asked, more interested in the story than Avator had expected him to be.

'No, no one. I suppose it was someone sleeping in the stables. Grooms, perhaps.'

'Yes, perhaps. Though, I have never heard of female grooms,' Forsith mused, reflecting Avator's thoughts of the night before. 'Besides, if they were talking as loudly as you say they were, I would have heard them too.'

'You were sleeping too soundly,' Avator teased.

'I was not!' Forsith protested indignantly. Then he added, 'I haven't slept soundly since I became responsible for the two of you. Besides, if I had been sleeping as soundly as you claim I was, how would I know that you were up and about?'

Avator knew that his guardian was teasing him, but there was an underlying layer of truth to that claim as well.

'So, if you were awake, why did you not hear the voices?' he asked.

'That's what surprises me too,' agreed Forsith. 'All I heard were horses neighing and whinnying.'

A wild, incredible thought suddenly crossed Avator's mind. 'Are you certain that you heard horses?' he asked.

'Yes, I am sure. The stables are right behind this property. The horses should have been sleeping, but I suppose the cold was keeping some of them up. The kereighes in this village, despite their good intentions, seem a little tardy in matters of upkeep of their animals and property. Just look at this roof! It should have been repaired anni ago.'

'What if the conversation I heard was the same that you heard?' Avator asked Forsith, ignoring his comments about the villagers and the roof and giving him an odd look.

'But I told you, I didn't hear a conversation. All I heard was…oh!' exclaimed Forsith, suddenly realising what the boy meant. 'Do you think it is possible? What am I saying? Of course, it is possible! Kereighes in your family have been known to have that talent.'

'They have?' asked Avator, surprised. He had not known that.

'Of course, they have! Although I don't think your father did. His father— your grandfather—definitely did. Haven't you ever wondered why there was such a preponderance of pictures and statues and tapestries and carpets depicting horses in the palace? It is not a very rare talent, but it is a precious one nevertheless.'

'Can we ascertain if I indeed have such a talent?' asked Avator, excited, as an idea began to form in his mind. If his newfound talent was proven, they could make a good living with a little clever effort. He had heard of horse-wizards— exceptional kereighes who understood horses in a way that ordinary eighes could not. They could tame the wildest horse and heal the sickest, it was said. They were wanderers, usually, but much sought after by all. The truly gifted ones could earn quite well. Forsith was, Avator knew, pretty good with horses already. If he could now talk to them, they could combine their talents and project Forsith as a horse-wizard. It wasn't entirely honest, but no one was going to be hurt, so what did a little deceit matter?

'We will proceed to verify your ability right after we finish repairing this roof,' Forsith replied enthusiastically, unaware of his ward's plans.

Evening had fallen by the time they finished working on the roof. They hadn't talked about the matter again, but it was obviously still on the minds of both as they made their way to the stables behind their host's house before dinner. Forsith had told everyone that Avator was interested in horses and wanted to see one at first hand. He gave the same story to the grooms at the stable. While Forsith talked to one of the grooms, Avator stood outside. He imagined that the horses were looking at him curiously. He felt rather uncomfortable and even foolish. What if his surmise was wrong? He would look like an idiot. Before he could change his mind, Forsith called him inside. Avator took a deep breath and entered. Forsith was standing next to a tall, brown stallion that was looking at Avator calmly.

'All right, Avator. Now we are going to see if you really *can* talk to horses,' Forsith said. 'I have learnt this horse's name and pedigree from the groom. You must ask the horse and find out the same information. I have sent the groom to fetch some water for us, so you have about two minuras. Be gentle but confident.'

Feeling nervous, Avator reached out to stroke the horse's muzzle. It did not shy away. Avator felt more confident. He remembered how Miehaf had talked to the horses to tell them the plan on the night of Avator's escape from Ustillor. He tried to copy the action. He leant closer to the horse and whispered into its ear, 'Hello! My name is Avator. I know that you can hear me and understand me. You are a very handsome fellow.'

To his great amazement, when the horse whinnied gently in response, he was clearly able to understand what the horse said. It said, 'Thank you, master Avator. I think you can understand me too.'

Avator realised that this was the third voice from the night before, the one that had ordered the others to be quiet. His heart thumping wildly, Avator spoke gently again, 'Yes, I can understand you. I would be grateful if you could tell me your name and your pedigree. I am being tested by my guardian, and I need to give him that information to pass the test.'

The horse nodded perceptibly as Forsith looked on with a curious mixture of pride and amusement on his face. Avator listened to the horse's neighs and conveyed the names of the horse, its sire and its dam to Forsith. Forsith nodded to indicate that he had passed the test successfully. Avator was overjoyed. He thanked the horse and fed it some lumps of sugar. The groom returned just then, so they drank the water, thanked the groom and left the stables. Avator stroked the horse affectionately one last time before leaving. As he left, he whispered a goodbye to all the horses. He could swear that several of them responded to his greeting!

He told Forsith his plan that night. The older kereighe was hesitant at first since it would be akin to conning folks for money, and they would still remain nomadic. In the end, he gave in when Avator argued that they *would* be performing the same functions as a horse-wizard. What did it matter that they would be doing it combining their talents? Also, although they would remain nomads, the new profession would allow them to earn enough money to survive comfortably. Besides, the boy pointed out, it wasn't as if there was much chance of their settling down in any case. Forsith was afraid that it would affect Avator's education, but the younger kereighe was insistent. His primary concern was for Avita's welfare. This plan would give them the best chance of looking after her without attracting attention to her problems. In the end, Forsith gave in.

They left Xylliot the next morning and started for the garrison city of Lembar. Forsith was unsure about beginning their fraudulent profession there, but Avator argued that it was a good place to start since the cavalry stationed there would be highly appreciative of the services of a horse-wizard. Forsith proceeded with the plan half-heartedly. On the way to the city, he procured and displayed upon his person the paraphernalia of a horse-wizard. At Lembar, he introduced Avator as his assistant and asked if there was work for them. To his surprise, the soldiers readily sought his services. Both Forsith and Avator were kept very busy over the next two days. When they finally left Lembar, they had earned enough to spend on new clothes and good food for several temporas. The highly impressed soldiers requested them to return soon.

Jubilant at their success, they continued on their way south, reaching the town of Engbom near the border of the desert on the sixth of Vyiedal. Avita was feeling tired and ill due to their long march and the cold weather. They decided to purchase a horse and a cart at Engbom. Thanks to their success at Lembar and other places, the surplus they would be left with, if they could find the transportation cheaply, would be enough even to procure supplies for a few days. They found a used cart in good condition for quite a reasonable sum. It had a covered back and an inbuilt box for storage. Then they went looking for horses. When they reached the trader who sold good workhorses, they were surprised to find the corrals almost empty. Horses for pulling carts, carrying loads or farming were greatly in demand, they learnt. The trader told them that he was practically sold out but was expecting more horses to arrive within a couple of temporas. Forsith and Avator were in a fix. They had already purchased the cart. They could not wait two temporas. And this was the only trader who sold workhorses. Avator suggested a look at the few horses that still remained. Sighing, Forsith agreed. They might find one cheap, he figured, if these horses were unwanted.

There were only four horses in the corrals. One was a mare who was too old for any work, one was a cross-eyed gelding, one was a terribly shy colt and the last was a partially deaf horse. None of them was ideal for work. It was no surprise that they had not been purchased yet. They would, in time, be sold off to horse farms at very low rates. Kereighe laws did not allow for horses to be killed, and all kereighes loved horses too much to hurt them anyway. Those horses unfortunate enough to find themselves unwanted, too, were provided for in one way or another, often at horse farms sponsored by the king or his nobles. As they walked out, Forsith was explaining this to Avator to comfort the boy, who felt sorry for the four unwanted horses.

'At least give us some apples before you leave!' someone remarked in a cheerful voice. Avator stopped dead in his tracks. Forsith gave him a puzzled look.

'What?' he asked. Avator pointed to the gelding with the crossed eyes.

'What did you say?' he asked the horse, stepping closer and pretending to examine it so that the trader would not realise what was going on.

'I said, at least give us some apples before you leave,' the gelding repeated.

'What's your name?' Avator asked the cheerful horse. He was genuinely taken with the animal's attitude. He had been rejected by potential owners, probably many times, yet he was cheerful and even asking for apples!

'My name's Habsolm,' the gelding drawled. 'And don't be fooled by my eyes,' it added. 'I can see very well.'

'Really?' Avator asked, amused.

'Yes, of course. For instance, I can see that you are a very discerning young kereighe, that your friend there is a very kind one and that you are going to purchase me or, at least, give me an apple.'

Avator chuckled. He liked the gelding. Forsith was giving him a funny look. He sobered up and told Forsith about the humorous horse. Forsith, too, smiled.

'He might be entertaining, but I'm not sure that he is suitable for pulling the cart,' he told Avator.

'I take back my opinion of the old fellow,' the horse Habsolm commented, hearing Forsith's opinion.

Avator kept a straight face and replied, 'But he is right. We need a horse to pull a cart. I like you, but I can't take you. You might see eighes' characters well, but can you see the road equally well?'

Instead of replying, Habsolm said, 'If you tell the trader that you were interested in me but then noticed the crossed eyes and changed your mind, he will sell me at half-price. That's still more than what the state agents will pay him when they whisk us off to the horse farms. And to answer your question, I can see the road well enough to pull a cart. Though you won't get me to prance along a narrow, straight line!' Habsolm winked.

Avator relayed that to Forsith. Forsith thought about it. If the funny horse was telling the truth, and they did succeed in procuring him at half price or less, they would have enough money left over to buy Avator a sword. He had one—the Simlin sword that Miehaf had given him—but it was too valuable to be used with any regularity. Avator had been practising with it for want of a substitute, but Forsith would have preferred to keep it hidden. He pretended to be dissatisfied with the horses. The trader shrugged; all who had seen these four had said the same thing. Then Forsith casually mentioned Habsolm and said that at first he had thought of buying the horse but had changed his mind upon seeing the horse's eyes. He noticed a slight shift in the trader's stance. From no hope of a sale, the trader had found a slim chance. He pounced upon it. He began to extol the other properties of the horse—its gentleness, its docility, its hardworking nature and so on. Every time he said something, Habsolm responded to the claim with a joke. Avator was hard pressed to look sober. Finally, the trader agreed to lower the price. Forsith drove a hard bargain and succeeded in beating down the price to half. The trader was almost relieved to receive even that much for Habsolm.

When the formalities of the sale were completed and they were on their way back, Avator said to the horse, 'The trader was in a mighty hurry to get rid of you.'

'Yes,' quipped Habsolm. 'Donkeys never can tolerate horses!'

Chapter 3

(14 Lokrin 5006 A.E. to 11 Yodirin 5006 A.E.)

Nishtar's orders placed Rauz Augurk in a terrible predicament. What Nishtar wanted him to do was not personally achievable. No individual, no matter who he was, could investigate into the truth behind a myth and discover the City of Stone. And Augurk was sure that Nishtar knew that. In fact, he was quite certain that his position as rauz was the reason Nishtar had dropped the impossible charge onto his shoulders. But how could he use his power for a task that was his burden alone? Dharvh rauzes were more custodians than masters of their countries. If it became known that Augurk was using his position for a personal endeavour, his subjects could turn against him. Did Nishtar not know this? Augurk could not risk everything for the sake of an insane mission. Neither could he refuse Nishtar. The thought of what the sumagus would say—and do—made him break out into a cold sweat. No, he could not refuse Nishtar. He was caught in a vice, and there was no salvation for him. He cursed the day he had become beholden to Nishtar. If he had not, he would not be faced with such a troublesome dilemma. He would not be rauz either, he reasoned. Yet it did not seem to be a fair trade to the beleaguered rauz of Ghrangghirm. Besides, he *had* taken Nishtar's help, he *was* rauz of Ghrangghirm and he *did* owe the sumagus. So all speculation to the contrary was meaningless.

After days of anguished cudgelling of his brains, he concluded that there was one thing that he could do to solve his problem. He could not publicise the situation, but there were some in his council whom he trusted enough to tell the truth. At least, some part of the truth. Angbruk, of course, was beyond a doubt the most loyal dharvh in his life. Then there was his friend and councillor, Durng. It was his cool head and foresight that had often helped Augurk where the combined might of the whole Council had not. Onelikh the Grizzled and his son Guzear the Bear-clawed could also be trusted, he thought. Father and son were as ferocious in battle as they were meticulous at planning and executing any event. He did not dare involve anyone else. He called these four dharvhs for a meeting. When they arrived for the meeting, the number of the participants told them that the matter was of paramount importance as well as confidentiality.

As soon as all of them had assembled in the private assembly chamber, Augurk began, 'I have asked you here today because a certain powerful person has entrusted us with a task that I dare not refuse. If we do not do as he says, he can wreak awful injury upon us. But the task that he wishes us to accomplish is equally dangerous. I would like to know your opinions in this regard.'

He then told them about the strange messenger and the message from Nishtar about finding the City of Stone. He also explained to them that Nishtar was one of the sumagi, the immortal and all-powerful magi, who ruled the sphere of Maghem.

'But he lives here, on Yennthem, and sometimes decides to involve himself in the affairs of mortals. Or involve mortals in his affairs. I do not know which this is, but I'm sure you can imagine the consequences of disobeying a sumagus,' Augurk concluded.

'The City of Stone is a myth,' Guzear immediately said. He was a well-known warrior and, though nothing to look at, had a commanding presence. He was broad and muscular, with dark hair and beard. On one of his hands, he wore the cured paw of a bear that he had killed anni ago after the bear had taken the hand. Thus, his nickname.

'Why would this sumagus—Nishtar, did you say?—want us to find it if it was a myth?' his father Onelikh countered. Onelikh was neither as broad nor as muscled as his son. His most distinguishing feature, though, was his well-kept salt and pepper beard, which, along with his temperament, gave him his nickname. 'It must exist if he says that we have to find it. But why does he want *us* to find it, my rauz?'

'I know no answer to that, Dar Onelikh,' Augurk lied smoothly. 'All I know is what I have told you. I am loath to make this matter public without knowing more about this mysterious city and what Nishtar wants with it. Until then, I would like to keep this mission a secret. And yet, how do we employ the necessary means to achieve this task without revealing the truth to all? That is the question that we now face.'

The others nodded sagely. They knew their race well enough to understand Augurk's concern with secrecy. If even one veradh decided that it was a bad idea, all of them could be up in arms in a tick, without consideration for the consequences. The dharvhs were young as a nation, and their clannish tendencies still determined much of their lives and choices. They would have to be very careful in handling this issue of the City of Stone.

Durng suggested in a slow drawl, like he was still thinking about the solution, 'There is one thing that we might do. It would prevent publicity of the mission while allowing us to search for information at the same time.'

'What do you propose?' Augurk asked.

'I think that we could send a handful of scouts to all corners of Ghrangghirm to look for this city. I assume that the place must be within our country. Why else would the sumagus Nishtar want *us* to look for it? The scouts will scour every corner and nook of the country for any hint of any information about this mythical place. They would be discreet about it as always, so no one will come to know of their search. I feel as if this might be our best option at present.'

Augurk felt a twinge of guilt. He knew that Durng's assumption was wrong. Nishtar had asked them to find the mythical city because of what Augurk owed him, but he could not tell Durng this without revealing the dark truth of his life that he had swore would go with him to Zyimnhem, the sphere of the dead. Though, it *was* possible that the place was somewhere in Ghrangghirm. It did seem logical—Nishtar would have picked someone else to torment if it had been in the countries of any of the other races. Augurk almost trembled visibly. He ardently hoped that it wasn't. He could not afford to go to war with any of the other races in order to repay his debt to Nishtar. Aloud he said, 'I think this is a good suggestion, Durng. What do the rest of you think?'

The others agreed that Durng's suggestion was a sensible one. Grateful for his friend's level-headedness, Augurk asked Angbruk to make the necessary arrangements. The scouts were given their orders the very next day, the fifteenth of Lokrin. However, despite searching assiduously for almost three mondans, the scouts failed utterly to discover even a shred of relevant information. When the last scout returned with news of failure, Augurk summoned his close circle of councillors once again with a heavy heart. They were all gutted on hearing about the failure of the scouts.

'It appears that we have no choice but to involve the rest of the councillors now,' Onelikh said, shaking his head.

The dharvhish councillors were incumbent and retired senior officials of the administration or the army, and their role was more advisory than functional. Only a few of them were instrumental in performing the most critical functions of state, although roles were not designated by title as they were in human and eighe monarchies. Fortunately, the title of Councillor was honorary rather than pecuniary, and only those serving the rauz in direct capacity were required to be paid. The vast majority of councillors contributed practically nothing to the running of the country; yet the rauz could not ignore them, or their veradhen would feel affronted.

'What good do you expect that clutch of doddering old fools to do?' Onelikh's son snorted. Guzear, at eighty-one, was in his prime, and extremely fit besides.[2] Anyone above the age of a hundred anni was old and doddering to him, although he never dared to say that about his rauz, or his father.

---

2 An eighty-one-annus-old dharvh is the equivalent of a forty and a half-annus-old human. For more details about the correlations in age between the different races, see Appendix 4 of Tornain Book One: The Prophecy of Kawiti

'Their age might turn out to be an advantage in this case,' Durng commented wryly. 'Some of them might have heard something from their fathers or grandfathers that can help us find this city.'

The discussion continued for some time more as the relative merits of involving the other councillors and keeping them in the dark were debated. In the end, a comment by Angbruk settled the matter. Although he had been quiet for most of the discussion, he suddenly said in support of Durng: 'At the very least, it will save us some trouble when we have to undertake more public steps to find the City of Stone.'

Augurk did not fail to notice that his brother had said 'when' rather than 'if'. But he knew that Angbruk was right. As was Durng. He had no choice but to bring his remaining councillors into the picture if he wanted to continue the search that Nishtar had mandated.

The decision to involve the full Council was taken by Augurk late at night on the ninth of Vyiedal, and he ordered Angbruk to implement it the very next morning. Unfortunately, it was past noon before all of Augurk's councillors could be awakened and brought before the rauz in some state of respectability and with their wits about them. The rauz was already in a bad temper by then due to the delay. He told them of the message that he had received concerning the City of Stone. A long and tedious discussion followed amongst the councillors, but none of them knew anything that could help Augurk. One of the oldest dharvhs was bold enough to question the very purpose of the message.

'Why must we be bothered over a message that is obviously senseless and useless to us? Why must we chase wild geese for some lunatic who knows no better than to disturb the peace of dharvhs who spend their days minding their own business?' he protested. A few others murmured in consent.

Augurk had had enough of his doddering advisors. He thundered at them, 'We must be bothered because *I, your rauz, say so*. And the message is not senseless because it comes from one who is a sumagus, an immortal. So, if any of you know anything relevant, speak up now. Else, go back to your worthless lives!'

A hush fell upon the gathering. They had never seen Augurk so angry. It reminded them how dangerous Augurk could be and why he had succeeded in defeating far stronger candidates to become rauz of Ghrangghirm. He was not to be taken for granted. They had also heard stories about the sumagi, the immortals, who saw all and knew all. The sudden realisation that they were standing on the edge of a sword stunned and awed them. But they truly had no knowledge to assist their rauz. All of them left Augurk's council chamber quietly, their heads hung with shame.

All except one decrepit, old dharvh who could barely stand on his own feet. He sat for a long time in the council chamber even after everyone, including the rauz, had departed. He was the oldest among Augurk's advisors and even among the dharvhs of the city of Drauzern. None remained of those who had played with him as lads or fought with him as soldiers. Even his sons and grandsons had perished. Yet he lingered on, like some desiccated tree in a corner of a forest, forgotten by all. He sat to one side of the vast council chamber, unnoticed, and tried to recall the tales that his great-grandfather had told him one night during a storm to lull him to sleep. He did not remember how long ago that had been, nor what the tales had been, but he was not willing to give up. Even when he finally scrambled up and hobbled home, his mind remained busy trying to recollect what that venerable dharvh had told him about the City of Stone and its awakening by someone.

Augurk, of course, learnt none of this. He was disappointed with and disgusted at his councillors. He called another meeting of the four who had begun to become his inner circle by then and were beginning to be known among the other councillors as the Special Advisory Council. They knew what had happened at the meeting of the full Council that day. Durng looked deep in thought; Angbruk looked impassive; Onelikh looked disappointed; Guzear looked stony faced, which was a surprise as Augurk had expected him to feel smug. Perhaps, he thought, Guzear was more concerned about the lack of direction they now faced than about being proven right.

'You all know where we stand right now. We have sent out scouts who made discreet enquiries and we have consulted the councillors of Ghrangghirm, but neither option has yielded any results. Apparently there is nothing more that we can do,' Augurk said, his tone heavy with the disappointment that he felt. 'But I can assure you that Nishtar will not accept this as an answer. So, we must find another way to discover this City of Stone.'

'I think I have a plan that might work, my rauz,' Durng suggested. 'But it will involve engaging larger numbers of dharvhs in this enterprise and substantial expenditure as well.'

'At this point, I can no longer afford to harp on either too much secrecy or too much economy,' the rauz said bitterly. 'Please tell us your plan.'

As Durng began to detail his plan, a ray of hope began to shine in Rauz Augurk's heart. Durng was the most sensible dharvh he knew. And his plan was a sensible one as well. There was a miniscule chance that it just might work. Augurk was not too sanguine, but it was the only plan they had at that moment. It was either that or informing Nishtar that he had failed. The latter was not really an option, not if he wanted to retain his life and all his limbs.

On the fourteenth of Vyiedal, he sent for bright young dharvhs from all corners of the country, some of whom he had first met as suitors for his daughter Meizha. They were the ones who would carry out Durng's plan. The inner circle had divided the territory of Ghrangghirm into divisions that would ensure equal distribution of work. Durng's plan involved a survey of the entire country for information about the City of Stone but without announcing the true object of the search. Rauz Augurk had revealed Nishtar's orders to his councillors—and soon everyone in the capital city would find out, no doubt—but he was reluctant to have the news spread like wildfire throughout the continent. His anxiety was not farfetched, he told himself. If all his subjects came to know, the rauz of Khwaznon would also learn sooner or later. After that, it was only a matter of time before the news spread to the fraels, the humans and the eighes. Who knew what would happen then? He wasn't sure whether Nishtar would appreciate the involvement of others, despise it or be entirely indifferent. It was best to be cautious in their approach.

Finally, on the fourteenth of Kielom, sixty intelligent and strong dharvhs stood ready to set off on Augurk's mission. These dharvhs had been selected from the army of Ghrangghirm as well as from the veradhen loyal to Augurk. Young and eager to make their name, these dharvhs had happily volunteered despite not being clearly told what they had to do. They were willing to accept any challenge, face any danger. Augurk and the inner circle entered the assembly hall looking grim and purposeful. They had several rolled up sheets of parchment with them. The gathered dharvhs noted with surprise that the rauz had not brought Shornhuz, his personal bodyguard, along. Everyone knew that Shornhuz was like the rauz's shadow and was almost never away from his master. They wondered what secret mission they were being sent on that even Shornhuz was not privy to, and their pulses quickened. Among those who had been chosen for the task were Shroog, Fongun, Ghruk, Witar, Hervoz and Veber. They had been suitors of Rauzditr Meizha. More than an annus had passed since the Hravisht-envar; they had shrugged off the competitiveness that had dominated their interactions during those days and were looking forward to rising to important positions under Augurk's patronage.

Augurk welcomed the young dharvhs and spoke briefly about the importance of their mission. He harped on how it could pave the way for their future success either in the army or in some capacity within the administration or even within their own veradhen. The gathered assembly cheered. Then one of the parchments was unrolled, and the sixty were divided into groups of three. When the grouping was done, each group was asked to choose a leader. When this task was complete, the assignment was announced. The ambitious, young dharvhs stood dumbstruck when they heard their mission, unable to decide whether to laugh or to groan with misery.

Because the plan had originally been Durng's, it fell upon him to explain it to the volunteers. 'The entire territory of Ghrangghirm has been divided into twenty blocks based on population as well as area,' he elaborated. 'Each of your groups will survey one area and conduct a census. You will gather basic information about the members of each and every family living in the block assigned to your group.' An almost audible groan arose from the young dharvhs. They were not excited. They felt that they had been sorely deceived with false promises of glory. Durng continued inexorably, 'But that is not the true purpose of your mission. It is only the pretext for gaining entry into the houses of all the citizens without being doubted or questioned. Your true purpose is to enquire about the City of Stone from every dharvh who seems even remotely likely to know anything about it. That is why you have been divided into teams of three. While one of you investigates the person you think might know something worthwhile, the other two will keep the rest of the family distracted to ensure that no one realises your true purpose. At the end of the census, you will report back to us with whatever information you can uncover about the mythical City of Stone. Of course, you are also welcome to submit the census data,' he ended with a smile.

His joke did not meet with much success. A few of the volunteers smiled politely. They were still utterly confused about what was going on. Then Angbruk addressed them. Looking more serious than usual, he said, 'You will now be told some things that are of the greatest significance imaginable to this kingdom and to our rauz. For obvious reasons, these matters cannot be disclosed to all. Consequently, we have resorted to the pretence of the census. Rauz Augurk will himself tell you why it is imperative for us to find this City of Stone and what the consequences of failure can be. We will provide you with all the resources that you require in order to carry out your orders successfully. You will liaise with me in this matter for the purpose of submitting information as well as for any assistance that you require while the work is in progress. Before our rauz explains the purpose of this mission, I must warn you that this task is fraught with risk, especially if your true purpose becomes known. Not all would want us to investigate the whereabouts of this mythical city. And if any of the veradhen feels that this enquiry is an affront to them for some reason, your very lives could be in danger. You will have to apply the utmost tact and cunning along with great courage to succeed. Needless to say, any who succeeds can expect great rewards.'

The prospect of great rewards was as tantalising to the young dharvhs as the thought of a secret mission. Angbruk sat down, allowing Augurk to take the stage. Augurk, too, looked deadly serious. The volunteer dharvhs turned towards him as one. A hush fell on the gathering.

'Have you heard of the sumagi?' Augurk asked them.

Some of them nodded hesitantly. Some said 'yes' in hushed tones. A few stood there looking petrified. They had all heard of the sumagi. The immortals who knew all and could do anything they pleased. An askance glance from a sumagus was enough to incinerate an entire village, it was said. They could read one's deepest thoughts and make one kill one's own children if they so wished. They could create cities out of thin air and even bring the dead back to life. They could travel between the hems at will, and they consorted with all kinds of magical beings. Some went so far as to say that they had regular communion with the Guardians! Tales of the sumagi's wrath were told to naughty children to make them behave. Tales of their great deeds were narrated on cold vernurt evenings by the hearth fire to inspire. They were the stuff of legends and of nightmares alike.

The expressions on the volunteers' faces told Augurk that he would not have to explain to them who the sumagi were, which made his task much easier. He spoke as casually as he could, describing how he had received a message from Nishtar, one of the sumagi, soon after his daughter's wedding. That message had asked him to find the City of Stone. He further told them what had been done already, how the measures had failed and what the consequences of failure to locate the city could be for all of Ghrangghirm. By the end of his speech, not one volunteer was sure whether it was the greatest opportunity he had ever had in life or the worst trap he could have fallen into. But their rauz's faith in them heartened them again. As Augurk continued to speak, they felt bold again.

'If you think that you cannot or do not wish to do this job, you can withdraw now. No one shall hold it against your honour. But once you commit, there is no going back. So, are you willing to take on this challenge?' Augurk demanded.

'Yes!' roared the volunteers in unison. They had no idea what the City of Stone was, but they were raring for a chance to prove their mettle. They would not back down, no matter what was thrown at them.

The five mondans that followed tested their intelligence, their resolve and their patience. They talked to thousands of dharvhs, young and old, under the pretext of the census. It was never easy to bring the conversation round to something as mythical as the City of Stone. Sometimes they were lucky enough to come across a gossipy old geezer who would prattle on about old myths and legends with only the slightest encouragement. At other times, they met with a wall of resolute silence. The dharvhs being surveyed looked askance at them, and they were assailed by self-doubt and disloyal sentiments towards their monarch. But none of them gave up. One by one, however, they completed their survey and returned to Drauzern with nothing but census data. The last group to return was that which had travelled to the lands of the Phushketh.

The volunteers met with Augurk and Angbruk again in the smaller assembly chamber where the previous audience had taken place. There was a marked difference in their expressions and demeanour. They were no longer excited or eager. Some looked frustrated. Some looked disappointed. Some looked hopelessly depressed. A few looked angry. All looked exhausted.

The sight of the sixty surveyors, all young and promising dharvhs of Ghrangghirm, their hearts and spirits broken, cut Augurk to the quick. It was all he could do to keep himself from apologising to them for putting them through such an ordeal. He braced himself and faced the gathering. After a few platitudes, he came to the point.

'What have you learnt about the City of Stone?' he asked.

'Nothing!' they all replied.

'Nothing? At all?' Augurk responded, his eyebrows raised.

'No one knew about it,' one of them said.

'No one had ever seen it or heard about it,' Veber added.

'An old dharvh I met said that he had heard about it from his grandfather, but he could not remember anything about it,' Ghruk said.

'I had a similar experience,' Hervoz said morosely. 'The old dharvhs who had heard about it said that it was not a real place. Never was. It is just a myth. They laughed at me and ragged me that I was wasting my time chasing myths.'

The others had similar reports; either they had heard nothing at all, or they had heard that it was a myth. No one in Ghrangghirm seemed to remember the city. Augurk thanked the groups for their efforts and sent them back, reminding them of the necessity for complete silence in this regard, and announcing their rewards. Unsurprisingly, even the mention of rewards failed to cheer them up. Augurk could empathise. He had done what he could. And had failed to achieve that which Nishtar had enjoined upon him. He shuddered at the thought of telling Nishtar that.

Chapter 4

AN EXCEPTIONAL BURGLAR

(4 Kielom 5006 A.E. to 8 Beybasel 5006 A.E.)

One morning, towards the end of the first tempora of Kielom, Rosa found one of her most precious possessions missing. She was also missing some utensils and rare herbs, but she couldn't care less about those. All she could think was that Sanfion's ring was gone! The loss of the ring was unbearable for her. It was one of only two belongings of her late husband that she still possessed; fate had taken everything else. Once the beautiful wife of a prominent courtier at King Rannzen's court, she was now an old, haggard, ugly, evil witch. She had given everything she had, including her sanity, to avenge her husband's death, yet it had all been futile. Kiel had taken her enemy before she could mete out justice to him. All she was left with were a wretched prisoner, an unrelenting hatred and the two mementos of her wrongfully murdered husband. One of which was now missing.

She searched frantically for the missing ring in every nook and corner of her dwelling, flinging things everywhere in an insane panic, moaning and panting, tears streaming down her face. She turned over the mattress on which she slept; she searched behind all her jars and pots and pans and bottles of animal parts, unguents, strange liquids and mysterious powders, not caring in her desperation if they fell and broke; she tossed her belongings all over the house but could not find it anywhere.

While she searched, Temeron cowered in a corner. He was the prisoner Rosa loathed yet never set free. A sallow complexioned human boy with a thin face and dark hair and eyes, he was emaciated with bony arms and legs sticking out at angles. He wore an expression of terror on his face. He had no idea what was going on with Rosa that day. She often had strange fits, he knew, but this was unlike any fit that she had ever had. Temeron's heart thumped as he hoped that the witch would not find his little stash hidden under the floorboard. Suddenly Rosa turned on him and screeched.

'You!' she screamed. 'You stole it!'

She pounced on him and began to rough him up, going through his tattered rags, searching for something. Temeron had no idea what she was talking about. He stayed as quiet as a mouse, hoping that the lech's rage would dissipate on its own. She was given to mad bouts of violent anger that vanished as quickly as they appeared. Her sharp nails scratched and cut him as she searched him, but these injuries were nothing compared to his usual wounds at her hands.

When she did not find whatever she was looking for, she slapped Temeron hard. 'Where is it?' she demanded, shaking him furiously. 'I know that you stole it!' she accused him. 'I know it. Now tell me where you have hidden it, or I shall give you the thrashing of a lifetime.'

But Temeron had no idea what it was that he was supposed to have stolen. He thought for a moment that Rosa was again searching for the book of magic that he had taken some time previously, but he changed his mind on seeing how frantic she was. It had been a while since that book had vanished into his secret cache. Even though Rosa had had no proof of his guilt, she had accused him of stealing the book and had punished him despite his protestations of innocence. The protestations had been false then. This time, though, he was truly innocent of the theft that Rosa was accusing him of. However, that did not stop her from thrashing Temeron. It took him several days to recover from the beating, though Rosa continued to keep him half-starved for several days more.

Rosa realised that her prisoner might not have stolen the ring when, a few temporas later, one of her regular clients came to her to buy some magic potion for protection against thieves and told her that her neighbour had been relieved of many of his precious belongings. Rosa gave her some worthless potion; she found it more expedient to earn a few coins than to tell the client that no potion could prevent a determined thief from carrying out his intentions.

Over the next three mondans, Rosa continued to hear about the exploits of this thief. He was extremely cunning, it transpired. The best of security measures failed to keep him out. No one could outwit him. Those who tried to remain awake to catch him failed to stay awake, no matter what they tried. He always outsmarted the traps that were set for him. The soldiers who had been sent from the capital to catch him were equally baffled; the thief never left any trails for them to follow either. He was just too good to be caught!

Temeron heard these things as well. Some he overheard from Rosa's clients; some he learnt from the conversations of passersby as he sat near the doorway or at the window of the shabby hut they lived in. No one paid him any heed as they gossiped freely about the thief, the stories of his exploits getting bigger and wilder until it was hard to distinguish reality from make-believe. Of course, these stories were enjoyed only by those who had not fallen victim to him and, that too, only until the thief decided to pay them a visit. Soon, it was difficult to find anyone who had not been at the receiving end of the thief's exploits.

One kereighe hired armed mercenaries to guard his safe. The mercenaries surrounded the safe and stood with naked swords in their hands night after night.

When morning came, the kereighe checked his safe to ensure that his valuables were still there. One morning, they weren't. The mercenaries swore that they had not moved from their positions, although they seemed to have a foggy recollection of what they had done between the horas of midnight and dawn.

Another, a well-known merchant, bought fierce hunting dogs. It became known that the dogs would attack and kill anyone except their handler. It was also rumoured that the merchant was starving them to give their ferociousness an added edge. One morning, the merchant woke up to find many of his valuables missing along with the dogs.

Yet another wealthy kereighe brought a sorcerer to ward his house against the thief. The sorcerer put up wards all around his estate, ensuring that not even a bird could enter the air above the property. The wards extended many feet underground as well, everyone whispered. Anyone who touched the ward without permission from the homeowner was instantly incinerated. The kereighe boasted that the thief would not be able to steal even a handkerchief from his house. Within a tempora he found himself waking up to a completely empty house, wearing nothing but a handkerchief around his neck. The wards were still intact, but nothing that wasn't fixed to the ground had survived the thief's raid.

Temeron heard these stories along with the rest of the kereighes and kereighees in town and marvelled at the skill of the thief. He felt sure that the thief knew magic. How else could he have managed the things he did? He did not feel sorry for the victims. They were nothing to him. He did not care if they suffered just as they did not care that he suffered. In his heart, he began to relate to this enemy of those whom he hated. So, when he saw the bands of soldiers patrolling the streets, searching for the miscreant, his mind was filled with apprehension. When the soldiers in their gleaming armours marched confidently past his window, his heart trembled with fear for the thief. When he overheard how the burglar had evaded the soldiers, he cheered silently. He hoped that the clever purloiner would never be caught. Capture meant inevitable death for the crook who had everyone trembling with misgivings.

Late one night, Temeron was awoken by a sound. He had just fallen into deep sleep after tossing and turning for a long time. It was Beybasel, and vernurt was on its way out, but the cold still clung to the small horas of the night. The lack of a blanket had kept the young boy from falling into a restful slumber. He closed his eyes and tried to pretend that he was comfortable despite the discomfort of tattered clothing and a threadbare covering that did nothing to keep the cold out. Close to midnight, he had just fallen into a deep sleep for real when a sudden sound like a door closing roused him.

He woke up with a start, wondering whether he had dreamt the sound. The new moon had passed seven days ago, but it was quite dark outside. Temeron looked towards the door, wondering if someone had knocked, but it was closed. A few momons of waiting brought no more knocks either. He turned towards the window, thinking that it might have been left open, and a shutter might have banged shut in the wind. But it, too, was closed. Puzzled, he sat up. He gazed around the small hovel, trying to figure out what might have caused the sound. Deep shadows lined the walls and the nooks, deeper where they mingled with furniture that cast large shadows. A large lump towards one side was Rosa on her mattress, sound asleep. Her snores gave away her position. Temeron surmised that the snores must have woken him and was about to lie back down when a tall slice of shadow peeled away from the wall, began to make its way towards the middle of the room and suddenly halted.

With a start, Temeron realised that this was not a shadow but a kereighe. He was practically invisible. The only indication of where he stood was a patch of darkness slightly darker than the rest of the darkness around him. Temeron was surprised that he had even managed to spy the figure. He was sure that this was the notorious thief that everyone had been talking about. He continued to stare at the thief spellbound. As he became used to the darkness, he was able to see the thief's features more clearly.

It soon became apparent to him that the thief was staring at him in disbelief as well. Why? The thief had a dagger in his hand, a beautiful jewel encrusted dagger. In fact, this dagger was Rosa's second-most prized possession, though Temeron had no way of knowing that. It was the dagger with which Sanfion had taken his own life, preferring that to being executed by the late king Rannzen, Temeron's father. Rosa had stolen Temeron to take revenge, leaving her own daughter in his stead. But things hadn't gone according to plan as the king and queen had been dethroned and killed shortly thereafter. The dagger was Rosa's last token by which to remember her dead husband. She had clung to it after the ring had been stolen. She had taken to keeping it on her person at all times; that had not prevented the adroit burglar from stealing it.

Unaware of all this, Temeron stared at the thief and wondered whether he was going to die at the hands of the miscreant for spotting him in action. But the thief did not move. The natural thing for Temeron would have been to scream to draw attention to the burglar. He did not. The natural thing for the burglar would have been to attack the boy. Yet he stood there, staring at the tiny figure, just as stunned as Temeron. Their eyes met, and each read the fear and desperation in the other's heart. Temeron was not yet six anni old, but his ordeals had made him older than his anni. He made a decision then—he would not give the burglar away. He would allow the thief to escape. Not only because he had developed a feeling of sympathy for the pilferer but also because the knife in the thief's hand looked valuable and would, he felt sure, be a loss for Rosa. He remembered the beating that he had received after Rosa had lost her precious ring. He knew that he would receive a beating again if the dagger went missing. He did not care. The lech was about to be injured in some way by someone, and the thought gave him a warm, happy feeling within.

After staring at each other for what seemed like an annus, both decided that it was time to take action. The thief took a step towards the door tentatively. Temeron gave a brief nod and lay back down. When, a few minuras later, he sat up again to check if the thief was still there, he found the house empty and everything as it had been before. There was no sign of anyone's entry or exit through door or window. He went back to sleep though sleep eluded him for horas as he pondered over what had happened and whether it had happened at all. He fell asleep close to dawn. He was soon woken up by a raging and screaming Rosa who was once again turning her house upside down in her search for the missing dagger. She accused Temeron of stealing it and beat him until he bled when he denied it. He took the beating quietly, as ever, while rejoicing in his heart over his tormentor's loss.

Chapter 5

A LIFE UNLIVED

(17 Zulheen 5006 A.E. to 24 Madal 5007 A.E.)

Eamilus was furious at Timror. Just because he had used his powers to find the herbs, the magus had called him stupid and lazy. True, Timror *had* expressly forbidden him from using his supernatural ability. But it wasn't as if Eamilus had disobeyed him out of wilfulness or stupidity. One of his goats was ill and had needed the herbs urgently for its medicine. Timror had sent him off to find them in the forest outside Abluvel, where the two of them lived, but he had had difficulty locating and recognising the herbs. Getting desperate to help his pet, Eamilus had decided to skip the lesson this one time and had focussed on finding the herbs rather than on learning whatever skills Timror was trying to inculcate in him. The result had been shockingly upsetting for the student.

Timror had been furious with him. He had berated Eamilus roundly, calling him names that had made the boy's ears go red. Stupid and lazy were only the mildest of the expletives that Timror had used. Eamilus had not even heard some of them before! In the end, Eamilus had had enough! He was sure that Nishtar would never have behaved thus. He had been putting up with Timror's eccentricity and rudeness for far too long, he decided. He would no longer tolerate the ill-tempered magus. He would go back to Nishtar!

He left for White Mountain that very day. He did not inform Timror that he was leaving; he was too angry. He felt bad about leaving his pets behind, but he told himself that Timror would either look after them or turn them loose. He stoked his anger towards Timror to stanch the guilt that he felt at abandoning his dependants. What had Timror really taught him? Nothing! He had had to learn everything on his own—through his own discoveries, his own experiences and by reading books. At Nishtar's school, he would have been properly taught, he grumbled. He felt that he must have fallen behind in his education by coming to Timror. Why had Nishtar sent him there? He must have been mistaken in thinking that Timror could be a good teacher.

It took Eamilus three days to reach White Mountain. As he climbed up to Nishtar's cave, he was surprised by the absence of the usual wards and traps that guarded the path against unwanted intruders. He knew how to sidestep them because of his earlier stay there, but there was no need. He could not believe that Nishtar had become so careless. Perhaps, Nishtar had learnt that he was coming and had cleared the obstacles. When he reached the cave at the top, he realised that Nishtar was not there. At first this puzzled Eamilus although it did explain the absence of the protections. Then Eamilus remembered the huts that he had built for his erstwhile master. That had been the last task that he had performed before leaving for Abluvel to study with Timror. The building of the huts all by himself without food or water for days had been a test. But it had not been the last one. Another had ridden on its back, another meant to test his control of his innate monstrous nature. He had passed thanks to Nishtar's training. He had managed to overcome the filthy beast that lay coiled up within him. Now he could harness any of the powers that his strange nature gave him. And it had all been because of Nishtar.

He figured that Nishtar was engaged in teaching that annus. He remembered with longing Nishtar's offer to remain with him for seven anni to learn. He wondered whether he had been right in refusing Nishtar. He wondered if his life would have been different if he had stayed on. He had refused because he had wanted to return to Haalzona to fight kocovuses, and seven anni in Blarzonia had seemed like exile. But where was his life poised now? He had not returned to Haalzona, and he was still in exile. Only, his place of exile was Qeezsh, and his teacher was Timror. Or had been, until he had left in a huff.

His mind was brimming with these thoughts as he walked down into the valley where he had built the huts. He found them easily enough, but Nishtar was still nowhere to be seen. A fence with a wicket gate marked the boundary of the school. Eamilus was certain that this place would have wards and traps around it. He climbed into a tree to survey the area. It took him some time to spot half a dozen wards and traps that he was familiar with. He was sure there were others, including invisible ones. How was he to identify those? He remembered reading that magic always left a trace, no matter how faint. One cannot bend nature without leaving one's imprint on it. Resorting to his special abilities, Eamilus looked for hints that would show that nature had been modified. Sure enough, there were half a dozen invisible traps. Only the tiniest bits of unnatural things gave them away: here, a leaf was twice as large as any other, there a patch of the bark of a tree was abnormally smooth, elsewhere the grass grew in a perfect square, and so on. None but the keenest observer would have noticed these. Having found the protections, Eamilus made his way towards the school, avoiding them without much difficulty. He was surprised when he realised that he knew just what to do to sidestep each one, even the ones that he was not familiar with. When did he learn so much about magical traps?

Eamilus reached the school without incident and without being noticed. He stood outside the gate, looking in. He saw seven boys in the courtyard. They all looked human, though their complexion was different from that of any human he had ever seen. It was an odd coppery colour. Their build, too, was subtly different.

But their smells told Eamilus that not all of them were human. In fact, they were not even the same species. Their clothing also proclaimed them to be from different parts of Elthrusia. There were three humans, all from the West. They wore woollen breeches and full sleeved cotton shirts, which was common to all the four human countries of the west; however, there were subtle differences between their garments. One boy's clothes were bright in colour, red and green. Another's shirt had puffy sleeves and a wide collar. The third wore a wide leather belt with his shirt tucked inside. Eamilus guessed that they were from Balignor, Cordemim and Storsnem respectively. Another boy, who wore a close fitting tunic and green leggings, had narrow features and longish hair tied at the nape. A fifth wore a vest over a high collared white linen shirt and soft boots. The remaining two wore elaborate shirts with lace at the neck, sleeves and down the front. They also wore tall boots with turned down tops, and their leather breeches tucked inside the boots. Although Eamilus was familiar with only the humans' smell, he guessed from the clothing that the fourth boy was from Wyrchhelim, the fifth was from Rosarfin, and the other two were from Emense. He was thrilled to learn how fraels, seleighes and kereighes smelled. It might come in handy some day.

The seven boys were wrestling in the courtyard. Upon a closer look, Eamilus realised that that wasn't entirely true. Six of them were trying to bring down one. The lone defender, one of the kereighe boys, was laughing as he flung his opponents to the ground with little effort while they desperately tried to subdue him. As Eamilus stood at the gate, he realised with a twinge that he would have been one of those seven had he accepted Nishtar's offer. Eamilus watched until all the wrestlers were tired, except the victor, whom six opponents had not managed to bring down despite a concerted effort towards the end of the bout. The six now sat around him wearing defeated and exhausted expressions while he still laughed and continued to challenge them. He suddenly saw Eamilus and called to his companions. All seven were immediately on their feet.

'Who are you? What do you want?' one of them demanded. This was the seleighe boy. He was tall and thin and displayed a haughty and superior stance in his manner of addressing Eamilus. He looked sharply at Eamilus's clothes and appearance, judging him silently and finding him wanting.

Eamilus introduced himself and enquired about Nishtar. One of the other boys, the Balignorian, opened the gate for him warily and asked him to enter. This boy was much shorter than the wrestler or the questioner, as Eamilus thought of them in his mind, and had the thick, muscled arms of one who worked with heavy tools. Probably a smith, Eamilus guessed. None of the others moved an inch from their places as he began to cross the courtyard towards the huts. Suddenly, the wrestler called out a challenge. He demanded to wrestle with Eamilus in exchange for information on where Nishtar could be found. Perhaps it was Eamilus's dishevelled and harrowed look that prompted him to bully the thinner boy. Perhaps he was still trying to work off his restlessness. Or, perhaps he was just looking to show off to his classmates or to Nishtar. Eamilus knew Nishtar enough to guess that nothing his students did would remain unknown to the sumagus.

At first Eamilus refused. He could find Nishtar on his own, he said, thank you very much. All seven boys began to taunt him then. Eamilus felt annoyed and finally agreed. All but the challenger formed a circle around Eamilus and their companion. Eamilus stood waiting patiently. The other boy bent low and attacked. Eamilus waited until the boy was almost upon him and then, swiftly sidestepping, tripped him up. Before the boy could recover, Eamilus effortlessly picked him up and dropped him upon the ground, face down. Then Eamilus flipped him over and pinned him down, barely batting an eyelid while his opponent panted and struggled to free himself. Eamilus's grip was like a vice. The wrestler was left with no choice but surrender. Before the defeated boy could stand up, Eamilus walked out of the courtyard, the other boys hastily making way for him. He no longer felt that he had been deprived; he was obviously no worse than any of Nishtar's pupils. At least in wrestling. And good manners. Maybe in other things too. He had been able to discover the magical traps and identify the boys' nationalities and races from their clothes. That was no mean feat for someone who had never encountered anyone from those countries in his life!

He did not turn around as he left Nishtar's school behind, so he did not see the master standing in front of his hut, his face aglow with pride for his dearest student. Nishtar had learnt of Eamilus's presence as soon as the boy had entered the school premises. He had been on his way to meet Eamilus when the two boys had engaged in their wrestling bout. Nishtar had hoped for a moment that Eamilus had come to tell him that he wanted to return, that he wanted to be taught by Nishtar. He sighed as he saw his erstwhile student walk away, his head held high with pride. What a student Eamilus would have made! He wondered why it was that he kept wishing that he had got the chance to teach Eamilus. Was it because his pride had been wounded when the boy had refused to remain with him? Or was it because he could see the potential in Eamilus and longed to channel it to enable the boy to reach the greatness that he was obviously capable of? Or was it because Eamilus was who he was?

Nishtar's heart ached to go after the boy and bring him back. To ask him how he was. To ask him to stay awhile with him. He checked himself. No, it would not do to give in to emotions. What was wrong with him? Nishtar chided himself and thanked his stars that he had no empaths among his students. If he had had any, his emotions might not have remained a secret. He was growing into a maudlin old fool, he scolded himself. What was he going to do next? Go around hugging his students? He felt disgusted at his own momentary weakness and forced thoughts of Eamilus away. The boy had chosen his destiny, and Nishtar was no longer responsible for what happened to him.

Eamilus returned to Timror on the twenty-third of Zulheen. He had had time to reflect upon his behaviour, and he was now thoroughly ashamed of how he had acted. He knew that Timror would be in his laboratory in the daytime and did not want to disturb him. So he went directly to his own chamber. He was happy to find that his pets had been looked after in his absence and that the goat that had been unwell was now fine. The animals greeted him with enthusiasm, gathering around him and pulling at his clothes. Eamilus felt doubly guilty. He petted them and apologised to them, even breaking down when one of the goats licked his nose affectionately.

Eamilus finally saw Timror at dinnertime. He had expected Timror to be angry. He was prepared for a harsh tirade like the one that had driven him away. What Timror did came as a complete surprise. It was the absolute reverse of what the boy had anticipated. The short, thin magus with sharp features, long hair and startling green eyes pretended as if Eamilus was not even there. He said not a word to the boy though Eamilus apologised profusely and promised never to run away again. Timror finished his meal and left for his own chamber. Eamilus did not know what to make of Timror's lack of response. Wasn't the magus bothered by what Eamilus had done? No, that was not so, said his voice of common sense. Timror *was* angry. In fact, he was so angry that it could not be expressed in words. That was why he had said nothing. What Eamilus had done was unthinkable and unforgivable; no words could suffice to chastise him. Eamilus felt so terribly ashamed, he wanted to disappear!

For days Eamilus continued to apologise to Timror while figuring out what to do with his time. But there was no change in Timror's behaviour towards him. The magus continued to act as if the boy did not exist. Meanwhile, Eamilus tried to study on his own. He realised just how mistaken he had been when he had thought that Timror had not been guiding him in his education. He sensed the subtle ways in which Timror had shown him the right paths to follow and had helped him where he had needed help. It was far more difficult to study and learn on his own than he had anticipated. However, he did not give up. He took control of his education and patiently waited for Timror to forgive him. That Timror had not thrown him out gave him hope that one day his master would acknowledge him again.

Every night, he talked to his teacher over dinner. At first, he mostly apologised but after a tempora of apologising, he decided that he had apologised enough. Thereafter, he told Timror what he had done during the day and what he had learnt. Initially, Timror completely ignored him, finishing his meal quickly and leaving immediately, irrespective of whether Eamilus had finished talking or not.

After a mondan of this, Eamilus noticed that Timror ate more slowly, allowing Eamilus to finish talking before he departed for the night. Encouraged, Eamilus began to write regular reports of what he had done during the day, as he had done during his initial time with the magus. He would submit the reports during their shared meal, placing them next to Timror's plate so that the magus could take them with him when he left. For one tempora, the reports remained untouched. Timror did not even look at them. Then, without a word, Timror began to collect them on his way out. The next night, he returned them with corrections. One morning, Eamilus was overjoyed to find a basket with a list inside it left on the table. It was a familiar object; it meant that Timror wanted him to forage for provisions in the forest. Eamilus happily accomplished the task set by his master, anticipating more of such familiar tasks in the future. He was disappointed in this, though. And all this while, the magus continued to ignore him.

Then, one night, just as Eamilus finished narrating what he had been doing that day (he'd been planting vegetables), Timror cleared his throat and sat back. Even though he had finished his dinner, he did not leave. Eamilus looked at him expectantly. Timror's eyes looked grave, though not forbidding.

'Let's go and sit outside,' Timror suggested. Eamilus followed him willingly.

They came up from the underground residence at the mound through which Eamilus had first entered Timror's lair close to an annus ago. They stepped outside and sat down upon it. The creepers covering the mound created quite a cushioned seat. It was the fifteenth of Niwukir, and somminar had settled in nicely. The air was warm and breezy. Crickets chirped in the hedges. A nightingale sang somewhere in the distance. The fragrance of flowers and budding fruits lent the atmosphere a lush suggestion. The stars were out in a body though the moon was only a narrow slice of silver so close to the new moon.

'So, you went to Nishtar, did you?' asked Timror.

'Yes,' answered Eamilus simply. He did not apologise. He did not need to. He knew that it was because Timror had forgiven him that they were talking again. He would not insult Timror by apologising again.

'Why Nishtar?'

'I couldn't think of anyone else. I haven't known that many people in my life. Those I knew before I met Nishtar—I don't think going back to them is an option. Yet.'

'I know *that*. I meant *why* Nishtar?' insisted Timror.

At first Eamilus did not understand what Timror meant. Then he realised what his master was asking. He answered, 'I was hoping, I think, that he would agree to take me on as a student.'

'Why did you come back?'

'I met his other students, and I realised that I did not need to be taught by him.'

'You trust him more than you trust anybody else,' Timror remarked. It was not a question, and Eamilus did not reply.

'What do you know about him?' Timror asked now. Eamilus told him what he knew.

'Do you know anything about who he was before he became a magus?'

'No,' answered Eamilus. He felt surprised that he had never thought about Nishtar's past before. He had always looked upon Nishtar as the powerful sumagus that he was, never really thinking of him as a man. 'Who was he?' he asked Timror.

'His full name is Nishtar Arvarles. He was born in the annus 1508 A.E. That makes him almost three and a half thousand anni old. He was born long before there were kingdoms on Yennthem, long before Rogran became the first king of men in the West. He was born close to where he lives in Blarzonia, although it was not called so then. It was then a rich, prosperous country and there were many wealthy and powerful manors there that were ruled by humans. Nishtar was born to the lord of one such manor—an only and precious child. He learnt much as he grew older, but nothing that encouraged the true potential that he had. His family were afraid that he would be taken from them, and they hid his true nature from him and from everyone else. As a result, he grew up to be a fearsome warrior and a shrewd manor-lord. He married and had a daughter. At the age of thirty, he discovered his true nature by accident. He had gone to meet some other manor-lords to discuss peace pacts, but he did not trust them. He wished he could learn what was on their minds and found that he could! It saved his life, since they had been plotting to assassinate him, and he turned the tables on them. But it awoke him to the reality of his inherent nature.

'He left home and journeyed to Maghem in his desire to reveal his inner self and to learn the art and craft of a magus. At first, none would teach him because he was too old to be a student. He was even treated as a rogue by some. But he persisted. After many trials and tribulations, he succeeded in becoming an accomplished magus. Like in everything else he had done in life, he was committed to excel in this as well. His dedication and his abilities so impressed Beben, a sumagus, that he took Nishtar as his disciple. At that time, no one knew of the sumagi. There were only two—Mesmen and Beben—and they kept their secret hidden from the other magi. Nishtar soon realised that his master was not an ordinary magus and set about to find the secret to Beben's immortality. When he almost succeeded, Beben realised that it would be better to have Nishtar on their side instead of leaving him free to search for such dangerous secrets on his own. He consulted Mesmen, the eldest of the sumagi, and revealed the secret to Nishtar, inducting him among their ranks. Consequently, Nishtar had to pledge to keep the secret of immortality concealed. He was the third magus to become a sumagus, and he is commonly acknowledged by the magi as the most brilliant of them all. It was much later, and through Nishtar's efforts, that the sumagi openly became leaders of Maghem.

'Either by his nature, his lineage or his upbringing, Nishtar has always been drawn to power. He gave up the sword when he became a magus, but that has done nothing to detract from his attraction to power. He lives a deceptively ordinary life, teaching pupils on Yennthem. However, there are many who believe that his true purpose behind staying on this hem is to control its mortals and thereby be at the heart of power here at all times. I do not personally think so, though where Nishtar is concerned, one cannot really say anything with any degree of certainty. He is morally rigorous and driven by unselfish purposes. At the same time, he has an incredibly complicated mind and a streak of ruthlessness. Even those closest to him cannot tell what he really wants or thinks. He can manipulate anyone if he so wishes, and he does not even have to control someone's mind to do so. He is extremely dangerous and extremely munificent at the same time.

'I have told you all this not to imply that you should fear or abhor or avoid Nishtar but because you should know who he is and was, so that you can make up your mind about him in the light of complete information. I, personally, admire and respect Nishtar tremendously. However, I will happily keep my distance from him unless there is need to do otherwise,' Timror finished.

Eamilus was silent. His mind was in a tizzy. He had never heard Timror give such a long speech before. He realised that Timror was genuinely intent on conveying all aspects of Nishtar's character to him. He was grateful for that, though he also resented Timror at one level for shattering his idealistic view of his erstwhile master. He no longer knew what to think about Nishtar, and he felt unhappy about it.

'Thank you for telling me all this,' he said, standing up. 'I am going for a walk now.'

Timror grunted assent and left. Eamilus walked in the beautiful night for horas, trying to come to a decision regarding how he now felt about Nishtar, but failed to reach a conclusion. His head was buzzing with thoughts that he could not calm down. He climbed into a tree and meditated for a long time. This finally helped him relax. When he returned to his chamber, it was long past midnight. He still had not made up his mind, but he had come to accept his ambivalence towards Nishtar. He crawled into bed and immediately fell asleep, at peace with himself.

Two mondans after Timror had told Eamilus about Nishtar's past, he said to his pupil one fine night, 'There is something else about Nishtar that you need to know. Since it concerns your past too, pay attention.'

After their dinner, Eamilus had been sitting in front of the hearth and playing with his rabbits, which had now multiplied to a dozen. He sat up when he heard these words. The rabbits, realising that his attention was now elsewhere, hopped away.

'Have you ever heard of Maheschom or Ealyse or Xanther?' Timror asked.

'Yes,' replied Eamilus, wondering why his teacher was mentioning mythical figures. 'We used to celebrate their birth anniversaries in Haalzona. It was said that they were ancient rulers of the kingdom though I do not remember much of their mythology. Aren't they just legends?'

Timror's eyes gained a faraway look, the way they did whenever he told a story to Eamilus, and he began, 'Legends are born from kernels of truth. The river of time washes everything away. Truth becomes legend, and legend becomes myth. The stories told nowadays about such figures may be myths, but at one time, these people were real enough. Diuras ago, there lived a manor-lord named Xanther in the land that later came to be known as Haalzona. He was rich and powerful and was often called *King* Xanther due to his vast possessions and great power. He was also a sorcerer. When he was twenty-one, he married Eaginna, the daughter of a powerful manor-lord from the north. He had nine daughters by her. When the youngest of them was born, he was almost forty anni of age. He was inordinately fond of the youngest child, though he loved the others greatly too. His daughters were named Mesthona, Porillyn, Dionyse, Ollivyra, Ealyse, Syliatta, Rabedhi, Liravya and Bezashy.

'Unfortunately, his wife died when little Bezashy was only three mondans old. Though Mesthona, the eldest, was only eight anni old at the time, she took charge of the household and her younger sisters. Four anni after Eaginna's death, King Xanther married again, hoping that Zarathie, his new wife, would be a good mother to his daughters while he had to travel far and wide to consolidate his power.

'Zarathie, however, was jealous of the beauty and grace of her young step-daughters. Once, while King Xanther was away, she buried them alive in the garden, unable to bear their presence any longer. When Xanther returned, she lied to him that they had run away. Believing her, Xanther cast a powerful spell to call them back. The next morning, nine flowering plants, laden with rich, fragrant flowers, sprung from the ground where the girls had been buried. These plants were unusual; they bloomed in all seasons without requiring any water or care. The nine flowers stood for the predominant qualities of Xanther's nine daughters: Iris, for wisdom; Magnolia, for nobility; Red clover, for industry; Bluebell, for humility;

Thyme, for courage; Bittersweet, for truth; Wallflower, for loyalty; Elderflower, for compassion; and Daisy, for innocence, hope and faith.

'The flowers were so beautiful and fragrant that Lady Zarathie just could not do without having them for her chamber. The gardener's boy tried to pluck the flowers but they climbed out of his reach. He called the gardener who, too, tried to pluck the flowers but failed. Many tried to pluck these fascinating and wonderful flowers, but every time someone tried to pluck them, they rose higher into the air, out of the reach of the person trying to pluck them. Zarathie herself tried in the end but failed. In her anger, she asked the gardener to destroy the flowers but, by then, King Xanther had understood the truth. He punished Zarathie and all those who had helped her commit the unforgivable crime. He spent days crying among the nine flowering plants, begging their forgiveness, and calling to them to return to him.

'One night, he had a dream. In the dream, he saw nine beautiful maidens. They called him 'father' and told him that they were not lost to him forever. They told him that they would return to their mortal forms when they were finally plucked. But only worthy suitors who deserved them would be able to pluck them. However, they warned him, if they were not plucked before the age of twenty-one, they would forever remain in their current form.

'King Xanther had pronouncements made throughout all the lands that any who could pluck one of these wonderful flowers would receive one of his daughters in marriage. Over seven anni, many tried and failed. Then, in his fifty-second annus, Xanther received an unusual visitor, a draconian named Ardumel from the region that later became known as Blarzonia. Though unsure of whether the young draconian was suitable for one of his daughters, he welcomed his guest as he had welcomed all others, and accorded him due hospitality. He was surprised at the young draconian's depth of knowledge and wisdom. The next day, Ardumel succeeded in plucking the Iris from the tallest plant almost without effort.

'As soon as he touched the plant, the flower came away into his hand. The plant shimmered and dissolved away, leaving in its place a lovely young draconian woman of twenty. Although she was now a draconian, there was no doubt in Xanther's mind that she was one of the maidens that he had seen in his dream. She confirmed that she was Mesthona, his eldest daughter. Because Ardumel was a draconian, that was the form that she had taken while returning to the world of the living. If Xanther had needed further proof that Ardumel was the most suitable husband for her, this was it. He unhesitatingly gave his eldest daughter's hand in marriage to the young draconian.

'The next annus, he received another unusual visitor, an equesar named Akhetash. Xanther's experience with Ardumel had opened his eyes, and when Akhetash succeeded in bringing Porillyn back to life, as an equesar maiden,

Xanther happily gave her to Akhetash in marriage. The next annus, Dionyse was revived by a young man named Castillon from the far south of eastern Elthrusia. The annus after that, Ollivyra was brought back by another extraordinary young man named Thybald from the far north of the region. Ealyse's destined groom turned out to be one of Xanther's own soldiers named Maheschom who had risen through the ranks very quickly due to his great courage and valour. Syliatta was claimed by a phrix named Ranhenh while Rabedhi and Liravya were returned to life by and wed to two young men named Trakurth and Seolaston from lands that subsequently came to be known as Mayndoda and Wyurr respectively. These eight anni were the most joyous and enlightening for Xanther as he came to meet such extraordinary representatives of the races that populated the East and found that he had known very little about them before. He was glad that he could give his daughters to such worthy husbands. In the annus of 1587 A.E., it was Bezashy's turn, and King Xanther, now almost sixty anni old, waited eagerly to see who would come to claim his youngest daughter's hand.

'However, no worthy suitor was found. The day of Bezashy's twenty-first birthday passed, and Xanther was devastated. That night he had another dream. He dreamt of one of the nine maidens who had come to him in his earlier dream. She was the loveliest of them all, and she glowed in the moonlight as she strolled in Xanther's garden. She was sad, and silver tears rolled down her cheeks. She was smiling at the same time. It broke Xanther's heart to see Bezashy thus. For, he had no doubt that that was who the maiden was. He begged her forgiveness, but she comforted him. She told him that all that had come to pass had been the work of destiny. He should not blame himself. She promised him that she would bloom in his garden forever, never dying, never fading.

'From that day forth, the daisy became a revered flower in all of the East. The eight suitors who had married Xanther's daughters all proved to be remarkable individuals, and either they or their direct descendants founded the eight countries of the East. Ardumel and Mesthona's grandson Conatin founded the kingdom of Blarzonia. Akhetash founded the tribal state of Qeezsh. Castillon and Dionyse's great-grandson Ishenar founded Illafanka. Thybald and Ollivyra's son Olveron founded Waurlen. Maheschom founded Haalzona. Ranhenh and Syliatta's granddaughter Herenna founded the hive federation of Mirhisd. Trakurth and Rabedhi's son Trabedh founded the kingdom of Mayndoda. And Seolaston and Liravya's grandson Barhamos founded Wyurr.

'Each of the sisters came to visit their father the annus after Bezashy's twenty-first birthday. They mourned their youngest sister and took with them one of the stalks of the magical daisy plant from Xanther's garden. They planted these in their own gardens, and the plants bloomed there as well. When King Xanther died at the ripe old age of eighty-six, the original daisy plant in his garden vanished, though the eight that had been born out of it continued to flourish in the gardens of Bezashy's eight sisters. When the eight countries were later established, the daisy plants were transplanted to the gardens of the eight founding families of the East and continued to flourish there. These countries were friends and allies and helped each other prosper. Every annus, on Bezashy's birthday, they sent bouquets of daisies to each other to remember her. This tradition continued through the diuras, although all forgot how it had begun or what its significance was, until all the kingdoms of the East fell to the forces of evil one by one. It is said, though, that as long as the descendants of the original founding families of the East survive, so will the daisies.'

Timror stopped after telling the long story. Eamilus had listened spellbound as the sad-sweet tale had unfolded, fascinated by the incredible history of his country's foundation. He suddenly remembered that Timror had said at the beginning of the tale that it was connected to Nishtar and to his past. He asked Timror about it.

'This story *is* connected to you and Nishtar,' Timror replied. 'The lines of the founding families remained unbroken either through sons or daughters until they fell. You are descended from Maheschom, father to son, in direct line. Which means that you are related to Xanther and his wife Eaginna through your ancestress Ealyse. Eaginna, Xanther's first wife was the only daughter of Nishtar Arvarles.'

Eamilus started. If Eaginna had indeed been Nishtar's daughter, and if he himself was a direct descendant of Eaginna's daughter Ealyse, it meant…it meant… Eamilus could not bring himself to acknowledge the enormousness of what it meant. Had Nishtar known all this when he had taken Eamilus in? Was that why he had been so fond of Eamilus, because Eamilus was his descendant? The boy's head reeled. Timror took pity on him and sent him to bed. But Eamilus could not sleep. Why hadn't Nishtar told him all this? Was he ashamed of Eamilus? No, that could not be true—had not Nishtar told Eamilus that he was proud of him? Then why had Nishtar hidden such a momentous fact from him? And why had Timror decided to reveal it to him all of a sudden? What was his agenda? The comment about the belief regarding the daisies haunted Eamilus quite as much. Timror had said—'as long as the descendants of the original royal families of the East survive, so will the daisies.' Could it be true? Eamilus fell asleep trying to recall if he had ever seen any magical daisies in the palace garden at Opeltra.

Chapter 6

REFUGE FROM STORM

In 5006 A.E., Bolsana faced a difficult vernurt. Coughs, colds and fevers assaulted almost every resident of the village. The healer found himself running out of medicines long before the season was over. Misa volunteered to get more from Atmut and set off in the cart driven by her mare, Marsil. On the way, she discovered that the entire region had been plagued by the same ailments. The apothecaries in Atmut were running dangerously low because of their own citizens' needs as well as increased demand for the medicines from nearby areas. They helpfully pointed Misa to nearby Hummold which, surprisingly, had escaped the epidemic. Misa hurried to Hummold. She was immensely relieved when she found well-stocked apothecaries there.

On the way back, Misa began to feel a little concerned about the weather. The sky was low with dark, threatening clouds. It was the end of Samrer, and chances of a snowstorm were low, but one could never tell. Even though she had the little cart with her, and Marsil was intelligent and reliable, there wasn't much that she could do if a storm arose. She still had a long way to go. She thought about Mizu. She had left him with the widow Molinee, and he would be safe. He would miss her, true, but he would not want for care or comfort. She hoped that there would be no storm. She missed him too.

Her hopes were dashed a mere forty miles from Hummold. A fierce snowstorm blew up so suddenly that she did not get the chance to take shelter. Everything turned white in a matter of moments. The wild wind howled around her and the little cart, threatening to overturn it and knock her down. The snow drove down in sheets, obscuring everything in her path. The cold was like a ravaging dog, biting with the ferocity of vicious hunger. Misa climbed out and took hold of Marsil's bridle. The mare was scared. Misa rubbed her head and whispered to her to calm her down. She tried to shield the mare from the oncoming blasts of snow with her body while manoeuvring her to a more sheltered spot. It was a difficult task given the terrible visibility and the freezing cold. Misa could not see two feet in front of her. She felt scared. The snowstorm was far more violent than any she had experienced. If she and Marsil did not get out of it soon, they would both be dead within the hora. She tried not to panic. She began to lead the tall, strong mare perpendicular to the direction of the winds, praying that they would soon find some shelter. The cart was too much of a burden for Marsil, so Misa let it go. It was a huge loss, but she had no choice. If she had to save herself and Marsil, she could not hold on to the cart.

Even with the cart gone, it was a fight for every breath of air that they inhaled, every step of ground that they trod. Soon, both mare and mistress were exhausted. The snow was coming down in furious eddies all around them now, and they could not see even half a foot ahead. Misa started walking with one hand extended to feel the way. Her hand suddenly touched the rough bark of a tree. Still feeling her way around the tree, she positioned Marsil along it so that the mare would be a little sheltered. She knew that any attempt at sheltering was practically futile. She hugged Marsil's neck and stood calmly, both of them shivering like they had the ague. This was it. This was the end! She had never imagined that she would die like this, far from all those she loved, in the middle of nowhere, like a homeless animal. She wanted to cry, but the tears froze at the corners of her eyes. She stood there, stroking the mare's neck and whispering through half-frozen lips that it would be all right. Around them, the storm raged like a wild beast intent on breaking out of its cage, the wind shrieked and howled like an insane monster on a rampage and the cold crawled into their very souls.

When she heard a voice calling out in the middle of the storm, Misa thought that either she had died or was hallucinating. Of course, no one would be calling out to her. She was miles away from the nearest town or village. No one knew where she was. In fact, even *she* did not know where she was. Who would be calling to her? Who would be out in this storm looking for her? Then she heard the voice again, closer this time, and louder. It was not a hallucination! She shouted back to whoever was calling. She hoped it would not prove to be a robber or murderer. That would be just perfect! When no one replied, she gave up hope. Perhaps whoever had been looking for her had not heard her cries and had moved on beyond the range of hearing. Her heart fell. Then it rose again as she heard a man's voice shouting quite clearly.

'Where are you? Can you hear me?'

She yelled back as loudly as she could, 'I am here! Next to this tree! I can hear you. Can you follow my voice? Please help me!'

Very soon, she could see a faint glow of light coming through the swirls of snow. Her heart soared. She shouted again and again, her voice growing hoarse with the effort. Marsil, sensing that something was afoot, neighed loudly. Then, to Misa's immense relief, a figure broke through the thick curtain of snow. It was an old man, she realised, though he could have been easily mistaken for a snowman. His hair and beard were white with caked snow, his clothes had taken on a layer of it too and the brim of his hat was deeply lined with the white powder. Without a word, he took hold of Marsil's bridle and began to lead the horse through the storm. Misa, holding on to Marsil from the other side, followed. She had no idea how the old man could tell where they were going, yet she had no choice but to trust him. It was better than trusting their luck with the storm. Besides, he was really old, and she was armed. What could he do to her?

Misa realised that they were going uphill. This surprised her, but she said nothing. Soon, to her immense relief, they were out of the thick of the storm. It was still snowing, and the wind was still blustering around them, but the storm was mild compared to what they had been stuck in only a while ago. She could also see a hut in the distance—a shepherd's hut. A wicket gate and a narrow path led up to it. So the old man was a shepherd. Where were his sheep, she wondered. Had they got lost in the storm? Had he been searching for them when he came upon her and Marsil? She hoped not. It seemed such a pity. They were at the gate now. It looked quaint. There was neither wall nor fence attached to it. Just a gate in the middle of a meadow. Misa smiled to herself. Perhaps the old shepherd was whimsical. The old man opened the gate and led them inside. Misa gasped.

They were no longer standing at the edge of a storm but upon a forested path. All signs of the storm had vanished. Behind her was dense forest through which the path meandered away into the distance. It was as if they had passed into a different world through that gate. Misa looked around her in wonderment. Was she hallucinating? Was all of this nothing but a trick that her dying mind was playing on her?

'No, this is not a hallucination,' the old man suddenly said, as if reading her mind. 'This is magic of sorts, an illusion. The storm is still out there if you prefer that to this landscape.'

'Thank you for saving us,' Misa said, not responding to his comment. What *could* she say?

'I'm glad that I could reach you on time,' said the old man. 'Now, if you don't mind, let us proceed to my cottage where a fire and hot soup are awaiting us.'

The two of them again started forward, Marsil walking contentedly between them. Neither of them said a word. When they reached the hut, the shepherd asked Misa to make herself comfortable while he stabled Marsil. Misa was reluctant to leave Marsil in a stranger's hands, but the old man said with a twinkle in his eyes, 'Don't worry, your mare will still be there—hale and hearty—when you want her back.' Misa couldn't very well protest. The man had rescued her and Marsil from inevitable death. She could not tell him to his face that she did not trust him!

The shepherd proved to be a generous host. He plied her with warm blankets, hot soup and fresh bread until she was quite herself once more. She thanked him with heartfelt gratitude and promised to repay his kindness if she could.

'If there is anything that I can do for you, please do not hesitate to tell me. I am eternally in your debt.'

'Dear lady, be careful what words you choose to express your gratitude. One never knows when one is called upon to keep one's word,' he said amiably. He was a thin and tall old man with a long beard that was white even without a layer of snow sticking to it. He looked completely harmless. Yet there was something intense and deep in his eyes that stopped Misa from labelling him a harmless old man. There was something latently dangerous about him. She suspected that he was a magus, a powerful one at that. No ordinary shepherd could have created the illusion of the forest. She was still grateful to him, though.

'I mean what I say, kind sir. If you ask me to keep my word, I will,' she responded.

'We will see about that. For now, tell me if you are feeling warm and comfortable.'

'Yes, I am. Thank you very much. I feel immensely better. Escaping from certain death probably has that effect!' she jested.

'I suppose you are right,' the magus agreed, puffing on a pipe now. Misa wondered when he had lit it. His hands had been empty only a momon ago. He smiled mischievously.

'I see that you have guessed who—or rather *what*—I am. I'm afraid that puts you at an advantage since I know nothing about you.'

Misa narrated a fictitious version of her life. The magus frowned. He looked annoyed. He stood up and, staring straight into her eyes, said, 'Please do not insult my hospitality. If you wish not to tell me who you are, say so honestly. I shall not insist on learning your identity. But do not lie to me.'

Misa was taken aback. She also felt guilty. She looked as upset as she felt.

'There, there,' said the old magus kindly, his annoyance evaporating. He sat back down and patted her hand. 'Do not get upset. I shall not provoke you further. I am sorry that I spoke harshly. If you wish to, you can tell me who you are. If not, your identity is your own. It is poor kindness that stands on expectation of any kind.'

Misa apologised for lying. She debated whether to tell the magus the truth about herself. She felt a strange desire to do so. She felt that she could trust him. For the first time in a long time, she was overcome with the desire to unburden herself. She had told Leormane, the chief of Bolsana, about her past. But he had almost dragged the tale out of her, and she had given in to his demand for the truth for her son's sake. With the old man, Misa felt that the truth was not only desirable but also preferable.

'You have saved my life. And though I know nothing more about you than that you are a magus, I owe it to you to tell the truth,' she said. 'If you betray me, then you can only take back what you have yourself given. So, I have no regrets,' Misa said. Then her story came gushing out, every painful detail and every happy moment carefully recapitulated for the man who had saved her.

She told him about her life as a seleighe princess in Azluren, about her parents, King Melson and Queen Felicia, about her brothers Melissen, Felicim and Felissom and her sister, Felisa. She told him how Melissen had trained her and Prince Feyanor of Ashperth in the use of arms and how she had taken to warrior training like a fish to water. She became grim when she narrated the circumstances of her marriage to Arlem, King of Samion, but a smile returned to her lips when she talked about how she had been happy with Arlem and his twin brother, Arslan, despite a rocky start to their relationship. She touched her belly unconsciously when she told the old magus about becoming pregnant. Shadow covered her face as she recounted the last days of Arlem's life and her escape from Fassinth, the capital of Samion, with Arslan's help. She shivered despite the warmth when she talked about the encounter with Holexar's soldiers in the Ersafin and the mysterious circumstances of her son's birth. The rest of her story was easily told; after wandering about for a long time and killing many of her enemies, she had disguised herself and her son as humans and settled down in human territory to escape her enemies.

The magus was a good listener; he did not interrupt her even once. He asked a few clarifying questions now and then but let her tell her story in her own way. She poured out her soul that evening while the storm raged outside and the sun went down into the west. When she finished her tale, she felt light, relieved.

'And that is the story of my life,' she concluded. 'What do you wish to do now that you know the truth about me?'

'What do you wish me to do, Your Majesty?' he asked.

The words sounded odd to her unused ears.

'Please do not call me that,' she said with a smile. 'No one has in over five anni. I am simply Misa now.'

The old man nodded and repeated his question, 'What do you want me to do, *Misa*?'

'Nothing,' she replied. 'I told you the truth because it felt like the right thing to do.'

'Then I shall do nothing,' the magus said. 'Though, I suppose, it is only fair that I tell you a little more about myself. I am, as you have guessed, a magus. My name is Oram Ashar. I am also a shepherd. I live out here within this bubble of mild climate because I am an old man and because my sheep remain healthier here. Yes, it is an illusion, but not entirely so. It is real enough in every way to those who experience it. I am known in the towns and villages around here as the

Old Man of the Hills. The people of these towns and villages often visit me for medicines for themselves or their livestock. None of them sees this magical forest around my house, though. I save it for special guests like you.' He grinned. Misa, too, smiled.

'As a magus, I have the power to influence thoughts, but I do not believe in intruding into mortals' lives unbidden. Everyone has the right to live his or her life and to make his or her choices. We are given this life to make of it what we will—a glory or a wreck—by our own devices. Today, I broke my rule about non-interference. I had a premonition that you needed help when the storm arose. So I went looking for you. It is not often that I have premonitions, so I was surprised when I had one about a complete stranger. I am glad that I did have it, though. It seems that I have brought you more than physical comfort, and I am glad of it.'

'So am I,' Misa responded. 'And I stand by my word that I would do anything in my power to repay your debt.'

'I will hold you to your word someday,' Oram said with a smile. 'But are you certain that there is nothing that I can do for you?'

Misa thought for a few momons before saying, 'Actually there *is* one thing that you could do for me. Not now, not for many anni perhaps. I would not ask you if it weren't for my son. I am already so indebted to you! Perhaps I have no right to ask this of you. But my son may need your help someday. He is too young now to know or understand all that I have told you. I hope to tell him when he is old enough to comprehend. He will need help then to reclaim that which is his by right. Would you help him?'

'I will help him then or at any other time that he needs my help, my dear,' Oram said. 'I shall help him because I asked you if you needed anything, and this is what you have asked for. I cannot go back on my word.' He felt a surge of affection for the dethroned and exiled queen of Samion. She was so brave and so fair and so alone in the world. He could not help admiring her courage. He wanted to help her. Not because she needed it but because it made him feel that he was doing something worthwhile. And in the long anni of being alive, he had found very little that had made him feel that way.

'Will you keep my secret?' she begged him. 'There is one other who knows who I am, and he will never betray my trust. This secrecy is necessary to keep my son safe.'

'I promise you that I will keep your secret until you permit me to reveal it or circumstances force me to do so for the good of your son. Will that suffice?'

Misa clutched Oram's hands gratefully. 'I don't know how to thank you for all that you have done for me today. I don't know why you have been so kind to me, but I will never forget it,' she declared.

'Honestly,' said Oram, 'even I don't know how I sensed your troubles today or why I feel compelled to help you. But I believe in destiny. And something tells me that it is destiny that has brought us together. Destiny works in mysterious ways to accomplish its purpose. I do not presume to predict what destiny has in store for either of us, but I feel it in my bones that our chance encounter today will have significant repercussions for both of our futures. Whether for good or evil I cannot say. I can only hope that it will be for good.'

'I hope so too,' Misa said, though she did not completely understand the old man's words.

'And now,' Oram said cheerfully, standing up and stretching, 'I think that the storm is over. I suppose that you would like to be on your way. I will guide you down the hill. I think I can also retrieve your cart for you. However, night has fallen while we have been engaged in our pleasant conversation. I would very much prefer if you spend the night here and depart tomorrow morning.'

Chapter 7

ORAM UNDERTAKES A JOURNEY

After his encounter with Misa, Oram found himself more disturbed than he had been in anni. He made up his mind to travel to the North to investigate what was going on there. He needed only a little time to set his affairs in order for the period of his absence. He arranged for his neighbour Okker to look after his flock during that time. Having ensured the safety of his animals, Oram packed a deceptively small bundle and set off on his long journey on the fourth of Beybasel in 5006 A.E. He dressed like an ordinary shepherd in woollen leggings, a woollen shirt, stout boots, a fleece vest and a coat that reached below his knees. The only unusual part of his appearance was his wide-brimmed hat; shepherds usually went bareheaded. A stout walking stick completed his attire. It was almost somminar, but the North was cooler than the rest of Elthrusia, especially outdoors at night. Oram anticipated having to spend several nights in haystacks or under hedges. A thick woollen cloak was added to his belongings to cope with that.

The first stop on Oram's route was Fassinth, the capital of Samion. As he travelled to the northern city, he remembered a similar journey he had undertaken at Nishtar's behest not that long ago. He had come North chasing rumours of sightings of Vyidie, the Guardian of Birth. Although it had been less than two anni ago, it felt as if ages had passed since then. So much had changed after that fateful meeting at which the sumagi had quarrelled and decided to go their separate ways! Oram had returned to his pastures, telling himself that he would be happy to remain a simple shepherd forever. But the encounter with Misa had changed everything. On his previous visit North, Oram had sensed that something was amiss; he had not had time or inclination to investigate. Now, after his conversation with Misa, he rued that he had not been more inquisitive about the affairs of mortals during that trip. It might have saved him this one.

Oram had long since realised that he had a special talent for befriending others, especially the ordinary mortals who lived ordinary lives. His ordinary looks, especially when he was dressed as a shepherd, lowered their guards. His status as a magus was enough to open almost any door, and his affable manner convinced others to open up to him. He was a good listener, and material temptations of food and drink provided at local inns were often a good accompaniment to long, informative discussions with those who were rarely seen but themselves saw everything. Cooks, gardeners, servants, guards, shopkeepers, aides, soldiers, traders, healers, inn-keepers, butchers, and others of their ilk were the primary sources of Oram's information. They readily poured out their stories to a patient and sympathetic listener who, additionally, was all too happy to help them with medicines, sage advice or domestic magic. They hardly realised that the exchange was rather unfair; the information they provided Oram was far more valuable than whatever they received in return.

In Fassinth, Oram almost failed to enter the city. Many questions and searches of his possessions and person later, he was allowed to enter with dire warnings about disturbing the peace. This peace, which the guards enjoined him to maintain on pain of severe punishment, turned out to be as mythical as the law and order that he was told to abide by. Through meticulous and careful efforts, Oram learnt that Holexar reigned in Samion with an iron hand and a bottomless pit of greed in his heart. Citizens were groaning under the burden of taxes—legal and extorted—on which Holexar and his cohorts were growing wealthier every day. The numbers of the poor were rising alarmingly as crops failed and jobs declined as eighes' ability to pay for work dwindled every day. Refugees from the countryside swelled the masses of the poor in cities and towns, fighting for the scraps of food available there.

Holexar was a vicious king who secured his rule through terror and blood. Even the smallest hint of rebellion was ruthlessly crushed. Those who were guilty of *treason*—real, imagined or framed—were made examples of. Their carcasses hung from gibbets in the city square where crows and vultures grew fat on their flesh. Citizens were forbidden from travelling out of the country on pain of death. Scores of nobles who had been loyal to the previous royal family had mysteriously died or disappeared or were rotting in the dungeons. Rumour had it that Holexar had poisoned the previous king, Arlem, though no one dared to say it in so many words. The queen had disappeared almost six anni ago, as had the previous king's brother, Arslan. Some said that both had been killed by Holexar. Some said that they had conspired and killed the king and had then fled the country. Everyone—from the topmost courtier to the lowliest peasant—was terrified of Holexar. Soldiers were in control of everything and did as they pleased. They reported to the king and to no one else. With no way to complain, there was no chance of redressal. Whispers questioned Holexar's mysterious origins. Half-spoken sentences and fear-filled eyes told of the decline of a prosperous country into a dictatorship dominated by want, fear and brutality.

What Oram saw and heard at Fassinth and elsewhere in Samion confirmed what Misa had told him: Holexar had murdered Arlem, and possibly Arslan as well, and had usurped the throne, levying the harshest measures to ensure that residents of Samion were too terrified to rebel. What Oram failed to learn was even more significant than what he did manage to learn: firstly, why had Holexar, who had served Arlem's father faithfully, suddenly turned on the royal family; secondly, when the war with Lyisl that had overthrown King Rannzen taken place; and, thirdly, how was Holexar (who had no wife or children) planning for succession. Not one whisper pertaining to these matters reached Oram's ears despite his extensive search for information. He decided that it would not be possible, at least at that time, to learn the answers to the first and third questions. The answer to the second question, though, could be found in Lyisl. So Oram made his way to Sepwin even though his original plan had been to retrace Misa's steps as she had fled from Samion. He was very curious about the birth of her son. He meant to discover the mysteries behind his birth and the following days during which Misa had remained unconscious.

Oram's experience in Sepwin was diametrically opposite to that in Fassinth. No one was bothered with questioning his purpose of visiting the city. The guards waved him into the capital along with a hundred other bedraggled and chaotic travellers. He faced another problem, though: whereas in Fassinth, he had received little but cohesive information, in Samion he was told too many disjointed tales. It took him a while to piece together the information, but when he did, a clear picture began to emerge. Two wars had been fought between Lyisl and Samion. The first had been an attack by Lyisl on Samion following incursions into Lyisl by soldiers of Samion. This war, which had taken place in Yodirin of 4998 A.E., had ended in disaster for the army of Lyisl. Oram wondered why Melicie had not told him about this war. Was it possible that she had not been aware of it? How could a queen remain unaware of such a critical event? He did not believe that she had concealed information from him deliberately. Something did not feel right. The second 'war' had been more of an invasion. It had taken place in Kawitor of 5001 A.E. By then, Oram knew, Arlem was already dead. He had been too ill for too long to have declared or planned it. It had to have been Holexar's doing. Which gave rise to the pertinent question: had the first war been Holexar's doing as well?

Oram further learnt that the throne of Lyisl had been taken over by Limossen, who had been the chief of its armies and had sided with the invading army of Samion. Most interestingly, this army had returned to Samion after putting Limossen on the throne of Lyisl. Conquest, apparently, had not been their goal. But why? Why would they march right into the capital and capture the throne only to leave Limossen master of the country? Unless, of course, Limossen was Holexar's puppet. That explained his complicity with the invading army and Limossen's capture of power in Lyisl.

King Rannzen and his family had fled. All those loyal to him had been put to death. The king had returned to reclaim his right, but he had returned alone and had been captured and executed. Chaos now reigned supreme in Lyisl as Limossen showed no interest at all in administration or law and order. The country, whose once-full coffers had been disastrously drained by Rannzen through his incompetence, was now on the verge of penury. Its army was a farce, and it was probably nothing more than lack of interest that prevented its neighbours from occupying it. Crops failed, but the king did not care; poverty and illness ran rampant, but the king was happy as long as he and his family were steeped in luxury. Small pockets of prosperity existed where local lords still held fast to their sanity and to their holding's worth, but these were under attack from the expanding anarchy and depredation.

One name cropped up several times during discussions of the first war as well as of Limossen's betrayal of Rannzen, who had been a loved though incompetent ruler. Lord Sanfion. Oram was told that Lord Sanfion had led the army that had attacked Samion in the first war. Later, though, he had tried to organise a coup with the help of Holexar. Oram wondered how such an alliance could have been struck. He suspected that it had had something to do with Sanfion's capture in Samion and his subsequent unconditional release. But if both Sanfion and Limossen had been allied with Holexar, why had the latter led the campaign to arrest the former? Had he been merely getting rid of a rival? And why had Sanfion, not Limossen, led the armies in the first war despite the fact that Limossen had been the commander-in-chief? There was more to the conspiracy than a simple coup with the help of a foreign army. Sanfion, Rannzen, Limossen, Holexar and Arlem all seemed to be pieces of the same puzzle.

As Oram learnt more and more, an image began to emerge in his mind, but there were still many pieces missing. Not least was the mystery of the vanished family of King Rannzen. Where had they disappeared? Had they died? Was that why the king had returned on what had been an obviously suicidal mission? Or were they somewhere safe, hidden, and far from the clutches of their enemies, as Misa and Mizu were? While enquiring about the late king's family, Oram learnt something that bewildered him even more. He had known about King Rannzen's son, but he learnt now that a daughter had been born to King Rannzen not long before the invasion by the Samionite army. In fact, she had been born on the first of Kawitor, 5001 A.E.

Oram's mind was in a tizzy. He remembered Nishtar saying that only three boys had been born on that date, the day mentioned in the prophecy of Kawiti, the Guardian of Immortality, the day when Astoreth and Zavak were expected to be born again. Had Nishtar been wrong? Or had his investigations thrown up a false clue? It would have made more sense, he thought, if Rannzen's second child had been a son. Oram's perplexity was increased manifold after talking to the healer who had been in attendance on Queen Iramina at the time of the child's birth. When asked by Oram, the healer, in a state of total inebriation, first said that the queen had given birth to a boy but immediately retracted his statement, declaring that she had given birth to a girl. Further probing proved the second assertion to be correct. But Oram could not help wondering how such an experienced healer could be confused about the sex of a child he had delivered, especially a royal one, even when drunk!

Oram also tried to find out what had happened to Sanfion's family after his arrest and death. He managed to learn that Sanfion had had a wife but no children. She had disappeared soon after Sanfion's arrest. Oram was beginning to feel that all his enquiries were going to end in the disappearances of his quarries. He did not like this. Too many important figures had disappeared from the scene. Too much discrepancy existed between what people thought was happening and what appeared to be actually happening. There was too wide a gap between the facade and the undercurrents in Lyisl. It was highly suspicious and worrisome. Though he was curious about what had happened to Rannzen's as well as Sanfion's families, Oram decided to go to Penin from Samion. His primary objective had been to find out about the days missing from Misa's memory, and he hoped to find some answers there. He could not afford to be dragged into the mire of chaos that was Lyisl's past and present. He decided to travel through the Ersafin, like Misa had done when she had escaped from Fassinth.

Yodirin was midway through by the time Oram found himself camping under some trees one night, close to the bridge across the Ulmyon River. Penin was not much further. He would reach it in three days. He sat by a warm fire, eating stale bread and cheese when a young trapper approached him. The trapper was a kereighe, he noticed, with very dark, brooding features and an aura dense enough to look almost solid. He was barely in his thirties (the equivalent of a human youth in his early twenties) but looked world-weary. Oram offered him the comfort of his fire and a share of his meagre supper. The youth accepted both gratefully. The two sat by the fire, eating their food in companionable silence. Oram was observing the youth closely. It appeared to make the latter self-conscious.

'I do not wish to impose upon you,' the youth said to Oram uncomfortably. 'If you wish, I shall leave.'

'Oh no!' Oram said. 'I do not feel imposed upon at all. By all means, stay. It is nice to have some company upon such a solitary and eerie night. I was just wondering what someone as young as you might have been doing here so late at night.'

'I live here,' said the youth simply.

'You live here in the forest?' asked Oram, surprised.

'Not in the forest, no,' the youth explained. 'In a village at its edge. Although, I do spend most of my time here, day and night alike. I like it here. It is beautiful.'

'It is dangerous too,' Oram reminded him.

'Yes, but where is the pleasure in enjoying something beautiful if you do not have to take a little risk to do so?' the youth said, smiling mischievously. 'I have seen such strange things in this forest at night! If I told you, you would not believe.'

'Try me!' Oram said, encouraging the strange youth to share his experiences.

'I have seen magical trees that glow at night but look ordinary enough in daylight. They burst forth into flowers that dazzle the eyes and fruits that are like balls of fire, as soon as the sun sets. As soon as it rises again, the flowers and fruits disappear, and the leaves and branches return to the normal colours of green and brown,' the youth described, getting animated at the opportunity to share his extraordinary encounters.

'Wow!' declared Oram. 'It must be wonderful to see such sights. What else have you seen?'

The youth replied, 'I have seen lilies that bloom upon the forest floor all of a sudden and have such a strong fragrance that you would faint if you breathed it in too long. Then they disappear just as suddenly.'

Oram felt a shiver run down his spine. He had heard a similar story when he had come to search for signs of Vyidie's presence a couple of anni ago. Nishtar had dismissed it as a hallucination by the person who had seen the lilies. A tiny ball of irritation at Nishtar's highhandedness flared in Oram's mind but was subdued almost at once. There was no point in being annoyed with Nishtar. He was what he was. At least, Oram was no longer paddling the boat where Nishtar pointed. The youth, in the meantime, was continuing with tales of miraculous things that he had seen in the forest.

'There is a hut deep within the Ersafin that was once occupied by three witches. Extremely powerful dark witches—lechs they are called to distinguish them from the benevolent ones. The three lechs no longer live there, but the hut still stands. It is said that they were so powerful that even after dying, their ghosts could return to Yennthem to do the bidding of their successor one last time, and that they could make even time stand still. I have seen that hut. It gives off such an aura of evil and pain that I have not dared to enter it.'

'What is the strangest thing that you have seen here?' Oram asked, trying to participate. He could not be sure that the youth wasn't making stories up for his benefit.

The youth thought for a minura before answering, 'The strangest thing I saw was the birth of a child. It was almost six anni ago. I had taken shelter in an oak grove when a seleighee came riding along and took shelter in the same grove. Then some soldiers arrived, chasing her, and she fought them single-handedly. But they were too many in number for her, and she was with child. She had almost finished them all off when she fell on the ground and went into labour. I realised that the

The youth held out an armguard to a stunned Oram.

baby was about to be born, and I wanted to help. But before I could go to assist her, someone else stepped in. A tall, warrior-like female, who could have been an eighee or a zedrel. She killed the two remaining soldiers and then delivered the baby, though the pregnant eighee was unconscious by then. The second eighee then led the unconscious one and her baby away on her horse—the unconscious eighee's horse. I thought it was all a dream, but the next morning, I found this on the ground though there was no other sign that anything had happened there that night.'

The youth held out an armguard to a stunned Oram. The sumagus could not believe his luck. Here was someone who had just described Melicie's encounter with the soldiers of Holexar perfectly. He had even told Oram what had happened *after* Melicie had fainted. Oram could not believe his luck. Was the youth telling the truth? Had he really been there that night? How else could he have known what had happened? But Misa had said nothing about a young trapper's presence that night. Had she not known about the youth's presence? Oram was more confused than ever. His eyes fell upon the armguard that the youth was holding out. It was made of some kind of alloy and shone white in the light of the fire. It was encrusted with glimmering pale green precious stones, possibly crystals of peridot, in the shape of a crossed lily and an arrow. It must have been extremely valuable. Why had the youth not sold it?

'It is exquisite,' Oram remarked, finding his tongue. 'It must be very expensive.'

'Yes, I am sure it is. But I haven't sold it because it is priceless to me,' the youth answered, catching Oram's drift. 'It is the only proof I have of what happened that night. Who would believe my story if I had no proof to back it up? Without evidence, the greatest truth is nothing more than fiction, is it not?'

'You are quite an unusual kereighe!' Oram remarked. 'You look like you are barely out of your adolescent anni, but you talk like a greybeard!'

'Well, things aren't always what they seem!' remarked the youth cheerfully, putting the armguard away.

Oram wanted to ask the youth for the armguard. He was sure that it was a clue—perhaps the most important one that he had found so far—and could lead to the solution of the mystery of Mizu's birth. But he did not ask the youth for it. Obviously, it was precious to the young trapper, and it would not be right to ask him to give it up. The two continued to talk for a while longer, discussing other strange things that the trapper had purportedly seen in Ersafin. When they began to feel sleepy, the youth volunteered to take the first watch. Though Oram had already taken measures to ensure that they would be safe at night, he kept this information from the youth to conceal his true identity. He agreed to take the second watch and went to sleep. When he awoke, it was already morning. The fire had burned out a long time ago. Oram sat up and looked for his companion of the night before. There was no sign of the young trapper. He would have given it all up as a dream but for the object lying on the ground next to the ashes of the previous night's fire. It was the armguard that the youth had shown him. This was uncannily like the youth's recollection of the morning after Mizu's birth. Oram gave an involuntary shudder. Underneath the armguard, scrawled into the ground, were a few words that obscured rather than clarified what had happened—'Faith is the proof of truth, not truth the proof of faith'.

Oram started on his way to Penin that day. Upon reaching there, he headed to the inn where Misa had found herself on gaining consciousness. He had been shaken by the mysterious nocturnal encounter with the enigmatic trapper. The sight of familiar activities in the town helped soothe his nerves. He received another shock, though, when he discovered that the landlady of the inn was someone whom he had met once before. Her name was Missus Kulter. She was one of those whom he had interviewed when he had been on Vyidie's trail. Was it coincidence? Oram was beginning to think that there was no such thing, that everything was part of the same puzzle, that every thread was part of the same tangled web. When they had last met, Missus Kulter had claimed to have a good memory for faces. This proved to be true when she recalled Oram easily.

'Aren't you the one who came to meet me at my sister's place by the sea? You wanted to know about the lady who had vanished after talking to me,' she said cheerfully.

'Yes, yes, you are right,' Oram accepted. This landlady had told him of a woman who had magically disappeared right in front of her eyes. Oram had suspected at the time that the vanished woman had been Vyidie. 'You told me that she had looked familiar because she had resembled some other patron of yours.'

'That's right. She had looked like the husband of an eighee who had come to stay here a few anni ago. They'd had a newborn baby with them. The wife had been unconscious, but the husband had carried the baby and led their horse, which was carrying the wife. He had left them here and travelled north, paying me enough for her care, for the infant's care, for the stabling of the horse and for room and board for several temporas. Later, he sent a message saying that he was going to Rosarfin but would return for them soon. The eighee with the baby stayed with me for a short while before following her husband to Rosarfin. I never saw either the husband or the wife again.'

'Can you tell me what the husband looked like?' Oram asked. He was now sure that the picture was becoming clearer. Misa, exhausted and stressed by her fight with the soldiers, had gone into labour but had fallen unconscious. Someone— the mysterious female mentioned by the trapper—had been watching or perhaps following her and had helped Misa give birth. Then this mysterious female, in disguise, or someone deputed by her, had brought Misa to Penin, pretending to be her husband, and had left her in the landlady's care, paying enough money to ensure that Misa and the newborn would be well looked after for some time. Whoever it had been had made excuses to depart hurriedly, probably to avoid being seen by Misa on regaining consciousness. But the actions of this mysterious eighe or eighee had been those of a friend. Why had he or she not wanted Misa to meet him or her? Oram was feeling very curious about the identity of this *friend* who had helped Misa in her time of dire need but had fled for fear of discovery.

Oram's wandering thoughts were brought crashing back to the ground by the landlady's description of the eighe who had brought Misa to the inn. 'He was tall but not too tall. He had very dark hair, dark eyes and a terribly dense aura. He looked very young. In fact, if he hadn't had the eighee and the baby with him, I would never have believed him to be married!'

Oram's head was beginning to ache now. The landlady's description fitted his strange supper companion of a few nights ago perfectly. Had the young trapper and the mysterious lady been in cahoots all this while? Or had the trapper been the one to help Misa? Who, then, had been the mysterious female whom Misa had also seen briefly before fainting? And where had she vanished? He decided to show the landlady the armguard that the trapper had left behind.

'Do you know this bracer?' Oram asked. 'Have you seen it before?'

'Yes, I remember this,' she answered. 'I think that the husband of the eighe was wearing this.'

'Are you sure?' Oram asked.

'Ye...s,' she answered, not sounding very sure. Apparently, her memory for things was not as strong as her recollection of faces.

'Is there any doubt in your mind? See, it's all right if you don't remember too well. After all, it was a very long time ago. And you have already helped me very much.'

'No, it's not that I don't remember,' the landlady said hastily. 'It's just that I suddenly remembered something else, something that I should have told you when you came asking me about that vanishing lady.'

'What?'

'You see, this bracer is very unique in appearance, and that is why I remember it so well. I am certain that the husband had been wearing a pair like this. But now I think that the lady who had vanished from the seaside had also been wearing the same kind of bracers. About that I cannot be entirely sure, though.'

'Are you certain that the husband had been wearing a *pair*?' Oram asked.

'Yes, absolutely. In fact, I had commented on how lovely they were and the husband had cryptically said that they were, weren't they, and what a shame it would be to lose one since there was only one such pair in existence.'

Oram thanked the landlady but did not stay at her inn. His mind was whirring and buzzing with confusing and conflicting ideas and information. He needed the peace and quiet of his own home to sort it all out. But before he could return home, he had one more stop on his journey—Kinqur. He travelled down to the capital of Emense the next day in hopes of gathering more information. However, all he could learn was that King Rannzen had never come to Kinqur to seek sanctuary with his neighbour. He was glad to find that all was well with the kereighe country of Emense, though a new pestilence had reared its head in the desert in its east—brigands! He completed his sojourn and started back home on the third of Patarshem, unsure whether his travels had enlightened or befuddled him.

Mizu awoke early on his birthday. He was completing six that annus and felt like a grown-up. He wanted to do grown-up things. Soon, though, he began to feel sleepy again. His drowsiness vanished when he saw the present that his mother had got him. It was in a long and narrow box wrapped in bright cloth and tied up with a ribbon. Mizu opened the box excitedly and found a flute inside. He clapped with joy. He had seen some of the villagers playing flutes and had been attracted to the music. He had wanted one for a while but had never told his mother because they were poor, and he did not want to burden her with his demands for things that were not necessary. But if he hadn't told her, how had his mother known to get one for him? Could she read minds? Maybe that was how she always knew what he wanted even though he never asked for anything.

The villagers had learnt that it was his birthday and brought him all sorts of gifts. Tyzer brought him some beautiful blue egg shells, Molinee had made some sweets for him, Fambert had carved a wooden horse with wheels, Verberon promised to teach him how to play the flute. Several villagers had flowers or treats for him. Leormane, the chief of Bolsana village, alone was conspicuous by the lack of gifts in his hands when he arrived. Misa had prepared some treats in anticipation of their visit, and they all sat around, enjoying the 'feast'.

'I couldn't decide what to get for you, so I've decided to let you choose,' Leormane said to Mizu, smiling. 'What do you want for your birthday, young man?' It was afternoon by then. Everyone had returned to their homes. Leormane had stayed back, saying nothing about his gift until after everyone had left. Misa wondered whether it was because he was embarrassed at being empty-handed or because he was looking for an excuse to stay behind after the others. He had become a fixture at Mizu's house, and nobody was surprised when he stayed behind. They were aware that he spent almost all of his free time with Mizu and Misa, usually with the former.

Mizu thought about all the things he wanted. He scrunched up his face in his attempt to concentrate and ran his hands through his soft, reddish brown hair. He was a little short for his age, and thin, but his strong jaw and mouth inherited from his uncle Melissen prevented him from looking delicate. He found it hard to think of something to ask of Leormane. He had received so many gifts that day! He couldn't think of anything that someone or the other had not yet given him. Those who had not brought any material presents had promised to teach him something or the other. He felt that his life was complete. He wanted for nothing. Then it struck him. There *was* one thing that no one had offered to teach him, something he very much wanted to learn.

'I want to learn swimming!' he declared, opening his big, gooseberry-green eyes wider than ever with excitement. 'You can teach me how to swim.'

Leormane's face turned ashen. He looked stricken, his eyes haunted. He looked towards Misa who was standing behind her son with an odd expression. She saw the pain in Leormane's eyes and almost asked Mizu to withdraw his request. She knew what was going through the chief's mind. He had never forgiven himself for his son's death from drowning while on a fishing trip with him. Mizu's innocent request had touched a raw nerve. She knew that if there was one thing that Leormane would not unhesitatingly do for Mizu, it was the thing that the boy had asked. She also knew that if she didn't allow Leormane to teach Mizu how to swim, she would affirm his guilt. He had not really been responsible for the accident that had taken his son's life. She wanted him to understand that. She looked steadily into his eyes and said, 'That is a lovely idea, Mizu. I am sure Leormane would love to teach you how to swim.'

For a brief momon, something like anger or resentment flashed in Leormane's eyes, but Misa did not flinch. He could hate her right then, but she would not back down. She would not enable his false sense of guilt. She was terrified of allowing anyone except herself to teach Mizu anything dangerous, but she had to do this for Leormane's sake. Mizu was leaping up and down excitedly and begging Leormane to take him swimming at once! Finally, with a sigh, Leormane gave in. He cast a glance of mixed terror and rage at Misa before departing with his terribly eager pupil. He had to pretend to be as excited as Mizu to avoid hurting the young boy's feelings. He wished he had never told Misa about his past. He could have made up an excuse to refuse Mizu if she hadn't known the truth; he could have said that he did not know how to swim. But if he refused now, she would think him a coward. He was terrified of letting anything happen to Mizu, but refusing to teach him would mean that he wasn't sure of his ability to protect the boy. Why had Misa agreed? She could have easily refused. Leormane wanted to give her a piece of his mind, but in Mizu's presence, that was impossible.

The stream was not far from the village, yet Leormane took the most indirect route he could, hoping that the delay would cool Mizu's enthusiasm. It did not. If anything, the little boy was even more eager to start learning. Against his better judgement, Leormane began to teach Mizu.

'The first thing to remember,' he said, trying to sound confident as he stepped into the stream, 'is that there is no reason to be afraid of the water. You need to think of the water as your friend.'

'Yes, of course! The water *is* my friend,' Mizu squealed as he squelched down the muddy bank and into the stream before Leormane could stop him. The chief of Bolsana grabbed him, terrified that he might slip too deep into the bed of the stream. But Mizu was completely unconcerned. Leormane tried to teach Mizu the importance of remaining relaxed in the water so that he could float. He soon realised that his student was far more at ease than he was. Mizu was floating comfortably very soon; he could float on his back as well as his stomach with equal ease at his very first attempt. Leormane was astounded.

'Did your mother teach you how to float?' Leormane asked Mizu, who was holding on to a rope tied to a tree on the riverbank and floating on his stomach, looking as comfortable as if he was in his bed at home.

'No,' he replied, 'but it's not that hard. What do we do next?'

Leormane had thought that he could spend the day in teaching the boy how to float. Since Mizu had mastered that skill in barely fifteen minuras, he decided to teach the boy how to breathe while swimming. This, too, came surprisingly easily to Mizu. Leormane began to suspect that Misa had already taught the boy swimming, or at least, some of the preparatory steps. But when he asked, Mizu again denied that he knew anything about swimming.

'Am I doing something wrong, Leom?' he asked, suddenly feeling shy and awkward. Leormane felt sorry for him. He assured Mizu that he had done nothing wrong. Mizu managed to learn the rest of the steps as quickly and as easily as he had learnt the initial ones. Leormane was stunned but said nothing. He acted as if all of it was completely normal, as if any boy would have learnt to swim just as quickly. When they returned to Misa after a couple of horas, Mizu had already become adept at swimming. He had even swum across the stream, much to Leormane's horror. He was still trembling when he and Mizu entered the house.

'So, how did it go?' Misa asked them.

'It was great!' Mizu exclaimed. 'Leom taught me how to swim. I can now swim across the stream.'

Misa raised her eyebrows. 'He's telling the truth,' Leormane acceded weakly. 'He really can do that.'

'B…but how?' asked Misa, astonished.

'I thought you might be able to explain that better,' remarked Leormane.

'What do you mean? And Mizu, what are you doing there?' she asked the boy who had headed straight for the kitchen.

'I am so hungry! I want to eat,' Mizu declared.

'Hold on!' Misa called back. Asking Leormane to wait, she handed Mizu a plate of assorted goodies that he had received from various women in the village.

She handed some to Leormane as well and sat by him as he ate out on the porch. Mizu, by her orders, remained inside.

'What did you mean—I would be able to explain better?' she asked the chief.

'I thought that it was because of...you know...his...um...heritage.'

'No, it isn't,' Misa answered. 'I have never known anyone to learn swimming this fast. Eighes take as long to learn swimming as humans do. Are you sure that...'

'That I wasn't hallucinating when he swam to the other bank of the stream and back? Yes, I am sure. My heart leapt out of my chest when he shot off before I could stop him. Do you know how scared I was? But he was perfectly comfortable, swimming like he had been doing it all his life. It was almost as if he already knew what to do and I was merely reminding him. It was so strange. I thought that you had already taught him how to swim, but he denied it, and he doesn't lie. I encountered khaypers and an obetulfer not long ago, yet this is the oddest thing that I have experienced in my life!' Leormane declared.

'I am sure it was,' Misa acquiesced. 'And it seems absolutely fantastic. Incredible.'

'Maybe it is one of his special abilities,' Leormane suggested. 'Like his ability at hide and seek or with farming. Maybe he has a natural talent at swimming.'

'Maybe,' Misa said, sitting down beside him, thoughtful. 'Are you all right?' she asked him.

'What do you mean? I am fine. A little shaken by Mizu's prodigious aquatic talents but all right otherwise. He is such an amazing little boy. I am so proud to be his...' Leormane suddenly stopped dead in the middle of the sentence. His face blanched, then reddened and finally darkened. He rose sharply and was about to leave when Misa put her hand on his arm.

'Don't go, please,' she said softly. 'I am sorry for putting you through such trauma, but you have to stop blaming yourself for what happened. It was *not* your fault.'

'And you were willing to risk your son's life to prove this?' he said, anger lending his voice an edge.

'I was not trying to prove anything,' Misa defended herself calmly. 'I just want you to be at peace with yourself. And I knew that you would never let anything happen to Mizu. You were a good father, and still are.'

Leormane started at her words. Misa continued, 'Yes, Leormane. You have been like a father to Mizu. No one has ever done for him as much as you have; no one has ever loved him as much. Sometimes, I wonder whether even *my* love for him can match up to yours. If anyone has the right to be called his father, it is you.'

Leormane closed his eyes and stood still, his whole body taut like a drawn bow. Then he gently removed Misa's hand from his arm.

'Don't ever try anything like this again! I will not be manipulated by you or your eighe mind tricks,' he ground out through gritted teeth, his breath forced and heavy. Then he turned and walked away.

Later that night, Misa awoke on hearing a knock at the door. Taking a knife in hand, she demanded, 'Who is it?'

'It's I, Leormane,' said a voice that was almost too hoarse to be recognisable. She put the knife away and opened the door. The chief of Bolsana stood outside, looking paler than the moonlight. He was a tall, distinguished looking man with acute features and a stern, proud demeanour that commanded respect. But now he looked broken. His face had crumpled, and his eyes looked hollow and red. 'Can we talk?' he asked in that haunting, hoarse voice. Misa shivered. She shut the door behind her and stepped out.

'I am sorry,' she said before Leormane could speak. 'If I had known what it would do to you, I would never have…'

Leormane raised his hand and Misa fell quiet. 'Don't apologise,' he said. 'I know that you wanted to help me. I was wrong to be angry at you. It is so, so difficult to live with this burden,' Leormane's voice faltered. He broke down.

'Shh!' Misa cooed to him, like she cooed to Mizu when the boy woke up from a nightmare. She made her companion sit down and held his hands in her own, talking to him soothingly until he had calmed down. He was visibly embarrassed by then.

'I don't know what to say,' he confessed.

'You don't have to say anything,' Misa said, letting go of his hands. 'Just tell me that your burden is a little lighter; it's all I ever wanted.'

Leormane smiled wanly and said, 'Yes, it is. And just so you know, I would be proud to be known as Mizu's father. I would be happy to—if only you would agree.'

'You know my answer, Leormane,' Misa said, rising. 'It won't change. Good night.'

When on Tyzer's eighteenth birthday, on the fourth of Chirshkom in the annus 5007 A.E., his mother Molinee thanked Misa for probably the hundredth time for saving her only son from the obetulfer, Misa could no longer bear the guilt that had been weighing down her heart since the day the incident had occurred. That evening, after the festivities were over, she took the older woman aside and told her the truth about what had really happened that day. The obetulfer had taken possession of Traozon, Molinee's husband, and had been trying to strangle Tyzer. Misa had had to kill Traozon to save Tyzer and to finish off the obetulfer for good. As Misa told her, Molinee started crying. Misa, too, was crying by then. She begged Molinee to forgive her, though she did not really expect the bereaved woman to do so. To her surprise, Molinee hugged her and sobbed into her ear, 'I forgave you long ago!'

Misa was taken aback. 'You mean that you already knew?'

Molinee nodded.

'And you have never blamed me for your misfortune?' Misa asked, overwhelmed by the large-heartedness of the woman whose kindness had been the cause of her settlement in Bolsana, the closest thing to home that she had in the whole world. 'How can you be so forgiving?' Misa sobbed.

'My dear,' Molinee cried, 'you saved my son! You did what you could. You saved the whole village! You did not kill my husband; that terrible monster did. How could I be angry at you?'

'But how did you know?'

Molinee gripped Misa's hand tightly and sniffled, 'Leormane told me. But don't be angry at him. I made him tell.'

Misa nodded mechanically, fuming within at Leormane. As soon as she left Molinee's house, she went to Leormane's. The chief of Bolsana village was playing with Mizu. The boy spent almost all his time with Leormane. Ever since the chief had taught him swimming, the two had grown closer than ever before, and they had been great friends even before that! When his mother entered, Mizu ran to hug her. She hugged him back and told him to go and play with Molinee. Mizu was puzzled but obeyed without question.

'We have to talk,' Misa said to Leormane through gritted teeth. Leormane guessed what she wanted to talk about and steeled himself.

'Go on,' he said.

Misa ranted at him for close to a hora about how betrayed she felt by what he had done. 'I trusted you with the greatest secret of my life, and you told Molinee anyway! How could you?' she screamed at him. 'You say that you care for Mizu and me, but you callously endanger our lives,' she accused him. She was a tall woman and she drew herself up to her full height to look down upon Leormane with hate and disgust. 'I thought you were my friend, but it appears that I was wrong!' she spat out. In her rage, she no longer looked handsome. Her fair complexioned face was red and blotchy, probably from anger as much as from her earlier crying, and her light brown hair was unkempt. Her eyes, which were normally a mysterious shade of bluish-grey, looked dark with pain. She looked ready to burst into flames. Leormane sat calmly, listening to her imprecations and accusations until she had tired herself out. Then he spoke. His voice was cold.

'I understand the violence of your reaction. I am truly sorry that you don't trust me enough to believe that I would never say or do anything to endanger you or Mizu. Yes, I did tell Molinee what had really happened to Traozon. But that was only after she accosted me with the partial truth and demanded to know the rest. Tyzer, you see, had begun to remember some of the things that had happened down in the tunnels. He clearly remembered his father attacking him. When I tried to bypass the subject, Molinee accused me of lying to her. And she was right. I *had* lied to her. For you. Not that I blame you for wanting to keep the hideous truth from her. I would never have consented to the idea if I had not believed it to be the right thing to do. But when Tyzer told her part of the truth and she confronted me, I had no choice but to tell her everything. Would you rather I had let her imagine that her husband had tried to kill his own son? I have not told her a word about your true identity. Believe me if you will; don't if you won't. I don't care either way. But I will have you understand today and remember always that I care about Mizu just as much as you do. I could never do anything that would harm him!'

Misa's words had wounded him, and the hurt and anger showed through in his eyes and his voice. Misa felt ashamed.

'I am sorry for whatever I said to you. It was uncalled for. But you should have allowed *me* to explain the truth to Molinee. You should have asked her to talk to me. When I learnt that you had told Molinee about Traozon's fate, I felt betrayed. I felt terrified that you had told her everything.'

'You were not here when she confronted me. You had gone to Atmut to get medicines. What was I to do? I had to tell her the truth. I had decided to tell you when you returned. But you have been strangely remote since your trip. And then, after some time had passed, it seemed rather redundant to bring it up without context, especially since Molinee never mentioned a word of it again. Have I ever done anything to hurt you? I would gladly die for Mizu, and you know that! Can't you trust me?'

'I do trust you!' Misa cried. 'I trust you with my life. But I cannot trust you with my son's, I am sorry. I told you before that he is the most precious thing in my life. And will always be. I cannot afford to do anything that might endanger him even accidentally.'

'What do I have to do,' demanded Leormane angrily, 'to prove to you that I will never let him get hurt?'

Misa was quiet for a while. Then she said, 'Promise me that if anything happens to me, you will look after him. Promise me that you will take him to Oram, the Old

Man of the Hills, to be educated, and that you will allow *him* to tell Mizu the truth about his identity. Promise me that you will keep him from harm and will care for him as if he were your own son.'

Leormane was taken aback by Misa's words. His anger evaporated and was replaced by concern. 'Are you all right?' he asked Misa, stepping closer to her and looking into her face to see if she was ill. 'And who is this Oram?' he added.

'First promise me,' said Misa.

'First tell me what is going on. What happened on your trip? Who is Oram? Why are you saying such things?' Leormane demanded stubbornly.

Misa sighed and gave in. She told him about her return trip from Hummold, about almost dying in the snowstorm and about her rescue by Oram. She told him how the incident had set her thinking about what would happen to Mizu if she died before he was old enough to reclaim his throne.

'You are not going to die before he is grown up,' Leormane protested. 'Stop this foolishness. Have you become senile? And how can you trust a stranger so completely but not me?'

'I do trust you, Leormane,' Misa said with a hint of irritation in her voice, 'but you cannot help Mizu the way Oram can. He is a magus. I *have* to trust him. He is powerful enough to aid Mizu in regaining his birthright.'

'And I am not,' Leormane said bitterly.

'Don't misunderstand me, please,' Misa begged, unable to make Leormane see her viewpoint.

'No, I understand what you are saying. You want what's best for your son. Believe me when I say that I want the same. If this Oram can help him more than I can, then I will do as you say. I promise to look after Mizu, to keep him from harm, to treat him as my son, to have him educated by Oram and to never reveal the truth about his identity to him. Are you satisfied?'

Misa nodded, relieved.

'I know that you want Mizu to win back his throne from his enemies,' Leormane added with a strange undertone, 'but are you sure that *he* wants that too?'

'That question,' said Misa haughtily, 'is irrelevant.'

Chapter 9

A ROYAL GUEST

Lord Aminor had just returned home after a long and tiring day. He settled down in his favourite armchair in his study with a refreshing glass of wine after telling his servants to prepare dinner. He dismissed the attendants, wishing for some privacy to think about his life. He liked to spend a little time in solitude every day, allowing himself to relax and meditate upon the ebbs and tides of his past, present and future. His thoughts often turned to his godson, Prince Amishar, and the prince's parents. He usually accompanied these musings with a glass of wine, although he was not a heavy drinker. The wine lulled his worries for a while, but he could not afford to have his senses too dulled; he needed to have his wits about him at all times. He was about to take the first sip of the evening when the tall, thin man stepped out of the shadows.

Lord Aminor reacted instantly. Before the man had taken five steps, the spymaster's dagger was at his throat. The intruder held up his hands and croaked, 'The moon is bright tonight!' Lord Aminor replied, 'But the stars are dim,' and removed his dagger from the man's throat. It was one of his own spies, though he did not recall the man. The spy, he observed, was barely out of his adolescent anni. He could not but admire the young man's cunning in managing to enter his house without being detected. It also meant that he needed better security. He wondered just how capable the young man was. Would he be able to penetrate the palace's security? He put that thought aside for the moment and asked for news.

'The news is regarding Feyanor, prince of Ashperth,' the spy reported.

Aminor's interest was aroused. It was not very often that he managed to receive news of Ashperth through his secret channels. Even when he did, the news often turned out to be trifling. Unlike the other human kingdoms, Ashperth was incredibly skilled at concealing information.

'What is the news?' he asked.

'Prince Feyanor of Ashperth has conquered the Ufharn Hills,' the spy reported.

Aminor, who had sat back down, almost stood up again. This was big news! He asked the spy for details.

'He fought the tribes of the Ufharn Hills and won over them. Then he returned their lands to them on condition of their acceptance of King Graniphor's suzerainty. They now fly the standards of the royal house in their territories.'

'How large was the army that conquered the tribes? Who led them?' enquired Lord Aminor.

'I do not have reliable reports of the number of soldiers deployed for the purpose, but rumours put the size from anywhere between eight and thirty thousand. Prince Feyanor himself led them though he was aided by his generals Korshernon, Dormap and Parned.'

'What were the terms of surrender?'

The spy told him the terms.

'Is there any dissent among the tribes?'

'None that I have heard of. Apparently, they are happy with how everything turned out.'

'Hmm,' said Aminor. 'Are you aware of the size of the main Ashperthian army?'

'No, but I have heard rumours that the force used by Prince Feyanor was a tenth of the total strength of the army.'

Which, Aminor calculated, put the total size of the army at anything between eighty thousand and three hundred thousand. There was too little information to decide which estimate was closer to the truth. Before dismissing the spy, he asked if the young man had any more information.

'No, but an official messenger is due to arrive from Ontar soon to apprise Their Majesties of Prince Feyanor's victory.'

Aminor tossed the spy a bag of coins. This was his reward, which was in addition to the generous pay that all the spies received. The young man grinned. He was thrilled to be affluent at that moment. He imagined visiting some of the poshest shops and establishments to splurge on himself.

'There's one more thing that I want you to do,' said Aminor. 'It is going to be extremely difficult and dangerous. If you succeed, you will receive thrice as large a reward as this. If you fail, you must immediately get in touch with me; if you cannot, you may even lose your life. Are you willing to risk it?'

'Yes, my lord,' said the spy, his youth making his heart race at the prospect of both danger and reward. 'I assure you that I will not fail. What is the task?'

'You must infiltrate the palace, and as proof of your success, bring back something that belongs to the king.'

The spy had already agreed, so he could not go back on his word. He went away in a daze, wondering whether the spymaster had gone mad.

He returned a tempora later, empty handed. He had not succeeded. He had managed to infiltrate the first two levels of palace security with difficulty but had been thwarted thereafter. He had decided to return before he was caught. Aminor heaved a sigh of relief. Although the despondent spy was afraid of being punished, he was not. He received, much to his surprise, a reward equal to what he had received when he had brought the message from Ashperth.

'What's your name?' Aminor asked the spy.

'Aymur' he answered.

'You are good, Aymur, but still too young. Do not be disheartened. Who knows that you might not succeed someday where you failed today? I just hope that on that day you are still working for Balignor.'

The spy bowed gratefully, swore his undying loyalty and left. Aminor smiled. He was thankful that the spy had not succeeded in penetrating the palace security completely. However, his incursion had shown that there was need for tightening of security in the outer layers. The lad Aymur had promise, Aminor mused. He had found out all there was to learn about Aymur after their first meeting. He was an orphan and had been raised by various relatives for some anni before joining the army at the minimum eligible age. He had come to the notice of his superiors by dint of his intelligence and industry and had soon found himself in Aminor's corps of spies. If he continued to work the way he had been working, he would rise to great heights someday, Aminor thought.

The messenger from Ontar reached Lufurdista on the twenty-fourth of Kawitor, within three temporas of Aymur's report to Aminor. The news of Prince Feyanor's victory was received with great lauding by everyone. King Amiroth immediately had it proclaimed throughout the kingdom. In the meantime, Aminor's spies reported to him that Feyanor was being hailed as the greatest hero in the West and as the greatest warrior since Rogran, among other things! Aminor smiled. He had met the prince once and had been taken by his maturity and poise though most people knew him only as a spirited, jovial man, albeit a good fighter. Aminor had never imagined that Feyanor could reach such heights of glory and adulation. He wondered how it would impact Balignor and Amiroth. He believed that Prince Feyanor was an honourable man and would not attack Balignor, at least as long as his sister was its queen. King Amiroth was another matter altogether. Hot-headed and proud, Amiroth was sometimes prone to jealousy, though he was noble, valiant and generous to a fault. At the moment, he was rejoicing in his brother-in-law's success. Would his joy continue? Or would it be replaced by envy and anger? Aminor hoped not.

Queen Lamella was overjoyed at her brother's success and fame. She suggested to King Amiroth that they should invite him to visit Balignor to honour him. She had not seen her brother since her marriage a decadus ago, and the idea seemed like a splendid one to both her and the king. A messenger was dispatched with an appropriate invitation. The messenger set off on the third of Madal and reached Ontar, the capital of Ashperth, in due course of time.

It was the middle of the rainy season and, unable to spend time outdoors, Prince Feyanor was playing a game of checkers with his wife, Princess Eileen, when the messenger from Lufurdista was announced. He immediately left the game and received the messenger. The messenger delivered the invitation with a deep bow and flowery words of congratulations to the prince. Prince Feyanor thanked him with a smile, hiding his impatience well. While the messenger waited, he read the invitation eagerly and replied, 'I am delighted to accept the kind invitation extended by King Amiroth and Queen Lamella, good sir. I shall start shortly after eshoinh ends.' He returned to his wife, excited, the game forgotten.

'What is it, my lord?' Eileen asked. 'Who was the message from?'

'It was from King Amiroth. He and Queen Lamella have invited me to visit Balignor to felicitate me.'

'You should definitely go, Your Highness. You have been driven to distraction by the lack of something to do,' she said, smiling. Prince Feyanor laughed.

'You know that's not true, my lady!' he protested. 'I have been spending time with you to make up for the long periods that I had to stay away.'

'And that has been driving *me* to distraction!' Eileen muttered, making a sour face.

'Why do you want me to go away, Princess?' Feyanor questioned, pouting in mock anger in return.

'Because I do not love you, my lord,' Eileen declared with a straight face.

'Yes, you do,' declared Feyanor, proceeding to suddenly pick her up in his arms. The servants, attendants and guards disappeared without a word.

'Put me down!' demanded Eileen, blushing.

'Not until you say that you do love me,' Feyanor stated.

Eileen rolled her eyes and said something about her husband that she would never have uttered in front of the servants or anyone else. For anyone, those words would mean a hangman's noose or an executioner's block or a dungeon cell on charges of treason. But the two of them had known each other since childhood, and Eileen dared to say to Feyanor things that no one else would dream of uttering. And Feyanor said to her things that he could not imagine saying to anyone else. In public, they maintained the decorum of royal life perfectly while in private they did not bother to rein their feelings in.

'No, I don't love you,' she repeated and stuck her tongue out at her husband.

'You may rail at me to your heart's content, madam princess, and say all sorts of bad things about me,' Feyanor teased, 'but I shall not set you down until you confess your love for me.'

'So, are you going to go to Balignor?' she asked him, trying to distract Feyanor.

'I most certainly am!' announced Feyanor. 'I haven't seen my sister in ages. But I won't go alone. You must come with me.'

'Of course, I will,' Eileen acquiesced. 'Now please put me down.'

'You won't get away so easily. Did you think that you could distract me by talking about Balignor? I am not so easily distracted, my darling wife!'

'You are the most stubborn man that I have ever met!' she exclaimed.

'And that's why I've managed to bring all of Ashperth under father's standard,' he said grandly.

'And developed a head bigger than a dragon's egg!' she sighed.

'But I still won't put you down until you declare your love for me,' Feyanor said, sidestepping her continued attempts at distraction.

Eileen laughed and gave in. She whispered in her husband's ear and kissed him. Feyanor let her down with a wide grin. No sooner had he set her down than the servants, attendants and guards returned as unobtrusively as they had left.

This was the first time that Prince Feyanor was visiting Balignor, and Balignorians felt exceptionally honoured. He was being hailed all over the West as a great conqueror and hero since he had subjugated the tribes of the Ufharn Hills. Everyone had been taken aback when Prince Feyanor had succeeded in accomplishing this seemingly unachievable feat. He was being hailed as the true successor of his illustrious ancestors.

The citizens of Lufurdista, rich and poor alike, were thrilled when they learnt that the heroic Prince Feyanor was not only bringing along his beautiful lady, but would remain in the city for a substantial period of time. A grand reception was planned for him by King Amiroth. The preparation for his visit turned into a festival with craftsmen coming from far and near to set up shop, performers and dancers coming to find approval by the reception committee, cooks and confectioners vying with each other to present the most delectable dishes at the royal tables and even ordinary citizens decorating their homes and hearths to the best of their ability. Girls and young women bought new dresses and ribbons and jewellery. Soldiers bought new, shiny gear. Children made pennants in all colours imaginable. For days, the visit of the great warrior was the only talk of the city. Bards walked the streets, singing of the prowess and glory and valour of the prince of Ashperth. The bustle at the palace was twice as much as that in the streets outside. King Amiroth personally oversaw the preparations. The most extravagant and exclusive gifts were bought and brought from across Elthrusia. Queen Lamella patiently counted the days to the moment that she would meet her beloved only brother again.

When the day finally arrived, Queen Lamella was no longer able to remain patient. She climbed up the tallest tower in the palace of Lufurdista to look for the travelling party; she went into the kitchen to ensure that all was in readiness for the grand feast that evening; she rechecked all the gifts and had the guest chamber where her brother would stay re-cleaned. But time passed slowly for her. She bustled in and out of the guest chamber repeatedly, young Amishar at her heels.

With great curiosity, he had been following everything that had been happening at the palace. He kept up a barrage of questions that sooner or later drove his listeners to run for shelter. He wanted to know everything. Who was coming? Why was he coming? Why was he a hero? What had he done? When would he reach? How long would he stay? Would he bring gifts? Why was a feast being prepared? Why were there so many gifts? How far was Ashperth? There was no end to the questions that the six-annus-old prince asked. He trotted behind his mother as she supervised the preparations.

Sometimes, though, he traipsed along by his godfather, Lord Aminor, who was having nightmares about the security of the city and the palace. He was responsible for the safety of the royal family and their guests while his friend, Lord Parkiod, the commander-in-chief, was responsible for security in the rest of the city. Though he tried to accommodate the young boy as best as he could, Lord Aminor could not give his godson as much time as the child wanted. Amishar, tiring of the serious conversations of the two men responsible for everyone's safety, often escaped to find his father and to cling to him. That was the most enjoyable time of the day for him. King Amiroth always had time for his son, no matter what he was engaged in doing.

Amishar was the apple of King Amiroth's eye. To the king of Balignor, his son was his entire universe. There was nothing that he would not do for his son. Nothing that Amishar did could be wrong. He carried the boy on his shoulders when he went to inspect the soldiers for the special parade. It amused and warmed the hearts of his subjects to see the immense and unconcealed affection that the great man felt for his only child. The servants and attendants and aides of the palace whispered amongst themselves that King Amiroth was indulging his son a little more than was necessary and that it would spoil the boy, but none had the courage to speak it to his face. The only one who complained of his indulgence towards his son was his wife. She exhorted him to discipline Amishar, but he merely smiled and told her that there was time enough for that when Amishar was older.

With only horas remaining for Prince Feyanor's arrival, Queen Lamella was on her way to the chamber where he and Princess Eileen would stay for the umpteenth time to check the arrangements. As she neared the chamber, a sudden, loud crash made her jump. When she rushed in, she found Amishar alone inside. At his feet, on the floor, were the remains of what had been an exquisitely hand-carved obsidian urn. It had been a four feet tall two-handled urn with a two-layered base, an inverted bell shaped body and a tall lid with rings in the handles. Geometric patterns had been etched on the lower layer and floral motifs had been carved into the upper layer of the base. The lid had been in the form of a vine in bloom, and the body had been a detailed lotus delicately worked in gold leaf. Now it was nothing but a pile of black and gold rubble. Queen Lamella had specially had it brought from Emense as a gift for her brother. She had wrapped it with her own hands in golden gauze and had kept it upon a pedestal in the chamber where he would lodge.

She sent for the king to show him what Amishar had done. When the king arrived, he found his son standing with his head bowed as his mother scolded him. When Queen Lamella complained to King Amiroth about the broken urn, he smiled and asked Amishar what had happened.

'I did not mean to break it, Your Majesty,' the young boy sobbed. 'I was looking at it, and it accidentally fell and broke.'

This was something that usually seemed to happen around Amishar. Often. He never meant to cause any harm, but great harm seemed to come to fragile and beautiful objects that came within his reach. The urn was only the latest in a long line of such accidental breakages. Amishar's father laughed and picked him up.

'Don't cry like a baby, Amishar!' he gently chided the boy. 'Great princes never cry. And don't worry your little head about what has happened. Go out into the garden and play there. Don't worry your mother any more. I shall send for you when your uncle comes.'

Amishar wiped his tears and smiled a bright, warm smile. His father's heart melted. What could he not do to ensure that that smile always stayed on his son's lips! When Amishar had left for the garden, he turned to his wife and cajoled her.

'Don't worry about the urn, my queen,' he said. 'I shall have another one brought from Emense for Prince Feyanor.'

'It is not the urn that I am upset about, my lord,' she complained, 'but your undue indulgence of our son. You should not spoil him so. You should discipline him.'

'How do I discipline him?' he pleaded. 'Every time he causes some mischief and I want to scold him, I see his dead face in front of my eyes, and I remember that it is only a miracle that you and he are with me today. How can I scold him then?'

Queen Lamella was about to reply when a servant came running to announce that the king was needed downstairs to start on his way to receive the guests. King Amiroth hurried away, leaving Queen Lamella to have the chamber cleaned once again. He barked final orders as he rushed towards the gates of the palace, where his horse awaited to take him to the city's western gates, through which the guests would enter Lufurdista.

Prince Feyanor and Princess Eileen reached Lufurdista just before sunset on the fourteenth of Supprom in the annus 5007 A.E. Their ship had docked at Naetel, the port at the mouth of the river Quazisha, thirty days ago. They, with their party, had then travelled by horse drawn carriage to the capital city. Their guards rode alongside. Many of Feyanor's men came behind the prince's contingent in carts, fetching all the supplies and gifts he had brought with him. When the procession reached Lufurdista, the entire city turned out onto the streets to welcome this great hero of men. He disembarked on the bank of the Quazisha just outside the capital city amidst thunderous cheer and fanfare. King Amiroth and Lord Aminor had gone to receive him with a special guard and a convoy suitable for such dignitaries. Upon alighting from the carriage, Prince Feyanor stepped forth and embraced his brother-in-law heartily. Refusing the glamorous coach that awaited him, he chose to ride into the city on a tall, black horse. Princess Eileen, though, thanked King Amiroth and stepped into the coach after curtseying with such grace and elegance that the women who had gone to wait on her during the entrance to the city almost sighed audibly.

Prince Feyanor entered the city gates accompanied by his brother-in-law, the king of Balignor, on one side and Lord Aminor on the other. Princess Eileen followed them in the exquisite covered coach drawn by a team of four horses. The coach was followed by a large retinue of aides and servants and carts carrying gifts. Behind them came the guard of honour: tall, proud soldiers of Balignor, riding on their powerful steeds two abreast, the plumes on their crests streaming behind them in the breeze, their armours glinting in the light of the setting sun. The citizens of the capital city poured into the streets to catch a glimpse of the valiant conqueror of invincible enemies and the procession that accompanied him. The main street was packed on both sides with jostling masses of citizens dressed in their best clothes, waving flags and pennants and showering flowers in the path of the approaching royals. Wherever Prince Feyanor and Princess Eileen passed, a shout of cheer went up among the crowd. The royals waved and smiled at the gathering, surprised and pleased at the exuberance of welcome.

Queen Lamella waited at the gates of the palace to receive the procession and to welcome the visitors inside. Young Amishar stood shyly by her, almost hidden behind her skirts. He had heard stories of the valour of their illustrious visitor, and now he looked upon this large man with curiosity and awe. Prince Feyanor was considered a large man even in Ashperth, a country that boasted of large men. He walked with long, powerful strides up the steps of the palace to where his sister stood to receive him. His long, wavy, titian hair reached below his shoulders. He had a large, full mouth, a square jaw, a straight, sharp nose and deep, green, intelligent eyes. He wore clothes of fur and leather and a long, heavy travelling cloak. Upon his head was a diadem of silver, crafted in a twisting, intricate pattern never before seen in Balignor. His deep voice matched his stature. He laughed easily and was affable in manner. He was a large, jovial, kind-looking man, Amishar thought. He wondered how a man who looked like that could have outwitted shrewd and dangerous hordes of enemies in treacherous battles. He was willing to believe that Prince Feyanor had valour so great that none could stand before him. At Prince Feyanor's side was his wife, Eileen, a tall, graceful, elegant, charming and beautiful lady. All who saw her felt a moment of breathless wonder that one such as her could exist among humans; she was as lovely, as charismatic and as stately as the eighe princesses that lore told about. All who were present felt enchanted by her. All but Amishar. The young prince was too awed by his uncle to even notice her.

Chapter 10

SHADOW OF DREAMS

(7 Madal 5007 A.E.)

Avita had turned six only a couple of mondans ago, but she looked older than other eighe children her age. She felt older too. And she understood that she was different in other ways as well. Ever since her encounter with the strange human boy in Kinqur, her life had changed, mostly for the worse. She was growing faster, as fast as human children. Forsith had explained this to her when she had asked why kereighes didn't believe her when she told them her age. She often had nightmares about being beaten by an old, scary eighee and bore marks of severe injuries all over her body when she woke up. Her guardians, Avator and Forsith, worried about her constantly. They were always on the move because if they lived anywhere for a length of time, folks became suspicious about her condition. Avator repeatedly told Avita not to blame herself, but she could not help thinking that it was her fault. If she had been like other kereighe children, they could have had a normal life.

Once they had visited a nice eighee who had given her lots of dolls to play with. Avator had taken her there to be cured. Avita wished she could visit that eighee again; she had liked her. Being with her had made Avita feel better even though she had not been cured. The nice eighee had given Avita a charm that she wore at all times. It helped heal her nightmare-born wounds faster. She knew that the nice eighee had said something about her condition being a result of her contact with the human boy. Avator hated the boy because of this. Avita did not; she could not. She often dreamt of him. She dreamt of him being beaten by the same old witch who haunted her own nightmares. She felt sorry for him and wished she could help him. Yet, in some inexplicable way, she felt that she *was* helping him because she was dreaming of him. It sounded insane when she said it aloud to herself during her waking horas. But in her dreams, it made perfect sense.

She was too young to understand what was wrong with her, yet she was certain that Avator and Forsith would be greatly worried if she told them about her dreams of the boy. They were trying to make a living by claiming that Forsith was a horse-wizard, and their plan was meeting with success so far. The kereighes of Emense who had availed of their services gave them much respect as well as a lot of money. Their new situation was beginning to stabilise. News of her dreams could unsettle everything again and ruin her guardians' plans, the little girl thought. So she told them nothing about these dreams.

On the seventh of Madal, she had a stranger than usual dream about the human boy who was responsible for her affliction. At first, as soon as she was asleep, she dreamt of fountains and birds and ribbons and horses and other things she liked. Usually, images of the human boy being beaten or abused or whipped intruded into whatever else she was dreaming of. That night, though, she turned around from looking at a rainbow and suddenly everything turned dark. In the darkness, he sat quietly and alone, looking at her with his big, dark, scared eyes. Though it was a dream, she *knew* that he was looking at her. Then his form began to alter. He still had dark hair and dark eyes, but he was no longer human. He was pale and tall. He had a dark aura around him. His features looked very familiar, almost as if she was used to seeing them every day but could not recall exactly where. He had become a kereighe boy. It did not strike her as odd that this should happen. She just knew, despite the changes, that it was the same boy. He looked trapped and scared and as if he wanted to say something to her. Avita tried to reach out to him but he was too far. She took a step towards him but he moved afar. She tried to get close enough to help him, but the more she tried to reach him, the further away he went, until the darkness around them swallowed him up.

She followed him and called out to him, afraid of never seeing him again, though she did not know why the thought of it was so unbearably painful. She searched desperately for him, but still he was not to be found. She began to panic as the darkness enveloped her and threatened to choke her. She batted at it with her hands but it was a cold, silent menace with a will of iron. It wrapped her in its coils and squeezed her until she was fighting for every breath! She screamed for help with her last remaining breath before the darkness overwhelmed her. Just as she was about to be deluged, she saw a flash of light somewhere in front of her, and the darkness began to dissipate. Reluctantly, hesitantly but undeniably it began to dissolve. Avita tried to take a step forward and found that she could. She pushed herself forward, towards the brilliance, away from the claustrophobic darkness.

She moved closer and closer to the source of the light, drawn to it like a moth. It looked like a large ball of fire. It was so bright that she had to squint to look at it. It felt warm and safe, like the sun. She walked towards it without fear until she was close enough to see that it was not a ball of fire but the aura of an eighe. An eighe whom she had never seen before but whom she knew very well at the same time. He was tall—taller than any eighe she had ever seen. He had dark, long hair and dark, penetrating eyes. His complexion was very pale and his lips were very red, almost as if painted on. His sharp features so perfect that Patarshp himself might have sculpted them! He wore strange clothes the likes of which she had never before. He was wrapped in armour from head to toe. The armour gleamed with a brightness that was alive. He was armed to the teeth with deadly weapons. He wore a martial looking helmet that was of the same golden white metal as the rest of his armour. He looked straight ahead, as if he saw no one. Avita was close to him now, close enough to touch. She reached out, not afraid of the immensely powerful eighe warrior she saw in front of her.

'Don't touch me,' the warrior said in a deep voice that folded Avita in waves of warmth. She knew that she could trust him with her life.

'Why not?' she asked him.

'Don't touch me,' he repeated. 'You might get burned.'

'I am not afraid,' Avita said boldly. She reached out. To her surprise, the warrior reached back, in a gesture that was all too familiar. It reminded her of someone, someone who seemed to have been left behind in her distant past. A boy. A kereighe boy. No! A human boy. A human boy who had suddenly turned into a kereighe boy. And with the certainty that comes only in dreams, Avita knew that this valiant and terrible warrior standing in front of her was the same boy.

'*Am eghim tremen!*'[3] she cried.

The warrior said nothing. He smiled and took her hand. His hand was hot, hot as fire, and it burned her. But she did not care. She felt safe. The fire spread from her hand up her arm and to the rest of her body until she burned as brilliantly as the warrior in front of her. Still she was not afraid. Suddenly he let go of her hand and stepped back. Avita fell. Down an unending pit of darkness she fell, clawing at the sides to stop her fall but failing miserably. She called out to the warrior to save her, but he was nowhere. She fell for a long, long time down the bottomless pit. After what felt like days, her fall ended abruptly as she landed on something hard.

Avita sat up, panting. She looked around. She felt confused. It was bright, like day. Had the warrior found her again? It gave her comfort. She tried to espy him. There! There he was, with his dark hair and eyes but without the weapons or the armour or the brilliant aura. He had turned back into a kereighe boy. But it did not matter. She wanted to call out to him but could not because she did not know his name. Then she realised that the kereighe boy she was looking at was not the boy from her dreams but Avator. Why had Avator appeared in her dream? And what was he doing? And if the warrior wasn't there, where was all this light coming from? She scrunched up her eyes in the bright light to focus. Avator was feeding Habsolm and chatting with him. Avita sighed as realisation washed over her. She was no longer dreaming. The bright light was the light of the day. She was awake. She wriggled out of her coverings and leapt off the cart.

She had not told Avator about her dreams before, but that morning, she resolved to finally confess. None of her previous dreams about the human boy had been so vivid or so unusual. She felt that that particular dream was important in some way. She should tell Avator about it. She approached her brother and Habsolm, who were still bantering.

---

3   'I know you!' (Eighon)

'Hello, miss!' Habsolm neighed. Avator turned around to find his little sister standing behind him, looking a little intimidated by the horse.

'Good morning, darling,' Avator said, giving her a hug. She hugged him back tightly. When she let go, Avator told her that Habsolm had greeted her.

'Hello, Habsolm,' she responded to the horse.

'Tell her that she looks very pretty. Her curls look just like a black cauliflower! I could happily munch on them,' the gelding said.

Avator cast a sharp glance at the horse and admonished him, 'If I ever find you trying anything of the sort, I will skin you alive!'

'I was joking!' Habsolm neighed in protest.

'What did he say?' Avita asked. She liked the jovial horse though she could not understand what he said. Avator was glad to translate when there were no potential clients around.

'He says that you look very pretty. Your curls look especially pretty, he says, and he likes them very much.'

'Really?' Avita asked, turning towards Habsolm with a big smile. The horse shook his head up and down, as if nodding in agreement. 'Thank you!' she said and tried to hug the horse.

Avator held her back. 'Easy!' he said. 'Or you'll scare Habsolm.'

Habsolm snorted, as if in derision. Avita laughed. She was feeling better. The dream had left her dazed and confused, but the conversation with Avator and Habsolm had cheered her up. She was feeling almost like herself again.

'Atta, I want to tell you something,' she began, deciding to tell her brother about her dream and all the other dreams of the boy before she lost her nerve. She could pronounce her brother's name clearly now, but she still called him by the nickname she had given him when she had been too young to speak his name properly.

'What is it, dear?' he asked, continuing to tend to the horse.

Avita hesitated. She badly wanted to tell Avator about her dream, but something was holding her back. She could not explain it; it felt as if something big and heavy was sitting inside her stomach and grabbing on to her tongue. 'Just say it!' she egged herself on mentally, but she was scared. What if Avator became angry because she dreamt of the human boy whom he blamed for all their problems? What if he became angry because she hadn't told him before? Would he think that her ailment was her own fault? Would he send her away? All these worrisome thoughts crossed her mind. But there was also something inexplicable, something that she could not put into words, that held her back.

Avator turned towards her and encouraged, 'Go on, tell me what you want to say.'

'I want to ride Habsolm,' she lied, saying the first thing that came to her mind.

'All right, but when you are a little older. I will teach you myself. Will that do?'

She nodded eagerly. He had not suspected her lie. Then, to change the subject, she asked about Forsith.

'He's gone to get some supplies,' Avator answered. 'We have to leave this town today.'

'Where are we going?' Avita asked.

'North, I think,' Avator answered. 'To another town or village.'

'Okay,' Avita said and turned away.

It was the first day of outomy. The rains were over, and the weather was cool and dry. It was beautiful outdoors. The residents of the town were out in droves. The thief that had plagued them for mondans had vanished as suddenly as he had appeared a few temporas ago. The citizens had heaved a collective sigh of relief and returned to their usual lifestyles. They loved the changed weather and were happy to be outdoors. But Temeron felt no desire to go out. He knew that the witch would not allow him out on his own. And going outside with her meant humiliation at the hands of kereighes of the worst sort, for she led him out on a chain and allowed anyone who wished to take a shot at him with a stone or stick. Temeron preferred to remain indoors and reinforce his meagre learning. He sat in his corner, trying to practice the letters and numbers he had learnt by bribing an old beggar with poppy paste. Rosa had wanted him ignorant and illiterate; if he had not taken advantage of the opportunity provided by the opium-addicted beggar's need for poppy paste, he would have remained so. He remembered only a little of what he had learnt, but he practised that little assiduously. And clandestinely. He knew what would happen if the witch found out that he could read and write.

His goal in learning to read and write had been to use one of Rosa's spells on her to hurt or even kill her so that he could escape her clutches. He had stolen a book of spells from her and hoped that there was something in it that could help him. Ever since learning how to read, he had tried many times to perform spells from the book. Unfortunately, none of the spells had worked. Yet he did not give up. He continued to practice his letters whenever he could get away with it in hopes of using that book one day to win his freedom. Like that morning. That morning, Rosa was making charms and hexes and paid scant attention to him. She had grown worse since the theft of her ring and her knife. She was more ill-tempered, morose and volatile than ever. Temeron did not mind. He knew that the reason behind her meanness was her loss, and that knowledge made all the additional torment and torture at her hands worth the while for him.

There was a knock on the door. Rosa went to check. Temeron pricked up his ears. He was not allowed to talk with Rosa's clients. He was immensely curious about them nonetheless. He greedily drank in everything they said. They were his primary source of information about the world outside his prison. He also tried to catch surreptitious glances of the visitors whenever he could. This time, too, he listened hard. Someone wanted to buy something from Rosa. A male voice could be heard telling Rosa that he wanted something that she had. Temeron turned to see if he could spot the speaker, but the *lech* stood in the doorway, blocking it.

'What do you want?' she demanded.

'Something that I would find quite useful if you were to sell it to me,' the visitor answered.

'I have many things that can be useful to many,' Rosa responded acidly. 'What exactly do you want? Or, if you don't know what you want…'

'Oh, I know exactly what I want,' said the kereighe. Temeron had never heard his voice before. That, along with Rosa's attitude, told Temeron that the kereighe was a stranger.

'Then spit it out!' Rosa snapped.

'What I want is a good slave,' the stranger responded.

'Well, then you have come to the wrong place. I am not a slave trader,' Rosa answered. She was about to turn around when the stranger mentioned Temeron. Rosa stood still in her tracks.

'You have a human boy staying with you, don't you? I want that boy. I have heard that humans make good slaves,' the stranger said.

'Who told you about the boy?' Rosa screeched at him.

He replied calmly, 'Many of the town's residents. They told me that you parade him around outside with a chain around his neck. It is an amusing sight, they tell me. I am willing to pay well for the slave.'

'He is not for sale,' Rosa replied coldly.

'But you haven't even heard what I am willing to offer!' the stranger insisted smoothly. He quoted a figure that Temeron thought was outrageously high. The witch could never have seen so much money in her life, he thought. Though he had little idea of how much money was a lot and how much was little, he was familiar with what Rosa's usual clients paid her. The amount quoted by the stranger was many times that. Temeron knew this because he had also learnt counting from the beggar who had taught him to read. He wondered who the stranger was and why he wanted to buy Temeron. Would the witch sell him? Would the stranger be a better master or worse? Would he keep him shackled like Rosa did? Would he hit him as much? His mind was in a tizzy with questions. In all his days of living with Rosa, no one had ever wanted to take him off her hands, even as a slave. He was deeply intrigued. He tried desperately to catch a glimpse of the kereighe who was willing to pay such a handsome price for him. However, the narrow doorway was completely blocked by the witch. Rosa refused the stranger's offer. He quoted an even higher figure. Temeron almost gasped. Rosa again refused.

When he quoted an even higher figure, Rosa did not reply immediately. Even Temeron could sense her hesitation. She was now seriously considering the stranger's offer. She could live off that amount for anni. She could live quite comfortably. And she would be rid of the vermin. The stranger did not know who the boy really was. He would take the wretch as a human and keep him enslaved all his life. He would treat the boy as badly as a human slave deserved to be treated. Wasn't that befitting of her plan of revenge? She pushed those thoughts away. No! She would accomplish her own revenge. She did not need to sell the boy. Besides, she had sacrificed everything for this opportunity to avenge her husband. She would not give in to temptations of comfortable living. She refused him a third time and slammed the door shut.

Temeron pretended not to have heard anything and hastily scrubbed away whatever he had scribbled on the grimy floor of the house. Nevertheless, Rosa suspected something. She gave him a round thrashing. What was worse, she began to look at him warily all the time, as if he were concealing some secret, and she was determined to find out what it was. He did have secrets but not the kind Rosa suspected him of having. She began to watch him like a hawk, much to his annoyance. Her increased vigilance meant that he would not be able to do many of the things that made his life a little bit better, like practicing his letters or trying to perform the spells or accessing his hidden loot under the floorboard.

She also reduced the frequency of her trips out of the house. Even when she did go out, she hurried back, often returning unexpectedly. As days dragged into temporas, and temporas became mondans, Rosa never relaxed her avid vigilance. By the time Sachir was moving into its last tempora, Temeron began to worry that he would never again get the opportunity to practice his reading or writing or be able to try casting spells again, that he would never learn magic. He was beginning to get desperate. Magic was his only key to freedom, he believed, and if he could not learn magic, how could he escape? He managed to hide his anxiety from Rosa, though, and continued to act as usual, all the while hoping that she would give up watching him. He silently cursed the stranger who had put Rosa on alert. Did she think that he would try to steal Temeron? The thought made him laugh inside. He dared not laugh aloud.

Then one day, she asked him outright, 'Who was the kereighe who wanted to buy you? Was he a friend of yours, you wretched vermin? Who wants to rescue you? Tell me!'

'I don't know anything about what you are saying,' Temeron replied truthfully. She lashed him then.

This interrogation began to happen so frequently that Temeron was tempted to make things up about his purported rescuer just to annoy the witch. He wondered why she was so desperate not to lose him. It was obvious that she did not care for him. Why, then, did she want to hold on to him so badly? She had not sold him to the stranger who had offered such a generous amount of money. What value did Temeron have for her? Was there really someone who wanted to rescue him? The boy's young mind began to fill with such questions. Finally, by the mid of Vyiedal, Rosa began to relax her vigil. Four mondans had passed, yet no rescue attempt had been mounted. She must have been mistaken, Rosa concluded. The kereighe must have really wanted a human boy for a slave. At peace about her prisoner, she returned to her old ways, much to Temeron's relief.

A mondan had passed since somminar had begun. Flowers and fruits blossomed on shrubs, plants and trees everywhere in Elthrusia. Birds built nests in anticipation of eggs. Butterflies flitted by in search of nectar. Bees busily hovered from flower to flower, collecting nectar to make honey. It was the season of joy and rejuvenation in nature. Crops were ripening and would be harvested soon. Everywhere there was good cheer and hope. Except in the heart of one little boy who was trapped in a dirty, dingy, ill-kept shack by a witch and was beaten and tortured regularly. That day his mood was darker than ever. He had begun to have strange dreams at night. He had dreamt of falling into a bottomless pit. He had heard the witch shrieking with laughter at his plight. And he had dreamt of an army of motionless soldiers standing on a beach. He had been searching for something in his dreams but had not found it. He had woken up late, feeling tired and ill and clammy with sweat. Because he had woken late, the witch had beaten him. She had grabbed his hair and dragged him out of bed. She had yanked out a clump of his hair with a slice of his scalp attached. She had also kicked him in the face. His cheek was cut, and he had lost a tooth. She had told him that he would not be fed that day.

He had been forced to do the cleaning and scrubbing of the house for some time now. In fact, ever since she had been robbed, Rosa had started to treat the boy as a domestic slave instead of merely as a prisoner. She kept him busy with chores, necessary and unnecessary, all day long. Temeron hardly ever found time for himself. He did what he was told with a very bad grace, often skipping work when he could get away with it. He lied to Rosa about many things. He fervently ill-wished her all the time. He had begun to fantasise about treating her the same way that she treated him, especially after he received a thrashing. Sometimes, it made him feel good, sometimes it made him feel worse. Some nights, he dreamt of the kereighe girl he had met on his only escape attempt, and that brought him comfort. These dreams were often vivid and seemed real even after he awoke. He wished he could see her again someday. Somehow, he felt, it would make everything all right.

That afternoon, after he had finished his morning's mindless scutwork, he had a hora or two free. Rosa had gone out to sell charms, hexes and potions. On other days, he would eat at this time and practice reading and writing surreptitiously. But that day he had not been given any food, and he was in a black mood. He sat by the window, listening to the kereighes passing by outside his window. He wished he had stones to throw at them. A bumblebee came buzzing along. Temeron waved it away. It flew a little afar but returned again. He again brushed it away. By then, two kereighe boys had started fighting in the street over a toy. Temeron wondered which of the two boys would win the fight and if they would kill each other over the toy. That would be an interesting sight, he thought. Their parents were hurrying to break them apart before they got injured. The bumblebee was buzzing near him again, and it distracted him long enough to miss what happened next. When Temeron looked, the fight was over. The boys were no longer there. His entertainment was finished.

Temeron was deluged by rage. Hot bile rose from his belly and embittered his mouth. His face flushed, and his head felt as if it would explode. He wanted to scream at the boys and their parents. He wanted to throw things at them. His whole body trembled. He was seized with a mad desire to break and tear and crush. The kereighes outside were, of course, oblivious to his fury. The futility of his anger made Temeron even madder. In his wrath, he turned to the only creature that was weaker than him—the bumblebee. He reached out and grabbed it. It stung him with all its might. The sting would have brought tears to anyone's eyes, but Temeron was already in too much pain to be hurt by the sting. It merely added fuel to the fire.

'You have ruined everything!' Temeron said to the bumblebee, which was now frantically trying to escape from his grasp. His voice was surprisingly calm despite his terrible anger. 'You are a worthless wretch. I must punish you.' He did not realise that he was repeating words that he had heard from his own tormentor many, many times in his young life.

He grabbed the wings of the bumblebee and ripped them off.

'How will you buzz around and annoy me now?' he demanded of the writhing insect. He chuckled like he had seen Rosa chuckle when he groaned with pain. He imagined how it would feel to tear out Rosa's hair, and the thought made him chuckle harder. If the insect were Rosa, how wonderful it would be! She would be in *his* power, not he in hers! He could do whatever he wished to her. He could make her suffer like she made him suffer. He thought of breaking Rosa's arms and legs as he pulled off the bumblebee's tiny legs. The suffering of the creature on his palm brought him joy. When he was done tormenting it, he crushed it underfoot and threw it out of the window. He imagined doing the same to Rosa. He imagined that he was standing at the top of a mountain and throwing her down a cliff. She would fall with a loud scream, and he would laugh and laugh. He began to laugh thinking about it. He laughed so hard that tears came to his eyes. He doubled over with laughter. His mad rage had given way to hysterical laughter. His eyes fell on the remains of the bumblebee that he had annihilated. Abruptly, his laughter stopped, and he began to cry.

What had he done! He had hurt an innocent, tiny insect. He cried and cried and cried, throwing his tiny fists against the floor and wailing his heart out. He apologised to the bumblebee incessantly. He wished with all his heart that he could change what he had done. He gathered the torn parts of the insect into his palm and stroked them gently, sorrowfully, his tears drowning them. He sat there a long time with the remains of the dead bumblebee in his hand, mourning its death. He held the witch responsible. If she hadn't hurt him so much that morning, he would not have been so angry. If he hadn't been angry, he would not have hurt the bumblebee. It was all *her* fault! Someday, he swore, he would make the witch pay. Not just for what she had done to him but also for what she had made him do to the bumblebee. Then, as it was almost time for Rosa to return, he wiped his tears and composed himself. From under the floorboards, where he kept the secret stash of his meagre possessions in the world, he took out a small jar that he had stolen a while back. Inside it were rotting remains of several cockroaches, grasshoppers, spiders, lizards and bees. He opened the lid. The smell of putrescence hit him. He did not flinch. He dropped the remains of the bumblebee into it, promising all the dead insects that he would avenge their deaths someday. He would then give them a proper burial. Then he closed the jar again and returned it to its hiding place.

When Rosa returned, she found him scrubbing her cauldron. The cauldron was bigger than the boy. He was panting and groaning as he tried to get all the slime and black, thick crusty remains out of it. Rosa smiled. How she wished that King Rannzen could have seen his son now! The thought made her hoot with laughter. Just like that, she slapped the boy, almost affectionately, and sent him rolling on the ground. 'You are a worthless wretch!' she spat at him. 'Now get on with cleaning my cauldron quickly. Make it shine, you whelp. Or I will have to punish you.'

As she trounced away, she did not notice the smile that had flitted onto Temeron's face. He was imagining that he was slapping Rosa away with a forceful blow. He would call *her* names and make *her* do painfully difficult work and, when she couldn't, he would thrash her. He would tear out her hair and break her arms and legs and then crush her under his foot.

The homecoming feast for Rauzditr Meizha, an annus after her marriage, was in sharp contrast to her wedding feast. It was a homely affair, with only family and close friends present to toast the completion of an annus of her married life with Rauzoon Valhazar. Rauz Augurk sat at the head of the dinner table as the amiable host. Rauzina Marizha sat on his left, a gracious hostess. She was a stately dharvhina, with a commanding air. Though shorter as well as stouter than average, she never appeared small. She could make even the strongest dharvh feel that she was a head taller than him due to her lofty presence. That night, she was all smiles and sweetness, beaming upon her guests with motherly affection and pride.

On Augurk's right sat Meizha and Valhazar. Meizha looked uncannily like her mother. With large eyes, a plump, upturned nose, full lips and straight hair, she looked the spitting image of the Rauzina, albeit a somewhat taller and slimmer one. She had never considered herself beautiful, though there were many dharvhs who thought her quite lovely. Foremost among these was her husband, Valhazar, who sat next to her. Valhazar was unlike most dharvhs. He was taller than average and was lightly bearded. He was also less stocky; in fact, he looked almost svelte! He wore his hair braided like all dharvhs of the Travedh veradh but, unlike them, he had braided it into over a dozen plaits, and these gave him quite a striking appearance.

Rauz Valhorz, his father and the rauz of Khwaznon, had been unable to attend due to his onerous responsibilities. However, the rauz's brother, Vanderz, had come with the rauzoon. He sat on Rauzina Marizha's left, duly deferential and attentive to his hostess. He had the same lean build that his nephew had but bore no other resemblance to Valhazar. In his youth, he had been called handsome. Age had not completely taken away his attractiveness, though the worry lines on his forehead and his deep set, intense eyes made detracted from it. He had a rich beard and short, straight hair, which was unusual for one of the Travedh. His features were angular and austere. Even when he smiled, the smile did not reach his eyes, especially when he looked at the young rauzoon who appeared completely oblivious of his uncle. On Valhazar's right sat two more nobles of Khwaznon, relations of Rauz Valhorz. They had accompanied the party to show honour to Rauz Augurk since Rauz Valhorz had not been able to come. A couple of Valhazar's close friends were there as well, more to enjoy themselves than to fulfil any diplomatic purpose. It helped that their fathers were well known figures of Khwaznon; their presence was seen to add to the honour shown to Rauz Augurk, possibly in an effort to make up for the absence of Rauz Valhorz.

Next to Vanderz sat Angbruk. On Angbruk's left sat Dastorv, a cousin of Rauz Valhorz, followed by Durng. Next sat Onelikh the grizzled and Guzear the bear-clawed. Shornhuz stood behind Augurk, his axe at the ready. It was said that his axe never left his hand, except when he ate or slept, and even then, it always lay next to him. The food was as exquisite as that served at the wedding feast, though not as varied or voluminous. Guests and hosts enjoyed the meal and toasted the anniversarial couple, wishing them a long and prosperous life together. Meizha blushed on hearing some of the toasts; Valhazar smiled mischievously.

After the meal, the two dharvhinas—Rauzina Marizha and Rauzditr Meizha—retired to the rauzina's chamber. Mother and daughter had much to talk about. The dharvhs congregated in the large domestic hall of the palace's residential area to smoke pipes. The hall was larger than most of the private chambers of the palace. It had a cavernous fireplace along the length of one wall, and comfortable armchairs and furs lay scattered around the floor of the room. A line of clay, wooden and horn pipes stood above the mantle, next to an enormous box of tobacco. Dharvhs liked to smoke, and Augurk's guests were happy to avail themselves of the comfort of a crackling fire and a heart-warming pipe-full. Moods were mellow as the dharvhs smoked and told stories. Even Shornhuz relaxed enough to put his axe down as he squatted near the door. Augurk was pleased at the gathering. The rains had ended almost a mondan ago, and the wind had turned temperate. The spirits of his guests reflected the weather.

Dastorv, who was the oldest of those present, was well known for his skill as a story-teller. The others prevailed upon him to regale them with a story. The tales that the dharvhs told were few, yet were enjoyed in repeated telling. Dastorv was pleased at having such an eager audience and began the chronicle of Vrenhor, who had united the dharvhs into a nation, a favourite legend of all dharvhs. Dastorv was a good narrator, and the others listened attentively, drawn into the tale by Dastorv's deep voice, skilful rendition and ability to bring the characters and situations to life. They listened spellbound and found the hair on their arms rising when the recital became quite thrilling, even though they had heard the story many times before and knew it as well as any dharvh. When Dastorv had finished, the audience clapped and cheered and begged him for another tale. This time he chose a far sadder narrative from the history of the dharvhs—that of the annihilation of the dharvhs on the way back from Blarzonia after conquering it. His listeners trembled with apprehension as he described the triumphant march of the dharvhish armies back towards their own lands after laying the country of Blarzonia to waste.

Uh irdhh yog yeldoh thand,
Uh irdhh laudenb medh herand,
Uh irdhh erabd jno waiand,
Mredth hnokth vhen ulkhar mhath,
Ehrnth vet vhen nyobh.
Urlon vhur hrudth dhen ulobh!
Vharod erghanm jno chhwel,
Jno Blarzonia druvth wabh
Zhorb revdh dhro Gharzel.

Uznodr thak zhorb shren,
Orgh vhur jyomkhth vhaeb lauden
Medh reubh lauden druvth vheten
Zhorb ulkhar irdhh loath!
Arthop yugh thak zhorb freg,
Medh zhadrark zhorb hoveg
Dhro dracoh umbhron medh rondel,
Vhar lugh hrudth dhen ulobh
Zhorb revdh dhro Gharzel.

'Pity!' a soft whisper from the back of the room broke the silence in which the assembled dharvhs were listening to the tragic tale.

Everyone turned to see who had spoken. Rauzoon Valhazar was lying upside down in an armchair, his feet upon the headrest, and his colourfully beaded braids touching the floor. His eyes were closed as he puffed away merrily, not the slightest look of grief upon his countenance. The senior dharvhs were taken aback by his lack of sententiousness on such an occasion. The tale being told was one of the most poignant tales in the history of the dharvhs and never failed to inspire awe and fear in their hearts. That a dharvh as young as Valhazar was completely unaffected by it was a shock to them. However, he was a guest of the rauz of Ghrangghirm, and a rauzoon at that. They mumbled their disapproval under their shaggy beards and continued with the telling of the story.

Zevn zhorb erash thak vegrth,
   Zhorb irdhh thak eddruvth,
Zhorb khlaheng zern thak fyogth
   Buvur zhorb Lyudzbradh shurth.
Chubd denvotoh ghaveth medh phrod,
   Waz halb medh waz regod,
Nutulth zoun chubd bhoghu medh kluel,
   Arthop loxewth medh zernbeh,
Zhorb revdh dhro Gharzel.

Vhar qerkhh drith vharod hunang,
   Shordth impher zern dhen gwaiv prang;
Zhorb Lyudzbradh luardth ang
   Zhorb dharvhs, vet Gharzel turghth.
Enh waianden yond sreghhth;
   Enh magus hrudth aowth
Reubh zhorb laudenbith goyell
   Sueth yugh plaxt dhro dharvhorth
Zhorb revdh dhro Gharzel.

Augurk noticed the dark looks on the countenances of Onelikh, Dastorv, Vanderz and Shornhuz, but wasn't unduly disturbed. In fact, he was rather amused by Valhazar's lack of due deference to established tradition. When Dastorv finished, everyone sighed as a token of respect to those who had lost their lives in the search for glory and honour. In the silence that followed, Rauzoon Valhazar was clearly heard to yawn.

Valhazar straightened himself and found the glares of most of his seniors fixed directly upon him. He had not meant to yawn so loudly and was now unwilling to hurt the sentiments of those with whom he had shared food, drink and a smoke. With eyes lowered to the ground, he apologised for his apparent misbehaviour. He asked pardon for his seeming lack of courtesy in the name of the tiredness caused by the long journey and the rich and excellent food served by his esteemed father-in-law. The ruffled dharvhs were somewhat mollified by his profuse and sincere apologies and forgave him, ascribing his impertinence to his youth.

Valhazar looked at his uncle and saw, to his dismay, that Vanderz had not been fooled by his elaborate excuses. He pretended not to notice.

Later that night, just as Valhazar was about to retire, Vanderz called him aside. The guests from Drauzern had returned to their homes, and the guests from Khwaznon had been accommodated in Augurk's and Angbruk's houses. Meizha and Valhazar were staying with Augurk at the palace, as were Vanderz and Dastorv. Vanderz asked Valhazar to step out onto the terrace on the pretext of viewing the glittering lamps of the capital city, which were beautiful to behold. Valhazar did not protest, even though he knew the true purpose of the summons.

Standing on the terrace, watching the twinkling lights of the city below, Vanderz lost no time in getting to the point.

'What were you doing down there, Valhazar?' he thundered at his nephew. 'We are guests here—and not ordinary guests either. Are you not aware what the consequences of such insulting behaviour can be?'

'Do not be angry, Uncle. I did not mean to insult anyone; but you are well aware that I do not hold with hypocrisy,' Valhazar answered politely.

'What do you mean by *hypocrisy*?' Vanderz demanded.

'I do not believe that the war with Blarzonia was a great political move. It was, in fact, the most idiotic thing we dharvhs have ever done. When we invaded it, Blarzonia had been an infertile, harsh land with no riches to offer for a long time. The internal wars of the natives had seen to that. To spend such effort and so many soldiers on conquering a land that could offer nothing useful was sheer stupidity. That is what I believe. I cannot pretend to feel otherwise.'

'That does not justify your behaviour! Dastorv is a noble dharvh and a relation of your father. He is much senior to you. We were greatly honoured by his agreeing to narrate the tales. Your behaviour was terribly insulting to him! And to Rauz Augurk since Dastorv is his honoured guest. Do you not know that the humiliation of a guest is the humiliation of his host as well? We cannot antagonise the ruling house of Ghrangghirm. The peace between our two countries is fragile, and you are well aware of that. Your marriage to Meizha should make that amity firmer and more lasting. Do not jeopardise it with your immaturity and irreverence!'

Valhazar replied after a pause, his voice icy cold, 'Uncle, I meant no disrespect to anyone, and I am pretty certain no one was seriously offended. Except you. I agree that I might have exerted greater control on the expression of my opinion. However, I have always been, and always shall remain, averse to being treated as a political pawn. I have genuine respect for Dar Dastorv's masterful craft and for Rauz Augurk, and I trust that they are perceptive enough to sense that. I am no longer a young boy, Uncle, so do not presume to treat me as one. And now, if you have spoken all you had to say, allow me to return to my loving wife and the comforts of a warm bed provided for me by my generous father-in-law.'

There was a sting to his last sentence that was not missed by Vanderz. He glared at Valhazar's back with a murderous look in his eyes as the rauzoon turned round and left the terrace, taking the stairs in no apparent hurry. Vanderz followed almost immediately, muttering curses and abuses at his recalcitrant nephew. Neither Valhazar's stinging comment nor Vanderz's reaction was missed by Augurk, who stood in the darkest corner of the terrace, unseen and quiet as a mouse. He had come to the terrace for a walk to digest the heavy dinner and had been standing in deep shadows when his guests had arrived. He had been on the verge of stepping out to greet them when the altercation between uncle and nephew had broken out. He had remained where he was out of a desire to spare them embarrassment and had, consequently, witnessed the entire conversation.

Augurk had been rather amused by Valhazar's reaction to Dastorv's second story. He rather admired the young dharvh's disregard for burdensome protocols and convention. The scene he had just witnessed showed him a side to Valhazar's character that he had never suspected. He frowned. He was apprehensive that Valhazar would end up making too many enemies to be in a position to succeed his father. Of course, dharvhs *won* the position of rauz instead of inheriting it, but a candidate needed the support of enough powerful patrons to be considered as a contestant in the Zhan-ang-Razr. At the same time, Augurk was happy that Valhazar genuinely cared for Meizha and did not think of their wedding as a political gambit. That night, Rauz Augurk went to bed with mixed feelings about his son-in-law in his heart. He was soon dreaming, though not about the unusual rauzoon of Khwaznon.

He saw himself walking down a dark plain. It was so dark that he could not see his hands in front of his face. The ground was uneven, and he stumbled frequently. There was complete silence; no sound reached his ears, not even sounds of his own breathing. Augurk was overcome by an inexplicable fear. Trembling, he fell to his knees and could not stand up again. Suddenly, the earth began to rock violently. Deep crevasses appeared everywhere and hot, molten fire rushed out of the cracks in the earth's surface. Augurk tried again to stand up and run, but could not. His legs gave way under him. As he watched, the ground in front of him collapsed and liquid flame gushed out in a pillar. Riding on the column of lava, a tall, fearsome figure emerged out of the bowels of the earth. The figure was that of a man, but the man was as tall as a mountain and his features were etched in burning brimstone. His eyes blazed with fire, his hair was a mass of flames and his breath was hot smoke. When he opened his mouth to speak, Augurk could see flames dancing inside.

This terrible figure pointed a glowing finger at Augurk and thundered accusingly, 'You have failed to keep your promise! You have not paid your dues to me. You will be punished!'

'Forgive me!' Augurk cried. 'I have tried—I sent out search parties everywhere, but no one found anything.'

'Liar!' the gigantic fiery figure roared. 'You dare try to deceive me! Now you must die!'

He raised his hand; in it, he held a thunderbolt blazing with white fire. Augurk cried out with fear at the sight of the thunderbolt. The fiery figure hurled the thunderbolt at the trembling, crouched figure in front of him.

'No!' screamed Augurk as the deadly thunderbolt rushed at him. He tried to roll away from the path of certain death, and landed on the floor of his chamber with a thud.

He sat up, panting. He had woken from his nightmare, but he was still shaking. The images and the emotions from the dream were still vivid in his mind. He pushed his hair back from his clammy forehead and stood up. It was still a long way to dawn. Rauz Augurk plodded over to a corner of the room where a jug of cool water stood next to an earthen basin. He splashed his face with cool water from the jug and sat down on his bed to contemplate. Sleep had flown from his eyes. He sat thinking about the mission that Nishtar had entrusted him with. It was true that he had sent out search parties and that all of them had returned empty-handed. Not even a scrap of rumour was to be found regarding the location of the City of Stone. In all of Ghrangghirm, no one apparently had knowledge of such a place. Yet he felt guilty. He felt that he had, indeed, not done enough.

He lay down while planning what else he could do. He decided to send the best of his spies to every corner of both dharvh kingdoms, particularly Khwaznon. He had not expanded his search to his neighbouring country due to political and diplomatic concerns. He knew that he still could not do so openly. Without permission from Rauz Valhorz, which would be predicated on the revelation of the entire matter to the rauz of Khwaznon, any investigation would necessarily have to be clandestine. Augurk did not savour the idea. He also did not look forward to sharing the news of the search with Rauz Valhorz. However, spies would not be noticed. And what the rauz of Khwaznon never learnt would not create a diplomatic issue between the two countries. He would charge his spies and scouts to search every inch of the lands. He would order them to enquire in the tiniest village and the deepest cave. As he lay planning how to execute this decision, Augurk fell asleep once more.

When Augurk awoke, the sun was higher in the sky than he would have liked it to be. He cursed his nightmare and dressed as quickly as he could. Then he hurried to meet his guests for breakfast. To his dismay, he found that they had already had breakfast and had proceeded towards the small enclosure in the palace's inner courtyard where entertainment had been arranged for them. Augurk hurried there. When he entered the enclosure, he was greeted with solicitous enquiries after his health. He was puzzled but gratefully replied that he was feeling better.

A large marquee and a stage had been erected in the yard. One side of the stage was curtained off; the performers waited behind this curtain for their turn. Cushions, furs and mattresses had been placed opposite the stage, at the front of the marquee, for the audience. A low table nearby held an abundant supply of food and beverages. On the stage, a group of acrobats was performing. They were followed by a troupe of dancers and then a party of Yomdelian actors. After these performances, the assembly broke for lunch.

During the meal, Augurk observed how well Valhazar was getting along with everyone. He was being very courteous and deferential towards all the senior dharvhs. Augurk looked for hints of irony in his gestures and voice but found none. Valhazar's respectfulness was genuine. Augurk expected Vanderz to be pleased about his nephew's improved behaviour but was surprised to spy a scowl on the dharvh's face. This was the first hint he had that the animosity between the two ran deeper than just friction caused due to Valhazar's flippancy the night before. While talking amicably with all his guests, Augurk found an opportunity to question Angbruk about the guests' reactions regarding to his late arrival. Angbruk seemed rather bemused.

'Valhazar gave us your message that you were indisposed. I was surprised that I didn't know, but found no reason to disbelief your son-in-law. We were all concerned for your health, so we were solicitous when you finally arrived,' Angbruk said. 'What's wrong?'

'Nothing. Everything is fine,' Augurk replied hastily.

Some time later, he managed to find himself next to Valhazar. The rauzoon bowed deeply and whispered that he wanted a word alone. Augurk looked around to check if any of the other guests were noticing them but found them involved with their food and conversations. The two walked a short distance away from the rest of the party.

'What is it, Rauzoon Valhazar? What do you wish to say?' Augurk asked. 'I hope everything is all right.'

'Oh yes! My rauz, everything is fine. I just wanted to apologise for last night,' Valhazar said. Augurk assumed he was apologizing for his irreverence towards Dastorv's story. But Valhazar's next words disillusioned him. 'It is indeed unfortunate that you had to witness the quarrel between my uncle and me. Believe me, if I had known at the time that you were present on the terrace, I would never have behaved thus.'

'How would you have behaved?' Augurk asked, still coming to terms with what Valhazar had just said.

'I would have been more...circumspect,' Valhazar said with a disarming smile. Augurk had thought that Valhazar was, deliberately or unwittingly, going to embarrass him. The young dharvh's answer pleased him. He understood that Valhazar was genuinely ashamed that he, Augurk, had witnessed a scene of such intimacy and indignity.

'How did you learn I was there?' he asked.

'Though I was angry during the altercation, I calmed down by the time I reached the bottom of the stairs. I decided to apologise to my uncle, so I waited for him there. Soon he arrived. He was still angry and was muttering abuses at me. That made me change my mind about apologising. Wrapped up in his anger, he didn't notice me. To avoid another encounter, I slipped into the shadows to wait for his departure before making my way to my chamber. Just after he left, I heard someone else coming down the stairs. So I stayed where I was. Soon, I saw you descend. Following so soon behind my uncle, you could not have failed to witness what had transpired such a short time before.'

Augurk nodded curtly. 'I accept your apology. However, I have been meaning to talk to you as well. I have a question to ask you—this morning, why did you tell the guests that I was ill?' he confronted Valhazar, expecting to see guilt or discomfort or mischief in the latter's eyes. The young rauzoon met his gaze frankly. 'When the rauz of a country fails to receive his guests on time, he is either indisposed or engaged in some critical affair of state. When we all met for breakfast this morning, no one had seen you, and you did not appear even until the end of breakfast. I discreetly found out through Meizha that you were not ill. So I suspected that you were engaged in some extremely confidential matter related to the governance of Ghrangghirm, one that you could not share even with your brother. Everyone was openly wondering what happened to you, so I made excuses on your behalf to prevent undue curiosity among the guests. I felt it to be my duty as your son-in-law. I hope I did not offend you or presume too much.'

Augurk was much impressed by the young dharvh's presence of mind and would have liked to talk to him for a while longer. However, he was hailed by Durng at that moment and had to return to the main party. Soon after, the second half of the entertainment began. This was the display of martial skills by the young dharvhs in the army of Ghrangghirm and was quite to the liking of the guests. First, there was archery. Guzear won this, despite his impaired hand. Wrestling was the next event, and Shornhuz truly shone in this. He defeated all the other contestants almost effortlessly. Just as Augurk was about to announce him the winner, Shornhuz challenged Valhazar, throwing all the guests into consternation. It was not unacceptable for such a challenge to be issued, for dharvhs did not discriminate based on position or class. The consternation was caused by the fact that Valhazar was so obviously inferior to Shornhuz in physique.

Valhazar stood up and, with a deep bow and a smile, said, 'Dar Shornhuz, I have amply witnessed your prowess at wrestling, and I have no desire to subject myself to it.'

Everyone laughed. Since the tournament was more for entertainment than for establishment of martial superiority, refusing a challenge was not considered shameful. Valhazar grinned at the gathered company as his seniors laughed and his friends teased him. He was about to sit down when Shornhuz challenged him again, 'Are you conceding that you are a coward, Rauzoon Valhazar?'

Suddenly the enclosure fell completely silent. All eyes were on the two dharvhs standing face to face. Valhazar was no longer smiling. There was a look of grim determination upon his face. On Shornhuz's face, there was a taunting smirk. Before Valhazar could respond to the challenge, Augurk stood up and announced loudly, 'Shornhuz, you have won the tournament and have defeated all the participants. The rauzoon does not wish to fight, and all of us present here respect his decision. Apologise to him for the insulting term that you just used for him.' The menace in Augurk's voice was obvious.

'I apologise,' Shornhuz said, bowing. 'I got carried away; I meant no offence.'

'And none is taken,' replied Valhazar cheerfully. 'I accept your apology and applaud you on your victory. I have declined today but, perhaps, someday you will do me the honour of going a few rounds with me.'

'I will do so with pleasure,' answered Shornhuz respectfully.

However, neither the anger in his gaze nor the underlying menace in his voice was missed by Augurk. He turned to look at Valhazar. He was sitting again now, applauding the champion with an inscrutable expression on his face. The young rauzoon's words, too, had meant more than they had said, and Shornhuz had understood that meaning, Augurk suspected. Augurk frowned. The more he became acquainted with Valhazar, the more he was intrigued. There were underlying currents of intelligence and strength in his son-in-law, along with a complex and layered personality and an acute awareness of all those traits, but what he meant to do with those qualities was anybody's guess.

Chapter 13

SUMAHO MAKES A DISCOVERY

(13 Lokrin 5007 A.E. to 16 Samrer 5007 A.E.)

Sumaho was happy that the sumagi were no longer working together. Ever since the rift among the sumagi, he had been left alone. No one had asked him to search for information on Astoreth or Zavak or anything else related to them. Nishtar, Vellila and Oram were in Yennthem as usual. Alanor was off gallivanting either in Maghem or in Yennthem; Sumaho had no idea and no desire to know where. Beben was away somewhere in his beloved ship. Sumaho had the entire castle to himself. He did not have to worry about being a good host or providing food and other comforts for his colleagues. Even though the castle was headquarters to all the sumagi, Sumaho generally thought of it as his own special domain since the library was an integral part of it. He was happiest when he had it all to himself. He could spend his days with his books, scrolls and parchments without a thought for anything or anyone else.

A new consignment of old and rare scrolls had just arrived from the east of Maghem that morning. Sumaho was thrilled. The new acquisitions would require special care and storage. He could spend horas repairing and cataloguing them. But first, he had to find a suitable repository. He had just the one in mind! It was a glass cabinet in the oldest part of the library, which contained other scrolls from the same period as the latest lot. His library was immense but surprisingly well-organised. Its millions of occupants stood neatly stacked in its tens of thousands of shelves. The oldest section, which was the innermost section as well, housed the oldest scrolls in recorded history of both Maghem and Yennthem. The further out a shelf was, the newer the provenance of its contents was. Sumaho hustled over to the cabinet he had in mind but was stymied by the lack of space inside. He had been so sure that there were a couple of empty shelves still in there. He sighed.

The lack of space in the cabinet meant that he would either have to create more space, literally, or move the existing cases outwards. He opted for the latter course of action. It would require less effort. Rolling up his sleeves, he placed his hands between two of the glass cabinets which held the oldest of the library's scrolls. He began to chant and blow upon the narrow crack between the two, while making pushing motions with his hands. Slowly, the shelves began to move apart, leaving a gradually widening space between them. When there was sufficient space for a new bookcase, Sumaho stopped. Happy with the progress of his plans, he was about to conjure a new glass cupboard in the empty space when he noticed something unusual.

Sumaho prided himself upon knowing every inch, every crack and every crevice of his library. Therefore, the sight of a round engraving on one of the stone blocks of the wall took him by surprise. It depicted a strange flower with five triangular petals. He felt almost angry at himself for not knowing about the existence of that engraving. But those glass cases had been in the library for a very long time, longer than he had been, he knew. It was quite possible that the mark had been placed even before Sumaho had come to occupy the castle and its enormous library. He had no reason to feel that it reflected upon him in a bad light. However, that knowledge did nothing to assuage his feeling of disturbance.

The engraving was small but intricate and detailed. The light from the torches reflected upon its edges and heightened its lifelikeness. Sumaho gently touched the engraving, admiring the workmanship of whoever had crafted that fantastic flower. He could not say what possessed him to do it, but he pressed down on the engraving. A loud grating noise sounded from deep within the castle and a section of the wall began to move aside, revealing a winding staircase going downwards. Sumaho stood spellbound. Was he dreaming?

The staircase was dark, cold and forbidding. There were no torches along the walls to light the way. Sumaho, who usually preferred to stay away from adventures and physically demanding activities, hesitated at the top of the staircase. Curiosity, nervousness and a sense of dismay were fighting within him. How could the library—*his library*—have a secret staircase hidden in the wall without his knowledge? The thought that he did not know his library as well as he believed gnawed at his heart. He resolved against his instinctive reluctance to explore the staircase and decided to see where it led. He had a hunch that something important or precious would be found at its end, or such elaborate measures to conceal it would not have been taken. As a precaution, he decided to send his thoughts to seek what was at the end of the stairway before venturing down himself.

He closed his eyes and sat in meditation in front of the opening in the wall. Concentrating, he channelled his thoughts into the dark passageway in front of him. His mind was completely focussed as his thoughts raced down the staircase. It was only a momon before they reached the end of the stairs. Something blocked their path there. Could it be that the stairs ended in a blank wall? Sumaho would not believe it. He tried to send his thoughts around whatever was blocking their path, but more than just a physical barrier stood in their way. And it was definitely not the end of the stairway. Sumaho could sense that there was something on the other side of the barrier. The intensity with which it was calling to him was replicated only by the call of his precious books and parchments. Sumaho drew back his thoughts and opened his eyes. His instincts told him that precious scrolls and literature were to be found at the bottom of the staircase. He hardened his resolve; he would not hesitate to go in search of them. Taking one of the torches from the main library, Sumaho stepped into the cold, winding stairway.

The staircase continued underground for what seemed to be miles upon miles but could only have been a few feet. Sumaho knew that space and distance in Maghem were completely illusory entities. He himself had never quite managed to master all the abilities of a magus to such expert levels as the other sumagi had. He was quite adept at manipulating space. But what he knew and understood best were books, scrolls and parchments. And he was happy to dedicate every single momon of his life to them. Distracted as he was by these thoughts, it took Sumaho a minura to realise that the staircase had abruptly come to an end. There was a sturdy wooden door that blocked his path. The door was neither locked nor bolted, but he still could not open it. He understood now why his thoughts had been unable to pass through. He had to exert every ounce of his abilities to make the door yield. By the time he managed to enter through the door, he was on the verge of exhaustion.

But what he saw on the other side made him forget all his toils. He found himself in a chamber that was hewn out of rock and was clearly far older than most of the castle. What truly awed him, though, was the sheer wealth of knowledge that the small, low chamber held. Every inch of its walls held shelves, and every inch of those shelves was overflowing with books and scrolls. A desk, a couple of benches and a chair stood upon the floor, and these too were piled with more literature. Even the floor was strewn with pages upon pages of ancient texts. Sumaho picked up the first page he saw. It was an illustration of the weapons that Astoreth had mastered. It showed the renowned and legendary hero in full war attire, carrying every single one of his weapons. Each weapon was sketched alongside in perfect detail and with a brief description of its provenance and prowess.

Sumaho was trembling with excitement at his discovery. He started checking every document one by one. To his surprise, all of them seemed to be about Astoreth, Zavak, the times they lived in, the eighes who came in contact with them or one or more of the elements mentioned in the prophecy. He could not believe that all the answers to the questions that had been plaguing the sumagi since Mesmen's disappearance had been right under their noses all the time. How thrilled Nishtar and the others would be when he told them! Sumaho picked up another document. It told about a woman warrior at the court of King Barhusa, a warrior who had achieved unbelievable feats and had saved the king's army by climbing Soytaren Mountain and bringing back the Mertis flower. The magical flower was described in detail. To Sumaho's surprise, it was the same flower that had been etched upon the stone in the library wall. The document mentioned the name of this great and noble warrior in bold letters. But before Sumaho could read her name, he felt a blinding pain at the back of his head. Then everything went black!

Ever since his trip to the eighe countries, Oram had been torn in two. It was against his principles to interfere without invitation in the matters of mortals. On the other hand, he could sense a dangerous conspiracy brewing in the eighe kingdoms that could undermine and even destroy them. And then there was the mystery of Mizu's birth. If he was piecing the clues right, then the same individual had helped Misa in the forest, had taken her to the inn disguised as her husband, had been seen by the landlady at the beach where she had literally vanished and had met Oram in the forest as the trapper to tell him about Mizu's birth. But who had it been? Oram had first heard the story of the vanishing lady at the beach during his search for Vyidie. If she had indeed been the Guardian, then it meant that…Oram could hardly come to terms with what it meant. If Vyidie was taking a special interest in Mizu's birth, then there was a possibility that Mizu was Astoreth reborn, wasn't there? But to believe that was to agree with Nishtar's stand on the matter. That was something Oram was determined not to do. He had declared that he would not pursue the prophecy, and he would not. However, he had also promised to help Misa and her son, so it behove him to try to find out who the mysterious lady had been and what Holexar was really up to.

For close to an annus, Oram kept debating with himself while he continued to live his life as a shepherd. Finally, in Kielom of 5007 A.E., he decided to pay a visit to Sumaho. There were two things that the Librarian could help him with. First was the armguard that he had been given by the trapper. If it indeed belonged to Vyidie, there was bound to be some record of it in Sumaho's vast repository of information. The other thing that he hoped Sumaho would be able to help him with was Holexar's past. Who was the seleighe? Where had he come from? Why had he had such a hold over the royal family since the beginning? No one seemed to know anything about the prime minister-turned-king of Samion from before his time at the court. Oram felt that the seleighe's motives could be understood better if his history could be known. Though the chances of finding anything about a contemporary individual in the library were poor, Oram was hopeful. He knew that Sumaho had such love for information that he had systems through which records of every birth, marriage, death, disappearance, crime, war, and all other events, big and small, arrived in the library sooner or later. If there was anything to be found about Holexar's life, Sumaho would find it, Oram was sure.

Therefore, that vernurt, once he had secured his flock and ensured that they would be well taken care of, Oram returned to Maghem to discuss his doubts with Sumaho. He arrived at the castle and was surprised to find that no torches lit its hallways, no fires burned in its fireplaces and dust layered the floor like a carpet. He first went to his own chambers and found that they were exactly as he had left them though no one seemed to have cleaned them in mondans. He passed through the entire castle on his way to the library, finding the same lack of care everywhere. He was aware that Sumaho was apathetic to the castle's general upkeep but could not believe that he had allowed things to go to seed so badly. He was feeling annoyed and decided that his mission would have to wait. First, he needed to have some words with Sumaho about the lack of maintenance of the headquarters.

The moment Oram reached the library, however, he realised that something was terribly wrong with Sumaho. He could believe by a long stretch of his imagination that Sumaho would allow the castle to fall into the filthy condition that he had found it in, but he could not accept that Sumaho would allow the library to gather one speck of dust. And what he saw was complete and utter desecration of all that Sumaho held dear. Shelves had been overturned; glass cases had been broken; books and scrolls were scattered everywhere and were even lying all over the floor; pages and parchments had been torn; dust and cobwebs covered everything. Oram was certain that Sumaho would have died before allowing the library to reach such a state. And since Sumaho was immortal, that was saying a lot.

Oram called out Sumaho's name but received no reply. He stepped inside and called again. He continued to progress further into the depths of the library, witnessing the same scenes of destruction everywhere and calling for the Librarian, but in vain. There was no sign of Sumaho. Oram then proceeded to search the rest of the castle. But Sumaho had vanished without a trace. Oram began to worry. His first instinct was to inform the others. They needed to know what had happened. Besides, one or the other of them might even be aware of what had happened to Sumaho, he mused.

He was about to call the others on the magic mirror in the banquet hall when another thought occurred to him. If any of the others knew about this, and had deliberately kept it from Oram, it was because of one of only two reasons: either he or she was responsible for this or he or she suspected Oram of being the perpetrator. If the first were true, letting the real perpetrator know that Oram had discovered the crime could endanger Sumaho further and even bring danger to Oram himself. If Oram was suspected of being the miscreant, his presence at the library would only confirm the suspicion. Of course, it was possible that none of the others knew anything about Sumaho's disappearance. If they knew nothing about this matter, it was possible that they would suspect Oram the moment he told them. All in all, Oram decided, it was better to keep quiet and search for Sumaho on his own.

Oram began his search by calling to Sumaho in the magic mirror. He had not really expected to find a reply, and he was right. He then proceeded to search all of Maghem. He had to employ the greatest discretion possible. It would not do to allow others to learn of Sumaho's disappearance following so soon after Mesmen's disappearance. The authority of the sumagi was already weakened by the perception that their leader had deserted them. The rift among them had added fuel to the fire. If it became known that Sumaho had disappeared as well, everyone would conclude that the sumagi were too weak to protect even themselves.

Out of fear and greed, the residents of Maghem would rise up in rebellion against the sumagi and their rules that regulated life in the hem. Oram could not allow that to happen. He had to find Sumaho but without allowing the news of his disappearance to leak out. The problem was that Sumaho could be anywhere! Their magical castle was too secluded for anyone to notice if Sumaho had received any visitors. Making enquiries was not only painstaking but practically futile. He searched for five temporas, but his search revealed nothing.

In the end, Oram decided to do something that he loathed from the bottom of his heart. He would have avoided it if he could. This ritual was best suited for finding those who were near death or comatose. Sometimes, it also worked for the living, since in sleep, a spirit is temporarily freed of the body. Oram had to concentrate his powers before he could attempt the ritual. For seven days and nights, he meditated without eating, drinking or sleeping, focussing his energy and his strength into his soul. When on the fifth of Samrer, he felt ready, he went into a deep trance in which he allowed his soul to reach out to Sumaho's.

Oram's spirit travelled through the grey shadows of Zyimnhem in search of Sumaho's soul. Though he touched only the surface of the hem of spirits, he felt an intense pull from the millions of souls trapped there forever. They had sensed one of their own and wanted him to join them. It was a pull that was hard to resist. He could not stay there too long or he would lose the will to return to the realms of the living. Oram began to worry that he would not find Sumaho even this way. The ritual had not worked for Mesmen either. He had almost given up his search when he sensed something pulling him.

This pull was different from that of the spirits of the dead. This was the pull of a living soul. Sumaho was alive, and Oram's soul was being drawn to his. Oram allowed himself to be guided by the hints of Sumaho's presence and soon found himself being drawn at a rapid pace towards a bright light. He braced himself and sped on, bursting into the light with a gasp. His spirit had found Sumaho, but it was just the beginning of the discovery process.

Oram felt extremely uncomfortable sharing the same space as Sumaho's consciousness. It was against nature. Very soon, one of the two would have to evacuate Sumaho's body, or devastating consequences would follow for both. Oram tried to focus on the surroundings. Sumaho had woken up as a result of Oram's soul landing into him. Oram sensed that Sumaho was very confused and not just because of Oram's presence within him. Something else was wrong with him. Something was making him uncoordinated and unfocussed. Soul transposition was always tricky; it felt like wearing armour that belonged to someone else and did not fit properly. Oram tried to see through his colleague's eyes, but Sumaho's ears worked instead. Oram quickly adjusted to Sumaho's body so that he could at least control Sumaho's eyes and ears.

Oram found that Sumaho was sitting under a coconut tree upon a sandy beach. The bright aquamarine waters of an ocean rose and fell in waves in front of him. Oram tried to make Sumaho turn his head to look around, but the magus began to walk towards the water. Oram quickly adjusted again. Sumaho sat back down. He turned his head to the right, and Oram saw the sun low on the horizon. Sumaho turned left, and Oram found a forest of coconut trees. He was obviously on an island, but there was nothing to indicate which one. Desperately, Oram made Sumaho turn once in every direction. He had only momons before he had to leave Sumaho's body. Suddenly, in the distance, Oram spotted another island that stretched out like the ridged back of an alligator. Finally recognising Sumaho's location, Oram let go of him and accelerated to return to his own body.

Normally it took Oram at least a tempora to fully recover from a transposition. This time, however, he had no time to spare for recuperation. He *had* to get to Sumaho before it was too late. When, in a couple of days, he was well enough to stand up on his own, he set out to find his one-time master. Sumaho had inducted Oram into the elite group of sumagi after being rescued by him from a mob of angry villagers. Sumaho had inadvertently got into a scrape without any idea of what the consequences could be. That was Sumaho! Oram had always been rather fond of the scholarly magus, not least because he had been a good master to Oram. He would not allow Sumaho to come to any harm.

Oram found Sumaho at the same place where he had found him during the transposition, albeit sitting under a different tree. Sumaho was in far worse shape than Oram had guessed from the transposition. He was thin and haggard, like he had not eaten in mondans. He was dirty and dishevelled, the bald patch at the top of his head was sunburned and peeling and the narrow ring of hair around it was matted and lice ridden, as was his beard. He was delirious and ill with diseases both physical and mental. He did not even remember who he was or how he had got there! Oram felt an overwhelming sense of pity and anger. Who could have done something so brutal? Oram vowed to find and punish the perpetrators of the heinous act. In the meantime, though, he had to nurse Sumaho back to health. He did not want to take Sumaho back to the headquarters; who knew how he would react on seeing the place? He picked up the small, frail body of the Librarian and returned to his cottage in Yennthem where he intended to look after Sumaho until the latter was fit to return to his own quarters. He also decided not to say a word to anyone about any of it.

Chapter 14

FIGHTING WITHOUT WEAPONS

(9 Sachir 5007 A.E. to 13 Vyiedal 5001 A.E.)

Towards the middle of Sachir, Eamilus declared to Timror that he wanted to learn how to fight. Timror asked him why. Eamilus was surprised by the question. He had assumed that Timror would understand why, given what he knew of Eamilus's past and his plans for the future. The exiled prince of Haalzona had been working his way towards his goal of reclaiming his kingdom from the kocovuses for close to two and a half anni, first with Nishtar, and then with Timror. For him, his entire education and training was for one purpose only. That Timror would question him about his reasons for wanting to learn combat was entirely unexpected. Nevertheless, he explained, 'I wish to return to my country in the near future and free it from the kocovuses. To do that, I need to know how to fight.'

'You cannot free a country full of kocovuses all by yourself,' said Timror. 'No matter how well you fight. What you need is an army.'

'Yes, but to lead an army, I need to be a warrior.'

'Wrong. To lead an army, you need to be a commander.'

Eamilus, now getting rather flummoxed, insisted, 'But if I want to be a commander, I have to know about warfare.'

'That is correct,' agreed Timror. 'However, knowing about warfare is not the same as knowing how to fight.'

'Are you trying to tell me that I don't need to learn how to fight?' asked Eamilus.

'No, not at all,' Timror said. 'I just want to understand why you need to learn combat. So far, none of the reasons given by you are adequate.'

Eamilus raked his brains. Why did he want to learn fighting? What Timror had said was reasonable; he did not need to know how to fight to lead an army. At the same time, for some reason that he could not pinpoint, he could not imagine achieving his goals without that knowledge. There was a flaw in Timror's logic, he knew. He just had to find that loophole to convince Timror to teach him the art of combat. He went over the arguments meticulously. He needed to learn about warfare so he could lead an army against his enemies. What would happen once he had an army? He would lead them against the kocovuses into battle. What would happen in the battle? His forces would fight bravely, facing down the enemy and destroying them. And what would he be doing in the battle? Leading them, of course. But how? He knew enough to be certain that he would have to lead his troops from the front. He had his answer!

'If I want to lead my army from the front, which I have to do if I wish to inspire them enough to stand against hordes of kocovuses, I must fight myself. I cannot stand back in safety and issue commands while my men die in battle. They will not last long if I do so.'

Another thought came to him. He was talking about the distant future. Timror's questions had confused him. There was a far more immediate and pressing reason for him to learn how to fight. Feeling more confident, he added, 'Besides, right now, I don't have an army. And who knows how long it will take me to gather one? Until then, I must face my enemies alone. How will I do so successfully if I cannot fight them and kill them? And who would follow me if I am not known as a valiant warrior, if I cannot destroy kocovuses on my own? I will never manage to have an army if I cannot fight. All the knowledge of warfare will be of no use to me then.'

'Finally you are thinking sensibly,' Timror said. 'All right, I will teach you how to fight. But before you learn combat, you must prepare yourself physically and mentally. You have to be strong within and without.'

'But I am already quite strong,' Eamilus insisted, afraid that the preparations would take a long time. He wanted to start learning combat immediately.

'Not without using your *special abilities*, you aren't,' snapped Timror. 'And you cannot rely on those when you fight.'

'Why not?' demanded Eamilus. He was beginning to wonder whether Timror was looking for excuses to refuse to teach him combat.

'Because it is the easy way to solve your problems. Because other people will accept you and follow you only if they see that you are as *human* as they are, that you struggle with the same weaknesses and fears that they do. Because resorting too much to your instinctive tendencies might push you over the edge someday. Because you cannot build a tower without building a strong foundation. Because you can already kill as a kocovus, but if you want to fight as a human, you must learn it as a human. Because a time might come when your abilities are not enough. And, because I will not teach you otherwise.'

Eamilus felt humbled. He accepted Timror's reasoning and asked what he had to do to prepare himself. Timror began by teaching him meditation and breath-control exercises. Since Nishtar had already taught him these, he needed only a refresher course. Timror quickly moved on to some other exercises. These involved sitting or standing in certain postures while maintaining breath control, or performing certain simple but specific sets of actions accurately and repeatedly. These exercises, Timror explained, would enable Eamilus to control his mind and body while making him both composed as well as physically and mentally agile. He also asked Eamilus to run every day and to perform certain routines that would build his stamina and strength. He was to spend two horas every dawn practising these activities. When Eamilus asked about starting training for combat, Timror replied, 'We will train when you are ready.'

Every morning, Eamilus climbed to the top of a nearby hill and religiously performed the exercises that Timror had taught him. He had thought that the exercises were easy when Timror had first demonstrated them for him. He now realised how difficult the simplest of actions became when they had to be repeated multiple times or when certain easy positions had to be held for a long duration. He began to tire quickly. He sweated as he stood on one leg with his hands raised above his head, trying to think about a candle flame. His muscles burned when he raised his hands and legs fifty times from a supine position. He panted as he ran down the mountain at the end of the routine.

At first, to complete the exercises without getting exhausted, he would often resort to his inner abilities. But he made a conscious effort to curb that habit, knowing that cheating would only delay the beginning of the actual lessons in combat training. Using only his *normal* human abilities, he found, tired him far more quickly and thoroughly than he could imagine. He began to understand why Timror had insisted on his learning combat as a human and on developing his strength first. Slowly but gradually, he could feel his stamina increasing, his muscles developing and his focus improving.

All through outomy, he rigorously followed this routine. As the temporas passed, Timror added to his daily exercises work that would augment his skills. He made Eamilus catch wild rabbits and fowl with his bare hands. He made the boy dig a well, draw water using only a rope and a bucket and use the water to irrigate crops that he had had Eamilus plant and that were a few miles away from the well. He made Eamilus chop log upon log of firewood and carry it in. Soon, Eamilus thought, he would be ready to learn how to fight.

Then, a few days before vernurt officially set in, Timror told Eamilus to clear a patch of ground close to their underground dwelling and ring it in. Eamilus was thrilled. He guessed that this patch of ground was to be the arena where they would train. He could not wait to begin. The very next morning, as soon as he had finished his exercises, he set to work with a will. By evening, the arena was ready. Timror told Eamilus that he would now have to clean and prepare the arena every day in addition to everything else he did. Eamilus did not mind. He asked Timror when they would begin to train, and his teacher told him that they would begin on the first day of vernurt.

The weather had already turned cool. At dawn, especially, the air had quite a nip. Despite this, Eamilus woke early on the thirteenth of Vyiedal, his excitement palpable. He performed his usual exercises, assuming correctly that he was expected to continue with them in the absence of instructions to the contrary. Although their rigour had increased over the mondans, he no longer found them as difficult as he had in the beginning. And he could see and feel the differences that they had wrought in him. He ate hurriedly and reached the arena long before Timror appeared. When Timror reached the arena, Eamilus noticed that his master carried no weapons with him. This surprised him, but he said nothing. When Timror asked him to assume a certain position that, he explained, was a defensive posture, Eamilus could contain himself no longer.

'What weapons will we be training with?' he asked. 'I don't see any with you.'

'None,' replied Timror with a broad smile. 'We shall train with our hands and feet, and every other part of our bodies. You will learn to fight but without the use of weapons!'

'But why? Why won't we use weapons?' Eamilus asked, confused.

'Because I am going to teach you a unique martial art,' Timror replied. 'In this type of fighting, you don't need a weapon. You *are* the weapon!'

He then proceeded to explain to his pupil how one could effectively counter as well as defeat enemies even without the use of weapons. He asked Eamilus to attack him. At first the boy hesitated. How could he attack Timror? The tiny magus surely could not withstand his assault, especially now that he was stronger than ever. But Timror began to insult him, calling him lazy and stupid, knowing that these adjectives annoyed Eamilus. The student, on the other hand, realised what the teacher was doing and was not affected by the insulting tirade. He also realised that Timror was serious about facing an attack. In the end, he attacked Timror half-heartedly. To his surprise, his blow went wide of the magus. Now more alert, he attacked in earnest but with no better result. As he continued to try to grab the magus, he failed repeatedly and began to grow hot and angry. He realised that he was about to turn and forced down his inner monster. The momentary distraction was all Timror needed. Suddenly Eamilus found himself soaring through the air and landing with a hard thud on his back.

When he got back on his feet, he felt as if a horde of buffaloes had run over him, or that he had climbed a mountain at a run. He thought that Timror would send him off to his room to recuperate, but he was mistaken. Timror insisted on continuing the training, making him return to the defensive position that he had begun the training with. This time Eamilus did not protest, although he still felt unsure about how the stolid posture could lead to the almost magical and lightning-fast way in which Timror had dealt with his attacks. As the training progressed, though, Eamilus's state of mind went from incredulous to sceptical to judgemental to appreciative to awed. By the end of training, his body was black and blue and bruised, but his mind was enlightened and his soul was humbled. He would never again underestimate the power of unarmed combat.

For a while now, Alanor had been feeling curious about Prince Feyanor. His journeys in the kingdoms of the west had provided him with many anecdotes about this brave prince. What finally caused him to make up his mind to see Feyanor in person was the remark by a random stranger that Feyanor was the greatest human hero since Rogran. This comment amused Alanor and piqued his interest because Rogran had been Alanor's father, and he had *not* been human, though that was something that Alanor had learnt only recently. Only Nishtar shared this secret. Rogran was generally acclaimed, and rightfully so, as the founder of the human kingdoms of the west.

Before Rogran became their first king, humans in the west had lived within small, self-reliant communities headed by wealthy landowners known as manor-lords. These manor-lords had ceaselessly fought each other over the smallest of pretexts. Rogran had united them into a nation and had established the first human kingdom, marking a turning point in the history of humans in western Elthrusia. If Feyanor was being compared to Rogran, Alanor thought, he *had* to see this young hero!

Alanor reached Lufurdista, the capital of Balignor, on the sixth of Kielom. Despite the cold weather, people were in a jubilant mood. What had added to the festivities, Alanor found, was the announcement that Prince Feyanor would take part in a special procession that day. The procession was to mark the triumph of Prince Feyanor over the tribes of the Ufharn Hills. This was part of King Amiroth's efforts to impress his illustrious brother-in-law, Alanor guessed, or of Queen Lamella's attempts to shower her brother with the greatest hospitality possible. It was also a good opportunity to watch Feyanor unobtrusively, he mused, and felt grateful for the ostentatiousness of the king of Balignor.

The people had been crowding the streets in front of the palace gates for over a hora when Alanor managed to join the audience. They thronged behind cordons on either side of the high street. To ensure the safety of the participants in the pageantry, these cordons were manned by hundreds of armed and alert soldiers. There was hardly enough standing room on either side of the street. Everybody chattered excitedly while waiting for the procession to begin. Alanor took advantage of the crowds to conceal himself in the front row in a position from which he could clearly see everything that was going on. He was a large man, and though age had given him white hair and a beard, it had not succeeded in taking from him his warrior's bearing and strength. Wherever he went, people noticed him, not least because of his aristocratic features. To avoid receiving similar attention at this gathering, he had disguised himself as a tourist from Cordemim, of which there were many. He looked nothing like himself now; no one who did not know him intimately would have recognised him.

The procession began with loud fanfare and a roll of drums at exactly noon. As soon as the fanfare sounded, people began to cheer loudly. The gates of the palace opened slowly and portentously. The first participants of the procession poured out into the street—young girls dressed as butterflies in glittering, frilly, colourful costumes. They skipped about to a merry tune played by a band that came behind them wearing gleaming livery and carrying dazzlingly bright instruments.

Behind them came the king's personal bodyguard, riding handsome and proud horses. Their uniforms were spotless, and their expressions were sombre and alert as they rode through the streets, perfectly in step even without looking at the path as they guided their mounts on. The next to step out were several of the prominent nobles along with their squires. They, too, rode magnificent horses. Soldiers armed to the teeth marched alongside them to ensure that no mishap befell them. This group was led by a distinguished looking man. This man, Alanor learnt from his neighbour—a gregarious young housewife with a young son—was Lord Aminor, the master-of-the-horse and the king's cousin. He was a very important member of the king's inner circle, she added. She also pointed out Lord Parkiod, the commander-in-chief, Lord Beleston, the prime minister, Lord Jumradam, the agriculture minister and several other well-known figures of the king's court. Alanor noticed that both Lord Aminor and Lord Parkiod were highly alert. Though they were part of the pageant, it was clear to a keen observer that their hearts lay in ensuring the security of the participants rather than in the showmanship. He also noticed that Lord Aminor's bearing was far more authoritative than that of any of the other nobles. Even the commander-in-chief appeared to be deferential towards him. It could be because he was the king's cousin, but Alanor suspected that the real reason was probably that Aminor was more important in the scheme of administration than his official title suggested.

Behind the nobles came the royal family and their guests in an open coach pulled by some of the finest horses the people had ever seen. Alanor suspected that these horses were from the kereighe lands. How they had come to be owned by a human king was a matter of great surprise to him. Anyone in Lyisl or Emense found selling horses to humans would invariably be executed, he knew. Someone had definitely been clever enough to evade the authorities!

There were five people in the coach—two men, two women and a child. The people burst into thunderous applause as the royal family passed by them.

They threw flowers in the path of the coach and cried out words of endearment towards the king, the queen, the young prince and his noble uncle Prince Feyanor. Alanor's neighbour was again happy to point out who was who. Alanor observed Feyanor closely. He was a powerfully built man, and rather handsome, but Alanor saw none of the attributes that he had expected to find in a man who was being hailed as *the greatest hero since Rogran*. Feyanor looked jovial rather than martial, friendly rather than awe-inspiring, easy-going rather than valiant. Alanor was disappointed.

Alanor's gaze passed on to the beautiful young woman seated next to Feyanor. She looked noble and calmly confident, smiling with an easy grace and waving with a casual elegance that had to have taken an agonizing amount of practice to be perfected. Alanor asked his neighbour who she was. The housewife informed him that she was Princess Eileen, Prince Feyanor's wife, her tone suggesting that Eileen was not as important as Feyanor. Alanor did not agree with her assessment. He saw strength and courage in her face, but also intelligence and patience. She was happy to remain in the background while her husband garnered all the accolades, but she was not unimportant. Far from it, Alanor thought. There was something else about her that he could not put a finger on, something that made him want to observe *her* rather than the rest of the royal family. As he watched, he noticed that she too was watching the crowds keenly, just as Aminor and Parkiod had been, but much more subtly. Just for a fraction of a momon, their eyes met. Alanor turned his gaze away but looked back almost instantly. She was no longer looking at him. In fact, she looked like she had never looked at him at all. But Alanor was not to be fooled. In the brief moment that their eyes had met, he had sensed something in her gaze. Recognition? No. Consternation? Not really. More like confusion. Like she thought she knew him but could not be certain. Oddly, Alanor felt the same way about her.

Alanor's musings were intruded upon by a gasp from his neighbour, the housewife, and several others standing in the crowd. He turned to look in the direction that they were pointing. Several men dressed in outlandish clothes were leaping off buildings and rushing towards the royal coach. The soldiers surrounding the coach ran to block the attackers, but were thrown down or shoved aside easily. A few punches were enough to knock them to the ground. Alanor, along with a few of the other spectators, had realised by then that this was all part of the show, but most of the members of the audience were still either panic-stricken or stunned. The possibility of a stampede was very real, and Alanor hoped that people would come to their senses before something untoward happened. As the outlandishly dressed men surrounded the coach, one of them yelled out—'I am a tribal from the Ufharn Hills, and I have come to avenge my people by killing the prince of Ashperth!'

Several girls and women screamed and gasped, though most of the crowd had figured out by then what was really going on. Alanor did not find it in good taste, and the expressions on the faces of Lord Aminor and Lord Parkiod said that neither did they. It was also exceedingly reckless and endangered thousands of people unnecessarily. King Amiroth looked highly entertained and proud of the show; Queen Lamella looked a little embarrassed; Prince Amishar looked spellbound. Feyanor's and Eileen's faces were inscrutable. Following the script of the pageant, the so-called men of the Ufharn Hills pretended to attack Feyanor. He drew his sword in style and pretended to fight them off. Several young women gasped again, and this time, Alanor joined them. Not because he was impressed by Feyanor's supposed valour but because he had recognised the sword that Feyanor now held aloft. It was a sword that he was intimately familiar with. At one time, his father Rogran had carried it. Then he himself had been its owner for a while. He had passed it on to his son Gimash all those thousands of anni ago and had never set sights on it again. Until he saw it in Prince Feyanor's hands.

Of course, at the time of owning the sword, he had not known that it was Fylhun. He had learnt the sword's identity, along with the secret of his father's origins, only a short time ago. He had been searching for Fylhun since then. He had managed to discover that from Gimash it had passed to his descendants, but he had not yet succeeded in discovering its exact whereabouts. Until that moment. His hands itched to hold it once again, to ride into battle once again, swinging it at his enemies. The mock fight that was going on in front of an awestruck audience seemed to him a travesty of its power and majesty. The sword that had been carried by the great Astoreth into battle against Zavak, that had pierced through Zavak's immortality, was now nothing more than a stage prop. Alanor felt his anger rising. He would see no more of this farce!

But the dense crowds made departure difficult. He had managed to move only a few steps away when something extraordinary happened in the pageant, something that made Alanor halt. The make-believe men of the tribes had all fallen by then, their 'leader' kneeling at Feyanor's feet, begging for mercy. Everyone urged the prince to 'kill' his enemy. But Feyanor hesitated. Then he sheathed his sword and, helping up the grovelling man, embraced him. The actor, though clearly surprised, played along. There was consternation among the crowds as well as among the actors at the deviation from the script. King Amiroth looked thunderous. Alanor decided to wait and watch what happened next. The silly pageant had suddenly become interesting to him. Standing to face the crowd, Feyanor announced, 'I am Feyanor, prince of Ashperth. I have fought the tribes of the Ufharn Hills, and I have defeated my enemies in their lair. They are some of the noblest foes that I have met. It has been an honour to pit my abilities against them. They are now sworn citizens of Ashperth, loyal to my father King Graniphor. There shall be no more bad blood between us!'

He embraced the actor playing the leader of the attackers again. This time the crowd cheered unabashedly. Alanor saw a hint of a smile on Eileen's lips. King Amiroth, though, looked unhappy. He probably felt that he had been belittled by his famous brother-in-law. Prince Feyanor released the actor and turned to his host. Kneeling before King Amiroth, he declared, 'My lord, King Amiroth, my illustrious and noble brother-in-law, let me bow to you in acknowledgement of your greatness! The welcome that you have shown me is unsurpassed. Where another may have given way to the affliction of envy, you have been gracious and welcoming. Where another might have succumbed to the dark venom of selfishness, you have openly celebrated my glory. It takes a great man to do what you have done. I am indeed honoured to call you my kinsman.'

The crowds went mad with cheering at Prince Feyanor's words. King Amiroth's scowl turned into a smile and he embraced his noble kinsman joyfully. Alanor turned around, shaking his head ruefully. There had been more drama in the interaction between Prince Feyanor and King Amiroth than there had been in the rest of the pageant! But he was beginning to realise that there was more to Feyanor than met the eye. He would have to get to know the man better, he decided. At present, though, he had something far more urgent and demanding to accomplish. Without waiting to see the rest of the procession, Alanor set off for Nishtar's school.

He travelled day and night with the barest minimum of food and rest. He reached Nishtar's school on the seventh of Beybasel. It was almost sunrise. Nishtar had just woken up. He was surprised to find Alanor at his door so early and looking so dusty and dishevelled.

'Is everything all right?' Nishtar asked anxiously, though Alanor would have preferred to be asked if *he* was all right. But that was Nishtar!

'Actually, I have something important to tell you. I did not want to talk over the mirror. One never knows who else might be listening.'

Nishtar nodded, asking Alanor to enter. Ever since the rift among the sumagi, Nishtar and Alanor had been working together. They had stopped using the magic mirrors to communicate except for the most routine and mundane matters. Anything pertaining to the prophecy or its elements was communicated either through pigeons or in person. Nishtar sensed that something really important must have happened for Alanor to have come in person instead of sending a pigeon.

Nishtar waited impatiently while Alanor freshened up and drank some water.

'You seem to have travelled from afar,' Nishtar commented.

'Yes,' agreed Alanor. 'I have come from Lufurdista.'

'That's far indeed!' exclaimed Nishtar, wondering what Alanor could have found there to bring him hurrying all this way.

'I've found Fylhun,' Alanor declared calmly once he was feeling more like himself.

Nishtar, on the other hand, started pacing the floor of his cottage restlessly as Alanor told him the full story of how he had discovered Fylhun in the hands of Prince Feyanor. When he had finished his tale, he asked, 'Do you want me to procure the sword?'

'No,' replied Nishtar, sitting down again, though his face remained excited and contemplative. 'Let the sword be for now. From what you tell me, Feyanor seems to be an interesting character. I have heard about him, of course, but most of the stories are about his heroism. He seems to be intelligent as well. It's too bad that he didn't study under me. Matters would have been so much more convenient if he had! Regardless, I think that the sword will be safe with him. We must keep an eye on him, but there is no need to get the sword from him yet. It would not be easy. The sword's disappearance would cause talk and, like you said, one never knows who is listening.'

'So, what do we do now?' asked Alanor, feeling that Nishtar's decision was a little anti-climactic.

'Now? I go to my students while you rest. You must be tired after your long journey. And later we will talk more about Feyanor and Amiroth and our friend Augurk who has not yet produced any results.'

Although Emense was rightfully well-known as a prosperous kingdom, its eastern half was a barren desert that contributed little to the country's wealth. This portion of the kingdom was also sparsely populated compared to the fertile western half. No rivers and few streams flowed in the desert in the east. These streams were rain-fed and dried up in the heat of the somminar mondans. Yet, there were towns and villages that had grown up around them. The populations of these hamlets were as transitory as the waters of the streams that were their life source. But these habitations had both kereighes and horses. And it was in these that Forsith and Avator decided to ply their trade of horse-wizardry soon after purchasing Habsolm from Engbom.

They reasoned that these towns and villages were more suitable for their purposes than densely populated cities. Often, there were no trained grooms or animal healers in these remote places. The services of a horse-wizard were greatly appreciated by the residents. As long as their horses received good care, the residents would not look too closely at the two claiming to be a horse-wizard and his assistant. It would be easier to get away with their deception. Their plan was to practice among the desert towns and villages until their *craft* was perfected, and they could confidently ply it even in big cities.

Although Forsith had had doubts about Habsolm, the horse proved to be a great asset. He was an ordinary looking but hardworking roan, not very large but sturdy. Though his eyesight wasn't too good, he had a keen sense of smell and hearing. His even and cheerful temperament also helped his masters deal more easily with horses that were too scared or in great pain. In the two mondans that he had been with them, Habsolm had become devoted to Avator, calling him *boss*. The young lad enjoyed the gelding's constant chatter and quips though Forsith thought that Habsolm was too chatty for a good horse. Avator did not relay Habsolm's responses on this comment to Forsith. The older eighe would not have liked them. Avita, too, liked the horse who sensed that the little girl ailed from something serious and was exceptionally gentle with her.

For over an annus, Forsith and Avator toured the desert territories. Their plan was working well, and they were beginning to get recognition for their work among the desert communities. One evening in early Zulheen, they had just finished their work in a village and were on their way out when a messenger came galloping in from a nearby town. Both horse and rider collapsed in front of the village centre. Forsith and Avator busied themselves with caring for the horse while others carried off the messenger to look after him. By the time they had finished tending to the horse, they were exhausted. The horse had been critical and had pulled back from the brink only after extraordinary efforts from the purported horse-wizards. It was too late to leave by then. They decided to stay the night at the village before moving on.

When Forsith and Avator reached their cart, they found Avita playing by herself under the watchful eye of Habsolm. They learnt from the gelding that the messenger had brought news of a robbery. He had told all the villagers that the outlaws came out of nowhere and attacked his town before anyone could understand what was happening. According to him, the bandits had had powerful weapons and fast horses. They had robbed the townsfolk of money, jewellery and silver. They had departed as suddenly and as swiftly as they had arrived. Some soldiers posted to guard the town had pursued them but had been either killed or injured. News about outlaws was not new to the so-called horse-wizards, but the proximity of the brigands' attack was. Forsith made off for the village centre to obtain more information while Avator remained behind to make preparations for the night's stay.

It was the middle of vernurt, and the desert was icy cold at night. Avator led Habsolm to a rented stable stall and covered him up with blankets. Then he booked himself and his companions in for the night into the only inn in the village. While he and Avita were having dinner, Forsith returned with more news about the outlaws. The incident had been repeated to him by the villagers with more details than Habsolm had furnished but had been essentially the same. The few additional particulars Forsith had learnt about the outlaws were, however, worrisome.

He had learnt that the outlaws were well organised. Many of them were deserters from the army of Emense and had fled into the desert for safety. There were multiple groups of outlaws, with the largest of them having between forty and fifty members. They were always armed to the teeth and were utterly ruthless. The king had sent soldiers time and again to curb the menace, but the soldiers had failed to apprehend the criminals. Only the Lord of Esvilar had had some success against the brigands, but his reach did not extend far enough into the desert to uproot them completely. The outlaws knew the desert like the backs of their hands and appeared and disappeared almost magically. Some were even beginning to say that they were ghosts or sprites rather than mortals. Forsith was deeply concerned. He wanted to leave the desert territories and move towards the towns and cities in the western part of Emense. Avator wasn't sure that it was a good idea.

'From what you tell me, it would appear that they only attack settlements. I see no reason why we would need to worry if we remain ambulatory,' he said to Forsith.

The older eighe was not convinced by Avator's argument. True, they had never heard of attacks on travellers, but that could be either because the outlaws left travellers alone or because they left no survivors. The latter seemed more likely to him. He posited his concerns to Avator.

'Whatever be the case,' he added, 'let us get away from the desert for now. It is getting too cold to spend night after night in the open here. And we have become adept enough to convince the kereighes of larger cities of our genuineness as horse-wizards. We can return again next annus.'

Avator did not protest. He had learnt to trust his guardian's judgement. Although not related to them by blood, Forsith had become his and Avita's guardian after their parents' death. After the fall of the royal family, he had stayed despite having no obligation to do so. He was an ordinary looking kereighe, rather short but well-built, though not muscular. He had nondescript greyish-black eyes and hair. His aura was slightly lighter than normal. But beneath his ordinary exterior, Forsith had an intelligent mind and a stout and loyal heart. He was a good judge of character. His decisions were usually well-reasoned and in the best interests of his wards. Avator knew this. He did not oppose Forsith when the older kereighe insisted on leaving the desert. He asked Forsith what the plan of travel was.

'We will begin our journey west tomorrow' Forsith said. 'We are deep inside the desert now, but we can reach the mouth of the Merosh River in three temporas. After that, we will travel south-west along the river and start approaching localities settled on its banks.'

The next morning, they started early and headed west. Before long, the village disappeared behind them although they had travelled no more than a few miles. The desert was notorious for playing tricks like that on travellers. Not long after, Habsolm began to neigh restlessly.

'What is the matter, Habsolm?' Avator asked him.

'I can smell horses—warhorses—coming this way. About a dozen,' he replied anxiously.

Avator told Forsith what Habsolm had said. They looked at each other grimly, their expressions reflecting the same thought—outlaws! Forsith quickly began to gather their belongings. He packed the most essential ones in a bundle and handed them to Avator. Taking Avita by the hand, he led her outside the cart. He gave Avator the two swords that the boy owned but kept his own.

'Take the horse and flee,' he said to Avator. 'Get out of the desert. Go to the mouth of the Merosh.'

'What about you?' Avator asked.

'I will meet you there within a few days of your arrival,' Forsith replied, averting his gaze.

'No,' said Avator calmly. He was feeling terrified, but he would not flee. 'I know what you are trying to do, and I cannot allow you to do it. Please do not take me for a fool, Forsith. I'd like to think that you have taught me better.'

Forsith smiled wanly. 'What other way is there?' he said.

Avator turned to Habsolm. 'How many horses did you say were coming?'

'A dozen or so,' answered the gelding, who was quite nervous now. 'And they are coming fast.'

'So we can't outrun them,' commented Avator. 'And we cannot fight them.'

'I can hold them back until you two are safely away,' Forsith volunteered.

'No, Forsith, you cannot. Your sacrifice will be in vain. Even if Avita and I flee while you remain behind to face them, you cannot buy us more than a few minuras. That will not be enough. I do not mean to insult your skill with the sword, Forsith; I am merely being rational.'

Forsith smiled.

'So, to continue,' said Avator. 'We cannot fight them, and we cannot flee them. Therefore, we have only one path left to us—we must join them.'

'What!' exclaimed Forsith and Habsolm together. The force of their exclamation scared Avita. Avator frowned. He calmed her down. Then he told her to sit inside the cart, making absolutely no noise. She nodded, understanding that something serious was afoot. Forsith placed the three swords back in their hiding place under the cart's bed and closed the coverings of the cart.

'Listen,' said Avator to Forsith and Habsolm in an urgent tone, 'we must convince the outlaws that we are worth more to them alive than dead. That is the only way we can save ourselves.'

'But how will we do that?' asked Forsith, wondering if the boy had become a little unhinged out of panic.

'We have convinced scores of kereighes that you, Forsith, are a horse-wizard. We need to repeat that deception. We will have a very brief opportunity to prove our worth as horse-wizards to the outlaws, and we must be able to convince them.'

'How will that work?' Habsolm and Forsith asked almost simultaneously.

'They have good horses. They probably have someone to look after them but, then again, maybe they do not. The services of a horse-wizard could be invaluable for a group of outlaws. After all, the desert is not the most hospitable climate for horses. And the chances of there being a talented groom among their numbers are low since a skilled caretaker of horses would not need to resort to marauding to earn a living. Not in a kereighe country, at least. Convincing the outlaws of our value as living kereighes rather than dead ones is our only option now.'

Forsith could not fault Avator's logic. However, he knew nothing about the outlaws' horses. How could he successfully pass himself off as a horse-wizard to these cutthroats without revealing that Avator could speak to horses? But he began to feel more confident as Avator outlined the plan in detail. On no account were they to allow the outlaws to know that Forsith was quite capable with the sword and that Avator could speak with horses. It could prove dangerous for them. They would present themselves as a horse-wizard and a smith.

'Habsolm, can you talk to their horses from this far?' Avator asked. The outlaws were still at a distance though they were quickly closing in. 'We need to find out as much as possible as soon as we can.'

'I'll try,' said Habsolm nervously.

'Good boy,' said Avator, stroking his neck. 'If you succeed, I will give you a bushel of apples for dinner.'

'And if I don't?'

'You will probably *be* dinner for the outlaws,' said Avator in all seriousness.

'All right then, no pressure at all,' joked the horse weakly. Avator could not resist a smile even in that tense situation.

While Habsolm tried to communicate with the outlaws' horses, Avator and Forsith finalised their plan. Avita, true to her instructions, was sitting inside the cart, quiet as a mouse. Habsolm called to Avator and relayed that he had succeeded in talking to some of the horses. They had a groom, he informed Avator, but not a good one. They also had not received good horseshoes in a while. Most importantly, they had no one in the outlaw camp who could speak to horses. Avator thanked the kaitsyas for that stroke of good fortune. He praised the gelding and told him to continue trying to obtain more information.

Very soon, the outlaws were close enough for Avator and Forsith to see their brown and white garb. They wore dun coloured turbans whose tails were wrapped around like masks over their faces. The gleam of their weapons wasn't concealed even by the cloud of dust around them as they galloped towards the stranded travellers. Their eyes shone as cruelly as their weapons, Avator thought, although at that distance, he could not yet see their features clearly. For a momon, he doubted his own plan. Would an attempt at escape have been a better idea, he wondered. Then he cast the doubts away and focussed on the situation at hand.

There were about a dozen outlaws, all on horseback. The horses were fine, proud creatures who had obviously seen better days. Avator wished he could talk to them, but he held his tongue. Forsith and he looked from one outlaw to the other fearlessly as the brigands circled them in, standing a few paces from them, observing calmly. One of them, obviously their leader, clicked his tongue and his horse moved ahead a few steps.

'You are either very brave or very foolish,' the outlaw addressed them. 'You did not run when you saw us coming. Do you know who we are?'

'Yes, you are outlaws. And we are neither very brave nor very foolish,' Forsith replied, trying to sound far more confident than he felt. 'We did not run because we were waiting for you. We want to join your ranks.'

The answer obviously took the outlaws by surprise. Those forming the ring moved uneasily. The leader's eyebrows shot up.

'This is the strangest plea of mercy I have ever heard,' he said. 'Why would I want to include an ordinary kereighe with a young boy, an old cart and a blind horse in my gang?'

Habsolm neighed abuses at the outlaw captain for being called blind, but Avator did not bother to translate. He and Forsith had planned out what to say to this obvious question.

'I am Eronsom, a horse-wizard,' Forsith said. 'This is Mordeph, my nephew. He is a smith. I heard about the attack on a nearby town yesterday. When I learnt of the fine horses that you possess, I could not resist wanting to see them for myself. Now that I see them, I feel that I would be most gratified to be able to look after them.'

'Why should I believe you? You may be a charlatan,' said the leader of the outlaws.

'If I am a charlatan, then how can I tell that the grey mare has had a foal not six mondans ago? Or that the chestnut lost a nail from its horseshoe just yesterday? Or that they have not had grain to eat for three mondans now and are being fed only hay? Some of them are beginning to catch cold but have not received treatment; though they look all right now, they might drop dead any minura if they remain uncared for. Would a charlatan know all this?' demanded Forsith with the utmost confidence laced with contempt.

Avator could see that their plan was beginning to succeed. The looks in the outlaws' eyes said that they were willing to accept that Forsith was a horse-wizard. Would they really fall for the ploy?

'Even if I agree that you are truly a horse-wizard, why should I spare you? I do not need a horse-wizard; I have grooms capable enough of looking after my steeds. It would be the work of a minura for my eighes and me to take your money, your cart and your horse and to leave you and your nephew dead for the vultures.'

'Or, you could let my nephew and me keep our money, our cart and our horse and allow us to accompany you to your camp,' Forsith responded. 'Because you *do* need my services. I can see that quite clearly. If your grooms had been capable, your horses would not have been in such a pitiful state. And such fine horses too!' he added with feeling. 'You can obviously kill us and leave us for the vultures, but perhaps we would be more use to you alive than dead. You ride like one who is accustomed to horses; I assume you care for them too. Would you rather let them perish than let us join your gang?'

'Even if I allow you to live, why should I spare the boy? I cannot believe that he is a smith. He is too young to be one.'

Avator snatched the medallion from around his neck and gave it to Forsith, who handed it to the outlaw leader. They had an advantage now, he knew, and had to press it. Forsith told the outlaw that Avator had made it himself. He also showed the outlaw captain Habsolm's horseshoes; they were among the last articles that Avator had made while at Lianma. The outlaw leader stared at the objects attentively and asked Avator's name, although Forsith had already told him both their names already.

'My name is Mordeph,' Avator replied. His voice was steady but deferential as he answered.

The leader turned again to Forsith and said, 'The runes behind this medallion are not the boy's.'

'No, they are his master's. He was a novice when he made this medallion and was not allowed to use his own runes. The horseshoes bear his own mark,' explained Forsith.

The horseshoes, which were also quite well made, did indeed bear the runes ᛗᛞ for Mordeph, which had been Avator's alias since their stay in Lianma. The captain still looked unconvinced. Avator wanted to be asked to fix the shoe of the chestnut horse. He was itching to speak but knew that Forsith had things well under control. He could ruin everything by speaking. To his relief, Forsith said, 'Let him fix the chestnut horse's shoe, and you can see for yourself whether we speak the truth or not.'

The outlaw captain nodded, and the brigand riding the chestnut horse dismounted. He led it to Avator. The boy set to work without a word. Though it was far more difficult to do the job outside of a smithy, he managed without any mistakes. The outlaw who had been riding the horse checked the work and nodded to the captain. The latter still looked unconvinced.

'What is in the cart?' he demanded.

'Our possessions, and my niece Menithyl,' Forsith answered honestly. In a burst of inspiration, he added, 'She has been cursed and is under the protection of the witch of Temtema.'

This produced the reaction that he had hoped for. The outlaws began to murmur uneasily. Avator felt nervous. He knew why Forsith had mentioned the witch. He wasn't sure, though, whether the result would be favourable or otherwise. He hoped it would be in their favour.

'Show me!' the captain ordered.

Forsith immediately removed the covering from the cart and gently brought out Avita. She looked scared but not inordinately so. She stared at the outlaws surrounding them with her big, beautiful eyes, wondering what was going on. Forsith showed the outlaws the charm that the girl wore around her neck.

'How much money do you have?' the outlaw captain demanded. Forsith told him.

'Hand over your money to me, and we will spare your lives. If you wish to join us, you can follow us to our camp. We cannot go at your pace. You will have to follow us on your own as best as you can,' the captain said.

Forsith agreed and held out the money. The captain gestured and one of the other outlaws took the pouch from Forsith. Although their weapons had been cleverly concealed, Forsith was worried that the outlaws would search their cart and find the weapons. One was about to look inside the cart, but the captain ordered him to stand back. Then, to a kereighe, they turned round and galloped back in the direction that they had come from. The travellers' sigh of relief was almost palpable.

'Can I sit down and rest, boss?' Habsolm asked shakily.

'You have done well, Habsolm,' Avator said. 'Rest a while before we follow the outlaws.'

'Follow the outlaws? Are you mad?' demanded Forsith. 'We just got away with our lives!'

'No, we did not,' said Avator confidently. 'The captain wants to test us. He wants to see if we were telling him the truth about wanting to join his gang. If we follow him to the camp, he will take us in. If we try to escape, he will hunt us down.'

Forsith recognised the wisdom in the boy's words and wondered when Avator had developed such acumen. They rested for half a hora and then began to follow the tracks of the outlaws' horses. They followed the tracks for two days; at that point, the tracks vanished. They were wondering what to do when one of the outlaws came walking up to them. It was the brigand who had led the group two days ago. His face was not concealed now. Avator saw that he was tall and had thick, black hair. He was no longer young but was still quite handsome. He walked with the confidence of a leader, and his charisma was unmistakable. He had shrewd, dark eyes that were hard with cunning and ruthlessness. His upper lip had been cut into two and had healed badly, giving him a snarling appearance that, somehow, did not detract from his handsomeness. His aura was a deep reddish-black. If Avator had not known him to be an outlaw, he would have mistaken the brigand for a noble injured in battle. But he was an outlaw, a robber, the boy reminded himself. A law-breaker. An ignoble lowlife. He had had to surrender to the robber for the time being, but he would escape as soon as he could, Avator told himself.

'My name is Igrag,' said the outlaw captain with a menacing grin. 'And you have passed my test. From today, Eronsom, you will look after our horses. Mordeph will set up and run a smithy. He will also work with us as a scout. If you have any questions, do not ask them. Welcome to my camp. May you be with us long!'

The threat in Igrag's final words was clear to Forsith and Avator. As Igrag led them through secret paths to their hideout, Avator could not help wondering about the vagaries of his fortunes. He had been born a prince, had been forced to flee and had become dependent on his uncle. Then he had become a smith's apprentice, a fugitive, another smith's apprentice, a wandering peddler, a vagabond and a horse-wizard's assistant in quick succession. Now he was an outlaw!

Chapter 17

(7 Zulheen 5007 A.E.)

Into the second tempora of Zulheen, vernurt was well entrenched. At a high altitude, the small village of Bolsana was exposed to the elements. But the people of Bolsana had prepared in advance for the cold weather. Firewood had been gathered in piles. Warm clothing had been sunned in advance. Food had been stockpiled. Though still harsh, vernurt was no longer a cause of apprehension for the residents of Bolsana. In the anni before Misa's arrival, they had dreaded the cold mondans that had never failed to kill—animals and people alike. Now, they were fortified enough to face the cold with confidence. The terror of vernurt was a thing of the past; the bitter cold had lost its bite.

In fact, the younger children did not even recall how heart-numbing and soul-withering the cold had been for the villagers. They were almost indifferent to it. Some of them even enjoyed the vernurt as, during the height of the cold season, it snowed in the upper reaches of the mountain on which Bolsana was settled, and they liked to play in the snow.

One of these children who loved the snow was Mizu. On the morning of the seventh, when he woke up at his usual time, he felt unsettled. He had not slept well. An odd sensation of discomfort had given him nightmares all night. He could not remember the strange dreams, but he had a vague sense of having battled someone or something all night. He felt worse than he had before going to bed the night before. Then he had been merely tired; now he felt uneasy in addition to being tired. He could not put a finger on what exactly was bothering him. At first, he ignored this disturbing feeling and went about his daily chores, hoping that it would vanish with the progression of the day. As the day wore on, though, the discomfort grew. Finally, he told his mother.

Misa suspected that he was coming down with a cold or a fever. He had had a few bouts of cough and cold during previous vernurts, and she had been anticipating something of the kind that annus as well. To her surprise, the vernurt that annus had passed without causing any health issues for Mizu so far. Perhaps it had been too much to hope for that the entire season would pass by without the boy falling ill. Misa checked his forehead, but it was cool. Mizu had no fever. He was not sniffing or coughing. He did not have a blocked nose or sore throat. Relieved, Misa dismissed Mizu's restlessness as a manifestation of his wanting to go outside to play and sent him out after wrapping him up in warm clothes.

Mizu, though, was surprisingly unenthusiastic about playing outdoors. When she asked him why, he could not answer. Misa began to feel anxious about what was happening to him, and Mizu could sense it. So he lied that he had changed his mind about going out and left before his mother could question him. He joined the other children of the village in playing catch-me-if-you-can. Little Mizu was fast, though not the fastest, and could often elude older children trying to catch him. They played for over a hora, running here and there and yelling and shrieking with joy. When they tired of it, Mizu suggested a game of hide and seek. Immediately, the others began to make excuses to return home. Hide and seek was still Mizu's favourite game. The trouble was that he was exceptionally good at seeking. Even his mother never managed to hide for long despite using what people called 'eighe magic'. Disappointed at his friends' disappearance, Mizu returned home.

Misa was a little surprised to see him home so soon. He told her what had happened. Since this was not the first time that the village children had deserted him to avoid playing hide and seek, she knew what would cheer him up. To distract him, she began to play a word association game with him while she went about her chores. She would say a word, and Mizu would respond with the first word that came to his mind on hearing that word. This was one of their favourite indoor games. It never failed to cheer Mizu up when he was upset with the other village children or wasn't feeling well—neither of which happened frequently—or when the weather forced him to stay cooped up inside the house—which did happen often enough in vernurt. Misa used it to increase her son's vocabulary, throwing new words at him every time they played. When he encountered a new word, Mizu did not respond with a word of his own. His mother then explained the meaning of the word to him before moving on to a different word. She came back to the new word later, giving Mizu another go at it. Mizu had never failed to respond to any word more than once. It also often gave Misa a clue about the young boy's thoughts, which helped her understand him more easily.

The game began as usual. Misa said 'good' and Mizu replied with 'boy'. Misa laughed and said, 'horse'; Mizu said, 'Marsil'. 'Cat' was met with 'tail' and 'cow' with 'bell'. These words and responses were favourites. Misa continued with other words as Mizu pranced around her, smiling and getting into the spirit of the game.

'Sun.'

'Clouds.'

'Red.'

'Fire.'

'White'

'Snow'

'Noon'

'Storm.'

The last answer made Misa stop and frown. She did not understand how Mizu could have associated 'storm' with 'noon'. Before they could resume the game, Mizu turned pale and sat down heavily with an 'Oh!'

Misa rushed to tend to him, but despite a thorough examination, found nothing wrong with him physically. 'What's the matter?' she asked him, concerned.

'Snow. Storm. Noon,' said Mizu cryptically.

'What do you mean?' asked Misa, puzzled.

'Snow. Storm. Noon,' Mizu repeated emphatically.

When Misa still did not understand, he insisted, 'Noon. Storm. Snow. *Today!*'

'Are you saying that there's going to be a blizzard at midday?' Misa asked, suddenly realizing what he was trying to convey. Mizu did not know what a blizzard was, so Misa explained it to him.

'Yes,' agreed Mizu on learning the meaning of the word. 'That is what is going to happen. Blizzard.'

Misa frowned. Why was Mizu saying that a blizzard was coming? How could he know? Had one of the villagers told him? Or one of his playmates? She checked the sky. Though the sun was hidden behind clouds, it did not look like a storm was brewing. Besides, it was too early in the season for snowstorms. Mizu must have been mistaken, she concluded.

'Who told you about the blizzard?' she asked.

'No one. I just know,' Mizu replied. 'That's why I've been feeling strange,' he added as he suddenly connected his discomfort to his unexpected weather forecast.

'How do you know?' Misa probed, curious.

'I just know,' Mizu maintained. 'I know here and here,' he added, touching his chest and his forehead.

A cold chill ran down Misa's spine as she recalled the last time she had seen Mizu use these gestures. He had been too young to pronounce any words clearly back then but had understood what the birds and animals around him had said. When quizzed by her as to how he knew, Mizu had pointed to his head and his heart just as he was doing now. She could not ignore his warning, she decided. It could be another instance of his uncanny ability to understand things intuitively. His instinctive understanding of things had once saved him from a group of monsters called khaypers that had attacked the village. She was willing to trust his gut feeling or whatever it was.

Ordering Mizu to stay indoors, Misa hurried to find Leormane. The chief of Bolsana was busy with the repair of an empty storehouse. Seeing Misa's worried look, he stepped aside to enquire what was wrong. When she told him what Mizu had said, he laughed. Misa did not join in.

'Are you serious?' he asked, incredulous. 'He's just a kid. Maybe he isn't feeling well and wants your attention.'

'No, I don't think that that is the case,' Misa responded firmly, shaking her head for emphasis. 'He sometimes displays an uncanny tendency to understand things that are not evident to others. Remember how he knew how to hide from the khaypers? And how good he is at hide and seek? Besides, isn't it better to be safe than sorry? We can always say that it was a drill if there is no blizzard. We do conduct drills of all sorts to keep everyone on their toes; they will not doubt us.'

Leormane frowned as he mused on Misa's words. He wasn't unfamiliar with Mizu's unusual abilities. But was he really going to ask everyone in the village to drop whatever they were doing and rush to their homes to take shelter against a blizzard that had precious little chance of coming? And what if the boy was right, said a little voice inside his head. Did he dare risk the welfare of everyone in Bolsana? He made a decision.

'Get everyone to return to their homes,' he ordered Misa. 'Tell them to stay indoors and prepare for a blizzard. If they protest or if they don't take this seriously, tell them that it is my command. I am going to fetch the men who have gone out to the fields, the river and the upper reaches of the mountain. There are still over two horas to noon. I can bring them back safely if I leave right now.'

'Hurry back!' Misa said. She was grateful to him for taking Mizu's prediction seriously. She was certain that Mizu was not mistaken. What would she have done if Leormane had not agreed to follow her plan? She was glad that she could depend on him at all times to do what was right. She never stopped admiring Leormane's steadfastness and dedication towards those he cared about. She stood watching him disappear out of the village before hurrying off to warn all the villagers about the impending blizzard. Some trusted her judgement based on the miraculous things they had seen her do and obeyed without a question; some had to be told that it was Leormane's order before they agreed to comply.

When she was certain that all the villagers were taking measures to protect themselves from the coming blizzard, she fetched Marsil from the stables into her house. Marsil was one of four horses owned by the villagers, and the other three had also been taken into their owners' houses. The mare appeared nervous and whinnied unhappily as Misa led her away. The sky had turned a much darker shade by then. The clouds were hanging low, and a strong wind was beginning to pick up. It was almost noon. Misa hurried home. She fastened and secured the windows and boosted up the fire in the hearth. She wrapped more warm clothing around Mizu, Marsil and herself. She also took other measures to ensure that they would remain warm, measures that would have been considered as eighe magic by the villagers.

By then, there was no doubt about Mizu's forecast. Soon a fierce, snow laden gale was howling and rushing at the little house, trying to knock it down and blow it away. The residents inside were safe, if nervous at the virulence of the storm. The house would endure, they knew, and the fire and warm clothes would keep them as comfortable as was possible. Misa placed a pot on the fire to make some soup. Hot soup would do very well on such a day. Suddenly, Mizu rushed to open the door. Misa caught him before he could throw it open, shocked by his unexpected behaviour.

'What are you doing?' she demanded.

'Leom!' Mizu declared, struggling to free himself.

Realising what he meant, Misa quickly opened the doors. A blast of frigid air loaded with snow blew into the house. The fire wavered and almost went out. Marsil neighed fearfully. Outside, visibility was lowering rapidly. Misa was debating whether to go in search of Leormane when the chief himself appeared, struggling against the rapidly worsening storm. Misa yelled to help him find the right direction. By the time Leormane stumbled inside, a layer of snow was deposited inside the house. It was as cold inside as it was outside. Misa had to redouble her efforts to ensure that all of them would not die of cold. It took a while for them to regain enough warmth. By then, the blizzard was raging outside with full force. It reminded Misa acutely of the one in which she and Marsil had been caught. Apparently, the mare remembered it too, for she neighed nervously every now and then and had to be comforted by her or Mizu, who was happy to coo to Marsil to calm her down whenever she began to fidget nervously.

'Why didn't you stay in your own house? You shouldn't have risked coming out here,' Misa scolded Leormane once everything had settled back down.

'I couldn't bear the thought of the two of you facing this by yourselves. I was worried,' he answered simply.

It seemed completely absurd to Misa that Leormane, an ordinary human vulnerable to the blizzard, would worry about her when she was more than adequately equipped to deal with any kind of weather. This generosity was one of the things she liked about humans, though not all humans were so kind. The folks of Bolsana, and their chief in particular, stood out even among those that were. At times, Misa could not believe her good fortune for stumbling upon them.

'Thank you for looking out for us,' she said to Leormane.

'It's Mizu we should thank for saving all our lives,' Leormane remarked. They turned to see how the young boy was faring. To their utter surprise, he was curled up against a supine Marsil and was fast asleep.

'I still can't understand how he can do these things, know these things. You've told me that it is not common even among eighes. Are you sure about that?' Leormane asked Misa in a whisper.

She frowned slightly as she answered, also in a whisper, 'Yes, I am. In fact, I have never even heard of anyone having an ability like this. I mean, there are those who can foretell the weather. And there are those who are instinctively good at finding things or people. There are also those who have a green thumb and can grow just about anything. Mizu's grandmother—his father's mother—had that talent. And I have heard of eighes who can speak to horses, though few among the seleighes have that talent now. But there are none, to the best of my knowledge, who can do all of these things.

'We call these talents 'gifts'. They are different from normal talents or abilities; they are deeper rooted, more defining of their possessors. All individuals of all races have a gift. Some are good soldiers, some are exceptional farmers and some are brilliant strategists. The strength of a gift varies from individual to individual. Some are able to discover and nurture their gift, some lose it through ignorance, indolence or irresoluteness. Rarely does someone have a gift to a noteworthy degree. Even rarer is one who has more than one gift. But Mizu...Mizu does all these things instinctively. And they are all different gifts on the surface. He's really good at each too. He says that he knows these things in his head and in his heart, which makes me think that what he does is something else altogether. I suspect that it's a single gift that manifests in the form of multiple ones. If that is true, then it's a gift that no one knows about.'

'How can you be sure?' asked Leormane, fascinated by Misa's long exposition about gifts and talents.

'We had to learn all kinds of things when I was...younger. The list of gifts was one of those. We have unique names for possessors of different talents. So, I'm absolutely certain that if Mizu can do these things because of a gift, his gift is one that has just been born or has been lost for thousands of anni.'

Chapter 18

IN IGRAG'S CAMP

(2 Beybasel 5007 A.E. to 24 Yodirin 5007 A.E.)

It hadn't been long since they had begun their lives with the outlaws, but Avita had already settled in. She found it strange that there were no kereighe girls there and hardly any kereighees. Most of the eighees at the camp were family members of the outlaws and came to meet their relations intermittently. None of them stayed for any length of time. This did not bother Avita unduly. She was used to being cared for by Forsith and Avator. Though Avator was often away from the camp, sometimes for days, Forsith was able to devote enough time to her despite his work. When he could not, she found ways to entertain herself. She could play on her own for horas, making pies, dolls or other objects from mud. She also liked to sing to herself. She liked to walk around the camp, quietly watching everyone busy at their chores.

She had begun to help Forsith with some of the housework now that Avator was often very busy. She did not mind living in the outlaw camp. She did not understand why Forsith did. He had tried to explain to her that the kereighes in the camp were not good kereighes and that they had to be very careful about what they said or did there. She had been rather afraid of them in the beginning but had grown used to them over the days. Forsith had repeatedly explained to her that she would have to answer to the name of Menithyl in front of everyone at the camp though he continued to call her by her real name in private. He was to be called Eronsom, and Avator was to be called Mordeph, he had explained. Even though she did not understand why they all had two names now, she complied with Forsith's instructions. It was like play-acting, and she did not mind. What she really liked was that everyone treated her as if she was normal. No one stared at her or pointed at her. No one called her names. No one teased her. Her life had changed for the better.

What had not changed were her recurring dreams of the human boy. She dreamt of him very often now. The dreams had become extremely confusing of late. Earlier, she had only dreamt of him and the old witch who hurt him but now she often dreamt of him as a grown up as well. Sometimes she dreamt that he was trying to read a book or eating scraps or catching insects; sometimes she dreamt that he was killing monsters or going on voyages or fighting with other warriors. Sometimes one type of dream melded into the other, leaving her perplexed and dazed. She felt tired and irritable when she awoke. At the same time, she did not want the dreams to end. She did not understand why she was ambivalent about her dreams. She thought of telling Avator or Forsith several times. Every time, somehow, she hesitated and changed her mind.

She was beginning to feel a sort of connection with the boy: not exactly friendship but a link of sympathy. She was interested in what was happening in his life and who he was. She wished she could meet him face to face so that they could talk. What would they talk about? Would he even want to? Avita did not know. But when she dreamt of him, she felt that she knew him. It never struck her as strange that she could feel such a strong bond with someone whom she had never really met and whose name she did not know. The more Avator became involved with the outlaws, and the more Forsith worried about him, the more Avita was left alone. She chose to find solace in the mysterious boy she dreamt of. He was her friend; he was the one who gave her hope, the one who shared her pain like no other could. At one time, she had dreaded her dreams, but now she looked forward to them and dreaded them at the same time. Unobserved by her guardians, Avita began to change.

At the beginning of Beybasel, vernurt still clung to the dry desert sand though it had begun to recede elsewhere. One such cold night, Avita dreamt that she and the boy were standing atop a mountain. She had never been there before, not just in real life but also in her dreams. She was acutely aware of his presence, like he was pulling her closer without actually touching her. She felt scared. She remembered what had happened the last time that she had held his hand. Did she? She tried to recall what had happened but could not be certain. Then why was she afraid of getting close to him? It would lead to untold misery, a voice whispered in her ear. What would happen? Something bad, the voice whispered again. She took a step backwards, but when she looked, she found that she was closer to the boy. Every time she tried to walk away, she moved closer to him. The voice warning her was now screaming in her ear to get away from him, to stay away from him. She was trying desperately to escape but could not. She turned around but found herself facing the same pale, desperately scared boy.

'Go away!' she screamed, terrified. She could not believe that she had wanted to see him in her dreams just a short while ago. Why had she wanted that? Now all she wanted was to get away from him. He reached out to her. It seemed to her that he had done so hundreds of times before. But it could not be true, could it? How could it? If taking his hand led to untold misery, why would he want her to hold his hand? Suddenly she was no longer afraid. She wanted to hold hands with him. It was the most natural thing to do. It was the right thing to do.

She reached out in response to his outstretched hand. Their fingers touched. But before she could get a grip, the earth began to tremble violently. The ground shook so hard that Avita could not remain upright. She fell on the hard ground, scraping her knees. She tried to stand up, but the undulating mountaintop prevented her from getting back on her feet. She looked to see how the boy was doing. To her horror, she found that the ground in front of her had split open, revealing a bottomless pit, and the boy was clinging to the edge of the chasm by his fingertips. He was calling to her for help. She crawled forward to pull him up.

But the voice that had warned her before spoke again. It reminded her that she should not touch him. 'See what happened when you did not listen!' the voice threatened. Avita had reached out to help the boy. Her outstretched hand was inches above his when the voice warned her. She froze. The disembodied voice was right! The earth had fallen away from under their feet because she had touched his hand. No, she could not risk doing so again. But what else was she supposed to do? How could she help him up without taking his hand? She looked around desperately for a rope or a stick or anything else that she could use to pull him up without touching him. But there was nothing except miles upon miles of quaking, undulating, barren rock. She scrambled back to the edge of the cliff where the boy was dangling by his mere fingertips and begging her to help him. In her desperation, she reached out to take his hand even as the warning voice shrieked at her to stop. 'Nooooooo!' it screamed as she grabbed the boy's wrist.

Then they were both falling. Down the endless schism. And the warning voice was hooting with laughter from the edge of the cliff. And then, suddenly, they were no longer on the mountaintop or falling down the cliff. They were in a place that was familiar to Avita from her nightmares. It was the hut of the witch who kept the boy a prisoner and tormented him. Even as Avita watched, the witch began to whip the boy. He writhed with intense pain and retched, throwing up bilious vomit. She tried to go to his aid, but she could not move. She tried to close her eyes to shut out the horrifying spectacle, but her eyelids were frozen open. She tried to cry out to the old eighee to stop hurting him, but no sound came from her mouth. She stood transfixed, a mute spectator to the torture of the boy who, she was beginning to understand, had become her co-inhabitant in a world that was completely imaginary and yet as real as the world outside of her dreams. He did not scream as the witch thrashed him and stripped the flesh away from his back. But Avita did. She screamed in agony and sat up sobbing.

Avator and Forsith were at her side, comforting and consoling her. It took her a while to calm down. She leant back and found that her bedclothes were soaked through. She tried to stand but her feet trembled. Her back felt as if it was on fire. She looked down to find that the moisture on her bedclothes was blood, not sweat. Without being told, Avita knew that she had had another episode of her mysterious ailment.

The outlaw camp was a veritable village. There were, contrary to reports, over fourscore of the outlaws living there in tents. The residents of the camp included servants, scouts, grooms, a tailor, a couple of cooks and a healer. Though none of them was especially talented at his work, each of them was capable of fighting and could hold his own in a raid. Apart from the permanent residents, there were dozens of outlaws who came and went, participating in a raid or two depending upon the gang's requirements, and then moving on to work with other gangs. They were the marauding world's equivalent of mercenaries. Another transient group was that of kereighees and kereighe children. They came to visit their relations every now and then, but none were stationed permanently at the camp. This worried Forsith for Avita's sake. He soon saw, however, that a strict code of conduct was followed by the outlaws and rigorously enforced by Igrag. One of the most important provisions of the code forbade the members of the camp from hurting or harming any of the other residents. The punishment for breaking the code could be severe even for the smallest infraction.

Forsith and Avator were welcomed into the community after a fashion and were asked to settle in immediately. It took them a very short while to become accustomed to their new life. Avator set up a small smithy in which he either made or fixed horseshoes, weapons and small objects of daily use. Sometimes he would use scraps to fabricate trinkets or toys, and some of the outlaws paid him for these. They had wives and children back home and liked to send something to them now and then that hadn't been obtained through looting. Avator's skill soon made him quite well-known as a smith among the outlaws. Forsith, too, was flourishing as a horse-wizard, and he was very careful not to let anyone guess the truth. Avita usually tagged along with Forsith or stayed in their tent by herself. She was a pretty but shy child, always charming but never feeling bold enough to venture forth on her own. Forsith did not mind. He had enough on his mind without having to worry about Avita running wild.

Though there was no dearth of money in the outlaw camp, provisions were a different story. The supply of consumables varied from tempora to tempora depending on what they found on their raids. This surprised Avator. He requested Forsith to suggest to Igrag that he, Avator, could be sent out with one of the servants to buy provisions from the nearby towns or from the city of Esvilar to the north. Forsith conveyed the message reluctantly. He wanted to remain as obscure as possible. Taking initiative would get them noticed. Igrag listened to him with an inscrutable expression, then thanked him and dismissed him. Some days later, one of the scouts, an eighe boy a few anni older than Avator, was sent with a servant to purchase provisions. Since the only cart in the camp was Forsith's, the cart and Habsolm were requisitioned for the purpose. The horse was not too happy to be driven by anyone except his owners, but Avator promised him some extra apples and also told him to keep his ears open for information. This made Habsolm far more eager for the job. Avator did not mind that another boy had been sent. What was important was that Igrag had acknowledged the value of their suggestion. Obviously, he still did not trust them enough to allow them outside. That would take time. Avator would be patient. Once the outlaws trusted him and Forsith implicitly, they would escape.

Avator's plan worked, and provisions were no longer scarce in the camp though their supply was strictly controlled by Igrag. Forsith petitioned for better fodder and grain for the horses, and this request, too, was accepted. Habsolm happily continued to pull the cart for the outlaws going to and coming from the markets. He listened to every word they spoke and relayed the information to Avator, who carefully tucked it all away inside his head. Soon, he knew more about the outlaws than Forsith did. He knew who was who, who was close to the captain, who was responsible for what jobs, who had family back home, who had been in the army and who hadn't, who was friends with whom and disliked whom, who Igrag's rivals were and many other small things that, in themselves, seemed insignificant but put together, formed a comprehensive picture of life in the outlaw camp. Avator had learnt the importance of information early in life and he was putting that lesson to good use.

One morning, towards the end of Yodirin, Avator was summoned by Igrag for a scouting mission. He was ordered to set off immediately for the city of Esvilar. He had to report to the head scout at the bottom of a hill outside the city. A chain of reporting had been created for news to be passed down to Igrag and the others; Avator's job was to take up a position determined by the head scout and report his observations to the next scout down the line from him. As he made his way to the stables, Avator noticed that all the scouts had been engaged, and all the able-bodied eighes were preparing for the attack. He guessed that a major raid was afoot. He wondered what the target could possibly be. He asked Habsolm, but the gelding knew nothing about this mission. Avator rode through the day and the night on a horse provided by the outlaws and reached Esvilar at dawn the next morning.

The head scout ordered him to go up the hill and keep an eye on the city. He was to be alert for signs of heightened activity or chests being moved. A spyglass was provided to him to make his work easier. He was at the front of the scouting line and was expected to report to the next scout in the chain in as much detail as possible every half a hora. Leaving his horse at the bottom of the hill, Avator climbed up and positioned himself so that he could observe the entire city without being noticed. What he saw made his heart pound.

A large contingent of soldiers was milling about. Esvilar was a large, prosperous city that owed its wealth to trade. It was the seat of a noble who was a prominent member of the king's court. It had its own port and harbour, being on the coast.

At all times, it was very well-guarded. That day, the number of soldiers seemed to have tripled. Esvilar was looking like the garrison-city of Lembar that morning! Avator passed down this message and continued observing the city.

As he scanned the movements of the troops, he wondered why the outlaws were planning to raid the city on a day on which it was especially well-protected. As a rule, the outlaws never raided this far north because Esvilar was such a well-guarded city. Why had they changed their strategy? The booty had to be massive enough to not only require such heavy protection but also to tempt the outlaws to take such a huge risk. Avator doubted they would be able to enter the city, given how dense with soldiers it was. Even if they managed to enter, they would be chopped down in no time by the soldiers.

He suddenly noticed a large group of soldiers moving towards the docks. The docks were situated on the other side of the city from where the outlaws were hidden, and Avator could not see very clearly what was going on there. Soon, though, the contingent returned, carrying what appeared to be large chests. They had been reinforced by another contingent at the docks. What was in the chests? The large number of soldiers suggested the king's money. Taxes? No, taxes would move from Esvilar to Kinqur. Salaries! Yes, that was what the outlaws were targeting. In a remote place like Esvilar, salaries would be sent down quarterly or half-yearly rather than monthly. This time, it must have travelled by sea due to the threat of the outlaws.

The two contingents made their way to the manor house with the chests. Avator was about to report this when something about the situation struck him as odd. If the city was so full of soldiers, the lord of Esvilar must have received news of an impending attack by the outlaws. How did he know? Had whoever told the outlaws about the incoming treasure been baiting them? If the lord of Esvilar knew of the planned raid, why was he allowing the money to be carried openly when it was given that the outlaws would have scouts observing the city? Why would he have the money stored in his own keep? That did not sound like the kereighe who had managed to hold his own against the infestation of brigands in his lands and had risen to prominence on the back of his unbreakable determination to establish the rule of law in his holdings. Something else was going on here. The whole parade of the soldiers going to the docks and fetching the chests was a sham. It was an act to convince any watching outlaws that the money had arrived and was stored in the manor house, a ploy to draw them in. It was a trap!

Avator started to make his way to the next scout when a voice inside his head stopped him. What did he care if they all died, it said. If the outlaws were destroyed, he would be free. Yet, something within him rebelled at the thought of allowing all those kereighes to go to their deaths when he could prevent it. Perhaps it was his dislike of failure. The notion of failure at any task always rankled with him. He had been tasked with scouting the city. If he deliberately allowed the outlaws to die, he would have failed at the task. More importantly, if some of the outlaws survived, his conscience was not the only one to whom he would have to answer. The consequences of his failure could be deadly for him and his family. Was freedom worth the risk? Failure was not an option any longer. The raid had to either be stopped or succeed.

Avator immediately sent a message to Igrag, warning him of the trap. Within a hora, he received the message that Igrag wanted to see him. Igrag and the others were camped a few miles west of his location in a rocky area. He was to report back in person immediately.

As he went to meet Igrag, Avator prayed to Supparo to enable him to keep his wits about him. Although he knew where the outlaws were hidden, he still could not spot them at first. Even after spending a few mondans with them, he was unable to gauge their places of concealment easily. He could not help feeling admiration for their cunning. Igrag was waiting for him under an outcrop. His deputies, Frengdan and Feerdhen, waited with him. Avator reported what he had seen.

'What makes you think that it is a trap?' Igrag demanded.

Avator explained his reasoning. Igrag frowned. Before Igrag could say anything, Avator added, 'Where did you get your information?'

'That is none of your concern, boy!' Frengdan snapped.

'You were sent to scout; you should mind your own business. Don't try to feed us your wild theories,' Feerdhen added.

Avator did not move. He would not move unless Igrag personally dismissed him. He stood there, ignoring Frengdan and Feerdhen's glares. Finally Igrag spoke, 'What you say seems reasonable, Mordeph. But my news is certain. The bounty is there.'

'Then there is another way to find out where it is being kept,' Avator quickly suggested before he was dismissed. 'This way, we can not only learn the treasure's whereabouts but also steal it with little or no bloodshed.'

'The puny smith is afraid of bloodshed,' sneered Frengdan. Feerdhen snickered. Avator bristled within but said nothing.

'Silence!' said Igrag, and they fell quiet. 'What is your plan?' he asked Avator.

Avator took a deep breath and outlined his plan to Igrag. The captain of the outlaws listened carefully to what the boy had to say, asking a few questions to clarify his doubts. When Avator had finished outlining his plan, Igrag nodded. 'It's a good plan,' he said. His deputies were sceptical, but he silenced them with a glare. 'At the very least, we can make sure that we are not rushing into a trap.'

'Send Qually and Lekker,' Frengdan suggested. Qually was one of the senior members of the gang; Lekker was the scout who had been travelling to the markets to purchase provisions following Avator's suggestion.

'No,' said Igrag. 'This is Mordeph's plan. He should go. And I shall personally accompany him. If he is right, he will be best placed to execute the plan. If he is wrong, I will be there to see that he gets what he deserves.'

Feerdhen began to protest, volunteering to go himself, but Igrag refused to listen. He told his deputies to wait for his signal to either rush to their aid or to fly back to camp. His instructions were soon relayed throughout the ranks.

Just before dark, a blind beggar and his young guide entered through the gates of Esvilar. Even they were not spared thorough scrutiny by the guards at the gate. However, they carried nothing that could be construed as a weapon, so they were allowed to enter. They passed through the main street and into lanes and byways, quickly arriving at the heart of the city. There they took up position near one of the eating houses. The owner of the eatery took pity on them and supplied them with some bread and stew. They thanked him and ate the food sitting nearby. They continued to sit there even after they had finished eating, begging from the patrons who came to the eatery. Some ignored them; others dropped a few coins into the bowl that the boy carried. Many of the patrons were soldiers and were in a hurry. They came to the eating house in groups of five or six. But one of them came alone. He ate quickly and moved away again, mingling with the crowd on the streets. In the hustle and bustle, no one noticed when the blind beggar and his boy disappeared from the front of the eatery.

The lone soldier was walking towards the docks—feeling uneasy at being by himself even though there were still kereighes on the streets and most of the shops were open—when he heard a feeble cry for help and looked about. He spotted a boy stooping over a kereighe in a side-lane. The boy appeared to be trying to rouse the kereighe who was lying in an unnatural position. They looked like the beggar and his companion whom he had seen near the place where he had eaten. He stepped closer to see what the matter was.

'Please, sir, please help my father!' the boy begged, gesturing towards the kereighe who was lying on the ground with his eyes closed. 'He is blind and depends on me for guidance. It is dark here, so I couldn't see clearly. I couldn't guide him right. He stumbled and fell and isn't getting up now,' the boy sobbed desperately, apparently blaming himself for his father's accident. The soldier felt sorry for the boy and leant closer to check if the older kereighe was still breathing. Before he realised what was happening, he had been knocked out with a mighty blow by the unconscious blind beggar.

Igrag and Avator pulled him further inside the dark lane. They tied him up and took his clothes. Telling Avator to watch the unconscious soldier, Igrag stepped out into the busy street. No one had noticed what had happened. That part of their plan had been completed successfully. Now it was up to him. He had been in the army before taking to a life of lawlessness. It wasn't difficult for him to imitate the swagger and speech of the soldiers. He noticed that many of the soldiers on the streets were wearing their helmets. He gratefully tugged on the one he had taken from the knocked out soldier. It covered almost his entire face and made his disguise even more effective. In a city full of soldiers who had come from outside, no one looked at him twice as he traversed the roads. The soldiers accepted him as one of their own. He moved from one area of the city to another, infiltrating groups of soldiers and trying to glean from them where the salaries were really being kept. Most of them seemed to have no idea of what he was talking about. They had come that morning to protect the city from outlaws, they said. An attack was imminent, they had been informed. Mordeph had been right, Igrag realised. It *was* a trap!

He could either return now, having ensured that it was indeed a trap, or he could try and carry out the rest of their dangerous plan. He decided to take the risk of carrying out their plan. The boy's plan had succeeded so far. Perhaps, it would succeed in entirety. The boy had promise, Igrag thought, as he continued his subterfuge. He soon found himself at the docks. To his enormous surprise, the docks were milling with troops. If the chests had already been unloaded and carried into the keep, why were so many soldiers still present at the docks? The keep *was* heavily guarded. That was only to be expected if the loot was stashed there. But why were the docks so heavily guarded as well? As he walked up and down, trying to mingle with the other soldiers, it gradually became clear to him. The trap had been laid well! No money had come that morning. The carrying of the chests down to the keep had been pretence, just as Mordeph had suspected. The real money, Igrag realised, was yet to arrive. That explained the heavy security at the docks. It also meant that a change of plans was in order.

He returned quickly to Avator. The soldier had not yet come round. Igrag told Avator what he had seen and learnt. 'We need to know when that ship is coming in,' Igrag said, 'and attack it.'

Avator frowned. 'Won't a ship be too obvious? I mean, the fake consignment came via ship. If they went to such lengths to fool you, why would they bring the real consignment in on another ship? Wouldn't the arrival of two ships the same day arouse your suspicion that the first one had not really been carrying the salaries? That might warn you off the raid. They're probably expecting you to attack at night. Why would they jeopardise their trap by brining in the salaries openly before you attack? Their plan is too clever. I don't think they would falter like this. I don't think the money is coming by ship.'

The boy's explanation did make sense. They would not use a ship to bring the actual money in, not after their ploy was using that ruse, especially if they knew that the outlaws were watching the port. But the massed soldiers in the docks still worried him.

'If no ship is coming to the port, why are the docks swarming with soldiers?' asked Igrag.

Avator was stumped. Was he wrong? No, he couldn't be. Everything else had fallen into place like pieces of a puzzle. All except this one piece that was refusing to fit. Why were there so many soldiers at the dock? He tried thinking like his adversary, the lord of Esvilar. From everything Avator had seen, he was an uncommonly cunning commander. If he, Avator, were in charge, why would he place so many soldiers at the docks if no ship was brining the salaries? Was it possible that, after all, a second ship was bringing the money? That made no sense whatsoever, especially since they must have been still waiting for the outlaws to attack. What if this was part of the trap, he suddenly thought. What if it was insurance in case the outlaws sensed that the morning's activities had been a trap? They probably suspected that the outlaws were keeping watch on what was happening in the city. If they figured out the trap and didn't attack, this was meant to fool them into attacking. A second ship would arrive, and the outlaws would think that this one was the one carrying the treasure. They would attack, meeting their doom. Avator could not help admire the genius of the lord of Esvilar.

He explained what he was thinking to Igrag. The captain of the outlaws frowned as he digested the information. He thought carefully and concluded that Mordeph was right. This was the only explanation. Curse the boy, he was right! This was another level of the trap. But if the money was not coming on the second ship, how was it entering the city? He was certain that it had not come overland. If it had come by sea, it had to be brought in some way. It would have to be removed from the ship before the ship reached the port. In mid-ocean, what could they do to send the money off the ship and secretly to shore? Boats! The money was coming in by boats! And the boats would not land at the port, of course. Everything in the city was a distraction for the outlaws; it would keep them busy while the real money was being brought ashore elsewhere. If the outlaws attacked, they would be killed; if they sensed the trap and refrained from attacking, the money would still be safe. It was a very clever ploy! But he had an idea of how to scuttle the brilliant plan. He was caught inside the city with Mordeph, but his gang was out there. He needed two things: uniforms and a way to return to his gang.

Briefly explaining his plan to Avator, Igrag said, 'The gates have closed for the night, and they won't allow anyone to leave, not even another soldier. I need you to create a distraction at the manor house laundry. Get the servants out of there.

Collect what we need. Then, run back and meet me at the main gate. We will need another distraction there.'

Avator understood what Igrag was planning. 'The same distraction will do, I think,' he said and strode off to do his part. The streets were beginning to empty by then. He found his way to the laundry and scoped the area. It was close to the manor house's kitchens. The kitchens were still very busy and no one noticed him as he rummaged about in the garbage outside. He found what he was looking for. He bloodied his clothes with discarded remains of the meat that had been prepared for supper. Then he staggered into the laundry, crying pitifully for help.

'Save me! Save me!' he cried. 'The outlaws are attacking.' Then he collapsed bodily into a vat of soapy water quite dramatically.

His announcement had the expected reaction. First, there was stunned silence. Then the servants began to scream and run helter-skelter. In the ensuing panic, he calmly collected some sheets and uniforms and returned to the kitchen. Dumping the sheets onto a pile of dry garbage, he set the pile aflame. When he was sure that the flame had taken hold, he returned to the main gate. The sentries were still alertly guarding the gates. Where was Igrag? A low whistle drew his attention to the captain of the outlaws, who was standing in the shadows a little way back from the gates. The boy hurried over to him and reported, 'The outlaws have attacked the keep from the rear and have set fire to a portion of it.' He pointed to smoke rising in the distance. Igrag nodded and rushed towards the sentries.

'The outlaws have attacked the keep from the rear and have set fire to a portion of it!' he announced. 'You can see the smoke rising there.'

The sentries looked where he was pointing. They cursed loudly and raised the alarm. Soon soldiers from every direction were rushing towards the rear of the keep. Igrag exhorted the sentries to join in the fray and they, not very enthusiastically, agreed. They did not want to be reported to their superiors if it was found that they had made no contribution towards the capture of the outlaws. They left three of their number behind and followed Igrag. The captain of the outlaws soon lost them in the rush and returned to the gate. It was a matter of momons for him to knock out the three surprised sentries. He and Avator opened the gate together. Igrag left first. Avator handed him a bundle that contained the stolen uniforms and then stepped back.

'What are you doing?' Igrag demanded, suddenly suspicious.

'I am going to close the gates again. If they find the gates open, they will know that someone has escaped. They will give chase. I can buy you time if I close the gates,' Avator explained.

'How will you escape?' Igrag asked, struck by the boy's intelligence.

'I am a young boy. How can I be in league with fearsome outlaws?' he smiled and said.

Igrag nodded. His opinion of Mordeph had changed drastically.

'Just one request,' Avator suddenly added.

'What?'

'Try not to kill too many soldiers.'

Igrag was surprised at the request. For a moment, he felt suspicious again, but his suspicions melted away when he thought of the risk that Mordeph was taking in staying back. Who knew when he would be able to return, if at all? Perhaps the boy was merely squeamish. He would get over it in time, Igrag figured. He promised he would try to avoid bloodshed as much as possible and sped away in the darkness of the night.

Avator pulled the gates closed and dropped the bars in place. It was difficult and heavy work, and he was panting by the time he finished. The sentries were beginning to stir by then. He had to disappear before they woke up. He hoped Igrag would keep his promise. If he could save some lives that night, it might be of use to him someday. For now, he had to lie low until the hubbub died down. It would not be difficult. His life on the road had trained him well for such an existence. Therefore, when the gates were opened after two days, and he finally managed to return to the outlaw camp, Avator was none the worse for wear. The expedition, Avator learnt, had been highly successful. All who knew of his role in the business cheered him and welcomed him back. All except Feerdhen and Frengdan, of course. He smiled bashfully, fully aware of the prominence to which one night's actions had raised him. As he was returning to his own tent, he noticed Igrag berating one of the outlaws angrily. The outlaw was vehemently denying something; he looked terrified.

'What is going on?' Avator asked Forsith as he entered the tent. He had expected a warm welcome from his family, but neither Forsith nor Avita showed him any degree of warmth. Forsith stood in the doorway, looking angry. Avita was sitting in a corner, cowed.

'What is going on?' he asked again, confused.

'This!' hissed Forsith, pulling Avita forward. A large red handprint was visible on Avita's cheek. 'That eighe was on guard duty last night. He was passing by our tent when Avita screamed louder than usual and woke up. I was up in an instant and noticed that handprint on her cheek. Just then the guard came in to check what was happening. He did not notice the handprint, though. I tried to persuade him to leave, but he wouldn't go until I gave him an explanation. Some of the other outlaws rushed in just at that moment, also woken by the scream. *They* noticed the handprint. Seeing Avita terrified and hurt and me trying to get the guard to leave, they assumed that the guard had hurt Avita. They hauled him off before I could intervene. And what would I have said if I had managed to intervene? Did you think of this when you chose to side with the outlaws?'Forsith berated his ward.

Avator couldn't control his anger either. 'You know very well why we joined the outlaws. I am not sorry for saving all our lives!'

'I understand *that* decision,' Forsith said, 'but I do not understand why you helped them rob Esvilar. What do you think you are doing?'

'What is necessary,' declared Avator and stormed out. He had to meet Igrag and tell the captain the truth. Even though these kereighes were outlaws and criminals, he could not let one of them take the blame for something that he had not done. Besides, there was no way that they could keep Avita's condition hidden for long. He found Igrag in his tent, looking grim. Without preamble, Avator told him about his sister's 'curse' and its manifestation.

Igrag sent one of his kereighes to set the accused kereighe free and then turned to Avator. 'I thought you said that she was under the protection of the witch of Temtema,' he said shrewdly, watching Avator carefully as the boy answered.

'She is. But she is not cured. The charm helps her to heal faster. It does not prevent the occurrence of her injuries. We have sought a cure everywhere but found none.'

'I believe you,' said Igrag. 'I can see in your eyes that you are telling the truth. It takes courage to tell some truths. I am sorry for your sister's plight.'

Avator nodded in acknowledgement and was about to excuse himself when Igrag continued, 'What you did at Esvilar was outstanding. I would not have imagined one as young as you capable of such things. You have potential, potential that can be better utilised in the army than in an outlaw gang. What future could you have here? What future do any of us have? A life of crime and a sword at the end of it are all that are destined for those who choose to live outside the laws made by others. If you say, I will release you from your pledge to serve me. You, your sister and your uncle can leave.'

Avator looked up at Igrag, trying to read the inscrutable expression on the captain's face. Was he truly offering Avator his freedom? Or was it another test? Avator looked him in the eye as he answered, 'Thank you for your kind offer. I will keep it in mind for the future. But we have nowhere to go. Where do you think my sister will be accepted? We may not have much of a future here, but we do not have much of a future anywhere else either. I feel a sense of belonging here that I have not felt elsewhere. If it is all the same to you, I would like to remain.'

Igrag nodded. The boy was truly remarkable. He had passed the test without batting an eyelid. Had he really meant the things that he had said? Or had he guessed that it was a test and responded accordingly? The more Igrag saw of Mordeph, the more intrigued he was. He decided that he would take a personal interest in the boy's development thenceforth.

Aloud, he said, 'Very well, then. Remain as one of us. As for your sister, I give you my word that none will say an unkind word to her or do an unkind deed. I shall decree it so. And there is a possible solution to your problems. There is a magus several miles from here who lives in a cave at the edge of the desert, in the shadow of the Lyudzbradh. He is known to be extremely wise and powerful. He might be able to help your sister.'

Avator thanked Igrag for the advice and for permission to remain with the outlaws. Then he turned to leave. His mind was in a whirl with all the recent developments in his life. Igrag called him from behind. He turned.

'Mordeph,' Igrag said, 'it might please you to know that we did not have to take any lives that night. When we turned up at the landing site of the boats, the soldiers were completely fooled by our disguises. By the time they realised what was happening, we had overcome them and had taken possession of the chests of money.'

Avator answered, 'I am glad that we were successful in our mission, and I am honoured that you kept my request in mind.' He showed no sign of either joy or relief. He again turned to leave. This time Igrag did not stop him. He remained staring at Mordeph's figure vanishing in the distance. He had tested the boy again, but the boy had passed again. He still did not understand why Mordeph had requested as little bloodshed as possible, but the boy's reaction to the news had given him no more clues. Either the boy was genuinely what he claimed to be, or he was exceptionally cunning. Only time would tell, Igrag decided.

Chapter 19

FEYANOR'S LESSON

(12 Beybasel 5007 A.E. to 2 Patarshem 5007 A.E.)

Five mondans had passed since Prince Feyanor's arrival in Lufurdista. The exuberance that had marked his arrival had settled down into mild joyfulness. One night, after supper, Amiroth, Feyanor and Aminor sat discussing serious matters of state in a small, open-air alcove attached to the dining chamber, while the ladies were chatting in the garden. Amishar was away playing somewhere on his own.

'There is bad news from Samion,' said Prince Feyanor gravely. 'Perhaps you have already heard?'

'No, Your Highness. No news of Samion has reached us here of late. The last we heard was that their king, Arlem, was ill,' Lord Aminor answered.

'That was a long time ago. Arlem has been dead for close to seven anni now. No one knows the whereabouts of his brother Arslan or his queen Melicie. Some say that they died too, and some say that they escaped. Arlem's prime minister, Holexar, has usurped the throne. War is brewing between Samion and Rosarfin.'

'That is bad news indeed,' conceded King Amiroth.

'More so for us than for you, my lord,' said Prince Feyanor. 'We are neighbours of Rosarfin and have ever had cordial relations with them. You might be aware that I spent a substantial part of my adolescence there and was trained by Prince Melissen himself. If they ask for aid in the war against Samion, we shall not be able to refuse.'

'But why should we become enmeshed in the wars of the eighes?' said King Amiroth.

Prince Feyanor shook his head. 'It is not that simple, Your Majesty. The times are changing. One can no longer disclaim responsibility because one belongs or does not belong to this race or that. No race is immune to the upheavals in the countries of others. Boundaries and divisions are breaking down and, I believe, need to.'

'Why do you say so, my lord?' asked Lord Aminor.

Prince Feyanor answered, 'Elthrusia has long been divided along racial lines. Today there are five major realms in this continent, four of which are based on racial identities. Each realm exists in an insular state, separate from the others.

Meanwhile, who knows what trouble has been brewing in the Shadow Lands beyond the Lyudzbradh? If we continue to exist thus separately…'

Prince Feyanor could not finish his sentence. A resounding crash came from within the chamber to which the alcove was attached. All three noblemen hurried back inside. They found young Amishar in the midst of the ruins of a clay horse that had been gifted to him by his uncle. The three men stared stupefied for a moment at this scene, and then Prince Feyanor burst out laughing.

'And this should teach us grown-up men not to be proud of our beasts of war!' he declared laughing, and scooped up young Amishar into his arms and onto his shoulders. The young boy gurgled with joy, his mishap of a few moments ago completely forgotten. Over the past mondans, he had become extremely attached to his ursine uncle. This hero of men always seemed to have ample time for his young nephew's games and enough patience for his unending questions. Prince Feyanor, too, was very fond of his nephew.

Excusing himself to the other two men, Prince Feyanor carried Amishar out into the garden to find his sister, Amishar's mother. But the ladies were not there.

'Where has your mother gone, young man?' he asked Amishar.

'I am sorry, sir, I do not know,' replied Amishar.

'Oh well!' declared Prince Feyanor and sat down on a stone bench, seating Amishar beside him.

'Tell me about the hill men,' Amishar suddenly demanded.

He had heard of the great exploits of Feyanor against the men of the Ufharn Hills, and he had been part of the tableau where the mock attack by them had been staged. He had been greatly intrigued and had been longing to ask his uncle for more information about the formidable tribals but hadn't managed to pluck up the courage to do so until then. Feyanor was amused by his demand. He was a little tired of talking about his latest expedition, but he obliged his nephew. He began to tell Amishar about some of the encounters in the hills where he had outwitted the hill men through the use of tracking and camouflage.

'What is tracking?' Amishar asked.

'Tracking means finding out which way someone has gone by looking at things like the grass and the trees and the ground.'

'How can one use these things to find out which way someone has gone, Your Highness?'

'You see, when a person passes through a place, he steps on the grass on the ground. The ground might retain a whole or partial footprint. Or the grass might be trampled down. Or a tree branch might be broken. Or some shrubs disturbed.

When one knows what to look for and how to read what one sees, one can use these things to track the enemy.'

'How does one know what to look for and to read it right?'

'It takes time and effort and a great deal of practice, young prince,' Feyanor said.

Amishar was silent for a while. Then he said, 'Can I learn to track if I try?'

Prince Feyanor was taken aback by this question. But he was pleased as well. The boy was eager to learn. He wished he could take Amishar with him and teach him all he knew.

'Yes, you can,' he answered.

'Will you teach me?' Amishar asked eagerly, jumping off the bench.

'Not so fast,' Prince Feyanor said, laughing. 'Don't you want me to finish my story first?'

'Oh, yes! Oh, yes!' said Amishar and sat back down.

'We had been following this large troop of the hill men for days when their tracks confused me,' Prince Feyanor resumed his tale. 'The troop seemed to have gone in two opposite directions, but that couldn't be right. One option was, of course, that they had split up and gone in two different directions to throw us off their track, or to compel us to divide up our strength.'

'So what did you do, my lord?'

'I ordered the men to set up camp at that spot. Then I sent scouts to spy out the location of the hill men. They returned that night with the news that the troop had indeed split up into two and were now encamped on two opposite slopes of a ditch.'

'Why did they do that?'

'You see, the path that we were following led into this low, narrow ditch. The hill men were expecting us to keep following the path into the ditch. They had planned an ambush for us at that spot and had stationed themselves on the two opposite slopes.'

'That seems to have been a good plan,' commented Amishar, nodding his head wisely. 'What did you do?'

'Once I knew their plan, I decided to outwit them. I split my own troops into two groups and had them cautiously climb round to higher ground behind the hill men. Then I had a few of my soldiers place effigies on the backs of the horses and lead them into the ditch. The hill men were waiting for us. On seeing the horses, they assumed that we had fallen into their trap. They attacked the effigies. Of course, nothing happened.'

'Weren't the horses hurt?'

'Yes, some of them were, but there are always casualties in war.'

'Then what happened?'

'The hill men became confused and descended into the ditch to check matters. Then *we* ambushed *them*. They fell into their own trap!'

'But didn't they find out that you were behind them on the slopes? Didn't they spot your men climbing up?'

'No, because we used camouflage.'

'What is camouflage?'

'Camouflage, my prince, is a type of disguise—you make yourself look like the surrounding area so that others cannot detect you.'

Amishar did not understand this explanation.

'Let me see,' said Prince Feyanor, thinking hard how to explain camouflage to his young nephew. 'Ah yes! Have you seen a chameleon?'

'Yes.'

'Have you seen how it changes its colour to green when it is sitting among the leaves of a tree, and then it becomes brown when it is on the tree trunk?'

'Yes, it becomes very difficult to see that it is there...oh! I see now,' said Amishar as the concept of camouflage became clear to him. 'But how did you and your men change colour?' he asked.

Prince Feyanor laughed aloud. 'No, we cannot change our colours like the chameleon,' he conceded. 'But we did something close to it. We wore clothes that were green and brown like the trees and we stuck leaves on our clothes and our helmets so that we looked like a walking forest. And when we moved quietly or remained still, we blended into the background.'

'Like a chameleon!'

'Yes, like a chameleon.'

Amishar was quiet and thoughtful for a while and then suddenly said, 'Camouflage can be used in other ways too, can't it?'

'What do you mean?' asked his uncle, puzzled.

'Well, a person could pretend to be someone else and make himself look like someone else too!'

'That is called a disguise, not camouflage. But, I guess,' added the prince of Ashperth thoughtfully, 'that it can be thought of as camouflage too. At least, sometimes.'

'When?' asked Amishar eagerly, glad that he had made a point worthy of the great man's consideration.

'Well, if the person can imitate the manners of the one whom he is dressed as, or if a person can infiltrate a group by imitating their dress, appearance and manners, then the person can blend in completely and not be noticeable. That is what spies learn to do.'

'What are spies, Your Highness?' Amishar asked, suddenly changing track.

'Spies are people who secretly find out information, especially hidden information, about others by using disguise and other cunning ways.'

'Why do they do that?'

'Because that is their job—they gather this information for whoever they are working for.'

'And what do the people that the spies work for do with this information?'

'That depends on what their aims are. Kings and rulers need to have information about their own country and about other countries to find out if someone is hatching a conspiracy or planning a war against them. It also helps them to know how the people are doing and if any problems are bothering them. It helps them be good rulers, my prince. Some people have bad intentions too, though. Spies don't always work for people with good intentions.'

'Spies are good at camouflage, aren't they?' Amishar asked, coming back to the original subject as abruptly as he had moved away from it.

'I suppose so,' replied Prince Feyanor thoughtfully, not sure whether his young nephew was unable to understand the difference between camouflage and disguise or exceptionally perceptive about the underlying common principle between the two. 'However, they need disguises more often than they need camouflage. But they do most of their work by using their cunning. And other types of deception as well.'

'And you are also good at camouflage, aren't you?'

Prince Feyanor laughed, unable to gather where the conversation was going by now and why the young boy was so obsessed with camouflage. 'I'd like to believe I am,' he said.

'Are you a spy?' demanded Amishar.

'What?' said Feyanor, taken aback.

'You can tell me if you are, Your Highness. I won't tell anyone.'

The prince of Ashperth did not know how to answer his young nephew's innocent question. He tried to change the subject and suggested that they go looking for Queen Lamella. But Amishar did not rise from the bench. He seemed absorbed in thought.

Finally, coming out of his reverie, he asked his uncle slowly and haltingly, 'Everyone says that you are a great man, a hero. But you do not behave like the heroes in the stories. You are always joking and laughing and enjoying yourself. At the same time, you know about things like tracking and camouflage and have defeated the hill men. No one has ever been able to do that, everyone says. If you really are a hero, then why do you behave like this ordinary, fun-loving man? Is that camouflage too?'

Again, the great warrior had no answer to give to his prodigious nephew. He was rescued by the timely arrival of Lord Aminor. He declared that King Amiroth was looking for his son and his brother-in-law. Amishar leapt off the bench and went to find his father. The two noblemen were left alone to walk back slowly. They had met at formal gatherings several times since Prince Feyanor's arrival in Lufurdista but had not found the opportunity to speak in private.

'I see that you have not married yet, my lord,' was the first thing Prince Feyanor said to Lord Aminor.

'Never really had the time or the inclination, Your Highness,' Lord Aminor replied uncomfortably.

'I see,' said Feyanor cheekily. 'I was not aware that the responsibilities of a master-of-the-horse were so numerous or so onerous as to leave no time for a personal life. However, there was another thing I wanted to ask you. When my messenger announced that I had achieved victory in my fight against the hill tribes, everyone showed surprise. Everyone, that is, except you. I am grateful for such a show of confidence in my abilities. Unless, of course, it was because you already knew of that victory, my lord?'

'I have ever had the utmost confidence in your capabilities, Prince Feyanor,' Lord Aminor said with a bow. 'On my part, I have never known mere messengers to be so astute as to observe all the members of the court closely while delivering a message.'

Feyanor nodded, conceding Aminor's point. They had almost reached the king and Amishar when Feyanor spoke again. 'I've heard that you are young Amishar's tutor as well as his godfather. It cannot be easy, I suppose,' he said with a hint of sympathy in his voice.

'The prince is curious and precocious and is a pleasure to teach,' Lord Aminor replied. 'I love him dearly and I enjoy being his tutor and his godfather.'

'I am sure you do, my lord. But that is not what I meant. I think you do know what I meant even though your answer is decorously evasive. However, what I actually wanted to ask you is whether you would be willing to go to Ashperth with me. I would really like that!'

Aminor was surprised. He could not imagine why Prince Feyanor would want him to visit Ashperth. He had understood by then that Feyanor had an espionage network far stronger than his own, and he felt curious about the Prince. He was nonetheless suspicious of Feyanor's intentions in taking him away from Balignor. He knew that his place was in Lufurdista, by King Amiroth's side. In his absence, things could go horribly wrong. At the same time, he was heartsick. The thought of a journey to a new place where he could rejuvenate himself was tempting. He was loath to believe that Feyanor's intentions were dishonourable.

'I will think about it,' Aminor replied sincerely.

That night, Lord Aminor could not sleep. He had been intrigued by Prince Feyanor ever since he had met the prince for the first time. The news that had come from Ashperth intermittently about his successes, coupled with the serious failure of his own intelligence system to unearth any significant information, had made Feyanor an even more intriguing figure for Aminor. He was sure that Feyanor, being King Graniphor's only son, would succeed to the throne of Ashperth. What kind of king would he make? Would he be a friend to Balignor or an enemy? Was there a reason for him to worry about what Feyanor would do as king? These questions kept him awake. He had become quite impressed by the unusual thinking and complex personality of the prince and wished he could know the man better. Going with him to Ontar was not only an opportunity to do so but also an honour. He wondered why Feyanor had made him that offer when they had been alone. That, too, made him curious. He made up his mind. The next morning, he informed Prince Feyanor that he was willing to go provided that King Amiroth did not object.

King Amiroth did not object though he was none too happy at the prospect of losing his most valued advisor for an extended period of time. However, he could not offend his illustrious relative. Besides, Aminor wanted to visit Ashperth, and King Amiroth loved his cousin well enough to allow him this. It was Amishar who raised the greatest objection. He was adamant that Aminor could not leave. The second-most powerful man in Balignor almost caved in then. But Prince Feyanor stepped in and talked to Amishar, explaining to him that his godfather needed to go on the trip so that he could learn new things that he could, upon returning, teach to Amishar. This did not placate the young prince entirely, but he agreed not to object to Lord Aminor's departure.

Prince Feyanor, Princess Eileen and Lord Aminor started for Ontar on the second of Patarshem amidst another great turnout of cheerers and well-wishers. Before they left, Feyanor took young Amishar aside. The boy was terribly upset. He had become much attached to his uncle. The prince's departure, along with that of his godfather, was making Amishar utterly miserable. He had asked his uncle to stay until his birthday, but Feyanor had declined due to reasons that he did not understand. He was trying his best to hide his pain, to put on a brave face, but he was still very young. Tears often trickled down his cheeks unbidden and were hastily brushed away.

When he and young Prince Amishar were alone, Feyanor said, 'Are you upset because I won't stay until your birthday?'

Amishar nodded.

'I am sorry, my dear Amishar, but I just can't stay any longer. I must leave. I wish I could have stayed, but I can't. However, I do have something for you—an early birthday gift, you might say. Will you accept it?'

Amishar nodded again, too upset to speak for fear of starting to cry again.

Prince Feyanor handed him a box inlaid with ivory in a design of vines, leaves and flowers. Amishar opened the box. Inside, upon a lining of velvet, sat a pair of identical hunting knives. They were not only extremely sharp but also exquisitely beautiful with ornamental handles. Despite being young, Amishar could sense that they were valuable.

'Thank you,' he said to his uncle in a quavering voice, on the verge of tears again.

'These are special hunting knives, Amishar,' Feyanor explained. 'They were made in Rosarfin and were given to me as a parting gift by Prince Melissen, my teacher and friend. I want you to have them. Take good care of them. They are very unique; there are just two of these in the entire world—these two.'

Amishar thanked his uncle again though he had not understood why his uncle's voice had subtly changed when he had mentioned his teacher Prince Melissen. But he brushed that thought aside. The gift of the hunting knives was like the final straw for him. Feyanor's departure was now all too real and incredibly agonizing. All of a sudden, he hugged the bear-like man and began to sob uncontrollably. Feyanor hugged him back with warmth, and if there were tears in the great man's eyes, no one saw them.

Chapter 20

FRIENDS FOR HIRE

(1 Kawitor 5008 A.E. to 5 Kawitor 5008 A.E.)

King Amiroth and Queen Lamella were utterly shocked when Prince Amishar refused to celebrate his seventh birthday. He had always enjoyed that one day in the annus when everyone pampered him and showered him with gifts. Even when he had been too young to understand what a birthday was, he had loved having his birthday celebrated. Although none of the birthday fiestas after the first one had been exorbitant, they had held a special place in the young boy's heart, not least because he had started learning something new on that day practically every annus. He loved learning new things, whether in the classroom or the gymnasium or the training arena.

However, that annus he looked dejected when his birthday came around. It was not because he considered himself too old to have a birthday, as his father thought, but because Lord Aminor was away. Amishar had not been interested in either his studies or his training since his tutor's departure. Despite his parents' encouragement, he sat around and moped. He said not a word about Aminor, but it was evident that he was missing his godfather. His affection for Aminor was well known by those close to the royal family, yet no one had expected him to take his godfather's trip to Ashperth so hard. Lords Parkiod and Beleston tried to cheer him up by trying to interest him in the running of the kingdom and the army, as they had seen Lord Aminor do, but he was no more than politely attentive. Anyone could see that his heart was no longer in his favourite activities.

'Why don't you write a letter to Lord Aminor?' his mother asked him, thinking that it would cheer the boy up. 'We'll have it sent to Ontar.' Amishar shook his head and walked away. In his own, childish way, he was too proud to take the first step. No letter had come for him since Aminor's departure. If his godfather did not care to think of him, he was not going to tell Aminor that he was miserable in his absence.

'Come, let us have an archery contest,' his father said to distract him with one of his best-loved activities, but the young prince wasn't interested. It reminded him too much of Lord Aminor, who had taught him how to shoot.

On his birthday, despite his protests, his parents arranged a small celebration, thinking that he would change his mind once he found himself being feted. To their utter disappointment, he showed no interest in the celebrations or in his gifts. He perked up when King Amiroth announced that his training would now include swordplay as well. He thought then that Aminor was about to return or had already returned. The master-of-the-horse had always been present at the start of any new training, either teaching it himself or supervising the teachers and trainers hired specially for the purpose. The announcement of the addition of swordplay to his training schedule made Amishar assume that his godfather would be there as usual. He could not imagine beginning to learn a new skill in Aminor's absence.

The young prince's face fell when he met his new tutor. It was definitely not Aminor. And, his father added when he asked, Aminor was not due to return any time soon. His young heart was breaking at the thought that he was about to start learning something as important as swordplay, but Aminor did not care enough to be there to inaugurate the training. The new tutor was a well-known trainer for the sons of noblemen and aristocrats. He bowed to the young prince and introduced himself. Amishar talked to him politely but showed no great interest in what he had to say.

Later in the day, his training began. The trainer was a serious man who neither joked nor told stories. He started the lessons systematically, taking the prince through the steps meticulously. Amishar tried to engage him in conversation but gave up when his efforts were met with annoyance. He also found that his new trainer did not like to be asked too many questions. Having been brought up to be respectful towards elders, Amishar did his best to obey his trainer. He soon found that the trainer was good in his own way. They trained with wooden swords, but it was still painful and laborious. Amishar worked hard that day and began to get used to the sententious style of his new teacher.

Amishar proved to have an inborn talent for swordplay. Even his new teacher had to admit that the prince was going to be an adept swordsman someday if he continued to work hard. Amishar found that he could forget about his loneliness when he was training and threw himself into it. He began to practice swordplay, archery, wrestling, athletics and gymnastics for horas on end. When he wasn't training, he was reading books and taking lessons with his academic tutors with such a zest that he more than made up for the lessons missed during his days of moping. When he wasn't studying, he was tagging along beside his father or the prime minister or the commander-in-chief, trying to 'learn' how to run a kingdom, much to their astonishment, as he had shown no enthusiasm for such matters only a short while before.

Lamella began to worry after three days of Amishar's newfound intense focus on learning. She decided that something had to be done. She told King Amiroth that Amishar was behaving oddly, not like himself at all. She suggested that he was lonely because of Lord Aminor's absence. King Amiroth was not too pleased to hear this and dismissed the idea curtly. He was there, wasn't he, to teach Amishar about administration and to oversee his education? Did he not love Amishar more than Aminor ever could? Why would the boy mope so for his cousin when his father was there with him? Even if he was missing his godfather, King Amiroth declared, the boy would get over it soon. But the queen would not be mollified. She was worried that her son would not grow up to be normal if he did not have a normal childhood, and she was determined to rectify the situation.

'Of course you are there for him but a boy cannot always spend time with grown-ups, not even his parents, my lord,' she told her husband, careful not to mention Aminor again. 'He needs friends, boys his own age to play with. They will bring him out of himself and cheer him up again.'

'What can I do about it, my queen?' he asked, wondering how he could help, and realising with relief that his wife wasn't asking him to bring Aminor back.

'There are so many ministers and officials at your court. Some of them surely have sons who are Amishar's age or close to him in age. Why don't you ask those boys over and introduce them to our son, my lord?'

King Amiroth agreed that it was a good plan. The company of young boys would distract Amishar, perhaps enough to make him act like himself again. Besides, he thought, it would be good for the prince if he was acquainted from an early age with those who would, one day, help him rule. So he invited his ministers and officials to send their young sons to meet and dine with the prince at a banquet two days thence. Greatly honoured, everyone who had young sons sent them to the palace on the designated evening. Close to fifty boys arrived at the palace to be introduced to Amishar. Most of them were a good bit older than him; only a handful of the guests were close to him in age.

They arrived with bright, hopeful looks and timorous smiles. They bowed a little awkwardly but deeply when they were introduced to the king and queen, some of them too awed to speak the simple words of greeting without faltering. They were less awestruck by the young prince, though no less admiring of his charm and generosity. They hovered around him throughout the evening, buzzing excitedly, each trying to keep Amishar's attention on himself. They all wanted to create as positive an impression as possible. The prince's favour meant a bright future, their parents had told them.

The dinner invitation, from the king and queen's viewpoint, was a success. At the end of it, the boys who were closest to Amishar in age were asked to visit him again soon to play with him. They gladly agreed before departing with the rich gifts that had been given to them by the royal family.

That night, Lamella talked to Amishar about his *new friends*.

'Did you have a good time, son?' she asked.

'Yes, Mother. It was quite enjoyable,' Amishar said, not wanting to hurt his mother's feelings. He had found the gathering quite tedious. The boys had been overly fawning, agreeing to whatever he had said. If he had said that the weather was pleasant and that they should go outside to play, they had agreed. If, at the very next moment, he had said that it was too hot to play outside, they had still agreed. They had come there only for the honour and the gifts, he knew. Even though he was only seven, he was perceptive enough to understand that none of the boys who had come to visit him cared for him as a person. They saw him only as the prince. Yet, he was unwilling to tell all this to his mother. She was eager for him to make friends. She would be happy if he became friends with some of those boys.

'How did you find your guests? Were they amiable, interesting and amusing?'

'Yes, Mother, some of them were quite amiable as well as amusing. I had a wonderful time. I really liked a few of them.'

Lamella was thrilled; her plan had succeeded. Amishar smiled and told his mother the names of the boys that had been asked by his parents to return to play with him. He knew that Amiroth and Lamella deemed them the most suitable companions for him. Lamella assured him that he would get all the opportunity he wanted of befriending those boys.

Before she sent him off to bed, Lamella hugged him. 'I am so happy that you are finally making friends. I am always worried that you will be lonely since you are an only child.'

'Father was an only child,' Amishar pointed out.

'Yes, but he had his cousin, Lord Aminor, for company. The two of them grew up together. Sometimes, I wish you had young cousins of your own. Then we wouldn't have to ask outsiders to come and be friends with you.'

'I'm sure that you won't feel bad about this once you see how much I am enjoying their company,' Amishar said to Lamella, his heart breaking at having to lie to her. The mention of Aminor made it worse. He had never felt the need for any other company except that of his parents and his godfather. Even now, he wished, he could do without being friends with those terribly dull and sycophantic sons of his father's ministers and courtiers. But he could clearly see that his spending time in the company of other boys his age meant a lot to his mother. She was certain that it would make him happy, and he did not want to disappoint her.

She looked joyfully into her son's face and saw no sign of the anguish the young boy was feeling at having to lie to her. His face was an impenetrable mask. He looked tired but cheerful, nothing worse than a seven-annus-old who had had a long, taxing day. His mother never sensed the turmoil within him from his smiling exterior. She did not know how much the young boy had taken his uncle Feyanor's lesson about disguises and camouflage to heart.

ASTORETH AND ZAVAK
(1 A.N.)

The two armies were camped on opposite ends of the battlefield. Both sides knew that battle would be joined the next day. Though rest was essential on the eve of battle, sleep was elusive that night. Especially for the two leaders of the opposing armies. A sense of destiny hung over them both as they turned and tossed, trying to snatch some much needed rest. The sounds of the semi-asleep camps permeated the night air and slipped in through the gaps in their tents' canvas, adding to their wakefulness. But they could not blame their soldiers. Everyone was on tenterhooks. On the brink of what was easily the most critical battle in the history of Pretvain, the warriors about to go into combat had every right to be restive. Who knew how many would survive? None perhaps. It was hard to guess how long the war would rage or what its outcome would be. The soldiers were obviously anxious. So were the leaders, though they would never have admitted it.

Soon after midnight, a heavy mist fell upon both armies. It covered everything, including the vast battlefield lying between the two camps. Everyone fell into a deep slumber and learnt nothing of the magic that lifted the battlefield and the two camps out of the mortal sphere and into a place that was between Yennthem and Vynobhem. Astoreth and Zavak too slept finally. And as they slept, they dreamt the same dream.

In their dream, they were boys again. They found themselves back in the garden of their father's palace, playing together as they had when they had been young.

Astoreth looked at the boy standing in front of him and gave a start.

'What's the matter?' asked Zavak. 'Seen a ghost?'

'I thought I was looking into a mirror, just for a momon,' Astoreth replied. 'You have looked so different for so long now that I had forgotten how alike we used to look.'

'Do you see me as I was all those anni ago?' Zavak asked, sounding amused. He peered into the pool to check his image. He saw a flaxen-haired and blue-eyed eighe lad staring up at him, the spitting image of the boy who stood by his side. 'You are right. I am indeed a twelve-annus-old eighe prince again, your identical twin!' Zavak declared. There was bitterness in his voice.

'Was it really so bad—being like me, being with *me?' Astoreth asked sadly.*

Zavak thought before he replied. 'No, not really. That was probably the last time that we were truly happy. We were still together, we had just started discovering our talents and we loved each other without reservation. No, it was not bad at all. Then everything changed.'

Astoreth nodded, sitting down on the grass. He looked at Zavak and patted the ground next to him. Zavak shrugged and sat down by Astoreth's side.

'You do know *that this is a dream,' Zavak said.*

'Yes, I know,' said Astoreth. 'But does that make it any less real?'

Zavak shrugged again. The two boys sat in silence for a while.

Suddenly Zavak said, 'Do you know who will really benefit from all of this strife between us?'

'Who?' asked Astoreth. 'I can't imagine anyone benefitting,' he added drily.

Zavak ignored his jibe and said, 'Moristol! He will be the gainer if we destroy each other.'

'Why have you always hated the poor fellow? What has he done to deserve it?' Astoreth said, sounding exasperated.

Zavak shrugged for the third time. 'You have always tried to see the best in everyone. See where that has led you. Betrayed by the one you loved!'

'And so are you. You never wanted to see the good in others, but you have come to the same end as I have. You and I are still not as different as you would like to believe. Our lives are still connected more deeply than you acknowledge.'

'No! You're wrong!' shouted Zavak angrily.

He stood up and began to walk away. Astoreth leapt up and ran behind him. When he caught up, he playfully tackled Zavak and the two went down. Zavak lashed back angrily, but Astoreth was limber, and the blow missed its target. The two fought for a while—Zavak in earnest at first and then giving in to the infectiously playful spirit of Astoreth. When they were exhausted, they lay back on the soft grass, panting.

'That felt surprisingly good,' Zavak declared.

'We really shouldn't fight,' said Astoreth.

Zavak knew that he did not mean their childish scuffle on the grass. 'Says the eighe who has the kaitsyas in his camp egging him on to destroy me,' he retaliated.

'Do you think that I can? Destroy you, I mean. I have heard that you are now immortal,' Astoreth commented.

'So are you from what I hear,' retorted Zavak. 'But we'll see, won't we.'

'Do you know something that I don't?' asked Astoreth suspiciously.

Zavak laughed. 'Are you really asking your arch enemy to reveal his secrets to you?'

'I am asking my brother to tell me if he knows something that can help us both,' answered Astoreth.

'Help us? In what way?' queried Zavak.

'We can still stop all this nonsense and go back to the way things were,' insisted Astoreth. 'We know now that we were both fooled and manipulated into this situation. Why can't we just give up all of this?'

'You don't understand, do you?' snapped Zavak. 'It is not that simple. I don't think that matters would have been much different even if we had not been manipulated in *the name of love. There was too much wrong between us even before that. Like I said, the last time that we were truly happy together was probably that day when we were playing here and we discovered our gifts as a magus and a dirsfer. I think that is why we are here now, in this dream.'*

'That was the day that father told us that he was fed up of our mischief and was sending us away to school,' Astoreth added. 'You were quite unhappy about the decision.'

'So I was,' Zavak agreed. And I was unhappy also about being a magus. It meant that I would have to go to Maghem, and I did not want to.'

'Yes, I remember. You did not want to leave me. You wanted us to be together forever,' Astoreth reminded him.

'I was young back then. And foolish,' Zavak said coldly.

'Weren't we both?' sighed Astoreth. 'In fact, I have a sneaking suspicion that we still might be.'

'Really? Why do you say that?' Zavak sneered.

'Think about it,' stressed Astoreth. 'We have spent so much time in gathering so much power, and now we are about to fight each other. We were so focussed on hating each other that we never saw the truth. Think for how long we were both manipulated by an eighee with a pretty face and a poisonous heart. If we had bothered to sit down and talk, things may not have come to this pass.'

'Perhaps,' agreed Zavak warily. 'But I am not so sure. And I have no regrets. I have lived the life that I wanted.'

'Did you really want that life? Or did you do whatever it took to run away from the life you did not want?' asked Astoreth astutely.

'Oh you think you are so clever with words!' mocked Zavak. 'Is that why Vyidie is so much in love with you? She's a bigger fool than you if your words impressed her so much.'

'I don't think that my words had anything to do with that,' Astoreth grinned. 'I think she was impressed by my archery skills and my nobility and all the other fine qualities that she is happy to enumerate.'

'You are a pompous ass!' declared Zavak smiling, his mood swinging back into a cheerful one.

'And you are a blind fool!' Astoreth retorted equally cheerfully.

'What I don't get is why you would refuse the attentions of a kaitsya for a mortal!' said Zavak.

'I know why you say that. You think that if I had accepted Vyidie's affections, your path to love would have been free of obstacles. That she would have turned to you if I had given her up for Vyidie. But I don't think that that would have happened even if I

hadn't rejected Vyidie's love. She never truly loved either of us; she merely pretended to. My breaking of our betrothal would not have pushed her into your arms for real.'

'Like I said before, you are a pompous ass full of yourself,' Zavak declared.

Astoreth said pointedly, 'I think I liked that boy who did not want to leave for Maghem better. He loved me and did not want to be separated from me. He felt the same way about me that I felt about him.'

'True,' agreed Zavak. 'We did love each other and never wanted to be parted. And you came up with that silly idea of a blood pact. Do you remember?'

'Yes, of course,' said Astoreth, sitting up. 'Do you think it will still be where we buried it?'

'Let's go and check,' said Zavak, joining him.

The two boys made their way to the place where they had buried the parchment containing the blood pact. It took them a while to find the exact spot. It had been so long ago! Grass covered the patch of ground. There was no sign of anything being buried there. The brothers worked silently as they pulled up the grass and dug with their bare hands. The parchment had been buried deep, and both were sweating and dirty by the time they managed to excavate it. The anni had not been kind to the parchment. It was falling apart, and the writing had almost vanished. A few pale brown scratches marked the signatures that had been scribbled in blood at the bottom. The two boys gingerly laid the parchment on the ground.

'I'm sorry to see its state,' said Astoreth.

'I wish we had not dug it up,' agreed Zavak.

As the two looked at the pitiful piece of their past, the same thought came to them. They looked at each other and knew what the other was thinking. Like they had so often all those anni ago when they had been mere lads. It seemed insane that they were back there, that they were acting as they had when they had been young boys together. But neither spared much thought for the reality or unreality of what was happening. For a few momons—or was it horas?—they were boys again, brothers again.

'Together?' Zavak asked. Astoreth nodded.

'This time, let us put it in a protective bubble,' Astoreth suggested. Zavak nodded agreement.

The two placed their hands upon the remnants of the parchment, and it began to change. It turned back into a fresh, whole, clean piece of parchment with the words of the pact clearly visible on it. The signatures, though, remained faded. Again, the two boys looked at each other and, without a word, understood each other's thoughts. They clicked their fingers and a bowl and a small knife appeared out of thin air. They cut their palms and allowed the blood to drip into the bowl. Then they mixed the blood and signed their names to the parchment, just as they had long ago when they had really been boys and had made the original pact. Then they again placed their hands on the parchment. The document shimmered and glowed for a few momons before regaining its normal appearance. It looked no different from a million other parchments, but it was. A protective bubble had been placed around it so that the ravages of time would no longer affect it. Then the two boys again buried it in the hole where it had rested for so long.

Suddenly everything began to dissolve away. The two boys reached out and held hands.

'I think we are waking up,' Zavak said.

'I think you are right,' agreed Astoreth. 'It has been good to see you again,' he added with feeling.

Zavak hesitated before conceding that he too felt the same way. 'I am glad that we met like this,' he said, 'no matter what happens tomorrow.'

And then, both were awake. They sat up, panting. Though not a nightmare, the dream had taken its toll. They were drenched in sweat. Their stinging palms made them look at their right hands. Both were surprised to see a scar where they had cut their hand in the dream. They looked up at the blank walls of their tents, trying to figure out what had happened. Something was different, they sensed. The sounds of the camps were no longer audible. Something had happened while they had been asleep and dreaming. Cursing their somnolence, they leapt out of bed. But before they could take a step further, each saw a shadow pass across the wall of his tent.

'Who is it?' both called out in their respective tents, the dream still hanging heavily on their consciousness. But no one answered. Quickly donning their garments and taking their swords, they stepped out into the silent night. Everywhere they looked, they saw soldiers sleeping. Those who had been on guard had fallen asleep leaning on posts or trees. Those who had found no support had collapsed onto the ground. All the animals were asleep too. Fires had died down. Even the bugs that buzzed around at night, biting and annoying, were silent. Nothing was awake save the two leaders of the opposing camps.

They knew enough to understand that something deeply magical had happened. It did not take either of them long to figure out what it was. The camps and the battlefield had not changed but their location had. The thought that someone had shifted the battle away from Yennthem brought a smile to either leader's face. They wondered who had done it—the kaitsyas or the magi? It did not matter. It would not change anything.

They remembered the shadow that they had followed out of their tent. Who had it been? No one stirred outside. Then they thought about the dream they had just woken from and were seized by a strong desire to see their brother for real. One last time before the end. Though the dense fog still covered everything, it was no difficulty for them to make their way into the camp of the enemy. They were surprised to find the other camp in the same state as their own. However, instead of taking advantage of the enemy's *weakness, they made their way to each other's tent. Each was intent on seeing the other and spared no thought for his hapless enemies lying in deep slumber at his mercy. Both stepped into the other's tent and peered around. Both were disappointed. The bed was empty! Wondering where the other could be, both wandered about the camp aimlessly for a while, hoping to spy their quarry, and finally returned to his own tent with a heavy heart. Nothing would have been achieved by a meeting, both knew, but the influence of the dream was still strong on them, and they felt that it would have been nice to see each other one last time before facing off in the battlefield. Both sighed and lay down again, wondering whether this time sleep would take them or elude them.*

PART TWO

Chapter 21

THE CAT THAT TALKED

(1 Kawitor 5008 A.E. to 23 Vyiedal 5008 A.E.)

On the day that Mizu completed seven anni, he asked for a birthday gift that Misa flatly refused. He wanted to learn how to ride a horse. Misa would not allow it. She was terrified that he would fall off the horse and be trampled to death. Bolsana had four horses including Marsil. The three besides Marsil were strong draft horses used for work, particularly in the fields. There was, of course, no question of allowing Mizu to ride any of them. If he was to ride any horse at all, it could only be Marsil. She would be careful not to drop him, Misa knew. But Marsil was a large horse, and Misa was still reluctant to risk Mizu's life and limb on an activity she considered him too young for.

She believed a pony the most appropriate for teaching a boy of Mizu's age to ride. But they were too poor to buy one, and she did not want to borrow money for something that was not a necessity of life. Besides, no one in Bolsana had enough money to spare her the substantial sum that a pony would cost. She was reluctant to even broach the topic with the villagers for fear that some of them would want to buy the pony for Mizu if they learnt about it. She could not allow them to waste such large sums of money on her son. They had barely managed to stand on their feet. And she did not want her son to grow up with a sense of entitlement, to think that he could have anything he wanted just for the asking. He was now old enough to be taught the importance of earning one's privileges. She forbade him from riding any of the village's horses and promised to buy him a pony when they had enough money saved up.

When Mizu asked Leormane to teach him how to ride, the Chief sided with Misa and refused. When Misa heard that Mizu had approached Leormane after she had refused him, she was furious. She made it very clear to her son that it was not acceptable behaviour to ask someone for something, especially after she had forbidden it. Only spoilt or greedy boys went around asking for things that they wanted, she told him. Did he want people to think that he was spoilt or greedy?

'What if Leormane had agreed to your request and bought you a pony?' she further scolded him. 'He would have had to borrow the money, and he would have spent a long time repaying the loan. Do you know what that means? It means that he would not have been able to buy good food or good clothes for anni, would not have been able to make repairs to his house, would not have been able to save up for his old age or for contingencies. Do you think it is right to make people suffer such things because we want something?'

'But I did not ask for a pony, only to be taught to ride,' sniffed little Mizu.

'And to learn to ride, you must have a pony. I have told you that. If Leormane had agreed to teach you on one of the village horses, you might have met with an accident while riding. Can you imagine what that would have done to him? He would have been devastated. He might even have hurt himself in his anguish at letting you get hurt because he cares deeply for you.'

By then, Mizu was blubbering. He was beginning to realise that what had seemed like a small thing to him was not a small thing at all. He had never seen his mother so angry or so upset. It added to his misery because he understood that he had hurt her.

'I am so, so sorry!' he whimpered through his copious tears.

'And I accept your apology,' Misa said kindly. 'But you must apologise to Leormane as well for trying to take advantage of his affections.'

Mizu agreed to apologise to Leormane. He also resolved never to ask anyone for anything that his mother had forbidden. Even if someone offered it on their own, he would not accept unless his mother permitted.

Leormane was taken aback when he found Mizu standing on his doorstep, looking like he had been crying.

'What happened?' he asked anxiously. 'Did anyone hurt you? I'll take care of it if someone hurt you.'

The chief's concern brought on a fresh bout of tears. Through his sobs, Mizu managed to get his apology out a few words at a time. Leormane sensed Misa's hand behind this, but he understood why she wanted Mizu to apologise. He sincerely accepted the young boy's apology. Then, to cheer him up, he suggested that Mizu should go and ask his mother if Leormane could take him for a ride on a horse if they rode together and were very careful about it.

Misa did not object to this. She was also feeling a little bad about scolding Mizu so hard. Leormane took Mizu along on a horse and rode through the village. At a very slow walk. While he rejoiced at the gesture, Mizu regretted that he would not really learn to ride until he was much older. He was already feeling better about it, though. His mother had explained that there was nothing wrong in wanting to ride; only the circumstances made it an issue at that time. He was an even tempered little boy and did not sulk over his unsatisfied wish. At the same time, he did not forget his great desire to learn how to ride either.

One day soon after, he was in the stables feeding apples to the horses. As he fed them, he talked to them about how much he would love to be able to ride them. Suddenly someone said, 'If you want to ride, why don't you learn?'

Mizu looked around. There was no one there. He looked into the corners but saw no one. 'Who's there?' he finally asked, curious about the seemingly disembodied voice. But there was no reply to his question. When he could find no one even after further searching, Mizu gave up and went home.

This mysterious occurrence continued for several days thereafter. Whenever Mizu visited the stables, the disembodied voice would tease and taunt Mizu about wanting to ride, but no owner of the voice was ever seen. Instead of scaring the young boy, it piqued his curiosity. He searched every nook and corner of the stables but found no sign of anyone's presence. Finally, one day, he declared, 'I give up. I can't find you. Where are you?'

'Up here!' said the voice. Mizu looked up but still saw no one. He frowned. Was someone playing a prank on him?

'More to the left,' the voice instructed. 'Not *your* left—your right. Ah! There, can you see me now?'

Mizu saw. A lean black cat was sitting atop one of the rafters, washing itself. It appeared to be beaming at him.

'What are you?' Mizu asked the cat.

The cat looked surprised. 'I'm a cat, of course! Don't you know what a cat looks like?'

'Yes, I do. But cats don't talk,' declared Mizu, insulted by the cat's insinuation that he was ignorant. 'So you can't really be a cat.'

'Are you sure that I am talking, that this conversation is not inside your head?' the cat asked saucily. It neatly leapt off the rafter and rappelled down a wooden pole to land on the ground near him with a soft thump. Mizu immediately tried to grab it, but it nimbly leapt up onto a ledge and hissed at him.

Looking affronted, it snapped, 'You humans just can't be trusted. Now, do you want to learn to ride or not?'

'Yes, I do,' answered Mizu, still wondering whether he was actually talking to the cat or it was all inside his head.

'I can teach you,' the cat declared brightly, 'for the right remuneration.'

'You are a cat!' Mizu declared.

'And you are a master at stating the obvious,' said the cat, stretching and scratching the ledge on which it stood.

'A cat can't ride, so you can't teach me how to ride,' Mizu clarified. For some reason, he wanted the cat to be think well of him. He could not say why, but it seemed important to the little boy. He was already embarrassed that he had not been able to find it even after searching for several days when he could find anyone or anything within momons. 'Plus,' he added, 'we don't have a pony. My mother had forbidden me from learning on a full-sized horse.'

'Suit yourself,' announced the cat and, before Mizu could say anything more, jumped out of the window and disappeared from view.

Mizu ran outside to locate it. There was no trace of the black cat anywhere. He looked in the shrubs and bushes near the stables, but no cat was found. He went home mystified but said nothing to his mother. He had never kept secrets from her, yet he just could not bring himself to tell her about the mysterious talking cat. He returned the next day, hoping that the cat would be there. He wasn't disappointed. It was sitting on the same ledge from which it had jumped away the day before.

'So you changed your mind about cats being able to teach you how to ride, did you?' the cat quipped as soon as he entered.

'I don't know what you mean,' Mizu said, trying to sound nonchalant. 'I come here all the time to look at Marsil and the other horses. I bring apples for them.' As if to prove his point, Mizu brought an apple out of his pocket and offered it to Marsil.

The cat let out a sound that could have been a sneeze or a snort. Of course, Mizu knew, cats could not snort. Then again, they could not talk either, could they? He was very confused.

'So, you said you could teach me to ride,' he quickly said before the cat puzzled him further or disappeared like it had done the day before.

'So I did. And I meant it. For remuneration, of course,' the cat said complacently licking its stomach.

'What is that? Re-mu-ne-ra-tion. I don't know what it means.'

'It means something in exchange for the trouble I'll take,' spat out the cat condescendingly.

'What do you want for re-mu-ner-ation?'

'Food, boy, food!' declared the facetious feline and again leapt out of the window, vanishing at once from sight.

Mizu returned the next day with some scraps of food and a saucer of milk. The cat was there as usual. He wondered whether any of the other villagers saw it. He had heard no mention of a cat that inhabiting the stables. That day, it began the conversation by teasing him about his curiosity.

'Remember what it did to the cat?' it commented and let out that strange half-sneeze, half-snort that Mizu was beginning to recognise as a sort of laugh.

'I brought food for you, like you asked,' Mizu said. He placed the scraps and the milk in front of the cat. It hissed. Mizu thought that it hissed quite frequently. He wished it was not so ill tempered.

'What is this?' it demanded angrily.

'Food,' replied Mizu, puzzled at its behaviour.

'You call this food? Scraps from the table and a saucer of milk! What do you think I am? Some mangy, homeless, feral, desperate creature from the gutters?'

Mizu thought that the cat was exactly that, but he did not dare say so. So he kept quiet. Obviously, the cat had a high opinion of itself. 'I'm sorry, what would you like to eat?' he asked instead.

But the cat did not reply. In high dudgeon, it scratched on the ground to cover the scraps with dust and disappeared through the stable window. Mizu thought about what to feed the cat throughout the day. He even went about asking everyone he knew what cats ate. They gave him curious looks as they answered his question. Some said that cats ate mice and rats; some said that they drank milk; some, again, mentioned birds; a few told him that cats ate fish. This gave the young lad an idea. The next morning, he left home early and went to the stream after finishing his chores. He had learnt how to fish from the older lads in the village and was quite good at it. It did not take him long to hook a fish. He took it to the stables with him.

'This is much better,' said the cat, devouring the fresh fish. It looked content as it sat licking its chops and washing itself. 'So, Mizu, you want me to teach you how to ride a horse and, in return, you will feed me. Is that our deal then?'

'How do you know my name?' asked Mizu. The cat gave him a look of such disdain that he immediately fell quiet. He was quite in awe of this talking animal.

'What about my mother?' he asked.

'What about her?'

'She does not want me to ride by myself on one of these horses.'

'Why not?'

'Because I might fall and get hurt.'

'She's right there. You might.'

'So?'

'So what?' asked the cat snappishly.

'I do want to learn, but I don't want to disobey her either,' Mizu explained. 'So, what is the way around it?'

'You can ask her permission,' suggested the cat in a voice that gurgled with suppressed laughter. But, of course, cats couldn't laugh.

Mizu's face fell. He knew that he could not ask his mother. Firstly, she would never agree. Secondly, she might not believe him about the talking cat. And finally, she could again get upset because he had not given up the idea of learning to ride. He sighed, his face crestfallen.

'I can't ask her, and I can't ride without her permission. Thank you for offering to teach me, but I don't think that I can,' he said sadly to the cat.

'Now, wait a minura,' said the cat hastily. 'What if I promise you that you won't fall?'

'I'm not sure that it will convince my mother to give permission.'

The cat again let out that half-sneeze and said, 'I did not mean that it would. But if a chance of accident is the only reason she won't let you ride a regular-sized horse, and I can ensure that there won't be any accidents, then there's no need for her permission, is there? If the cause of the lack of permission is made redundant, so is the need for it, isn't it?'

Mizu felt his head swimming. The cat's complicated arguments were too much for the little boy! They seemed to make sense. Yet, a small voice inside his head told him that there was some fallacy in the animal's logic. In the end, Mizu's desire to learn to ride allowed him to submit to the cat's reasoning about not asking for Misa's permission.

'All right, it's a deal,' he agreed.

'Good, let us begin,' the cat said and nimbly leapt onto Marsil's back as Mizu watched. Marsil did not move an inch. The cat jogged over to Marsil's neck and rubbed its head against her mane. It stood up on its hind legs, placing its front paws on the mare's head, and licked her cheek and ear, purring audibly. Marsil, too, responded with soft neighs and whinnies. It looked to Mizu as if the two were having an affectionate conversation. When the *conversation* was over, the cat instructed Mizu to groom Marsil. Mizu had seen his mother do it many times before and had even helped her sometimes. Therefore, it proved to be an easy though laborious task for the little boy. He used a stool to stand on while he brushed and combed the tall horse's mane and back. When the task was done, the cat left, asking Mizu to meet it in the stables at the same time the next day.

The cat made Mizu groom Marsil for several days until Mizu could perform the task without getting tired, and Marsil was as comfortable with the boy as she was with his mother. Then the cat taught Mizu how to tack Marsil. It proved to be a slightly difficult task for Mizu by dint of Marsil's size and the heaviness of the gear. Marsil was very patient as the boy fumbled to complete the task. When she became restive, the cat calmed her down. It also taught Mizu how to talk to Marsil so that she would remain calm. Finally, when Mizu learnt how to clean, groom and tack Marsil, the cat declared that he was ready to progress to the next level of his training.

Much to the young boy's disappointment, it proved to be something as mundane as walking the horse. He would take Marsil out without anyone noticing and walk her about for a while before returning her to the stables and cleaning her hooves out. The cat instructed him to talk to Marsil during these walks so that she would become familiar with his voice and presence. Once the cat felt that this stage was accomplished successfully, it taught Mizu how to mount. Because of being small, Mizu had to shorten the stirrups and use a stool to mount Marsil. As soon as he learnt to mount, he was eager to be off riding, but the cat would not allow that. It ensured that Mizu could sit well-balanced upon Marsil's back and that Marsil did not object to him riding her before it would allow the boy to ride.

Mizu's clandestine riding lessons continued for several mondans. Since most children in the village were left to their own devices for most of the time, no one paid any particular notice to the fact that he was spending so much time in the stables. When Misa asked him what he was doing there, he replied that he was spending time with Marsil, which was not entirely a lie. He felt guilty about withholding information from her. But he was sure that if he told her the truth, she would stop him from continuing his lessons with the cat. He was really enjoying his riding lessons. He had also become fond of the mysterious cat that had turned out to be a wonderful teacher. It was snappy and arrogant but also patient and clever. Mizu was sure that it was not really a cat, but he did not probe what it was for fear that it would depart and leave his riding lessons incomplete. He was also almost certain that his mother would not approve of his hobnobbing with an animal that wasn't supposed to talk but did.

Finally, he was ready to show others what he had learnt. Vyiedal was almost over when the cat told him that his training was complete. Supremely excited, Mizu quickly readied the mare and trotted out into the village. At first, no one noticed. Then someone screamed. Someone else ran to fetch Misa. By then, a crowd had gathered to watch Mizu riding the horse. He made Marsil trot, canter and even jump over barriers. He sat there, cool as a cucumber, and controlled the horse as if he had been doing it all his life. Marsil responded beautifully to every command of his. The two put on quite a show for the whole village. Misa, who had arrived running a few minuras previously, stood at a distance watching him, anger and pride struggling for mastery in her heart.

How had he managed to learn to ride on his own? Had someone from the village taught him? Was that why he had been spending so much time in the stables? Why had he not told her? He had lied to her! He had never lied to her before. Who had encouraged him to lie to his mother? What if he had an accident? What if he got hurt? Misa's mind was buzzing with worries and she was grateful to finally snatch Mizu off Marsil's back when the demonstration ended. She grabbed his hand and dragged him off to their home, asking Tyzer to stable Marsil for her. She had never hit Mizu, but he cringed in front of her anger.

'Tell me everything,' she demanded, 'or I swear that I will never let you leave the house again.'

Mizu remembered the only other time he had seen her this angry. He was sensible enough to know that the truth was his best option. He told her all about his riding lessons from the cat. He also told her about the cat's arguments to convince him that he did not need her permission. She listened without a word, her grim expression response enough. He finished his tale and sat with his head bowed.

'If you ever disobey me again, if you ever lie to me again, or if you ever conceal things from me again, I will never trust you ever again,' Misa told him firmly. 'Trust is a fragile thing. It is difficult to gain and easy to lose. I don't care that you are my son; if you lose my trust, you will have to earn it back like a stranger, and it will not be easy. You may have succeeded in learning to ride without meeting with an accident. But you have disobeyed me, lied to me and concealed things from me. Even if the cat's promise held any weight, you have acted wrongly. Thrice as wrongly as you had when you had asked Leormane to teach you to ride. For that, you will have to face suitable punishment. But first, come with me and show me this talking cat that taught you how to ride.'

Mizu led Misa to the stables, but the cat was not there. It did not come even when he called for it. Even a thorough search everywhere failed to locate it. He had not expected to. He had never been able to find it before.

'I told you the truth about the cat,' he said to his mother in a small voice, worried that she would not believe him.

'I believe you,' she said, as much to her own astonishment as Mizu's. And she did. What surprised her the most was that Mizu, who could find anything and anyone, had failed to find the cat. She did not disbelieve its existence. Mizu could not have learnt to ride Marsil without help. No one in the village would have helped him after she had expressly forbidden him from riding. But the cat couldn't have been a real cat. Whoever had heard of a cat talking? It had obviously been a magical creature. She wondered what it had been. Evidently, it had not meant the boy any harm. But what had been its motive behind teaching the boy to ride? Its interest in her son brought a familiar twinge of worry. She fought it down. She told herself that it was probably helping Mizu in exchange for food, as the boy had said, though she didn't really believe it. Anyway, it was gone now. And she had to acknowledge that it had done a marvellous job. Mizu could ride as well as she did. However, she made him promise never to ride Marsil without her permission until he was older and bigger.

'I am sorry that I hid my riding lessons from you and that I lied to you,' Mizu apologised, tears in his eyes. He was upset not only because his mother was angry but also because he was missing his little friend, the cat. He had a feeling that it would not return. He had never even thanked it properly for its help!

'It's all right as long as you don't do anything like this again. I was scared for you, Mizu. I was worried that you might hurt yourself. I always am. And you *will* have to endure your punishment; there is always a price for everything. But all said and done, I am proud of you,' Misa said, finally smiling. She hugged Mizu. The boy was overjoyed despite the impending punishment. He had never been punished before. He had no idea what it entailed. But his mother had forgiven him, and she was proud of him. That was all that truly mattered. Mother and son patted Marsil and fed her an apple together. As they left the stables, hand in hand, neither noticed a pair of green feline eyes watching them avidly from atop the highest rafter of the stables.

Chapter 22

AUGURK'S FAILURE

Rauz Augurk sat deep in contemplation on his throne in the empty council chamber. Twelve days into the new annus, he did not feel the cheer that still permeated the lives of his subjects. Almost an annus and a half had passed since his first search parties had travelled forth in search of the City of Stone. When no sign of the stone city had been discovered in Ghrangghirm, he had sent scouts and spies—some of his best ones—to search in Khwaznon. Almost all of them had returned. Only two scouts had not returned yet, and they were feared dead. Augurk hoped that they had survived and that at least one of them had managed to find something about the City of Stone. He knew that it was wishful thinking, yet that thought was his only comfort. As he sat thinking of what might befall him if the city was not found, one of the missing scouts was announced. Augurk sat up eagerly, surprised at the almost miraculous fulfilment of his wish. The very next moment, he reminded himself that the spy might have found nothing. He should not be too sanguine. He composed himself as a bedraggled, worn-out dharvh entered the chamber.

'Speak!' said Augurk even before the spy could greet him. 'Have you found the City of Stone?'

'Forgive me, my rauz, but I return only to disappoint you,' the scout said forlornly. 'I have travelled to the farthest reaches of Khwaznon, even up to the great sea, but have found no trace of any city such as the one I was told to look for. Please forgive me!'

He had evidently expected some severe punishment to befall him. His surprise, when his sovereign merely sighed aloud and asked him to leave, was palpable.

'At least Blurz is still left to return,' Augurk muttered to himself. 'He might have some news.'

Augurk had inadvertently spoken aloud. The retreating scout, hearing these words, suddenly stopped. He hesitated but then turned around and approached Augurk once more.

'My rauz, pardon me for being so forward, but I heard you mention Blurz. Unfortunately, Blurz shall not return. He is dead,' he said.

'How do you know that?' demanded Augurk.

'I encountered the unfortunate dharvh just five days before he met his end. He had been searching towards eastern Khwaznon, and I was going forth on my sojourn to the south. We accidentally met one night at an inn and fell to talking. I told him of my failure. He, too, had found nothing. However, he had heard rumours of a mysterious place in the valleys of the Lyudzbradh near the borders of Wyurr. He told me that he intended to go there, though he sounded quite anxious. He was in two minds about investigating the rumour, I suspect.'

Augurk blanched on hearing the name of the dreaded Lyudzbradh but contained himself. He asked the scout, who had paused, to continue with his narrative.

'Unfortunately, I was taken ill the very next day and could not continue my journey. I never saw Blurz alive again. Five days later, on the morning of the day I was planning to depart, news reached the inn that an unidentified dharvh had been found dead a few miles from the town. His clothes had declared him to be a resident of Ghrangghirm. Knowing me to be from the same country, and having remembered seeing us talking together, the innkeeper asked me if I could identify my compatriot. I had met several dharvhs from Ghrangghirm at that inn and wasn't sure if I could recognise the one whose body had been discovered. However, I went to check on the dead dharvh to oblige my host. To my shock and horror, I discovered that it was Blurz. I found nothing among his belongings to indicate where he had been or how he had met his end. Those who had initially spotted his body told me that he had been found on the path to the mountains in the east, facing towards the town. After giving him his last rites, I continued the next day towards the south. I did ask the innkeeper to send the information on to Drauzern before I departed. I do not know why the news has not reached you yet.'

'Why did you not tell me this before?' demanded Augurk angrily.

'I was unaware that you had not received information of Blurz's death, my rauz,' replied the scout anxiously.

Augurk sighed and dismissed the scout. He sank into a dark mood. He did not regret the death of Blurz. He had never liked the dharvh anyway! Blurz had been a squint-eyed, mean braggart who had managed to eke out a living as a spy only through sheer luck. Augurk guessed that Blurz's luck had finally run out when he had decided to confront the Lyudzbradh. Augurk silently cursed the dead scout. Only a fool like him would have dared to travel to the dreaded Lyudzbradh alone.

Blurz's death worried him for another reason. His body had been found facing *towards* the city, away from the mountains. He had not died while *going* towards the Lyudzbradh; he had met his end while *returning* from it. The realisation that Blurz *had* returned alive, even though he had not managed to reach his goal, disturbed Augurk. Had he discovered something? What if the rumours that Blurz had heard had been about the City of Stone? It was the only relevant fragment of information that had been uncovered by any of his scouts. And Blurz had been undeniably and uncannily lucky quite often. Had his luck held one last time before deserting him? Was this mysterious city located in the Lyudzbradh?

Even the undaunted ruler of the dharvhs felt a cold shiver run down his back at the thought of what that entailed. He felt caught between a rock and a very hard place, almost literally. Nishtar would not forgive him if he opposed Nishtar and refused to pursue the investigation. On the other hand, if the City of Stone really *was* located among the reaches of the Lyudzbradh, there was not one dharvh who would be willing to go looking for it. The only one who had uncovered the rumour was dead, and they had no other clues. Augurk sighed again. He did not know what to do next. For, there was nothing that he *could* do.

He blamed Nishtar for the whole debacle. What had possessed him to choose Augurk for discovering the stone city? Augurk was sure that Nishtar himself knew where the city was located and was merely trying to plague him for some mysterious reason best known to Nishtar alone. He toyed with the idea of enquiring directly from Nishtar where the city was located, but he did not dare. There was nothing for him to do in the matter, he concluded. He had done his best, but he had failed. He was not going to make the mistake of challenging the mountain that had been the dharvhs' greatest dread for as long as anyone could remember. He was ashamed of his weakness, but he decided that he was more afraid of the Lyudzbradh than he was of Nishtar.

Though he had felt certain at first, Rauz Augurk took half an annus to finally come to a decision regarding the City of Stone. For mondans, he vacillated between his dread of the Lyudzbradh and his terror of Nishtar's anger. He could not decide what was worse. At times, he believed that the mountain scared him more. At other times, he was certain that the sumagus was the more fearsome of the two. Food and drink no longer gave him pleasure. Sleep eluded him at night. He grew distracted. Only his iron will kept him focussed on matters of governance without giving a hint of the state of his mind to his councillors. Even Rauzina Marizha received no inclination of the unnerving dilemma plaguing Augurk. She sensed that he had something on his mind but never guessed its significance or extent.

Only Angbruk knew how seriously worried the ruler of Ghrangghirm was, though he did not understand why. He was as different from Augurk as chalk from cheese not only in appearance but also in demeanour. Where Augurk was tall and muscular, he was short and plump. Where Augurk had angular features, he had thick lips, a flat nose and beady eyes. Where Augurk was charismatic and ambitious, he was quiet and stolid. However, his life and loyalty were completely and unstintedly Augurk's. He said nothing though he saw how his elder brother suffered. He wished he could help Augurk, but it was not his burden. Augurk alone could decide what to do about the search for the City of Stone in the light of the incident with Blurz, the unfortunate spy.

Finally, Augurk made up his mind. He would not endanger his subjects by forcing them to traverse the Lyudzbradh. He knew that his response would anger Nishtar. However, he would not allow his dharvhs to suffer in consequence of his choices. He steeled his mind and sent his reply to Nishtar in as brief and as courteous a missive as he could devise. He sent the message off by pigeon. The bird would take no more than two days to reach the sumagus. And Nishtar would reply promptly—Augurk was sure of that. He was not mistaken. He wrote to Nishtar on the second of Vyiedal. On the sixth, a pigeon arrived with Nishtar's reply. Augurk winced as he saw the dark scrawl. The writing suggested that when he had written the note, Nishtar had either been in a hurry or in the grip of a strong emotion, probably anger. The latter was far more likely, Augurk thought. The letter dripped with hot venom, metaphorically speaking. Augurk would not have been surprised if the venom had been literal.

'Rauz Augurk,' it began, the 'Rauz' underlined for effect. 'It greatly disappoints me that one such as you has refused to uphold his responsibilities. Long ago, the dharvhs were entrusted with the safekeeping of the City of Stone, but they failed in their duties and the city passed into myth, unknown and unheard of, while the dharvhs continued to engage in their wars and squabbles. And you of all dharvhs! *You* dare refuse me! I wished not to impose upon you, nor to remind you of what you owe me. So, I *requested* you to find this remarkable city that your ancestors were entrusted with guarding. And you *dare* throw my request in my face and declare that you *dare* not go up against the Lyudzbradh! You *dared* enough to do that at one time, or have you forgotten? Perhaps, the luxuries of the seat of rauz have obliterated from your memory what once transpired between us? I am sure that must be the case. For, I cannot imagine that you would have dared to refuse me if you remembered! I have asked you once; I will not ask you again. If you fail me, you have worse to fear than the nameless terrors of the Lyudzbradh!'

Augurk trembled in his shoes upon reading Nishtar's message. Looking at him, no one would have imagined him capable of feeling fear. He was large and imposing and grim. Any dharvh he glowered down at—and most were close to a head shorter than him—melted under his gaze. But Nishtar's missive rendered him as terrified as a child in a thunderstorm. He had anticipated the sumagus's anger, but its intensity shook him to the core. It was all too clear that he had no choice in the matter and never had had. He had tried to hold on to the tiny fragment of a semblance of control that Nishtar's initial approach had allowed. But now, even that shred of pretence was gone. He had been ordered—nay, threatened—to find the City of Stone though it might cost him everything he had worked so hard for—his reputation, his throne, his subjects, even his life. And he could not refuse

Nishtar, for the sumagus had himself predicted the outcome of doing so. Augurk was willing to believe that Nishtar was as ruthless as he claimed to be.

That night, Rauz Augurk could not sleep. He spent several horas brooding upon his hopeless predicament and, just before dawn, walked up to the terrace for some fresh air. Shornhuz was on duty, as usual, and was about to follow him. Augurk indicated that he should remain at his post outside Augurk's door. Shornhuz nodded and obeyed. Augurk was so disturbed that the serenity of the hora was wasted on him. It was his favourite time of the day, but he no longer felt refreshed by the rapidly brightening sky in the east. To him, the reddening horizon was a presage of the bloodshed that Nishtar's proclamation was about to propel him into. Augurk heard footsteps behind him. He was all alone and, for a momon, wondered whether Nishtar had sent an assassin to murder him. He turned round. Angbruk was standing there, looking pale and anxious.

'What is it, Angbruk?' Augurk asked, trying not to sound as demoralised as he felt.

'I went to see you, but your chamber was empty. The guards said that you had come up here. Is everything all right? They said you had received a message by pigeon,' Angbruk said hesitantly.

Augurk sighed and passed him the message that had come from Nishtar. Angbruk read it quickly in the golden light of the early morning. He looked blank.

'Why is the sumagus threatening you?' he asked. 'And why *you*? What connection do you have to him?'

Augurk could sense and sympathise with Angbruk's confusion. For anni, he had borne a heavy secret in his heart, a secret that could shake the very foundation of his rule. He had not, could not, share it with any. However, today he would have to, he realised. Angbruk had followed him through thick and thin with utter devotion and without any questions. He deserved to know the truth, to know that all dharvhs were in danger of Nishtar's wrath because of what he, Augurk, owed the sumagus. 'Let us take a walk,' he said to Angbruk.

The brothers walked out of the palace and towards the outskirts of Drauzern, avoiding Shornhuz who would have wanted to follow his rauz. It was too early for many dharvhs to be around. The streets of Drauzern were almost devoid of traffic as Augurk and Angbruk trotted silently towards the east. Drauzern was a densely populated city settled upon the lip of a shelf. The slope of the cliff was not steep, but a wall protected citizens from accidentally going off the edge. It was a wide wall with steps leading up to the ramparts. Soldiers patrolled there at night; during the day, guards kept watch from squat cabins built along the wall at intervals. The sun was well on its way in the sky by the time Augurk and Angbruk reached the wall. They climbed up and sat with their feet dangling over the outer edge.

Angbruk felt uneasy. What was going on? Why were they there? Though anxious, he waited patiently for Augurk to speak.

Finally Augurk said, 'Do you remember the time I became rauz?'

Angbruk frowned at the strange question but nodded. 'We are all proud of you,' he said. 'You changed the way the dharvhs looked at our veradh. It was almost unbelievable that you defeated such strong contenders for the throne. But you succeeded against all odds.'

Augurk nodded absent-mindedly. 'Yes, I succeeded against all odds. And that's why we are in this situation today.'

'What do you mean?'

'I succeeded in the Zhan-ang-Razr because I had help. From Nishtar. I would not have succeeded without his aid,' Augurk said in a tone of resignation. Somehow, as he confessed this, a weight seemed to lift off his chest.

'I don't understand,' Angbruk said, looking puzzled. 'Nishtar helped you? Why? How? Where did you meet him? How did you meet him? And what has that to do with our situation today?'

Augurk sighed and said, 'Listen then. This is a story that I have never told anyone, not even the rauzina. This secret was supposed to go to the grave with me. But given our current problem, I am compelled to share it with you. I trust you, but I must stress upon the need to keep what I am going to tell you completely secret.'

'I swear I shall never say a word to anyone,' Angbruk promised.

'I have been rauz for close to forty anni now. In all this time, our lives have been full of bustle. But I am sure you remember our life in Etroval despite that: how dull and pointless it had seemed. And then we ran away!'

Angbruk nodded, a smile stretching his lips slightly. He remembered all too well how their lives as youngsters had been. For anni, Augurk had been chomping at the bit to leave the sedate life of the veradh behind. Ever since he had been sixteen, Augurk had talked of nothing except joining the army. He had been only a lad then, no older than an eight-annus-old human boy[4]. But he was already tired of the lack of action that their life promised. Their father, an ardent pacifist, and a master miner, had refused to allow his son to take that path. He had trained his sons to be miners and would not hear of dissent. Then, one fateful day, an accident in the mines claimed their mother's life. Their father was too devastated to look after the boys properly, so their grandfather stepped in as their guardian. This did not sit well with their father, but their grandfather was too stubborn to give up

---

4 Augurk's chronological age would have been sixteen anni at the time. For more details about the correlations in age between the different races, see Appendix 4 of Tornain Book One: The Prophecy of Kawiti

his wards. The two fought over custody of the boys. Augurk solved the problem by running away. He was thirty-three at the time, just old enough to enlist, and Angbruk was twenty. Though too young to be in the army, Angbruk followed his elder brother without hesitation.

'I remember the night we ran away,' Angbruk said to Augurk. 'You were so angry at father and grandfather that you even refused to leave a note, though I wanted to.'

'You were very young. You did not understand how serious matters were. We had to disappear without a trace, or they would have taken us back,' Augurk commented, remembering that night with fondness. The journey to Drauzern had not been easy and, Angbruk had been too young to help in case of danger. They had been fortunate and had managed to reach Drauzern without incident and without being caught by the dharvhs of the Mermurdh, their veradh.

Augurk had immediately joined the army and had risen through the ranks by dint of determination, hard work and merit. By the time Angbruk was old enough to enlist, Augurk already had charge of a thousand. Those who knew him were full of praise for the young soldier and had high hopes for him. Angbruk had been assigned to a unit that was under Augurk's command. He had felt the pressure of performance on him but had been happy to progress at his own pace. Augurk and Angbruk had returned to Etroval when they had learnt that their grandfather was on his deathbed. They had been greeted with cordiality by all the residents of the veradh and, though their father had never forgiven them, he had had to concede that Augurk had brought glory to the veradh by following his own path. Angbruk was neither rebuked nor celebrated though he was welcomed back with equal enthusiasm. He had been content to know that he could return to Etroval and find a home there despite following his own dreams.

Two significant events had happened during their stay in Etroval: their grandfather had passed, leaving Augurk and Angbruk as his heirs, and Marizha's father had visited with her wedding invitation. Like several other young dharvhs of the veradh, Augurk had competed for her hand. He had won, though, by the time the marriage finally took place, he had returned to Drauzern. They had had a daughter after a few anni. At the time of Meizha's birth, Augurk was fifty and Angbruk was thirty-seven. Augurk had been in the army for close to two decadi by then. Ten anni later, when the rauz had declared that he was abdicating due to reasons of health, tumult had shaken Ghrangghirm. Some of the most powerful dharvhs in the country had contented for the most coveted position in the kingdom. Augurk had been one of the very last to declare his nomination. In fact, he had almost failed to enter his name in time. He had vanished for a while right after the announcement of the Zhan-ang-Razr, the kingship tournament, and had not been seen until the last day for submitting nominations. During the contest, though, he had easily defeated the other contenders, some of whom had been clear favourites, and had succeeded to the throne of Ghrangghirm. Forty anni had passed since then.

'Do you remember grandfather's legacy?' Augurk asked Angbruk, breaking into the latter's thoughts.

'Yes, he left us everything he had. He named us as his heirs. Father was terribly angry though he should have anticipated it after their bitter quarrels,' Angbruk responded.

'Yes, but what you don't know is that grandfather told me a secret before he died. A secret that I buried deep within my mind for anni. Can you guess what that secret was?'

Beginning to add all the pieces together, Angbruk guessed what it possibly was, but waited to hear his brother spell it out.

Augurk continued, 'He spoke about an old man who lived upon a mountain near the coast. An old man with the power to make any of your dreams come true. And he told me how to reach this old man's lair in the north.'

'Nishtar?' Angbruk asked by way of confirmation. Augurk nodded.

'I never intended to follow up on this revelation. The thought of crossing the Lyudzbradh was too terrifying despite the secret paths that grandfather had told me about. I could have gone around the mountains, but that would have entailed a far longer journey through kereighe lands. I decided it was best to leave the matter alone. I pushed thoughts of this old man and his powers to the back of my mind. I focussed my entire attention and energy on excelling in the military. And I had all but forgotten about this old man when the rauz announced that he was abdicating. I had been rising steadily within the army, but there were many who might have easily defeated me in the Zhan-ang-Razr. I knew that. But I did not want it to be so. I wanted to win at any cost. So…so…,' Augurk appeared to have some difficulty in saying it aloud.

'So you went to meet Nishtar to ask for his help with the tournament,' Angbruk supplied. Augurk nodded, looking tired.

'Why?' Angbruk asked.

'Why? Because there was no other way for me to win.'

'No, I mean, why were you so desperate to win?'

'Because I knew that it was the only way to keep the country together,' Augurk said matter-of-factly. 'Dermizh had pulled us together, back from the brink of destruction, but there were forces straining to break away and plunge the kingdom into anarchy again. There still are. None of those who could have defeated me had any vision for Ghrangghirm as a nation or for dharvhs as a race. I knew them all personally. They wanted to become rauz for personal glory and power. Some others, though they had the vision, did not have the strength to achieve that vision. Either type of rauz would have failed to keep the forces of anarchy at bay. Everything that Dermizh had achieved would have been lost. We dharvhs of Ghrangghirm would have reverted to the days of barbarism and anonymity. Don't you see? I *had* to win. Not for myself. For Ghrangghirm. For all dharvhs!'

Angbruk nodded, understanding his brother's complex motivation.

'So I went to Nishtar for help. It was a horrifying journey. I still have nightmares about it, so I won't talk about what happened on the way to the White Mountain and back. Suffice it to say that I met Nishtar and convinced him to help me. His aid allowed me victory in the Zhan-ang-Razr. He also gave me the baculus.'

'And so you won and became rauz,' Angbruk said with a sigh. 'And after all these anni, Nishtar has decided to collect his dues.'

Augurk nodded. 'I am sorry,' he whispered.

'What for?' Angbruk asked, surprised.

'For bringing this on you and on our subjects. You should not have to pay for my choices.'

'But no one is paying for *your* choices!' Angbruk protested. 'We are facing the consequences of our own decisions. I chose to follow you no matter what. So, if you face danger, I face danger. I have always understood that. I have no regrets.'

'What about the subjects? What did they choose to deserve this?'

'They chose to cling to a system that forced you to do what you did,' Angbruk said simply.

Chapter 23

HEIR APPARENT

As the days went by, Prince Amishar became more accustomed to his new 'friends' who visited him regularly to play with him. Though his training and studies remained his true interest, he began to see the value of having cronies. They made him feel good about himself. They were almost always willing to do whatever he wanted. They would fall over one another to do his bidding. They agreed with whatever he said without question. They made him feel important. Of course, they expected to be rewarded in return. Amishar knew this well and never disappointed them. The more they fawned on him, the more contemptuous of them he became. At the same time, a desire began to grow in his heart to impress them with his heroics. He wanted them to look up to him as a brave and strong leader. They kowtowed to him because he was the prince, but he wanted them to adore him for his qualities. His young heart yearned for genuine admiration from his sycophantic companions.

The palace gardens were assigned as the province of their games. This suited Amishar, who was adept at inventing games requiring the display of physical prowess. Soon, the din caused by their energetic games startled and distracted several ministers and officials trying to work, ladies-in-waiting taking their rest and servants hurrying about their business. When the level of noise did not subside for days, Queen Lamella had the gardeners give them access to the royal orchard, which was at some distance from the main palace, to allow them to play their boisterous games without disturbing anyone.

For the prince's protection, a group of bodyguards was assigned to accompany them during these sojourns. But their presence made Amishar unhappy. It was difficult to pretend that he was a fierce warrior with so many guards around. What would his companions think? They would think that he was too weak to look after himself. He requested that the guards be posted at a distance. They could not be themselves, Amishar argued, with too many sentries constantly monitoring them. The guards intimidated the other boys. Lamella reluctantly agreed, and King Amiroth required even more persuasion to be convinced of the merit of this suggestion.

One day, in the beginning of Kielom, the boys were playing hide and seek among the trees in the orchard. The orchard was full of tall trees that bore fruits.

The trees also provided excellent hiding places, and the boys enjoyed themselves for a hora. When they were tired of this game, they competed with each other for downing fruits using slings. Soon, though, they tired of this game too, especially after some of the gardeners started casting them sour looks. Of course, they could say nothing to their prince, but that did not prevent them from looking like they had bitten into raw berries. Someone then suggested a tree-climbing contest, and this idea was enthusiastically accepted by all.

Each boy chose a tree to climb. The goal was to climb as far as possible and tie a ribbon on a branch as a mark. Once everyone was back on the ground, the marks would be checked to determine the winner. The boy who climbed the highest would be declared the victor. One of the boys was scared of heights and volunteered to act as referee. On his whistle, the remaining boys began to climb. They were active, nimble boys, and they climbed fast. Soon, most of them were several feet above the ground. The first boy to stop climbing was on a mango tree. He had reached the topmost sturdy branch of the tree. The branches above would not carry his weight. He checked to see if he could climb a little higher but found it too risky. He tied a ribbon as high up along the branch as he could and shimmied back down to earth. To his disappointment, none of his comrades had returned yet.

All the boys returned from their climbs within the next fifteen minuras. All except Amishar. When they realised this, the boys began to search for him. Ten minuras of searching revealed that the prince was perched on a tree towards the centre of the orchard. He had infallibly chosen to climb the tallest tree in the orchard and was very high up in its branches. The boys called out to him and asked him to return. They conceded that he had already climbed higher than any of them. But Amishar had no wish to return so soon. He shouted back at them that he would return only after climbing to the very top. The boys looked at one another nervously. If the prince fell, they would lose their heads. They were responsible for his safety, they knew, though no one had explicitly told them so. They continued to plead with Amishar to climb down but to no avail. Finally, they gave up and sat down around the tree, waiting for the prince's return. It was fully half a hora before they saw him cleverly climbing down the strong branches of the tree, grinning. Relieved, they applauded him and praised him for his agility. Amishar flushed with pride and thanked them. When they returned to the palace, he gifted them beautiful belts and knives. The implicit understanding was that not a word of that afternoon's escapades would reach the king and queen directly or indirectly.

In the solitude of his chamber, though, Prince Amishar moped. He did not really enjoy the company of the nobles' sons. He had begun by being friends with those who were closest to him in age, but they had proven too shy around him. He had then befriended some of the older boys. These boys were confident enough to act natural around him, but that was all it was—acting. Amishar felt sure that they did not really care for him. He could have dispensed with them if he had wanted to, but something about their behaviour appealed to him. Though they were all older than him, they bowed and scraped to him because he was the prince of the country. He could not deny that he liked the attention even though he did not like any of the boys. He knew that his godfather, Lord Aminor, would not have been happy about this. Amishar wasn't sure what was wrong about the way he felt and acted towards these companions of his, but he knew in his heart that his actions would have displeased Aminor. He still missed his tutor but not as keenly as he had earlier. He had written a letter to his noble relation once but had been too shy to have it sent. News had come from Aminor about his stay in Ashperth, but no messages had come for Amishar personally. He scowled at the thought and thought of other things to distract himself. He was doing very well both inside the classroom and outside. King Amiroth had promised him that in somminar, he would be taught how to swim. It was now vernurt. He could hardly wait for the season to change.

In the meantime, he continued to show off for his sycophantic friends. His antics continued to grow more dangerous by the tempora. On the last day of Zulheen, Amishar and his 'friends' were having a picnic on one of the terraces of the palace. It was in the oldest part of the palace and had high walls around it. Lamella had agreed to a rooftop picnic on the condition that they would remain within the confines of this secure terrace. The boys had had their food and were dozing in the vernurt sun when a shrill whistle caught their attention. They looked up to find Prince Amishar standing upon one of the terrace walls. It was at least ten feet high! A fall from that height would invariably result in broken bones, if not worse. They could not see how the prince had climbed up; there were hardly any handholds or footholds on the terrace wall. They begged the prince to come down. One of them went off to fetch a ladder. Another wanted to call an adult but was immediately grabbed and subdued by the others. A third boy was smart enough to drag a couple of the mattresses on which they had been resting to the base of the wall to break Amishar's fall, in case he toppled off the wall. Amishar laughed contemptuously and leapt. He landed adroitly on his feet and then took a bow like an acrobat. His companions stood in stunned silence for a momon and then erupted in claps and cheers. That evening, they went home with rich trinkets and toys.

Just a mondan later, Amishar performed what was his most dangerous caper so far. The boys had been wandering around the royal dairy when they spotted a bull penned in separately from the rest of the cattle. They enquired about it and learnt that it was given to bouts of bad temper and had to be segregated every once in a while to allow it to calm down. Amishar decided that he would tease the bull. His companions could not dissuade him. He threw stones at the bull from outside the pen when none of the dairy workers was watching. His companions copied him eagerly. At first the bull ignored them. Then, when the irritating boys did not desist, the bull lost all patience. It charged. It trampled down the pen's fence and chased after the boys. All of them scattered before the enraged bull but Amishar stood his ground. He waited until the furious animal was almost upon him and then started running, turning around to check if the bull was following. This time, though, there were adults nearby. They noticed at once what was happening. Immediate action was taken, and the bull was captured before it could harm the prince. The king and queen were informed about the incident. They were furious at the dairy workers until Prince Amishar confessed to the truth. Their anger reverted to him now. He was banned from going outdoors for two temporas. The offending bull was ordered to be slaughtered. Amishar felt sorry for the bull that, after all, had not been to blame for the incident. He pleaded with his father to spare the bull. It was only after Amishar promised never to repeat his antics and to stay indoors for two more temporas that King Amiroth agreed to spare the poor animal.

During the days of his confinement, Amishar applied himself to his studies with the utmost zeal, not allowing himself time to pine for the outdoors. Thinking that he might be missing his friends during these days, King Amiroth asked Amishar if he would like to include his friends in his training and study routines. However, the idea did not appeal to the young boy. He did not wish to have the nobles' sons as witnesses to his efforts to learn. He was afraid that he would make mistakes, and they would laugh at him behind his back. He told his father that he preferred to take his lessons alone. The king never mentioned this idea again.

It was close to two mondans later, after somminar had well set in, that Amishar's swimming lessons began. He was then gladder than ever that he had insisted on training alone. He had been looking forward to these lessons. But everything went terribly wrong right from the beginning. As soon as he stepped inside the pool, his teacher right by his side, Amishar panicked. His heart seemed to leap into his throat, and his chest felt constricted. He could not breathe. The water, it seemed to him, was rushing up to drown him. He began to thrash about in an effort to escape. He lost his footing and plunged inside the water. In the few momons that he was underwater, he felt that his head would explode, that he would die. His teacher immediately dragged him out. However, Amishar was on the verge of tears. He was terrified and did not calm down for a long time. His trainer was baffled. He had never seen anyone react this way. It was almost as if the prince had some congenital fear of water. He apologised to the king, who was equally baffled, and promised to try again the next day. Amishar was coaxed into attempting swimming a second time even though he had received a major shock on his first attempt. The results were no different. Thereafter, Amishar refused to enter the water again. His swimming lessons came to an abrupt end with the decision that they would be resumed when he was older and, hopefully, less afraid of the water.

(5 Kielom 5008 A.E. to 15Yodirin 5008 A.E.)

After sending off his angry missive to Augurk, it took Nishtar four temporas to calm down and acknowledge that he had been a little too hard on the rauz. After all, he confessed to Alanor, Augurk was a dharvh. And the terror of the Lyudzbradh was so ingrained in dharvhs that expecting Augurk to launch an expedition into the mountain range was expecting entirely too much. He should have been more reasonable in his reply to Augurk's letter, he conceded.

'So, are you going to apologise to him?' Alanor asked, wondering where the discussion was headed.

'Of course not!' answered Nishtar with a hint of surprise in his voice, as if he could not believe that Alanor would even suggest such a thing!

'Of course not,' Alanor agreed, trying to keep a straight face. He had asked Nishtar the question merely to test the magus's reaction. Nishtar's lack of awareness regarding his own follies never failed to amuse him. 'So, what do you have in mind?'

'I have been thinking about what Augurk wrote to me. I believe he needs a little help. It might be time to involve someone besides the dharvhs in the matter of the stone city. Especially since Augurk has found indications that it might be located among the mountains of the Lyudzbradh. The dharvhs' aversion to a continuation of the search is an obstacle that is almost impossible to overcome. Therefore, we will have to find a way to go around it.'

'Quite,' agreed Alanor. 'But who else can be involved? I don't think that there is any race either in the east or the west that does not fear the mountain range.'

'True, but the men of the west and the fraels only know it by reputation. They have not had to live in its shadow and, therefore, though it inspires fear in them, they may be willing to accept the challenge nonetheless.'

'So which of the two races are you planning to involve in this search?' Alanor asked.

'I think you know the answer to that question, Alanor,' Nishtar responded with a grim smile.

'So, you intend to engage the royal families of the West in this quest?' asked Alanor, his thoughts going unbidden to one hero who had recently garnered great renown. He somehow could not reconcile the idea of Feyanor being cowed into joining the search for Patarshp's city with the man he had seen in the streets of Lufurdista.

Guessing Alanor's line of thinking, Nishtar said, 'I don't have anyone particular in mind. In fact, I am not going to communicate with them over this matter at all.'

'What exactly *are* you thinking?' asked Alanor, feeling a little puzzled.

'I am thinking of giving our friend Augurk a little nudge to propel him in the right direction. If he were to find out that the humans can be enlisted to help, I believe he would be happy to approach them. I am sure that he would rather part with some of the fabled wealth of the dharvhs than send his soldiers marching off into the unknown terrors of the Lyudzbradh. He would have no compunction in sending human soldiers off into the same unknown terrors, I think, if he strikes a deal to that effect with the human kings.'

'And how do you plan to achieve this *nudge*? Are you going to tell Augurk that Simhurd, the founder of the kingdom of Krovad, was the last person who released the city's powers?'

'Yes, but not so clearly. If Augurk learns that I know a good deal about the city, he will assume that I already know its location and that I am merely tormenting him by asking him to find it. I'm not sure that he does not already think so. I will not give him more cause for such thought. It might cause his stubborn pride to overcome his fear of me.'

'Then what do you intend to do?'

'Oh, Augurk will have to be informed of this, no doubt. But we will have to leave out the details. Just let him know, preferably indirectly, that the last person to awaken the city was an ancient human king of the West. I think that he will be happy to take the hint and will put it to good use without further prompting.'

'And just how do you plan to let Augurk know about this indirectly?' Alanor asked, both intrigued and exasperated by Nishtar's complicated thinking.

'I am not,' Nishtar responded calmly. '*You* are!'

And so it was that Alanor found himself on the path to Drauzern, disguised as an ordinary wandering magus making his way in the world by casting fortunes and reading omens. It took him seventeen days to reach Drauzern. Next morning, he began to walk the streets of the capital city, offering his services to the citizens. Though Eskielar, the festival of Kiel, had been over for more than two temporas, some of the houses still had the Song of Kiel written upon their main entrances. Eskielar was a dark festival, and while it was widely observed, it was marked by

grim and ascetic routines rather than exuberant festivities. One of the rituals
involved the writing of the Song of Kiel on the main entrance of the house. It was
said to ward off Kiel's gaze on the day of Eskielar. Although there was no proof
that it actually caused Kiel to turn away from the doorstep, many often did not
erase the song for temporas afterwards, hoping to appease the Guardian of Death
for as long as possible. Alanor stopped in front of a house to read:

> *Vh plorb thur, O ghir aghhribesh Kiel,*
>> *Derdar dhro Loarn, Gezh dhro Zyimnhem,*
> *Wrekh druv thur cheun bunyond len vhek bunordh*
>> *Eblirar, eblirar, eblirar?*
> *Hane novdhr dhen foythun howadoh waz zhorb gyudhh?*
>> *Hane novdhr dhen foythun zyimnoh waz Zyimnhem?*
> *Wrekh druv thur shord lybhed jno vhek bunordhmog*
>> *Ishbarar, ishbarar, ishbarar?*
> *Mred Vh druvth kilhet jno jaghh vher morvag?*
>> *Mred neharoh ogdreth zhorb rooghash dhro vhek puvoh?*
> *Wrekh druv thur qoshb vhek swekh gwaivoh twoz vhu*
>> *Ulacrar, ulacrar, ulacrar?*
> *Druv dhen cheun novdhr shav ghaveth medh shurthesh,*
>> *Uh wajegr buvur vhek yashthhad zukzar zhorb adenb.*
> *Vh mred ogdreth waz crevh daverdoh dhro byghh, vhek dedel*
>> *Xotrar, xotrar, xotrar.*
> *Kiel, Gezh dhro Loarn, Derdar dhro Zyimnhem,*
>> *Hroaz shrodh medh enjhe vhek barkhel enh gorvd.*
> *Druv dhen shord fandh medh fandh jno vhek bunordh*
>> *Eblirar, eblirar, eblirar?*

Alanor continued to roam through Drauzern, offering to read fortunes and
omens. Some accepted his offer, paying him a few coins in return. Alanor had
never truly enjoyed casting or fortune telling, but he did his best to be accurate.
Even though the fortune telling was only part of his disguise, he felt that he owed
it to his 'patrons' to make a genuine effort, especially since they were paying him
their hard-earned money. He gradually made his way to the houses of Augurk's

councillors. Augurk was sure to have enquired about the City of Stone among his councillors. Alanor had no idea if any of them had been able to help him. Augurk's lack of success indicated that they probably had not. Nevertheless, the best way to get his information to Augurk would be through one of them, he decided. He continued to visit one councillor's home after another until he came upon a councillor who was extremely old and withered. Alanor was surprised that the old dharvh was still alive! He was even more surprised to find that this councillor took his duties very seriously. He had found the perfect candidate to convey his message to the rauz!

Alanor made sure to visit this councillor just after sunset. The old councillor was amused when Alanor offered to read into his 'long and prosperous' future and invited the magus in. Once he was inside, Alanor made sure that he intrigued the old councillor and his family enough with his forecasts and predictions to garner an invitation to dinner. Dinner was followed by a clever wrangling of an offer to spend the night. As he sat puffing on a pipe and chatting with the old councillor later that night, Alanor used his powers of suggestion to get the dharvh talking about the City of Stone. Even the councillor could not have said later how the discussion had moved from soup to the hidden city. He found himself recalling how, when he had been very young, his great-grandfather had told him the story of the city to comfort him during a storm. Though he had forgotten most of that incident, a little help from Alanor jogged his memory abundantly. He soon discovered that he could remember everything that had happened that evening, including the story that the venerable old dharvh had told him.

Feeling excited, he narrated everything to a raptly listening Alanor.

'It is a splendid story, old father,' Alanor congratulated him. 'And you have a terrific memory.'

'I do, don't I?' the old dharvh agreed, rather surprised at his own mnemonic prowess. 'Do you know what is odd though? When the rauz asked about the city, I tried so hard to remember the story that my great-grandfather had told me, but I could not. I wonder why that was.'

'Sometimes these things happen,' Alanor said, nodding his head sagely. 'If you try to recall something very hard, it slips your mind and then, when you are not thinking about it at all, the memory comes flooding back.'

'True, true,' the old councillor agreed, convincing himself that such must have been the case with his memories of the tale told by his great-grandfather.

'You know, you could go and tell the rauz now that you have remembered the story. I am sure he would be fascinated to hear it!' Alanor suggested.

Alanor deliberately spoke as if he thought that the story rather than the city had been the main interest of the rauz. He felt sure that the old councillor would not forget the story again and that he would definitely go to Augurk the next day. Still, to be completely certain, Alanor used the power of suggestion on the old dharvh to fix the idea in his mind. Next morning, he rose early and left before he was noticed, feeling certain that Augurk would get the nudge that Nishtar had intended for him. As he hurried from Drauzern, Alanor fantasised about Feyanor being Augurk's chosen hero and the glory such an expedition would bring the prince. He knew that too many generations had passed for him to feel a bond of kinship with any of the present day human kings of the West. He also knew that as a sumagus, he should be impartial. But he could not ignore the prince of Ashperth who had strangely impressed him. Or his wife, who had strangely intrigued him.

A mondan had passed since Augurk had received Nishtar's angry missive. Despite his initial terror, he had not undertaken any action. The truth was that he had not yet succeeded in deciding what further course of action was best. Augurk was not indecisive by nature, so his inability to decide the right course of action in the matter of the City of Stone caused him great frustration. Nishtar had made it abundantly clear that he would not be disobeyed. Yet, there was no way to obey Nishtar without giving birth to a danger of rebellion. No dharvh would willingly set foot upon the Lyudzbradh, especially for a reason that was vague and seemingly insane. Augurk sat with Nishtar's message open by his side in his chamber. He had read it again and again in his despair. Nishtar had not only spoken about him with derision but had made no secret of how he felt about dharvhs in general. For a moment, Augurk felt his ears turning warm with anger. How dare Nishtar insult him and his race! But there was little that Nishtar dared not do, he knew. He was the one who lacked the gumption to either stand up to Nishtar or to throw caution to the winds and march off in search of the City of Stone. He could not do the latter, he told himself, because he had responsibilities towards his subjects as rauz. But he knew the truth; he was afraid of risking his position and his life for a possibly futile and definitely dangerous mission. He sat in a dark mood, reflecting on his dues to the sumagus and to his subjects.

At this moment, like a reflection of his dark thoughts, a shadow fell across his chamber. Shornhuz entered to announce that one of Augurk's councillors wanted to meet him. With a sigh, Augurk asked Shornhuz to escort the councillor in. He wondered what was so important that this dharvh had come to meet him in his private quarters instead of in the council chamber. But he was rauz and could not refuse to meet his councillor unless he was in the middle of something important. He was almost glad to find an excuse to stop thinking about Nishtar's letter.

An old and decrepit dharvh hobbled into the room, trembling like a leaf and looking as if he would collapse any minura. Augurk hurried to provide him with a chair. He sat down gratefully and smiled a toothless smile at the rauz.

'How can I help you, venerable one?' Augurk asked.

'My name, rauz, is Onnish. I am here in response to your query about the City of Stone.'

Augurk gave a start. He had enquired about the city amongst his councillors a long time ago. He had an ominous feeling that Nishtar had something to do with the presence of the old dharvh in his chamber. However, he could not see how that could be. He shook off the feeling and asked Onnish to continue.

'A while ago, you asked your councillors whether any of us knew anything about the City of Stone,' said Onnish. 'To our great and everlasting shame, none of us could be of any service to you that day. I am ashamed to state that I too was unable to recall anything upon the subject at the time. However, yesterday I miraculously remembered something that I had once heard.'

Augurk stood up, agitated and suspicious, but willing himself to stay calm. Was it really possible that after all this time, someone had come forth with real information? It was hard to believe. He now clearly recalled the old councillor who had lingered on in a corner of his council for anni without ever making any contribution. No one remembered when, or how, he had become an advisor to the rauz of Ghrangghirm. But there he always was, more fragile than a sheet of parchment and more wrinkled than a raisin. Augurk suddenly felt sorry for the old dharvh. He wondered how old Onnish was, and whether he had any near and dear ones still living. He said nothing, however, and allowed the old dharvh to continue. Onnish was now mumbling something about a storm and talking almost to himself. Augurk sat down and listened patiently, hoping to discover some helpful scraps in the rambling speech of the elderly dharvh.

Onnish was saying, 'The storm was terrible indeed. At that time, I was only a child. We had a large family. My father was there and my grandfather and even my great-grandfather. He had been in the army of Vrenhor, or so he claimed. He was a gaffer to be sure. And my grandmother—she was a shrew! She would start throwing things at him as soon as he opened his mouth to spin one of his yarns...'

Augurk shifted restlessly. He was too wound up to sit through the meandering tales of the old dharvh and too polite to cut him short. After rambling on for a while about the various members of his family, Onnish finally returned to the subject of the storm.

'I could not go to sleep—I was so scared—that night. And then my great-grandfather started telling me the tale of a city that was unlike any other. It was made entirely of stone, he said. And he had heard from *his* grandfather that only once had it been awakened since its inception. Terrible things had happened afterwards. I was so interested in his tale that I forgot all about the storm, and then I fell asleep,' finished Onnish.

'Did he tell you who awakened it?' Augurk asked, barely able to contain his excitement. It was as if a shaft of light had suddenly entered the gloomy dungeon of his life.

'Yes, why, yes, he did. I am quite sure he did,' agreed Onnish enthusiastically.

'And who was it?' asked Augurk, unable to wait any longer for the old councillor to reveal the information on his own.

'Well, he did tell me at the time but I have forgotten now,' Onnish responded, not taking any offense at his rauz's impetuous actions. After all, the rauz was a young dharvh, and the young always are impetuous! He continued in his mumbling drawl, 'Though, I do seem to remember that it was some western human—a king, I think. But it was so long ago that I cannot be absolutely certain, of course!'

Augurk did not press the old dharvh for more. What he had told Augurk was very little, but it was significant. It was almost a miracle that the old councillor was even alive! That he actually remembered the tale was nothing short of destiny. Augurk had finally found a path again. A plan began to take shape. They were in the first tempora of Zulheen. He would wait till the vernurt was over before putting his plan into action.

Throughout that mondan, he continued to brood upon his new plan. The more he thought about it, the more appealing it became. Finally, two days before vernurt officially ended, he shared his strategy with his brother.

'I'm not too certain about this plan,' Angbruk said, frowning. 'Why must we involve the humans? Why can't we do this on our own?'

Augurk replied impatiently, 'First, the humans might have some information about the city that we do not since it was a western human king who awakened it the last time. Second, they would not be as afraid of the Lyudzbradh as we dharvhs are, never having had to live under its shadow. Third, I won't have to risk revolt by sending dharvh soldiers forcefully into the mountains. Fourth, the loss in lives and property would be the humans' alone, though we will have to pay them a hefty compensation for it. I mind that far less than I mind the deaths of my subjects. Fifth, this will make the humans sit up and take notice of the dharvhs.'

Angbruk was not entirely convinced by Augurk's reasoning. He suspected that his brother was clutching at a straw to save himself from drowning in the debacle caused by Nishtar's demand. All the reasons seemed like excuses to cover his desperation at not knowing how to resolve the situation. But he could see that his brother was correct about one thing—no dharvh soldier would agree to go on an expedition into the Lyudzbradh willingly, and forcing them could very well lead to revolt. On the other hand, doing nothing about the problem was also not an option. He had come to understand from his brother's terror of the sumagus how dire the consequences of disobeying Nishtar would be. In the end, despite his misgivings, he fell in with the rauz's plan.

Three days later, on the first day of somminar, late in the evening, four of Augurk's most trusted spies were summoned and were given a task the likes of which they had never performed before. They were to set out for the four human kingdoms of the west on a special mission. Before the sun rose the next morning, the four had bidden farewell to their homes and loved ones and had set off for their destinations, not knowing what the conclusion of their mission would be.

Rauberk sat in a corner of the inn, watching the clientele seated on the wooden benches or standing around, laughing and joking and milling about on the floor. These men were from all walks of life; the respectable and the disreputable sat at the same table and drank to their hearts' content in the house of intoxication. Rauberk, though, was far from being drunk even though he had consumed enough ale to knock any man senseless. To him, the ale of humans was too weak to cause him anything more than the slightest drowsiness. He missed the taverns of Drauzern. He had left Drauzern two mondans ago and had come to Lufurdista in search of news that connected the king of Balignor to the City of Stone. He had been living in the city for close to two temporas now, gathering information that might help his rauz. So far he had had no luck. He had been told what to do if such proved to be the case. He was to attempt another gambit. In order to decide whether the alternative plan was worth implementing, he needed information. Information that could not be obtained from common folks.

The difficulty of getting someone close to the king to spill their guts had stumped him. However, the night before, he had met a man who had bragged of being familiar with members of the administration. The man was a regular customer of the inn where Rauberk was staying. More precisely, he was a regular of the taproom of the inn where Rauberk was staying. In a highly inebriated state, he had informed the dharvh that he was in close contact with one of the keepers of records of the court. He had promised to introduce Rauberk to this personage the next day in lieu of what he had imagined to be lucrative rewards.

Rauberk waited in a corner of the bar of the Dancing Clowns at the appointed time. He was sceptical about the promise made by his previous evening's drinking companion, but it was his only lead. After a while, he spotted the drunkard entering the inn in the company of a bent old man. Perhaps, he had been telling the truth after all, thought Rauberk. Perhaps the thought of rewards or the chance of winning a few free drinks had convinced him to drag the official to the Dancing Clowns.

The old man was small and shrivelled. He peered around him nervously through round glasses. He had a shuffling gait and sunken cheeks. This official of the royal court held a comfortable position, which required little labour and afforded him a handsome lifestyle. He maintained records of all proceedings of the court and stored the records away in an underground chamber that was hardly ever visited by any of the higher officials. It was not a glamorous position or one that brought him into close communion with the king, but it suited him just fine.

He did not feel happy about the place where he found himself. He should not have agreed to accompany this rascally distant cousin of his wife, he mused. The man was no good and was almost always drunk. But when he had sauntered up to his house and invited him to a drink at a nice place, and his wife had eagerly encouraged him, he had had no choice but to give in. Now the official regretted the moment of weakness. He tried to think of an excuse to leave early as his disreputable companion shepherded him across the hall to a corner. A short man— no, a dharvh—sat there alone at a table with a large, frothing jug. The official's wife's distant cousin greeted the dharvh with familiarity. The dharvh welcomed the official upon hearing who he was and introduced himself as Rauberk, a travelling dharvh in search of customers needing strong armours. At first, the keeper-of-the-books was sceptical of the dharvh's character. Rauberk's generosity in plying him with mug after mug of delicious ale washed away all his suspicions.

By the time the drunken official had managed to weave his way out of the inn, supported by his even more drunken relative, Rauberk knew that his evening had been well-spent. Under the influence of alcohol, the old man had told him all that he needed to know. He paid the innkeeper for the ale and hurried to his room, where he scribbled a note and sealed it up. He then stealthily made his way to a house located at the corner of the lane. He knocked thrice and waited. A small panel was opened and immediately closed again. A few moments later, the door opened and Rauberk entered. A crooked looking man stood inside.

'What do you want?' he demanded of Rauberk.

'I have a message to be sent,' answered Rauberk, holding out the note he had hastily composed.

'Where to?' croaked the man suspiciously.

'Drauzern,' answered Rauberk. The man still did not take the note from him.

'Whom to?' was the next question.

'Augurk, rauz of Ghrangghirm,' Rauberk answered. 'Resident at the palace in Drauzern,' he added before the man could ask. He was still standing with the note in his outstretched hand.

The man did not take the note even then. He glared suspiciously at the dharvh for a few momons while Rauberk waited patiently. Then the man slowly stretched out his palm. Rauberk dropped a few gold coins into it.

The man clasped the coins to his chest with a hungry intensity, snatched the note from Rauberk and hobbled away, rasping, 'The note will be sent. See yourself out!'

Chapter 25

HALIFERN COMES OF AGE

(4 Beybasel 5008 A.E. to 25 Beybasel 5008 A.E.)

In the south of Elthrusia lived the fraels. They were a solitary race and as different from their neighbours—the humans and the dharvhs—as chalk from cheese. Fraelish life was almost entirely built around the forests and groves that they inhabited. Their lands were dotted with groves and woods that housed between a hundred and a few thousand inhabitants. Only a few forests were large enough to provide sustenance for larger numbers. These large settlements, known as Cities, were the heart of their society and culture. Short, though not as short as dharvhs, and lithe with sharp, narrow features and a brown complexion, fraels lived in and with nature. They were nimble climbers and agile jumpers. They lived in tree houses, ate fruits, herbs, roots, wild vegetables and game, and tried to ensure that no plant, animal, bird or insect died in vain. They were excellent archers and fencers but never considered either of those activities as professions. It was part of who they were just as much as giving back to nature by planting trees and breeding game. They had small families and spent their entire lives in the same colony, hardly ever venturing far outside. Fraels who lived near the borders of their countries sometimes traded with the humans or the dharvhs; as a rule, however, fraels disliked interaction with other races.

The two countries of the fraels—Harwillen and Wyrchhelim—were ruled by Councils. In both countries, adult male members of the Leading Families comprised the Council. Each City had between one and six Leading Families—depending on the size of its population and the number of smaller settlements that fell under its control—whose males could join the Council subject to requirements of age and approval, the latter often no more than a formality once the frael reached the accepted age. The Council was headed by the Committee, which consisted of the five seniormost Elders. Though all fraels above the age of a hundred[5] were often called elders in common parlance, the title of Elders of the Council was used only for the heads of the Leading Families, irrespective of age. The members of the Leading Families were called Princes and Princesses though there was no monarchy among the fraels. The Councils made all the decisions pertinent to the lives of citizens using discussion and balloting as ways of settling issues.

---

5   Fraels age half as fast as humans. For more details about the correlations in age between the different races, see Appendix 4 of Tornain Book One: The Prophecy of Kawiti

On the fourth of Beybasel in the annus 5008 A.E., Prince Halifern of the fraels of Harwillen completed forty anni and came of age. Coming of age was an important landmark in the life of a frael. Before coming of age, fraels lived with their parents and were bound in obedience to them. When they came of age, they were expected to begin their independent lives. They would adopt professions, live on their own and choose their life partners. There were hardly any professions to choose from—fraels' primary source of sustenance was the bounty of nature—and almost all of them chose to become hunters or gatherers. Nonetheless, some did venture into other occupations. Farmers, cobblers, weavers, dancers, bards, acrobats and fishers were common enough; more uncommon were traders, miners, potters, teachers and herders.

Halifern belonged to one of the Leading Families of Numosyn, the most prominent of the Cities of Harwillen. It was the seat of the Council of Harwillen and home to three Leading Families. With a population of over two hundred thousand, it was also the second-most heavily populated settlement of Harwillen. And although Harwillen had no capital city, Numosyn was often referred to as its capital by outsiders. It was, by fraelish standards, the poshest and most sophisticated City in the country. The three Leading Families of Numosyn were headed by Ellahas, Rovinon and Rohyllar. Rohyllar, who was a member of the Committee of the Council of Harwillen, was also Halifern's father. Neither father nor son was excited at the prospect of Halifern coming of age, albeit for very different reasons.

Rohyllar was worried that his wayward son would now be able to pursue his strange preference in life for books and would bring shame to the family name with his unorthodox and heretical opinions. Once Halifern was officially accepted into the community as an adult, he would no longer be under his father's command. This thought greatly bothered Rohyllar. These same reasons were a source of joy to the young fraelish prince. His anxiety about coming of age lay elsewhere.

The lengthy ceremony that culminated in the acceptance of a frael as a mature citizen of the country began at the end of the mondan in which he or she was born. The birthdays of all who had turned forty that mondan were celebrated on the last day of the mondan by their settlement in a public ceremony. The ceremony was followed over the next annus by several traditions associated with the gaining of independence by a young frael, including a number of tests. If a frael successfully completed all the rituals, he or she was declared an acceptable member of society. Since these tests were ceremonial rather than functional, most young fraels took them as a last opportunity to live a carefree life before taking on the responsibility of their own lives. And that was precisely what was bothering Halifern.

Halifern did not like ceremonies of any sort, particularly those where he had to take centre stage. He liked books rather than hunting and could spend horas poring over thick volumes instead of enjoying the outdoors with his friends. It wasn't that he wasn't adept at typically fraelish activities like hunting and merrymaking; he simply preferred to spend his time otherwise, much to his father's chagrin. Halifern was a frael with average looks, average build and average height, with dark brown hair and eyes and a complexion the colour of almonds. Nothing about his physical appearance stood out. What made him unique were his qualities—he had unusual intelligence, tremendous curiosity, terrific agility and superb skill at weaponry. He was also modest and hated showing off, a quality that most fraels found inscrutable. All of his friends had, at one time or another, mistaken his modesty for weakness and had challenged him to a fight, only to find themselves wishing that they hadn't. Halifern was actually looking forward to his independence though definitely unhappy about the rituals of acquiring it. He was particularly apprehensive about the first step, which was to take place along with the mondan-end celebrations.

So, on the twenty-fifth of Beybasel, Halifern found himself surrounded by over a hundred compatriots, both male and female, who had attained the age of forty within the last mondan. Although he belonged to one of the Leading Families, he was by no means the most popular or well-known of the young fraels gathered in the large clearing where all public ceremonies and functions were conducted, which suited him fine. He knew quite a few of the others. his childhood friends Loyohen, Erofone and Siltare; his cousins Wornychh and Uposnesee, the latter resplendent in a shimmering dress that made her look very grown up, flirting with the young fraels; his neighbours Senteyon, Fwelhyn and twin sisters Fruschya and Wyzisia; and Weryntza, the youngest sister of his secret friends Waroned and Woroned.

They were there too, though as part of the crowd of onlookers and well-wishers. The twins were better than average looking with sharp features, cheerful smiles and a graceful bearing. However, they were unpopular among their compatriots because they were tall—too tall for fraels, many said. They pretended not to know Halifern when their paths crossed. Being friends with them would have earned him a share of the hostility that they attracted, and they would not let their only friend suffer for their sake. Hence, the secret nature of their friendship. However, when they were allowed to wish their near and dear ones good luck for the contest, they winked at Halifern from a distance and signalled their best wishes to him. Halifern hoped wholeheartedly that their wishes would hold good since the first step towards officially being recognised as part of fraelish society was a singing and dancing contest, something that Halifern dreaded with all his heart!

Fortunately for Halifern, the candidates weren't expected to sing more than a few lines, or it would have taken days for the ceremony to be completed. Halifern had been practising his lines for a while. Unfortunately, just as he opened his mouth to sing in front of the huge gathering of parents, relatives, friends and well-wishers of the hundred odd fraels and fraelinas coming of age, the lyrics fled from his head, and the tune began to play tricks on his voice. He managed to finish his piece without breaking down like Fruschya, but he was well aware that had the judging been on genuine merit, he would have found himself out of the running for citizenship. Both Uposnesee and Senteyon were among the score odd singers who were truly talented and enthralled the audience.

Following this came the more anticipated of the evening's events—the dance. Halifern, by dint of being nimble and agile, was a far better dancer than he was a singer. As all the fraels began to rush around to try and grab partners, he stood in a corner of the large, open-air enclosure, trying—and failing miserably—to gather the courage to ask one of the beautifully attired, confident and chattering fraelinas to dance with him. Suddenly, to his utter surprise, he found a fraelina standing in front of him. Weryntza was looking at him with a mischievous but sympathetic smile on her face. She was not pretty, though her friendliness often compelled people to overlook her homely features. She had tousled brown hair and brown eyes like all her siblings; though, dressed in elegant clothing, she barely resembled her brothers. 'Would you like to dance with me?' she asked Halifern.

Before Halifern could gratefully accept, he was approached by another fraelina—one vastly different from Weryntza. Fwelhyn was lithe and lovely, feminine and elegant, mesmerising and charismatic. She was deservedly considered a great beauty, but that evening, she looked positively stunning. Fraels between the ages of twenty and a hundred and twenty stopped in the middle of sentences and turned to gape at her when she passed by. Halifern knew her, being her neighbour, but had never spoken to her before. Like all the fraelish youth of his acquaintance, he had had a crush on her at one time. Now, he stood stunned as she stepped very close to him, almost pushing Weryntza aside, her fragrance and her presence almost overwhelming him. He knew without looking that all eyes were on them.

'Will you dance with me?' Fwelhyn asked Halifern in a soft, lilting voice that could still a beating heart.

Halifern was sorely tempted to accept, despite knowing that he was no match for her graceful and talented dancing. He looked into her large, lovely black eyes and immediately had the sensation of falling into a pool of icy water. There was no warmth or friendliness in them. He took a step back involuntarily. Aware of being watched, he thanked her politely and refused, explaining that Weryntza had asked first, so he would accept *her* offer. Fwelhyn smiled and withdrew, though there was nothing gracious in that smile. A cold shiver ran down Halifern's spine, dampening his spirits further.

Shortly thereafter, the dancing began. Weryntza was not a bad dancer and was definitely better than Halifern, but she kept her exuberance in restraint.

'I'm sorry that I'm not a better dancer,' Halifern apologised. 'I can see that you are not having any fun.'

'It's all right. I'm basking in the honour of being the one that you chose over Fwelhyn. I would have enjoyed myself if you had been ten times worse as a dancer,' laughed Weryntza. Halifern laughed with her, glad that she shared her brothers' sense of humour. 'By the way, for the life of me, I cannot imagine why you refused her,' she continued. 'You could have knocked me down with a feather when you told her, all polite and formal, that you would rather dance with me than with her because I had asked first. Why did you do that?'

'Because you did ask first!'

'But you had not yet replied to me when she asked, so you need not have refused her. So, really, why did you opt to dance with me?'

'I could ask you the same thing,' Halifern tried to dodge.

'That one's simple. I felt sorry for you. You were standing all forlorn and hoping that you could get one of the pretty fraelinas to dance with you but hopelessly devoid of courage to ask any of them.'

'Ouch!' said Halifern, pretending to be hurt, 'I thought it was my charm and magnetism that drew you to me as a dancing partner.'

'Well, that too, if you insist,' teased Weryntza as they leapt and stomped to some lively tunes. 'And the fact that my brothers would have cuffed me if I hadn't come to your rescue. They just adore you!'

'And I happen to reciprocate the feeling though I find it hard to believe that they bully *you*.'

'They try. I'm not saying that they succeed!'

This time, Halifern laughed with genuine merriment, twirling his partner with such vigour that she almost flew into a couple dancing nearby. They apologised and moved a little aside, finding themselves next to Fwelhyn and a muscular frael that Halifern did not know.

'You still haven't told me why you chose me over her,' Weryntza reminded Halifern, nodding her head towards Fwelhyn.

'Because you are nice and she isn't,' Halifern replied simply. She nodded, understanding what he meant.

'Not that I'm not glad that you chose me,' she said, 'but Fwelhyn isn't going to forget this insult.'

'I'm not terribly bothered about that at the moment,' answered Halifern. 'What worries me more is why she would even want to dance with me when she could have her pick of the lot? Any frael would feel blessed to get the chance to spend two full horas in such close proximity with her.'

'Don't shortchange yourself,' Weryntza replied loyally. 'You aren't so bad looking. Plus, you have other merits, I'm sure, though I have no idea what they might be.'

'Then how can you be sure that I have any merits at all?'

'My brothers praise you a lot, so I guess there must be something to you, though I'm not too sure that Fwelhyn is aware of those either.'

'Which is why I can't imagine why she would be interested in me.'

'Are you really that dumb?' demanded Weryntza.

'Ouch!' said Halifern for the second time that evening.

'Well, I don't much care if the truth hurts you, *Prince* Halifern. There's more than one fraelina here tonight who would be happy to receive your favours, if you haven't noticed,' Weryntza commented tartly. Then she added to herself in an audible undertone, 'I can't believe how dumb some so-called smart fraels can be!'

Halifern was too stunned by her revelation to even say 'ouch' this time. He could not come to terms with the fact that others' attitude towards him could have changed simply because he was now of age and would soon be a member of the Council. He thanked Weryntza for pointing this out as the dance came to an end and another began. Halifern remained rather distracted though he valiantly tried to do justice to every dance that he had to perform with Weryntza, more for her sake than for his own. When the dancing was over, a formal announcement was made to the effect that all those taking part in the coming of age ritual had successfully completed the first stage and, from the next day, had to begin the second stage, which consisted of building a tree house and moving into it.

Halifern had regained his good humour by then. He thanked Weryntza and kissed her lightly on the cheek. 'My hero!' he declared with exaggerated melodrama. She laughed good-naturedly and winked. Her brothers then collected her, again pretending not to know Halifern. The crowd parted as the twins passed through them, flanking their sister. The other fraels glared at them with open contempt and despisal as they walked away, literally head and shoulders above the rest.

Chapter 26

FLIGHT AT NIGHT

Misa was haggling over the price of coal at the market in Colbenos when a fight broke out nearby. Colbenos was the nearest town to Bolsana, and it hosted a market every Maghem evening. Sellers from villages all around came to trade their wares. Every other tempora, one of the villagers from Bolsana travelled to Colbenos to procure commodities that their own village or other nearby villages did not produce. This tempora, it had been Misa's turn. She had sold the surplus wool from Bolsana early in the evening and was now trying to purchase the items on her list at the lowest possible prices. Busy with her bargaining, at first she paid no attention to the two men fighting nearby. Quarrels and fights were not uncommon at this market; conflicts arose over prices, quality or competition. The press of the vast crowd and the shouts of sellers and buyers often made the situation worse. Fights were quickly broken up by marshals hired by the town committee.

This fight, however, proved to be about something else. When the marshals pulled the two combatants aside and fined them, Misa noticed that one of the two men was the landlord of the inn where she had taken a room for the day. He was an easygoing, rotund man, and his involvement in the fight aroused Misa's curiosity. She did not know the other man. As the landlord was walking away, she accosted him and asked if he was all right.

'I am not badly hurt. Thank you for asking, Madam Misa,' the landlord replied politely.

'What happened? Why did that man attack you?' she further asked.

The landlord looked guilty for a moment before he replied sheepishly, 'Actually, I hit him first.'

Misa's startled expression brought on a slight scowl and a defensive attitude. 'He accused me of being a liar!' he exclaimed. 'Me! Have you ever known me to lie?'

Misa did not know the man well enough to answer with certainty, but she took the prudent course of affirming the man's truthfulness.

'But why would he call you a liar?' she enquired, still curious.

'I told him what I saw last night when I was suddenly woken up in the middle of the night, but he wouldn't believe me. Then he called me a liar,' the landlord explained.

'And what exactly *did* you see that he found so hard to believe?' queried Misa.

'I saw some suspicious cloaked figures walking quietly through the streets. They were taller than any people and had a sinister air about them. They knocked on my inn's door, but I did not let them in. Then they moved on down the street. I saw them through the window.'

Misa felt a cold chill running down her spine. Had her enemies found her again? The landlord had said that the sinister strangers had been taller than humans. What else could they be if not eighes?

'Did you see any of their faces?' she asked him again.

'No, it was too dark, and they were hooded. Actually, to be honest, I did not see them too clearly at all. I did not have a lantern, and I only saw their shadows. That does not make them any less real, madam, does it?'

'No, of course not!' Misa agreed with him to assuage the landlord's hurt pride. So, he had seen only shadows. A trick of the light could have made the figures' shadows appear taller. They might not have been eighes at all. But could she afford to risk everything on that assumption?

'Do you have any idea which direction they were coming from?' she asked the landlord.

'I cannot be certain,' he answered, a little surprised at her interest in the subject. 'But the road they were on goes from the north of the town to the south, towards Vittor. I guess they must have come from the north.'

Misa thanked him for the information, repeated her concern about his health and bid him farewell. Her mind was awhirl. The mysterious figures had come from the north, the landlord had thought. She considered him a reasonable man, not given to flights of fancy. What he had said could not be discounted. What if Holexar's spies had decided to search among the human kingdoms now? True, they had moved further south, away from Bolsana, but how long would it be before they would find out where she was hiding, especially if they had a tracking crystal like the one that they had used originally while pursuing her? She hurried through the rest of the items on her list, not bothering to bargain much. She felt guilty spending more of the villagers' money than she needed to, but she was in a tearing hurry to return and could not afford to bargain at her leisure. The other option was to leave some of the items off the list, but she was unwilling to hurt the villagers to that extent. Every item on that list was essential. The villagers would face difficulties without them. She hastily completed her purchasing and returned to the inn where Marsil and her cart were stabled. She made up an excuse to leave that night instead of the next morning as originally planned, much to the landlord's surprise. Even then, it was close to midnight when Misa was finally able to leave Colbenos, a familiar haunting feeling of fear gnawing at her stomach.

It was dawn. Mizu stood upon a rock at the edge of a sandy beach. Behind him, and to his right and his left, the white, pristine sand stretched endlessly, disappearing into the penumbral milieu. In front of him, the infinite expanse of the deep blue sea embraced the horizon. Where the sea met the shore, the land was dotted unevenly with rocks rising up from the seabed. Tall waves crashed upon the rocks. A strong wind blew from the sea towards land, bearing with it a familiar salty tang. Mizu looked towards the slightly ruddy spot in the distance. Upon the dark breast of the sea, it glowed like an ember. The sun was coming to claim its own. As the glow in the east grew, the breakers became more and more violent until Mizu was in danger of being swept away. His feet were beginning to slip upon the slick, seaweed-covered rock. Yet he longed to remain there. He felt peaceful. He knew that nowhere else could he be so completely alone yet so completely tranquil. Suddenly, a loud 'bang' sounded somewhere.

Mizu opened his tired, sleepy eyes. For a momon, he could not understand what he was doing in a small, dark room, or who was moving about noisily. Where had that beautiful beach disappeared? Slowly, recollection came to him. He was on his bed in his house. He had been dreaming of the beach. He felt that he had had the same dream before, but he could not be sure. He focussed on the present. The two women moving about the room agitatedly were Molinee and his mother. His mother! Mizu leapt off the bed and ran to her. He wrapped his arms around her knees, burying his face in the folds of her clothes. How he had missed her for the past few days!

In Misa's absence, Molinee had looked after Mizu. Molinee was a middle-aged woman with a plump face and plain features. She was always good to him and even pampered him. But he had pined for his mother almost continuously. Now she was back—earlier than expected—and everything was all right again in his world. He looked up at her; she was the centre and the circumference of his young universe. If she smiled, he felt that the world was beautiful. If she frowned at him, his sky darkened with thunderclouds.

Misa bent down and embraced him tightly. The blissful Mizu did not see the pain that crossed her face. The next moment, however, she stood up straight and said, 'Mizu, we are going to leave tonight as soon as we can. I need you to help me pack everything.'

Mizu nodded determinedly even though he felt puzzled by the sudden decision to leave. He wondered whether they were going on a vacation. He wanted to ask Misa, but her expression was too grim to encourage queries. Mizu busied himself in packing the things that he could. He wasn't yet eight anni old, and he tottered slightly as he tried to carry large piles of objects to his mother. Molinee helped too, sniffling all the while. Intermittently, she would stop packing and sob heartily. Or she would hug Mizu and shower him with kisses. Mizu wondered if something bad had happened to her. He looked at his mother. She was not crying. She looked tense and angry, but she was reining in her emotions. Mizu admired her immensely. She could be very loving and warm, but she could also be hard and cold as steel. She packed silently, not wasting time on tears or words. Mizu wanted to be like her when he grew up. Their meagre belongings were soon packed.

Their mare, Marsil, was standing outside, their cart hitched to her. The three of them—Misa, Molinee and Mizu—piled everything into the back of the cart. Marsil stood patiently as the cart was loaded. Misa picked Mizu up and seated him among the belongings. Then she turned to Molinee, who was crying volubly by now.

'Molinee, I cannot thank you enough for all that you and the other villagers have done for me. But I must go. Men may come searching for me. I cannot stay here any longer.'

'Misa, you don't have to go!' begged Molinee, taking Misa's hands in her own. 'Let them come. We will hide you. You have been our saviour! The things you have done for us! We could never repay your debt. We will help you in your hora of need. We cannot abandon you like this.'

Misa smiled gently. 'You are not abandoning me, Molinee. No one is! This is what I must do. If you wish to help me, then inform everyone tomorrow that I have left. If anyone ever asks about me, say that you know nothing. Tell them the truth: that I lived here but have left. Those who are looking for me are dangerous and ruthless. If I stay here, they *will* find me, even if they have to kill every single villager to do so. But on the open road, they will never catch me. They are also adept at sensing the truth. You cannot lie to them. They can torture even children to get the information that they want. The only way I will be safe and everyone here will be safe is if no one knows anything. If you know nothing, and tell them the truth about me no matter what they ask, they will leave you alone. Any knowledge of my whereabouts can be a source of danger, and I have already endangered all of you by living here this long. Please do not ask me to remain. I must go!'

'Won't you at least tell Leormane?' Molinee asked hesitantly.

'No, he will try to convince me to stay back. He might succeed. I cannot allow that. Tell him that I am sorry. Tell him that I heard of sinister strangers from the north. He will understand. Tell him that I am in his debt eternally and that he deserved better. Above all, tell him that I shall hold him to his promise.'

There was a strange sense of urgency and desperation in Misa's voice that caused the weeping Molinee to reconsider her position. She protested no more. She hugged the younger woman and ambled off towards her own house, turning again and again to wave. When she was gone, Misa walked up to the house. It stood in a little glade just outside the village, partly hidden from view by thick shrubs and trees that grew around it. They had built it with their own hands. Misa appeared to just stand there, doing nothing. Mizu was beginning to feel sleepy again. He did not notice anything unusual, but suddenly the house was ablaze. Hungry blue flames rose from the earth and swallowed up the little thatched hut within minuras. Before his very eyes, the house was razed into a mound of ashes. His mother stood nearby, making not the slightest effort to save it. And then, when nothing stood where their house had been, with a crackling sound, bushes sprang up out of the ground, creepers crawled over the mound and trees shot up in the clearing until there was no sign that anyone had ever lived there. Mizu sat with his mouth open, amazed beyond words. He wondered whether he was dreaming again.

They had reached the border of the village when someone stepped into their path.

'Leom!' Mizu yelled. He loved the chief and was always happy to see him, no matter what the time or the circumstances.

Leormane ruffled his hair and told him to run down to his house and fetch a box lying on a table there. Before Misa could stop him, Mizu leapt out of the cart and sped off. Misa turned to Leormane to protest, but he stalled her.

'I knew I would find you here when I saw you return a hora ago and heard Molinee weeping like she had lost someone precious to her soon after,' he said.

'Were you keeping a watch on my house?' Misa asked uncomfortably.

'Yes,' Leormane replied. 'I like to keep an eye on Mizu when you are away from the village. Why are you leaving?'

'I heard of tall, mysterious figures passing through Colbenos at night, passing via the road from the north. I think they were spies of Holexar.' She told him what the landlord had said to her.

'He might have been mistaken,' Leormane said. 'They might have been people; after all, he only saw their shadows. That too, at night and without a lantern.'

'Maybe,' Misa agreed. 'And maybe not. If there is the slightest chance that they were Holexar's spies, I have to go. That seleighe is too cunning. I think he has guessed how I escaped his clutches and has sent spies to find out if I have taken shelter with humans. They might start at Vittor since it is the capital of the nearest human kingdom bordering the eighe lands, but they will not stop there. They will scour every inch of the land until they find me. They might even have a tracking crystal like the one they had used in their initial pursuit. If they do, they are bound to locate me sooner or later. If I am here when they catch up with me, they will raze Bolsana to the ground to capture me.'

'Your theory sounds rather far-fetched to me,' commented Leormane sceptically. 'Are you sure that you are not being unnecessarily paranoid?'

Misa hesitated then and considered what Leormane had said. She did have very little and very vague information to go on. Finally, she replied, 'No, I'm not sure. I might be correct about the spies. Or I might be acting unreasonably. I cannot know for sure. But I cannot afford to take a risk either. If I am correct, then my presence here will doom not just Mizu and me but everyone in Bolsana. On the road, I can escape anyone who comes after me. If I am wrong, not much harm is done. I don't really have any other choice! You do see that, don't you?'

Leormane nodded sadly. He could not deny the truth in Misa's words. He would not risk the lives of the villagers either. He said, 'So you must leave. But why were you leaving without seeing me? Do I mean nothing at all to you?'

'Oh, Leormane!' Misa cried. 'You are my dearest and closest friend. I was leaving without seeing you because I was afraid that you would convince me to stay.'

Leormane nodded, surprised by her answer.

'You know that I would die fighting to protect you and Mizu if your enemies did find you here, don't you?' he asked. 'But you are right. It would be futile. Everyone in Bolsana would die in the end. We do not have the manpower to withstand the might of Holexar. Even if we manage to fight off his soldiers once or twice, they will never stop attacking until we are finished.'

'That is what I am afraid of,' Misa acknowledged. 'I don't want anyone to die needlessly for me. It is too great a burden to bear.'

'And I won't ask you to bear it,' Leormane said kindly. 'I know that you must go, and I won't stop you. But I will go with you if you ask me to.'

'I know you will. Tempting as that is, I cannot in all conscience ask you to abandon Bolsana for my sake. Your place is here. They will wither and die if we both leave. You must carry on the task that we began together. And remember your promise!'

'I will,' Leormane replied, answering both her exhortations.

At that moment, Mizu returned, carrying a small, colourful box with him.

'Is this the box you wanted?' he asked Leormane.

'Yes, it is. It's for you, my boy. It was supposed to be your birthday present, but take it now. Open it on your birthday. I hope you like it.'

'Thank you,' said Mizu in a small voice. He was beginning to realise that they were not going on a vacation; they were leaving for good. Tears came to his eyes, and he hugged Leormane's gift to his chest. The chief of Bolsana lifted him up and hugged him tightly, the small boy returning the embrace with equal warmth.

'Be a good boy and take care of your mother,' Leormane said to him, putting him back inside the cart. Mizu nodded, tears beginning to roll down his cheeks.

'We must leave now,' Misa said miserably.

Leormane nodded silently and stood aside. Misa led the cart away, guiding the mare down the path that led to the foothills of the Aravel Mountains. Leormane stood watching after them until they vanished in the darkness of the night, wondering whether he would ever see them again, whether Misa had ever considered spending her life with him, whether he would ever have to fulfil the terrible promise that he had made to her.

Mizu was dreaming of a magnificent beach again. He was certain that it was the same one he had dreamt of many times before. This time, however, he was not alone. The seashore behind him was crowded. Statuesque and elegant men, the likes of whom Mizu had never seen, stood in the gloom quietly, their faces lowered and hooded. They were dressed as soldiers in a uniform that glowed eerily red in the twilight. He wondered who they were and why they were there. They seemed to be waiting for something or someone. He walked up to the soldier nearest him and raised his eyes to the man's face. Surprisingly, he could not discern the man's features. Either it was too dark, or the man's countenance was hazy. Mizu touched his hand. The soldier did not react. Mizu walked up to several of the others and tried to engage with them. The results were no different. None of them seemed to notice his presence. They stood with stony stances and featureless faces, shrouded in an atmosphere fraught with an intangible but intense sense of grief, failure and despair.

'Mizu! Wake up!' a voice called to him suddenly.

He opened his eyes to find Misa standing at his side, bow on her back and arrows in her hands. She was going in search of game again. Instructing Mizu to stay alert, and to blow his horn if he needed her, she helped him up onto the lowermost branch of the tree to which Marsil was tied. Once she left, he began to entertain himself by discerning the various sounds of the forest so he wouldn't fall asleep. Mizu liked the forest. He could hear Marsil chomping on the grass at the foot of the tree. The trees were soughing and rustling in the soft breeze. He could hear a multitude of birds chirping and warbling to welcome the day. His mother preferred to hunt at dawn because that was when the predators returned to their lairs, but the herbivores awoke and began to roam the forest in search of fodder.

They had been on the road for close to three mondans since leaving Bolsana. Mizu did not understand why they had left, but he did not ask his mother. He had asked her once. The question had upset her, so he did not ask again. He tried to obey her and to stay out of her way when she looked pensive or anxious. Although he did not know where exactly they were, he could sense that they were moving towards the west. How he knew it was a mystery to him, but he was sure. He was also sure that if they kept going west, they would ultimately come to the ocean. The thought of seeing the ocean quickened his pulse. It also made him think about his spooky dream. Despite trying hard to remember it, he could recall it only vaguely. He wanted to tell his mother about it, about having similar dreams repeatedly, but he just could not bring himself to do it.

Mizu yawned loudly. His sleepiness was catching up with him. Shaking his head like he had seen Marsil do, he sat up straighter, wondering how else he could stay awake. He would have liked to play his flute; he really enjoyed it when the birds kept him company as he played his favourite tunes. But his mother had told him not to make any noise when she was hunting, so he had to desist from his newfound pastime. He thought about opening the box that Leormane had given him, but it made him miss the chief of Bolsana village too much. He still could not believe that they had left the village permanently. Even though Misa kept telling him that they would return there someday, he felt in his heart that he would never see the place again.

Suddenly, he heard neighing. He looked towards Marsil, but *she* was not neighing. She was busy feeding on the soft grass under the tree. Mizu wondered whether he had imagined the sound. Then he heard it again. This time, even Marsil heard it. She stopped chomping and stood still, flicking her ears this way and that. As he tried to locate the source of the neighing, Mizu heard another sound. It was the softest of sounds, meant to deceive even the sharpest-eared animal in the forest. It had not eluded Mizu, though. It was the tread of a predator on the dewy earth. And it was coming from the same direction as the neighing.

Marsil whinnied uneasily below him, trying to move away from the oncoming predator. Mizu looked around frantically to spy the predator and the prey. The sun had not risen completely yet. In the semi-darkness, things were still hazy. Almost like in his dream, Mizu thought. Then he saw it! A small white colt trapped in brambles at the corner of a turn in the narrow dirt track that their cart had been following. Only a few feet behind it, crouching in the undergrowth, was a wildcat. Mizu raised his horn to his lips but stopped short of blowing it. There was no need to worry his mother. She would come running, thinking that he was in danger. Moreover, there was no time to be lost. The poor colt would be dead by the time Misa reached them. Mizu made a decision.

He slid off the tree. Hastening to their cart, which was standing nearby, he grabbed his catapult. Then, taking careful aim, he let fly a shot. The young boy's aim was true. The stone struck the wildcat on the nose. With a yelp, the animal sprang backwards and looked around warily, trying to detect where the attack had come from. It could not see Mizu hidden behind the wheel of the cart or Marsil behind a tree. There was no one else around. So, it lifted its nose to sniff out this unexpected opponent, but both Mizu and the mare were downwind from it. Failing to sense any enemies, the wildcat began to stalk the colt again. Before it could advance, another of the missiles from the unseen enemy hit it below the ear. It leapt to one side, yelping in pain, but was loath to discard a prey as easy as the trapped colt. It looked and sniffed all round again and, once more failing to detect anyone besides the colt, crouched a third time, getting ready to pounce. The colt was now neighing loudly and trying desperately to free itself. Mizu took careful aim and let go a larger stone. It hit the crouching beast on the nose again. This time, it did not wait to take a chance with its prey. It yowled loudly and hared off.

Mizu waited a while to make sure that it was indeed gone and that there were no other predators around. When he was certain, he crawled out of his hiding place and approached the trapped colt. The colt stood patiently, as if it knew that Mizu was a friend. Cooing to it, as he had seen his mother do to Marsil when the mare got upset, Mizu bent down and freed the colt from the brambles. It did not look badly hurt, but there were quite a few scratches on its legs. It made no attempt to escape as the boy gently pulled the brambles apart to free it. Even when it was free, it did not bolt. Rather, it stood snuggling against Mizu, almost like a pet dog. The colt stuck its small snout in Mizu's hand and made snorting noises, much to the boy's delight, and followed him back when he returned to the tree where Marsil waited.

When Misa returned with a dead stag that would suffice for meat for days, she found a strange scene awaiting her. A white colt stood nestling against Marsil, who was licking its mane maternally. Mizu stood near, rubbing the colt's nose and mumbling things into its ear. She sighed and smiled. Then she frowned. The colt bothered her. It did not look wild. Where were its owners? Even more importantly, *who* were its owners? How had the colt reached their camp? Mizu saw her approaching with the kill. He rushed to tell her about his rescue of the colt. Misa listened as she skinned the stag and roasted the venison over an open fire. After they had eaten, she wrapped the rest of the meat in broad leaves and stored it at the back of the cart. Then she turned her attention to the colt. It whinnied joyfully as she bent down and stroked its head. She opened its mouth and looked at its teeth. It was rather small for its age, she figured. Then she noticed the slightly crooked shape of the shoulders. It looked almost exactly like a normal colt. Almost, but not quite. Suspicion began to creep into her mind. She picked the colt up and found it to be surprisingly light. Her suspicion was confirmed. She turned to Mizu with a grave look on her face.

'Mizu, this is no ordinary colt. Can you see the slightly unusual shape of the shoulders?'

Mizu looked closely at the colt's back and nodded.

'He is also smaller than colts his age normally are. And very light. Do you know what that means, Mizu?' Misa asked. The boy looked carefully at his new friend. What could the features pointed out by his mother mean except that the colt was a little different from other colts its age? Maybe it was a little deformed though it looked perfectly normal to him. Mizu shook his head, puzzled. His mother sighed and said, 'Mizu, this is the colt of a rayainmora.'

'A rayainmora?' asked Mizu, bemused. 'What is a rayainmora?'

Misa explained, 'A rayainmora, which is also known as a pegasus, is a very rare animal. It is related to a horse, and it looks a lot like one, but it has wings.'

'I don't see any wings on this colt,' Mizu remarked, sounding even more confused.

'No, he does not have wings,' Misa agreed. 'But that is because he is still very young. When he grows up, he will sprout wings.'

'Will he be able to fly then?' Mizu asked in disbelief. Even in his wildest dreams, he had never imagined that winged horses existed, let alone belonged to him. He had already started thinking of the colt as his!

'Yes, rayainmora can fly,' Misa informed him.

'Really?'

Misa nodded. She sat down underneath the tree, stroking the head of the colt that was now nuzzling against her neck. The colt was quite a handsome one. She knew that Mizu wanted to keep it. But they could not keep a rayainmora. Not where they were headed. She tried to reason with herself. They could not take the colt along, in case its parents were searching for it. On the other hand, if they had abandoned it, or were dead, to leave the colt behind would surely kill it.

'What should we name him?' Mizu asked, breaking into her thoughts.

'I am not sure we can keep him, Mizu,' she said gently. 'What if his parents come to look for him?'

'But if we leave him behind, and they don't come, some wild animal will eat him!' pleaded Mizu. 'Today is my birthday, isn't it? Can't you think of him as my birthday gift?'

Misa knew that he was right. She made up her mind.

'All right,' she said, 'we will wait here for three days for his parents to turn up. If they turn up, he can go with them. If they do not, we will keep him.'

'Thank you!' cried Mizu and gave his mother a tight hug. Then he hugged the colt and told it that it was going to stay with them. The colt neighed and licked Mizu's nose. Misa laughed.

'In case we get to keep him,' Mizu asked, raising his face to hers hopefully, 'what should we name him?'

Misa looked at the pure white colt now again nestling against Marsil, who seemed quite happy to play mother to him.

'We shall name him Marsillon, after Marsil. Everyone will believe him to be her colt. No one will suspect the truth,' Misa said. To herself, she added, 'Until the day he sprouts wings!'

Chapter 27

A MYSTERIOUS BENEFACTOR

(2 Patarshem 5008 A.E. to 15 Reklan 5009 A.E.)

One morning, at the beginning of Patarshem in the annus 5008 A.E., Temeron woke up and discovered an unusual object next to his pillow—a brown paper packet. He had never seen it before. He looked around to spot the witch, but she was nowhere to be seen. Perhaps she was brewing something in the backyard. Temeron touched the packet gingerly. It rustled a little; the paper was crisp and smooth to touch. He crawled as quietly as he could towards the back of the shanty to peer into the backyard through a crack in the rear wall. His shackles restricted his movements, but he had discovered ways to get around the limitations. Even when he had to work all day at Rosa's beck and call, he still strived to find time to do things that *he* liked and to disobey Rosa without getting caught.

Of these tiny rebellions, the pride and joy of his heart was the concealed hole in the ground under one of the floorboards. He had painstakingly pried that floorboard up after sensing that the ground underneath it was hollow. It had taken him temporas to complete the task, working secretly and without any tools. But the effort and patience had paid him well in the end. The secret hole was where he stashed his precious treasures, the few things that he could truly claim as his own in the world. They would have been trash for anyone else, but for him, they were priceless.

Another act of defiance was keeping track of the witch's activities without being seen to do so. Temeron had discovered a few holes and cracks in the shack's walls to spy on Rosa as she worked in the backyard or out front. He now saw through the crack in the rear wall that she was indeed brewing. That was good. She would not hassle him that day if he kept quiet. He had learnt well how to keep quiet and avoid drawing Rosa's attention. He returned to his corner.

He unwrapped the brown packet carefully. Inside it was a big, soft, yellow block of cake. He knew it was cake because he had been fed cake once before, though the pieces he had eaten had been partly burned, hard as rock and crumbly. This cake was fresh and moist. And it smelled delicious. His mouth watered. He had never had anything like this in his whole life. He stared at the delicacy, mesmerised by its look, feel and smell. It was like a block of sunshine made tangible—warm and sweet and soft and golden and smelling of all things wonderful. He could not bring himself either to eat it or to put it back into the packet. Where had it come from?

Who had left it by his bed? The thought made him want to laugh. Who would have left it? There was no one in the world who cared enough for him to leave him food. It must be a dream, he decided. He pinched himself to check. It hurt. No, he was not dreaming!

He frowned. The cake was beginning to worry him. Where *had* it come from? Had it fallen out of the witch's bag? No, that was not possible, he told himself. He doubted if anyone would have given *her* something as wonderful as this. He was certain that she had not bought it either since she never bought anything fresh. Then another thought occurred to him. Maybe the witch had left it there deliberately, knowing that he wouldn't be able to resist a bite. Why would she do that? Why would she feed him something fresh and nutritious? Maybe it was a trap! Maybe she had poisoned it. Maybe she wanted him to die. That he could very well believe. He almost threw the cake away then.

He stopped at the last moment. The idea that the witch was trying to kill him did not ring true. Why would she want to finish him off when she enjoyed seeing him suffer? Even if she did get tired of tormenting him, she would not kill him quietly with poison, he was sure. She would torture him to death, milking every momon of joy that it could provide her. Besides, if she did decide to poison him, she would still not waste money on good food. She would simply force the poison into his mouth, as she had forced rotten, stinking, raw blood once. No, the chance that the cake was poisoned by the witch was slim, he decided.

By the time he reached this conclusion, Temeron had begun to feel very hungry. Rosa had been starving him again. On a ravenous stomach, the mouth-watering aroma of the cake was too much for the seven-annus-old boy. Temeron threw caution to the winds and greedily fell upon the cake. It tasted as good as it looked and smelled! He had never eaten anything remotely like it in his entire life. He gobbled up as much of the delicacy as he could. When his stomach was close to bursting full, he stopped. More than half the cake still remained. He wrapped it carefully again in its brown covering and stashed it underground with his other belongings. Feeling more satisfied than he could ever remember feeling, he set about doing the chores that Rosa expected him to complete every morning, more cheerful than he had been in a long time. He even forgot to think of the ways in which he would have liked to punish the witch for what she did to him. His mind was full of the wonderful gift and its secret giver. No matter how long or how hard he thought, he could not figure out who had left the cake for him or why.

The cake lasted him for six whole days. After his initial splurge, he ate it only a tiny piece at a time. He wanted it to last as long as possible. Also, he could not eat it when Rosa was around. He was clever enough not to refuse the scraps Rosa fed him to keep her from getting suspicious. By the time he finished it, the cake was hard and crusty, but he still ate it with relish. He did not throw away the cover either. He smoothed it out and practised his letters on it. He was used to practicing on the floor and wiping the writing away to hide it from Rosa. This was much better. He could practice on the paper and then hide it. Rosa would not learn that he was practicing writing, and he would not lose any of his work either. He felt grateful to whomever had given him such a wonderful gift. He thought often about his mysterious benefactor and wondered if the cake had been given to him by accident. Whatever the case, it was the most wonderful thing that had happened to him in his miserable life. No, not *the* most wonderful. The second-most wonderful. The kereighe girl whose dreams reduced his pain and hopelessness was the most wonderful thing in his life. This gift came right after her in importance. Temeron was sure that the mysteriously delivered cake was a one-time miracle, but that did not reduce his gratitude towards the giver of the gift.

Within a few days, his belief that the gift from the mysterious benefactor was an isolated incident was proven wrong. Another morning, he woke up to find a similar packet next to his pillow. His heart thumping, he looked around to check on Rosa. The witch was inside the house that day but had fortuitously not seen the packet. He hid the packet under some rags near his bed and went about his daily chores, his mind fixated on the packet. Was it another cake? That would be wonderful! Did he really have a friend out in the world who cared enough to give him food? It was hard to believe. He began to fantasise that he really did have a friend. Perhaps it was his father or his mother? Perhaps they had been searching for him all these anni and had finally found him. Perhaps they wanted to rescue him but were afraid of the witch. Yes, that was it! His parents had been looking for him ever since he had been taken by the witch and had now, finally, managed to track him down. Because it was difficult for them to rescue him immediately, they were trying to help him by giving him food. Who else could it be if not his parents? Someday, soon, they would rescue him too.

The little boy convinced himself that this story was the truth. When Rosa left to sell her potions, powders, charms and hexes at the local market, he took out his concealed treasure and eagerly opened it. He was a little disappointed to see that this time the packet did not contain cake. However, there was good quality bread and, to his utter surprise, a big chunk of rich succulent meat cooked to perfection. He had only ever eaten half-spoilt, raw or dry meat before. He gobbled down the meat for fear that if he kept it long, it would spoil. The meat filled his stomach, so he wrapped up the bread and hid it away. He received another packet a few days later. This time, it contained some fruits.

One day, while he was practicing his writing, he had an idea. He tore off a piece of one of the packet covers that he had saved and wrote on it, 'I hav got wat yu left fer me. Thunk yu. Who are yu?'

That night, when he went to bed, Temeron left the note where the gifts were usually left by his mysterious friend. The next morning, the note was still there. He wasn't disappointed, though. After all, the gift-giver did not visit every night. Temeron continued to leave the note out for his benefactor at bedtime. One morning, the note had disappeared, but a packet had appeared in its place. Temeron joyously opened the package. Inside it was another cake. He left another note to thank his benefactor. The next morning, the new note was gone, but the old one had been returned with corrections. Temeron was thrilled. He continued to leave longer and longer notes every time he received food. Invariably, they were returned with corrections. This continued for temporas.

Then, one morning, Temeron was disappointed to find that a package had been left for him that did not contain food. It contained, instead, a top. He had seen boys in the street play with tops but had no idea how to spin it. He tried for horas that afternoon and finally managed to learn the technique. Now he had something to play with during his horas of idleness, not that he had too many of those. He began to spend those horas enjoying his new toy where he would have spent them torturing insects or thinking of ways to take revenge on the witch.

Towards the end of Reklan in 5009 A.E., Temeron received something completely unexpected. He had completed eight anni on the first of Kawitor that annus, but he did not know that. He was taller now, and stronger. He understood far better what was happening around him. When he opened the flat, hard, square package, he immediately knew that it was a book. It was only the second book that he had ever opened, but one glance was enough to tell him that it was very different from the one that he had stolen from Rosa long ago. That had been a book of spells. This one had lots of writing and many beautiful pictures. He could not wait to read it!

That afternoon, after Rosa went to the market, he took his new book out of its hiding place and began to read. The cover of the book said at the top in bold: 'The Monkey King and Other Stories'. A name was given at the bottom—Orobis Nemsha. Temeron had no idea why her name was mentioned. He flipped through the first few pages to discover what stories the book contained. The first one bore the title: 'The Marvellous Tale of the Monkey King'. Temeron felt excited. No one had ever told him a story. He began to read the marvellous tale of the monkey king with tremendous eagerness. He was unused to reading, and progress was slow for him. But that detracted neither from his enthusiasm nor from his enjoyment. The story told of a monkey who was raised in a king's palace. He was mocked and laughed at, but he was very intelligent and managed to escape. He was a fugitive for anni. During this period, he travelled from country to country and learnt much. He had a natural talent for quick thinking and solving problems, and this kept him out of harm's way as he travelled from place to place, having amazing adventures.

Temeron was so engrossed in reading the story that Rosa was back before he'd had a chance to hide the book. He barely managed to conceal it under his mattress. His expression made Rosa suspicious. She beat him and starved him, but Temeron said nothing about the marvellous world he had uncovered and which now sat under his filthy, bug-ridden, tattered mattress. He could not wait for her to leave again so that he could continue to read about the artful monkey! That night, he managed to conceal the book in its hidey hole before going to sleep. He had figured out that his benefactor usually left the packages at night while they slept or early in the morning before they awoke. He resolved to stay up that night to see who it was that left him such wonderful things. He would thank his friend personally. He would ask his benefactor to take him away. A person who helped him with food and gifts was bound to look after him better than the witch did. He tried hard to stay up all night, even pinching himself whenever he felt sleepy, but to no avail. He fell into a deep slumber close to midnight and awoke only the next morning.

He continued to read the story of the monkey king that afternoon. After wandering for many anni, the monkey realised that he was now grown up. No one in his country recognised him. He wanted to see his parents who, like him, had lived in the palace zoo. He had learnt to speak like humans. He disguised himself and returned to his hometown. This was as far as Temeron could read that day. He did not want to repeat the mistake that he had made the previous day. He hid the book before Rosa returned. He also wrote another lengthy note to thank his generous friend. That night, he again tried to stay awake but again failed. The note was gone the next morning. It was returned the morning after, as usual, with corrections.

And so Temeron's life continued. He still had to work very hard in the house. He still had to endure Rosa's torments and beatings. He still had to face the other kereighes' taunts and kicks. But he endured all of it with greater fortitude. He finished reading about how the clever monkey tricked the humans into making him a king and how he ruled long and wisely and freed all the animals kept in cages in the palace. He read about many other wonderful beings and adventures and wished he could go on such grand exploits. His mind began to grow and be filled with something more than hatred and anger, just as his body began to be nourished by good and nutritious food. Several times, he tried hard to catch his mysterious benefactor in the act of leaving the packages but never could. In the end, he decided that if his benefactor wanted to remain secret, he would respect his friend's wishes. That was the least that he could do for someone who had done so much for him.

During the time that Sumaho spent in Yennthem with his protégé, he recovered greatly in both mind and body. His spirit took longer to heal. His eyes still bore a haunted look, and his memory played tricks on him at times. Oram nursed him with great gentleness, patience and diligence. Sumaho was grateful to him for his care. He still could not remember what had happened to him or how he had ended up on the island where Oram had found him. Fortunately, he did remember much of what his life had been like prior to the incident. Most of his abilities began to return after a while. He started improving every day, growing stronger in body, mind and spirit. He was happy to spend the days with Oram, living an 'adventure' as he called the mundane life of a mortal. Oram was happy to host him. However, when Sumaho began to feel 'a little chilly' in the cosy cottage, Oram was thrilled. It was well known that any place besides the stuffy castle that was the headquarters of the sumagi was too cold and too damp for the Librarian. The complaint about the cottage's temperature was the greatest sign of Sumaho's recovery. Oram decided that it was time to return to Maghem. On the penultimate day of 5008 A.E., Sumaho returned to his home accompanied by Oram

To his utter amazement, Oram found the headquarters exactly as he had left it. It could mean only one thing—no one had been there in more than an annus. It was unbelievable! He and Sumaho had been in Yennthem. Nishtar was busy with his students. Vellila was in Vittor, flourishing under King Dorstoph's patronage. What had Beben and Alanor been doing that they had never visited the castle in all this time? Perhaps, Oram thought, they *had* visited it but, like him, had decided to leave things the way they were. Perhaps they had thought and acted exactly the way he had. It still surprised him that no one had talked to him about Sumaho's mysterious disappearance yet. Was it possible that they still had no idea? Oram found it hard to believe but had to admit that since Mesmen's disappearance, and particularly since the rift, they had all been shepherding their own flocks. So, perhaps, it wasn't exactly impossible that none of them had visited the headquarters in the past annus.

Sumaho's reaction at seeing the devastated condition of his beloved library was predictable and heartbreaking. He cried out in anguish and ran hither-thither, picking up armfuls of scrolls or hugging piles of books. It was several minuras before he was calm enough to even speak coherently. When he could, he tried to express his opinion of whoever had done such a deed, but he was so angry that his cheeks quivered, his eyes filled with tears and no words came from his lips. He sat down heavily on the dusty floor and sobbed unreservedly. Oram felt uncomfortable having to witness Sumaho in such a weak state. Even when he had been in the worst of shapes during the past annus, Sumaho had never given way to tears. Oram's heart went out to the Librarian.

'Don't worry,' Oram comforted his colleague. 'We will work together to restore the library. It will be back to its original condition in no time at all.'

'Do you think so?' Sumaho asked hopefully, raising his tear-stained face to Oram like a child.

'Of course,' Oram assured him. 'But I will need you to guide the efforts. No one knows this place better than you. I can work to restore everything if you tell me what goes where. Can you do that?'

'Yes, I can,' Sumaho said with resolve and stood up. He wiped his face and composed himself. Then, in a voice filled with determination, he said, 'Come on, let us get to work!'

While they worked, Oram could not help noticing that Sumaho was looking far stronger than he had in temporas. Perhaps the proximity of his beloved books was aiding his recovery. The mind was a strange, powerful thing. Oram was glad that he had decided to bring Sumaho back to the castle despite misgivings as to the sagacity of the plan. He also noticed that Sumaho was remembering more and more about the time preceding the attack, although he still could not recall what had happened to him or to his library. The two worked hard day and night to return the library to its previous glory. Thankfully, Sumaho informed Oram, nothing was missing. While this news delighted Sumaho, it worried Oram. He had been so focussed on getting Sumaho back on his feet that he had not spared much thought for how or why the library had been damaged. He had assumed that someone had ransacked the library for valuable books or manuscripts and had attacked the Librarian because Sumaho had come upon the burglar in the process of the theft. If nothing had been stolen, why had the library been ravaged? The obvious answer made Oram grimace.

Based in Maghem, the castle was accessible only to magi and, at that, only to privileged magi. Since the castle was the headquarters of the sumagi, no one could enter without permission from one of them. The only ones who could freely come and go were the seven sumagi. If Oram's suspicions were true—and it was beginning to seem more and more that they were—then either one of the sumagi or a magus who had been permitted by one of the sumagi to visit the castle had caused the destruction and had been responsible for Sumaho's ordeal. What was more, the main target had been Sumaho. The destruction of the library was a diversion for the sumagi for when they visited the headquarters. It was meant to make them think exactly what Oram had been thinking. This was hard to accept, yet strangely easy to believe. Oram did not want to concede that his theory was correct. But something happened soon after that compelled him to.

The library was almost completely restored by then. As each section was reinstated to its former glory, Sumaho's recollection of the days preceding his disappearance increased rapidly. By the fourteenth of Kawitor, the task of restoring the library was almost complete and Sumaho had remembered everything up to the moment of going to bed on the night before the devastating event. Oram and Sumaho were working on the last remaining section, the oldest part of the castle. As they finished up the work and repaired the broken glass cabinets, they found a stack of books, scrolls and parchments stashed away together, unsorted. Sumaho frowned as a vague memory stirred. These were newly arrived. Or had been when he had last seen them. He had been meaning to put them away in the appropriate glass cases, but something had prevented him from doing so. What? The need for more space! Yes! He would have faced the need to enhance the space by moving the shelves apart. Had he done so or not? He seemed to recall that he had. What had happened thereafter? Had he created another shelf and put the scrolls away? No, he thought, he had not. Something had interfered with his plan. What had caused him to stop work? Something that he had found. It had distracted him. Something behind the shelves. But what?

'Oram!' he called out, suddenly sitting down as the memory overwhelmed him.

Oram rushed to his side. 'Are you all right?' he asked anxiously.

'I just remembered something,' Sumaho said without bothering to reply to Oram's question. 'That day, I was moving the shelves aside to build a new case for these ancient scrolls that had just arrived. I wanted to put them here, in this part of the library, because they are very old, and all our oldest scrolls are kept here. But there was no space in the existent cases, so I decided to move them aside to make space.'

Oram listened patiently to his companion's rambling story, hoping that his memory was finally whole and that he would learn what had really happened. Sumaho was saying, 'After I moved them aside, something distracted me, something I found on the wall behind the cases. Now, you know that these cases are very old. They have been here since before I came to stay, so I had no idea that there was something on the wall behind them. It was a carving. Of an odd flower. When I pressed on it, a staircase opened in the wall. I went down the staircase, I think. I vaguely recall that there was something at the end of the staircase, something important, something to do with books. But I can't remember much more.'

Oram encouraged him, 'This is wonderful! You have remembered a great deal in the last few days. Can you remember on which day you found this staircase? Or what happened afterwards?'

'I remember the day. I think it was the thirteenth of Lokrin. As for what happened after I discovered the staircase, I have already told you what I can remember,' said Sumaho. 'Although,' he added slowly, deliberately, with a look of concentration on his face, 'I think that I found something down there.' He felt the back of his head almost subconsciously, his face scrunched up with concentration. 'I also think I was hit on the back of my head!'

What Sumaho said confirmed Oram's theory that foul play had been at work. The best way to find the culprit was if Sumaho were to recall his attacker. Yet, that way was closed to them. Sumaho had remembered much on his own, but there was no certainty that he would ever remember everything. The only solution left, in Oram's opinion, was for him to try to recover Sumaho's memories of the assault.

'Would you like me to try to recover your lost memories?' he asked Sumaho.

'How?' asked the Librarian.

'I could put you in a trance and read your subconscious mind.'

'I'm not sure that's a good plan,' said Sumaho nervously.

'I won't force you if you aren't comfortable,' Oram said. 'It is difficult and dangerous, though highly effective.'

'Didn't Nishtar discover this process? He's exceptionally good at it. Maybe we could ask him,' Sumaho suggested. He had great faith in his one-time mentor's abilities.

'We could, but we would have to explain everything to him. Then we would have to wait for him to come here. Or we would have to go there. If you are willing to endure it, I could do it today. Don't worry, I'm not too bad at it,' Oram tried to convince Sumaho. He was now desperate to keep the incident of Sumaho's assault from the other sumagi. Until he could be certain that none of them was responsible for it, he could not afford to let them learn that he knew anything about it.

'Do you think that you could really make me remember?' Sumaho asked, unsure of whether he preferred to wait a few days to allow Nishtar to try the process or to take the risk of allowing Oram to do it that very day. The prospect of having to go to Yennthem if Nishtar could not come to Maghem was daunting.

'If the memory is there in your mind, I can fetch it back,' Oram said confidently. 'I won't hurt you, I promise. If it starts getting painful for you, I will stop.'

'All right then,' Sumaho acceded. 'I suppose I can trust you not to make things worse.'

That afternoon, Oram first gave Sumaho a sedative to help him relax. When Sumaho was feeling sufficiently calm, Oram put him under a trance. Then he placed his hand upon Sumaho's forehead and tried to enter the older man's mind. Because Sumaho was a magus, his willpower was stronger than that of most mortals. His mind resisted Oram's efforts at first. Slowly but gradually, Oram overcame its opposition and reached Sumaho's subconscious. He had always liked Sumaho but had wondered what Nishtar had seen in the magus that had prompted him to share the secret of immortality with him. Sumaho was more powerful than an average magus, true, but there *were* magi who were far more capable and powerful. Now Oram saw what Nishtar had seen those thousands of anni ago without having to read Sumaho's mind. Behind Sumaho's shrivelled appearance and grim, peevish manner lay a brilliant mind that was dedicated solely and completely to scholarship of the highest order. It possessed a wealth that was unrivalled by all the treasures of the world. Sumaho's mind was like a library on its own; it was filled with knowledge about every subject under the sun. This one magus knew more than all the magi in existence put together. Oram was struck anew by Nishtar's foresight and felt humbled at his lack of faith in the magus who had, in turn, enabled *him* to be immortal.

Oram continued to delve deeper into Sumaho's mind, trying not to read the magus's thoughts any more than he had to in order to reach those memories that had been lost. When he had peeled back all the conscious layers and several of the subconscious layers of Sumaho's mind, he expected to find the forgotten memories. What he did find made him reel. Where there should have been thoughts and memories, there was nothing except fragments of incoherent ideas. It was almost like stepping upon a rock in the heart of a river and suddenly realising that it was the back of a crocodile. Someone had systematically destroyed every memory that pertained to what Sumaho had discovered that day. Some fragments had remained either because Sumaho had a powerful mind or because the work had been done in a hurry. These fragments had enabled Sumaho to remember the little that he had. No wonder Sumaho had been in such a wretched state when Oram had found him! A part of his mind had been entirely destroyed. No mortal—not even a magus—would have survived such an attack. Only Sumaho's immortality had kept him alive. It was nothing short of miraculous that he had not gone mad permanently! His near-total recovery was astounding, a testament to the Librarian's mental strength.

Oram withdrew from Sumaho's mind, wondering how he was going to give the horrifying news to him that someone had violated his mind and had destroyed his memories ruthlessly. One thing, though, was now clear to Oram. No ordinary magus could have done this, which meant that one of the sumagi was responsible. Unless it was someone who was as powerful as a sumagus but about whom none of the sumagi knew. Oram did not want to consider the possibility. Sumaho's mind was in no state to provide any clue as to who it could be. Oram realised that if he wanted to find the culprit, he would have to do it the old-fashioned way!

Chapter 29

THE ORDER OF THE LILY

(5 Ach 5008 A.E.)

Lord Aminor had never seen Ixluatach celebrated with such fanfare! The Ashperthian people were widely believed to be more sententious than Balignorians, and his stay at Ontar had reinforced this belief. However, the pomp and cheer with which they welcomed Ixluatach far overshadowed the observance of the day by Aminor's countrymen. Ixluatach was the last day of the annus, the day of the ach dedicated to celebration. The entire day had passed in a whirl of colour, sound and movement. Lord Aminor could not recall experiencing such merriment in a long time. Event after event had followed since early morning, yet there had been no excessiveness in any of the arrangements at the palace in Ontar. Everything had been tasteful, elegant and immensely enjoyable. Now he had joined the royal family on a pavilion on a terrace to watch fireworks.

He sat on King Graniphor's left. Princess Eileen sat on the king's other side. The seat on the king's immediate right, however, was empty. Prince Feyanor was busy looking after the arrangements. He would join them just before the fireworks started. It was not yet dark. While they waited, King Graniphor told Aminor stories of the early days of his rule when Ashperth had undergone great political turbulence. Celebrations had been muted then. Now, there was no dampener on the celebration of the new annus. People were singing and dancing for their monarch's entertainment in the streets below, though King Graniphor paid attention to them only partly.

He was talking of how much he missed his daughter. He wanted to know from Lord Aminor everything that he could tell about her. Although he had heard the same news and anecdotes several times before during the nobleman's stay in Ontar, the king of Ashperth seemed not to tire of hearing about his only daughter. He looked wistfully at the celebrations in the streets and murmured, 'I had really hoped it would be you.'

Lord Aminor blushed. He knew what the king was talking about. His stay in Ontar had made one thing abundantly clear to him: the royal family of Ashperth had preferred him over King Amiroth as a husband for Lamella and had never quite reconciled themselves to the fact that Aminor had stood aside for his cousin. It had made things rather uncomfortable for him at times, but he had become used to it over the mondans.

All things concerned, he thought, his stay at Ontar had been extremely *revelatory*. He had learnt much that his spies had missed, although he had also come to realise why he could not blame them for their failures. For, he now knew, no news of Ashperth reached beyond its borders unless Prince Feyanor wanted it to. At the same time, nothing happened in any of the other human kingdoms without Prince Feyanor hearing about it sooner or later—usually sooner. Aminor was spellbound by the efficiency and superiority of Ashperth's intelligence system. He also suspected that whatever he had learnt about it had been only because Feyanor had been willing to allow him that knowledge.

Aminor's reverie was broken by the announcement of a ceremony called 'The Trade of Blossoms'. As soon as the announcement was made, King Graniphor sat up straighter with a wide smile. He was obviously looking forward to it! Lord Aminor had never heard of this ceremony and asked King Graniphor about it. The king explained that it was a tradition peculiar to Ashperth. It was a relatively new tradition, he explained, but one that had become immensely popular. He was about to explain it in detail when General Korshernon came up to the pavilion, carrying a bunch of flowers. Aminor could not help wondering whether the normally sententious general had allowed his sense of decorum to slip under the influence of alcohol on this merry occasion. He wondered what the king would make of it.

General Korshernon bowed to King Graniphor, Princess Eileen and Lord Aminor. He then presented the king with a sprig of white lilies, much to Aminor's surprise. Princess Eileen received a purple lily. To Aminor's greater surprise, General Korshernon proffered *him* a yellow lily, which he accepted with hesitant thanks. The king then had a servant remove the cover of one of three piled trays standing on the right side of the platform. It was heaped with roses. The king presented the general with a beautiful white rose from the tray, which the general accepted with a deep bow. Princess Eileen uncovered another tray next to the one with roses and presented General Korshernon with a stalk of forget-me-nots. Not having any flowers to give, Lord Aminor simply bowed and thanked him again. This, he realised, was the 'Trade of Blossoms' that had been announced and not some aberrant behaviour by Ashperth's second-most powerful military figure. Aminor noticed a third covered tray. Waiting for the prince, he guessed. A novel tradition indeed!

Several of the noblemen and ladies of Ashperth came up to the royal pavilion to wish their king and princess a happy new annus and to exchange flowers. They also wore flowers—mostly yellow lilies—in their sleeves, buttonholes, lapels or headgear. Some wore lilies of other colours. When the king and the princess could no longer hold the multitude of flowers in their hands, they deposited the flowers on trays standing on the left side of the pavilion. As the ceremony continued, and more important personages came to pay tribute to the king, the blossoms began to pile up on one side of the terrace and diminish on the other. The people down on the streets were also waving flowers for their monarch. A page was sent to collect these. Soon the terrace was intoxicatingly fragrant with the aroma of thousands of blossoms. Aminor noticed roses, irises, dandelions, crocuses, marigolds and many other varieties, though lilies were, by far, the most numerous. The preponderance of lilies intrigued Lord Aminor. When he mentioned this to King Graniphor and Princess Eileen, asking whether lilies had some special significance for Ashperth, they merely laughed.

'In Ashperth, flowers have their own language, my lord,' King Graniphor said mysteriously. 'And they speak openly on this night to those who know how to listen.'

Before Aminor could ask the king what he meant, Prince Feyanor was announced. The lamps were being lit, an indication that it was dark enough for the fireworks to begin, when Prince Feyanor walked onto the pavilion to join his family and his guest for the evening's prime attraction—the fireworks. The prince, Aminor noticed, boldly wore a tiger lily on his jacket's lapel. Feyanor saw Aminor eyeing his unusual accessory and smiled mischievously. He made straight for the third tray, which had been uncovered as soon as he had arrived. He grabbed handfuls of flowers from the tray and threw them among the crowd gathered below, amidst great cheering. However, before the flowers had all gone, he made a sign. The servants disappeared with the tray. He winked at the spymaster then and handed him the last of the yellow lilies in his hand before taking his seat at his father's right, leaving Aminor speechless.

The fireworks display was breathtaking! The illuminators had surpassed themselves in creating a display that burst into all colours and shapes imaginable and filled the sky with scenes of grandness and splendour. There were exotic flowers and birds, knights riding horses, stars shimmering in constellations, elephants trumpeting in processions, trees blossoming and then shedding their leaves with the passing of the seasons, the Ashperthian flag fluttering in twinkling lights in the night sky and many other delightful tableaus. Lord Aminor was astonished at the wonder and beauty of the show and applauded as loudly as the people on the streets.

As the show drew to a close, everyone began to disperse rapidly. Aminor stood up to follow King Graniphor and the royal family back to the palace, but Prince Feyanor placed a hand on his arm.

'Would you care to walk down to the palace with me, my lord?' he asked politely.

Lord Aminor was a little mystified but could not very well refuse. He declared that it would be his honour and began to stride at the prince's side. He congratulated the prince on a brilliant celebration of Ixluatach, particularly the astonishing fireworks. Feyanor acknowledged the wishes graciously. They followed the king and the princess into the palace grounds, but then Prince Feyanor dismissed his guards and walked off towards the gardens. Since Feyanor had not given him leave to go his own way, Aminor was obliged to accompany the prince into the royal gardens, wondering what was going on.

As soon as the two were completely alone, Feyanor said, 'I believe that you have something to ask me, Lord Aminor?'

Though taken aback, Aminor replied confidently, 'It was merely the matter of the language of flowers that caught my attention, Your Highness. But, perhaps the right person to satisfy my curiosity is your gardener?'

'Perhaps,' answered Feyanor. 'On a completely different subject matter, may I ask you about your relationship with my sister, Lamella?' Aminor almost stumbled as Feyanor continued, 'And with King Amiroth, my brother-in-law, as well, of course.'

Aminor could not help feeling that Feyanor was playing a game with him. What it was and why it was being played, he could not guess. His days in Ontar had taught him one thing about Feyanor—the prince hardly ever did anything without good reason. So, Aminor tried to answer the question as best as he could. He talked about his loyalty and affection towards Amiroth and his admiration and fealty towards the queen of Balignor.

'A wonderfully diplomatic and uninformative answer!' Feyanor exclaimed. 'I must congratulate you on your restraint and self-control, Lord Aminor. But I would be greatly obliged if you told me the truth regarding your feelings for my sister. I will not press you to share your true feelings about Amiroth; frankly, I couldn't care less about whether you like him or not.'

Aminor blushed deeply. He spoke in a cold tone, 'Prince Feyanor, I am grateful for your hospitality and the honour you have shown me during my visit, but I will not stand here and have you insult my king.'

'Would you fight for his honour, Lord Aminor?' Feyanor taunted.

'If I have to, my lord,' conceded Aminor unwillingly.

Feyanor laughed. 'You are truly devoted to King Amiroth, I see. I am glad. With you by his side, his reign is definitely secure. Then, again, you are the plinth on which it rests, isn't it? At least, that is what I have been led to believe.'

'I am not sure who has led you to believe such baseless rumours, my lord,' Aminor replied with a light smile, recovering his humour.

'Now you insult *me*, Lord Aminor,' Feyanor said in a tone of casual hurt. 'I am utterly certain that my spies are far better informed than yours!'

It took all of Aminor's self control not to gasp. He did not know how to respond to Feyanor's comment. He remained silent.

'I will take your silence for acquiescence,' Feyanor continued. 'So, tell me, Lord Aminor, what would it take for you to overthrow King Amiroth and seize the throne of Balignor?'

'Are you accusing me of treason or instigating me towards it?' Lord Aminor demanded coldly, thoroughly discombobulated by the prince's sudden, strange and contradictory statements and questions, and trying to avoid giving way to rapidly growing agitation.

'Neither, actually. I am just curious as to why a man of your talents is satisfied to remain second in command to another who is so obviously inferior.'

'I know my position. If I have any talents, they are for the use of my king and my country,' Lord Aminor declared haughtily. 'My king is inferior to none. I am sorry to hear that you have such a poor opinion of the man to whom your sister is married. She is, of course, utterly devoted to him. I suspect she would be wounded if she knew how you felt about King Amiroth.'

'I agree with you! Indeed she is devoted to him. But I wonder if she is as devoted to him as you are? Or even as devoted as you are to *her*?'

'I do not gather your meaning, Prince Feyanor,' Aminor said through clenched teeth.

'No?' asked the prince pleasantly, apparently unaware of Aminor's growing anger. 'Well, what I mean is simply this: if you had to choose between your king and your queen, whom would you choose?'

Aminor wanted to turn round and leave. He knew it would be rude. He knew it would be an insult to Feyanor. But he could not stand there and endure any more of the prince's insane questions. He wished, for the first time since coming to Ashperth, that he had not. He felt trapped, but he was certain that he could not leave Ashperth without Feyanor's permission. He wondered what the prince was up to. Was Feyanor planning to invade Balignor? Was that why he had lured Aminor away—so that Balignor would be weak? What could he, Aminor, do to rectify the situation? The only thing that he could do at that moment, Aminor realised, was to continue to play the game that Feyanor had initiated.

'My king has the foremost right to my loyalty among all men and women,' he replied.

'And what about your love, my lord? Does he have the first right to your love as well? Do you truly love him more than you love my sister?'

'Your Highness, I see no reason why you and I should say things that would only dishonour a noble lady who has ever been true to the husband that her family wedded her to.'

'You are a master at deflecting questions, Lord Aminor! But tell me this, and tell me as directly as you can—if you had to choose between king and country, which would you choose?'

This one was easy for Aminor even though he could not help feeling that he was stepping into a trap, 'The only thing dearer to me than my king is my country.'

'So, if you had to choose between the two, would you choose your country?'

'Yes,' replied Aminor with a hint of tiredness in his voice.

'Then, if I told you that the best way for you to serve your country was by siding with me in an invasion of Balignor, would you agree?'

'What!' exclaimed Aminor. 'How dare you ask me to betray my king and country?'

'I am asking you to betray your king, yes, but not your country. Please do not insult my intelligence—pun intended—by saying that it is Amiroth who truly rules Balignor. Since you already do the work, why not take credit for it too? Besides, I am sure that those who know the truth about who you really are in the scheme of things in Balignor would have no objection to you as king. They would immediately surrender to me upon learning that you have sided with me. So much bloodshed would be spared!'

'You would do this to your own sister?' Aminor said incredulously. 'You would make her a widow by your own hand?'

'I would rid her of a worse husband and provide her with a better one. I am sure that she will be heartbroken for Amiroth and will despise you and me. But we both love her enough to win her over in the end, especially if we work together,' declared Prince Feyanor flippantly. 'So, what do you say to my proposal?'

'Only this, my lord,' said Aminor, drawing his sword. 'I am sorry for breaking all laws of hospitality, but I will not let you harm my king and country.' He knew that it was an act of utmost stupidity, yet he felt as if he had no choice. He would never fall in with Feyanor's conspiracy to attack Balignor! And he knew that he could not lie his way out of the situation—Feyanor was too clever not to see through any attempt at deception. He had to do the one thing that he would never have chosen to do had there been a choice. Besides, it was probably the only way to distract the prince and force him to stop playing his dangerous game.

It seemed to Aminor that Feyanor was anticipating just such a move, as the prince drew his own weapon coolly and engaged him. Lord Aminor found his anger disappearing as he concentrated on facing the man widely reputed as the best swordsman in all four human kingdoms. The two were calm, collected and skilful warriors. The duel ranged for a while. Aminor fleetingly wondered why no guards came rushing to their prince's aid, but he pushed the thought away. He had to concentrate fully on his opponent, who was justifying his reputation with every stroke and swing of his sword. Aminor had managed to hold his own so far, but he had a sneaking suspicion that it was because Prince Feyanor was not even trying very hard to defeat him. The truth of his conjecture was brought home to him when a sudden move by Feyanor found him disarmed and with his opponent's sword at his throat.

'And what should we do with you now, my lord?' Feyanor said in a strange, almost amused, voice. Aminor did not reply. The prince suddenly laughed heartily. He lowered his sword and embraced Aminor warmly, much to the latter's astonishment.

'You are brave, noble and honourable, though a little more cunning would not be amiss in one who carries such responsibilities as you do. Also, a sense of humour. You are far too serious, my lord, though you are a wonderful man!' he continued after releasing Aminor.

Aminor acknowledged the compliment with a stiff bow. Still bemused, he asked, 'May I know what is going on, Your Highness? I am beginning to think that all of this is some elaborate game designed with some ulterior motive.'

'You are correct in thinking that, my lord. I beg your pardon for provoking you as I did. Unfortunately, it was necessary to test you.'

'To test me? What for?'

'You will soon learn,' Feyanor said, returning Aminor's sword. 'Please follow me.'

The prince led Aminor further down the garden to a part of it that Aminor was unfamiliar with. A low stone wall separated the area from the rest of the gardens. Feyanor unlocked a gate set in the wall and beckoned Aminor in. It had evidently been an enclosed garden or park once. Now, it was impossible to say when it had last received the attentions of a gardener. The spymaster of Balignor was surprised at its unkempt state. It was almost wild with trees and shrubs growing rampantly everywhere. The grass underfoot had not been trimmed in a long time. The smell of rotting leaves permeated the air. A gazebo stood in one corner of it. It looked old and dilapidated.

'This was my mother's favourite garden, my lord,' Prince Feyanor said in a sad voice, as he walked into the gazebo. 'It has not been tended since her death.'

Wondering whether Prince Feyanor was about to entrust him with some family secret, Aminor gingerly followed his host into the rotting building. However, Feyanor said nothing more about his late mother. Instead, he pressed a knob hidden among the ornate woodwork of a post. A section of the floor slid open, revealing a staircase winding down into the bowels of the earth. As soon as they entered, the trapdoor slid shut again. A row of torches stood along a wall.

Feyanor took one of these and started down the stairs, followed by his guest. The stairs soon gave way to a walled passage. The passage turned and twisted underground for furlong after furlong in mind-boggling tunnels lined by identical blocks of stone. At many places, other passages joined up to it through identical stone arches. The passages were a bewildering maze. Feyanor walked on with a surety that could have come only from complete familiarity. Aminor followed without a word, trying to remember as much as he could. He wasn't sure he would be able to find his way back alone if he had to.

Finally, the two stepped inside what looked like a waiting room. It was a low-ceilinged, square room lined with the same stone blocks as the tunnels. Several men were already there. Some sat quietly on wooden benches while others stood talking to each other in murmuring knots of twos and threes. Aminor knew some of them and remembered seeing some others earlier in the evening. Several were complete strangers. What struck him the most was that all of them wore yellow lilies upon their clothing. So this was what the preponderance of lilies was about! He heard giggling from an open archway and realised that women were also present.

'Greetings, my friends!' Feyanor cried out as he entered. All present turned towards him as one at his cry and greeted him with a resounding welcome. More people poured in from nearby rooms as it became known that the prince had arrived. The waiting room was not big enough to accommodate everyone. They passed into a larger hall through one of the many archways that lined the walls of the waiting room. This chamber was similar in construction to the waiting room but was three times as large and had a raised platform to one side. Feyanor climbed onto it, accompanied by some of his closest followers, both men and women. He gestured for Aminor to join him. Aminor, who had been observing everything quietly from a corner, reluctantly complied. He was beginning to suspect that this was a secret organisation with Feyanor at its head. He also guessed that this same organisation was behind the prince's incredibly strong intelligence capabilities. The lilies were some kind of symbol used by the group. He stood a little behind Feyanor on the stage and surveyed the gathering while everyone waited for Feyanor to commence the proceedings. There were over a hundred men and at least half as many women of all ages and social statuses in that chamber. However, they stood without class or gender distinctions, shoulder to shoulder, like equals.

'Greetings!' Feyanor roared again, grinning broadly. 'I wish all of you a very happy new annus!' They replied as one. The roar of their voices made the stone ceiling reverberate and the underground hall rumble. Feyanor then turned to Aminor and said, 'Lord Aminor, welcome to the headquarters of the Order of the Lily.'

'Thank you, but may I ask what the Order of the Lily is, Your Highness?'

'Be patient, Lord Aminor, you will soon find out,' said someone behind Aminor. General Korshernon. Some of those present snickered. Aminor shifted uncomfortably.

'Now, now, General, don't tease our guest,' Feyanor admonished him, sounding quite unserious. 'He is quite handy with a sword.'

General Korshernon smiled and bowed to Aminor, coming to stand near his prince. Aminor acknowledged the apology with a nod. Feyanor then turned to the gathered crowd and introduced Aminor.

'This is Lord Aminor from Balignor. Many of you already know him; some of you do not. He has been a guest here in Ontar for some time. He is the maternal cousin of King Amiroth of Balignor. However, that is not the only qualification to recommend him,' the prince declared. Feyanor then proceeded to talk in great detail about Aminor's merits and accomplishments, sparing no secret about his role in the administration of Balignor. Aminor blushed upon being praised so lavishly and also at realising how thoroughly Feyanor knew every secret of his espionage network. He observed that all those present were listening to Feyanor eagerly, with a matter-of-fact expression on their faces. He understood then that Feyanor was not really *praising* him, just stating the facts for his followers. He felt even more intrigued about the prince and his followers. He was glad, though, when Feyanor finished his declaration without mentioning either Lamella or Amiroth. Everyone applauded generously, and Aminor bowed to acknowledge.

'Now, Lord Aminor,' said Prince Feyanor, 'I think that you deserve to be told about the Order of the Lily. We are, as you have invariably guessed by now, a secret organisation. Our numbers are not limited to the small gathering you see here today. Those you see here are only a fraction of our members. They are the ones who were in Ontar or its vicinity and could travel here tonight. Our members are scattered throughout the four human kingdoms of western Elthrusia. We come from every rank and file of life, and while in our ordinary lives we are divided by considerations of wealth and status, here in the Order we are all equal. The only thing that sets us apart is our capability. We are always on the lookout for people who can join our cause. It is not easy since complete secrecy is at the heart of the order's success. We cannot choose just anybody to join us. Those who become members are special in some way. We know everything there is to know about all our members. There are no secrets in the Order of the Lily. This is our greatest weakness and also our greatest strength. The members are avowed to do everything they can for the fulfilment of the order's goals and to help its other members. Any member of the order can expect to find the entire order's strength and support behind him or her when need arises. Therein lies our power. I invite you today to join us as our newest member. Will you swear loyalty to us? Will you stand with us? Will you be counted as one of us?'

There was thunderous applause again. Aminor felt bewildered. Why had he never heard of this order before? What did they do? Were they a threat to Balignor? Who were the members who were present in Balignor? Did he know any of them? Had they leaked all Balignor's secrets to Feyanor and the others? What was the goal of the order that was so sacrosanct to the members? Myriad other questions roiled inside his mind. How could he answer Feyanor's question without knowing anything? Feyanor's grand description of the order had contained very little useful information. Aminor needed to know more before he could take a decision. So, instead of replying, he placed his queries before Feyanor, trying to sound as inoffensive as possible. Feyanor seemed not to mind. In fact, he smiled amiably and said to the gathering, 'Did I not tell you how intelligent, discerning and patriotic Lord Aminor is?' There was no hint of irony in his voice. Many present murmured in approval.

'Do not worry, Lord Aminor,' General Korshernon replied on his prince's behalf. 'We do nothing that would lead you to betray your king or country. Our goal is to ensure that mankind remains secure and strong in this world where there are many powerful races coexisting in a delicate balance of power and competition for survival.'

'The Order of the Lily was founded by my father,' Feyanor continued, 'as a counter-intelligence measure against his enemies during the days of his exile. Their purpose was twofold—to provide him with information about his adversaries and to protect his daughter, my sister, who was being raised on the mainland in secret. When my father returned to power, he wished to disband the order, but I dissuaded him. The order was reincarnated as an intelligence network with the goal of watching for enemies of all mankind. Our loyalties lie not with Ashperth alone but with all four kingdoms. We provide secret aid to any who requires it in the cause of truth, justice and good. We know everything that goes on in the four kingdoms though we act only when the situation becomes desperate. We do not hunger for power or control, only for the welfare of men in a world where we are merely one of a score of races, and not necessarily one of the most powerful. We wish to protect mankind from other races that could easily overpower us if they so wished, especially if we weaken through internal strife. Do you understand?'

'I think I do, my lord. But what would happen if I were to face a conflict of interest? If I had to choose between the order, on the one hand, and my king and country on the other?' Aminor demanded.

'Let me assure you that you will never have to choose between Balignor and the order. Whatever is in the best interests of Balignor will be in the best interests of the order. That will be what the order will wish to enforce. It is possible, however, that you may have to choose between your king and the order. That would happen only if the king wished to act in a manner that would harm Balignor. I think you know the answer to your question now.'

'Why did you invite *me*, Your Highness?' Aminor asked, still not responding to Feyanor's original question.

'I have had my eye on you for a while now, I confess,' Feyanor replied candidly. 'But you have been so close to King Amiroth that I have hesitated. The order now plans to expand its network beyond the human kingdoms, and we could do with a man of your calibre among our ranks in this venture, my lord.'

'Was that why you invited me here to Ashperth?'

'That, among other reasons. I did not lie to you in Lufurdista when I gave you my reasons for inviting you. You cannot say that you have not been happy here!'

'Indeed I cannot, because that would be a lie,' Aminor acknowledged. 'What will happen if I agree to join the order?'

'You will be formally inducted into the order tonight. Thenceforth, your primary loyalty will be to the order.'

'And if I refuse?'

'Unfortunately, my lord, if you refuse, we cannot just let you walk out of here with what you have learnt about us. You will have to fight me again, this time to the death.'

'I have one more question, my lord.'

'Ask.'

'What happens to me if I join the order and King Amiroth finds out and accuses me of treason?'

'First, we will rescue you. Then we will get all our members in the vicinity out of harm's way. Following that, we will find and plug the source of the leak, for no one learns of our activities by accident. We will lie low until things calm down. We will try to convince King Amiroth that we are merely a rumour, that we do not truly exist. If we fail to do that, and King Amiroth takes up cudgels against us, we will be forced to fight him. I sincerely wish that we never have to resort to such measures.'

'And what happens if you fail to rescue me?'

'Then we will pray for Kiel to have mercy on your soul, Lord Aminor. And, of course, we will avenge you. But let us hope that things do not come to such a pass. Do you have any more questions to ask?'

'No, not at present.'

'You will be informed in far greater detail about the order and its activities if you choose to join this illustrious band of brothers.'

'And sisters!' shouted one of the women in the crowd.

'And sisters,' Feyanor corrected himself. 'You will be formally inducted and taught the rules and protocols of the order, given passwords and codes, shown how to recognise and communicate with other members and provided with a list of all our members and all information about them. So, what do you say?'

Aminor took a deep breath. He looked at Feyanor standing in front of him, radiant with confidence and power. He looked at the men and women standing behind him, staunch and loyal members of the Order of the Lily who would follow their leader to any end. He looked at the crowd before the platform, proud men and women who served Feyanor and the order unflinchingly. Everyone seemed to be holding their breaths, waiting for Aminor to reply. It was unnerving, but Aminor was finally composed. He knew what he was about to do and what its consequences would be. But he was ready. He turned to Feyanor and met the prince's gaze. Then he said in a clear, audible voice, 'Yes.'

Chapter 30

AN INTRIGUING OFFER

Rauberk sought an audience with King Amiroth of Balignor as soon as Augurk's letter bearing permission to proceed had arrived. The mention of the rauz of Ghrangghirm had made it easier to gain access to Amiroth's court. Rauberk's presence caused a good deal of excitement and conversation. Never in living memory had there been any interaction between humans and dharvhs beyond the occasional trade of goods. All who saw and heard of the dharvh messenger wondered what had brought him to the court of Balignor from as far as Drauzern. On his part, Rauberk was awed by the grandeur of the palace as he was led through to meet the king. He wondered why humans spent so much wealth on things like carpets, fountains, paintings and decorations that served no real purpose. However, he kept his thoughts to himself. His mission was too delicate and precious to risk over a carelessly spoken word. He praised the beauty of the palace to the attendant accompanying him to the audience chamber. The attendant appeared uncomfortable. Perhaps he was unused to being spoken to by visitors to His Majesty King Amiroth. Rauberk shut his mouth.

Rauberk had seen King Amiroth before but only from a distance. He was impressed anew when he saw the proud king sitting at the head of his court, surrounded by his courtiers, looking relaxed and dignified at the same time. Humans gained kingship through inheritance, father to son, Rauberk knew. But he had no doubt that Amiroth was a worthy ruler and the most suited to assist Augurk. He bowed deeply and, after the commonplaces of greeting due to a king from a foreign emissary, broached the reason for his visit.

'I come here from far Drauzern on behalf of Rauz Augurk of Ghrangghirm,' he declared. This announcement was followed by a brief extolling of Augurk's virtues. Then he continued, 'My rauz has authorised me to place before you a proposal that can benefit both your country and ours.'

'I am pleasantly surprised to find an emissary of Rauz Augurk in my court,' Amiroth said politely. 'It surprises me even more to hear of this proposal since Rauz Augurk and I have never met, though I have heard much about him.'

'He, too, has heard much about you, my lord,' Rauberk lied unabashedly. 'So has decided to put this proposal to you of all the human kings even without having met you face to face. He has no doubt that you are the most capable and the most suitable king to present this proposal to.'

'Indeed! I am honoured by his faith in me, sir,' said Amiroth. The diplomatic exchanges laden with subtext were beginning to tire him. He asked Rauberk about the proposal. He had a feeling that Aminor would not have done so, would have known the best way through the maze of diplomatic caution and obliqueness. He might even have known about the proposal beforehand. Not for the first time since Aminor's departure to Ashperth, King Amiroth ardently wished he had his cousin by his side.

Rauberk answered without hesitation, 'My rauz has for some time now desired to discover a certain place that has been lost to us due to the vagaries of time and history. It is not possible for us dharvhs to discover this place due to reasons that Rauz Augurk can himself best explain when he meets you. He wishes you to undertake an expedition on his behalf to discover this legendary place. He assures you that no expenses shall be spared to recompense you for your trouble.'

'What is this place that he wishes me to discover?' Amiroth asked.

'The City of Stone, Your Majesty,' Rauberk replied with a bow. His announcement was met with consternation and disbelief. Never before had such an expedition been heard of! Amiroth was immediately suspicious. He had heard of this City of Stone but had not known it to exist for real. It was a mythical city about which none seemed to know anything except that it was a city, that it was made of stone and that it was a legend. He questioned Rauberk closely regarding Augurk's reasons for wanting the city found, for choosing him to lead an expedition and for any possible treachery. Concluding that the messenger knew no more than he had already told the court, Amiroth dismissed him, declaring that he would think about Rauz Augurk's proposal and send for Rauberk when he was ready to answer. He offered the dharvhish messenger the hospitality of the guest quarters in the palace. Amiroth did not trust the messenger. He did not trust any dharvh, in fact. He was in two minds. On the one hand, the whole matter reeked of conspiracy and treachery. On the other, it could be an opportunity to gain fame, wealth and glory. He wished for the umpteenth time that day that Aminor were there to help him decide. He keenly missed his cousin's sound advice.

One mondan! Rauberk paced his room agitatedly. The king had been mulling over his proposition for over one mondan now! What was there to think so much about? Rauberk had last seen King Amiroth on the fifth of Reklan. Today was the seventh of Madal. He was running out of patience. Although, it was not as if he had been patiently waiting all these days. He had politely declined the king's hospitality and had continued to live at the Dancing Clowns. He knew, though, that men were keeping an eye on him. The obviousness with which the men spied on him made him laugh at times. But he was also beginning to understand the world of humans. Until his visit to the western kingdom, he had always believed men to be a weak, cowardly race. He had changed his mind in the past few mondans. Though men were physically weaker and far less adept at metalwork and mining, they had their own merits. They built beautiful houses and spun wonderful cloth. They made melodious songs and danced to the rhythms of enchanting music. They wrote erudite books and told spellbinding tales. They herded cattle and grew crops and sailed the seas and tamed wild beasts for work and entertainment. And they were skilled in arms, far more skilled that Rauberk had ever imagined. They could work in unison like a well-oiled machine in battle. Men had their weaknesses, but their strengths and determination and the will to rise above their limitations more than compensated for those.

A knock on the door caused Rauberk to focus on the business that had brought him to Balignor. Rauberk opened the door. The king's messenger was standing outside. The messenger bowed to Rauberk and read out the king's summons. Rauberk had been asked by King Amiroth to attend his court that day. King Amiroth would reply to the request made by Rauz Augurk. Rauberk eagerly accompanied the messenger to the court. His heart was filled with anxiety. What would happen if the king refused? Would it lead to animosity between their countries? How would the rauz react? Would he approach another king? Would he declare hostilities on Balignor? Rauberk did not know. His job was only to do what his rauz ordered him to do.

King Amiroth sat flanked by Lord Parkiod, the commander-in-chief, and Lord Beleston, the prime minister. Other important ministers were also present. The king of Balignor was a handsome man with sharp features, intense black eyes, black curly hair and full lips that did not detract from his masculinity. He was not tall and had a lean build that belied his strength. He looked every inch the grand ruler that he was. Rauberk bowed to him and the others and thanked King Amiroth for the invitation. He expressed the hope that King Amiroth had been well in the meanwhile and that the day would prove to be a harbinger of a new era of human-dharvh friendship. Then he waited for Amiroth to speak.

'I have considered the proposal sent to me by your rauz in great depth,' King Amiroth said to Rauberk. 'What he asks me to do is neither easy nor profitable to the race of men. Besides, it is still not clear to me why he seeks this City of Stone. What treasure does he hope to find there? And why does he believe that I can help him in finding this city? There are many such unanswered questions that have bothered me, causing me to delay answering you. I have sought the answers among the ancient texts in my keeping but have found little to justify either the possibility of success or the necessity of performing such a task.

'I have been advised by my counsellors against embarking upon such a perilous and possibly fruitless expedition simply for the sake of helping another monarch with whom we have never had any intercourse in the long anni of the existence of both races. There is wisdom in their words. It would be foolish to neglect such good advice. How do I know that I am not being led into a trap? Even if this is not a trap, what do my people and I gain out of it?'

'You gain the thanks and friendship of the dharvhs for ages to come,' said Rauberk, his heart sinking faster than a nail in a bucket of water. He was on the verge of panic but forced himself to retain a calm demeanour.

'And we are grateful for such friendship,' King Amiroth answered with a nod. 'But in order to embark upon a dangerous journey from which they might never return, my men might not be motivated by the thanks and friendship of the dharvhs alone, valuable though it is. What has your rauz to say to that?'

Rauberk almost sighed with relief. He now knew where the conversation was headed. His desperation eased as he realised that Amiroth was not about to refuse. He was merely enquiring about a suitable financial reward in a highly indirect manner. Rauberk was prepared for such a question from King Amiroth.

'Your Majesty, my rauz has authorised me to offer each of your soldiers a full set of dharvh-made armour and weapons of his choosing. Besides these, they will be entitled to two bags of gold each. Any commanders of these men will be given ten such bags besides two sets of armour and weapons of their choice. You, my lord, shall have as many sets of armour and a hundred bags of gold and gems besides five bales of Simlin.'

King Amiroth smiled. He had expected no less from the dharvhs. They were rumoured to be wealthy beyond imagination. His expectations had not been disappointed. He suspected that the mission was not an ordinary one. He had been warned by his ministers and councillors of the treachery of the dharvhs and of the dangers he would court unnecessarily if he accepted Augurk's request. However, the expedition promised adventure, wealth and glory. He had long been itching for some such challenge, especially since Feyanor's conquest of the Ufharn Hills. He also remembered Prince Feyanor's assertion about the need for amity among the races. He had been testing the messenger merely to discover how important this mission was to Augurk and how far the rauz of Ghrangghirm was willing to go to convince him.

He addressed Rauberk, 'Something tells me that what you offer me is nothing compared to the treasures that the mythical city holds. Is this all that the dharvhs measure their thanks by?'

Rauberk felt angry. What he had promised Amiroth was beyond the dreams of any king of men. Did Amiroth not realise the worth of what he had been offered?

Or did he hold the honour of the dharvhs lightly? Rauberk checked his temper and spoke politely to Amiroth.

'What does Your Majesty desire then?'

'A third share in the treasures that will be Rauz Augurk's once the city is discovered,' said King Amiroth without hesitation.

Rauberk stood speechless. He was completely unprepared for a demand of such magnitude. He knew that the burden of the mission's success or failure now rested entirely on him. If he withdrew to consult his rauz, the king of Balignor would know that he, Rauberk, had not the authority that he claimed to have. It would weaken their position in the negotiations. If he accepted, he risked losing much more than his employment as a spy. If he refused, he still risked losing his life at Amiroth's hands. He was caught on the horns of a dilemma. He stood in the centre of Amiroth's court in utter silence, deciding which path to choose. Finally, he squared his shoulders and addressed Amiroth.

'On behalf of Rauz Augurk, I accept your demand for a share of the city's spoils, my lord, provided that the exact distribution must be Rauz Augurk's decision. And this share—whether a third or less or more—will be in lieu of the gifts promised before.'

King Amiroth laughed and applauded loudly. Rauberk was taken aback by the unexpected behaviour.

'Bravo, Dar Rauberk!' said Amiroth. 'You are indeed the perfect dharvh for the job. Do not think that I am unaware of the risk you took in accepting my demand on behalf of your rauz. I respect you for the courage that you have shown. Be pleased to know that I have no desire for a share in either the treasures or the secrets that the city holds. I will help your rauz to discover the City of Stone in exchange for the original *gifts* that were promised to me. Even though I do not believe that the city exists, I shall go upon an expedition to your lands and not turn back until I have fulfilled my commitment to Rauz Augurk.'

'However,' Amiroth added, 'the expedition might turn out to be extremely arduous, dangerous and prolonged. I cannot leave without sufficient preparation, which will take a few mondans. Inform your rauz that he must be patient for that period of time.'

Rauberk was once again struck by the unpredictability of humans. He gladly agreed to the terms set by King Amiroth, upon which the king had it proclaimed that he would sally forth in search of the City of Stone in answer to the call of Rauz Augurk of Ghrangghirm on the first of Lokrin in the annus 5009 A.E.

Chapter 31

MIZU AND AMISHAR

(9 Reklan 5009 A.E. to 19 Madal 5009 A.E.)

Mizu woke up with a start, panting hard as if he had been running. This confused him for a moment. Then he remembered. He *had* been running, though in his dream. Something had been chasing him—a strange creature that looked like a cross between a bird and a lizard and breathed fire. He had been trying to escape it. He still felt terrified. He reached out and felt his mother's arm where she slept next to him. A warm sense of comfort and security filled him. The residual fear of the nightmare melted away. Misa still slept soundly, oblivious to the rest of the universe. She looked so relaxed! Ever since leaving Bolsana almost four mondans ago, she had seemed anxious almost all the time, especially when passing through villages. That anxiety mellowed to cautious vigilance when they passed through forests, which they often did. When they had to sleep in a field, as they had done the previous night, she became tense and grim.

Mizu did not wake her. Trying to forget memories of the awful dream, he crawled out from under the cart. The sun was beginning to rise out of the horizon behind them. He could see it peeking above the roof of the hut attached to the field in which they were sleeping. Perhaps the farmer who owned the field lived there. At the moment, the field was lying fallow, which was surprising at that time of the annus since eshoinh had already set in. A hedge separated the field from the dusty, unpaved road a few feet away. The tall hedge also hid the refugees well. At a distance, Marsil and Marsillon were standing quietly. They were awake too. Mizu looked up at the rapidly lightening sky. Just a momon before, it had been inky dark. Now it was a bright cerulean like Yodiri's eyes. Yodiri's eyes? Where had that thought come from? What did he know of what Yodiri looked like? Mizu shook his head. He had these strange thoughts sometimes, thoughts that he could not remember thinking, that were like fragments of someone else's memories or forgotten dreams.

He looked back at the sun. It was behind them. Always behind them as they pushed on relentlessly west. Another image came to him unbidden: the vast ocean and the faceless soldiers standing on its shore. For a mondan now, he had been feeling sure that if they kept going west, they would come to the ocean. Remembering how unhappy his questions regarding the reasons for leaving Bolsana had made Misa, he had not asked his mother about their destination.

'Why didn't you wake me?' Misa's voice broke into his thoughts.

He turned around and hugged her, not replying to her question. Instead, breaking his resolution not to ask her about their goal, he asked, 'Are we going to a particular place?'

'No, we are not,' she replied with a slight heaviness in her voice and a stiffening of her shoulders.

'Are we going to go on towards the west?' the boy asked again.

'I'm not sure about that either,' his mother replied. 'Maybe we will change direction after some time. For now, west is the direction we will continue in.'

'What is to the west?' he asked her, thinking about the ocean that he often dreamt of.

'The kingdom of Storsnem,' she replied.

'And beyond that?'

'Balignor.'

'And beyond that?' he asked innocently.

'The wide ocean,' she replied with a smile. Mizu realised with a start that his guess about the ocean had been correct, but he said nothing to his mother. Liking the new game, he again asked, 'And beyond that?'

'Beyond that…Ashperth,' she said in a strange, wistful voice and looked away.

Puzzled, Mizu didn't bother her with any more questions. He wanted to ask her if they were headed for Ashperth, wherever that was, but did not. Obviously, she would tell him when the time came, he decided. He did wonder, though, what would happen if they continued west beyond Ashperth. But he didn't ask.

Mizu lay on a sturdy branch of a tree, his feet dangling below, looking at the stars. He loved watching the stars. They looked like hordes of fireflies flittering high up in the sky. His mother often told him about the stars and how to find one's way using them. She also told him about constellations—clusters of stars that looked like animals or things. Some people said that one's future could be read in the stars. She had also told him about the zodiac. The zodiac was a group of constellations associated with the Guardians. Some believed that one's zodiacal sign revealed much about one's character. To Mizu, the stars were a marvel of nature, tiny lamps to light the night. Of course, they were actually large balls of fire. Mizu started. Where had that thought come from? Had his mother told him that? Had anyone else? He did not think so. Then why did he think such a strange thing about the stars?

He tried to ignore that idea and enjoy the night. The breeze was cool and sharp. His mother sat on the ground near the tree on which he perched, cooking a pair of wild fowls over a blue fire. She had shown him the powder used to make that fire—arghyll powder—and taught him the words to bring the fire to life from the powder. The powder and the words were from the North, the land of the eighes. He didn't like the fire. He had seen it consume their house in Bolsana. He was afraid of its power. He preferred the distant twinkling light of the stars to the blazing glow of arghyll fire.

Suddenly, the stars were gone. Mizu blinked, but they did not reappear. What had happened while he had been distracted, thinking about arghyll fire? A low rumble solved the mystery. Clouds! Dark clouds. Eshoinh had begun a few temporas ago. It often rained heavily those days. When it did, they stretched a canvas between trees to shelter the horses. Mother and son slept inside the cart. Mizu liked eshoinh. The rain was a source of joy and wonder to him. The way it came down in drops but stung hard nonetheless. The way it made the leaves of trees glisten. The way it seemed to draw new life out of the earth's heart. A streak of lightning spiked across the sky, momentarily cloaking a section of the forest in dirty yellow light.

Mizu climbed down from the tree and went to help his mother. It was time to prepare for the upcoming downpour. He hoped that the game was cooked. He was beginning to feel quite hungry. Whenever they travelled through forests, Misa always hunted for food. Lately, he had begun to accompany her. She had also taught him how to trap animals, kill them humanely and skin them. He was even starting to learn how to cook game, though Misa never left him to tend to the cooking food by himself. Now, he saw, the birds were done. Misa was already putting the fire out. She dropped a few grains of the arghyll fire in a jar and placed it in the cart, extinguishing the rest of the campfire. She wrapped the meat in large leaves and left it inside the cart as well. Then mother and son busied themselves in erecting the shelter for the horses. They worked side by side in companionable silence. By the time Marsil and Marsillon were tied up under the canvas sheet and relatively safe from the rain, the wind had begun to blow in earnest. Fat drops of rain were coming down fast. Misa and Mizu climbed into their cart, where they settled down to the delicious meal of roasted wild fowl in the dim light of the arghyll fire in the jar.

'Where do the stars go when we cannot see them?' Mizu asked suddenly.

Misa laughed. She enjoyed answering the strange questions that her son put to her.

'The stars do not go anywhere, Mizu. They stay up in the sky as usual.'

'Then why can't we see them?'

'You mean, like now? Or like in the daytime?'

'Both times.'

'See, the light of the stars comes from very far. So they do not shine very strongly. The sun is much nearer to us. Its light is much more powerful. So, in the daytime, we cannot see the stars because the sun is so bright that its light makes the stars pale into the background—like a firefly in a lighted room. Do you understand that?'

'Yes!'

'When it rains or the sky is cloudy, we cannot see the stars because the clouds are nearer to us than the stars. They block our view. Understand?'

'No, not really.'

Misa held up her hand and asked Mizu if he could see it. He answered in the affirmative. Then she held a piece of cloth in front of it and asked him again if he could see her hand. This time he understood.

'Oh! I see now,' he said eagerly.

'Good!' Misa said. They had finished eating by then. The rain had turned torrential with bursts of lightning forking across the sky. Mizu jumped when thunder cracked loudly. To distract him, she began to quiz him about the stars.

'How do we detect directions using the stars?' she asked.

'We use the North Star,' Mizu answered confidently. 'Its position is fixed, so once we locate it, we can use it to judge the other directions.'

'How do we find the North Star?'

'We use the Great Bear to find the North Star. An imaginary line drawn through its first two stars towards the Little Bear will lead us to the North Star. The North Star is the last star of the Little Bear.'

'Well done!' said Misa, surprised at the cogent explanation. 'Why else is the Great Bear significant?'

Mizu replied without pause for thinking, 'Also known as Madu's Bear, it is the third sign of the zodiac. Though mostly associated with Madu, its dates are the twenty-fourth of Matisal to the first of Sachir. It is said that it is the bear that Madu rides when she visits Yennthem. It is also sometimes called the Big Dipper, which refers to Madu's emblem.'

Misa was impressed with her son's recollection. He was repeating the information almost exactly as she had conveyed it. By then, the rain had turned into a storm and was sweeping inside the cart. The meagre light inside the jar was flickering madly, casting wildly dancing shadows on the cart's walls. As long as he was focused on the answers, Mizu did not notice the terrible weather. So Misa continued the quiz, hoping that the storm would end soon.

'What are the other signs of the zodiac?' she asked.

'Apart from the Great Bear, there are fifteen signs of the zodiac. They are the Lyre, the Ram, the Bull, the Flying Fish, the Furnace, the Cup, the Hydra, the Arrow, the Phoenix, the Peacock, the Unicorn, the Balance, the Compass, the Shield and the Chisel.'

Before Misa could ask her next question, Mizu suddenly enquired, 'Why do you believe that the zodiacal signs cannot tell our characters?'

Misa was taken aback by the query, but she tried to explain as simply as she could. 'You see, Mizu, how the stars work to tell the fortunes of individuals and nations is not simple. It is knowledge that cannot be acquired by all. It requires hard work and great intellectual discipline to acquire that knowledge. Even then, it is unpredictable and hard to grasp. The stars, like destiny, have paths and intentions of their own. Most people know this, so they try to tell themselves that they too can share in this esoteric art by believing that the zodiac can tell one's character or that a birth chart can predict one's future. Besides, if that were true, everyone born in the same time period would be all alike, and how ridiculous is that, isn't it?'

Mizu did not understand the explanation about the study of stars being an esoteric art, but he appreciated the last bit about people being different. There were so many kinds of people. No two were just the same. Even those who shared his own zodiac sign, the Compass, were very different from him. So it could not be true, of course, that the zodiac signs could tell about a person's character.

He was beginning to feel very sleepy by then. He was also drenched to the bone, he realised, and terribly cold. He wished that the rain would stop. He liked rain but not being cold and wet. His heart also went out to Marsil and Marsillon, whose shelter was probably insufficient protection in such weather. Almost as if the rain had understood him, suddenly it stopped. However, the wind continued to blow fiercely, dark clouds continued to rumble threateningly and lightning continued to shatter the night sky again and again. As soon as the rain stopped, Misa relit the campfire. She laid Mizu down in front of it. He was dry and toasty within half a hora, but he had fallen asleep long since, snuggled in his mother's lap, dreaming of the stars.

The next morning, Mizu woke up feeling strangely hot and sore. He was puzzled since he had never felt this way before. He turned to his mother lying next to him. She was still asleep. He shook her gently. She awoke at once. One glance at his flushed face and glazed eyes told her that Mizu was in the grip of a high fever. She put Mizu to bed in the back of the cart and started boiling herbs. She made him drink the foul smelling concoction despite his protests. She washed his head in cold water and covered him up with blankets. Mizu was seriously ill for a tempora. During this time, he drifted in and out of consciousness many times a day. He vaguely remembered being made to drink the herbal mixture several times a day even though he hated it. When he finally recovered, he felt very weak and dizzy. He could not recall if they were at the same place where the storm had drenched him or had moved elsewhere. Neither could he recall when his mother had left his side though there had been no dearth of food or firewood during the past tempora.

Another tempora passed before Mizu was well enough to stand on his own feet again. They had continued to travel in the meantime, with Mizu sleeping for long periods at a stretch. When they finally set up camp, Mizu noticed that they had reached the borders of another village, this one on the bank of a river. In the distance, Mizu could also glimpse a city. He had never been to a city before even though he had seen a few from a distance. He wondered whether they would travel through this one or bypass it like they had the others. He sat up in the cart and saw that his mother was feeding the horses in the distance. Marsillon had grown very fond of his adoptive mother. He hardly ever left her side, except when he and Mizu went roaming in the plains or woods together. He still looked no different from a normal colt, though his coat was whiter and shinier than ever.

Misa finished feeding the horses and came to check on her son.

'How are you feeling today?' she asked him, checking his forehead. He looked much better, she decided. The fever had not returned in the past tempora.

'I am fine,' Mizu said.

'Would you like to go for a stroll? The weather is pleasant today. I think that you can manage a little exercise if you don't go far. I must go to the village you see over there to buy some supplies.'

'Are we going to stay here for a while?'

'I don't know. Maybe we will stay until you are completely recovered.'

'What place is this?'

'I don't know the name of this village, but that city you can see in the distance is Lufurdista, the capital of Balignor. Now get dressed and run along to the river. Take Marsillon with you. See if you can catch some fish for us today.'

Misa knew that the long confinement had begun to chafe on the young boy's nerves. He had been longing to be up and about for days now. The permission to go fishing with his best friend in tow would please him. Mizu did not take long to get ready. Soon, he was on his way. He led Marsillon along the riverbank in search of a good spot for angling. He had learnt fishing while at Bolsana. During their travels, he had become quite the fisherman. Soon, Mizu was comfortably settled under a shady tree with his rod baited and stuck at an angle in the ground in front of him. Mizu was a patient but keen-eyed angler with good instincts. His patience and skill were soon rewarded. By the time the sun had risen high in the sky, Mizu had half a dozen catches.

The day was hot and Mizu had not yet recovered his strength completely. As he sat there planning to ask his mother to fry the fish for dinner, he began to drowse. A gentle breeze was blowing. The fragrance of grass and water-soaked earth floated on it. Crickets chirped in the solitude of the riverside. There was a lull in the ambience. Mizu began to doze. Soon he was fast asleep in the shade of the tree, dreaming about roasted fish, fried fish, stuffed fish and a dozen other varieties of fish preparations. He saw himself sitting down at the head of a great table laden with succulent, exotic and delicious food.

To his right and left sat richly attired and lavishly adorned fine looking lords and ladies. They bowed to him respectfully when his gaze fell upon them. Surprised, he looked down to see that he, too, was dressed in rich velvets and silks. He had a shining belt that girdled his silken robe. From it hung a jewelled dagger in a soft leather sheath worked in gold thread. On his head was a narrow diadem wrought in finely crafted silver. He also realised that he was no longer a child but a great lord. Splendidly liveried and perfectly trained attendants rushed about busily, helping people sit down or stand up, serving food or wine, and playing music. There was laughter and merriment all around. But, like the faces of the soldiers on the sea shore, the faces of these people were indiscernible. Suddenly, a loud burst of laughter arose from the far end of the table. Mizu turned to see who had laughed so loudly, and the whole panorama vanished.

With a start, Mizu awoke. He realised that the laughter was real. As he turned to locate the source of the mirth, he received a jolt. The people from his dream had come alive! The very next moment, he realised his mistake and almost laughed aloud at his silliness. On the other side of the river was a group of five or six boys. It looked like they too had come fishing. They seemed to be about his own age, though he could not be sure from a distance. They were dressed in fine, rich clothes. This had made Mizu mistake them for the people from his dream. They were obviously from the nearby city of Lufurdista. They seemed not to have noticed Mizu. He did not mind. He was content to watch them without being seen.

One of the boys, Mizu realised, was doing something very funny. It was this that had caused his companions to laugh out loud. This boy had climbed into a tree that was bent over the river. He was gripping a branch that hung close to the river with his knees and was dangling upside down from it. He was clapping in the water, trying to catch the fish with his bare hands. At first, Mizu too smiled, struck by the absurdity and comicality of the situation. The boy was evidently trying to play the fool to entertain his friends. The next moment, Mizu was struck by something else. In a flash, he saw that which was completely invisible to the boys on the other bank. The boy dangling from the branch was in great danger.

Having grown up in a village and in the woods, Mizu could easily ascertain, even at this distance, that the branch supporting the boy was not strong enough. With each dive, the branch weakened further and lowered a little more. At any moment, it would snap and propel the boy into the water. That might not have been dangerous since the spot was quite near the bank. However, at that very spot, there was a current just below the surface of the water. It would suck the boy in, drown him and carry him downriver in momons unless he was a very strong swimmer. Mizu sensed all this in a momon even though the other boys were completely unaware of the danger.

Mizu shouted to the daredevil boy, 'Get off that branch now. Don't jump into the water! There is a hidden current there!'

The boys on the other side heard his voice but could not understand what he was saying. Mizu went as close to the river's edge as he could and shouted out his warning again. The boy dangling from the branch stopped his tomfoolery and stared at Mizu. Perhaps he heard Mizu's warning or, perhaps, he was tired of his game, but to Mizu's immense relief, he heaved himself back upright to return to the bank. However, just as the boy started moving back, the branch snapped. The boy hurtled into the dangerous water below. His companions were struck speechless at first. Then, with a unanimous scream of terror, they fled towards the city. Mizu wasted no time in deciding what to do. He knew that even an experienced swimmer would have had difficulty if he'd been caught in the whirlpool. This boy, he realised, knew nothing of swimming. He was thrashing his arms around, trying to keep his head above the water as he was swiftly dragged downstream. Mizu knew he would drown soon.

Mizu was about to jump in when a thought stopped him. What if the current was too strong for him? He could not hope to swim through it to the other side, supporting the other boy, if it was. He quickly undid his fishing line from the rod. He tied one end to his waist and the other to a tree, working as fast as he could and hoping that the delay would not be fatal for the other boy. Ordering Marsillon to stay put, he leapt into the water and swam towards the drowning boy with strong, swift strokes. Soon he was at the other boy's side and had hauled him up by his collar.

But now, Mizu realised, he was in danger as well, just as he had suspected. The pull of the current was very strong. Mizu began to doubt if he could swim back to shore, let alone drag the half-drowned boy with him, even with the help of the line. For a momon, he wondered if it would be a better idea to cut the line and make for the opposite shore. He dismissed the plan. They would never make it. His original plan was still the better one. He grabbed the boy with one arm,

When the two had recovered sufficiently, the rescued boy stood up and extended his hand to Mizu.

the line tied to his waist with the other, and began to paddle furiously, winding the line on his arm as they moved towards shore. On the shore, Marsillon neighed restlessly, understanding that his friend was in danger. Thanks to Mizu's strong strokes, the two boys progressed towards the shore slowly but surely. Mizu's only fear was that the fishing line would not hold. Miraculously, it did. Soon the two boys flopped onto the shore, exhausted with the ordeal. Marsillon came trotting up and licked Mizu's face. Mizu stroked the faithful, intelligent horse's neck gratefully, whispering into his ear. The other boy lay prostrated on the bank, coughing up the water he had swallowed.

When the two had recovered sufficiently, the rescued boy stood up and extended his hand to Mizu.

'Thank you for saving my life,' he said. 'I am in your debt forever. They say in my country that if a man saves your life, the only way to repay him is by saving his or by giving up yours for him.'

Mizu was both awed and embarrassed by such a grand speech. He studied the other boy quietly. The rescued boy had a lean build and was slightly shorter than him. He had sharp features, black eyes and black hair that now stuck damply to his face and forehead. Mizu was unused to such grandiloquence. Nor had he encountered such finery as he now noticed the boy wearing. 'It was nothing,' he replied shyly.

'I am Prince Amishar, son of King Amiroth of Balignor,' said the rescued boy. 'I am sure my father would be pleased to meet you. What's your name?'

'I am Mizu,' replied the rescuer awkwardly. 'I live with my mother, Misa.'

'Do you live in Durnum?' Amishar asked.

'What is Durnum?' Mizu asked.

'It's the village over there,' Amishar answered, pointing to the group of huts near which Mizu and his mother were camped. He was surprised that this strange boy did not the name of the village where he apparently lived.

'No, we don't live there. We have just arrived here,' Mizu said.

'Are you planning to stay here now?' Amishar asked politely, realising why Mizu did not know the name of the village.

'I don't know,' Mizu replied. 'My mother has gone to purchase supplies in the village. We probably won't stay long here. We are always travelling. We never stay anywhere for long.'

Amishar was intrigued by this boy. He had never before met a boy who lived with his mother alone, or who was always travelling. He wanted to know where Mizu's father was but felt that it would be rude to ask. With a great effort, he suppressed his curiosity.

Mizu wondered what to do with his unexpected guest, for that was how he saw Amishar. He debated whether to say goodbye and return to his mother or to invite Amishar to lunch. As the two boys stood facing each other, smiling, but neither sure about what to do next, hoof beats sounded on the other side of the river. The boys turned to see a group of horsemen galloping towards the river. They were led by a proud, lordly man dressed in robes as fine as Amishar's. His countenance was clouded by deep anxiety. As he raced to the riverside, King Amiroth noticed the two boys on the opposite bank. Relief washed over him. He turned his horse and, without waiting for his followers, rode into the river. The powerful horse was barely able to wade against the strong current, but the masterful rider skilfully guided him across.

The reunion of father and son was indeed touching. There were tears in the eyes of the king of Balignor. For the third time in his life, he had almost lost his beloved son. He forgot the rest of the world in his delight and relief at finding Amishar alive and safe. He hugged Amishar and kissed his face and his hair, Amishar returning the affection in equal measure. For the moment, they were merely an ardent father and an adoring son, not the king and the prince of the most powerful kingdom of men. When Amiroth released Amishar from his embrace, the latter told him about Mizu and how the boy had rescued him, risking his own life. When he turned to introduce Mizu to his father, however, he found that Mizu had vanished.

'Where did he go?' said Amishar, puzzled.

'What did he tell you about himself?' King Amiroth asked.

Amishar repeated all that Mizu had told him, which was not much. By then, the other horsemen, who had crossed the river using a bridge that was a mile upriver, had joined them. King Amiroth told them to spread out in search of a boy about Amishar's age and to bring him and his mother to him. He was grateful to the boy and wished to reward him.

In the meantime, Mizu had returned to their camp. He found his mother pacing anxiously. He told her about what had happened and how he had left the father and son in a loving embrace.

'Did you bid them farewell before you left?' Misa asked.

'No, I...I did not...want to disturb them,' Mizu said, uncomfortably. The truth was that on seeing Amishar with King Amiroth, he had felt, for the first time in his life, an acute longing in his heart for his missing parent. He had shared such a relationship with Leormane, but he knew that the chief of Bolsana was not his father. He wished he had a father who loved him as much as King Amiroth loved Amishar. It was this thought that had prompted him to escape unannounced from the riverbank.

Misa sensed that there was more to the matter than Mizu was letting on, but she did not push him to talk about it. She took his hand and walked to the riverbank. King Amiroth and Amishar were standing under a tree there, waiting for the others to return from their search. Misa curtseyed to King Amiroth and introduced herself. Then she apologised on Mizu's behalf for absenting himself without waiting to be introduced to him.

'No matter, Madam,' said King Amiroth generously. 'I am immensely grateful to your son for what he has done today. Words cannot express how precious my son is to me or how indebted I truly am to your son. The loss of Amishar is a loss I would not have survived,' he declared with great feeling in his voice.

Misa smiled and said, 'Then, Your Majesty, I am glad that my son did what he did. Any harm to the esteemed prince of Balignor would have been tragic indeed.'

'Madam, I wish to express my gratitude with more than just words. I award your son a thousand gold coins, which will be fetched immediately from the treasury!'

His announcement was met with a gasp from his followers, who had returned while he and Misa had been talking. He frowned at them. They blanched, bowed hurriedly and mounted their horses to rush to do his bidding.

Misa, too, was thunderstruck by the announcement. A thousand gold coins! That was a rich gift indeed! It could go a long way in securing Mizu's future and education. But could she afford to take it? News—and rumour—of such a reward would spread far and wide, inflating a thousand to ten times as much. It would shine a light upon them, bringing down the attention of robbers, crooks and maybe even her enemies upon them. No, she could not accept such a gift.

She curtseyed deeply to King Amiroth before the king's followers could hasten to obey him and said, 'Your Majesty, you honour us with such a kingly gift. I am struck speechless by your generosity. However, I am afraid to accept it. For, I am a single woman with a small child and fear what dangers such a priceless reward might bring upon us.'

King Amiroth pondered on her refusal. Then he said, 'You speak the truth, Madam. Such a reward would bring great danger upon you. Therefore, to protect you and your son, I will assign soldiers to guard you.'

Misa's heart sank. The situation, she thought, was going from bad to worse. She spoke as softly and politely as she could, trying to refuse this offer as well without offending the king. 'I do not know how to thank Your Majesty for this kindness,' she said. 'But my son and I live a nomadic life. We are here today; a tempora hence, we might be on our way to Atmut; a mondan hence, we might be in Storsnem. I would not want to force your soldiers to give up their homes and wander along with us. I do beg your pardon, but I cannot accept this wonderful offer either, my lord.'

King Amiroth frowned. His attendants began to look nervous. Misa began to wonder whether she had angered King Amiroth. Then he smiled, and everyone relaxed.

'I have found the perfect solution, Madam Misa,' he declared. 'I will give you land in Durnum village. You will find Durnum village a safe and prosperous location to settle in. You will no longer have to wonder like a nomad. You can farm the land and build a house here. I will ensure that you want for nothing that you need to establish yourself in the village.'

Misa knew that to refuse this offer would be an unbelievable insult. She had already turned down two rewards. To be refused a third time would be greatly humiliating for the king. She wondered whether he would forgive it despite his professed gratitude to Mizu for saving his son. She did not feel happy about the indirect pressure that King Amiroth was applying on her to change her lifestyle simply because he wanted to repay Mizu for saving his son and would not be denied his satisfaction of accomplishing it. But, for Mizu's sake, she could not afford to antagonise the king of Balignor. She bowed to signify her acceptance. She knew that she would have to settle down sooner or later if she wanted Mizu to have a normal life and education. Near Lufurdista was as good a place as any for that purpose. Besides, the patronage of the king of Balignor could ensure her and Mizu's safety far better than a solitary life on the road could, she surmised.

'I have no words to thank Your Majesty for your magnanimity. I accept with great gratitude the lordly gift that you have bestowed upon such humble folk as us,' she said.

'Wonderful!' declared King Amiroth happily. 'I give you ten acres of land in the east of the village. It is good land but unoccupied by dint of being in the immediate proximity of the forest. I assume that the location would not inconvenience you since you seem used to travelling through forests. I will also have materials, men and tools sent to help you clear the land for farming and to help you build your house.'

'Thank you, my lord,' Misa said with gratitude. 'It will be enough if you send only materials and tools. I can manage on my own. What you are doing for us is beyond belief. I do not wish to inconvenience you further. I do not have words to thank you enough.'

'As you say, Madam,' agreed King Amiroth. 'But there is one other thing that I must insist on.'

'What is it, my lord?' asked Misa cautiously.

'You and Mizu must come and dine with us in the palace. Queen Lamella, the daughter of the great King Graniphor of Ashperth, will be delighted to make your acquaintance. Since you will be busy with your new living arrangements today, we shall schedule the invitation for another day. But we must have a celebration soon.'

Misa agreed with another deep curtsey, looking grateful and humble. However, a strange look had come into her eyes at the mention of Graniphor of Ashperth. None save Mizu, who had shyly stood by his mother during the entire conversation, noticed this. He remembered how she had averted the topic of Ashperth the last time it had arisen as well, and wondered why.

Chapter 32

HALIFERN AND THE TWINS

(2 Madal 5009 A.E. to 16 Lokrin 5009 A.E.)

Halifern searched diligently and rigorously for a tree to build his house in. The difficulty in choosing was not due to a lack of options. It was due to his dislike for the available options. Like all the other coming-of-age rituals, house-building was more ceremonial than necessary. Many young fraels simply moved into empty houses of relatives or built a house in the same tree where their parents or friends resided. Halifern was not one of these fraels. He had a definite purpose in mind when he began to search for a suitable tree. He wanted one that would satisfy three criteria—first, it had to be far from his parents' house; second, it had to be wide enough for him to build a substantial library inside; and third, it had to be segregated enough for him to go unnoticed by his neighbours if he so wanted. He received many offers of help from his family, relations and friends. He politely turned them down, claiming that he wanted to do this the *proper way*—that is, by himself.

After mondans of searching, at the beginning of Madal in 5009 A.E., he finally found a tree that suited him perfectly. It was close to the eastern border of Numosyn, near the nurseries. The section of the forest where it stood was densely wooded but sparsely populated. The fraels who lived there were mostly planters. This meant that Halifern would be left alone by them for the most part, although complete isolation was unheard of in the lives of fraels. It was said that they were so gregarious that even bitter enemies would call a truce if stranded together for more than a hora. The tree Halifern chose was a tall and thick one with dense foliage and adventitious roots, giving it an appearance of ruggedness and inhospitality. It was perfect for Halifern. He began boring into the thick trunk after calculating the correct measurements for building his house.

He soon discovered that house-building was an easy task only in theory. He began to wonder whether he would ever get the place ready in time. He started working at night as well as by day to complete at least one habitable room so that he would not fail the test. One night, he was working on carving out his bedroom, the second thing he was building after the hallway, and the first 'room' that would be acceptable to the Council, when he heard taps coming from the doorway. Surprised and annoyed, he went to check whether his mother had come to persuade him again to give up his crazy idea and return to their home tree. An elderly relative, who had lived in the same tree for decadi, had died a few anni ago, and her house had been lying vacant. Halifern's parents had been certain that he would move into it once he came of age. They were still hoping that he would do so. To persuade him to return, his mother had already visited him four times since he had declared that he had found a suitable tree and was moving out. Each time, the conversation had proceeded along similar lines and ended in the same dissatisfaction for his mother. Halifern did not want another repetition of the discussion. To his delight, however, his visitor turned out to be not his mother but Waroned.

'Welcome to my humble abode,' Halifern said to his friend, stepping aside for the tall frael to enter. 'Where's Woroned? I thought you never went anywhere without each other.'

'We don't,' confirmed Waroned. 'He's upstairs.'

'Upstairs?' asked Halifern, puzzled.

'Yes, above your *humble abode*. Though it is no abode at all, to be honest. You don't seem to be getting along terribly fast, are you?' he added, looking around at the barely chiselled out hallway with its gnarly walls and knotty floor.

'Let us put it this way,' said Halifern. 'I am definitely not going to become a carpenter. But what is Woroned doing up there?'

'Examining it as prospective property,' answered the subject of the question, now entering behind his brother. He had to bend his head to enter. 'My!' he exclaimed. 'What a lovely house you have, Prince Halifern!'

Halifern made a face. The twins had an exaggerated and zany sense of humour. Perhaps it was their defence mechanism against all the hostilities that they faced routinely, Halifern thought. He watched them as they debated the merits and demerits of the tree as the location of a house. They were much taller than regular fraels; they were tall even for tall fraels! In fact, they could have easily passed off as humans but for their lithe figures, pointy ears and sharp, frael-like features. They had long, tapering and nimble fingers and bony arms and legs. Most fraels disliked them because they were so tall. Halifern found this prejudice absurd. They were outcasts of a sort, tolerated but never respected. They looked exactly alike, and hardly anyone could tell them apart. They were the only boys in their family. All five of their sisters were average looking but cheerful and hard-working fraelinas like their mother. Their father was a reticent but even-tempered frael. No one in the family was as mischievous-minded or had as bizarre a sense of humour as Waroned and Woroned. Their idea of funny did nothing to endear them to the general populace. Halifern was probably their only friend even though he was seven anni younger.

'Why are you two so interested in this tree's suitability as a dwelling?' he now asked the twins, who were always bickering about something or the other.

They hardly ever seemed to agree on anything except how to cause mischief. Now, Waroned liked the tree, but Woroned did not.

'One cannot just build a house without taking all factors into consideration,' Waroned said sagely.

'Thank you for your concern,' said Halifern. 'But I have already made up my mind.'

The twins laughed aloud and clapped him sympathetically on the back. 'Poor fool,' said Woroned. 'He thinks we are doing all this for him!'

'You aren't?' asked Halifern.

'Not at all,' replied Waroned cheerfully.

'For whom are you doing it then?' Halifern questioned, puzzled.

'Us!' they said together.

'We're going to be your neighbours,' added Waroned gleefully.

'No we're not!' objected Woroned.

'No you're not,' agreed Halifern.

'You don't want us to stay here?' asked Woroned, sounding hurt, even though he had himself just refused to live there.

'I don't want *anyone* besides me staying here,' Halifern asserted, knowing full well that he wouldn't get a moment's peace if the twins decided to settle in the same tree.

'I thought you were our friend,' said Waroned, sounding hurt.

'And I thought you two had a house of your own,' shot back Halifern.

'We had to give it up for our little sister,' explained Woroned sadly. 'She just bullied us into giving it up for her. And being the youngest, she always gets whatever she wants.'

'You got bullied out of your house by your baby sister! That's precious!' Halifern laughed.

'She's no longer a baby,' warned Woroned. 'I think she has her eye on you. If I were you, I'd be careful.'

'Wh…what do you mean, she has her eye on me?' Halifern now asked, suddenly serious again.

'It means that she has made up her mind to marry you,' explained Waroned earnestly. 'Why do you think she wanted to dance with you that night? Your turning down of Fwelhyn has convinced Weryntza that you are madly in love with her.'

Halifern looked stunned. He did not know what to say. He had never had any romantic feelings towards Weryntza. But before he could reply, the twins burst into laughter. They hooted and howled, holding onto their stomachs.

'Oh! The look on his face! Now *that's* precious!' wheezed Waroned.

'My knees are weak with laughter,' groaned Woroned.

'Wait till I tell Weryntza what you said,' riled Halifern. This had the desired effect of immediately sobering up the twins.

'Now, why are you really here?' demanded Halifern. 'I am, as you can see, a little busy.'

He had expected another wisecrack but, to his surprise, Woroned replied seriously, 'To be honest, we really were wondering whether we could live here. You seem to be the only frael outside of our family who doesn't mind our presence. Everyone else hates us.'

'They don't hate you, they just can't bring themselves to accept that you are different,' said Halifern sympathetically. He guessed that the ostracism against them had increased. They were probably being forced to leave Numosyn. 'Folks are always suspicious of that which is different, and we fraels are particularly so. It's no one's fault really,' he said philosophically. His sage remark did not cheer up the twins.

'Do you know what they are saying these days?' said Waroned sharply.

'What?' enquired Halifern.

'That we are as tall as humans because…because… our mother…,' Waroned could not finish. He was trembling with rage. His brother placed a hand on his shoulder to calm him down.

'But that's outrageous and slanderous!' exclaimed Halifern, stung by the malice behind the rumour.

'Our parents are reasonable fraels, but they want peaceful lives,' said Woroned. 'Besides, we still have two unwed sisters.'

'You don't need to worry about Weryntza; she has already decided to marry me,' Halifern tried to joke weakly. It had the desired effect. The twins smiled wanly.

'Is that the best you can come up with?' teased Waroned, clicking his tongue.

'So, can we stay here?' asked Woroned.

Halifern pondered the question for a while. Then he said, 'I have a solution to this problem. I don't know if you two will agree, but I have a plan that might help all parties concerned.'

'We agree,' said the twins without waiting for Halifern to elaborate.

'But you haven't even heard the plan yet!' protested Halifern.

'We trust you,' said Waroned. 'After all, you have been our only friend for far too long.'

'Yeah!' added Woroned. 'When everyone at school bullied us because of our height, you were the only one who made us feel worth anything. This height has been such a curse!'

'Are you joking? I always thought it was a gift. You had the longest reach of any of us. I envied you so much.'

'You must have been dropped on your head as a baby,' declared Woroned.

'Right from the roof of the treehouse to the ground,' added Waroned, grinning manically. 'I can just imagine the scene!'

'Do you want to listen to the plan, or would you rather talk about the causes of my insanity?' demanded Halifern.

'I prefer the latter,' answered Waroned at once.

'But you're such a good friend that we will do the former,' rejoined Woroned.

'Good!' said Halifern. 'Now listen. You can stay here, with me. But not in a separate house. You will stay *upstairs*.'

The twins looked up at the roughly hewn-out wood of the tree.

'Um…in case you haven't noticed, Halifern, there is no upstairs,' said Waroned.

'There will be,' said Halifern, his eyes shining. 'Once you help me build it. With a secret trapdoor set into its floor.'

Halifern then outlined his plan in detail to his friends. The idea greatly appealed to their unusual sense of humour. The three friends debated and discussed the plan of the house until it seemed to Halifern that they would never get started on the actual construction. Finally, when they did, he was glad he had had the unexpected idea. Under the twins' able carpentry, the house took shape quickly enough. In the end, it had three levels. The bottom level was partly Halifern's study and library and partly a suite of guest rooms. The one above it comprised Halifern's living quarters. The third level was the secret dwelling of the twins. When Halifern inaugurated his beautiful house nine days before the deadline, everyone was astounded, not least Halifern's family.

Later that day, the three friends sat on a platform that formed part of the ceiling of the secret top floor, celebrating. After congratulating each other, they lay staring at a canopy of stars through densely leafed branches.

'You know, we can't live like this forever,' said Woroned. 'Sooner or later, someone will realise that we are still here in Numosyn and will discover our secret house.'

'Yes,' agreed Waroned. 'It might get you into trouble too, Halifern.'

'Which is why I have another idea,' said Halifern.

'What?' asked the twins together.

'You should leave. Not just Numosyn but fraelish territories altogether.'

'What!' said the twins, sitting up. 'Do you support the others now?'

'Don't worry, I do not,' Halifern soothed their ruffled feelings. 'We all know that you will never be allowed to live in peace here. So, if you are game, I'd like you to live among the humans in disguise.'

'Why?' asked Waroned.

'Because I'd like to know what is going on in their countries through sources that are neither as xenophobic nor as secretive as the Council's. Someday, I will have to join it. I want to do more than just turn up and unquestioningly agree to everything the Elders say. I'd like to know about events in the dharvhish lands as well, but you two are too tall to disguise yourselves as dharvhs. Besides, I think I can trust Rauz Augurk to keep me in the know about important events.'

'So, you want us to be spies?' asked Woroned.

'And if I do?' returned Halifern.

'I'll gladly accept,' answered Woroned warmly.

'Me too,' chimed in Waroned. 'But what do we get in return?' he added, just to rag Halifern.

Playing along, Halifern quipped with a pained expression, 'Am I not marrying your sister?'

Chapter 33

DREAMCATCHER

(18 Madal 5009 A.E. to 21 Madal 5009 A.E.)

After the success of the raid on Esvilar, the outlaws began to consider Avator as one of their own. Igrag kept an eye on him at all times, trying to gauge the boy's potential and intentions. Forsith, though liked and respected for his skill with horses, remained in the background and preferred to do so. Unlike Avator, he sought anonymity rather than prominence among the outlaws. And he sought it not just for himself but also for Avita who, as the only permanent kereighee in the camp, stuck out like a sore thumb. She also preferred to be left alone even though she did not dislike the outlaws as much as Forsith did. She entertained herself when neither of her guardians could keep her company. She had always been very even-tempered. Of late, however, she had started becoming somewhat irritable, sometimes pouting or snapping when things weren't as per her preference. Her guardians attributed it to her continued ailment. What child could have borne so much trauma so patiently? They did everything in their power to make her comfortable, hoping that it would restore her joyful nature.

Avita, on the other hand, was feeling increasingly guilty about hiding the matter of her dreams from them, and this was part of the reason for her growing irritability. Two anni had passed since she had first dreamt of the human boy as a warrior. Her dreams had only grown more confusing and intense since then. She had begun to understand that they were important in some way and that she should tell Avator about them. She sensed the strain that her condition put on him and Forsith. One day, in the fourth tempora of Madal in 5009 A.E., she finally opened up to her brother.

They were alone in their tent that day because Forsith had gone to check on a pregnant mare early in the morning. Avita came and sat by Avator as he was about to leave on his own duties. He saw the extremely guilty and scared look on her face and asked her what was wrong. At first, she said nothing. She continued to stare at the floor, leaning against her brother's arm, and biting her lips. Avator said nothing, waiting for her to open up on her own. Suddenly, Avita started talking very fast. She was afraid that if she spoke slowly or hesitated for even a momon, she would never get her courage up again. She blurted out everything about the dreams: how they had started as nightmares of the boy being tormented by the old witch and how they had changed into complicated ones that she could make neither head nor tail of.

Avator listened patiently and without interrupting her as long as she talked. His face remained inscrutable even after she finished speaking. Avita had been afraid that he would scold her for concealing something like this for so long. But he didn't. Avator said nothing at all. After they had been sitting silently for several minuras, he stood up and left the tent. He was deep in thought. What Avita had told him had disturbed him enormously. He recalled the words of the witch of Temtema. He had brushed aside her conclusion that Avita had formed a spiritual bond with the human boy when their hands had touched all those anni ago in that narrow alley in Kinqur. Now it was clear that she had been correct. Avita dreamt of the boy because of that connection. Something else was equally clear to him now. Avita's wounds were directly related to her nightmares of the boy being beaten. Whatever injuries were sustained by the human boy were also sustained by Avita through the spiritual connection.

Avator felt angry and bitter. Why did it have to happen to them? Did they not have enough to deal with already? Life was so unfair! He wanted to blame someone for all their problems and, finding no one else, he directed his anger towards the human boy whom he had seen but once in his life. *He* was the root of all their problems, Avator told himself, though he knew well enough that it was not the truth. If only he could find that boy…what would he do? He did not really know. Several unsavoury thoughts crossed his mind, but he couldn't be sure that their impact on Avita would not be severe. He suspected that anything that happened to the human boy would happen to Avita too. He wanted to scream out of frustration and helplessness. That, of course, would do absolutely nothing to alleviate Avita's problems. He tormented himself with ideas of how he would like to repay the human boy for bringing such misery to her until his head began to hurt. Finally, as reason reasserted itself, he gave up his hateful fantasies with a sigh and made his way towards Igrag's tent.

The leader of the outlaws was exercising when Avator reached his tent. He had to wait outside until Igrag was finished with his routine. When he entered, the captain of the outlaws was wiping himself down with a wet towel, cleaning off the sweat that the vigorous exercise had generated. Avator could not help but admire the eighe's powerful physique. He was stunned at the number of scars on his body, though, and wondered how strong one would have to be to endure so much and still remain unbroken in body and mind.

'You should exercise,' Igrag said to Avator, putting on his shirt. 'You are rather scrawny. You won't remain a scout forever, you know. You'll need to build up your strength.'

Avator, who was lean but neither scrawny nor weak, nodded in acknowledgement of the advice. Then he came straight to the point. He had begun to understand Igrag well enough to know that the outlaw captain preferred the direct approach, especially when being told about problems. Avator told him in brief what Avita had said to him about her dreams. He also added what the witch of Temtema had said when they had visited her long ago.

Igrag listened to him and asked, 'What help do you want from me?'

'You told me once that you knew a powerful magus who might be able to help my sister. Could you tell me his address so that I can take my sister to him?'

Igrag was thoughtful for a few momons. Then he said, 'I will tell you his address. In fact, I will send one of my eighes to lead you there. But Eronsom must remain here at the camp. Do you accept?'

Avator knew what Igrag was doing. The captain still did not trust them enough to let all of them leave camp together. He did not blame Igrag. As leader of the outlaws, it was his job to be suspicious. If Avator refused or insisted that Forsith should accompany them, Igrag would conclude that they were planning to escape. The generosity of sending one of his outlaws to accompany them was also more than just a measure of support. The kereighe would make sure that Avator and Avita did not make a run for it once they were out in the open. Avator was more interested in consulting the magus than in escaping. He gratefully accepted Igrag's offer without letting on that he had seen through it.

When Forsith heard about it, he was grim. He did not like the idea. He was suspicious of Igrag's designs in sending the children to this magus with one of his outlaws to look after them. Avator tried to allay his suspicions by pointing out that if they acted as if such an arrangement was quite acceptable to them, Igrag would never suspect their actual intentions. Forsith was not convinced by this argument, but he said no more. He knew that Avator was determined to leave no stone unturned to help his sister. Nothing he said would stop the boy from visiting this magus that Igrag had recommended. He helped the two children pack for their journey.

The place where the magus lived was two days' journey from the camp. Qually, one of Igrag's most trusted lieutenants, accompanied them there. The magus lived in a cave upon the seacoast. When Avator's party reached his dwelling, it was almost sunset. To their surprise, there were many eighes waiting to meet the magus. The petitioners stood or sat in a long queue upon the beach outside the cave. Avator, Avita and Qually joined the rear of the queue, awaiting their turn. As they waited, they watched the sun dip down in the west until it melted away into the Talsear Ocean, leaking red into the rolling waves. Suddenly, everything turned dark. A couple of kereighes—acolytes of the magus—emerged from the cave and lit torches for the benefit of the waiting visitors.

A few more had joined the queue behind Avator, Avita and Qually by then. The magus was taking varying lengths of time to deal with each visitor. Qually began to get bored and restless waiting for their turn. He began to fidget, making Avita more nervous about the impending encounter. Finally, Avator suggested to him that he could find a suitable spot and make camp since it appeared that they would be spending the night there. Though not too enthusiastic about the idea, Qually acceded that Avator was right. It would be a while before the children would get to meet the magus. Who knew how long the consultation would take? Igrag had instructed him to keep an eye on them without being too invasive. He decided to settle down nearby, behind some rocks higher up on the shore, above the tide line. He could keep an eye on the children from there without having to stand in queue himself. He lit a fire and sat down to eat his dinner. Avator and Avita had their dinner waiting outside the magus's cave. One by one, the supplicants were accompanied inside the cave by some of the acolytes while others turned away newcomers, requesting them to return the next morning. Gradually, the queue grew shorter.

By the time their turn came, Avita was sleepy, but she bravely walked into the cave with Avator and two acolytes. It was a long, narrow cave that meandered underground. Several chambers had been dug out of the stony ground to the right and left of the original tunnel. While Avator was asked to wait in one such chamber, Avita was led by one of the acolytes into another one nearby. At first, Avator was reluctant to let his sister out of sight, but the other acolyte explained that the magus would be able to concentrate only if he met Avita alone. Avator could stand outside the magus's consultation chamber if he wasn't completely comfortable with waiting in the other chamber, the acolyte told him. Avator accepted his offer and took up position outside the chamber where the magus was about to have his interview with Avita.

Filmy lace curtains were drawn across the mouth of the chamber, yet neither light nor sound and not even smell emanated from within. The magus's powers were responsible for that, Avator suspected. However, he managed to catch a glimpse of the inside of the chamber when the curtains were drawn slightly aside to let Avita in. He noticed that the chamber was moderately proportioned, well-lighted and strewn with comfortable mattresses and cushions. He waited patiently outside, hoping desperately that finally Avita would get the help that she needed. An acolyte asked him to describe the problem as elaborately as possible so that he could note down the details. He wanted the information from Avator, he said, because Avita was very young. She might not be able to explain her complaint properly to the magus. He reassured the boy that strict confidentiality would be maintained.

Inside, the magus welcomed Avita cordially and asked her to take a seat. He was middle-aged and completely nondescript. He could have been one of the thousands of eighes one passed on the street every day. However, he had a warm and genuine smile, Avita noted. She smiled back hesitantly. He offered her some fruits and sweets. She shook her head. Forsith had taught her not to accept food from strangers. The magus did not press.

'Do not be afraid of me,' he said kindly. 'Please sit.'

Avita sat at a little distance from the magus with her knees drawn up to her chin and her arms around her legs. The interior of the cave was now dark and smoky and smelled of freshly cut grass. When had the light dimmed and the fragrance changed? Hadn't she entered a brightly lit chamber that smelled of incense? The mattress she sat on was very plush and snug. It radiated a mild, welcome warmth that loosened her arms and legs as she sank deep into its softness and slowly uncurled herself to be more comfortable. She could hear the sound of waves even though they were deep underground. The waves rose and fell in a steady, unwavering, humming rhythm somewhere far, far away. Avita began to feel very drowsy.

'What is your name?' the magus asked her in a soft, gentle voice.

Avita hesitated. She now had two names. Which one should she tell him? She decided to use her new name.

'I am Menithyl,' she said.

'A beautiful name for a beautiful girl,' remarked the magus with a smile. An acolyte entered with a parchment. He handed it to the magus and left without a word.

'Do you mind if I read this first?' the magus asked Avita. 'It contains a statement from your brother about the reason for your visit.'

Avita nodded to indicate her permission. While the magus scanned the parchment, Avita looked around. It was an ordinary looking stone chamber lit with torches and lamps in brackets on the walls. She wondered if the magus lived in that chamber or just met his visitors there. It looked very cosy. She hoped that he would quickly finish reading whatever Avator had written. She was having a hard time staying awake!

The magus finished reading and turned to her. 'So, Menithyl, why don't you tell me why you have visited me today?'

'I thought that my brother explained that in that scroll you just read,' Avita answered, confused. If Avator had already explained, why was he asking her?

'Yes, your brother did explain the problem, but I want to hear from you why you have come here today. After all, you may know the situation better than he does, may you not?'

Avita did not understand what he meant, but she did not argue. She began to tell him about the dreams and the injuries. She told him about the human boy that she dreamt of and how she had first met him. She had only a vague memory of that meeting since she had been so young at the time. But she recalled his face very clearly, and her dreams had reinforced the image in her mind. As she spoke, she began to feel more confident. The magus was a good listener. While she rambled on in her childish fashion, he did not interrupt. When she became confused, he asked her simple questions to guide her back to the story. He neither hurried her nor showed impatience when she repeated something that she had already said. He encouraged her by nodding and by making sympathetic sounds. By the time Avita was done telling her story, it was well past midnight.

The magus sat deep in thought for a while. He scribbled on a piece of paper and counted something on his fingertips, like he was calculating. Then he said to Avita, 'I suspect that the witch of Temtema was correct about the cause of your complaint. If you allow me, I would like to put you in a trance and read your mind. I promise that anything I learn about you will be kept strictly confidential.'

'I don't understand,' Avita said, sounding scared.

The magus explained gently. 'I will put you to sleep. You will sleep very soundly and comfortably, without dreams. While you are sleeping, I can read your mind and learn everything about you, even things that you may not know yourself.'

'How can you do that?' Avita asked out of curiosity.

'I can do that because I am a magus,' he explained.

'I mean, how can you learn what I don't know about myself?'

'Our mind,' the magus explained, 'is like a scroll that goes on and on. Everything that happens to us, whether we remember it or not, whether we understand it or not, or whether we realise it or not, gets recorded onto it. For example, can you remember who was the first eighe you saw after you were born?'

Avita shook her head.

'No,' agreed the magus. 'But the scroll in your mind has that information. Magi can read that scroll. That is why I can find out things that even you may not know consciously. And that is why I need your permission. What your mind holds is very private and very sacred. It belongs to you and to no one else. I cannot read your mind if you don't give me permission. I will also never tell anyone what I learn about you today. Do you understand now?'

Avita did not understand completely, but she felt curious about mind-reading. She also sensed that the magus did not want to hurt her, that she could trust him. She nodded to give her permission. The magus made her lie down on the comfortable mattress and close her eyes. He hummed a tune softly and wafted some vapours towards her. Before Avita could yawn, she was fast asleep. When she opened her eyes, she thought that only momons had passed. In truth, over a hora had gone by. The magus was kneeling next to her, gently calling her name. She sat up slowly, feeling more rested than she had in a long time.

'What happened? Couldn't you put me to sleep?' she asked timidly.

'You did very nicely, my dear,' the magus said with a warm smile. 'You slept very soundly. Everything went smoothly.'

'Good. So tell me everything,' Avita remarked excitedly.

The magus looked grim and did not respond to her question. Avita felt worried. Had something gone wrong? If everything had gone smoothly, why was the magus looking worried?

The magus clapped and one of the acolytes entered. The magus asked him to fetch Avator. After Avator was seated, the magus told him what he had told Avita about reading her mind. Avator was not in favour of such an idea. The magus explained to him that he was not asking for Avator's permission to read Avita's mind, that Avita had already given permission and that he had already read her mind. Avator frowned. He did not like this. Why had he agreed to come? What if the magus had learnt the truth about them? What if he told the outlaws?

Avator noticed the magus gazing at him intently and asked, 'So, have you managed to figure out how to cure my sister?'

'Her problem,' the magus said, choosing his words carefully, 'is not a disease that it can be cured. I will repeat what the witch of Temtema told you: she has formed a spiritual connection with the human boy whom the two of you encountered in Kinqur. Why or how is inexplicable. What is happening is that their minds can connect with each other and influence their lives. The dreams are the obvious conduit for this connection, but I think that they are only a fragment of this complex concatenation. She feels not only his emotional pain but also his physical ones and vice versa.'

'What do you mean?' Avator asked baffled. 'And what can I do to help her?'

The magus tried to explain. 'This connection that your sister has with this human boy makes her go through whatever he is going through. So, if he is hurt, she feels the hurt. If he is wounded, she gets wounded. The reverse would be true as well, I think. If she is injured or worried, he would be injured or worried. If she is happy, he would be able to feel that happiness. That is why your sister has been growing as fast as a human—because he is. That is why she wakes up with injuries—because he suffers those same injuries. She is still too young for this link to be manifested outside of her dreams; as she grows older, it will grow stronger. She already dreams of him in forms other than the one you saw him in. She might even come to be able to communicate with him telepathically, and not just in her dreams either. She might be able to sense where he is, see through his eyes, hear and smell what he hears and smells and even influence his actions. The reverse would be equally applicable. He will be able to have the same effect upon your sister.'

'This is insane! How is it even possible?' Avator demanded, agitated. At his side, Avita looked scared. She hadn't understood much of what the magus had said. What she *had* understood had told her that she had been right about the importance of her dreams and of the human boy in her life.

The magus tried to comfort Avator, 'I only told you what I learnt from your sister herself. I do not know how something like this is possible. I have never before encountered anything like this connection. There are many things in existence that are without explanation. It is a hard blow, I know. You must accept it as best as you can.'

'So you can't help her?' Avator asked, his voice heavy with pain and disappointment.

'I did not say that. I cannot make the bond go away, true, but I can help her in another way. I think that the key to this riddle lies in her dreams and in who that boy is. I can give her a dreamcatcher. It will help her control her dreams and remember them better. That might someday provide a clue to how this connection can be broken. The dreamcatcher will also prevent her from receiving the injuries that the human boy suffers.'

Avator nodded. The magus had been his last hope. Now it was gone. He could do nothing for his sister. He had failed! Tears stung his eyes, but he gritted his teeth and forced them away. The magus was talking to Avita now, showing her the dreamcatcher and explaining what it was. It was an ordinary looking circular talisman with symbols carved into it. She was to wear it in her hair when she slept at night. She liked the idea of being able to control her dreams. When the magus had explained the use of the dreamcatcher to her and had answered all her questions, he sent her out. Avator guessed that the magus wanted to discuss remuneration. He took a pouch of coins from his belt, wondering whether he would have enough to pay. He was about to ask the magus what he owed him when the magus said something that stopped him in his tracks.

'You can pay me when you become king. There is no need to deplete your small stock of wealth yet!' the magus said calmly.

'What do you mean?' Avator asked, pretending not to understand while his heart hammered against his chest with tension.

The magus answered, 'I learnt many things from Avita, including her true name—things that even she does not know that she knows. I know who you truly are. Worry not; your secret is safe with me. Anything I find out from my patrons is confidential. I am proud to say that I have never violated the trust of any of my clients, no matter who they might have been or what they might have done. I must say, though, that I am highly impressed with your fortitude.'

'Thank you,' responded Avator. 'I do not know what to say. You are truly a highly powerful magus, as Igrag said. I am sure that you understand that our lives are in your hands. I have no choice but to trust your word. But if there was any way to ensure that our secret would remain secret...'

'Are you trying to threaten me, Avator, or bribe me?' the magus asked in an amused tone.

'Whatever works, I suppose,' Avator said candidly.

The magus smiled his warm, engaging smile. 'You don't have to worry, young prince. Rather, young king, since your father is no more. I am a magus. I neither care for wealth nor fear death. However, I do admire your courage. It was a bold gesture, especially when you know that you have neither the money to pay me nor the means to kill me. I am not offended,' he continued, raising a hand to silence Avator, who had been about to apologise. 'I shall keep your secret not because you can bribe me or threaten me but because it is a matter of honour. Avita permitted me to access knowledge that was buried deep within her subconscious. If I speak of it to anyone, I would violate her trust. She came to me for help. I am honour-bound to keep whatever I learn from her confidential.'

'Thank you,' Avator said, in two minds about what the magus had said. Part of him wanted to believe the magus, but part of him was suspicious.

'I would like to give you two bits of advice, though, if you are willing to listen,' the magus said.

'Please tell me what you would have me do,' Avator said respectfully.

'I merely suggest that you should not try to hide your identity from your sister. She has subconsciously picked up enough clues to piece together the whole story someday, just as I did. By the time she does, she will be older and less inclined to forgive your concealment of the truth from her. She is a special girl, and she deserves to know her reality. Maybe not right away, but sooner rather than later.'

'As you say, she is a special girl. That is why I want to keep her away from all of this. Revenge is *my* business, not hers.'

'Revenge is never any one individual's business. There are always others involved. Some are involved in your revenge even today, and some will become involved in the future. Your sister cannot remain uninvolved. If you don't involve her, someone else will.'

Avator did not respond to this. 'What is the other suggestion you have for me?' he asked, changing the subject.

'There is a magus who lives in the north of Blarzonia, upon White Mountain. His name is Nishtar Arvarles. He is extremely powerful but, more importantly, he is the greatest teacher in Yennthem. At least, that is what one hears. I am sure that if you studied under him, it would greatly help you in achieving your goal.'

Avator thanked the magus for his advice and promised to consider it, more to conclude the conversation than out of a genuine desire to take the magus's suggestions. Avita was waiting outside for him and, when he joined her, asked him what he and the magus had talked about. Avator told her that they had been talking about the future. This satisfied Avita, who was feeling hungry now though she had already had dinner. They joined Qually, who had fallen asleep. He had some leftovers, and they quietly finished it off. Qually asked nothing, and Avator said nothing. He knew, though, that he would have to answer to Igrag. He sat thinking almost until dawn, trying to decide what to tell the outlaw captain and to make up his mind about whether he was happy about meeting the magus or not.

Chapter 34

AN UNUSUAL FRIENDSHIP

(22 Madal 5009 A.E. to 14 Chirshkom 5009 A.E.)

King Amiroth was true to his word. Thanks to the resources provided by him, and the use of what a bystander might have called eighe magic, Misa had a sizeable tract of land cleared and a house with four solid walls and a roof built within three days. Mizu helped her to the best of his ability. His assistance was invaluable in preparing the fields for cultivation. He had a gift for farming, which Misa had first noticed in Bolsana. Mizu was entirely unaware of this gift though it allowed him to excel at his agricultural chores. Therefore, when King Amiroth's emissaries came to fetch the two of them three days after Amishar's rescue by Mizu, they were astounded to see the progress that Misa had made.

They had brought a horse for Misa and a pony for Mizu to ride to the palace. Misa would have chosen to ride Marsil, but she did not wish to leave young Marsillon alone in a new place. So mother and son made their way to the palace of the king of Balignor, dressed in their best clothes, accompanied by a small retinue of soldiers and followed by the inquisitive gazes of all the villagers. Mizu was an accomplished rider, but the unfamiliar crowd and the extraordinary circumstances made him terribly uncomfortable. He looked with awe at his mother who rode at his side, proud and cool as a vernurt morning.

What he did not know was that she was feeling far from relaxed despite her calm exterior. It had been anni since she had last been inside a palace. What worried her more were the questions she might have to answer. It was one thing to lie about or refuse to talk about her past to ordinary villagers. To lie to the king and queen of Balignor was another matter altogether. She wished she could excuse herself from the occasion. Then she chided herself. Was she not the queen of Samion? Why then was she feeling nervous at meeting Amiroth and Lamella, who were human royalty? Had not Feyanor, Lamella's brother, been her closest friend at one time? Why then did she feel nervous about the meeting? Life had finally provided her with a golden opportunity; why was she dreading it instead of embracing it? All her internal remonstration with herself, however, could not assuage her anxiety completely.

Unaware of the turmoil in his mother's mind, Mizu wished that the ceremony would be over quickly. He was afraid of embarrassing his mother in front of the king, queen and prince. The king, queen and prince! He had never imagined that he would ever think of them as real persons whom he knew! Royalty had always been mythical to him, just like the kaitsyas or magi. And now he was going to not only meet them but dine with them as well. As he came within view of Lufurdista palace, however, he forgot about his discomfort. He was rendered speechless by the glorious vision before his eyes. It was unlike anything he had ever seen!

The palace towered over everything in the vast city. Its domes, towers and turrets of golden sandstone rose high and proud into the evening sky. The setting sun was scattered into a thousand rays by the golden mirrors on the central turret and surrounding spires, bathing the palace in gold. The sun appeared to have descended on it! Banners displaying the coat of arms of the royal line—a golden sun with a bronze eagle flying beneath it upon a sky-blue background—fluttered in the breeze proudly. Tall trees laden with fragrant flowers or luscious fruit surrounded the premises and lined smoothly paved pathways. Tall statuary stood in lush gardens or marble pavilions everywhere. Everything gleamed, glowed and glittered!

The Lord Chamberlain welcomed Mizu and Misa and led them to the reception chamber in the residential quarters where the banquet had been arranged. He announced them to King Amiroth, Queen Lamella and Prince Amishar before bowing and departing. Mother and son bowed deferentially to the royal family and stood at the door quietly. Amishar hastened forward to welcome them, followed immediately by his parents. The king again thanked Mizu and shook his hand. The queen embraced him with maternal affection. She then took Misa's hands in her own and thanked her for raising a son as brave and as morally upright as Mizu.

'If you hadn't raised him to be so, my son would be dead today,' she declared, her eyes misting at the heartbreaking thought.

Touched and a little embarrassed by all the gratitude, Misa simply replied, 'He only did what anyone in his place would have done, Your Majesty. We are both very glad that the prince is safe.' This was the first time that she had met Lamella, daughter of King Graniphor and sister of Prince Feyanor. She had heard much about Lamella from her brother in her youth when they had been students together, but fate had intervened in the lives of both before she could meet Feyanor's beloved sister. Queen Lamella was as different from her brother as a rose from a stone. She was a beautiful petite woman with an oval face and delicate features. Her only similarity with her brother was the auburn hair that they had both inherited from their father. While Feyanor had inherited their father's build and features as well, Lamella looked more like her mother, the late Queen Allaren.

Before Lamella could respond to Misa's comment, dinner was announced. The royal family proceeded to seat themselves along with their guests. No one besides the five was present for dinner. Misa felt the full attention of the king and queen on her. Their gaze held an odd mixture of gratitude, politeness and curiosity. The questions, she anticipated, would come sooner or later. Mizu, she was relieved to see, was maintaining a dignified air despite the grandeur and novelty of the experience. He must have been feeling overawed by everything, yet his demeanour was courteous and composed. He acted with perfect etiquette and flawless manners. She was so proud of him!

Mizu was amazed by the luxury and magnificence of the palace. The inside had proven as rich and splendorous as the outside. The high ceilinged rooms were decorated with rich tapestries, dazzling mosaics and murals, soft carpets and beautifully sculpted statues. Aides and attendants in fine livery were everywhere. Alert soldiers with wickedly sharp weapons stood at attention to protect their sovereign and the royal family. The monarch's slightest wish was a command, and servants almost fell over each other to obey and serve.

When dinner was served, he was equally astonished by the feast. It was beyond anything he had seen in his dream. The table groaned with scores of aromatic and succulent dishes of every conceivable variety and flavour as attendant followed by attendant brought in trays and plates and tureens and placed them in front of the diners. Mizu had never seen this much food in his life! It was enough to feed the entire village of Bolsana for three days, he thought. King Amiroth explained that this banquet was in honour of Mizu and to celebrate the safe return of the prince to his parents. This announcement stunned Mizu so much that he was hardly able to eat a morsel.

Dinner was accompanied by desultory conversation and polite niceties from all sides. Once the food was eaten and the wine was drunk, the king and queen asked Misa to join them for a tour of the grounds while Amishar showed her son around the palace. Misa acquiesced with an elegant curtsey and left with Amiroth and Lamella. Amishar grabbed Mizu's hand and dragged him off impatiently. He couldn't wait to show off his chambers, his books, his toys and his weapons to his new friend. They were followed by a bevy of attendants and guards as they trotted through the palace with Amishar pointing out the various chambers with the nonchalance of a shepherd showing off his flock and Mizu drinking in the splendour, spellbound. He pinched himself to make sure he was not dreaming again. Soon they reached Amishar's chambers. The prince's rooms were bigger than any house that Mizu had ever seen. Several families of Bolsana could have easily lived in them! He was awestruck by the sheer number, variety and finery of the prince's clothes and toys. For the first time in his life, he began to understand that he and his mother were poor. However, it caused him neither jealousy nor frustration. He was quite content to be poor and only marvelled at his new friend's good fortune at being immensely wealthy.

What did send a sharp pang through his heart was that his friend had a father while he did not. It was brought home to him when Amishar asked him about it outright.

'Where is your father?' the prince asked out of curiosity. He had kept quiet on the matter before out of politeness, but in the furious struggle between curiosity and courtesy in his heart, curiosity had finally overcome courtesy.

'I don't have one,' Mizu replied hesitantly.

'Why not?' Amishar asked puzzled. 'Everyone seems to have a father. Did your father die?'

'I don't know,' Mizu answered, feeling uncomfortable in the extreme.

Amishar sensed his discomfort and, feeling abashed, tried to assuage Mizu's uneasiness. 'It does not matter,' he said grandly. 'You can think of my father as your father. He is, after all, the father of all his subjects—at least, that's what my teachers tell me. The king is like a father to his subjects. Now that you are his subject, he is like a father to you too.'

He paused hesitantly, not sure of himself for the first time in his life as he saw no indication of enthusiasm for this idea on Mizu's face. He decided to change the topic of conversation and continued, 'He likes you a lot. He was talking about how brave you are and how noble and courageous your mother is.'

'I am grateful for the honour I have been shown,' Mizu said, trying to sound grand. It was all very new to him, and he was trying to speak as he had heard his mother speaking to the king and queen.

'Don't be shy!' Amishar said, pushing him into an armchair that was so plush that Mizu sank into the upholstery. 'Be comfortable. I really wish we could be friends.'

'You must already have many friends,' Mizu commented, trying to act comfortable even if he didn't feel so.

'No, none,' said Amishar sounding rather wistful.

'What about those boys who were with you at the riverbank that day?' asked Mizu, beginning to feel curious about Amishar. 'I thought they were your friends.'

'Only in name. They keep me company simply because I am the prince. They always agree to everything I say to keep me happy so that I give them expensive gifts.'

'And do you?'

'Do I what?'

'Give them expensive gifts?'

Amishar shrugged. 'It keeps them happy.'

'Why do you keep them around if you don't care for them?' Mizu asked, genuinely baffled. He had never come across a boy like Amishar before. He wondered if all princes were like Amishar.

'Because my mother doesn't like me to be by myself,' the prince replied earnestly. 'I used to roam about alone after my cousin, Lord Aminor, left for Ashperth, but mother wanted me to have friends. These boys are sons of noblemen, so my parents thought that they would be suitable companions for me. But now that I have met you, I don't need them any longer. You and I will be friends, won't we?'

'But I am just a poor boy from the village while you are a prince,' Mizu responded. 'How can we be friends?'

'Why not?' declared Amishar. 'If we like each other, why should we not be friends? Do you like me?'

Mizu nodded shyly. Despite Amishar's unusual behaviour, Mizu was beginning to feel interested in him.

'Good. I like you too,' announced Amishar, clapping his hands. 'And not just because you saved my life. I think I would have liked you even otherwise. I think we were meant to become friends. Don't you think so?'

Mizu thought that under normal circumstances, the two of them would never have met, but he was too polite to say so. Amishar seemed not to notice his reticence.

'Should we go and play in the garden?' the prince asked and dragged off his new friend before Mizu could answer. The garden was as breathtakingly beautiful as the palace had been. Mizu liked it even better than the opulent indoors. Amishar showed Mizu the archery range that had been specially built for him, the horse that had been bought for him by his father and all the other facilities for his training.

'All this is because I have to become a great warrior. You know, I am good at everything except swimming. I just can't swim! How do *you* manage?'

Mizu, who could not lay claim to such accomplishments, simply answered, 'I have always liked swimming. Maybe, that is why I am good at it. I could teach you if you want.'

'Will you? That would be fun. And you can come here and train with me. I think that's a great idea. We could do everything together. Whatever I have, you can share. We will be the best of friends! What do you think?'

'Perhaps you should ask your father,' suggested Mizu, who was beginning to feel overwhelmed by the prince's generosity, enthusiasm and energy.

'He won't mind, I'm sure. He never refuses me anything. I will have to convince my mother though. She is very strict. But she likes you. I don't think she will object.'

'And I will have to ask my mother,' added Mizu, suddenly feeling a sense of kinship with the prince on learning about his mother's strictness. 'Though I have no idea what she will say.'

'Let us hope for the best,' said the prince cheerfully.

Almost on cue, an attendant arrived to announce that Their Majesties and Madam Misa were asking for the boys. It was getting late. Misa wanted to return to Durnum. The boys followed the attendant to where their parents waited in the entrance hall of the residential quarters. After formal goodbyes, mother and son started back for their new house, again accompanied by a retinue of guards. Misa was rather absent-minded. She was thinking of the answers she had given King Amiroth and Queen Lamella in response to their queries about her past and about Mizu's absent father. The enquiries had been made out of politeness, true, but she had not been able to avoid them. She felt that she had succeeded in answering them without revealing anything of import. For the time being, she was still safe and anonymous. The lies would pose a problem if she had to seek their help in regaining Mizu's birthright. That was a problem for another day, she told herself. Mostly, she was relieved that the visit had passed satisfactorily.

When they were back in their newly built house, she asked Mizu about his tour of the palace with Amishar. She hesitated when Mizu told her about Amishar's offer to be friends and to share everything.

'If you don't want me to, I will not be friends with him,' Mizu said. 'But I do like him. He is friendly and straightforward and generous.'

'But he is a prince. He is extremely wealthy, is he not?'

'Yes, he is,' Mizu agreed in a small voice.

'You might feel bad about your own lack of wealth. You might aspire for something that is beyond your reach, leading to terrible consequences. That is what worries me,' Misa confessed.

'I know we are poor,' said Mizu, 'but I am not unhappy about it. Amishar may be wealthy, but I do not feel jealous of him. I think that despite being surrounded by so many things and people, he is actually lonely.'

Misa was surprised by her son's keen insight. Still not sure, she reluctantly agreed to let him be friends with Amishar. She could not deny that the friendship would help Mizu in many ways. It would provide him with opportunities that an ordinary life would not. Amishar was heir to the throne of Balignor. Such a connection could be of great benefit to Mizu later in life. Besides, she scolded herself, princes *were* her son's true peers.

Her doubts about Amishar's wealth and status coming between the two boys were proven unfounded as the boys' friendship matured over the next few mondans. Amishar was charming and unassuming despite being a prince, though he took much of life for granted. He was as innocent as Mizu in his own way, and Misa saw in him things that reminded her of his illustrious uncle Feyanor: the same manic energy, the same charm, the same keenness to accomplish things. He eagerly participated in the mundane and ordinary activities that were part of Mizu's life. It was all new and exciting to him. More importantly, Mizu remained the same. He felt neither jealous of nor inferior to Amishar. To him, his poverty and Amishar's wealth were just facts of life, not things that interfered with how he felt or acted.

The king and queen were very fond of Mizu as well. King Amiroth, in particular, often gave him rich gifts. Sometimes, Misa returned these, apologising that the presence of such priceless objects in her house would attract burglars and, as a single mother, she did not wish to risk such harm. The offer to provide security was met with polite refusal. Amiroth could not understand Misa. It still bothered him that Misa had never visited the palace since that first dinner banquet. Whenever she was invited, she found a justifiable reason to excuse herself at the last minura. He did not want to force her hand since she was the mother of the boy who had saved Amishar, and his gratitude was still profound.

Every time he saw Mizu, he was reminded of what he would have lost that day had it not been for Mizu. With time, he began to like Mizu for his own qualities rather than the fact that he had saved Amishar. Mizu was humble though not obsequious, intelligent though not impudent, courageous though not foolhardy and eager to learn though not impetuous. He had a strong sense of self-respect though he was always grateful for the affection and kindness shown to him. He decided that the friendship with Mizu was good for his son. It would not only provide Amishar with a likeable and loyal companion but would also teach him about the lives of common people, which would help him be a better prince and, in future, a better king.

As promised, King Amiroth set out for Drauzern on the first of Lokrin in 5009 A.E. He was accompanied by a large entourage. There were troops of soldiers, of course, but also a few of his ministers, some military officers, several administrative officials, carts loaded with supplies, goats, sheep, bullocks and horses, and an army of aides, common labourers, blacksmiths, valets, cooks, servants, grooms, butchers, drivers, entertainers, jacks-of-all-trades and an assortment of others who had come either because their usefulness was anticipated or because they hoped to profit from the venture in some way. The king's route lay along the southern bank of the Quazisha, above the Wenymod Mountains, across the Chensey, across the Helawel and along the northern edge of the Norowichh Forest until arriving at the Great Desert of Laudhern.

Queen Lamella, Prince Amishar, Lord Beleston, Lord Parkiod, Lord Jumradam, other dignitaries of the royal court and household and hordes of ordinary citizens saw off their king at the border of the capital city. Mizu, as usual, accompanied Amishar. King Amiroth repeated his instructions for the running of the kingdom. Lord Aminor was expected to return soon but, until then, Lord Beleston was regent. The young prince bravely promised to look after his mother for his father, and Mizu promised to keep Amishar out of trouble. Queen Lamella cried and asked King Amiroth to return as soon as he could and to keep her informed about his progress. Then, wishing the king luck in his venture, they returned to the palace to their duties. Whether the king remained in the capital or not, the kingdom had to be run.

King Amiroth and his immense retinue proceeded at a leisurely pace along the southern bank of the Quazisha, headed for their first major camp at a distance of five hundred and sixty miles to the east, on the banks of the river where it flowed closest to the Wenymod Mountains. There they would recoup and replenish supplies, especially barrels of water. Going was slow due to the size of the expedition. But spirits were high, and a thirst for adventure coursed through the veins of the explorers. So, the long journey passed without tedium.

A tempora into the journey, the king and his retinue were still less than a hundred miles from Lufurdista. They had set up temporary camp for the night when two messengers were announced. They were from King Hanmer and King

Dorstoph. Amiroth decided to meet Hanmer's messenger first in deference to King Hanmer's seniority. The messenger bowed and delivered two rolls of parchment. One of these, he said, was a letter and was to be read first. Amiroth accepted both and asked the messenger to refresh himself while waiting for a reply. Hoping that the letter contained a positive reply to his request for passing through Storsnem on the way to Drauzern, Amiroth opened the scroll that the messenger had pointed out as the letter. It was written in King Hanmer's well-known circumlocutious style. It began with salutations and enquiries into the welfare of Amiroth and his family members. Then it mentioned the primary reason for which King Hanmer had written.

'I have heard of the purpose for which you travel east, my lord, although you mentioned it not in your missive in which you sought permission to pass through Storsnem on your way to Drauzern,' King Hanmer's letter said. 'Tales of a search for the City of Stone have been heard in my kingdom too. One would have to be a fool to discard these rumours as idle. I feel I am justified in presuming that your expedition to the east is connected to the rumours. Some might say that it is unwise to embark upon such a venture. It is not for me to comment on the wisdom or otherwise of your decision. I am sure that you have good reasons for doing what you do. I shall not create any obstructions in the progress of your expedition. All I say is this: ask yourself whether you are doing this for your glory or for the glory of your kingdom. Once before, a king sought that which you now seek. Do you know what the consequence was? The scroll that I have sent along with this letter has remained buried under reams of priceless documents that have been in the collection of the ruling house of Storsnem for centuries. I would like you to have it, for I believe that you would do well to heed the tale it tells. One more thing, my lord. Do not trust the dharvhs. They have secret motives of their own for all that they do. You may never know what danger they are leading you into until it is too late. It is indeed courageous of you to undertake such a perilous quest. But remember always who your friends are. Be careful not to walk into traps laid by the enemies of men. For, your success or failure can change the course of history for all mankind.'

Disturbed and intrigued by King Hanmer's letter, Amiroth looked at the other missive. It looked like an old scroll tied with a fraying red ribbon. For its protection, it was sealed inside a narrow cloth tube with the personal seal of the king of Storsnem. He broke the seal and gingerly drew the scroll out. The ribbon broke as he was trying to untie it. Grimacing, he unfurled the scroll as gently as he could. It was an ancient scroll, very fragile. King Amiroth carefully laid it on his desk to read the strange tale that it told. His mind filled with questions as the tale of the vagaries of fortune faced by his illustrious ancestor unfolded. When he was done, he painstakingly rolled it back up, sealed it inside the cloth tube under his seal and sent the scroll away to Lufurdista for safekeeping. He then sat down to compose a reply to King Hanmer:

'My noble kinsman, I am eternally grateful to you for the precious gift that you have given me. I am honoured for the wisdom that you have shared with me in your letter. I shall not insult you by denying that you have presumed correctly; indeed, I travel in search of the City of Stone. I assure you that I have not forgotten what I owe to my country as its king. The glory of Balignor takes precedence over the glory of Amiroth, as it always shall. I shall keep your warnings, and the lessons to be learnt from our great ancestor's life, in my heart and before my eyes as I progress upon my path. I thank you for granting me permission to pass through your realm with my retinue. I promise you that we shall cause no disturbance to you or your people. I hope that my actions will bring glory not only to Balignor but to all our kingdoms in the west.' Amiroth read his reply and, satisfied with it, handed it to the messenger who had brought Hanmer's message.

He then met with King Dorstoph's messenger. He, too, had a letter from his master. This letter was far more direct. 'I have learnt of your expedition to Ghrangghirm,' it said. 'I have no objection to allowing you to pass through Cordemim on that account. However, for the sake of my peace of mind, I consulted the Sorceress on this matter. She appeared unhappy though not surprised when I told her about your intentions. She looked into a bowl of some fragrant liquid to scry. She talked as she looked into your future. "Will you not stop to wonder why you undertake such a hazardous campaign, King Amiroth?" she said, almost as if you were sitting there. "What will you gain from it? Will you not consider returning home to your wife and son? Do you not remember what you once lost but found again by a miracle? Would you have that miracle be in vain? What will you gain, my lord, by staking all?" Then she looked up and said to me with tears in her eyes, "Tell your valiant kinsman that it would be better if he were to return to Balignor and leave the dharvhs to take care of their business. But if he must go, he must take care not to turn from the path that he has chosen, for as his success will bring with it great glory for men, so will his failure bring great doom to them." And then she went into a trance and foretold,

> *"You seek that which has never been found,*
> *Above nor underneath the ground,*
> *But once by a man who knew*
> *Not what he was set to do!*
> *There they wait with bated breath*
> *To be awoken from their death*

Once more by feeble hands that fail,

Led by feeble hearts that quail!

And perilous is the path you walk;

So beware all honeyed talk

For, they come guising venom dark,

And strangers often leave their mark."

'A shadow seemed to fall upon all present as she said these words, and the glow in the room seemed to flee into the shadows around the edges of the room. My heart was chilled, and it was with difficulty that I could draw courage enough to recover my countenance. I shall not hinder you from passing through my lands, but I exhort you to pay heed to the Sorceress and return to Balignor.'

This letter disturbed Amiroth far more than the other had. He read and reread the prophecy that the Sorceress had made about him. He wondered what she had seen in his future. Had she seen his death? His heart turned suddenly heavy with foreboding. For a moment, he considered taking the Sorceress's advice and turning back. Then his pride asserted itself, and he steeled his resolve. He replied to King Dorstoph, thanking him for permission to pass through his lands and for his heartfelt concern that had prompted him to seek the counsel of the Sorceress on Amiroth's behalf. He thought that King Dorstoph had gone to her due to concern that Amiroth might be on his way to attack Cordemim; however, he did not express that opinion in his reply. He assured King Dorstoph that he would be utmost careful.

It took Amiroth's contingent over another mondan and a half to reach the first major camp. There they camped for five days before pushing on for the second camp, on the bank of the Chensey. Another five days passed while they restocked, and five more days passed in getting the entire expedition across the wide river. They continued to move east until they camped for the third time and then crossed the Helawel. The fourth leg of their journey took them along the northern edge of the Norowichh forest to the banks of the Sumarin, to their fourth major camp. They reached there on the ninth of Beybasel in 5009 A.E., a hundred and sixty-three days from when they had started from Lufurdista.

Chapter 36

HEAVY IS THE HEAD

(9 Lokrin 5009 A.E. to 16 Lokrin 5009 A.E.)

Lord Aminor returned to Lufurdista on the ninth of Lokrin, eight days after King Amiroth's departure, and after a long absence of an annus and six mondans. Much had changed in Balignor and in Lufurdista in that period of time. Some of these transitions had come to his notice in Ontar, courtesy of the Order of the Lily, including the offer from the dharvhs and its acceptance by King Amiroth. The small, quotidian differences had not reached his ears and, by their unexpectedness, stood out all the more. For a few momons, he felt a little dissatisfied that things had carried on unhindered in his absence. The shock to his sense of indispensability hurt his ego mildly. The very next moment, he was overwhelmed by the concerns of his fellow ministers and officials, and his sense of self-importance was restored. Things had gone on in his absence, true, but he had been missed terribly.

He wished that he could have returned earlier. He had learnt about the proposal of the dharvhs and Amiroth's answer long before the king himself had sent for him. The order had been efficient, as promised by Feyanor. Aminor had wanted to stop Amiroth then. He had wanted to return immediately. His oath to the order had stopped him. To allow Amiroth to learn that he knew anything of the matter before he was officially informed by Amiroth would have given the order away. So, he had remained in Ashperth, waiting for Amiroth to send for him. He had left almost immediately after the messenger from Balignor had arrived. But he had been too late! By the time he reached the capital city, Amiroth was already away on his expedition. Lord Aminor sent a message to King Amiroth, informing the latter of his return. He debated whether to request the king to reconsider his expedition but decided against it. Amiroth had already set the wheels in motion. To try to persuade him to change his mind would be an obvious insult to the king. He hoped that nothing would go wrong with the expedition and prepared himself to handle the onerous responsibility of acting as regent while the king was away, garnering glory for Balignor.

He soon realised that despite the order's updates, he had much to learn about what had been happening in Balignor in his absence. For two days, he ploughed through mountains of paperwork to get a sense of how the kingdom had fared during his absence. He was pleased to find that the treasury was full, that taxes had been collected on time, that crime was no worse, that expenses were not unduly high, that the army was still well-trained, that trade was flourishing and that everything was practically as he had left it. Except for the expedition at the request of the dharvhs, a nagging voice at the back of his mind said. However, the reports were not enough to provide a complete picture. So, from the first Kaidiu after his return, Lord Aminor began to visit the various ministers to learn about the kingdom's condition in detail from their personal testimony.

His first port of call was the prime minister, Lord Beleston. The old man was overjoyed to see him. He was a small, wrinkled man with entirely white hair and beard. He embraced his one-time pupil and welcomed him back with a sense of obvious relief. He looked like he had aged ten anni in the days that Aminor had been gone. Lord Aminor thought that he looked more stooped than usual and was definitely surprised to see the pair of eyeglasses he took out of a silken pouch as they pored over important documents, discussing the minute facets and the many considerations that the writing on the page could not convey.

'You have no idea how difficult it has been without you,' the prime minister complained. 'Actually, you probably *do* have an idea, since no one knows the king better than you.'

Aminor laughed. It was good to be back. The two of them talked for horas, discussing everything of importance. Aminor even had dinner at the prime minister's residence that night. By the time he left, his head was spinning with the amount of information he had received. Some of it, he had already learnt through the order; some of it was new; some of it would have to be conveyed to the order. He again spent several horas with the prime minister the next day. The day after that was spent with Lord Parkiod, the commander-in-chief. Lord Parkiod was very different in both appearance and demeanour to Lord Beleston, but he appeared equally relieved at Lord Aminor's return. With an impressive height and an equally impressive physique as well as a ramrod-straight bearing and neatly trimmed facial hair, he was the epitome of a soldier. However, he too hugged Lord Aminor with evident joy and a most unsoldierly declaration of affection when his close associate visited him at his home. The two often worked very closely to ensure the country's safety and security. Sometimes, it involved undertakings of which no one but the two ever became aware. Lord Parkiod was the closest thing to a friend that Lord Aminor had in Lufurdista. He was one of the few men whom he could trust with his life. Though highly competent, Lord Parkiod was relieved at his friend's return nonetheless and was eager to apprise him of all that had passed in the kingdom during his absence. It was only by the end of the tempora that Lord Aminor was able to respond to Queen Lamella's invitation to visit her and Amishar.

Lamella was as happy as Lord Beleston and Lord Parkiod had been to see Aminor. During his absence, she had come to understand how important Lord

Aminor was in Balignor's governance. With the king gone, the other ministers had been doing their best, but with Aminor's return, it was as if they had found a helmsman again. She fully appreciated this and welcomed him graciously, sparing no effort at hospitality. Young Amishar was there too. He was no less overjoyed than his mother at Aminor's return but lacked the intensity of attachment that he had once displayed towards his godfather. The boy had grown taller during the mondans of Aminor's absence and looked leaner and stronger. Unlike his father, Amishar would grow to be a tall man, Aminor thought. Like his uncle. He noticed that the young prince also looked distracted. Aminor wondered why but did not ask in front of him. After a while, the prince asked for permission to leave, and his guardians excused him.

The queen asked Aminor scores of questions about her father and brother and about Ashperth and Ontar and the palace and its residents. Her thirst for information about her birthplace seemed insatiable. Aminor sat answering her questions for horas. In the end, he was compelled by considerations of time to conclude his visit without fully satisfying her queries. It was already rather late. His stay in the queen's chambers for a longer duration might have given rise to talk, especially in the king's absence. He was also feeling exhausted after a busy tempora and needed rest. He begged to be excused on grounds of tiredness. The queen blushed to think that she was taxing him too much. She hastily apologised and bade goodbye, expressing the hope that they would get the opportunity to talk about Ashperth another day soon. Aminor bowed, genuinely hoping that they would. His stay in Ashperth had renewed his self-control, but his love had grown no less. To his own surprise, this realisation did not perturb him as it once had. He had become more comfortable with his feelings. He no longer felt tortured by his emotions. He wished the queen a good night and was about to leave when he realised that he had forgotten to ask about Amishar's distractedness.

'It's because I did not allow him to bring his best friend, Mizu, with him tonight,' Lamella answered when he asked. 'The two of them are almost inseparable! But I forbade Mizu's presence here today. I wanted Amishar to be here by himself to welcome you back.'

'Mizu?' said Lord Aminor. 'I do not seem to recall that name, my lady.'

'He's a new friend of Amishar's, my lord, a boy his own age from the village on the other side of the river. He and his mother have come to Balignor from the east not very long ago. But you should ask Amishar about his friend; he will tell you more than you might want to know!' Lamella smiled.

Aminor smiled and replied, 'I will.' He was already wondering who this boy was and why he hadn't heard about him before.

The next day, Zyimdiu, was a day of relaxation for most people. Aminor, though, had much to do. He had to meet with some of the other officials and ministers. He had to make certain policy decisions. He had to adjudge some pending matters. He had to send the king an update on the state of things in the kingdom. He had to send messages to Feyanor. And he had to learn about Amishar's new friend, Mizu. He finally managed to get around to the last task by evening. He was eager to find out how the prince's education and training had continued in his absence and asked Amishar to meet him at the shooting gallery that had been created for the young prince's training at one time. He realised as soon as he entered the gallery that the prince still practised there. He also noticed signs of archery practice by someone who was not quite as skilled as Amishar. Before he could ponder this matter further, the prince arrived. Alone. Obviously, he had remembered his mother's injunction about not bringing his friend along while meeting with Aminor.

'How have you been, my dear Prince Amishar?' Lord Aminor asked.

'Well, I suppose, my lord,' Amishar replied rather shyly.

'Why do you *suppose*?' Aminor asked, surprised.

Amishar blushed. 'The truth is that I have been getting into trouble a little. Well, a lot, to be honest,' the young prince confessed, sitting down beside his godfather. He was beginning to feel more comfortable as he remembered Aminor training him to shoot. 'But that was only to begin with. I missed you, you see. Then father got some of the nobles' sons to come and be my friends. They were terrible.'

'Did they mistreat you, Your Highness?' Aminor asked sharply.

Amishar shook his head. 'No, not at all, my lord. They were always very ob… obse…'

'Obsequious?' Aminor finished for the boy. Amishar nodded.

'Yes, that. And they were very dull. I gave them lots of gifts. That was all they cared about anyway. I used to do all kinds of tricks to show off to them, and they would say how brave I was. How clever. That sort of thing. Then I fell into the river, and they ran away, but Mizu saved me.'

'Who is this Mizu? One of the nobles' sons?'

'No, he stays in the village. Durnum village. He and his mother were passing through that day. He was at the riverside with his horse when he saw me fall in. He jumped in and pulled me out.'

'I am glad that he was there to save you,' Aminor said with feeling. He really was grateful to this unknown boy. He felt shaken by the incident that Amishar had narrated so casually. He could not believe that news of such import had failed to reach the order. It should not have happened. Prince Feyanor would have been hugely concerned about his nephew's near-fatal accident. Aminor resolved to enquire into the lapse in intelligence with regard to this incident. He hugged the prince, who felt ostensibly embarrassed. So he let Amishar go and asked him to continue his story.

'Mizu and I are friends now. He can swim very well and knows a great deal about plants and animals, but he has had no training in archery or wrestling or swordplay. So we practise together. I try to help him improve. I got rid of the nobles' sons. I haven't been in much trouble for some time now.' There was a definite hint of regret in Amishar's voice as he sad this. Aminor laughed.

'How old is this Mizu?' he asked.

'He is about my age.'

Aminor was surprised. For such a young boy to have saved another boy must have taken great courage. He was becoming more and more intrigued by Amishar's new friend.

'Where is he from? What do his parents do?' he asked.

'I don't know the name of the village he lived in before coming here. It is somewhere in the east. East of Balignor, I mean. Maybe in Storsnem or Cordemim. His mother has a farm here. Father gave it to her as a token of thanks for Mizu saving my life. He doesn't have a father. I think his father died a long time ago. He does not know anything about his father. His mother is very nice. She is scary, too. Not scary, not really,' he corrected himself. 'Strict. I am a little scared of her, though. She works very hard. They both do. They have two horses.'

Aminor allowed the young prince to babble on about his new friend while he tried to piece together the information that he had received. It had indeed been fortuitous that the boy had been present at the time Amishar had fallen into the river, but had it been pure coincidence, or had it been something more? Who were these people? Amishar seemed to know nothing very definite about their past and did not seem to care either. He, as regent, and as Amishar's godfather, could not afford to be so complacent about mysterious strangers. Why hadn't he heard about them from the order? Perhaps, he thought, Amishar was too young for the order to feel that his activities merited scrutiny. He, though, could not ignore the newcomers. He had to know more, preferably from the horse's mouth. He decided to pay Mizu and his mother a visit.

He said to Amishar, 'I would like to personally thank this boy. The next time you go to meet him, I would like to go with you, Your Highness. To give him a gift. What do you think he would like? Would he like some toys? Maybe a bow and some arrows? Or a saddle and bridle for his horse?'

Amishar enthusiastically agreed. 'I think that he would like that. He really loves his horse. But you will have to get it quickly. I am planning to go there tomorrow.'

So, the next day, Lord Aminor accompanied his godson to Mizu's house across the river. He had heard a good deal more about the boy and his mother in the meantime, mostly from Amishar himself, but also a little from servants and other sources. All he heard indicated that the boy and his mother were good, honest, hard-working, ordinary folk. He wondered what he would find at their house. He was surprised to find that the prince had not exaggerated about their qualities. The boy's mother, Misa, had not had prior intimation of their arrival, but the house was clean and tidy enough to receive visitors nonetheless. After pleasantries were exchanged, the boys went off to play, leaving the adults to talk.

'I hope that you are finding things comfortable and to your liking here,' Aminor said politely, all the while observing Misa, her small house and its belongings, like a hawk.

'My son and I are very comfortable here, thank you, my lord. King Amiroth and Queen Lamella have been extremely generous to us. I could have hardly expected such warmth and kindness from such important personages. I am very grateful,' Misa replied. She observed her visitor closely without giving a hint of doing so. She knew that Lord Aminor was the king's cousin, but they looked nothing alike. Aminor was taller than King Amiroth though not quite as handsome. He had brown eyes and hair, again, unlike the king. The only feature they had in common was a long, straight nose. Perhaps they had both taken after their fathers, she thought.

'And the prince? I hope that he is well-behaved towards you, Madam,' Aminor said.

'He is a very well-mannered young boy though high-spirited, my lord,' she answered. 'He and my son have become good friends. Prince Amishar has inherited his father's warmth and generosity.'

'Indeed he has,' Aminor agreed with a smile. 'And knowing him as well as I do, especially since he will be king someday, I am a little concerned that he trusts everyone too quickly. Trust needs to be placed with care, especially by those whose trust can be so…rewarding.'

Misa stiffened. She sensed that Aminor was not convinced that she and Mizu were dependable and scrupulous. On the one hand, this realisation intrigued her. So, there *was* someone in Lufurdista smart enough to be on the lookout for potential trouble. On the other hand, it disturbed her. Aminor, from what she had heard, could cause her a lot of difficulties if she got on his wrong side. She needed to convince him of the truth—that she and Mizu meant the prince or the kingdom no harm.

'You are absolutely correct, Lord Aminor,' she stated. 'I am happy to see that the young prince has someone like you to guide him. He has missed you greatly. I hope that your trip to Ashperth was pleasant and successful. I am aware that my son and I must appear like suspicious strangers to you, especially considering the royal family's favourable attitude towards us. I do not blame you for not trusting us. I would like to assure you, though, that we are merely ordinary people. We do not mean the prince or the kingdom of Balignor any harm.'

Aminor was surprised by her honesty and perspicacity. She had a refined air and pride of bearing that told him that she was no ordinary peasant woman, although her material conditions suggested a commonplace background. He *had* to learn more about her.

'Thank you for your candour. I shall also be candid then,' he said. 'Perhaps you would not mind answering some questions in the spirit of clearing the air for the sake of the prince. Amishar told me quite a lot about you but was rather vague regarding certain details,' he said.

'Please ask what you wish to, my lord,' Misa said, her voice polite but impersonal.

Aminor began by asking where they had come from, why they had been in the vicinity and where they had been going. He enquired about Mizu's missing father and about her background. He had many questions, some straightforward and some indirect. Misa understood what he was trying to do. She answered all his questions. Some she answered truthfully, some in half-truths and some in blatant lies. She knew that Aminor was too clever to digest all her lies easily. She also knew that there was no way that he could prove that she had lied. Finally, the master-of-the-horse thanked her again, this time for her hospitality, and bid her farewell.

Amishar went with him. He was very excited, and asked his cousin what he had thought of Mizu. Aminor gave satisfactory answers to his queries, showing enthusiasm in the prince's new friend. In truth, he had hardly paid attention to the boy, who had seemed harmless and innocent enough. His whole focus had been on the mother. His mind was churning the answers that Misa had given to his questions. He was sure that she had lied in answer to at least four or five questions, possibly more, but he could not prove it. He did not trust her. The boy seemed trustworthy, though. Mizu had been overjoyed with the gift of the saddle and bridle. He was as innocent as a boy his age was expected to be. Aminor liked him. His mother was a different matter altogether.

He decided that he would have to resort to his order resources to learn more about her. Yet, he wasn't sure if that would be appropriate. He could be chasing wild geese. If so, he would end up abusing the order's resources. He was still new enough to be concerned about how he would be perceived by the other members. Perhaps, he tried to convince himself, there was nothing to worry about. Perhaps the boy and his mother were exactly who they claimed to be. Perhaps it was sheer coincidence that had brought them into the royal family's life. He sighed.

He decided that it would be better to use his own resources first. If his people found anything suspicious, he would involve the order. He sighed again. It was not easy being responsible for the safety and welfare of an entire kingdom! He wondered how Feyanor made it seem so easy. He sighed a third time in as many minuras at the thought of the prince of Ashperth and the complications into which he had entangled Aminor by making him a member of the Order of the Lily.

Chapter 37

MIZU'S NEW LIFE

(10 Supprom 5009 A.E. to 18 Kielom 5009 A.E.)

As unexpected as the decision to stay in Durnum had been, Mizu was glad that they had settled down there. They finally had a house again and did not move about all the time. The generous king of Balignor had given them a substantial tract of land, which Misa cultivated. The river was near their house, so Mizu could go for a swim whenever he wanted. The prince of Balignor visited them every now and then, and Mizu and his mother had been invited to the palace a few times. Amishar and Mizu were well on the way to becoming close friends, spending a lot of time together, particularly since King Amiroth had set off on his expedition. Mizu's life was complete in many ways. In the daytime, he helped his mother in the fields, did chores around the house and caught fish for food. In the evenings, he either visited Amishar, received the prince or played with Marsillon. The colt was an annus old now and looked large enough to be ridden. But Misa had told him that Marsillon was still too young to carry a rider, even one as young and light as Mizu. At night, Mizu studied with his mother. She taught him many things. He loved to study and to listen to her stories.

One evening, Mizu was playing by himself when he heard someone crying. Because their house was on the outskirts of the village, not many people passed that way. Mizu was surprised by the sobbing. When he went to check who was crying, he found a boy, younger than himself, sitting in a nook behind his house and sobbing. His dirty face was streaked, and he was sniffling balls of snot. He tried to run when he saw Mizu approaching but tripped and fell. The boy immediately started bawling even more loudly. Mizu pulled him up and comforted him. He took the boy inside and cleaned his face. He gave an apple to the youngster. The small boy ate the apple greedily. Then he sat down, looking around.

'What's your name? Why were you crying?' Mizu asked him.

'My name is Laroosa,' he said. 'I was crying because Zibar stole my toy and beat me up.'

Mizu did not know Zibar, but the boy sounded like a bully to him.

'Who is Zibar?' he asked Laroosa.

'He is the village chief's son. He thinks that his father owns the village. He bullies everyone who's not in his father's good books, even grownups!' Laroosa complained. He seemed to have overcome his initial fright of Mizu and looked quite cheerful now.

'Doesn't anyone tell his father?' Mizu asked, surprised.

'His father never scolds him. If anyone young tells the chief, he finds himself beaten up. If a grown up complains, he has his chickens stolen or his cow set loose or his window broken or his vegetable patch dug up or something like that,' Laroosa said with a sour face.

'But it's awful!' Mizu exclaimed. Laroosa smiled wanly, glad of the sympathy.

'Let's go,' Mizu declared, standing up. Before the other boy could protest, Mizu grabbed his hand and almost dragged him away. He stopped only when he found the bully Zibar. The son of the chief of Durnum was a large boy with flabby limbs and a round, almost stupid face. His eyes, however, held a shrewd and cruel glint. When Mizu saw him, Zibar was sitting under a tree and laughing while two of his cronies were annoying an old woman. They had taken her stick away and were tossing it to each other while she hobbled about, trying to retrieve it. Two more of Zibar's cronies stood by him, also laughing. He seemed to have collected some of the largest boys in the village to his side. Or, perhaps, they had gravitated to his side on their own because he provided them the opportunity to exhibit their meanness without fear of retribution. Mizu rarely felt angry, if ever, but now he did. Hot bile rose from the pit of his stomach and soured his mouth. His heart beat faster, and his face felt hot. His head felt like something was gripping it in a vice. He wanted to fall upon Zibar and his cronies and beat them to a pulp. He balled his fists and gritted his teeth, ready to fall upon his enemies. Suddenly he stood stock still and blinked. Enemies? Where had that thought come from? For that matter, the feeling of intense anger too was alien to him. And with this thought, the rage dissipated. He still felt angry, but the emotion was far more reasonable and controlled. He decided to teach the bullies a lesson.

'Are you going to fight them?' Laroosa whispered doubtfully at his elbow. Mizu shook his head. It wasn't that he was afraid of them; it just didn't seem like a good idea to him.

'What will you do?' the younger boy asked.

Mizu looked around, seeking inspiration. The tree under which Zibar and his cronies sat caught his eye. It had dense foliage. Some kind of hard, green berry grew on it. Mizu had an idea.

'Wait and watch!' Mizu said to Laroosa before scooting off in the opposite direction to the bullies. He circled around from a distance. The group under the tree did not notice him. They were too busy laughing at the old woman whom Zibar's cronies were tormenting. Thanks in part to his mother's training, in part to his own talents, Mizu was completely silent as he climbed into the densest part of the tree. There he hid, invisible to those below, as he filled his pockets with scores of the berries. By then, the two that had been tormenting the old woman had given up their cruel game and joined the others under the tree. The old woman hobbled away with her chipped stick, panting and cursing her tormentors.

The five boys below the tree were still laughing about how they had harassed the old woman. Silently, Mizu took his sling out of a pocket. Aiming carefully, he shot a berry at one of Zibar's cronies.

'Ow!' said the boy as the berry hit his head hard. He looked about, trying to see who had hit him while rubbing the spot where the berry had struck him. Mizu hit him with another berry. He yelped, looking up at the tree suspiciously. When he detected no one there, he frowned, puzzled, and rejoined the conversation. Mizu pelted him and another boy this time. Both leapt up.

'What's going on?' demanded Zibar.

'Someone's pelting us with berries,' complained the boy who had been Mizu's first target. Zibar guffawed.

'Sissy!' he poked the boy. 'As if a berry could hurt.'

Right on cue, Mizu pelted Zibar with half a dozen. They struck him on his nose, chin, right eye and head. Bellowing with pain and holding on to his bleeding nose, one eye closed, Zibar thundered to his cronies to climb into the tree to catch whoever had dared to attack them. The others too had received generous doses of pelting by then. On receiving Zibar's order, they tried to climb into the tree. They were too large and heavy. They kept slithering and falling all over themselves as Zibar screamed at them and Mizu pelted them mercilessly with berries as hard as stones. It was growing dark and they could not see anything clearly, which added to their misery. Finally, they gave up. Despite Zibar's threats, they turned tail and ran. Zibar, the fattest of them, was slower than the rest and fell behind. Huffing and puffing, he followed his cronies as fast as he could, holding on to his large belly and groaning loudly. When the bullies had disappeared, Mizu descended from the tree, satisfied with his handiwork. Laroosa, who had been hidden all this time, joined him. The two had a good laugh. Then they left for their respective homes, Mizu happy at having made another friend.

The next day, when Mizu went into the village to fetch milk, he spotted Laroosa. The young boy was sitting on the porch of a house, looking glum. When Mizu approached him, Laroosa cast a sharp glance of panic at Mizu and fled inside. Mizu was puzzled by his behaviour. However, he did not follow the boy inside. He went to the dairy, filled his pail and paid the farmer. He was on his way back when five large shapes blocked his path. Zibar and his cronies grinned evilly. The looks on their faces told Mizu that they had learnt who the perpetrator of their previous day's misery was. He was trapped. There was no way that he could trick or fight those five boys.

'So you think you are very smart, eh?' Zibar sneered. 'Who did you get your brains from—your father?'

He stepped forward and tried to snatch the pail out of Mizu's hands. Mizu nimbly moved out of the way. Zibar's hand swiped at air. Angry, he snarled, taking a step forward. In a flash, Mizu grabbed the pail and threw all the milk into Zibar's face with as much force as he could. Before Zibar could recover or his cronies could understand what had happened, Mizu fled. He was much faster than the five. Though they chased him, he soon outdistanced them. He was breathing hard when he reached home. His mother wasn't there. He closed the door and windows and waited, fearing that any minura the bullies would descend on their house to punish him for standing up to them. But though he waited for over a hora, no one came. Misa returned close to evening, tired and dirty. She was surprised to see the house all locked up. Before she could demand an explanation from Mizu, however, there was a knock on the door. Mizu looked on anxiously as his mother answered. The chief of Durnum stood there.

He was a larger version of his son Zibar, though he had an oily manner that was incongruous with his flabby body. He looked thunderous at the moment.

'Is your son in, woman?' he demanded.

Misa answered coldly, 'What do you want with him?'

'I am here to punish him for assaulting my son, Zibar,' the chief declared.

Misa eyed Chief Zillock frigidly. In her opinion, he was nothing more than an overgrown worm who had become chief by dint of nothing more than obsequious flattery and opportunism. She was not cowed by his assertions of power and position. Misa believed him to be cowardly, stupid and incompetent in the extreme. She suspected that there was some truth to what he was accusing Mizu of. Yet, she was disinclined to let him talk to Mizu. If Mizu had done any wrong, she would deal with it. The chief of Durnum would not get the satisfaction of punishing her son. He had hated her from the day she had come to Durnum, probably because the king had shown her favour. She would not allow him to take his envy and ill will out on Mizu.

'Can you prove that my son assaulted yours?' she demanded in return, not moving an inch from the doorway.

'There are witnesses,' he replied smugly.

'And those witnesses can verify that my son, young and thin and small, assaulted your son who is older, larger and stronger?' Misa asked sweetly.

Zillock turned beet red. He looked like he would love to strangle her right there. He took a step forward. Misa stood her ground. Before anything else could transpire, someone spoke from beyond the doorway, 'Is everything fine here?'

Mizu was at the doorway like a shot on hearing the voice. He had never been happier to see its owner. Prince Amishar stood outside the house, two guards with him. He was scowling.

'What's going on?' he demanded, when no one answered his first question.

Zillock spoke before Misa could. 'Your Highness, I am honoured to have you in my village. What can I do for you?'

Amishar replied without changing his tone, 'I come here quite often, Chief Zillock, and you know it. The question is what are *you* doing here?'

'I came here because this boy, Mizu, assaulted my son Zibar.'

Amishar raised his eyebrows. He had seen Zibar. He did not believe that Mizu could hurt anyone, even a bully like the chief's son. At least, not without reason.

Amishar answered Zillock, 'Mizu is my friend. I know him well. He would never assault anyone and definitely not without justifiable cause. If he hurt your son, there must have been a very good reason for it. Zibar must have deserved it.'

Zillock smiled greasily and said, 'I take your word for it, Your Highness. It must be some sort of misunderstanding. I am extremely sorry.' He bowed obsequiously and departed without delay, looking daggers at Misa and Mizu over his shoulder. His look made it very clear that the matter was far from over.

Over four mondans had passed since King Amiroth had left on his expedition to Ghrangghirm. Amishar was missing him badly. At first, it had felt like an adventure—being the 'head' of the household in his father's absence. He pretended that he was now the king but soon grew tired of it. He tried to tell himself that brave warriors did not give way to emotions, repeating in his mind the words his teachers and guardians had often told him. However, he was a very young warrior and had never stayed apart from his father for longer than a day or two. He was as deeply attached to King Amiroth as the king was to him. The only times that Amishar truly emerged from gloom were the times he spent with Mizu.

One such evening, the prince was in a mischievous mood. He had been getting into trouble that entire tempora. Despite his mother's warnings, he had not yet sobered down.

'Let us go to Father's chambers,' he suggested to his friend.

Mizu, who always felt self-conscious inside the palace, was hesitant. 'Aren't they locked up since his departure?' he asked.

'Yes, so they are,' agreed Amishar. 'Don't worry, the guards will let us in.' He sounded confident enough to convince Mizu to tag along. The guards, however, were under orders from Lord Aminor not to allow anyone in. They refused to let the boys enter the king's chambers. Nothing Amishar said could make them budge. They dared not disobey Aminor. Amishar scolded them and threatened them but to no avail. They were polite, humble and apologetic in the extreme, but they did not unlock the door. They requested the prince to talk to Lord Aminor if he wanted permission to enter King Amiroth's chambers. Amishar was reluctant to do so. The two boys had no choice but to return to the garden. Amishar was cross at this setback though Mizu was secretly glad. The prince continued to fume and grumble for a while. Mizu sat by patiently, knowing that Amishar was never angry for long. Soon, Amishar calmed down. He suggested that they play catch. Mizu happily agreed.

The two boys played energetically for a while in one of the gardens. Amishar showed less adeptness at catching and throwing than usual. Mizu wondered what was going on in his friend's mind to distract him. He was missing easy catches. Or he was letting the ball roll away too far then chasing it down. Or he was throwing the ball too askew, apologising and throwing it again from where it had landed. Mizu was apprehensive that the prince was planning some sort of mischief. Sure enough, at one time, Amishar threw the ball so high that it sailed far over Mizu's head and landed in a balcony on the first floor of the palace. Mizu had become familiar enough with the palace grounds by then to realise that the balcony was attached to the king's chambers.

Mizu sighed. Amishar was as stubborn as a mule. Once he got an idea into his head, it was close to impossible to get him to change his mind. Mizu knew that Amishar wanted to visit his father's chambers because he was missing King Amiroth but would never acknowledge that out of pride. Mizu was sure that if Amishar only asked his cousin, Lord Aminor, the regent would allow Amishar in. He was also sure that Amishar would be too embarrassed to acknowledge his emotions, so he would never approach Aminor.

The prince apologised without sounding at all apologetic. 'I am so sorry about that, Mizu. Entirely my mistake. Wait here, I'll be back in a jiffy.'

Mizu felt that it was his duty to try to stop his friend from getting into trouble. 'Where are you going?' he demanded.

'To get the ball,' Amishar replied innocently.

'Forget the ball, let's play some other game,' Mizu suggested.

'All right,' agreed Amishar, much to Mizu's surprise. 'Let's play hide and seek!'

Mizu felt suspicious about Amishar's ready agreement to his suggestion since no one was ever willing to play hide and seek with him. Mizu was extremely clever at seeking. Apparently, that spoiled the fun for other players. But the temptation to play his favourite game was too strong for Mizu to resist. Surprisingly, Amishar sought first. Since Mizu was very good at hiding as well, it took Amishar a while to search him out. Then it was Amishar's turn to hide. Mizu closed his eyes and began to count. When he opened his eyes, Amishar was nowhere to be seen. Mizu looked carefully around. He was certain that Amishar was not hiding close by. He wondered how he knew that, but he had always had an uncanny ability to find hiders. He continued to run his gaze around slowly, trying to identify Amishar's hiding place. He stopped when his eyes fell upon the balcony where their ball had landed a short while ago. It looked the same as before, but Mizu could sense that something had changed. He could not be sure what, but he was absolutely certain that something was different. He was also certain that Amishar had climbed up into the balcony and had managed to enter the chambers to which the balcony was attached. He sighed and made his way towards it.

In the meantime, Amishar was lost in his father's memories. He had indeed tricked Mizu into playing hide and seek, knowing it to be his favourite game, so that his friend would not be able to stop him from breaking into his father's chambers. He had nimbly climbed into the balcony using the trees and creepers that grew outside. He had tried all the windows in hopes of finding one loose enough to open. He had been lucky. He had quickly climbed inside, leaving the window only slightly ajar to allow in light and fresh air. It was dark inside. It took Amishar a while to get accustomed to the dim light. When he did, he found it difficult to control himself. Memories of all the times he had spent in there with his father flooded him. His father's smell still lingered in the air, or so it seemed to him. The room looked strangely forlorn in King Amiroth's absence, like it was waiting for someone to breathe life into it. Amishar sat down heavily on the luxuriant bed, a lump forming in his throat. He swallowed hard to push it down, but it threatened to burst out through his stinging eyes.

To distract himself, Amishar began to rummage among his father's belongings. His first targets were the chests that contained the king's clothes. Most of the chests were too big, their lids too heavy for the young prince to lift. However, he managed to push open the lid of one of the smaller ones by a few inches with great effort. Grabbing the first thing he could, Amishar let the lid fall shut. What he had extricated from the chest was a blue silk robe embroidered in gold thread and precious stones. He pressed his face into it and breathed deeply. He was rather disappointed that it did not smell of his father. However, he put it on over his own clothes. It was too big for him and fanned out on the floor around him like a peacock's tail. The sleeves fell to the floor; Amishar rolled them up. Some of the king's shoes were on a nearby rack. Amishar picked up a pair and inserted his feet into them. He could no longer walk properly. He shuffled back into the sleeping chamber and looked around for more things to fiddle with. His eyes fell on the weapons lining one of the walls. He could not reach most of them, but he managed to take a long dagger off the wall. He attached it to his belt like a sword.

His eyes then turned to the most precious thing in the room. In fact, the most precious thing in the entire kingdom. It sat inside a glass case on a tall chest of drawers. Amishar dragged a stool over to the chest of drawers to climb up. He gingerly raised the glass lid of the case. Inside, on a plush velvet cushion, sat King Amiroth's crown! He lifted it out of the case gently. Sitting down on the stool, he placed the crown on his head. Being too big for him, it slid down around his neck. He lifted it and placed it at an angle behind his right ear. Instead of falling round his neck, it now tilted rakishly across his face. He was about to adjust it further when a noise behind him alerted him to the presence of someone else in the chamber. He leapt off the stool and turned around to see who it was, gripping the handle of the dagger at his belt. It was Mizu. He had grown tired of waiting for his friend on the lawns below and had finally climbed up despite his misgivings. Amishar relaxed.

'How do I look?' he asked his friend eagerly.

'Like a clown,' was the first response that came to Mizu's mind. He was feeling rather annoyed with the prince. But the look on Amishar's face stopped him short.

'Like your father,' he replied instead, feeling glad when Amishar's face turned radiant with joy. 'But we'd better get out of here fast, before anyone catches us,' he added. 'Or we will both look like idiots.'

Supprom was almost over when Timror received four visitors. They wore robes and hoods like him, but they were not magi. One of them was a blacksmith, one was a herder, one was a soldier and the fourth was a thief; three were men, the herder was a woman. They arrived separately during the morning. Each was familiar with the entrance to Timror's lair and went straight through to the chamber where Timror had first met Eamilus. Then they passed through into his kitchen where they received a warm welcome from their host.

'What news?' Timror asked his first visitor, the blacksmith, after offering him food and water.

'Things are as usual on the other side. No unusual activity of vynobnie has occurred,' the blacksmith reported. 'By the way, only I have come from the other side. The others are busy keeping watch. Something seems to be going on with the dharvhs. And with the eighes. We're staying alert though vynobnie presence is probably not behind any of it. How are things here?'

'Bad,' said Timror. Before he could elaborate, the soldier arrived. He had come from Haalzona.

'Haalzona has fallen. There is no resistance any longer. The kocovuses have completely overrun the capital. Now there is no more hope for men,' the soldier declared grimly, sitting down and gratefully accepting a mug of ale. The blacksmith started on hearing this news, but Timror remained calm.

'You know about this already,' commented the soldier on seeing Timror's unsurprised response. Timror shook his head.

'I guessed,' he said.

At that moment, the thief arrived. He had come from distant Waurlen. His news was a little more cheerful than the soldier's. 'The hrenks have not managed to discover the underground human settlements. They stomp over the hidden tunnels but cannot find the entrances. Folks were worried that the roofs would cave in, but they have held up,' he announced.

The herder was the last to arrive. She had news from Illafanka, but they could not decide whether it was good news or bad. 'A prisoner, a female mertkhezin, has escaped. A countrywide search was going on to find her. No trace had been found by the time I left.'

'Whose prisoner was she—humans' or her own kind's?' asked the thief.

The herder snorted. 'Are there humans in Illafanka who would want to or be able to imprison a mertkhezin?'

A sudden noise distracted them. 'What's that?' asked the thief.

'That's my student practicing,' Timror informed them.

'Practicing what?' the blacksmith asked suspiciously. Timror said nothing. The others followed the source of the sound outside to the arena where Eamilus was breaking stone blocks with his bare knuckles. They stood at a distance, hidden behind rubble, watching him.

'You taught him the secret art!' the herder cried out.

'Shh!' said Timror, sure that Eamilus would hear her. 'Quiet!'

'He is good,' commented the soldier.

'Yes, he is,' agreed the thief. The blacksmith snorted.

'Why did you teach him?' the herder demanded of Timror as the other three continued to watch Eamilus practice.

'I have my reasons,' Timror replied guardedly, not caring to explain himself. Before the herder could pursue the matter further, Eamilus crumbled three very large, very solid blocks of stone to dust. The three men watching him gasped with surprise.

'Wonder how he would fare against a real opponent,' the blacksmith smirked, not willing to concede that the boy was actually quite impressive.

'Would you like to try a bout with him?' Timror suddenly asked.

The blacksmith hesitated. 'I wouldn't mind going a round,' the thief declared. 'Me neither!' the soldier added.

In the end, all four of Timror's visitors agreed to fight Eamilus. They stepped out into the arena. Eamilus stopped and stared at them. He had never seen people with Timror before. He wondered who these people were. Timror did not bother to introduce them. Instead, he told Eamilus that the four would duel him. Eamilus bowed and acknowledged the challenge as part of his training.

The blacksmith was the first to step into the arena. He was large and strong. His arms were muscular. He did not last very long against Eamilus. The boy used the blacksmith's size and strength against him, causing him to lose his balance and easily flipping him over. Suddenly the blacksmith found himself flat on his back on the ground, wondering how he got there. All present were surprised. Except Timror. He beamed.

The thief was the next to take up the challenge. He prided himself on his quick reflexes. He had always believed the blacksmith to be less than competent. He felt sure that the boy could not beat him as he had beaten the blacksmith. He could not have been more wrong. Though he lasted longer in the arena than the blacksmith had, he was no match for Eamilus who, true to his training, was not even relying on his superhuman abilities. His pride humbled, the thief stepped out of the arena, wondering how the boy could have caught his kicks and punches in midair and then used the momentum to thwart his attacks.

The soldier was the third to face Eamilus. His fate was no better than that of his companions. He soon found himself flying through the air and landing on top of them at the ringside.

The herder was the last to fight Eamilus. She had seen her predecessors getting beaten by the boy and went into the arena mentally prepared for a real fight and not a training routine. She lasted the longest against Eamilus. However, he hardly broke into a sweat as he faced her attacks, countering them adroitly. He stood his ground defensively, trying not to hurt the woman, until she tired, and he had to use little force to conquer her.

All four guests of Timror applauded Eamilus sincerely, impressed by the boy's skill and agility. Eamilus, his heart thumping proudly at his accomplishment, could not resist throwing a challenge at his master with an inviting gesture. Timror was taken aback. But his companions cheered loudly, and he could not back out. The duel was a pleasure to watch. Both contestants were lightning fast and sure of their moves. They cleverly attacked, sidestepped, defended and counterattacked each other. For a long time, neither could touch the other. The outcome hung in the balance. Then, slowly but surely, Timror began to gain an upper hand. Until suddenly, a completely unexpected manoeuvre by Eamilus took him by surprise and he found himself on the ground, staring up at the sky, Eamilus's face looming over him with a grin of victory. When Timror signalled that he accepted defeat, Eamilus helped him up and bowed to his master.

Timror was proud as well as astonished. Dusting off his clothes, he embraced his pupil while the others yelled encouragement.

'I'm proud of you,' Timror said to his student. 'You have learnt well!'

'I guess I had a good teacher!' Eamilus returned, grinning broadly.

Eamilus saw no more of Timror's guests that day. However, he remained curious about them. Who were they? Where had they come from? Why had they come? How could all of them fight the same way that Timror could? The questions kept puzzling him. The mystery was heightened by Timror's instructions not to join them for dinner that night. He tried to eavesdrop on their dinnertime conversation using his superior hearing. When he couldn't hear anything, Eamilus figured that Timror had put up a block. This only heightened his curiosity. He did not give up. He continued to prowl at a suitable distance from the main residence, planning to follow anyone who left. He checked his map of the tunnels leading out of Timror's underground house and selected a cranny that Timror would have to cross on his way out irrespective of which exit he took. Hiding there, Eamilus waited patiently. Horas passed. Finally, his patience was rewarded. He saw the five hooded figures pass by. When they went down one of the tunnels, Eamilus followed them quietly at a distance, easily keeping track of them through their smells.

He followed them out of the underground warren of tunnels and into the ruined city. They were completely silent as they walked in a line through the dark night. Eamilus was surprised by how fast they walked. He almost lost them a few times. He managed to keep up with them only through the use of his keen senses. They finally stopped in front of a ruined house in the east of Abluvel. They looked very alike in their hooded robes, but Eamilus had no difficulty in recognising the person in front as his master. Timror whispered something. A gap opened in one of the stones through which they entered in single file. Eamilus followed them to the mouth of the gap. Not having any idea what could lie beyond, he hesitated to enter. Even as he watched, a portion of the stone rolled back, and the gap closed without any indication that it had ever been there.

Eamilus returned to await Timror. When the magus returned, it was close to midnight. Eamilus sat wide awake in front of Timror's chamber. One glance told Timror what was on the boy's mind. Without saying a word, he entered his room and shut the doors. Eamilus was wondering whether he should give up his vigil when Timror emerged again, a sheet of parchment in his hand. He thrust it at Eamilus and then vanished inside again. Eamilus unrolled the parchment. It contained a riddle:

> *Darker than day, brighter than night;*
> *Enemy of birds, bats' delight;*
> *Dark for minuras, for momons bright;*
> *See if you can an unseeable sight.*

Eamilus puzzled over the riddle for a while. It was well past midnight by the time he was able to figure out the answer. Solar eclipse. The first line referred to the twilight darkness during a solar eclipse. The day became dark, but not as dark as night. The second line was easy and, in fact, gave him his first clue. Birds were agitated but bats were pleased during the period of unexpected darkness during an eclipse. The third line puzzled him for a long time until he remembered a strange phenomenon that happened when the shadow first began to move away from the sun. There was a burst of brilliance that lasted only a few momons. Once he had figured out all this, the last line easily fell into place. An eclipse was not seeable through naked eyes, but the sight of it through reflections was still an unforgettable sight.

The answer to the riddle puzzled Eamilus even more. What was he to do with it? He was certain that Timror had understood his purpose in waiting outside his door. He could have just ignored Eamilus or asked him to go back to bed if he hadn't wanted to share information. Why would he give Eamilus a riddle to solve if the answer wasn't relevant? Did he want Eamilus to ask him about the matter on the next solar eclipse? Did the nightly trip have something to do with alchemical work regarding a solar eclipse? Were Timror and his companions trying to cause a solar eclipse? The ideas kept getting more absurd. So, discarding them, Eamilus focused on what he had witnessed that night. As he went over the night's events minura by minura in his mind, he understood the significance of the riddle. The solution was a password.

He immediately returned to the spot where he had seen Timror and the other four vanish inside the rock. He stood where Timror had stood and uttered the password. Immediately, the secret door opened for him. A narrow staircase led down. He stepped inside. The door rumbled shut behind him. Though it was pitch dark, Eamilus had no difficulty seeing. There were torches in brackets along the walls and provisions to light them. He lit one and began to descend. He had expected booby traps or magical obstructions similar to the ones he had encountered on his first visit to Timror. To his surprise, he found none. The staircase led to a small underground chamber that could have held no more than a dozen people. On one side of the chamber was a sort of long stone table on which several things were kept: a fat book, quills, inkpots, scrolls and blank sheets of parchment. Similar fat books lined shelves cut into the walls of the chamber at the opposite end. A curtain hung beyond the stone table. Unable to resist his curiosity, and certain that his teacher meant for him to discover this place, Eamilus moved back the old, thick curtain.

There was nothing behind the curtain except one of the walls of the chamber. This wall, though, was smoother than the others. Eamilus lightly touched it; it felt different too. Magic, he thought. Or science. Timror had long since taught him that the line between the two was a thin one. He spoke the password again. Nothing happened. No, it could not be that simple, he guessed. But why hadn't Timror given him a clue to the secret of the wall? Perhaps he did not want Eamilus to learn the secret. Or, perhaps, the boy suddenly thought, he already knew whatever he needed to in order to reveal the secret. Given what he knew of his master, he surmised that the secret of the wall had to be something unexpected but not complicated. Hidden in plain sight, as it were. What could it be? He thought about Timror and his four visitors. There had to be some connection between them; there was the matter of the chamber in which he now stood. Was there any other connection? Yes! They could all fight in the same style that Timror had taught him. But how could that help?

He scanned the smooth wall again. He thought he spotted some sort of a knob near the ceiling, but he could not be sure. Besides, even though the chamber wasn't very high, the knob was still too far for anyone to reach. The tallest of Timror's guests could not have done it, and Timror himself was exceptionally short. Unless…! Eamilus had an idea. He looked at the rest of the room closely— at the stone table, at the far shelves, at the bare walls, at the torch brackets. Then he smiled. It was simple but clever. Only very few could climb to the ceiling using the meagre and almost invisible hand and footholds that were there. He was, he realised, one of those few, though he could have just flown to the ceiling as well. Nonetheless, he used the art taught to him by Timror to reach the nearly invisible knob at the top of the wall. Immediately upon pressing it, some kind of writing appeared on the wall. Eamilus floated down and read.

'*We, the Brotherhood of the Secret Watchers, hereby solemnly swear that we shall forever continue to keep watch on vynobnie on both sides of the Lyudzbradh. We shall hide our true identities and secretly gather all possible information that may pertain to unnatural or supernatural activity in the continent of Elthrusia. We shall meet every fourth mondan and record our findings. We will never become directly involved in the fight between yennts and vynobnie but will remain at a distance, observing and recording. Our purpose is to act as beacons, providing warning and information to mortals so that they can enable themselves to deal with the evil forces of the Lyudzbradh as they see fit and if they so desire.*'

The writing vanished almost as soon as Eamilus read it. His mind was in a whirl. He had had no idea how complex the world really was, how many forces were operating in it in layers and currents. But he was beginning to form a pretty good idea. At the same time, he felt an overwhelming sense of anger. He rushed back, prepared to confront Timror. It was close to dawn. He was surprised to find his teacher waiting for him.

'I assume you have some questions for me,' Timror said wearily.

Eamilus did not waste time in prefacing his angry questions. 'Did you know about the impending attack on Haalzona? Did you warn my father? Do you know what happened after I left? Why have you never told me about any of this before? Why did you send me to that place tonight? What do you want from me?'

He felt himself trembling and sensed that he was about to lose control. With great effort, he pulled himself together. He sat down to keep himself calm and composed. He continued to glare at Timror even as he sat, waiting for answers.

Timror answered solemnly, 'We knew about the kocovus army and about Lilluana and Rohzun but not about their exact plans. We did try to warn King Eamarilus, and several times at that, but he refused to heed our warnings. He thought they were rumours and ignored them, especially after your stepmother's death, when he lost all interest in running his kingdom. After the attack of the kocovus army on Haalzona, we lost touch with our sources there for some time, though we have managed to get more information recently.

'Yes, things are very bad there, and yes, I have known that for a while and have chosen not to tell you. Because, it would serve no purpose. You cannot do anything about it. Yet. You are not ready though you might think you are. I sent you to the hideout tonight because I knew that you had followed us there. I did not intend to insult either your intelligence or my training by assuming that you would forget about what you saw or fail to gain entry by yourself. Letting you know about the cave was the safest course of action for everyone concerned. The answer to your last question is, nothing. I want nothing from you besides that which a teacher can expect from his student. Remember, *you* came to me to learn from me. I never sought you out. And even though I could have refused you, I did not. Not through some ulterior motive but because Nishtar had sent you. Also because I was curious about you, given the talent you had displayed while gaining access to my house. I regret nothing that I have done.'

With those words, Timror left his student alone.

Chapter 39

A FRIEND IN DREAMS

(9 Vyiedal 5009 A.E. to 5 Kielom 5009 A.E.)

Within six mondans of receiving the dreamcatcher, Avita's life was utterly changed. She still dreamt about the human boy, but she could stop or change the dream whenever she wanted to. She was sleeping better too. Even when she dreamt of the boy getting beaten, she was no longer wounded. Sometimes she felt guilty about it. What if the boy was suffering more because she was no longer sharing his pain? But she was healthier and happier than she had been in anni. Her guardians, too, were thrilled with the changes in her. Avator asked her every morning about her dreams. Usually she told him the truth. Sometimes, when she had dreamt of the boy as the warrior, she lied. Avator trusted her answers and was satisfied with her improvement.

Then, one day, Avita had an idea. If she could control what not to see, mightn't she control what to see? Would it be possible to focus her dreams so that she could talk to the boy in her dreams? That night, she went to bed rather excited at the prospect of trying this. For a long time, she could not sleep. She was feeling too much on edge about what she wanted to attempt in her dreams. The lack of sleep frustrated her. She tossed from side to side, becoming increasingly wakeful. By the time she finally relaxed enough to fall asleep, it was past midnight. The dreamcatcher allowed her to retain a measure of consciousness even while dreaming. Her thoughts and feelings remained relatively clear. She dreamt of rivers and forests for a while, then she dreamt of Avator and the outlaws. She began to feel impatient. She wanted to dream of the human boy. As soon as she thought about him, her dream changed.

She was now standing in a garden. She did not know the garden from any of her previous dreams. It was a beautiful place. Tall trees rustled in the breeze. Bamboo groves swayed elegantly. Flowers of many bright colours were in full bloom everywhere. Birds were trilling in the shady trees. The grass was soft and luxurious. A cobbled path lined by tall hedges meandered through the garden, joining its various sections. Arches bore thickly flowering vines. Tall fountains in shapes of fantastic animals tinkled merrily. The sun shone down warmly. Sweet fragrances wafted upon a gentle breeze. Avita liked the garden. There was an ornate iron bench there. She sat down. At first she was alone. Then she felt another presence in the garden with her. She turned around and saw a figure in the distance walking towards her. She had no doubt that it was the human boy.

In the blink of an eye, he was there, sitting on the bench next to her. She could see him clearly now. She smiled at him. At first, he looked taken aback. Then he smiled back at her. The two sat there for a while, smiling at each other. Avita was afraid to move lest the dream vanished. Finally, she plucked up enough courage to speak to him.

'Hello!' she said. The boy's smile vanished. He opened his mouth to say something but closed it again.

Maybe he was shy, Avita thought. She was about to ask him his name. Before she could, everything began to wobble. She stood up, panic-stricken. What was happening? She could hear a voice calling her name. Who was calling? She tried to focus, to hold the dream together, but it vanished in a burst of light and sound. Avita opened her eyes. Forsith was standing over her, shaking her, looking bemused.

'Are you all right?' he asked her, concerned.

'Yes, why? What's wrong?' she asked sleepily.

'You were giggling in your sleep!' Forsith remarked. 'Are you sure you are all right?'

'Yes, I am,' Avita insisted. 'I was dreaming of dolls,' she added by way of explanation. She was annoyed at having been awoken. And just as she had been about to talk to the boy too!

Temeron, too, awoke with a start. It was early morning. Rosa was still asleep. He had had a strange dream about a kereighe girl. He had met her in a lovely garden where they had sat upon a bench side by side. He knew that it was the same girl that he had met during his failed escape attempt, the girl with the ribbons in her hair, the girl who in some magical way helped him heal faster and feel better no matter how badly Rosa treated him. She was older now, but he had no doubt that it was she. He thought about his strange dream. He had been dreaming of something else, he seemed to remember, though he could not recall what he had been dreaming of. All of a sudden, he had found himself in the wonderful garden. He had seen a girl sitting on a bench in the distance. The very next moment, he had been sitting next to her. In the blink of an eye. Like magic. Of course, dreams were hardly ever logical, he knew, and he had always had strange dreams. However, for the past six mondans, his dreams had turned even odder, even more out of his control than usual. The dream about the girl in the garden had been the most unusual of all. She had smiled at him as if she knew him. Did she? Was it possible that she felt the bond between them just as he did? His pulse quickened at the thought. He wondered if he would dream about her again that night and, if he did, what he would see.

That night, again, Avita could not wait to fall asleep. Remembering the previous night's experience, she tried to relax. Almost as soon as she was asleep, she began to dream. She dreamt that she was on the beach of a dark, stormy ocean. The waves were tall and hungry. They attacked the rocks on the shore with a desperate vehemence. Avita found herself standing at the edge of the raging waters, but she was not afraid. She liked the stormy ocean. It made her feel calm. She felt a sense of kinship with the crashing waves. But she wanted to meet the human boy. She wanted to know who he was and why she dreamt of him. She thought about him like she had done the night before. However, her surroundings did not change into a garden as they had the previous night. She remained where she was. Surprised, she focussed on thoughts of the human boy with greater intensity.

Footsteps sounded behind her on the rock. Avita turned sharply. Her foot slipped, and she toppled backwards. In her panic, she forgot that she could control whatever happened in her dream. However, the boy reached out, grabbed her dress and pulled her in. The force caused the dress to tear. The boy blushed, ashamed. Avita, pulling herself together, wished for her dress to be mended, having remembered that whatever was happening was within her control. The boy stared wide-eyed as the tear in her dress vanished before his very eyes. Avita smiled and said, 'Thank you for grabbing me before I fell.'

The boy nodded. The two stood there, smiling shyly, wanting to talk but hesitating. The boy was the first to break the silence.

'You are the girl I met in the alley, the one with the ribbons, aren't you?'

Avita nodded. 'Yes, I am. My name is Avita. What is yours?'

'My name is Temeron. Is this a dream, or is this real?' Temeron asked. Even as he spoke the question aloud, he sensed what a ridiculous query it was. It wasn't as if he was really meeting her, was it? It was a dream, and he knew it. Yet, in his heart, he was desperate for her to say that it was somehow real. He did not know why but it mattered more to him than anything ever had.

Avita frowned. She had never thought of her dreams about Temeron that way. To her, there had never been a clear distinction. More importantly, it did not matter whether there was a distinction or not. It was what it was. And she was fine with it. She tried to explain it to Temeron. 'I think this is a dream, but I am a real girl in the real world, just as you are a real boy. Again, that we are talking to each other is real, even though this place and whatever else happens is not. Earlier it used to be different, though.'

'What do you mean?' Temeron asked, confused.

Avita wanted to explain it to him as clearly as she could. It was difficult, considering that she herself did not understand it very well. She decided to tell Temeron everything that had happened to her since their chance encounter in the

That night, though, when she sat down upon that familiar bench, he was already there.

alley in hopes that that would enable him to understand. But before she could, a searing pain shot through her stomach, and she bent over double. Temeron knelt by her, anxious and terrified.

'What's wrong?' he asked in a worried voice. 'How can I help?'

Avita was having difficulty breathing. Sweating profusely, she managed to gasp, 'I think someone, perhaps the witch, just kicked you in the stomach.'

Temeron looked startled. Before the conversation could continue, the dream began to wobble. Avita did not want the dream to end. She had so much to say to Temeron! She tried to hold on to the dream with all her mind, but it was to no avail. The pain in her belly prevented her from concentrating. Soon she found herself awake, holding on to her stomach. It no longer hurt as badly as it had in the dream. But there were tears in her eyes. Not from the pain but from the frustration of having awoken. She wished she could have talked longer to Temeron. Temeron! How wonderful it felt to finally know his name. Where was he in real life? What was his life like? She wished she could find him, help him. Dawn was a long way away yet. As the pain receded, she fell asleep again, hoping to dream of Temeron once more. But no more dreams of Temeron came to her sleeping eyes that night.

In fact, it was almost a mondan before she dreamt of him again. She had grown irritable and anxious when night after night, she had tried to summon dreams of Temeron but had failed. She had almost given up hope of seeing him again when one night, she once more found herself in the garden with the bench. Realising that she wasn't strong enough to control her dreams absolutely, she had stopped trying to call Temeron to her dreams. That night, though, when she sat down upon that familiar bench, he was already there. Her heart soared!

'Were you already here, or did I call you?' she asked him.

Temeron looked puzzled by her question. She sighed and sat down next to him.

'How have you been?' he asked her.

'Worried that I might never meet you again,' she answered truthfully. 'How about you?'

'Fine, I suppose. The last mondan has been strangely uneventful.'

Avita sat up at his words. 'So you remember?' she asked.

'Remember what?'

'Our last conversation.'

'Yes, of course I do. We were on the rock on the sea shore. We told each other our names. You said something odd about this being both a dream as well as real. Before you could explain, the dream vanished.'

'Yes! That's correct!' exclaimed Avita. Her face fell the very next moment. 'Someone had kicked you in the stomach.'

'Yes, but how did you know? Even I didn't know—in the dream I mean. You were bent over with pain; that was the last thing I saw before waking up and finding that the witch who keeps me a prisoner was kicking me.'

'I always know,' Avita said hesitantly. She did not know just how to explain this to Temeron either.

'How?'

Avita said slowly, choosing her words carefully, 'From the time that we first met in that alley, we have had a connection. I don't remember too well because I was so young, but my guardians have told me that I fainted after our hands touched. We both did. From that time onwards, I have dreamt about you. I used to dream about an old eighee beating me, and I used to wake up with bruises, cuts and worse injuries. My brother, Avator, and our guardian, Forsith, took me to many healers and magi, but they did not know what was happening to me. Then we met this really nice witch. She gave me a charm to wear, and I felt better. I healed faster. Then, about half an annus ago, my brother took me to another magus. He read my mind. He told us that I have a spiritual connection to you. That is why I dream about you and get those injuries. He gave me a dreamcatcher so that I can control my dreams and so that I won't get wounded in real life when I dream of you being hurt.'

Avita paused after her long, complicated speech. Temeron was silent too. She did not know how he would react after listening to her explanation. When he spoke, he said something surprising.

'Do your guardians love you?'

'Yes, very much,' she answered, wondering why he would ask that.

'That explains a lot,' he said.

'What explains what?'

It was Temeron's turn to explain. 'I live with an old lech, a malicious and crazy witch who is always beating me, abusing me and hurting me in any way she can. She also encourages others to injure me. I have been living with her for as long as I can remember, though living is probably not the right word. I am her prisoner and her slave. One day, I tried to escape. I met you. As your guardians have told you, I also fainted after our hands touched. The witch found me and brutally beat me. That was nothing new because she had been doing it for as long as I can remember. What was new was that I started healing faster from that time onwards. And I felt that someone loved me. Whenever I was hurt, I felt comforted by someone's love. I used to wonder why, though I suspected that it had something to do with you.

Now I know. Because your guardians loved you and comforted you, I felt loved and comforted. I think that I healed faster because you shared my injuries not just in your dreams but physically as well. I owe you a great deal.'

'No, you don't,' said Avita, trying to take his hand to comfort him. He recoiled with horror.

'What's wrong?' she asked, tears in her eyes.

'What if you are hurt again if you touch my hand?' said Temeron.

'No, I won't be,' said Avita confidently. 'In my dreams, we can hold hands without fainting.'

'Are you sure?'

'Yes,' replied Avita, though not very confidently. There had been dreams where bad things *had* happened, but that had been before the dreamcatcher. She believed that now that she had greater control of her dreams, they were safe.

Temeron hesitantly reached out and took Avita's hand. Both looked nervous and waited for something awful to happen. Nothing did. Both relaxed and resumed their conversation.

Avita told Temeron about Forsith and Avator, about their life in Lianma before she met him, about the witch of Temtema, about their nomadic life, about her guardians pretending that Forsith was a horse-wizard, about the outlaws, about using false names while living at the camp, about the visit to the magus who had given her the dreamcatcher and about her strange dreams in which she saw him as a kereighe boy or a kereighe warrior. When she was done, she asked Temeron to talk about his life.

Temeron told her about the numerous ingenious ways in which Rosa punished and tormented him all the time, about his discovery that he was actually a kereighe, about his pursuit of magic, about the beggar who had taught him to read and write, about the thief whom he had not given up, about the stranger who had wanted to purchase him from Rosa, about his collection of insect parts, about his secret benefactor, about his hatred for everybody except Avita and about his strange dreams besides the ones that he had of Avita.

Avita listened patiently and said, 'Why don't you ask your secret friend to help you to escape? You could run away and stay with him.'

Temeron shook his head. 'No, I think that he would have rescued me by now if he could. The witch is very powerful as well as cruel. I don't want her to hurt him. He is the only one who does anything good for me. Besides, the last time I tried to run away, things did not go very well.'

'Because you came across me,' Avita said in a small voice. 'I am sorry about that. If you hadn't met me, you might have escaped.'

'I'm not so sure about that,' said Temeron introspectively. 'I think the witch would have managed to find me. And even if I had escaped the witch, I might have landed in an equally disastrous situation. Who in Kinqur would have helped a human boy? Besides, I'm glad that I met you. You are my greatest comfort. You helped me bear the pain and heal faster. I don't know how I would have survived without you.'

'But I no longer share your injuries because of the dreamcatcher,' said Avita, feeling mortified. If he had been healing faster because she was receiving the same injuries, he was probably taking longer to heal now. She felt guilty.

'You still feel my pain, don't you?'

'Yes, but if I don't share your wounds, you will not heal faster. If I stop using the dreamcatcher, it will help you.'

'No!' cried Temeron vehemently. 'Never even think of doing that! If it takes me longer to heal, so be it. I won't be able to forgive myself if you are hurt because of me. Besides, if you stop using the dreamcatcher, we won't be able to talk like this. This is worth far more to me!'

'I too want that we should be able to meet and talk like this. I keep waiting to dream about you,' said Avita, blushing furiously.

'Really? Why?' asked Temeron, genuinely taken aback.

'I have no friends here at the camp. Avator used to play with me earlier, but he is too busy these days. Our guardian, Forsith, tries to spend as much time as he can with me, but he is very worried about what Avator is doing with the outlaws. He thinks I don't understand, but I do. They are not as good friends as they were before. This pains both of them though neither will admit it. That is why even though they both love me very much, we have not spent much time together for a while.'

'I would like to be your friend,' Temeron said shyly. 'I also don't have any friends.'

'You are already my friend!' Avita exclaimed joyfully. She was feeling truly happy. She had never had such a long conversation with anybody. And never had she been able to pour out her heart to anyone with as much ease. It seemed odd that she should feel such closeness with someone who was practically a stranger. And that, too, in her dreams!

'Do you think that we will remember all this when we wake up?' she asked Temeron.

'I am sure we will,' he replied confidently.

'That is good,' Avita said. 'Do you think that if we tell each other where we stay, we can find one another in the real world?'

'I suppose so. But I don't know where I live. I just know that it is a town. Do you know where you live?'

Avita shook her head. 'It is the camp of the outlaws and it is in the desert. That is all I know.'

'Then how will we find each other?' Temeron asked.

Avita was about to say something in response when the dream began to wobble. As she slowly woke up with the morning light falling on her face, she thought about Temeron's final words to her—'Until next time!'

It was past mid-Vyiedal when Timror confessed to Eamilus that he had taught the boy all that he could. This surprised Eamilus since he still had not learnt to fight with weapons, and he knew next to nothing about alchemy. He asked Timror about it.

'I can't teach you either,' Timror said.

'Why not?' asked Eamilus, surprised.

'Because you are not destined to be an alchemist. What you know about it is enough for a warrior. Perhaps more than enough. Why would you want to waste anni of your life pursuing the wrong profession? And as far as weapons are concerned, I cannot teach you how to wield them because I never learnt myself. Boy, I never trained as a warrior, not in the traditional sense. Very few magi do.'

Eamilus was about to say that Nishtar, he knew, was adept at the use of weapons but remembered Nishtar's life story just in time not to say anything. 'Where can I learn the use of weapons then?' he asked instead.

Timror was silent for a moment. Then he answered, 'Go west, to the human kingdoms there. Find a teacher there who can teach you. That would be the best option.'

The thought of leaving Timror pained Eamilus. Despite the slight chill that had come between the two since Eamilus's discovery of the Brotherhood of Secret Watchers, the boy felt sorry that his education with the eccentric magus was at an end. He had learnt much from Timror though at one time, he had imagined that staying with Nishtar would have benefitted him more. He no longer thought so. However, he still needed to learn the use of weapons, and Timror could not teach him that.

Eamilus took leave of his teacher one dark, windy night, after extracting the promise that Timror would look after his pets in his absence. Vernurt had set in only recently, but the weather had taken a turn for the worse early that annus. Eamilus's plan was to remain on the eastern side of the Lyudzbradh for that night. Even though he had learnt about all the safe passes of the Lyudzbradh, and he was afraid of nothing that could be found upon the mountains' slopes, he did not look forward to crossing the Lyudzbradh on a night like that. The weather continued to worsen by the minura until Eamilus was caught in a full-blown storm. He decided to travel to the south of Qeezsh, where the widest passes were, and cross as soon as the storm subsided.

He wrapped his cloak tightly around him and swiftly flew south, doing the best he could to stay on track despite extremely poor visibility, buffeting gales and lashing rain. When he reached what should have been the mouth of Cornen Pass, he found himself staring up at a solid wall of rock. He assumed that he had misjudged the distance and continued to travel further south in hopes of coming across the pass soon. However, he was lost beyond a doubt. Although he was soaked to the skin, he ignored the physical discomfort and began to gauge his bearings. The sky was completely overcast; there was neither moon nor stars to help him. He checked the direction of the wind. It was on his left if he faced the Lyudzbradh. This meant that he was still travelling south. He must have overshot the pass, he guessed. But how far south had he come? There was a slight hint of putrescence in the air, like that of bogs and rotting things, though most mortals would not have been able to smell the faint scent. Only one country could smell like that—Illafanka. However, the smell was not as strong as it should have been had be entered that country. So, he reasoned, he was not yet that far south. He had to be in Wyurr! Wyurr was ghrimben country, he knew, but he wasn't unduly worried.

He could have tried to make his way back to Cornen Pass that very night, but he was afraid of losing his way again. He did not want to waste time and energy travelling up and down the foothills of the Lyudzbradh. For a moment, he considered crossing the Lyudzbradh where he found himself. After all, it hardly made a difference to him where he crossed—through a pass or over a mountain! He gave up the idea as being foolhardy. It was not that he was afraid for his life; it was just that he had learnt from Timror that only fools take unnecessary risks. Eamilus decided that he could rectify his error the next morning. All he had to do was travel north till he found Cornen Pass. It was located at the point where the borders of Qeezsh, Wyurr, Ghrangghirm and Khwaznon met.

He looked into the sky and sensed that the storm was not about to let up any time soon. He was not afraid of the turbulence or of the dark. If anything, he was completely at home in the darkness of night, and he actually found the wildness of a devastating storm rather invigorating. Eamilus began to look for shelter among the crags of the mountain. He found one, along the mountain's slopes, in a narrow crevice in the mountainside, skirted by a ledge overhanging a deep precipice. He squeezed inside comfortably and settled in for the rest of the night. The narrow mouth of the crevice kept the rain water from entering, keeping him relatively dry. Eamilus did not bother to light a fire. He curled into a ball and went to sleep.

Eamilus was awoken suddenly. He lay still and tried to figure out what had woken him. His sharp ears detected a rustling sound along the mountainside. Almost simultaneously, his nose detected a strong, foul odour. He knew what the smell meant. A ghrimben was nearby. Most likely, it had seen his tracks or smelled his presence and was creeping up the mountainside to take him by surprise. He listened carefully but could not sense more than one ghrimben. In all probability, it was a lone runner, possibly an outcast. That would explain its need for secrecy and stealth. Ghrimbens were not known for their courage. While attacking, they usually relied on the strength of numbers to terrify and bring down prey. They were small, bony vynobnie with splayed but nimble hands and feet, large bulbous eyes, coarse pasty skin, exceedingly ugly faces, very little language skills and absolutely no personal hygiene. They were little better than packs of carnivorous hyenas, except that they killed for pleasure as much as hunger and destroyed everything in their path.

The loner must have been very hungry, Eamilus thought, to be willing to attack even him. Usually, the predatory creatures that roamed the Lyudzbradh and the Shadow Lands relied on their sense of smell to tell them the nature of their prey. Eamilus's kocovussy ancestry often helped him avoid such predators. There were few creatures, if any, that would dare to attack a kocovus, even one that had a hint of human odour about him.

And then Eamilus detected another smell. At first, he thought that it was a tiger. If so, there was something odd about the tiger. It smelled strangely like a human. For a moment, Eamilus was puzzled. Then realisation dawned. He smiled to himself as he readied himself to face his twin enemies. He felt certain that the two were hunting independently. The only question was, who was hunting whom? Or were they both hunting him? Eamilus bared his fangs and claws, arched his body into a tight crouch and waited. The sounds continued to approach. It was still dark outside. The rain hadn't stopped, although it had slowed down to a drizzle. Eamilus crouched lower as the ghrimben came nearer. He sat staring at the open mouth of the crevice. He counted the moments under his breath until his attacker would crawl over the ledge at the mouth of the crevice. Suddenly, he saw the ghrimben's red, glowering eyes peeping over the ledge.

The ghrimben, too, saw him at the same instant. With a scream of anger (or was it greed?), it leapt towards him. Eamilus knew that he had to meet his foe outside, where he could defend himself better. He leapt out of the gap at the charging ghrimben. But, before he could even touch the creature, a large form came hurtling out of the darkness above him and launched itself at the ghrimben. The ghrimben was strong and fierce, but it was no match for its attacker. The fight between the two growling and roaring creatures was brief and ended with a long, final shriek that melted away into a strangled gurgling. The ghrimben lay still. Eamilus stood outside the crevice, watching the spine-chilling scene. In the gathering light, he could clearly see the large, hulking tiger that had leapt on the ghrimben from the slopes above him.

The enormous beast turned round slowly. Behind him, the dead ghrimben lay in a heap. The fiery coat of the tiger glistened in the rain. Its eyes glowed like coals in the semi-darkness. Blood dripped from its wet, reddened maw. It was a magnificent creature, all sinew and strength, fire and rage. It looked like a leaping flame come to life as it took slow but deliberate steps towards Eamilus. The boy stood spellbound at the majesty and beauty of this wonderful beast, almost forgetting where he was, hypnotised by the fiercely burning eyes. He saw the tiger crouch but could not move. The tiger leapt at him and the spell suddenly broke. Eamilus was galvanised into action. He bared his fangs and claws and leapt aside. The tiger landed where he had been standing just moments before and whirled round with unbelievable speed. Eamilus now stood in front of the ghrimben's corpse, his back to the precipice, facing the terrible beast.

'Stop!' he suddenly cried, withdrawing his claws and fangs. 'Stop, homanim!'

The tiger, which had been about to leap again, stopped in its tracks.

Eamilus continued, 'I know that you are a homanim. I know it by your smell. I wish you no harm. I am just a traveller who has lost his way and will be gone with the first light.'

The tiger stood its ground, neither attacking nor showing any signs of relenting. Eamilus continued, 'If you wish only to protect your territory, let us both forget this incident and go our separate ways. I truly wish you no harm. I am without weapons, but I am not completely defenceless. If you wish to fight me despite my assurances, I am not afraid to fight. The choice is yours, homanim!'

Eamilus and the tiger stood staring into each other's eyes for a long time, as the sun began to peep out of the eastern horizon, behind Eamilus's back. The two stood there, on the narrow mountain ledge, like two statues carved out of stone. Suddenly, the tiger began to tremble. It crouched into a ball and then began to stretch out. It lengthened until its form was entirely changed. In its place stood a tall, well-muscled, broad-shouldered man who wore thick, fur-lined clothes of orange and black. His bronzed skin glowed in the light of the early morning sun. His face was heavily bearded but not unclean. He carried no weapons. As he stepped forward, Eamilus found the same grace and majesty in him that he had noticed in the tiger. The man-tiger in front of him had lost none of his magnificence in the transformation. When he spoke, his low, deep voice was calm and confident.

'You are brave although you are young. What are you doing on this mountain?'

Eamilus replied courteously, 'I lost my way in the dark during the storm. I wished to find Cornen Pass but missed it. I took shelter here for the night.'

The man-tiger stood contemplating Eamilus. He saw before him a young boy who had the bearing and eyes of an older man. He was tall for his age and sinewy though lean. He was striking rather than good looking, with lines and angles in his face that suggested the kocovussy side of his lineage. Mostly, his expression and bearing were proud and rebellious, as if he dared the world to do its worst to him, confident in his ability to survive whatever was thrown at him. 'What is your name?' he asked.

'Eamilus.'

'Eamilus, you are wise for one so young. You have answered me without telling me anything. I could ask you to trust me, but I will not. In this day and age, it is wise to trust no one, not even those you know, let alone strangers. I will not ask what you do not wish to tell. But I am surprised that you seek to cross the Lyudzbradh. I know of very few who would wish to do so or dare to do so.'

'You will pardon me if I say only that I cross the Lyudzbradh through necessity, not choice. However, I am not afraid of any creature that roams these mountains. And, if I may ask, who are you?'

The man-tiger smiled and replied, 'I am Uzdal Lyudz. High up on this mountain is my lair. Look around you; this is the Valdero forest. Though this country is Wyurr, no ghrimben sets foot in Valdero. If any dares to, it never returns to tell the tale.'

Uzdal looked with open disgust and hatred at the prostrate figure behind Eamilus.

'I will not ask you the purpose or destination of your journey,' Uzdal said to Eamilus, 'but I would be happy to entertain you in my lair if you agree to it. It is not often that I come across such interesting and brave yet strange young men.'

Eamilus was in no hurry to leave. He was curious about this homanim named Uzdal. He had never met another homanim before, and he wanted to learn more about the man-tiger. He accepted Uzdal's invitation. The two climbed in silence for a while. Uzdal, Eamilus noted, was as agile as a mountain goat. He climbed the steep mountainside with as much ease as if it had been a straight road. What would have taken a normal man two full days of climbing took these two barely two horas. The sun was beginning to rise above the line of mountains when they reached Uzdal's lair at the top of the mountain.

As Eamilus caught up with Uzdal, he stopped to look down into the valley on the other side. A strange sight met his eyes. A wide plain stretched out for miles; a barren, dusty plain. And, at the centre of the plain, stood a vast city. Eamilus could detect no signs of life in it. Even as he stood staring at the mysterious city, it began to vanish. Soon, there was no sign that such a place even existed. All he could see were mountains, deep valleys, green trees and a barren plain in deep shadow. He had never seen anything stranger in his life.

'That, Eamilus, is Patrisha, the city of Patarshp,' Uzdal explained from behind him. 'It is a magical city made of stone and appears only when the first light of the morning touches these mountain peaks and is reflected back into the valley.'

'What is that place?' asked Eamilus, awed.

'No one knows. In fact, I doubt if anyone even knows about its existence. Even I know barely anything more than its name. Now come, let us have something to eat and drink.'

As Eamilus followed Uzdal into the man-tiger's lair, a strange desire came into his heart to learn more about and to unburden his heart to this newfound friend of his. He realised with a start that he had already begun to think of Uzdal as a friend even though the two had just met. Somehow, he felt, he could trust Uzdal. He was mightily impressed by this man-tiger who hunted ghrimbens in their own country and lived at the edge of a mysterious and magical city of stone. He felt a strange longing to stay with Uzdal for more than just a meal.

Eamilus found it surprisingly easy to open up to Uzdal. He found himself telling Uzdal all about his life, including what had happened with Earilus. Perhaps because Uzdal too was only half-human, Eamilus felt that he would understand. He asked Uzdal if he could stay with him for a few days, full of hope and enthusiasm. Uzdal, on the other hand, was very uncomfortable at first. He liked this strange boy, but he was so unused to having company that he almost refused Eamilus's request. However, he was curious about the boy. He had seen Eamilus in kocovus form and had his nose not told him that the boy had a human side to him as well, he would not have hesitated to attack Eamilus. Soon, though, he began to sense a kindred soul in the boy and was glad that he had agreed to let Eamilus stay for a while with him.

The next morning, Uzdal awoke early as usual. After a quick breakfast, he went hunting, Eamilus in tow. To the boy's surprise, Uzdal turned into a tiger to hunt. He soon realised why. It gave him greater strength and ferocity; it also gave his prey a fair chance to escape. Or, at least, as fair a chance as nature had meant deer to have, Uzdal explained, as he carried the carcass back to his cave. He stripped the skin off and left it to dry, cut off chunks of flesh that he either cooked and ate or salted and cured for future use. The rest he threw out for scavenging birds and animals. Eamilus asked him if he had ever eaten raw meat.

'Often at one time,' he replied. 'These days, only if I am too hungry or too far to return to my lair.'

They had a filling meal. Then Uzdal lay down for a siesta. Eamilus was taken aback. Uzdal grinned and declared, 'All cats love to sleep, boy! Especially in the daytime!' Then he closed his eyes and dropped off to sleep. Eamilus walked around outside the lair, exploring the mountain and the forest. There was nothing near the lair to indicate that a human being lived there. It was almost as if Uzdal was just a tiger and nothing more. Eamilus could not imagine living like that, though he had learnt that kocovuses often lived like animals in the wild. Unlike him, Uzdal seemed perfectly adjusted to the duality of his nature.

As he sat thinking these thoughts, a crow flew into the cave and began to caw loudly. Uzdal awoke immediately, an angry gleam in his eyes. He merely stopped for a fraction of a momon to tell Eamilus, 'Ghrimbens have entered in the south. I am going to kill them.' Then he sped off, transforming even as he leapt down the mountain. Eamilus lost no time in following him, himself transforming to keep up with the massive tiger's speed and stamina. They reached the intruding group of ghrimbens in no time, the crow flying overhead to show them the way. There were five ghrimbens in the group. Uzdal fell upon them and began to maul them with his sharp claws and teeth. Eamilus joined him. Within a couple of minuras, the fight was over. The ghrimbens would not have stood a chance even had Uzdal been alone. With Eamilus aiding him, it was practically a massacre. Uzdal was surprised at Eamilus's fighting, though the boy had told him the day before, when they had first come face to face, that he wasn't without defences. He realised that Eamilus was far more dangerous and capable than he had imagined even after listening to the boy's life story.

'Did the crow tell you about the intruders?' Eamilus asked him as they made their way back by a circuitous route to ensure that no other ghrimben had entered the borders of the Valdero.

'Yes,' answered Uzdal. 'I feed the scavengers with the remains from my hunts and they, in turn, supply me with information about threats to my forest.' Uzdal stopped in front of a tree and frowned. He changed his hands into claws and scratched on it before moving on. He did this several times during their excursion, Eamilus noticed, marking his territory. Wherever they went, birds raised a hue and cry and monkeys screeched. Uzdal growled at them and even climbed into a tree once to scare them. Eamilus laughed on seeing the man's antics. By the time they returned to the lair, Uzdal had taken Eamilus on a tour of a large portion of Valdero forest. It was quite a large forest though its borders were almost indistinguishable from the forests to its north and south. Some more mountains besides the one on which Uzdal lived were encompassed by the Valdero, and Eamilus even spotted a few villages upon their foothills. However, Uzdal's mountain was the heart of Valdero.

'It will not be easy,' Uzdal commented, 'but I will never allow the vynobnie to spoil my forest with their presence as long as I am alive.'

'Why do you call it your forest?' Eamilus asked, curious.

'Because it is my home and because my father left it to me!' answered Uzdal, surprised that it could be unobvious to someone.

'Your father—he owned this forest?' Eamilus asked, confused. He had never thought of forests as belonging to anyone.

Uzdal almost snorted. 'My father was an Abyu or true tiger, one of the greatest beings that ever roamed these forests. He was a tiger, but he was unlike any other. He was descended, father to son, from the first Abyu of Yennthem. He had wisdom and sentience superior to most mortals though in form he was but an animal. This forest was his through his birthright. It has been sacred to all animals since the beginning of existence because of the presence of those higher beings, the Abyus. It is said that Vyidie herself created them, so they are considered the most supreme of all beasts. At the time of his death, my father pronounced that I was to inherit this forest though I am not a true tiger. Since then, the Valdero is my forest.'

Eamilus listened, fascinated. He had heard of the Abyus. It was said that only one Abyu existed in every generation, and any who was fortunate enough to encounter it was blessed forever by its wisdom.

'Was your father the last of the Abyus?' he asked Uzdal.

'No, I have a brother, a half-brother. He is a true tiger, but he resides further north, close to the eastern coast of Wyurr.'

'What is his name?'

'Baruzdal, meaning son of Uzdal.'

'So, your father's name was Uzdal too?'

'Yes. I was his younger son. My step-brother is older than me by a decadus.'

Eamilus was stunned. He wondered how long these true tigers lived. It would be fascinating to meet Baruzdal, he thought, though he did not voice that thought aloud.

'And your mother—what was her name? Was she a female Abyu?' he asked, his curiosity leading him to be more talkative than usual. By then, they had returned to Uzdal's lair. The man-tiger stopped when he heard Eamilus's question. He hesitated for a momon before answering. 'No, my mother was human.'

He pointed to the villages at the foothills of the nearby mountains and said, 'Do you see those? The Lyudzbradh is one of the most inhospitable habitats in Elthrusia, yet there are those who have settled here because they have been cast out by so-called civilised society. There are many such villages along the length and breadth of the Lyudzbradh. The residents of these villages lead very difficult lives. My mother was a human woman and came from one of those villages that you see there. She used to come to the forest to gather wood. She was a widow with a growing son and elderly parents. She was their only support. One day, while gathering wood, she had an accident and fainted. My father found her and brought her to his lair, this same one that I now live in.'

Uzdal paused, as if trying to recall the times that he had spent there with his parents. Then he sighed and continued, 'He tended and cared for her. When she came to, she was scared and thought that he would kill and eat her. Then she sensed how different he was. She began to feel grateful towards him for saving her from the other dangerous beasts of the forest. She had broken her leg, and it took her close to two mondans to recover. During this time, her gratitude slowly changed to affection and then to love. When she recovered, instead of returning to her village, she went to a witch and underwent very powerful transformations to become a tigress. She returned in that form to my father. The two of them were very happy together. They had a cub—me. But I was born human. Though this surprised them, they cared well for me. I grew faster than a normal human baby, however. In fact, I grew at the rate that a tiger would grow. When I was two anni old, my mother died as a result of the complications of the powerful magical spells that she had undergone. My father was heartbroken. He, too, died soon after. The night he died, I changed into a tiger for the first time. It was very painful, but I had no one to turn to for help. My step-brother, who had lived in Valdero until then, left for the north. He wanted to continue to live here, where our father had lived, and his father before that. But Valdero was mine by my father's decree, and he could not remain. Since then, I have been protecting my inheritance from those who wish to spoil it.'

Uzdal was silent for a long time after finishing his story. Eamilus, too, sat quietly. The pain in the man-tiger's tale had touched him. Did everyone have such sad stories or were homanims particularly subject to tragedy, he wondered. It had grown dark by then. Uzdal announced that they would go for a stroll in the forest and rose. Eamilus followed him outside. Before Uzdal could transform, Eamilus blurted out, 'How do you deal with it?'

Uzdal turned and asked, 'Deal with what?'

'This—being a tiger *and* a man. Don't you ever feel confused, like you don't know which is the right thing for you to do? I mean, whether you should live like a tiger or whether you should live like a man?'

'It did once, when I was young. Now it does not. Because I have understood that I am neither a tiger nor a human; I am both.'

Before Eamilus could ask anything further, Uzdal turned into a tiger and leapt away. The boy had not understood what Uzdal had meant, but he was beginning to realise that the older homanim was better adjusted to his state of being than he was if he wasn't plagued by the kind of questions that Eamilus was plagued by. Staying with Uzdal would help him resolve some of those questions, he hoped, as he also transformed and followed his new friend into the forest.

ASTORETH AND ZAVAK
(9 A.N.)

Only minuras were left for sunrise. Astoreth stood on the banks of the flowing river, steeling himself for what he was about to do. He had made up his mind, and nothing was going to change it. Not the knowledge that he had already done everything necessary to make himself the most powerful mortal possible. Not the fact that it wasn't essential to go through the rebirth ritual to harness his powers at will. And definitely not the possibility that things could go horribly wrong during the ritual. He had been born a dirsfer while Zavak had been born a magus. He had learnt magic so that he could be the equal of his brother. He had roused his consciousness to the highest level and had extended it to bond with every fragment of energy and power in creation, in effect, learning to control everything around him. Yet, his powers were not entirely infallible. Though the probability was slim, they could still betray him. The only way to bind all that power to him forever was through the rebirth ritual. And nothing was going to stop him from performing it.

In another part of Pretvain, at the same time, Zavak was contemplating the same ritual. He stood in front of a raging bonfire, gathering his thoughts and calming his mind. He had started in life with the advantages of a magus, but they had not been enough. He had wanted to be more powerful than every magus in the world. What was more, he had always had a penchant for magic. It had not been too difficult for him to master the most difficult forms of magic that had drawn the power of the world to him. For anni, he had undergone every transformation that would bind to him the powers of the elements, of the spirits of Nature, of all the energy in the universe until he could bend them to his will. Yet he was not infallible. And though he was confident in his abilities, he wanted to ensure that his powers would stand him in good stead at all times. And so he would have to undergo the rebirth ritual. Not because he felt that he was not powerful enough, but because he had to be more powerful than everyone else.

Unbeknownst to the other, each prepared for the ultimate sacrifice, going through the paces of the routine that would prepare their souls for rebirth in this very life. The ritual was notoriously tricky. It was the most complex and difficult ritual in the entirety of magic. Few, if any, had ever dared to perform it. None had lived to reap its benefits. One had to let go of everything one had, including one's body and one's life. If one succeeded, one was born anew, one's body fully restored, and with all one's powers not only intact but intensified. If one failed, one's soul was lost for eternity. This was the final step in the accumulation of magical powers. Any who succeeded in completing this ritual became invincible. In theory. In practice, none had lived to confirm or deny the theory. One could choose to complete the sacrifice in any of the elements; both brothers had chosen their preferred elements.

Astoreth finished the preparatory part of the ritual and, when the first rays of the sun coloured the river pale pink, stepped into the flowing water. He discarded every last shred of his clothing as he walked deeper and deeper into the river until he was floating at the very centre, naked as a newborn baby. Then he let go and sank like a stone. The water rushed into his nostrils, and they burned. It seeped into his throat and his lungs, and they burned. Every fibre in Astoreth's being wanted to swim up, to escape, but he forced himself not to struggle. He allowed the water to claim him for its own. As everything began to grow dark, he wondered why everyone was so afraid to die. As his body turned lifeless, the mud of the riverbed sucked it inside.

Zavak, too, completed the preparation and, just as the first golden rays of the sun touched the earth, stepped into the roaring fire. The fire burned away every shred of clothing on his body. But it burned more than that; it burned his skin and his hair and every particle of his body. The agony was unbelievable! He could feel the flesh melting off his bones and plopping into the pyre long before his nerves were rendered senseless by the blaze. The fire ate through his flesh and through his bones and into his organs, sparing nothing. And still Zavak did not hesitate for a momon. Not once did he wish that he had not taken such an extreme step. He never had second thoughts despite the searing torment. An unearthly scream could be heard upon the air, and Zavak wondered whether his feelings had betrayed him. But it was only the sound of the hot air rising up around the hungry bonfire. By the time the fire died down, all that was left of Zavak was a heap of ashes and charred fragments of bones. The fire had taken over a hora to consume him.

When he opened his eyes, it was mid-day. Zavak was lying on the ground next to the pyre that had consumed his body. He sat up slowly and tried to recall what had happened. Gradually, all his memories, his knowledge, his thoughts, his feelings and his powers returned to him. They filed him until he was the same Zavak as before. Only, he wasn't exactly the same. He was better than before. He looked the same—tall and fair with flaxen hair and eyes as blue as the outomy sky—but he felt different. His aura had changed too. It was now more red than gold and its edges were rimmed with black so dark that even the intense brightness of the aura could not overcome. He felt stronger, more determined, more confident of himself. The magic had worked! He was the most powerful mortal in existence! There was none who could come in his way, none who could stop him! He could achieve all that he wanted to. Now his father would regret choosing Astoreth as his heir. Now he would see how much more capable Zavak was than he had always believed! Zavak stood up and reached for the clothes that he had laid out before stepping into the fire. As he dressed, he thought of what he would do first. Strange as it seemed, the only thought in his mind was how Astoreth would react when he learnt about Zavak's ultimate achievement.

When Astoreth opened his eyes, he was lying in the mud on the riverbank. It was noon, and the sun was directly overhead. He slowly stood up, washed himself in the river and put on the clothes that were laid out upon higher ground to prevent them from getting wet. Slowly, the events of the morning came back to him. His reflection showed him the same eighe who had stepped into the river at dawn. For a momon, he panicked as he wondered whether he had swum ashore, his instincts getting the better of his conscious efforts. Then he remembered the darkness that had enveloped him underwater. No, the water had accepted his sacrifice and had returned him renewed and more powerful than ever before. He could feel that he had changed in some subtle way. Only his aura was noticeably changed, though. It shone brighter and purer white than ever before, almost like an intense burst of starlight. He was now the most powerful mortal in existence! He was stronger than Zavak though he could not imagine why that thought made him feel strangely melancholy. He wondered what Zavak would say if he learnt that Astoreth had embraced the power of magic! He also wondered if he would have turned to magic if the rift between him and Zavak had not pushed them apart.

Now that Zavak was as powerful as any mortal could hope to be, he wanted to go beyond the ambitions of any yennt. His father had thought him unworthy of the throne of Effine. Well, he would just have to find another kingdom for himself. And not just any kingdom. He would be the ruler of all Yennthem. And why just Yennthem? He could be the ruler of Maghem too if he wanted. And even Vynobhem. He was powerful enough. And if he could bring three of the hems into his dominion, why spare the other two? He was as powerful as any kaitsya, and he could rule over the entirety of Creation. He needed two things first—an army and a sword worthy of him. And he knew just where to find them!

PART THREE

Chapter 41

FROM PRINCE TO THIEF

By the time Avator turned sixteen, he had been living with the outlaws for close to two anni. He, along with Forsith and Avita, had become an accepted member of the group and was allowed not only to go into neighbouring towns and villages on his own but also to receive a share of the loot that the outlaws brought in. Even though he was still primarily a scout, his suggestions were taken seriously by Igrag. He took care not to put forward too many suggestions lest Igrag begin to pay too much attention to him. His sixteenth birthday came and went without much notice by anyone. Forsith gifted him a saddle for Habsolm, whom he usually rode. Avita, who was over eight anni old then, gave him a scarf that she had knitted. Habsolm gave him a 'free' ride, meaning that he did not demand to be fed apples in return for allowing Avator to ride him. He had proven very helpful to the young kereighe boy over the mondans, providing him with critical information about the outlaws. The outlaws still had no idea of who the three really were or what Avator could do. Forsith was still considered the horse-wizard and Avator, or Mordeph, as he was known, was their smith and scout. Forsith's cover had been maintained, in large part, due to Habsolm's information.

Just over a mondan after Avator's sixteenth birthday, he had to accompany the outlaws on a mission a short distance south from the camp, towards the edge of the desert. The outlaws had received intelligence that a rich caravan of merchants was about to pass that way. They planned to target the caravan. It would be heavily guarded, they had learnt, though they had no idea how heavily. They were prepared for the worst as they rode in a south-western direction to intercept the caravan. The scouts, as usual, went ahead to keep an eye on the target. Avator took up a position by the side of the path along which the caravan was expected to pass, hidden behind mounds of sand. A few other scouts took up similar positions further up the road. Soon, Avator heard the signal to indicate that the caravan was close by. He passed the message further down the line. A hora later, he could see the dust raised by the caravan on its way to Esvilar. Almost simultaneously, he heard the signal to indicate that there were few guards with the caravan. He signalled to indicate that the caravan was now in his sights but hesitated to confirm the lack of guards. He knew that the scouts of the outlaws were well trained in their work but were often not too cunning. He wanted to be sure that the caravan was indeed poorly guarded before passing on the message. After all, he was a scout, not a messenger. His job was to gather information, not just to pass it along. Igrag's source had predicted a heavy presence of guards, and his sources were rarely wrong.

Avator waited patiently hidden beside the road as the caravan passed by him. Several animal call signals from scouts further down the line asked him to report on the status of guards, but he didn't respond. He had to be sure before he signalled. There were at least a score carts in the caravan along with riders mounted on horses or mules. All the travellers were dressed like merchants or caravaneers. Only a few soldiers on horseback were evident. Avator reluctantly agreed that the previous scout's report had been correct. But the scene before him did not feel right somehow. He could not believe that it was going to be so simple. He still remembered how they had been tricked in Esvilar. The same mastermind had given them much trouble over the subsequent mondans. During raids, they had lost several members to the cunning tricks of the lord of Esvilar. This caravan, headed for the city of Esvilar, also belonged to him. Was it too much of a stretch to assume that he would make sure that it was well-protected? Avator thought not.

He observed the travellers closely. There were hardly any eighees or eighe children. This was not unusual. What was unnatural, though, was the number of riders compared to the number of carts. There were too few. Usually, because the carts were laden with goods, the merchants accompanying their consignments had to ride on horseback beside the carts. There were anywhere between three to six riders accompanying each cart in a normal caravan. Then there were the guards. This caravan should have had between a seventy to a hundred or more riders. So why were there so few of them? And why were there so many horses without riders? The extra horses could not have been for sale because it made no sense to risk the loss of saleable animals by making them walk through the desert to their destination.

Avator also noticed, with growing suspicion, that the carts were covered. He knew that this was nothing unusual either. Travelling in the desert required protection from heat and dust. However, given his overall sense of misgiving, the covered carts bothered him. He tried to peer into the carts as they passed him. A glint of metal inside one caught his eye when an improperly fastened canvas covering briefly flapped open just as the cart was trundling past. Fortuitously, it happened in front of Avator. Anyone else would have assumed that the glint indicated that the cart contained metal goods, which were one of Esvilar's main imports. But not Avator. His time with Miehaf as the master-smith's apprentice had given him, among other things, an extraordinary and intimate knowledge of metals and metal objects. He knew immediately that it was not the glint of tools or utensils. It was sunlight reflected off the edge of a sharp sword. His suspicion was now confirmed. It *was* a trap. The carts—at least some of them—were carrying soldiers rather than goods.

Avator signalled a warning as soon as he safely could. He sensed hesitation in the scout down the line, but in the end, the scout passed on the message. The next scout passed it further on. Avator began to follow the caravan at a discreet distance, as he had been instructed to do. Several of the scouts from up the line caught up with him on the way back to the main body of the outlaws. Avator had no idea what Igrag would do with the information that he had provided. Some of the other scouts were sour that he had contradicted their report. He was sure that they were hoping for him to be proven wrong. They soon caught up with the caravan and the other scouts. No one had any information on Igrag's plans though the scouts down the line confirmed Avator's findings. The boy smiled as he saw the thunderous looks on the faces of the scouts who had failed to detect the hidden soldiers. He was still concerned about how Igrag was planning to deal with the trap.

Suddenly, a band of outlaws attacked the caravan from the opposite side of the road. They rode down a hillock with loud yells, brandishing their weapons. The travellers in the caravan acted as expected, rushing to the back in panic, trying to hide or escape. Avator frowned. This was not how the outlaws usually attacked. There were too few of them. And why was *Qually* leading them? What was going on? The scouts were concealed by the roadside, watching patiently. Avator felt his heart beating fast; he wanted to join in the action. When the gang of robbers neared the front of the caravan, a troop of soldiers erupted from the first cart and fell upon them. Others emerged from half a dozen carts in the line and soon had the robbers almost surrounded. Realising that their attempt had been foiled, the outlaws turned tail and sped away, pursued by the soldiers, many of whom had now mounted the riderless horses.

The small gang of outlaws disappeared over the hills behind which they had ostensibly been waiting, followed by the soldiers. As soon as the guards reached the hills, another band of outlaws emerged from behind a hill half a mile south of the spot from where the first band had emerged. Unlike them, these robbers came quietly but swiftly. The travellers had been riveted on the guards chasing the outlaws away, beginning to relax, when they noticed the second, larger band coming towards them. Before reaching the caravan, the band split in two, with the smaller section continuing on towards the travellers and the larger section pursuing the soldiers. The group that attacked the caravan was led by Frengdan and Feerdhen; Igrag led the group that went after the soldiers. The realisation that their trick had not worked gave rise to redoubled panic among the travellers. But it was too late. They never stood a chance. Few of them were armed. They were no match for the marauders. Before long, they had been rounded up like cattle. The scouts were ordered to round up the horses while the rest of the group gathered the loot.

In the distance, the soldiers could be seen returning, now fleeing before those whom they had originally pursued. Even as they galloped towards the halted caravan, they saw the other group of bandits headed in their direction. Realisation dawned too late that the tables had been turned on them. They were caught between the two troops of the outlaws. The soldiers fought desperately but futilely. The outlaws, though fewer in number, were far more ferocious and ruthless. Soon, the battle was over. The triumphant outlaws arrived at the site of the caravan, their clothes and faces splattered with blood. The travellers were standing together, cowering. Their carts had been emptied of their precious cargo, and their horses had been requisitioned to carry the goods. They had been stripped of all valuables that they had been carrying on their persons. Even the few children travelling with the caravan had not been spared; their jewellery and toys had been taken. A few of the travellers had tried to resist and had been rebutted harshly. Cuts and bruises were evident on most of them. One woman simply refused to let the outlaws take her jewellery. She shrieked and fought back, scratching Lamissur who was trying to wrench her bangles off her wrists. This infuriated Lamissur and he ran her through. She fell down dead. Lamissur then proceeded to relieve her of her valuables. No one else protested after that.

Avator turned away, feeling sick to the stomach. He wanted to *be* sick, but he knew that the others would take it as a sign of weakness. He could not allow that. He had to pretend to be as callous and hardened as the rest. He went to stand by the horses captured from the traders. Horses always brought him comfort. He could not talk to them in front of the other outlaws, but he could listen to their worries and fears and could comfort them. In a small measure, he felt, this was his self-imposed retribution for causing such strain to them. He would ensure that they were looked after well. For their owners, he knew, there was nothing he could do.

Avator was quiet after returning to the camp. He lay down on his bed, trying to push thoughts of the dead eighee out of his mind. But his mind continued to replay the scene of horror in lurid detail. The shock and pain that had been on the dying eighee's face was branded onto Avator's young mind. He could never forget her. He had seen death before. He had even seen the outlaws killing eighes before. But those had been soldiers or armed eighes. He had never seen any of them slaughtering unarmed innocents. Forsith saw him and came over to check.

'Are you all right? Did you get hurt?' he asked, full of concern for his young ward. He had heard what Avator had done to help the outlaws but found it hard to believe. Why would Avator want to help them? But then he remembered what the boy had done at Esvilar, and his concern had deepened.

'No, I'm not hurt,' Avator said, sitting up. He looked tired and drawn, far older than his anni.

'What happened?' Forsith asked kindly. Avator told him about Lamissur and the murdered eighee.

'What else do you expect from these barbaric outlaws?' declared Forsith, outraged but not entirely surprised at the outlaw's cruelty. 'They have neither a vestige of honour nor a shred of nobility in their blood. I don't understand why we continue to live with them!' He remembered the day they had joined the outlaws. It had been to escape being slaughtered by them. Avator might have forgotten it, but he had not. They had been as capable of killing innocents in cold blood then as they were now.

'What else would we do?' snapped Avator. 'Remember, we came here because we had no choice!'

'Yes,' responded Forsith, rather hotly, 'and the plan was to escape as soon as we gained their trust. I think we have, don't you?'

'What do you mean?'

'I mean, they surely trust us now if they form their strategies of attack based on what *you* tell them!'

'I was just doing my job! And if you want to accuse me of something, say it clearly,' Avator said sharply.

'No, I am not accusing you of anything. I am merely pointing out that we had planned to escape once we'd gained their trust, but we never talk about it.'

'Because we *can't* escape! How would we escape? Habsolm couldn't carry one of us, let alone three. If we stole horses, we would be found before we had gone two miles. They are not like my foolish uncle Nersefan who tried to trap us and failed. They are cunning and ruthless. Besides, where would we go even if we managed to get out of here? There's a vast desert out there that is their veritable fiefdom. And weren't you the one who wanted us to live a settled life? Believe me, for the likes of us, life doesn't get more settled than this. No one pries into our past. No one points fingers at my sister. She's been more at peace here than anywhere else. Tell me, even if we ignore all that, where could we go that these outlaws wouldn't find us long before we reached safety?'

'We could go to Esvilar,' Forsith said, beginning to grow saddened by the change in Avator.

'Even if we manage to steal horses and get to Esvilar, how would we have escaped? You know very well that Igrag's reach cannot be escaped even there.'

'We could go to the lord of Esvilar and seek his help and protection,' argued Forsith.

'Excellent!' retorted Avator. 'We tell him what? That we spent the last two anni with the outlaws and please now give us sanctuary?'

'If it is impossible to escape, why did you plan for us to come with these outlaws in the first place?' snapped Forsith in frustration. 'Your brilliant plan seems to have failed. Or is it something else that has changed?'

Avator stood up, too angry. He spoke coldly and with deliberation. 'The plan was meant to keep us alive. And if you are sorry for it, I am not!'

He turned away and began to walk out. Forsith, a tad ashamed of his outburst now, called after him. 'Avator! I didn't mean to accuse you of anything. I just wanted to remind you of who and what you are. Of late, I feel that you seem to have lost your way.'

'Thank you for reminding me,' Avator replied coldly, without turning back, 'but I know who I am and what I am doing.' He began to walk away.

'Avator!' Forsith called again.

The boy turned round sharply and declared in a flat voice, 'Don't call me by that name any more. I am no longer Avator, your ward. I am Mordeph, smith and scout in Igrag's gang of outlaws. My sister is Menithyl. And you are Eronsom. Like it or not, that is who we are now.'

Then he turned and walked out, ignoring Forsith's calls. His throat felt constricted, his chest felt heavy and his eyes stung, but he would not cry. He did not honestly know what had upset him more—his tiredness, the sight of seeing Lamissur kill the eighee without a momon's hesitation or Forsith's accusation. But he suspected that the truth in Forsith's words probably had more to do with it than the shock of seeing an innocent eighee's death. Avator would not admit it to himself, but Forsith had been correct in assuming that something had changed in Avator. It was not what Forsith thought it was. Avator himself could not have put a finger on what it was. But something had definitely changed.

Chapter 42

PRINCE HALIFERN'S ADVENTURES

(1 Kielom 5009 A.E. to 11 Beybasel 5009 A.E.)

Just over four mondans after inaugurating his new treehouse, Prince Halifern was faced with the third and last leg of the fraels' traditional journey into adulthood. Each frael was required to live outside civilisation for a quarter of an annus to prove that he or she was indeed at one with nature. It was hardly a challenge for any frael. In fact, most of them took this as an opportunity for a last irresponsible fling before settling down to the serious business of living one's life as an adult. Halifern was invited by his friends Loyohen, Erofone and Siltare to go on a hunting trip with them. At first, Halifern hesitated. The fraels were supposed to live on their own during this period to prove that they were truly capable of independence. However, it was quite common for them to band together with friends to spend the four mondans of exile. In the end, Halifern gave in to his friends' wheedling and agreed to join them. They decided to travel through the forests of Norowichh along the borders of Harwillen and Cordemim. The plan was to go as far north as possible without crossing over into the human kingdom.

By the tenth of Samrer, they were into the third mondan of their tour and had managed to explore about halfway into the Norowichh Forest. They were camped on the banks of the river Helawel, one of the most important rivers of the fraels. Their day started with a swim and fishing. Then they cooked and ate the fish that they had caught along with some roasted root vegetables that they had gathered. In the evening, they whiled away the horas by climbing trees, performing acrobatics and competing in impromptu archery contests. As dusk fell, they gathered round a bonfire where they ate more of the fish while singing and dancing cheerfully. All in all, it was a normal day with hardly any variation from the other days that they had spent in the Norowichh.

Halifern was getting a little tired of this routine, but his friends were far from spent. When Halifern wanted to read quietly, they dragged him into their games. They scolded him, threatening to tell the Elders that he had brought books along. The young fraels were supposed to be bonding with nature. Books had no place in that relationship. Halifern felt a little worried but dismissed his worries and joined them. They were his friends, after all. They wouldn't betray him. When they gathered eggs for a meal, Halifern studied the birds, their habits and their calls and noted them down on parchment. His friends teased him, but he didn't mind.

They, on their part, were quite tolerant of Halifern's eccentricities. They ragged and baited him, but it was all in good fun. No offense was meant. None was taken.

The next day, they decided to explore the opposite bank of the Helawel. Since it was past afternoon by the time they crossed over, they decided to postpone the exploration until the next morning. Vernurt held sway. Night came fast and sudden in the forest. They did not want to be caught away from the safety of the temporary camp that they had made on the riverbank.

They awoke bright and early the next morning, eager to continue their excursion. They broke camp after an early breakfast and set off to prospect the forest. They had never been to this side of the Helawel before. The variety of trees that grew here amazed them. They spent days roaming through the sylvan woods. Being fraels, they could easily find their way around without maps or directions. The beauty of the forest enthralled them. The dense vegetation promised big game. Pretty soon, they came across spoor of a large animal. They were sure that the trail was that of a tiger. They eagerly followed the trail for three days in the deep forest, never once seeing the beast they were pursuing, nor ever losing track of it. By the time the tiger's traces vanished, they were well inside the Norowichh and, though not lost, definitely off the route that they had planned. They wandered the forest for days before they could figure out the path back. Niwukir had already given way to Beybasel by then. They had twenty-two days left for their return home.

One evening, while they were making their way back to their original route, they came across a group of human woodcutters from one of the villages in the border area. Territories between the human and frael countries were not clearly marked in the forest. It wasn't very unusual for those living along the border to cross over accidentally in search of livelihoods. The fraels thought that the humans had crossed into their territory. What they didn't know was that they, rather than the humans, had missed the border and were trespassing. Halifern wanted to leave the woodcutters alone, but his companions were in a mischievous mood. They climbed into the trees quietly, unseen by the woodcutters busy with their laborious task. Then, when it was just getting dark, they started roaring like leopards. The terrified woodcutters dropped their axes and loads of wood and fled. Hooting with laughter, Erofone, Siltare and Loyohen descended from the trees. Suddenly, their laughter dried in their throats as a roar of a different kind rang through the forest. It was the roar of a tiger! The three fraels stood rooted to the spot, turning their heads this way and that to locate the dangerous predator. When they saw nothing, they rapidly climbed back into the trees that they had just descended from. Soon after, Halifern emerged from behind some shrubs, laughing. When the others realised that their friend had played a trick on them, they chased him through the growing darkness. He was quicker than the other three, and they could not catch up with him. Finally, giving up, they called a truce and made camp for the night.

The next morning, they again caught sight of a tiger's pugmarks and decided to pursue it. They were sure it was the same animal they had failed to track down earlier. This time it would not escape, they swore.

'Perhaps it heard Halifern roaring and came to investigate,' Siltare joked.

'Maybe it thought that a tigress was calling,' Loyohen ribbed his friend. Halifern smiled and said nothing.

They followed the tiger's trail into even denser forest, determined not to give up this time. They doggedly pursued the spoor into unfamiliar, dangerous territory. Next afternoon, they came across the carcass of a deer. The half-eaten body of the animal seemed to have been abandoned in a hurry, as if the predator had been disturbed at its meal and had left hurriedly to conceal itself. The four friends decided to wait there that night, assuming that the beast would return to reclaim its prey. Since there was no certainty of when the beast would return to the spot, they climbed into a stout tree to spend the night.

They decided to keep watch by turns. Erofone took the first watch. He would wake Siltare up after three horas. Loyohen was settled upon to take the third watch. Halifern chose the last watch to stay awake during the last horas of the night into dawn. He curled up against one of the broad branches of the tree and comfortably fell into a deep sleep.

Halifern awoke suddenly. He sat up and looked for Loyohen. But there was no Loyohen to be seen. Nor were Erofone and Siltare present. Halifern's sharp eyes detected no movement around him whatsoever. For a fraction of a momon, he wondered whether his friends hadn't transported him during his sleep to another part of the forest. This was a trick that they had played on him once before. A quick glance around told him that it was not so. He was still in the tree that they had chosen as their shelter and lookout point. Carefully, he unsheathed his narrow sword and soundlessly descended from the tree. Something was different about that area, he sensed. At first he could not fathom what was wrong. It struck him suddenly. There was no deer carcass! Fear gripped him as he suspected the worst: the beast had come, his friends had attacked it without waking him and the hunters had become the prey. His stomach felt stuffed with lead.

He was startled by the sound of a low, moaning sound. He turned in the direction it was coming from, expecting to find one of his friends injured. But what he saw completely bewildered him. A human female—a woman—was sitting under a tree, crying. She was young, he noticed, and good-looking by human standards. He wondered whether she was a resident of neighbouring Cordemim. He approached her cautiously and called to her.

'Hi there! Who are you?' he asked. He spoke in Volegan, the common tongue. Most fraels knew some rudimentary Volegan, but Halifern was quite fluent in it, and rather proud of his linguistic ability.

The woman jumped up. She looked terrified of the voice in the dark and stared around wildly. Halifern noticed that her face was tear-stained.

'Who…who is it?' She shrank away, the fear in her voice apparent.

Prince Halifern stepped out of the shadows and approached the crying woman.

'I am a frael,' he said. 'I was in the forest searching for prey. I mean you no harm. Who are you?'

'I am a poor woman from a neighbouring village,' the young woman answered. 'My family were travelling through the forest, but I got separated from them. Before I could find them, darkness fell. I searched for them even after dark but became hopelessly lost. Please help me find my way back!' she begged.

Prince Halifern felt sorry for her. Humans never were good at finding their way about without roads and landmarks. Unlike fraels, they could not see in the dark or climb trees with ease or go long distances without feeling fatigued. They were neither limber nor swift. Most fraels felt nothing but contempt for humans, but Halifern took a sympathetic view of the race. They had other qualities, which the fraels lacked. They were planners and were a persistent lot. They could endure hardships and still survive. They were skilled at arms. They kept farms and grew crops and were not entirely dependent on the bounty of nature for their livelihood. They practised all manners of crafts and trades. Most importantly, they valued books and learning. Halifern felt a certain admiration and curiosity towards humans that he effectively hid from his race.

'I will help you,' he reassured the lost young woman. 'But can you tell me what has become of my friends? We were four, but now I see none of the others. Did you see any of them?'

'Your friends left a while ago,' she answered. 'They came down from that tree,' she pointed to the tree in which the four friends had been roosting, 'and rushed away excitedly after some tiger. I was scared and hid myself.'

It was difficult for Halifern to believe that his friends would behave thus. They would never chase after a dangerous animal like a tiger in the middle of the night instead of merely shooting at it from their vantage point in the tree. And they would definitely not leave without waking him first so that he could join them. Would they? Wouldn't they? Had he not been thinking similar thoughts when the woman's crying had first caught his attention? Had he been convinced of his theory? In balance, Halifern decided, his friends would *not* have left him alone. However, he said nothing. He asked the woman where she lived. She named a village near the edge of the forest, on the side of Cordemim.

Halifern debated whether to help the woman or not. She was obviously lying when she said that his friends had left, but why? And how did she know that they had been pursuing a tiger? Even if they had been talking amongst themselves about it, what were the chances that she knew Hentar, their language? He had promised to help her out of a sense of gallantry, but he was now thinking that his chivalry might have been misplaced. He looked at the tearful face of the woman and chided himself. Such an innocent and wretched person could neither mean any hurt nor pose any danger. She was really pretty too, he realised. It would be indeed a shame if she came to harm. He had to help her. That was the right thing to do. He was torn between wanting to search for his friends and helping the lost woman. If she was telling the truth, his friends would certainly return for him. They would never know where he was if he left with the woman without informing them. There had to be a good reason for their absence, he reasoned. He could not, and would not, believe that they could desert him in the middle of the forest and disappear.

'Let us wait for the others to return,' he said to the woman. 'Then we will take you to your village.'

The woman didn't seem too pleased with the arrangement. However, she sat back down without complaint, huddling against the tree on which she had been leaning. Halifern leapt into the same tree and perched on a low branch. The two sat quietly for a while, each absorbed in his or her thoughts. Then the woman softly said, 'I know that I am imposing on your kindness, but I am very hungry and thirsty. Do you have anything that I can eat or drink?'

Halifern apologised for forgetting his manners. 'I am sorry. You should not have had to ask.'

He gave her some water. She gulped it down thirstily. Halifern gave her some apples that he had in his pouch. She accepted them with thanks, though it was obvious from the tepidity of her enthusiasm that they were not her preferred victuals. Halifern felt sorry for her as she opened her mouth wide and hungrily bit into one. Suddenly Halifern's keen nose was assailed by the strong odour of rot. He became rigid with shock. There was only one place in Elthrusia where such fetidness could be found. Only one country where the earth stank with the rot of ages of dead creatures sunk into squelching, treacherous bogs. And only one country whose swamp-dwelling creatures bore that stench upon their breath—the marshy kingdom of Illafanka. Nothing else in existence could compare to that foul odour. Sometimes at night, the sea breeze bore that stench to the shores of the fraelish countries, and those who smelled it shivered with fear of the terrible creatures that lived in that cursed land. They fed on the flesh of fraels, phrixes and other smaller races but not of larger races like humans, eighes or kocovuses, though no one knew why they preferred one over the other. It was said that a mertkhezin could swallow a phrix whole and a frael in two gulps. They were too weak to capture and kill their prey when the latter were conscious, so they used a special weapon to render them immobile first.

Halifern climbed back into the tree, taking care not to disturb the woman. She looked absorbed in her meal. The apples were soon gone. She sighed and leant back against the tree. A whisper susurrated through the leaves of the trees standing motionless in the silence of the night. It seemed to say something to Halifern. He closed his eyes and leant back, trying to listen to it. He realised that the whisper was actually a song. The woman sitting below him was singing. He could not make out what she was saying, but it was strangely soothing and beautiful. Since when did humans sing like that, Halifern vaguely wondered. He believed that he could spend his life sitting at the feet of that beautiful woman, listening to her song. He was about to climb out of the tree to go to her when he heard a faint buzzing near his ear. He swiped at the bug that was annoying him. His hand brushed against thin air. There was no bug. The sound was inside his head, he realised. It was trying to tell him something. He felt irritated. He wanted to listen to the beautiful woman singing. He did not want to listen to bothersome inner voices. The voice was telling him something. What? That she wasn't a woman. That she wasn't, in fact, human at all. That humans *could not* sing like that. That only one kind of creature *could*. And that he was in terrible and mortal danger of life.

The sound inside his head began to grow louder. Halifern clearly understood the warning. He suddenly came out of his reverie. He covered his ears with his hands and leapt into a higher branch of the tree. The woman's whispering voice still pursued him. Without removing his hands from his ears, he fled as fast as he could. He leapt from tree to tree and branch to higher branch. The mertkhezin's song unrelentingly followed him. He did not understand how that was possible. He turned round to check whether he was safe and received a shock when he found his predator pursuing him only a short distance behind, continuing to sing her venomous song. He tore strips off his cloak and tied them round his ears. He leapt off the trees onto the ground and ran as fast as he could. He ran for what seemed to be horas. When he stopped, he was exhausted. He could flee no more. He fell upon the ground and passed out.

When he regained consciousness, he found himself lying in a glade near the edge of the forest. He was across the Sumarin though he had no recollection of crossing the river. There was no sign of the terrible temptress of the night before. He dragged his tired body up from the ground and out of the forest. He guessed what had befallen his poor friends. His heart was laden with grief for them. If only he had taken an earlier watch! He looked round for signs of habitation when he heard sounds of conversation, but what he saw increased his anxiety. In the distance, on the other side of the river, he espied a large group of people coming in the direction of the forest. He could tell that they were western humans. He stepped back into the shadows of the forest and began to wonder what such a large group of people was doing there. He also realised suddenly that they were quite close to the borders of the dharvh kingdoms. Was war afoot? There were too few soldiers for a war, he realised. What, then, was going on? His training told him to leave them alone and to try to return home, but his curiosity would not let him. He knew that with the mertkhezin still around, the humans were in great danger. He felt no threat to himself any more. Now that he knew where danger lay, he would be able to protect himself. He was more worried for the humans he could see in the distance. He decided to watch them clandestinely and see matters through to the end. Whatever that end might be.

It was early morning of the tenth day of Beybasel. More than seven mondans had passed since King Amiroth had left his kingdom. His contingent had reached their fourth major campsite, on the western bank of the River Sumarin, the day before. The expedition east was progressing as planned, and morale was still high. While his troops were busy setting up camp, looking for a ford to cross the river and replenishing supplies, King Amiroth was thinking about his family, particularly his son. Amishar was a precocious little boy. King Amiroth missed him. He wondered what Amishar had done the previous day. Probably spent it with Mizu, the boy from the village with the odd mother, he mused. A smile lit his lips involuntarily. The two were almost always together. They were practically inseparable. At first, he had worried. Though, if he were to be honest to himself, he had been more jealous than anxious. He had felt that the newcomers in Amishar's life were taking Amishar away from him. He could not bear to be away from his son for more than a few horas, and here he was, hundreds of miles away from home, on his way to search for something that probably did not even exist. The king of Balignor, sitting inside his tent alone in his camp by the river Sumarin, sighed.

A commotion outside his tent brought him out of his reverie. He stepped out to investigate.

'What is the matter?' he demanded.

The sentry who stood guard at the mouth of his tent bowed to him. 'My lord, the men that had gone to fetch water from the river have come running back to report a strange find.'

'What have they found?' King Amiroth asked.

'They found a young woman lying unconscious on the riverbank, Your Majesty. She looks bedraggled and injured. Her clothes are muddy and torn in places. It appears that she crossed the river during the night but fell unconscious on this side, exhausted with the strain.'

King Amiroth frowned. There were no villages for miles around. Where had she come from? And why was she in such a deplorable condition? He ordered to have her brought into the camp and tended to. The sentry bowed and left to fulfil his commands. Amiroth returned to his tent, vaguely uneasy about the new development. He knew that he was not very far from the borders of fraelish countries. He did not want unnecessary strife. On the other hand, if the woman had come from downriver, there was a possibility that the fraels were involved in the incident. He had no power to take action against the fraels in a country that was not his; nor could he allow malfeasance to go unpunished, for he was an honourable man. He was in a conundrum. He hoped that the matter was simply a misunderstanding and that he would not be called upon to take any action. Maybe the woman had merely had an accident, he mused.

They had settled into the fourth major camp by then. They would spend five days there, procuring rations from the nearest villages and towns, which were rather far from the area where they had set up camp. Scouts brought news of a potential place to cross the river, a ford further upriver, not more than seven or eight miles from the camp. The men and beasts could cross on foot when the tide was low; the carts would have to be rowed across on rafts during high tide. Amiroth spent the day taking stock of their progress and rations. They had been moving slowly, particularly due to the heavily laden carts accompanying the large contingent of soldiers and workers. These carts carried not only ration but also equipment to survive outdoors even in hostile conditions. Further, there was excavation equipment and weaponry. It was a complex affair moving all those men and carts safely through the countryside, especially when travelling through uninhabited or forest regions. But, all said, his expedition was making good progress. Soon they would be in dharvhish territories. Then the real expedition would begin. King Amiroth went to bed that night and dreamt of glory and riches for himself and his country.

The next morning, Amiroth was about to start on an inspection of his camp when a sentry entered to announce that the rescued woman wanted to meet him. King Amiroth nodded his permission. He sat down on a plush ottoman in the public section of his tent where he met his officials and ministers to discuss matters of administration. The curtains at the entrance of the tent opened, and the woman entered, accompanied by the sentry. She was quite young, he noticed, and rather good looking. She had fair skin, almost translucently pale. Her hair was light brown, as were her eyes. She was lightly built and had sharp features. Her large, round eyes still reflected the trauma of the ordeal she had passed through. She bowed to King Amiroth and stood quietly, uneasy, shy and frightened. Amiroth spoke kindly to her.

'Madam, please take a seat. Do not be afraid. You are entirely safe here.'

'Thank you, my lord,' she replied in a small, timid voice and took the seat offered, sitting rather rigidly, as if unsure of her surroundings.

'I assure you again that you are completely safe here,' King Amiroth repeated, not sure what else to say to her. He felt slightly uncomfortable in her presence though he could not say why. She had changed into clean clothes and had freshened up, but a strange smell lingered around her, as if the dirt and slime from the riverbank had seeped into her skin and refused to let go.

'Thank you, Your Majesty,' she said in a small voice. 'I am grateful to you for saving me from that... monster!' she suddenly said with feeling, hugging herself like a small child and trembling.

King Amiroth felt alarmed. He had never been faced with a situation like this before. He wished Lamella had been there. Or Aminor. Or even Lord Beleston. They were better equipped to deal with emotionally fragile women.

'Please don't be upset!' he said helplessly. 'Please tell me who you are and where you are from. I promise that I shall do all I can to help you.'

The woman stopped trembling and tried to smile. 'My name is Samiesna, Your Majesty. I come from a village on the other side of the river. I entered the forest two days ago to collect firewood, but I got lost. I wandered about the whole day but could not find my way back. In fact, by nightfall I found myself deep within the forest. I spent the night trembling with fear of wild animals. The next day I again tried to find my way home but became even more hopelessly lost. That night, I came upon a lone, wandering frael who promised to help me in the morning to find my way home. He comforted me and even offered me food. He lulled me into a sense of security and then...suddenly... attacked me!'

Samiesna trembled again, ostensibly at having to recall the horror of being attacked. King Amiroth ordered a sentry to fetch her water. She sipped the water gratefully and continued her story, 'I tried to flee, but he was too fast. I managed to save myself by jumping into the river. I don't know why he did not follow me. I swam upriver for a long time and was completely exhausted. The last thing I remember is dragging myself onto the riverbank. When I opened my eyes, I found myself surrounded by your men. I think that the presence of your camp must have deterred the beast from pursuing me.'

'I do not know how to remedy the wrongs that have been done to you by the frael that you mentioned, Madam, but I assure you that you will remain completely unmolested here. I hope my men have been duly respectful towards you,' King Amiroth said, feeling sorry for the young woman.

'You are kind, my lord. I want for nothing in your camp. I am thankful to you for all that you have done for a poor woman like me.'

'Please do not make much of it. Anyone else would have done the same. Please let me know if there is anything more that I can do for you,' Amiroth said kindly.

'My lord, I do not wish to be a burden on you. But if you could arrange to have me escorted back home, I would be eternally grateful to you! After my ordeal, I am afraid to travel alone,' Samiesna requested, blushing at her own boldness.

Amiroth declared, 'Madam, what you ask is nothing. Nothing at all! I shall immediately have someone take you home.'

Samiesna thanked him warmly and tearfully for his kindness. Slowly, she began to walk out of the tent. King Amiroth, who had risen to bid her farewell, remained standing. He watched her walking away, half-formed thoughts jostling in his mind. A gust of breeze entered the tenth through the open curtains. It tossed Samiesna's soft hair astray and brushed against Amiroth's face. On the breeze came a soft, murmuring whisper. Though Amiroth could not discern what the sound was, he was sure that he had never heard anything as melodious. Suddenly he knew that it was Samiesna singing. What a song it was! The king of Balignor stood spellbound, bewitched by the sound that had taken many to their dooms before him. In a captivating melody, Samiesna sang:

> With what joy did my eyes alight
>> Upon the face my heart has long sought;
> I declare I can no longer fight
>> The craving in me that once I had fought!

> Life was a prison for long, long anni,
>> But now I have fled from its cold constraint.
> Now, to my past I shall bid goodbye
>> And embrace my future without restraint.

> For, in my future, I am sure I see
>> Millions of enchanting wonders unfold!
> I have been brought to you by destiny
>> To sing as long as my breath shall hold.

> Enchanted by the power of music,
>> We will give birth to new lore;

Music will create a world of magic
     Where you and I shall dwell forever more.

Away from the bustle of worldly ways,
     Away from the stabs of worldly pains,
We will blissfully spend all our days
     In a world where nothing else remains.

Where magic turns into sweet music
     For your heart's deserved adulation,
And sweet music turns into magic
     To bind your heart in eternal fascination.

The song came to an end, its echoes still floating on the breeze. 'Goodbye, my lord,' Samiesna whispered from the tent's entrance, turning round to face Amiroth one last time.

'Goodbye, Samiesna,' Amiroth whispered back, transfixed by a sensation he had never experienced before.

But, even as he said those words, King Amiroth felt a strange reluctance to carry out his own avowed actions. He did not like to see Samiesna go. He wanted her to remain with him. He felt that he had never seen a woman as beautiful, as gentle, as graceful as her. And he did not want her to leave. His face lit up when she smiled. Suddenly the tent seemed to be filled with a bright glow. He knew then that he was in love, that he had never known before what love truly was. He forgot his beloved son who could hardly wait to grow as tall as his father. He forgot his beautiful and loving wife who was waiting anxiously for his return. He forgot all those men who waited outside for his order to move eastward. All he remembered was that this lovely woman was going to leave him, and he did not want that to happen.

'My lord,' said Samiesna, in a voice that was more musical than any he had ever heard. 'Before we part forever, I would like to say one last thing. You have done much for me. I am forever in your debt. But I am poor and have nothing to offer. How can I ever thank you truly?'

'You do not have to thank me,' said King Amiroth with feeling. He walked to her and took her hand. 'I do not know what magic this is, but my life seems to have found new meaning today in your presence.'

Samiesna blushed prettily and whispered, 'My lord, I too do not know what magic this is, but for me there is now nothing undoable for your sake. If you ask me to forget my family and stay, I shall stay.'

'Then stay, sweet lady, stay,' whispered Amiroth and took her in his arms. She placed her cheek upon his bosom and sang softly, slowly. Yet her voice flew on the air to the farthest corners of the massive camp. Within the tent, Amiroth sank deeper and deeper into her enchantment. Outside, the entire entourage heard her and fell under her spell.

Soon after deciding to watch over the human camp, Prince Halifern climbed into a tall tree to keep an eye on them. He spotted the mertkhezin lying unconscious on the other bank of the river, on the side of the human camp. She was in her human form. He wondered if, by some miracle, she had drowned and died. It was too much to hope for! Some soldiers came down to the riverbank with buckets, probably to fetch water, and found her. At first there was great consternation among them, but eventually they were taken in by her deception. Halifern wanted to shout out the truth to them, but he was too far to be heard from across the river. Before his very eyes, they carried her into the camp. Halifern felt desperate. He wanted to rush into the camp and warn them. However, there were too many soldiers for his comfort. How would they react if he burst in and declared that they had just rescued a dangerous creature? He doubted they would believe him. They would probably think that he was a frael spy. How else would he have known that they had rescued anyone? And he *was* spying on them, if truth be told. Perhaps the mertkhezin was really ill or hurt and would not be able to harm them, Halifern told himself. He decided to wait and watch instead of rushing in.

As he continued to keep an eye on the camp, Halifern noticed a frenzy of activity. He saw the men carrying in loads of supplies, filling vats with water and chopping down trees that were hauled upriver, probably to make rafts to cross the river at a ford. They were planning to move on soon, he guessed. They were not from Cordemim, he was sure. Their clothes and accents were different from those of the men of Cordemim. Halifern smiled to himself as it struck him that most of his compatriots would never be able to tell the men of the different countries apart. He was glad that the men were moving on. Their presence was faintly disconcerting. He was sure from his observations that they were planning to move east towards Ghrangghirm. Why were they going there? He had already ruled out war as an intention. But there were too many soldiers in the contingent for the expedition to be a peaceful one either.

He felt caught between concern for them and concern about them. He knew Augurk, the rauz of Ghrangghirm, and did not want any harm to befall him.

Nor did he want any harm to come to the humans for whom he had begun to feel a sense of responsibility. The fact that he had not yet warned them of the danger that the mertkhezin posed gnawed at him. He wondered what had happened to her. Had she left without him noticing it? He thought it highly unlikely. She had deliberately inserted herself into the camp. She wasn't going to just leave, he reasoned. Had she died? He hoped against hope that she had.

Though it would have been prudent to return to Numosyn, he continued to watch the humans, as much out of curiosity about the race as worry about the mertkhezin. He thought he heard singing coming from the camp the day after the mertkhezin had been 'rescued' by the humans. It was too far away to be sure, but Halifern's heart sank. His instincts told him that it was that awful creature singing. He cursed his hesitation on the day the humans had found her. His doubts had doomed them, he rued. He was afraid that the humans had fallen under her spell. If only he had had the courage!

For a long time, he debated what to do. He could leave them to their fate. That was what his people would have advised him to do. But he felt guilty leaving the humans to the mertkhezin's mercy. He could guess from the grandeur of some of the tents that important persons were present in the camp. If so, it was doubly dangerous to allow them to fall into the mertkhezin's clutches, if they hadn't already. And though he was unsure of the right course of action, Prince Halifern decided to attempt to warn the humans. Perhaps it was too late, but his conscience would not allow him to rest until he had done the right thing.

He entered the river a little above the camp, unseen by the guards. He swam at an angle to reach the other side just beyond the perimeter of sentries. Once on the other side, he took to the trees. He climbed into the dense foliage and kept watch on the group of people busily working below. Several standards fluttered here and there in the camp. Their emblems confirmed that they were not from Cordemim or Storsnem. Perhaps they were from one of the human kingdoms further to the west, Halifern mused.

The camp was a large one. The tents were arranged in concentric circles, with small but better tents at the centre surrounded by larger, plainer ones. Halifern guessed that the central tents belonged to the commanders, and the outer ones were barracks for the soldiers and workers. No one noticed him. They were going about their business of daily life without any undue hurry or tension. Towards evening, he ceased his unremitting watch to forage for food. When he returned to his position, darkness had begun to fall. He could see fires lighting up all over the camp. One area was especially illuminated. It was a large, sturdy, elegant and prosperous-looking tent. He guessed that it was the tent of the leader of the party. Sounds of merriment were coming from within. One voice was especially alluring.

Prince Halifern steeled himself. He was not looking forward to encountering the cunning mertkhezin again, but he knew that he would have to do so if he wanted to warn the humans. He descended from the tree and, wrapping his cloak tightly around him, began to circle the camp to spot a point of entry. He saw some sentries standing with their backs to the forest and took advantage of their neglect to slip inside. He tiptoed between the tall tents silently, working his way towards the big one at the centre. When he was near enough to it, he stepped out of the shadows and approached the sentries guarding the tent.

'I come in peace!' he cried in Volegan, startling the sentries and throwing them into consternation. They rushed to surround him, their arms drawn, but Halifern stood unmoved.

'I am Prince Halifern of Wyrchhelim, and I have come to talk to the leader of your party,' he declared, trying to sound confident and nonchalant.

The sentries stood still, confused. They could not understand how a frael had suddenly appeared at the centre of their camp. They did not feel inclined to obey him, even though he had declared himself a prince. Nor could they ignore him. They did not dare lay hands on him for, if the frael truly was a prince who came in peace and they attacked him, it could have disastrous consequences for them. At last, one of the sentries decided to inform their master of what was going on. He could decide what to do with the mysterious frael. He entered the tent where a feast was laid out in honour of Samiesna. The king and his beloved lady were entertaining all the captains of the host. The sentry bowed to King Amiroth and whispered to him that a strange frael was outside to meet him. He did not fail to mention that the frael called himself prince something or the other.

Frowning, Amiroth excused himself. He did not notice Samiesna's eyes, now flashing rather than soft, following him. Neither did he notice the short, sharp intake of breath and the momentary clenching of teeth that disturbed his beautiful companion's composure for a few momons. He stepped out of the tent to encounter Prince Halifern.

'I am Amiroth, King of Balignor, and commander of this expedition. Who are you and what do you want? Why have you crept stealthily into my camp?' he demanded of the frael who, in his opinion, looked nothing like a prince.

Halifern bowed to him and introduced himself. 'I apologise for the abrupt and unannounced entry,' he said, 'but the circumstances called for secrecy. I have some urgent communication for you.'

'Prince Halifern, I would have been honoured to have you as my guest under other circumstances,' said Amiroth. 'But the manner of your arrival arouses suspicion. You will not mind if I first enquire the purpose of your visit before I ask you to join me at my table?'

'I do not, indeed, take offense, my lord. It is prudent not to trust strangers in this time and age. I am glad to find that you are so discerning. I hope you have been using the same discretion with regard to *all* strangers, Your Majesty,' Halifern said pointedly, with an edge to his voice that was not lost on Amiroth.

'What do you mean, Prince?' King Amiroth demanded.

'Three days ago, your men found a woman by the river and brought her here. She is still here, is she not, my lord? Do you know who she is?'

'How do *you* know about her?' demanded Lord Amiroth.

'There is not time enough to tell you that now. She is not who you imagine her to be despite whatever story she might have told you. She is a mertkhezin. Do not shelter her, my lord. She killed my three companions, and she would have killed me had I not managed to escape by the skin of my teeth. She means you and your men harm. Kill her this instant, King Amiroth, and save everyone.'

'Silence!' thundered King Amiroth, shaking with anger. 'You insolent frael! You dare insult a lady so pure and wonderful! *You* attacked her in the forest, did you not? And when you found that she had escaped and found shelter with those who would protect her, your trickery brought you here to convince me to murder her! Frael, do not think that men are fools. I shall not be taken in by your trickery!'

Prince Halifern felt sad and baffled. He understood that the king of Balignor had fallen under the mertkhezin's spell. But why had she entranced *him*? It wasn't likely that she wanted to eat him. Mertkhezi were notorious for putting their prey under their spell, but they never ate humans. And the control usually took the form of numbing all other sensations so that the prey wouldn't fight as the mertkhezin gobbled it up. This kind of control, where the prey remained in full possession of all faculties but was completely devoted to the mertkhezin, was rare. It was used only when prey was required to be transported over long distances. Why bother to carry dead flesh when the living one could be made to go willingly to its intended eaters? And the mertkhezi who could exert this kind of control were extremely powerful. What was happening here? What game was the mertkhezin playing?

Halifern again tried to convince King Amiroth that the woman whom he had rescued was actually a dangerous vynobin, but it was in vain. The king of Balignor was deaf and blind to everything besides the charms of the woman who had cast her spell on him.

As if on cue, Samiesna stepped out of the tent. She saw Prince Halifern and screamed. Halifern swiftly drew his knife and lunged at her, hoping that her death would release King Amiroth from her spell. Amiroth was faster. He leapt forward and blocked Halifern's attack with his sword. Halifern drew his own sword and retaliated. A brief but furious fight ensued. Though Halifern was quite exceptional in skill and agility, he did not wish to hurt Amiroth and fought only to defend himself. He now desperately wanted to escape, certain that he could do nothing to help the humans. However, it was too late. At a word from Amiroth, his sentries closed in upon Halifern and captured him. They overwhelmed him and dragged him down to the ground. Then they tied his arms and legs and pulled him up to face the king's judgement.

King Amiroth held his sword to Halifern's throat and growled, 'Now, frael, you will be punished for your impudence. I will cut you into pieces and leave your body behind to be eaten by crows.'

'If you do so, my lord,' said Halifern calmly, 'it could cause trouble between humans and fraels. It could even lead to war. Would you risk that for a woman who is a stranger to you? Would you rather not be friends with a race that is known for its loyalty and courage? Would you plunge your nation into war for the sake of your personal interest?'

'You are clever, frael,' said King Amiroth, lowering his sword. 'And correct. If I kill you, there might be war. I will not send my men into battle for the sake of revenge on a worthless worm like you. But I cannot allow you to go unpunished either. Oh! I know! You will be my prisoner. As long as I have you, your people will not dare to attack me. And I can punish you suitably at my convenience.'

He then turned to his men and ordered them to secure the prisoner. He also announced that they would break camp and move onwards to Ghrangghirm in three days, as planned originally, and that the prisoner would travel with them. Halifern pricked up his ears at the mention of the dharvh kingdom. Amiroth's announcement confirmed his guess about their destination. He wondered again why they were going there. Unfortunately, for the present, he was helpless. He stood defeated in spirit as well as might. He held no grudge against King Amiroth. He could sense the mertkhezin's thoughts in his words. He wondered just what she had in store for him. He knew that he was about to endure pain and hardship, that he had failed to save the humans from a horrifying fate. And all because he had chosen to flee to save his life instead of killing the mertkhezin when he had first encountered her.

Chapter 43

THE RESCUE OF PRINCE HALIFERN

(12 Beybasel 5009 A.E. to 1 Niwukir 5009 A.E.)

Sitting a little apart from the rest of the army, King Amiroth watched his men with pride and satisfaction—they were good, loyal, honest men. They would follow him to the ends of the world. They were going about their duties in the camp, ensuring that preparations would be complete for them to leave by the day after. They worked with more cheer and zeal than they had felt in many temporas past. Occasionally, men broke into song as they worked. Amiroth felt a strange sense of destiny hanging over the camp. By him sat Samiesna, looking intently at him. Her light eyes seemed ablaze with some internal fire. But King Amiroth sat unaware of her gaze.

Angbruk smiled wryly as he walked through the ranks of tents and the antlike bustle of the humans. He was followed by two guard-dharvhs who stared openly at the actions of the men. Angbruk had seen men before. To his companions, however, men were a novelty. Angbruk made his way directly to the clearing where King Amiroth sat with Samiesna. He nodded briskly but courteously to King Amiroth and thanked him on behalf of his brother, Rauz Augurk, for undertaking the expedition. King Amiroth acknowledged the greeting and asked him the purpose of his visit.

'My rauz wishes for the king of Balignor to know how grateful he is for this token of friendship between men and dharvhs. He wishes to enquire after Your Majesty's comfort and ensure that everything is well with you and your entourage. He is eagerly awaiting your arrival at Drauzern, where he can welcome you properly.'

'Thank you and thanks to your rauz for your words and your hospitality. Please do inform him that my men and I are progressing well and want for nothing at present. We will camp here for two more days before setting forth for Drauzern. We are refurbishing our supplies and making arrangements to ford the river a little way upriver on the fourteenth,' King Amiroth replied.

Angbruk bowed again and said, 'I shall intimate my rauz of your progress. I am glad that you and your men want for nothing. Although you do not have any supply problems at the moment, please do inform me if you anticipate any such difficulties or if you wish for something that you currently have not managed to procure, my lord. My rauz will be happy to provide you what you need.'

'Actually, there is one thing that he could help me with,' responded Amiroth. 'It will be very kind of him if he could send some suitable transportation for the lady here—we have a difficult journey ahead of us, and I would like to see her comfortable on the road.'

'It shall be done,' Angbruk acquiesced. He looked at Samiesna out of the corner of his eyes and was not pleased. There was a keenness about her aspect that disturbed him.

Two of Amiroth's sentries escorted Angbruk and his guards out of the camp. As he was passing the spot where the animals were housed, Angbruk noticed a small cage with something huddled up inside. He could not see clearly what animal it was. It did not appear to be a cow or goat or sheep or horse or any other kind of animal that could be expected to accompany a contingent like this. The cage was too small for even the small animal, and Angbruk stopped to check on the animal out of curiosity.

'What beast is that?' he enquired of the men accompanying him.

'That is no beast,' one of them answered. 'It is a prisoner who attacked Lady Samiesna and was later captured. It is an insolent frael by the name of Halifern,' the sentry said contemptuously.

Angbruk knew that his brother was on friendly terms with a frael named Halifern. Of course, it was possible that this was some other Halifern altogether. He thanked the sentries for the information and hastily proceeded on his way out.

Eamilus had left Uzdal half-heartedly two days ago and had started west to find himself a master who could teach him how to fight with weapons. He had travelled in a straight line towards the human kingdoms of the west, across the great desert of Laudhern and some grasslands beyond it. That morning, however, Eamilus had once again found himself within the safe concealment of shady trees. He sat munching upon an apple among the branches of a tall tree close to the outskirts of Norowichh Forest in Cordemim when he heard the sound of trumpets. In a flash, he was up the trunk into the thickest branches. His sharp eyes detected movement beyond the edges of the forest. He cautiously made his way towards it, staying hidden among the foliage.

He saw a large party of soldiers marching in a clearing in front of a lively camp. Eamilus watched them avidly, full of curiosity as well as wariness. The camp seemed to be full of soldiers. Some were practising manoeuvres, some were chopping firewood or fetching water, some were washing and drying clothes, some were tending to horses, all were busy in some activity or another. Their complexions announced them to be from the west. Their standards and uniforms proclaimed them to be from Balignor. Eamilus wondered what such a large troop from Balignor was doing in Cordemim.

Though he had never been to this side of the Lyudzbradh before, his studies with Timror had taught him enough to know exactly where he was. To the immediate south was Wyrchhelim, which was frael country, and to the east was Ghrangghirm, which was dharvh country. Were the soldiers going to invade the dharvhs? Eamilus had no way of knowing whether the army he saw below was large enough for the purpose.

The sight of his own kind after so long filled his heart with a strange and bitter ache. He longed to approach them and flee them at the same time! What attracted him the most, though, was the sight of soldiers practising with swords or javelins. Joining an army could be an effective way of learning weaponcraft. He considered approaching the camp about joining up. Then he discarded the idea; who knew what they were up to? He was better off looking for a teacher, as he had originally planned.

By afternoon, the smells and sounds of the camp filled the quiet air of the forest where Eamilus sat. It disturbed the nesting birds, who flew up into the sky with cackles of complaint. Eamilus sat still, as he had in the morning. He had not moved a muscle, yet he felt no discomfort. He had begun to understand the basic character of the camp. His keen ears picked up sounds of a tongue that seemed familiar to his own but was definitely not Gamberra. Timror had taught him Volegan, and he spoke it fairly well. The accent of the Balignorians was unfamiliar, so it took him a while to get used enough to it to clearly understand what the men were saying. From his observations, and from what he could hear of the men's conversations, Eamilus gathered that these men were the party of an important person who was travelling to Ghrangghirm. The smell of cooking food and the revelry of the men reached Eamilus sitting atop the tree. It stirred an uncontrollable longing in him to move closer to the men. But his prudence dictated that it would be a dangerous move while it was still light. He would have to wait for the night; after all, darkness was a kocovus's best friend!

When night came, Eamilus descended from the tree and made his way to the camp. It was the first night after the new moon. The darkness was deep enough for Eamilus's purpose. He glided like a shadow among the penumbral tents and carts of the camp as he sought his way around. He avoided the large tent at the centre of the camp. It was, he rightly guessed, the leader's tent and was heavily guarded. He restricted his prowling to the outermost edges of the camp. He could hear men snoring or breathing deeply as he passed by their tents. Here and there sentries kept guard. They strolled round and round and then about on their fixed paths between and across the circles of tents.

After watching them for some time, Eamilus was able to figure out the pattern they walked in. He was also able to calculate accurately when a place would be free of guards for a few momons. His sense of curiosity prompted him to take advantage of this. He waited till there was a gap in the outermost circle for a few moments and slipped into the inner circle. He moved so fast and so silently that no guard noticed him. One by one, Eamilus began to cross the circles in which the camp watch was organised. In his childish excitement, he failed to notice that he had drawn close to the centre of the ring.

All his senses were now alert, and he was playing a game with himself of tracing as many different smells as he could to their origins. As he focussed, he could trace two score different human smells to the sentries patrolling in the circles immediately to his front and behind. A new smell tingled his nostrils as he breathed in deeply. The smell of animals. He quietly made his way in the direction of the smell. As he neared the animals' pens, he could easily discern the horses, cows, goats and bullocks tied in separate pens for the night. Then a new smell assailed his senses, and he was immediately alert.

He knew it was not human. Neither was it the smell of any animal—domestic or wild—that he was familiar with; nor was it the smell of any of the various strange creatures and beasts that roamed the foothills of the Lyudzbradh and sometimes lost their way and wandered into the forests of the hinterlands. There was also something familiar about it, as if he had encountered someone who smelled that way before. Cautiously approaching the smell, his claws and fangs at the ready, Eamilus realised that the smell was coming from a figure huddled up inside a tiny cage. It seemed pathetically helpless and in pain. Returning to his human form, but still alert, he approached the prisoner.

Hearing very light, almost imperceptible, footsteps Halifern twisted his neck round to look at the approaching figure. What he saw surprised him immensely. A boy of fifteen or sixteen was approaching his cage bent in a strangely feline crouch, as if ready to fly at the slightest hint of danger. As he watched, the boy came closer and stood near the cage. From the boy's features and clothes, Halifern identified him as an eastern human. Taking care not to make any sudden movements, he turned round as much as possible to face the boy who was looking at him keenly but intrepidly. The cramped cage made any movement extremely difficult and painful.

'Who are you?' whispered the boy in Volegan.

'Who are you?' Halifern rasped back in Gamberra, the language of the eastern humans. His throat was parched and cracked, but hope gave him unexpected energy.

'I am Eamilus,' the boy answered simply, changing to Gamberra with ease and confirming Halifern's suspicion about his origin.

'I am Halifern,' responded the prisoner similarly.

'Why are you in the cage?' Eamilus asked.

'It's a long story,' Halifern sighed painfully. 'But I can assure you that I didn't do anything to deserve this.'

'You are a frael?' the boy suddenly asked with unexpected excitement. He had remembered where he had encountered that smell before: at Nishtar's school, when he had run away from Timror. One of the students had been a frael, and Eamilus had vaguely retained the memory of how the boy had smelled. Halifern felt slightly uncomfortable. He didn't enjoy the idea of being treated as an object of curiosity. The boy's next words caused him to change his mind.

'Do you want me to release you?' Eamilus asked.

'Can you?' Halifern almost begged.

Eamilus did not reply. He lifted his face and focussed his senses of smell and hearing to detect the nearest guards. Then he grabbed the lock hanging from the cage door and gave it a sudden but forceful wrench. The lock broke with a loud snap. The guards heard the sound and rushed to check on the prisoner, but when they reached the cage, they saw nothing amiss. The cage stood where it had and Halifern lay inert within. They breathed sighs of relief and resumed their patrolling.

As soon as they were gone, Eamilus emerged from the shadows at the foot of the cage. Halifern was too weak to leave his prison on his own. Eamilus helped him out.

'Can you walk?' he urgently whispered to Halifern. Halifern tried, but his legs gave way after just a few steps. Eamilus caught him before he could fall. Halifern's heart sank. He would not escape.

'I'm sorry, I'm too weak and injured,' he moaned to Eamilus.

'Don't fret,' Eamilus said. He stood there, eyes shut, doing nothing. Halifern assumed he was wondering what to do. When Eamilus opened his eyes, he seemed somehow altered. There was a ruddy glint in his eyes that sent a shiver down Halifern's spine. He wondered whether he was imagining it. Before he could make up his mind, Eamilus had grabbed his arms and hauled him onto his back. The frael's weight seemed to hardly bother the boy, young though he was.

'Hold on tight!' he instructed Halifern. 'And keep your eyes closed.' There was a slight rasp in his voice.

Halifern did as he was told. He held on to Eamilus's shirt with all his strength and shut his eyes tightly. Within moments, he felt himself moving, the wind brushing against his face. He did not understand what was happening. It seemed to him that he was flying through the air but that, of course, was impossible. He

felt his rescuer come to a stop and set him down under a tree. After what felt like
horas, Halifern peeped out from behind half closed eyelids. He saw that he was far
from the camp where he had been taken prisoner. He was within the Norowichh
again, though closer to the other end of the forest. How had that happened? He
was certain that he had been carried out of Amiroth's camp not very long ago. It
was still night. How had he managed to come that far? Had Eamilus, a mere boy,
flown him there? If he had, then he couldn't be a human boy. What was he if he
wasn't human? The darkness dripped off the leaves of the trees and prowled round
with oppressive presence. Halifern wondered whether he hadn't landed himself in
worse trouble than before. And yet, curiously, a deep-rooted feeling within him
told him that he could trust Eamilus.

'Where are we?' Halifern asked faintly. Eamilus confirmed his guess that they
were at the other end of the Norowichh.

'They won't find you here,' he added. 'By the way, why were you imprisoned?
You said it was a long story. You can tell me now. If you don't mind, I'd like to be
sure that you really didn't deserve to be imprisoned.'

Before Halifern could respond, he fainted. Eamilus realised how fragile the
frael's condition was. He splashed some water on Halifern's face to bring him
round, and then made him drink some of the fresh, cool liquid. Halifern was also
starving, he sensed. He wasn't sure what fraels ate, so he gathered some fruits and
berries and brought these to Halifern. The frael ate these gratefully and slept.

'If you don't find that heinous frael, you will pay for it with your hides!' King
Amiroth thundered at his men.

Early that morning, Halifern's disappearance had been discovered, and a frantic
search had been instituted. Men rushed in all directions on foot and on horses to
discover the fugitive and recapture him. King Amiroth was in a towering rage. None
of the soldiers had ever seen him so angry. They cowered before him and jumped
to obey his orders for fear of retribution. Their king appeared to be drastically
changed, but none of them dared to challenge his vehement hatred and viciousness.
He might be different, and they might now fear where once they had loved him, but
he was still their master. They were honour-bound to obey him without question.

When a frantic but thorough search from dawn to dusk failed to reveal any
trace of Prince Halifern, or how he had managed to escape, King Amiroth was
ready to behead every man who had been sent out to capture the fugitive. He
barely had patience enough to listen to the sentry who entered his tent, trembling
with fear at the wrath of his king.

'What is it, you worm?' Amiroth demanded.

'A couple of days ago, another sentry and I escorted the dharvhs who visited us on their way out of the camp. When we passed the prisoner, one of the dharvhs enquired about him.'

'And you choose to inform me about this NOW!' roared King Amiroth.

'I…I am s…sorry, Your M…Majesty,' the soldier stammered out of fear. 'But I did not realise that this was important in any way. They thought that it was some strange beast. Even after learning that it was a frael, they said nothing. So I thought that it was not a matter of importance.'

'Get lost before I throw you into the river with rocks tied to your hands and feet!' thundered Amiroth.

The sentry fled in terror. King Amiroth paced his tent for a long time after receiving this information. None dared enter his tent except Samiesna. She was with him always. She was as inseparable as his shadow. All present accepted it either because they were under her spell or were too loyal to question their king's actions. Even now, they accepted it as natural that she should be with him though he was more agitated and enraged than ever.

'What is the matter, my king?' she asked him sweetly, leading him to sit down. She poured out a cup of sweet wine for him and fanned him gently. King Amiroth began to relax.

'The prisoner, that villainous frael who dared to attack you, has escaped. My idiotic men have failed to find him. All that they have managed to do is remember that the dharvhs who came to visit me had shown some mild interest in him. I can't imagine how he could have escaped!'

'Forget him, my lord,' said Samiesna with a smile. 'It does not matter that he has escaped. You have saved me, and we now have each other. That is all that matters, is it not?'

'You are right, my dear,' Amiroth agreed, taking her hand. 'Perhaps I should ignore the frael. After all, you are now beyond his reach. But I can't help wondering why the dharvhs were interested in him.'

'Perhaps they were just curious, perhaps they had never seen a frael before,' suggested Samiesna.

'Perhaps. On the other hand, they were the only strangers in the camp since the frael's arrest. What if they were here to rescue him? What if they had been his friends instead of emissaries of Rauz Augurk? Or, even worse, what if Rauz Augurk himself had sent them to rescue him?' Amiroth began to get worked up again.

'It seems a little farfetched,' said Samiesna, 'but what do I know? You are worldly wise, my lord, and understand such matters better than anyone.'

King Amiroth sent for his captains. The captains entered the tent with timorous steps. Amiroth sat at his usual place, Samiesna at his side, holding his hand. The inside of the tent was dimly lit. There was no servant in sight. The king of Balignor looked grim, as if he was angry and worried. His eyes were dark with hatred. The captains were shocked at the transformation in their kind, generous king, but they held their tongues. He looked up when they entered and in a strained voice, issued instructions that filled them with confusion.

'The dharvhs have humiliated and betrayed us,' he told them. 'Just as the Sorceress foretold. They have snatched the frael who mistreated Lady Samiesna from under our noses. They are in league with the fraels against men. We are now in danger of our lives. I have decided that we shall immediately return to Balignor. Break camp this instant and begin the journey home. Send a messenger to Augurk to intimate him of my decision. As of this moment, there is to be no more friendship between men and dharvhs, for one cannot be friends with those who seek to betray and humiliate one! Who knows what they truly want? Perhaps, they plan to destroy the strength of men by murdering me! We shall march within a couple of horas towards Balignor. If anyone is not ready to move by then, let him perish. These are my orders; I want them obeyed without question. Disobedience can have only one consequence. Now go and spare me your worthless faces!'

After the captains left, King Amiroth turned to Samiesna and said, 'I hope you will agree to come with us, my lady. I don't think that I can survive the journey back if you do not!'

Samiesna blushed daintily. But when she answered, her voice was keen, 'Of course I will go with you, my lord. I would not dream of doing otherwise!'

The morning after his rescue, Halifern developed a raging fever. Eamilus wasn't well versed with medicine, but he knew enough, courtesy of Timror, to cure Halifern's fever. He lifted the frael into a makeshift hammock and looked after him over the next couple of days until he got better. He was in a dilemma the entire time; he had freed Halifern from the humans upon the frael's assertion that he didn't deserve to be in the cage. But what if the assertion had been wrong? What if he had saved someone who didn't deserve to be saved? There was no way for him to learn the truth until Halifern recovered.

When he recovered, Halifern was so grateful to the boy that he could not stop thanking Eamilus. For the first time, he noticed how young Eamilus truly was. He had thought that the boy was fifteen or sixteen. Now he realised that the boy was probably closer to thirteen!

To the frael, who still sat under a tree, the boy seemed to loom.

'Thank you, Eamilus, my friend,' Halifern said, taking the boy's hands into his own. 'You have saved my life.' Eamilus flushed red. He could not recall the last time anyone had called him a friend. Despite his closeness to Uzdal, he had never known just where he stood with the older man. And Uzdal had never called him 'friend,' perhaps because of the difference in their ages. Halifern, though also older, seemed to treat him as an equal. He felt a sudden and heartfelt fondness for the frael whom he had rescued, though he was not yet sure whether it had been the right thing to do or not. For all he knew, Halifern would try to stick a knife in him the moment his back was turned!

'You do not need to thank me,' Eamilus said shyly. 'It seemed like the right thing to do.'

'Nonetheless, I am eternally grateful to you,' Halifern responded with a smile and a bow of gratitude.

'Then tell me why you were imprisoned by those soldiers. And do not try to lie; I can sense when someone is lying,' Eamilus stated.

Halifern was rather surprised at the boy's words. He realised that Eamilus wasn't sure about his decision to save Halifern and needed to set his conscience at peace. He could not blame the boy. He had taken a great risk in rescuing Halifern and deserved to know the truth. So Halifern sat down and told him everything that had befallen him from the time that he and his friends had found the deer carcass. Eamilus listened intently and without interrupting until Halifern was done telling his tale.

Then Eamilus nodded and said, 'I believe you. I am glad that I found you.' There was an undertone of relief in his voice that Halifern did not miss.

'I am glad that your doubts are assuaged and that you have taken me at my word,' Halifern acknowledged. 'But in the spirit of honesty, I must ask you something too, and I expect you to tell me the truth as well.'

'Ask,' said Eamilus, looking rather uncomfortable.

'You are not an ordinary human boy, Eamilus,' said Halifern. 'In the past few days, I have seen you do things that no ordinary human, let alone a mere boy like you, could have accomplished. There is something different about you, and I shall be honest with you—it causes me anxiety. Who or what are you, and what were you doing in the human camp when we met?

Eamilus stood up, looking uncomfortable. Despite his young age, he was as tall as Halifern. To the frael, who still sat under a tree, the boy seemed to loom. But he controlled his panic and forced himself to maintain a calm exterior.

'I don't blame you for feeling anxious,' Eamilus said miserably. 'But unlike you, my condition is not the result of a misunderstanding. I am not, as you say, ordinary. But can we not leave it at that?'

Eamilus looked as wretched as he felt. He had felt unsure about demonstrating his abilities to Halifern, but there had been no other way of saving the frael. He had hoped that Halifern would have ascribed those memories to his high fever. However, things had not worked out as he'd wished. As he saw the grief and pain in Eamilus's eyes, Halifern's heart went out to this young boy who took the risk of saving others without a second thought but was reluctant to talk about his past for reasons that could only be dark and unhappy. He was about to say that Eamilus could keep his secret to himself when the boy began to speak again.

'You are right to be scared of me, Halifern,' Eamilus said, looking away. He had mistaken the frael's silence for refusal to let matters be. He felt obligated to answer since Halifern had answered his accusations honestly. 'I am dangerous. That is why I am also in exile. Please forgive me if I do not tell you where I hail from or what makes me different from others; suffice to know that I am a homanim. Do not ask what other blood is mingled in mine, for I cannot tell you. I am who I am. There is no help for it while I live.'

There was a strange bitterness in Eamilus's voice when he said these words, which it was not lost on Halifern. Suddenly he realised that he was sitting not before a young boy but a far older and wiser man. The trials and travails of life had aged Eamilus far, far beyond his anni. At heart, he was a boy no more. His childhood had been lost somewhere along his life's journey. Halifern felt sorry for Eamilus. He wished he could help his rescuer.

'Can I do anything for you?' he asked earnestly. Eamilus shook his head.

'Will you be safe if I leave you?' Eamilus asked.

'I guess so,' Halifern replied doubtfully. He was back in the forest in fraelish lands and was definitely safer, but he was still too weak. He did not know whether he would be able to look after himself.

'If you are not sure, I can stay with you and look after you. Or, if you wish, I can take you home,' Eamilus offered.

Halifern considered the offer. The thought of returning home was tempting. But he could not return before the four mondans of the trial period were over.

'What is the date today?' Halifern asked.

'The sixteenth of Beybasel,' Eamilus replied, surprised.

'Then I cannot return home for another nine days,' said Halifern. He explained about the coming of age ceremony, which led to other anecdotes about his life. Eamilus listened with interest. He asked several questions about fraelish society. His astuteness surprised Halifern. When he commented on this, Eamilus replied cryptically that he had had good teachers. He was beginning to feel very curious about this race about whom little was known by outsiders. A desire arose in the boy's heart to see this interesting race at close quarters.

'So, what will you do until the first of Niwukir?' he asked Halifern.

'I will have to stay in the forest and make my way home slowly.'

'You are not well enough to fend for yourself; you know that as well as I do. Let me help you.'

'You have already done so much for me! How can I allow you to do more?' protested Halifern, though in his heart he was glad. It would give him the chance to get to know his benefactor more closely.

'It is no trouble. You have called me your friend. I will help you.'

By the time they reached Numosyn on the first of Niwukir, Halifern and Eamilus had truly become friends, though Eamilus still refused to reveal anything about his past. He wanted to leave his new friend at the edge of the City, but Halifern would not hear of it.

'Won't you at least see my home and rest awhile before you continue on your way?' Halifern persisted. Eamilus agreed. In truth, he was quite glad that he would get an opportunity to glimpse into the lives of fraels and satisfy his curiosity about their lifestyle.

He had expected Numosyn to be like Opeltra, the only city he had known. He was mistaken. As he entered a grove of immense trees, he wondered where he was being led. After a while, he realised that it was more than just a grove of trees; it was a forest. In truth, it was a part of a forest that had once covered the entire region where the fraels now dwelt. Norowichh had been only the northern edge of it. The old forest had thinned out over time, but in many places the tall, ancient trees still stood in large clusters or groves. In places, they spread across areas large enough to seem like forests. Eamilus stared open-mouthed as he realised that this forest *was* the City of Numosyn. As they walked deeper into the woods, the trees got thicker, until each tree was thick enough for a whole house to be hidden inside. Eamilus looked up towards the tops of the tallest trees, which were hidden in clouds perennially, and wondered what it would feel like to stand there, high above the world, and find oneself cloaked in soft, white, whispery clouds.

Halifern followed his gaze and guessed his thoughts. 'It feels wonderful,' he said. 'To live so high up. Do you want to see?'

Eamilus nodded, spellbound by the beauty of the forest and the soft music that was now floating down from the invisible treetops.

'Is she all right?' Avator asked Forsith in a whisper, looking at the sleeping form of Avita. It was still evening, yet she had already gone to bed. Avator was concerned about his sister.

'She said she was fine,' Forsith answered, his voice low as well, not wanting to disturb the sleeping girl.

'But you don't think she is?'

'The season is changing. Vernurt is giving way to somminar. Maybe she is just a tad under the weather.'

Something in Forsith's tone told Avator that their guardian suspected something else.

'Is there something I should know about?' he asked Forsith. 'Has someone been bothering her? Have her injuries recurred?'

'No,' replied Forsith curtly, answering all his questions at once.

'What are you not telling me?' Avator asked, slightly irritated.

'It's been a few mondans since she got that dreamcatcher from the magus you took her to on Igrag's advice. I can't say for sure, but her behaviour has been changing subtly ever since. She is more withdrawn and distracted, she goes to bed as early as she can, she refuses to wake up on time, she is irritable once awake and she lies about her dreams. I didn't think she would do that once we found out that her dreams were the cause of her injuries, but she does. I've seen her smiling in her sleep and asked her about it. She says she dreams about dolls or flowers, and they make her happy. I don't believe her. She's dreaming about something else that she won't tell me about. It worries me no end. She wasn't like this before she started wearing that thing,' Forsith said bluntly. He did not want to appear to blame Avator, but the boy had asked to know the truth, so he would speak his mind.

'Are you saying that the dreamcatcher is responsible for this?' Avator's voice held a note of deep concern.

Forsith shrugged.

Avator looked worried. Was Forsith correct? Had Avita's behaviour changed since she had started wearing the dreamcatcher? Had the visit to the magus done her more harm than good? No, he could not say that unequivocally. Avita's nightmares had reduced significantly in numbers and frequency. She no longer woke up with injuries. She was still growing like a human, and she still felt ill after her nightmares, but the magus had never claimed that she would be completely cured. The improvements in Avita's health were noticeable. Had there been changes in her behaviour as well? Forsith had noticed changes; he himself had not. A twinge of guilt twisted his heart. Perhaps he had not been paying as much attention to her as he should have. He was often busy with his work for the outlaws and hardly spent any time with her these days. He resolved to be more attentive towards her thenceforth.

'I think that the dreamcatcher has helped her a great deal, Forsith. Maybe she just feels lonely or bored,' Avator suggested. 'I know that I have not been spending as much time with her as I should have. Unfortunately, there are no others in the camp of her age with whom she can play or talk. Maybe she does see pretty things in her dreams now, things which make her smile. The magus said she would be able to control her dreams. Maybe she smiles because she has fun doing that and lies about her dreams because she thinks that we will not understand how she feels. She has always been so quiet and reserved!'

'Maybe,' Forsith agreed without enthusiasm. He was, obviously, not convinced.

'You don't believe that, do you?' Avator asked, correctly reading his guardian's stiff way of holding himself.

Forsith looked at the young kereighe boy sitting in front of him with his eyes full of concern for his sister and felt a stab of guilt. Avator was just sixteen, barely old enough to look after himself, but his spirit had already matured into that of an adult eighe. For anni, he had been trying to find a cure for Avita's strange malady. The thought that the only solution he had found could be harming her worse than the original problem was heartbreaking for him. He and Avator might no longer see eye to eye about their way of life, but they both still cared enough about their young ward. Younger ward, Forsith reminded himself. Another stab of guilt pieced his heart. Avator had gradually taken on the mantle of the head of their unusual little family, through his natural instinct for leadership rather than out of any sense of entitlement, but he was still not old enough to have to bear that responsibility. Both he and Avita were his charges.

'I have been thinking about this for a while now,' Forsith continued more gently than before. 'I think that the dreamcatcher is giving her obsessive dreams.'

'Obsessive dreams?' Avator asked, puzzled.

'Dreams that are addictive, that show her deepest wishes fulfilled,' Forsith explained. 'Sort of like an opiate. That could explain her behaviour. Like an addict, she is drawn to her dreams with a desperate inevitability. She aches for these dreams when she is conscious and tries to remain ensconced in them as long as she can when asleep. She feels guilty about these dreams, too, and so she lies about them. It all fits.'

'You think that the dreamcatcher acts as an opiate?' Avator asked uncertainly. 'The magus said that it would give her greater control over her dreams.'

'What if he was lying? What if it removes her from her awful nightmares by giving her obsessive ones instead?' Forsith countered.

Avator wasn't willing to accept that the dreamcatcher was hurting his sister. He had placed so much trust in the magus, and in more ways than one! The very thought that he mightn't have been trustworthy sent shivers down his spine. No! Forsith had to be wrong about the magus and the dreamcatcher. There had to be some other explanation for Avita's odd behaviour.

'Do you think it could be because she is…growing up…growing older… becoming a grown-up?' Avator asked abruptly, trying hard to find the right words to express the sudden thought that had come to him.

Forsith could not resist a tiny smile. He shook his head. 'She's too young,' he said to his ward. 'She is not even nine. Even if we consider that she is growing as fast as a human—and she didn't start doing that until she was four and a half—she is still too young.'

Avator could not think of any other explanations. He knew that Forsith's suggestion was the most rational one. Yet, he was unwilling to accept it without further proof. The dreamcatcher had helped stop the injuries to Avita's body where nothing had been able to help her before. He would not ask her to stop using it without being certain that it is was bad for her. The way ahead lay in learning more about her dreams, he figured. He decided to talk to her about her dreams the next day. He hadn't spent much time with her lately and felt guilty about it. He decided that he would take the morning off and spend it with his sister. He could take her on a picnic to a nearby village with Igrag's permission. Or he could take her riding. She was fond of Habsolm, and the horse would be pleased to spend time with her. Or he could practice reading and writing with her. Forsith had begun to teach her and according to him, she was quite bright.

However, it wasn't until a couple of temporas later that Avator was finally able to find time to spend with his sister. He had tried his best to keep an eye on her in the meantime and had found that Forsith's observations had not been exaggerated. He was still loath to believe that the dreamcatcher was responsible for these changes in Avita. He decided to go ahead with his plan of talking to her to get to the bottom of the problem.

He woke Avita soon after sunrise on the day of his holiday. By then the entire camp was up and about.

'Wake up sleepyhead!' he said affectionately, shaking her. She squeezed her eyes shut and pushed her face into the pillow. Avator was not to be outdone. He tickled her ear, forcing her to get up. To his surprise, instead of being amused, she was annoyed. She pouted and snapped at him. Avator flushed. Realising that she had made a mistake, Avita immediately apologised. Nevertheless, it had cooled Avator's enthusiasm for the day's plans. He still tried to act cheerful for her sake.

'I've taken the day off to spend time with you,' he said to Avita. 'What would you like to do?'

'I don't know. Anything you want,' said Avita, not sounding interested or pleased.

'Would you like to take Habsolm and the cart and go to visit one of the nearby villages?' Avator asked, knowing that she rarely left the camp. But Avita did not like the plan.

'How about going up the watchtower?' Avator asked hopefully. A new watchtower had been erected in the camp. It provided quite a panoramic view of the surroundings. Most of the younger eighes in the camp loved to climb up into it. If the outlaw on guard duty happened to be in a good mood, he allowed the youngsters to stay, otherwise he chased them away.

Avator had not really expected Avita to like this plan. To his surprise, she agreed readily. They packed a picnic lunch and climbed up into the shady cabin of the tall watchtower. The outlaw on duty there was a cheerful and easygoing kereighe who had no objection to allowing the two to squat there. They climbed onto a cushioned bench against the cabin's walls. The view was spellbinding! Miles upon miles of empty, undulating desert stretched out in every direction. Barren, brutal and breathtakingly beautiful, it gleamed like burnished gold in the sunlight. Hillocks and dunes broke the monotony of the arid plains of yellow sand that rose upon the flowing wind and blew from place to place with the winds. The landscape was ever-changing and yet, strangely immutable. Avita, who had never been to the watchtower before and had never seen this panoramic view of the desert, fell in love with it.

'It's beautiful!' she declared, breathing in the warm, dry breeze. She had seen many strange places in her dreams but never anything so stark and yet so stunning. Before she realised what she was saying, she uttered, 'I've never seen anything this beautiful in my dreams!'

She wanted to bite her tongue. Now Avator would ask her about her dreams. She began to fidget. She did not want to lie to him. Neither would she tell him or anyone else about Temeron. They would not understand. They would want her to stop dreaming about him. She could not do that. She remained tense, waiting for Avator to say something. He did not.

Avator had heard her comment about her dreams. He had also noticed her discomfort. She was clearly unwilling to talk about them. So he said nothing and pretended not to have noticed the comment. He knew that if he asked her anything just then, she would become upset and would clam up. He would learn nothing. He watched as she grew restless at first but relaxed again when he did not question her. It also told him something important; her strange behaviour was undoubtedly connected to her dreams. After a while, it was time for their picnic lunch. The guard in the watchtower joined them for their meal, so they did not talk much while enjoying their light meal. Afterwards, when the guard had returned to his post, Avator casually asked his sister, 'Do you still have nightmares these days?'

Avita answered a little stiffly, 'No, not really. Very rarely, in fact.'

'So the dreamcatcher is doing its job, I must say,' her brother commented, sounding relieved.

'Oh yes!' she agreed quite enthusiastically.

'Are you glad that we went to the magus who gave you the dreamcatcher?'

'Yes, definitely.'

'I'm glad about that,' he concurred. 'Until now I wasn't sure whether the dreamcatcher was actually helping you or not.'

'Oh it's very useful,' Avita declared. 'I don't get hurt anymore after my nightmares. I can control my dreams better. And I can remember everything that happens in them.'

'What does that mean—being able to control them?' Avator asked, sounding innocently curious.

Avita took the bait. 'It means that I can dream of anything I want to and change any aspect of any dream,' she replied.

'So,' said Avator, apparently trying to understand more clearly, 'you can choose to dream about flying if you want to?'

'Yes, I can,' replied Avita with a smile. She had never dreamt of flying, but that was an interesting idea. She would have to try it that night.

'And you can sleep without dreams if you want?' Avator further asked.

This time Avita thought for a few momons before answering. Her brother was obviously trying to understand how the dreamcatcher helped her. There was no harm in telling him a few things as long as she did not mention Temeron. 'I'm not sure about not dreaming,' she replied. 'I have never tried that. But I do get dreams that I haven't thought up. So, maybe, it doesn't allow me to choose whether to dream or not, only to choose what to dream about.'

'So what do you do if you start dreaming of bad things, say, a monster or a witch?' The question was too close to Avita's original nightmares, but Avator had deliberately risked it, hoping that she would let it pass among the other questions without getting suspicious.

'If I get such a dream,' Avita replied earnestly trying to explain the working of the dreamcatcher, 'I change it.'

'How do you change it? I'm not getting this clearly,' Avator confessed.

'Well,' Avita tried to explain. 'It depends on the dream. If I am dreaming of a monster or witch, like you said, I might change the monster into stone or the witch into a good one—like the witch of Temtema! Or I might leave that entire dream behind and dream of something else like gardens.'

'I get it now!' Avator declared. 'It lets you dream about what you want to and to change the dreams that you don't like.'

Avita nodded with a smile, glad that her brother had understood.

'So you are really happy with it? I am glad that I listened to Igrag,' said Avator, now much wiser than he or Forsith had been before about what was happening to his sister, though he would have liked to know more. Forsith had been partly right—that Avita's behaviour had to do with her dreams—but Avator now knew that Avita herself, rather than the dreamcatcher, was responsible for those dreams. If her dreams were obsessive, it was not because of the effect of the magus's device. It was because Avita was choosing to dream such wish-fulfilling dreams. The important question was, what *was* she dreaming of that was so addictive to her? He did not probe the matter, however, knowing that it would alert her to his intentions and upset her. He let the topic go. He could pursue it another time. Part of his agenda had been met. He was certain that the dreamcatcher was not hurting his sister, at least, not directly. The rest could be dealt with in due time.

'Eronsom has been worried about you,' he said instead, using Forsith's pseudonym since the guard was in the vicinity.

'Why? I am fine, really,' Avita protested.

'Of course you are! It's just that you are such a quiet girl. He is probably thinking of me at your age. I was much more outgoing. Maybe he thinks that you are not boisterous because you haven't been keeping well.'

'It's nothing like that,' Avita said, wondering how far Forsith's suspicions went regarding her reticence. She decided that she had to be more careful in future if she wanted to avoid her guardians' suspicions. They could not be allowed to realise that anything was different.

Brother and sister had a wonderful day. When they returned, Forsith had a delicious dinner ready for them. They ate heartily and sat playing board games until late into the night. Avita began to itch to go to sleep soon after sunset, but Avator's words had put her on her guard. It would not do to continue such unusual behaviour. Much as it bothered and annoyed her, she would have to sleep at regular horas and wake at regular horas.

Temeron had gone to bed early that night as well. He too could not wait to meet his new friend in his dreams. He knew that Avita was the one who had control of the dreams, but he looked forward to seeing her every night. On the nights that he did not dream of her, he slept badly. He fidgeted in his sleep and woke up several times through the night. When morning came, he was irritable and ill-tempered. This often led to beatings. He bore them without complaint, all the while focusing on Avita and what they would do in their dreams that night. He could not stop thinking about her, about the things she told him. He had no one else to talk to, and she was a very good listener. She was always happy to see him. She liked to spend time with him even though it was only in the dreams. His miserable life continued as before in reality, but his dreams had given him a new goal. Someday he would learn magic, escape from the lech and find Avita. It did not matter how long he had to wait. He would be patient. But he would unfailingly find her. His life, he felt sure, would remain meaningless as long as they were apart. Only when he found her would he be complete.

Rosa, who had noticed that Temeron had begun to sleep early and wake late, began to revile him, calling him lazy and stupid and many other names. When her abuses got no response, she lashed him with a leather belt. He gritted his teeth and bore it, though it cut his flesh and drew blood. Rosa beat him until she was tired, then went to bed. Temeron lay still. He did not want to tend to his wounds. All he wanted was to fall asleep so that he could dream of Avita. His whole body was racked with pain, but he ignored it. He screwed his eyes shut and waited for sleep to rescue him. He did fall asleep eventually. However, he did not dream of Avita for a long time. He began to panic. He saw himself in a dark cave, surrounded by the hoots and screeches of invisible creatures. He was terrified. He ran, but the cave was endless, no matter which direction he ran in. Wherever he ran, the terrifying creatures chased him. He could not see where he was going and several times he stumbled and fell. He began to pant with exertion when he suddenly heard the most beautiful sound in the world. Avita's voice. She was calling to him. His heart soared with joy.

He felt that no evil or hurt could touch him now. He closed his eyes and thought about her. When he opened his eyes again, he was no longer in the dark, scary cave but in the beautiful garden where they usually met. She was sitting on their usual bench. Though she looked rather serious, she appeared happy to see him. Forgetting about all his pains and sorrows, Temeron took his place by her side on the bench, ready to tell her all about the awful cave he had been dreaming of just before.

Chapter 45

Augurk's Choices

While King Amiroth's soldiers were completing the second day of their march back to Balignor, Angbruk was telling Augurk about what he had seen in the human camp.

'Are you sure that it was a frael?' Augurk asked, agitated. Irrespective of who the frael was or what he had done, Augurk did not want to be responsible for conflict between the humans and the fraels. If the fraels found out that he was responsible for Amiroth being in a position to capture one of them, they would drag him into the conflict too. And that was entirely undesirable.

'Yes, they told us that it was a frael. Even I could see it clearly then,' Angbruk confirmed. 'They said that his name was Halifern and that he had attacked some lady whom they seemed to be very devoted to.'

'What? How is that possible?' Augurk exclaimed. 'The Halifern *I* know would never attack anyone unless there was good reason to do so. Maybe it was some other Halifern. Even so, what was a lady of the court doing with them in the wilderness? As far as I know, the queen is back in Lufurdista.'

'This lady was not the queen,' Angbruk confirmed. 'I saw her myself. Her name is Samiesna. The queen of Balignor is named Lamella, isn't she?'

Augurk nodded. Angbruk continued with a mild frown, 'However, she appeared to be much favoured by the king. In fact, he requested you to send suitable transportation for her.'

'Did you agree?' Augurk asked.

'Yes, of course I did. But I felt uncomfortable in her presence. There was something odd about her, a sharpness that went beyond just her features.'

Augurk frowned. It was unlike Angbruk to be so imaginative. He trusted his brother's judgement. If Angbruk said that there was something wrong about this lady, he would believe it. And what about the frael? It was bewildering that a frael would be caught so far from his home. It wasn't completely unheard of for fraels to attack humans, but it was rare. They generally kept to themselves. Their dislike for other races took the form of avoidance rather than aggression. Then there was the name—Halifern! Augurk was sure that there were many fraels by that name; he couldn't be certain that the frael seen by Angbruk had been his friend, but he could not be certain that it wasn't either. Halifern was very curious about other races. This rare interest could have drawn him to the humans, Augurk thought. Yet, he found the idea of his friend Prince Halifern attacking anyone incomprehensible. It was all very disturbing.

'There is only one thing to be done,' declared Augurk. 'We will immediately set off for the human camp. They might be on their way here now, but we will be faster. I must see this frael and this lady for myself. If it is indeed the Halifern I know, we must rescue him without King Amiroth becoming aware of it. Also, send some dharvhs with a covered litter for the lady. We should not forget our promises to our guests. After all, it might all turn out to be a big misunderstanding.' However, even as he said this aloud to Angbruk, Augurk had misgivings.

It took Augurk, Angbruk, Shornhuz and Veber four days to reach the human camp, travelling by the most direct route and walking for fourteen horas a day at the fastest pace possible. A formal welcoming party with a litter for Samiesna followed them at a normal speed. However, they found the camp deserted. Everywhere there were telltale signs of a large party having camped not long ago. Black patches on the ground showed where fires had been lit; the ground pockmarked with holes attested to the large numbers of tents that had been erected; marks of hooves and wheels told where the horses and the carts had been stabled. The weather had been dry, so the traces of the expedition's departure were clear upon the road. However, they did not trail towards Drauzern but away from it. King Amiroth was gone! And, apparently, back towards his own kingdom.

Baffled, Augurk and his companions started on their way back at once. The next day, they met a messenger from King Amiroth on his way to Drauzern. They had missed him on their way to the camp because they had passed each other during the horas of the night. The messenger confirmed that King Amiroth had cancelled the expedition and had returned to Balignor. The explanation provided by the king seemed bizarre and perfunctory to Augurk. He wondered what the real reason had been. He felt angry. He felt humiliated. He wanted to attack the humans. But he kept his calm because he knew that it would prove futile. It would gain him nothing. Amiroth had been bound by nothing save honour to help him. He had even come almost as far as Ghrangghirm with his troops in good faith. What could have happened to change his mind all of a sudden? Augurk had a feeling that the woman mentioned by Angbruk had something to do with it. With Amiroth, the last hope of discovering the City of Stone had also gone.

Augurk made a decision. He would face Nishtar's wrath but do his bidding no more. He sent a message to Nishtar, informing him of the return of Amiroth's expedition and declaring his helplessness in pursuing the matter further. He mentioned nothing in it about the frael or the mysterious lady, guessing that the reasons for Amiroth's departure would be of no interest to Nishtar.

He knew that Nishtar would not sympathise with him over Amiroth's betrayal. The magus had not told Augurk to seek Amiroth's help. In Nishtar's opinion, Augurk believed, it was Augurk's sole responsibility to discover the whereabouts of the lost city. 'I have done everything that I could to fulfil what you asked of me,' he wrote. 'Unfortunately, my efforts have been to no avail. I have failed despite my greatest exertions. I beg you to release me from this charge. But if you cannot forgive me, if you deem me worthy of punishment, so be it. I only beg you to spare my subjects, for they are not responsible for my failure,' he added at the end.

On the seventeenth of Niwukir, fifteen days after he had sent his message to Nishtar, Augurk received the sumagus's reply. It disturbed him to the core. He had feared that Nishtar would be enraged at his refusal to continue the search for the City of Stone; he realised that he had underestimated the extent of Nishtar's obsession with the legendary city. Nishtar's wrath almost leapt out of the page at him with every word he read. He was drenched in sweat and trembling by the time he finished reading the letter. He had to sit down. For, Nishtar had declared that he would destroy everything that Augurk had built up using Nishtar's help—his monarchy, his family, his very kingdom. He had spared no details of what he would do to Augurk and his country, mocking Augurk's request for his subjects to be spared in the harshest tone. Augurk knew that Nishtar was capable of fulfilling every one of those threats! He had brought doom upon Ghrangghirm.

For one whole day, Augurk remained terrified. Then his pride asserted itself, and he decided to face his end with honour. He had indeed done everything that he could, and if Nishtar chose to believe otherwise, then he was not really as omniscient as he was believed to be. Another day went by in a state of depression for the rauz of Ghrangghirm. He was so affectionate to his family and friends that it alarmed them. Angbruk asked Augurk outright if he was contemplating suicide. This checked Augurk's state of grieving. On the fourth day, Augurk rose with a new resolution. He had sensed what the problem was. Too long he had worried about how his people would be affected if he sent them to the Lyudzbradh. He did not want them to die among the mountains, searching for the stone city. Death, however, seemed inevitable for them; if it did not come from the mountains, it would take the form of Nishtar's wrath. Augurk's mind was finally made up.

He hastened off a message to Nishtar declaring his intention of sending an expedition in search of the City of Stone. This message was very different from the pleading messages that he had sent before. It was, as Nishtar noted to Alanor, the declaration of a dharvh who had faced the worst in himself and had found his worth and honour. Six days after Augurk had resolved to take matters entirely into his own hands, an expedition set out from Drauzern with the secret purpose of discovering Patarshp's city. There were thirty dharvhs in the party, and it was led by Witar. The members of the expedition were chosen based on their courage, intelligence and determination. They were some of the best soldiers of Ghrangghirm. And their orders were to find the City of Stone or die trying.

Chapter 46

EAMILUS AND HALIFERN

(2 Niwukir 5009 A.E. to 24 Sachir 5010 A.E.)

The day after Prince Halifern returned home, he was summoned by the three Elders of Numosyn: Ellahas, Rovinon and his father Rohyllar. They had heard rumours about the arrival of strangers in their lands with Halifern and were unhappy. They also noted that Loyohen, Erofone and Siltare had not returned with Halifern though they had left together and had planned to spend the four mondans together. They wanted to discover the mysteries behind these worrisome matters. Halifern met them in the Council's main chamber. Wary but confident, he bowed to the panel of three and sat facing them calmly. He had anticipated what the summons were about and was prepared to answer honestly.

'We are glad that you have completed your independent stay successfully. We welcome you as a full-fledged citizen of Harwillen,' Rohyllar said formally, no hint of pride or affection in his voice. He was a tall frael with wide shoulders, black hair and a wooden look that was further underlined by his stiff bearing. His complexion was darker than that of his son, who took after his mother, and no one who didn't know them would have guessed him to be Halifern's father. Halifern nodded to acknowledge the ceremonial announcement. It, he knew, was only the opening.

'We have heard,' Rovinon picked up the conversation, 'that a human has accompanied you here. Is it true?' He was as unlike Rohyllar in appearance as two fraels could be. Shorter than usual, he was as thin as a reed and had snow white hair and a long, hooked nose. He was as brown and as wrinkled as a raisin though he was not as old as he looked at first sight.

Halifern wanted to declare that it was only half true since Eamilus was only half human, but he decided that it would be prudent not to. Fraels, he was well aware, could be paranoid about any stranger in their lands; a stranger known to be a homanim would undoubtedly disturb them greatly.

'It is true,' he answered simply.

'How dare you bring a strange human amidst us!' thundered Rohyllar, shamed and angered by his son's irresponsible and reckless behaviour.

'He is merely a boy,' Halifern replied calmly. 'Besides, he saved my life. I could not be so rude as to ask him to leave as soon as I knew that I was safe within my City.'

'May I ask how he saved your life?' Ellahas asked smoothly. He was a rather handsome frael, not very tall but always well-dressed and suave. He was neither very dark nor fair and had neatly combed straight black hair shot through with grey at the temples, which gave him a dignified air. He had sharp, thin features that make him look noble rather than pinched; surprisingly, he sported a narrow moustache, something that was almost never seen among fraels.

Halifern had hoped to avoid being cornered into such a position, but it was impossible to tell how Eamilus had saved his life without telling about his misadventures with the mertkhezin and the western humans as well. So, without too many details, he told them of the attack on him and his friends, his friends' suspected deaths, his escape and subsequent capture by King Amiroth of Balignor and of his rescue by Eamilus. He left out many pertinent details to make the episode sound completely coincidental. The elders weren't fooled. They probed his answers until he had given them a more detailed picture of his unfortunate adventures. However, he said nothing about Eamilus's true identity though they asked him many questions about the boy.

'Your son is a fool, Rohyllar,' snapped Rovinon. 'He would have brought war upon us through his foolishness.'

'Which was fortunately averted by his miraculous rescue by this boy Eamilus,' Ellahas added, ostensibly to defend Halifern. But the hidden sneer was not missed by the younger frael. Ellahas was suggesting that the whole thing was a plot or scam by Halifern to fulfil some ulterior goal. He ignored the jibe and agreed that it was true that his concern for the humans had been responsible for putting all Harwillen in danger, but that danger *had* been averted.

'And what if this human king decides to attack us now because you have escaped? Would you surrender yourself to avert war?' Rohyllar demanded, clearly unhappy with his son.

'If King Amiroth decides to attack, and I'm not so sure he will, and if my surrender can cause him to withdraw, then I will,' Halifern replied coldly. 'But you cannot hold Eamilus responsible for what King Amiroth may or may not do. He is not from Balignor and has no connection with King Amiroth.'

'Where *is* he from?' Ellahas asked smoothly, with a smile that suggested that this was the opening he had been waiting for. Halifern felt his hackles rising, but he kept calm.

'I met him in Cordemim,' he answered, neither lying nor telling the truth that he wasn't sure where Eamilus was from. He hoped that the Elders knew so little about humans that Eamilus's complexion would not reveal that he could not be from the west.

'Are you aware of what a human army was doing near the borders of Ghrangghirm and Wyrchhelim?' Rovinon asked.

'No,' Halifern replied honestly.

'What if the humans and dharvhs are planning to attack us jointly?' Rovinon raised this question to his two companions.

Before either of them could comment, Halifern answered, 'Rauz Augurk is my friend. He would never attack Harwillen. Besides, I did not know that we were interested in the activities of humans or dharvhs.'

'We are now, thanks to you!' snapped Rohyllar angrily. 'You have an unfortunate tendency of making friends with individuals of other races. That can bring nothing but trouble. I have never approved of your friendship with the dharvh rauz, and now you have brought a strange human here. I am tired of your irresponsible and foolhardy conduct!'

The censure of Halifern by the Elders continued for some time more. The young frael bore their recriminations patiently, replying as he deemed appropriate and refraining from comment otherwise. At the end of the tirade, they ordered him to return to his house and tell the human boy to leave at once. Halifern pointed out how ungrateful that would make them look and what a poor impression of the fraels it would leave on the boy who had risked his own life to save one of their own. They grudgingly agreed to let the boy remain in Numosyn. Since Halifern was so adamant on having the boy to stay, he was ordered to make sure that his human guest caused no nuisance or discomfiture to any frael. They could not hold Halifern responsible for the deaths of Loyohen, Siltare and Erofone, they admitted, but declared City-wide mourning for the three. It was obvious that Halifern was the victim in much of the mishaps that had befallen him, though they acknowledged it only reluctantly. Somehow, they held, Halifern had brought it upon himself although they could not point out just how he was responsible. He was fined two hundred horas of community service for putting the country at risk of war with humans.

While Halifern was being berated, Eamilus had been wandering about discreetly, enjoying the wonder and beauty of Numosyn. He had never seen such a place before, and he was struck by its elegant sylvan loveliness. Unlike the Valdero, the forests of the fraels were not untamed and dangerous; they were graceful, picturesque and gentle. As he walked, angry words reached his ears. He could hear Halifern being scolded by the three Elders. He felt sorry for Halifern. He also realised that his presence could get Halifern into more trouble than he already was in since fraels were notoriously xenophobic. Besides, his destination lay elsewhere. He had been sidetracked by Halifern's need for help, but he had to return to his quest. He decided to leave that night, under cover of darkness. He had a feeling that Halifern would try to convince him to stay on if he learnt of Eamilus's intention to leave.

On his way back to Halifern's treehouse, Eamilus spotted some fraels practicing archery in a glade. He was astonished at their skill. Nearby, some others were practicing with swords. Eamilus felt jealous of these fraels though, he knew, they were no match for him in strength or deadliness. He returned thoughtfully and remained rather distracted. Halifern returned soon after. The two had a quiet, companionable meal, both remaining preoccupied with his own thoughts. In the evening, Halifern went out again. He did not return for a long time. Eamilus felt unhappy about leaving without saying goodbye but knew that it was the best course of action. Slithering down the tree as quietly as a squirrel, he made his way towards the border of Numosyn.

He hadn't gone more than a few steps when someone spoke to him from behind, 'Going exploring?'

Eamilus turned round and smiled sheepishly. 'Sort of,' he answered Halifern.

'But you weren't planning on returning, is that it?' Halifern asked. Eamilus nodded.

'Why do you want to go? Are you uncomfortable here?'

'No, not at all. But all the same, I don't think I should stay here.'

'Why?'

'I have to be someplace else. It's important,' Eamilus said, feeling rather uncomfortable. He did not wish to tell Halifern the truth because it would hurt the frael; nor did he want to lie because it would be unfair to him.

'I can't stop you if you have made up your mind to go, but I would have liked you to stay. I can't ever repay you for what you have done for me, but I would have tried to make you welcome here.'

'I know. I too wish that I could have stayed. Unfortunately, I have to go.'

'Is there nothing that I can say that will change your mind? Stay for a few days, at least!'

Eamilus stood there, biting his lower lip, rent by hesitation. He knew from the earnestness in Halifern's voice that the frael really wanted him to stay. Yet he had already made up his mind. In the few days that he had known Halifern, the two had become friends despite the differences in their ages, races and circumstances. Eamilus found Halifern's world enchanting, but he did not want to burden his friend. He did not know what to do. He stood there, unable to agree to remain and equally unable to walk away. As Halifern watched Eamilus, it was brought home to him just how young the boy was. He was tall for his age, and mature. It was easy to mistake him for an adult. Halifern stood as tall as Eamilus. In the dark, the two could have been mistaken as two fraels or two boys of the same age. But the truth was that Eamilus was thirteen anni old whereas Halifern was forty-one. Despite his maturity, Eamilus was still only a boy. Halifern felt sorry for him.

'Is there nothing here that you might want to stay for?' he asked Eamilus kindly. 'I would like to be a better friend to you than I have been so far. If you won't stay, then tell me, what can I do to repay you for saving me?'

Eamilus joked weakly, 'I have no idea of the price of a fraelish prince's life. But there is something that I'd really like very much, if you don't mind.'

'Please, anything!' insisted Halifern.

'I do not know how to use weapons although I find it fascinating. I saw some of the fraels here practicing today. I would very much like to see more of it, if it would not trouble you.'

Halifern was taken aback. He understood that Eamilus wanted him to demonstrate his prowess with weapons. It was a strange request indeed, but he was honour bound. Then he had an idea. 'Eamilus,' he said, 'do you know that the fraels are the best warriors in Elthrusia even though we have no armies? Yes, we are highly skilled at archery and swordplay, though we learn it and practice it out of love for the art rather than because we plan to fight wars. And of course, the bow and arrow provide us with food, so they are our favourite weapons. Would you like to live with us for a while and learn how to wield arms? I would be happy to teach you if you are willing to take me as a teacher.'

Eamilus stood rooted to the spot. He could not believe the offer that Halifern was making him. It was the one thing that could have changed his mind. When he had asked Halifern for a demonstration, he had not imagined that the frael might be interested in teaching him. In fact, it had simply been out of a desire to learn a little, if possible, by observing Halifern. 'Yes,' Eamilus answered with deep feeling and gratitude. 'I will stay and learn from you!'

The fraels stood round in a milling circle at the foot of Halifern's treehouse. Most of them bore an expression of curious interest as they craned their necks to look up at the upper reaches of the tree. A few looked irritated. Nothing was visible though grunts and swishes were clearly audible. Suddenly, two figures came flying down the bole of the wide tree. They weren't actually flying, but they moved so fast, swinging from one branch to another and climbing down the thick trunk, that they created an illusion of flying. Eamilus was pursuing Halifern, and Halifern was trying to find a branch sturdy enough to stand upon. The fraels standing below murmured anxiously. Their mood lifted when Halifern found a strong branch and stood his ground. Now Eamilus was at a disadvantage. No matter how fast and cleverly he swung his sword at Halifern, the frael was always faster, always smarter. Eamilus could find no opening. And all of a sudden he was on the back foot, retreating while Halifern attacked him relentlessly. The watchers below let out a collective gasp as a low swing by Halifern compelled Eamilus to leap off the branch. But Eamilus did not fall. He simply grabbed another branch and steadied himself. For an infinitesimal momon, he watched the frael lazily. Then he sped off towards the treetop where his speed and strength gave him an advantage. The audience expected Halifern to pursue Eamilus up the tree and sighed in anticipation of a long duel.

Halifern, however, did something surprising. Sheathing his sword, he unslung his bow from his shoulder. Taking three arrows from the quiver at his hip, he paused briefly to take aim upwards. Then he shot all three arrows one after the other. Two dull thuds and a resounding twang told that one of the arrows had hit the target. Everyone waited with bated breath as Halifern swiftly climbed and disappeared among the foliage. He soon returned, this time with Eamilus. The two wore identical smiles. Eamilus's torn sleeve showed where the third arrow had struck. It had torn through his sleeve and impaled his sword by its handle to the tree. The crowd that had gathered below to watch the duel cheered loudly before dispersing.

When the duellists reached the ground, only three fraels remained standing there, looking severe and disapproving. Halifern's smile vanished. Eamilus looked serious and inscrutable. He bowed to the three fraels and asked permission to be dismissed. When the oldest of the Elders nodded, he climbed back up, casting a backward glance of sympathy at Halifern, who stood facing the three with respectful defiance. All three members of the fraelish Council looked grim. They had never felt the same way about Eamilus as Halifern did. Astute as he was, Eamilus wasn't sure whether they deprecated Eamilus for himself or because of being an outsider. He hoped that his and Halifern's display of that day would not lead to Halifern being punished, though the latter was quite capable of defiance and that, rather than anything else, was often the trouble.

Eamilus had grown to respect and like Halifern in the time since he had first stepped into the world of the fraels. He understood that Prince Halifern was different from other fraels. Unlike them, he valued seriousness, knowledge and scholarship. Even though he loved to hunt and to engage in lively bouts of martial exhibition, he spent horas trying to learn about the world outside of the fraelish lands. He had talked to Eamilus often about the different subjects that the boy had learnt from his masters. Eamilus had happily shared all he knew even as he had learnt all he could about fighting with weapons. He was now as proficient as he could expect to be. That day, he had almost managed not to lose to Halifern.

He wondered whether it was time to leave. His heart grew heavy at the thought of parting from a good friend.

Halifern, meanwhile, was engaged in an argument with the Elders.

'You can see, can you not, how much Eamilus has improved? He almost defeated me today!'

'Yes, we saw,' said an acid faced Rovinon. 'We saw how the kocovus almost defeated you.'

'He is not a kocovus, he is a human,' Halifern protested angrily, his fists balled up.

'Humans don't move that fast,' stated the Elder flatly.

'And a kocovus would have torn me to pieces long since,' snarled Halifern.

'Control your son, Rohyllar,' said Ellahas grimly. 'He appears to be willing to rebel and turn against his own people for the sake of an outsider. This won't brook well for his candidacy when he becomes eligible to join the Council.'

'Behave yourself, Halifern!' Rohyllar scolded, ashamed at the humiliation that his headstrong son had caused him. Theirs had been a Leading Family of Numosyn for generations. Ellahas had always been jealous of him and had looked for ways to show him down even when they had been young fraels hardly old enough to think of anything beyond the next meal and the newest jig. Never had he got an opportunity as ripe as the one Halifern had provided by bringing the strange boy into their midst. No one knew who the boy was or where he came from. Rohyllar had watched the two grow closer with anxiety.

'Listen to your father, boy!' sneered Rovinon. Halifern turned red. It was no secret that father and son were not on the best of terms. Halifern was a disappointment to his father; Rohyllar was a myopic, stubborn opposer of change to his son.

'Keep quiet, Rovinon! You should know better than to get into an argument with someone young enough to be your son,' Rohyllar chided him. Rovinon had always been excitable and flighty, getting carried away by petty issues. He was quick to challenge others to a duel at the smallest of excuses and, even though he was a member of the Council by virtue of belonging to a Leading Family, no one took him seriously.

Turning to Halifern, Rohyllar continued, 'The Council is worried by your growing intimacy with a strange and powerful creature who looks like a human but seems to have traits that are known to be possessed by those vilest of creatures— the kocovuses. We have always considered him dangerous but have taken no action against him in consideration of your fondness for him. However, now that he has acquired prowess in arms, we can no longer sanction his presence in our midst.

We have decided that he has to go. If you do not tell him, we will. The Council's decision is final. We will not endanger our entire City for the sake of one frael's foolhardiness.'

'He saved my life, Father—does that count for nothing?' Halifern pleaded. He was shocked to hear the Council's decision.

'We will not talk of that episode,' Rohyllar said darkly. And, with that, all three turned around and walked away. Halifern stood silently, dejected, his head bowed with grief and shame. How could he tell the boy who had saved his life to leave? He slowly began to make his way up his tree. He had been sharing his residence with Eamilus since the boy's arrival. Eamilus had adapted to the ways of the fraels with amazing ease and speed. Halifern hesitated midway to his treehouse, unsure of whether he was ready to face Eamilus yet. Finally, with a heart that had sunk into his shoes, he climbed up slowly and unwillingly.

Late that night, Eamilus met Halifern to discuss with him a decision that he had taken after the duel that evening. He found Halifern reading a piece of old parchment intently. He recognised it as one of the set that Halifern had received from some human scribe in the west. It contained the legends of the ancient kings of the western kingdoms. Halifern had, at times, read out to him from these scrolls. Eamilus felt curious about the lives and attainments of those men. He felt particularly interested in the life of Alanor who, like Eamilus, had spent anni away from his home and people because he had unwittingly done something wrong.

'Halifern, I wish to speak to you about something important,' Eamilus said.

'I, too, have something important to tell you,' Halifern responded. 'You go first.'

'I came here with you over half an annus ago,' Eamilus began. 'I have learnt much under your careful and untiring tutelage since then. I am grateful to you for your generosity and for your friendship. So it pains me to say this—I feel that it is time for me to leave. You stopped me once before. This time, I must truly go.' He sat silently once he had said these words. It had been hard, but he had done it.

Halifern put down the scroll and gazed at Eamilus. He wondered whether the boy had heard the Elders and had decided to leave. Eamilus looked perfectly calm. Halifern decided that Eamilus knew nothing of the Council's decision. Finally, Halifern nodded, signalling his acquiescence. The two friends sat in silence, both wanting to say much but not knowing how to. Finally, Halifern began to sing:

Olom fechh dylohel, sroth pratals bec outomy sef cazuf,

Olom fechh shez ryawal bec vernurt voinsh emin feen,

Olom shihar traizars chhorn emin ducai yaz wahys

Yaz tefy sissan trafezulayf hallh uryz emin ishts,

Olom Em quez feyor gyfah frazi dopel

Alt brooh wed kilss fechh dopelhich yessahs hyfralef achhai,

Olom fechh hermas threfs bec yechhaz himral dil puffot

Huful Em selye Em anef nin wed roff yoryn veyt lewoh –

Alom, emin mial ernom, Em chelm uleh chuf emin yoelf

Wed sol, olom alt sufy sef chhai nes emin fesh,

Wed sol, olom Em kliss sufy uchhai Em quez wed kliss,

Wed sol, olom keyuch hychhar ans nin chhempaef hoon,

Wed sol, olom yechhaz hychhar sif nin trechhef vyallop,

Wed sol, olom hychhar sufy sef emin mial ernom.

'What does it mean?' Eamilus asked. He had begun to learn Hentar, but his grasp of the language still extended only to the most basic expressions that allowed him rudimentary interaction with others.

Halifern translated the song for him in Volegan, the common tongue. Although Halifern could speak Gamberra fluently, by mutual agreement they spoke either in Hentar or Volegan so that Eamilus could conceal his identity as an eastern human from the fraels. 'It is a traditional farewell song,' Halifern added, by way of information.

'It is a beautiful song,' Eamilus commented, 'but you are a terrible singer.'

'I know,' Halifern said with a smile. 'You should hear my cousin Uposnesee sing it. She brings tears to the listeners' eyes every time.'

After an awkward pause, Halifern sighed and said, 'I will miss your company when you are gone. Where will you go from here?'

'East,' Eamilus replied simply. For a momon, he considered telling Halifern all about his life. Then the mood passed. He remembered Nishtar's lessons in self-control and pulled himself together.

'Since you are going east, could you do something for me? It is a delicate matter that I do not dare trust anyone else with. Will you do it for me?' Halifern asked.

'I am proud that you trust me so highly,' said Eamilus. 'What do you need me to do?'

'I want to send a letter to Augurk, rauz of Ghrangghirm. You have to deliver it to him. Will you?'

'Of course I will,' Eamilus agreed.

'When do you plan to depart?' Halifern enquired.

'The day after tomorrow, on the first of Supprom.'

'I will have the letter ready by then,' Halifern confirmed.

'Good,' said Eamilus. 'So, now I've said all that I had to say. But what was it that you wanted to tell me?'

'It is not important,' Halifern said. 'It no longer matters.'

Chapter 47

BLOOD AND HONOUR

In the second tempora of Niwukir, Avator accompanied the outlaws when they raided one of the desert villages. The villages had, by then, become used to these raids and usually kept aside a 'tribute' to avoid being indiscriminately looted. It was no different this time. The scouts had gone ahead to check for guards and had announced that all was in order. The main body of the outlaws had then ridden in to claim their tribute. The villagers had handed over the tribute without a murmur of protest; they valued their lives more than their wealth. Avator felt sorry for them, but there was nothing he could do to help them.

On the way back, the outlaws came across a heavily guarded caravan leading hordes of cattle towards the south. The owner of the cattle likely wanted to sell them in the small seasonal towns there. Several of the outlaws wanted to attack the caravan and snatch the cattle though Igrag was not too keen on the plan. The outlaws were few in number because they hadn't expected to encounter a large group of soldiers on the raid. They had taken with them just enough provisions to last them the trip to and from the village. But those who wanted to rob the cattle prevailed in the end. After much debate, they agreed that they would not resort to frontal attack. Instead, they would use stealth and secrecy. To this idea, Igrag acceded.

The outlaws dismounted, leaving the scouts in charge of their horses, and disappeared into the rapidly descending darkness of sunset. The scouts led the horses to the spot where they had been instructed to camp for the night and settled down. They had been ordered to stay put with the horses until the others returned, but Avator decided to disobey the order. He took off as soon as the sun rose, following the faint trail left behind by the outlaws who were now trailing the caravan on foot. He realised that a couple of anni ago, he would never have found the trail, let alone be able to follow it. His time with the outlaws had taught him *some* useful things, he decided. He sighted the robbers around noon but kept his distance. He wanted to know what they were up to. It had been extremely foolish to disobey Igrag's orders, he knew, but his curiosity had got the better of him. He had willy-nilly come to admire Igrag's merits as a tactician. This was another opportunity for him to study the outlaw captain's cunning at work, he told himself.

The outlaws had been discreetly following the caravan all this time. They had managed to sneak up close to it without being noticed. They continued stalking their prey till nightfall, when the caravan stopped. The guards spread out, torches were lit, campfires came to life. The soldiers patrolled the borders of the caravan ceaselessly. The animals that had moved as a large herd during the day were now penned into several enclaves, all guarded actively. Avator could not imagine how Igrag planned to steal some of the cattle and get away with the theft under the circumstances! Avator was still at a distance from the outlaws as he observed them. Since he needed not to get caught by them or the soldiers, he could not light a fire. He noticed that the outlaws had not lit any fires either to avoid detection. While waiting, Avator passed the time by pondering what he would have done in Igrag's place. Several plans came to his mind. Not one of them was foolproof. He hoped that he wouldn't miss whatever Igrag did due to the darkness.

He almost *did* miss the outlaws' plan, it was so smoothly and silently managed. He noticed just in time that one of the outlaws sneaked into an enclosure, perfectly timing his actions so that the guards' backs were turned at the moment that he made his move. In the blink of an eye, he crossed the distance between the spot where the outlaws were hidden and the enclosure and slipped inside. Soon after, another outlaw slipped into the enclosure in the same way. By dawn, at least nine or ten of them were concealed amongst the cattle. When the caravan broke camp, the cattle were again herded together. The outlaws moved between the animals, staying low, unseen and unheard. The caravan started on its way again. The outlaws on the outside began to follow them discreetly. Avator, too, resumed his pursuit.

Around noon, some of the cattle started showing signs of restlessness. They began to move towards the edges of the herd. Avator could not overhear what the herders looking after the cattle said to each other. However, two of them trotted off towards the front of the caravan. They soon returned with buckets of water and a trough. While the rest of the herd moved on, the cattle that had been agitated were stopped for watering. Avator smiled. He knew how the outlaws had managed to make some of the cattle too thirsty to go on. Salt!

As the rest of the caravan moved on, dust from the scores of animals' hooves obscured the road. Taking advantage of the poor visibility, the outlaws who had been following the caravan attacked. The two herders were too terrified to fight; the moment they saw the outlaws emerging from the roadside, they fled. Laughing, the outlaws took charge of the score odd cows and bulls that had been left behind. Igrag ordered his eighes to leave the scene quickly and disappear. However, it had been easier to get the cattle than it was to disappear with them. The animals refused to obey orders from strangers. They stubbornly stood around, mooing loudly. The outlaws prodded them and smacked their rumps and finally got them moving. However, they moved rather slowly, unsure of who was herding them. Sometimes, one or the other tried to break and run and had to be brought back. They were proving more trouble than they were worth. Avator, who had begun to return almost as soon as the outlaws had taken possession of the cattle, laughed silently at the spectacle when he turned back to check on them from a distance. The outlaws were not going to have an easy time getting to camp! He hurried on towards the other scouts' location.

Suddenly he heard horses, many horses, coming down the path. He turned back to see what was happening and he froze with fear. Two dozen or more soldiers were bearing down on the small group of outlaws who had stolen the cattle. He had no idea where the outlaws who had gone with the herd were or if they were even alive, but one thing was certain—they would not be coming to the aid of their comrades. Which meant that the half dozen that had taken charge of the cattle were doomed. Avator did not know what to do. He was too far to go for help. By the time he reached anybody, Igrag and the others would be dead. He stayed where he was, unable to make up his mind whether to go to their aid or to run back to camp.

In the meantime, the outlaws too had realised what was happening. They drew their weapons, ready to fight to the death.

'No!' Avator heard Igrag roar above the thundering of the soldiers' horses. 'Run! I will hold them back. They don't know how many we are. Get away from here. Find the others and rescue them if need be.'

Avator could not believe his ears. Igrag was asking his eighes to flee, leaving him behind to face what was certain death. He wondered what the bandits would do. They stood there, hesitating, not happy at the prospect of leaving their leader to certain death. Igrag again ordered them to leave, and one by one, they melted away into the dusty desert. Qually was the last to leave, reluctant till the end. By then, the soldiers were almost upon Igrag. He stood in the middle of the road, sword in hand, a resolute expression on his face. He knew that he was waiting for death, yet he was not afraid. Avator could not help admiring him. The cattle that had been the cause of the debacle stood by the roadside, forgotten. Suddenly Avator had an idea.

He had been used to helping out a farmer at his dairy during his stay in Ustillor several anni ago. He was not as familiar with cattle as he was with horses, but what he knew would suffice. He hastened to the animals and began to chase them into the middle of the road, clicking his tongue to make the noises that the cows and bulls would recognise. They obediently moved into the path, effectively blocking Igrag from the soldiers' view. Avator ran to the captain of the outlaws and tugged at his sleeve. He gestured for the eighe to follow him into a ditch by the roadside. Igrag was taken aback by his sudden appearance but understood his plan and raced to the ditch instantly. By the time the soldiers had managed to get through the mass of cattle, both Igrag and Avator were nowhere nearby.

Neither of the two spoke for a long time. They continued to walk swiftly but cautiously towards the camp where the scouts and horses were. That was where the other escaped outlaws would head to as well. The two were almost there when night fell. Instead of pushing on, Igrag decided to make camp by the roadside under a sheltering rocky outcrop. The two still had not said a word. Igrag lit a fire with arghyll powder. The two sat near it, warming themselves. Though it was somminar, the desert could still be cold at night. Igrag was the first to break the silence.

'You disobeyed your orders to stay put,' he said, not very harshly but in a tone that made it clear that he wasn't too happy about it.

'I am sorry,' responded Avator. He wanted to add that if he hadn't, Igrag would be dead by then, but he held his tongue.

'If you hadn't, I would be dead by now,' Igrag continued, almost reading his mind. 'I thank you for that.'

Avator noticed that Igrag's aura was glowing unusually brightly. Sometimes it happened if an eighe was agitated, but Igrag appeared perfectly calm. He continued to speak, 'However, I cannot allow disobedience to go unpunished. It was the merest of coincidences that your presence came in handy; we might have succeeded in our venture easily enough. When we return to the main camp, you must face the consequences of your actions, both right and wrong. Do you understand, Mordeph?'

Avator nodded, surprised and angry at what he felt was Igrag's ingratitude. The captain softened his stance and added, 'Do not think that I am ungrateful. On the contrary, I owe you my life. I am in your debt. But discipline is extremely essential for our survival. If I do nothing about your disobedience, others will be encouraged to follow suit and, perhaps, without such desirable results. As an individual, I cannot thank you enough; as a leader, I cannot turn a blind eye to an obvious breach of discipline. A leader's life extends only as far as his last obeyed command.'

Avator nodded again, not totally convinced that he saw eye to eye with Igrag. He wondered, though, why the captain was bothering to explain all this to him. Igrag was not angry, he sensed. Perhaps he meant what he was saying, that as a leader he had to ensure that no one broke the rules. Their life was a precarious one. Even Avator could see how important it was to follow the discipline of the gang if they were to survive. Perhaps the explanation was Igrag's way of apologising for whatever punishment he would have to mete out as leader to Avator. 'I understand,' he said simply to Igrag.

The two continued to sit in silence for a while longer. Then, unable to suppress his curiosity, and sensing that Igrag might be in a pliable mood, Avator said,

'I often wonder what such a capable warrior and tactician like you is doing among outlaws instead of being in an important position in the army.'

Igrag stared at the boy for a while, surprised at the lad's audacity. No one had ever dared to ask why he had become an outlaw. No one asked *any outlaw* that question. There was an unwritten code that forbade one from asking another outlaw about his past. If someone wanted to tell others, he told the story of his own accord. Most of them were happy enough to narrate the tale of their journey into lawlessness; some were even proud of their stories. Some, like Igrag, preferred not to talk about it. Igrag was surprised that Mordeph would ask him such a personal question despite being familiar with the norms of silence in this regard. He found Mordeph difficult to figure. There was something very unusual about the boy that he just could not pin down. Then he smiled. He was in a mellow mood. Besides, the boy *had* saved his life.

'I wasn't always an outlaw,' he said to Avator. 'In fact, I was in the army once. I was a very highly placed official in the army of Lyisl.'

Avator started. Lyisl! His homeland! His home that he had left behind so many anni ago that he hardly remembered what life in the palace as the prince of Lyisl had been like! Sure that Igrag would have noticed his surprise at the mention of Lyisl, Avator hastily said to cover his surprise, 'Then how did you happen to come this far, into this desert?'

Igrag frowned slightly at the interruption but continued with his story. 'I was well-liked by the soldiers because I had worked my way up through the ranks. The nobles in the army, though, did not like me. I was not one of them. No matter how good I was, they never accepted me wholeheartedly. In fact, most of them knew that I was better than them. They were jealous. They did everything they could to prevent my rise, but they failed. King Rannzen, bless his soul in Zyimnhem, was happily unaware of what his courtiers were up to. He was never a military eighe. For all his good intentions, he was completely incapable as an army's commander, and his generals did as they pleased.'

Igrag noticed that the boy was looking pale.

'Are you ill?' he asked Mordeph.

'No, just hungry. Please continue,' Avator said hurriedly. This was the second time that someone had accused his father of being incompetent. The shock of hearing an outlaw captain in the desert of Emense, who had once been in his father's army, say those things about his father was too much of a shock. Avator pulled himself together. He had never been in greater danger, he realised. No way could he allow Igrag to realise who he was.

Still dubious about Avator's sudden pallor, Igrag continued, 'One day I learnt that I was to be promoted. I would be made a general. I was very happy. I felt that finally I was getting my due. I was mistaken. There were some in the court who had the king's ear. They lied about me to him. They told him that I had committed some heinous crime; they planted the evidence and had me thrown out of the army. I would have been arrested and beheaded but for Lord Sanfion. There was a truly noble eighe! He knew the truth. He and his cousin, Lord Carahan, were always nice to me. They helped me escape. I came to Emense, but I could not find employment. I had no papers to prove my credibility as a soldier. And I had never known another skill or profession besides soldiering. Finally, I came out to the desert to make a living in whatever way I could. I met others like me, kereighes who had been dealt a raw hand by luck or their enemies or their own stupidity. Not all of them were victims of misfortune; some of them were hardened criminals. I brought them together, and we have been together since. Others have joined us over the anni, like you and your family. All the eighes in my band have their stories, some sad and some disgusting. But they are all my eighes. I'm their leader. I do what I have to do to ensure that we all survive.'

'Even if it means sacrificing your own life?' Avator could not help asking out loud. He had been moved by Igrag's story. He had never before imagined this aspect of his former life. He had always had an ideal picture in his heart of what life as a king or a noble was like. That was the ideal he wanted to achieve, the image he was striving to attain. Igrag's story had driven a stake through that vision, shattering it into a hundred pieces.

'Even that,' said Igrag, nodding. 'If push comes to shove.'

'But your death would leave them leaderless. All that you have done will be undone.'

'True, but that is inevitable, is it not? I will not be around forever,' Igrag said philosophically. Then, on a lighter note he added, 'And you may not be around every time to save the day while disobeying your orders!'

'Perhaps I will,' Avator replied with a smile, sharing in the joke.

Neither talked much during the rest of the night. They kept watch in turns until dawn. Then they resumed their journey, joining the rest of the gang soon after daylight. Those who had gone with the herd had miraculously managed to escape unscathed as well. Everyone cheered on seeing Igrag; they had given him up for dead. Seeing him alive was a pleasant surprise to them all. The entire group made its way back to camp, tired and chastised but relatively cheerful at having escaped misfortune in one piece.

Forsith and Avator had had one of their rows before the boy had left on the raid. The two were still angry with each other for being obtuse and not seeing the truth, but the older eighe still cared enough for Avator to cook him a hot meal upon his return. Avator did not see Avita in the tent, so he asked Forsith where she was. Forsith informed him that she was playing by herself somewhere in the camp. He didn't sound too happy about it. Before Avator could say anything further, the young girl returned and sat down on her bed without a word. She showed no liveliness at Avator's return. When he asked her about her day, she answered perfunctorily. Then she buried her face in her pillow and began to sob.

Concerned, Avator left his food and hurried to her side.

'What is the matter?' he asked her. 'Why are you upset?'

'Nothing,' she replied in a hoarse voice. She did not want to tell him what had happened. She wanted to wait to tell Temeron. Avator would not understand. Temeron would.

But Avator would not be dissuaded. He continued to coax and cajole her until she gave in. Finally, she told him, 'Lekker called me a freak and threw stones at me. They didn't hit me, though.'

Avator saw red. If he had not been so angry, he would have noticed something unusual in what Avita told him, but he was too furious to notice anything. He stormed out despite Forsith's and Avita's attempts to hold him back. He ran through the camp until he found Lekker. The older boy was chatting and laughing with a group of his cronies. In a flash, Avator was upon him. Lekker was older and bigger, but Avator was fast and really angry. Neither opponent had a clear advantage. The fight could have easily gone either way if the bystanders had not pulled the two apart as soon as they realised what was happening. The two were hauled in front of Igrag. The captain looked thunderous on being told what had happened.

'You both know that one of the most important rules in this camp is that we do not fight with one another. I will happily have both of you hided for this. But I'd like to know what you have to say for yourselves first,' declared Igrag angrily. He turned to Avator and asked, 'First you disobey your orders. Now you fight another member of the camp. What do you think you are doing?'

Avator looked him in the eye and answered, 'Lekker called my sister a freak and threw stones at her. What was I supposed to do? Take it lying down?'

'He's lying!' Lekker protested. 'I never did anything like that.'

'Can you prove it?' Igrag asked Avator.

'Menithyl can testify,' Avator said confidently.

Avita was sent for. Igrag asked everyone to leave his tent before she arrived. He wanted to speak to Menithyl alone. Soon after, Avita entered, accompanied by Forsith. She looked terrified. Forsith stood by her side, looking grim. Igrag had been talking to the two quarrellers in a gruff voice, but when he spoke to Avita, he was kind and gentle. He asked her to step closer to him. When she was standing at his side, he asked her to tell him what had happened between her and Lekker. She looked nervously at Forsith, who smiled and nodded to encourage her.

She answered Igrag in a small, shy voice, 'I was playing near the well, making mud dollies, when Lekker came by. He stamped on my dolls and broke them. When I tried to move my dolls away, one of them jumped up and splattered onto his clothes. He then called me a freak and threw stones at me. I covered my face and crouched down. None of the stones hit me. They fell all around me but did not touch me. He then called me a freak again and walked away. Then I went home.'

Igrag looked from Avita to Forsith, an expression of perplexity on his face. Avita's story seemed rather incredible. It was hard to believe that a mud dolly could jump up onto someone's clothes on its own or that stones thrown from such a short distance would all miss. He knew that there was something odd about the girl; Mordeph himself had told him about it. Still, the story seemed fantastic. Yet, there was no lie in her eyes. And Eronsom was calm enough. If the girl had been lying, and he knew it, he would have looked guilty. Igrag decided to accept her story; after all, stranger things happened every day. He sent Avita and Forsith away and asked the quarrellers to be brought back inside.

As Avator was entering the tent to report to Igrag, Forsith and Avita were leaving. He looked towards Forsith to gauge from his guardian's expression what had happened with Igrag, but Forsith did not look at Avator as he walked past. Clearly, he held the boy responsible for Avita's current problems. Avator smiled at Avita encouragingly, and she responded shyly before being purposefully led away by Forsith.

'I have talked to Menithyl,' Igrag said, once the quarrellers, witnesses and other outlaws were all back inside his tent. 'She confirmed what Mordeph said: Lekker called her a freak and threw stones at her.'

'She's lying!' Lekker cried out. 'She's making it all up. She doesn't even have a scratch!'

'How do you know that if you never hit her?' Igrag growled. He jumped up and collared the lad. 'If I had any doubts about her story, they are now gone. I think that you did try to hurt the child, you rascal!'

He shoved Lekker hard, and the lad stumbled and fell. He lay on the ground cowering in front of Igrag's rage. He knew that of all the rules of the camp, one was sacrosanct: no one was to hurt or injure any other member of the camp deliberately. He trembled with fear. The punishment would be severe, he knew.

Before Igrag could pronounce his sentence, Lamissur stepped forward. 'I would like to intercede on behalf of Lekker,' he said to Igrag, much to the astonishment of all present.

'Why?' demanded Igrag.

'Because he is a fool and a liar, but he is still my nephew. I beg you to take pity on him and treat him as a fool rather than as a delinquent. He never thinks before he acts. Reduce the severity of his punishment, and I shall always be grateful to you.'

'He may be your nephew, Lamissur,' said Igrag, 'but he is also a member of my gang. And the same rules bind everyone. There was malice in his actions, malice that was uncalled for. I would sentence him to twenty lashes and banishment for his actions. But since you have interceded on his behalf, and you are a faithful member of the gang since long, I will reduce his sentence to fifteen lashes if you promise me that he will never repeat such a deed.'

'I promise you that he will never give you cause for complaint in future,' declared Lamissur. 'But I beg you to reconsider and reduce his sentence further. He is, after all, a mere lad.'

But Igrag was not to be moved. Lekker was led away, his face pale and his eyes looking hollow like that of an animal being led to the slaughter. Avator stood calmly, his face inscrutable. He knew that he could not escape punishment, but he had begun to understand something important about Igrag and the outlaws. They did not live by the rule of law, yet they had their own codes and rules of conduct, which were no less important and sacred to them than laws of the land were to respectable citizens. In that was a kind of honour and nobility that could not be found even in courtiers, especially in those who pretended to be better than they were and abused the power that their positions conferred on them. He remained calm as Igrag turned to sentence him.

'You may have done what you did under provocation. However, your conduct is not made excusable by that. Moreover, you disobeyed your orders earlier when we were out on a raid. No matter how beneficial your disobedience may have turned out to be, it cannot be pardoned. I sentence you to ten lashes and a day's starvation! And your share of the raid will revert to the camp.'

Avator paled slightly but did not protest. He bowed to acknowledge Igrag's sentence and was led out to receive his punishment. Lekker had been sentenced first, and he received his punishment first. He bawled like a baby and fainted before the third lash had touched him. Lamissur affectionately carried him away when his punishment was over. Avator was next. As the whip stripped away skin from his back, leaving behind bloody welts, he gritted his teeth and endured. He was determined to prove to Igrag that he belonged, that he was one of Igrag's eighes. Nearby, Igrag watched quietly and wondered again about the unusual kereighe lad. From another place in the crowd, Forsith watched his ward receiving his harsh punishment and wondered how their lives had taken such a tragic turn. He wondered if there was anything that he could do make things better. To his dismay, he could think of nothing.

Chapter 48

GIFTED

Only two days remained to the new annus. It was the fourth day of the Ach, and as per custom, a day of grieving—for the departing annus as well as for those that one has lost. This day was particularly significant to Rosa. She fell into a dark mood of despair and resorted to intoxication to drown her sorrows. In her state of senselessness, she could do anything and not remember afterwards. Temeron had learnt to avoid her on this day. Over the anni, he had managed to figure out what made the lech notice him and what enabled him to remain unmolested. Though he had no calendar, he figured out that the day was Torimach by observing outsiders, the eighes and eighees on the street. Everyone wore either black or white—the colours of mourning—and looked particularly solemn this day. Temeron immediately shrank into his corner and disappeared amongst piles of junk. True to routine, Rosa soon began to drink and to inhale intoxicants. As her senses dulled, she began to cry and moan loudly for her husband and daughter. Temeron sat quiet as a mouse, neither moving nor speaking. He observed her with his big, black eyes, alert to every move she made.

'How I wish I hadn't switched them!' Temeron suddenly heard Rosa say. She was pretty far gone in her intoxication by then and beyond the mood in which she usually battered him. He was in no danger unless he drew attention to himself. Knowing this, his thoughts had begun to drift. He became alert immediately when he heard these words. What was the lech talking about?

Rosa repeated her lament about switching someone though, Temeron noticed, she did not open her mouth. Was he hearing things? Had the fumes from the witch's intoxicants befuddled him too? No, he was sitting too far away to be affected. How could she be talking without opening her mouth?

'Oh, my poor, poor daughter!' Rosa moaned again. This time, too, her mouth remained closed. 'I so, so hate this boy's very guts. I wish I could kill him and be done with it!'

Temeron shrank back. He knew that Rosa was talking about him, even though she wasn't *really* talking. Was she thinking these things, he wondered. Then how was he able to hear her? He felt a sudden thrill. He could hear the witch's thoughts! Just then, Rosa began to wail loudly again and mourn for her dead husband and her lost daughter quite vociferously.

After a while, she fell quiet again. However, she continued to think rambling, venomous thoughts about Temeron, which he was able to hear clearly. In between her ramblings, she suddenly thought, 'He is getting tall and fat. Where is he getting food?' Temeron stiffened. He had been utmost careful about hiding his benefactor's gifts. He was sure that she knew nothing about them. But the regular nutrition must have shown in his improved health. She had noticed him getting healthier and was not happy about it. 'I will beat him today if he eats any food,' Rosa resolved. Temeron made up his mind to starve that day and for the next couple of days too. 'If he tries to step out of his corner, I will beat him, and if he doesn't complete his chores I will still beat him,' Rosa planned. The thought made her chuckle gleefully. That broke her marginally coherent line of thinking, and she again began to wail and keen for those whom she had lost. Temeron sat as still as a kingfisher upon the riverbank. He was stunned. Normally, she forgot all about him when she was intoxicated.

He was immensely relieved that he had managed to hear Rosa's plans for him. His assumption of safety had been a false one. He would never have known the danger he was in had he not heard her thoughts. Now he could plan beforehand to avert the danger. There had to be a way to get around her plans for him. He had to do his chores but without being seen to do them. What could he do? He continued to wait to hear more of Rosa's thoughts, hoping they would give him clue. He did hear more of what was going on in her mind, but he learnt nothing useful. Her thoughts had become completely incoherent by then. All she did was think about her husband and her daughter and how much she hated Temeron. Slowly, as the intoxication took a deeper hold of her, Rosa fell into a stupor. Still Temeron did not move; he knew that the slightest sound could wake her. When he was certain that she was in a deep slumber, he ventured forth from his corner. Watching her falling asleep had given him an idea.

He hurriedly began to complete the chores that he was expected to do. They usually took him a few horas, but he did not have a few horas that day. He decided to complete only the most noticeable tasks. If the witch was still asleep by the time he was done with them, he would think about doing the others. Besides, the house was so dirty that no matter how hard he cleaned, it never really looked clean. All he had to do was clean the places where Rosa slept or worked and the things that she used. She would not pay attention to the rest of the house. He worked quickly and quietly, thinking about what had happened that morning. Was it a result of his attempts to learn magic? Had he finally managed to master some spell that gave him the ability to overhear the witch's thoughts? If so, it could be very useful to him. Feeling excited about his achievement, he quickly finished up and scurried back to his corner before Rosa awoke.

When Rosa became relatively conscious, she remembered only fragments of what she had been thinking earlier. Unfortunately, one of the things she did remember was her plan to beat Temeron. She looked at him in his corner and was satisfied to find that he was sitting there quietly, terrified out of his wits. Good! This meant that he had not completed his chores. She was about to get a lash to flog him when she noticed that the shelves of her magical ingredients were clean, as was the kitchen. In fact, as far as she could see, the whole house was clean. She hurried to check if he had cleaned her big cauldron. He had. She ran through the house, trying to find one excuse to beat the boy but found none. In her frantic and opiate-befuddled mood, she failed to realise that she did not really need those reasons to thrash him; she never had. They were mere excuses to vent her frustration and hatred. She also failed to notice that Temeron was looking far from terrified. In fact, he looked downright smug. She was still not completely in her senses. The fact that Temeron's chores had been completed though he had not moved from his corner stupefied her so much that she forgot to beat him. Giving up on trying to make sense of the mystery, she returned to her intoxication and mourning.

Temeron hoped that he would be able to hear her thoughts again. While sitting there and watching the witch run about bewildered, he had begun to think of the nature of their relationship, if it could be called that. As far back as he could remember, he had been beaten and tortured by the lech. She had turned him into a human, he knew, so that others would also ill-treat him. She obviously hated him. She had told him as much. But why? What had he done? And always the witch would talk about her lost daughter and her dead husband. Did he have anything to do with that? How could he? And why did she call her daughter lost, not dead? And that very day she had talked about 'switching them'. What had she meant? Who were Temeron's parents? Where were they? Had they ever tried to find him or rescue him? He no longer fantasised that his parents were secretly helping him with food and other gifts. Rosa had once or twice mentioned his father. He had gathered from those mentions that she hated him too. Why? He had been too young to understand these things earlier. But as he was growing older, these questions were beginning to occur to him. He decided to talk to Avita about it that night.

But it was a long time before Temeron could sleep. Rosa continued to swing between intoxication and part-consciousness before finally succumbing to her abuses of herself throughout the day. Temeron had failed to hear any more of her thoughts, much to his chagrin. He had begun to think that it would become a regular event, but he was disappointed. He was starting to wonder whether he had actually heard her thoughts at all. Maybe the fumes *had* befuddled him. In any case, things were back to their usual dismal state for him.

Finally, late at night, after all the folks outside had finished their business of the day and gone home, and Rosa was deeply unconscious, Temeron crawled out of his corner. He did not bother to eat; he was not hungry. All he wanted to do was sleep so that he could meet Avita and tell her what had happened that day. But sleep eluded him. He was too much on edge. It was only very late at night that he managed to fall asleep. Not long after, he dreamt that he was on a beach. The place was strangely familiar, as if he had been there before. He could not recall when or why. Of course, many places in his dreams felt like that! Then he remembered. It was the same place that he and Avita had first talked, telling each other their names.

The waves were roaring loudly as he walked down the beach, looking for Avita. She was not there! Why was she not there? Temeron panicked. He called for her. The roar of the waves drowned out his voice. He called even louder, but the waves still overwhelmed his voice. He ran, looking everywhere for her and calling as loudly as he could. Suddenly, a dark figure approached him from the distance. Was it Avita? As he ran towards it, it kept getting further and further away. Finally, he gave up and sat down. He was panting hard from his exertions. Then he heard someone crying. He looked up. Right in front of him was a rock. On the rock sat Avita with her back to him, sobbing. Temeron's heart thudded with mixed feelings of joy at having found her and worry at hearing her cry! He called out her name. This time, his cry was clearly audible.

Avita whipped round. Seeing that it was Temeron, she leapt up with glee. Scampering down to him, she hugged him tightly before laughing out loud.

'Why are you crying? Are you all right?' Temeron asked, concerned.

'Of course I am all right!' she answered happily. 'At least, I am now. You're here.'

'Why were you crying when I saw you?'

'I have been waiting so long tonight. I thought you would not come.'

'And that upset you?' Temeron asked, unable to believe his incredible fortune that someone cared so deeply for him. Avita nodded shyly. They held hands and climbed up the rock again. They sat watching the waves that were much calmer now.

'Do you know that today is the penultimate day of this annus?' Temeron asked her. 'The day after tomorrow is the new annus. Not that it matters to me,' he added bitterly.

'The day after tomorrow is my birthday,' Avita declared. 'I will be nine anni old.'

'Then that day should matter to me,' Temeron said solemnly. Then, as something struck him, he asked in a worried tone, 'Will you be able to meet me that night?'

'Of course I will!' she replied. 'How can I celebrate my birthday without meeting you? When is *your* birthday?'

'I don't know,' said Temeron, looking away. He wished he knew.

'If you don't know, maybe you should pick any day you like, and that day could be your birthday,' Avita suggested enthusiastically.

'Maybe,' said Temeron, not sounding too sure.

'What day would you like to pick?' Avita asked, not wanting her friend to be without a birthday.

Temeron answered without hesitation. 'The same day as yours is. It is the most important day of the annus for me. Yes, I'd like to celebrate my birthday on the same day as you. That is, if you don't mind,' he added hesitantly.

'No, I definitely don't mind,' Avita declared. She then asked Temeron how he would like to celebrate his birthday.

Temeron was quiet. He did not know how birthdays were celebrated. He had learnt that word from the beggar who had taught him to read and write and, although he knew what it meant, he had no idea what folks did to celebrate it. He wished he knew so that he could tell Avita. He wished he could tell his friend something about himself besides details of his miserable life with the witch. The monotony of those incidents was relieved by descriptions of what his mysterious benefactor left for him. There was hardly anything else for him to talk to Avita about. Then he remembered what had happened that day. He told her.

'You were so clever to fool her,' Avita commented, laughing. 'It's wonderful that you can now hear her thoughts. Maybe you will find out a way to escape.'

'No, I cannot hear her thoughts any longer. It was only that one time in the morning. I'm not even sure that I actually did manage to overhear what she was thinking.'

'I'm sure you did!' Avita said loyally. 'Maybe you'll hear something again another day. Don't lose heart.'

'Maybe,' said Temeron without too much conviction. 'I'm not even sure if I want to, to be honest. She is mad. She keeps saying the strangest things.'

'What strange things?' asked Avita.

He told her about the recurring themes of Rosa's thoughts and about the switching of somebody. Avita thought seriously about all this. Then she said, 'Maybe she hates you because you remind her of her lost daughter. Maybe she *is* your mother and she had another baby, a girl, who died or was lost. Maybe she blames you for it.'

'I hope not,' Temeron said with feeling. 'Nothing would be worse than that. How could a mother hate her child as much as she hates me?'

'That is true. But I cannot think of any other reason. Maybe she hates your entire family for some reason and not just you. You did say that she mentioned something about your father once,' Avita suggested.

'Maybe. I hate her too. I wish I would grow up soon and be able to do magic so that I could kill her and escape,' Temeron hissed.

'Don't talk about killing her!' Avita cried. 'You should just escape. You will become as bad as she is if you kill her. Worse than her. She has kept you alive all these anni, hasn't she?'

'Yes, she has,' Temeron said bitterly. 'But this life is worse than death. You have no idea how I suffer!'

'Don't I?' Avita said gently, taking his hand in hers. They looked into each other's eyes. Temeron lowered his face.

'I am sorry. I did not mean that,' he apologised. 'I forgot that you suffered as much as I did for such a long time. I hate myself for that.'

'Don't!' Avita said. 'I do not regret it since it made you feel better faster. I would not give that up any more than I would give up our meetings. We must find a way to face all this together.'

'I wish I knew why I am in this situation,' Temeron grumbled.

'All is not bad in your life,' Avita comforted Temeron. 'You have a secret friend who gives you food and toys and books. Tell me the story of the vanishing fountain again.' She wanted to distract Temeron from his dark musings. Temeron did as she told. The tale of the vanishing fountain was from a book that Temeron had received many mondans ago. It was one of Avita's favourite stories. She had no access to books where she was. The outlaws had practically everything except books. She loved to listen to Temeron's stories from the books that his mysterious benefactor sent him.

When he finished, Avita curled up by his side and placed her head on his shoulder. 'I wish this would never end,' she sighed.

'I wish so too,' said Temeron. 'But it is only a dream; it must end. I wish I was free so that I could come and find you.'

'That would be nice,' Avita responded. 'We could go searching for your parents together.'

'Yes, that would be nice. Someday, I swear, I will be free. And I will come for you. I promise you that,' Temeron said with resolve.

'Then I will wait for that day,' Avita said simply. The two then fell quiet, watching the waves crashing upon the glistening beach. They knew that it was almost dawn. Soon their dream would be over. They would be dragged back to their separate realities. They wanted to hold on to these last moments of togetherness as long as possible.

Chapter 49

BEST OF FRIENDS

Prince Amishar's favourite haunt these days was the village of Durnum because Mizu, who lived on the eastern outskirts of the village, was his only friend. Amishar visited Mizu every other day. On the days that Amishar did not go to Durnum, Mizu visited him at the palace. Over the last half annus, Amishar's visits with Mizu had increased both in frequency and duration. Despite noticing this, Mizu said nothing. He knew that his friend had been unhappy in the palace ever since his father's departure for the dharvh lands; though Amishar loved his mother and Lord Aminor, the palace seemed empty to him in his father's absence. He wanted to escape it by spending time with Mizu rather than with anyone else from the palace. Mizu tried to cheer his friend up whenever the prince came to visit. He had many chores to do around the house now that he was older, yet he made sure that his guest never felt ignored or unwanted. It was a fine line that Mizu managed to walk.

On his ninth birthday, Mizu received an offer of a day off from his chores from his mother. He refused. He did not want to increase her workload just because it was his birthday. She smiled, having anticipated his response, and gave him his alternative gift—a new pair of riding boots. Mizu was thrilled and wanted to show them to Marsillon. Laughing, Misa permitted him to go off to the stables. He was in the stables, showing Marsillon his wonderful birthday gift while grooming him, when he heard Amishar call from the stable doorway.

'Hey!'

'In here,' Mizu replied. At the prince's request, he had long since stopped using honorifics while talking with Amishar. It had smoothened their interactions tremendously, allowing Mizu to feel more comfortable around Amishar.

Amishar walked into the stable. Coming from the light, at first he could see nothing. As his eyes adjusted to the darkness of the stable, Amishar saw Mizu standing next to Marsillon. A cocoon of light seemed to envelop them. He blinked and his friend came into sharper focus. Amishar dismissed it as a trick of the light. Mizu was brushing down Marsillon briskly and the colt, now turning into a fine, strong stallion, appeared to be enjoying the treatment.

'He's grown into a fine horse,' Amishar commented, sitting down on a bale of straw to watch his friend.

'Yes, and he's getting very restless and headstrong day by day. I think Marsil spoils him,' commented Mizu. Marsil was known to all as the colt's mother.

Amishar laughed. He could feel a sense of brotherhood with Marsillon in this. People often accused *his* mother of spoiling him. They assumed that being a woman, she was naturally soft-natured and that having almost lost her son more than once, she was too indulgent towards him. Nothing could have been further from the truth. She was quite strict in matters of discipline; it was Amishar's father who had always spoiled him. The thought of his father threatened to turn his mood sour, so Amishar changed the topic.

'Where is *your* mother?' Amishar enquired. 'I didn't see her on my way here. Is she in the fields?' Amishar liked romping about among the crops, but Mizu's mother scared him. She was a woman whom one couldn't help feeling respectful towards. The young prince had no intention of getting into her bad graces, for she would, he was sure, chastise him the same way that she would her own son.

'She was in the house when I left. Maybe she has gone into the woods to get firewood and herbs. We need some medicines for the crops to keep the bugs away from the grain. She might catch a few rabbits as well.'

'Wow! Rabbits! You are in for a treat tonight, it seems,' commented the young prince whose own table never wanted for any delicacy.

'She always cooks something special for me on my birthday,' Mizu replied nonchalantly.

'Is it your birthday today?' demanded Amishar, sitting up. 'I didn't know. I'm sorry. If I'd known, I would have brought you something. Happy birthday!'

'Thank you, and a very happy birthday to you too. I should have wished you as soon as you came in.' Mizu confessed.

'How do you know it's my birthday?' Amishar demanded. He could not remember telling Mizu.

Mizu frowned. He tried to remember when and how he had learnt of Amishar's birthday. He could not. 'You must have told me some time, I guess,' he replied. 'Or maybe I learnt from Ma. I can't remember.'

'So, have you got a present for me?' asked Amishar eagerly, not particularly bothered about the source of Mizu's knowledge of his birthday. He had already received many rich and valuable presents that morning, but the most precious one had been the permission to visit Mizu. He had not visited Mizu for a whole tempora because his mother had wanted him to spend time with her. He had been afraid that she would not allow him to leave the palace that day either. He had pleaded with her, and she had finally given in.

'It's in the house,' Mizu answered Amishar's question about his gift. Mizu had finished tending to the horse by then. The two boys walked down to Mizu's house with their arms around each other's shoulders, singing a ditty that they had recently learnt.

> *There is an island far, far away—*
> > *A place all brown and green;*
> *That island is, I dare say,*
> > *The prettiest place I've seen.*

> *There is a forest far, far away—*
> > *Lush and dark and dense;*
> *That forest is, I dare say,*
> > *Full of thrill and suspense.*

> *The forest is on the island*
> > *That is far, far away,*
> *And the most beautiful land*
> > *I've seen, I dare say.*

> *There is a tree far, far away*
> > *That turns golden at nightfall;*
> *That tree is, I dare say,*
> > *The tallest tree of all.*

> *The tree is in the forest*
> > *That is far, far away,*
> *And is the greenest*
> > *I've seen, I dare say.*

> *There is a nest far, far away—*
> > *So round and so neat;*

That nest is, I dare say,
  A delight and a treat.

The nest is in the tree
  That is far, far away,
And is the tallest tree
  I've seen, I dare say.

There is a bird far, far away
  Feathered in colours that glow;
That bird is, I dare say,
  Lovelier than a rainbow.

The bird is in the nest
  That is far, far away,
And is the prettiest
  I've seen, I dare say.

The bird is in the nest,
  The nest is in the tree,
The tree is in the forest
  Of unsurpassed beauty.

The forest is on the island
  That is far, far away,
And is the most beautiful land
  I've seen, I dare say!

Once they were inside the house, Mizu gave Amishar a lumpy object wrapped up in cloth, clumsily tied with a ribbon. It was quite heavy. Amishar unwrapped the covering to find a beautiful, polished stone bowl inside. The stone was ochre in colour, shot through with swirling veins of red, with a flawless sheen. Amishar had no idea why Mizu would gift him a bowl.

'You do know what this is, don't you?' Mizu asked, suspicious at the lack of enthusiasm in his friend.

'Um…no?' Amishar said.

'It's a fish bowl! You fill it with water, put some pebbles and water plants at the bottom and keep live fish in it. I've got you some fish too.'

Mizu showed him the pretty red fish he had caught from the river. Then he helped Amishar arrange his fish bowl properly. The prince was delighted with his gift. He asked Mizu to keep it for the time being; he would have someone from the palace fetch it later. The excitement over, the boys wondered what they should do next.

'Let's go down to the river,' Mizu suggested. Amishar agreed readily. He liked the river even though he wasn't a strong swimmer. Mizu was teaching him, but he still had much to learn before he could become as good a swimmer as Mizu. He could not help but be astonished at how easily Mizu could teach him when compared to the struggle that his previous teacher had had. Somehow, with Mizu in the water with him, Amishar felt safe, as if the water would not think of hurting him. He guessed it was because Mizu had saved him from drowning.

The two friends raced each other to the river, which wasn't far from Mizu's house. Amishar won by a couple of feet and was jumping up and down with joy when Mizu suddenly tackled him from behind. The two boys went rolling on the ground, both laughing.

'Let's wrestle,' said Amishar when they had both stood up.

Instead of answering Amishar, Mizu tried to rush him again. This time, the prince was ready. He sidestepped and then tripped Mizu up, easily brining him down. The two boys wrestled on the riverbank earnestly, Mizu hardly able to keep his feet on the ground for longer than two minuras at a time. Amishar was learning to become a warrior. He took his training very seriously even at such a young age. Wrestling and archery were his favourite. Even his training partners found it difficult to beat him at those; Mizu was no match for him. Once, though, Mizu was able to hold his own against Amishar when he put his skilled opponent in a headlock from behind and forced him down on his knees. He was grinning from ear to ear when, with a sudden jerk, Amishar moved backwards, throwing Mizu off balance. Mizu had to lean forward to retain his hold. Taking advantage of this, Amishar grabbed Mizu's arms and neatly swung him over his head onto the ground. Mizu landed with a thud and a newfound respect for his friend.

The boys lay on the riverbank, panting, recovering from their brief but furious bout of wrestling. Suddenly Mizu cried out, 'Look at the sun! It's almost mid-day! Let's get going or it will be time to go to the fields before we are done with our meal.'

He dragged a partially unwilling Amishar into the river. The water was cool. It felt comfortable on their bare skin. In the water, Mizu was the superior of the two. He swam like a fish, paddling fast and even gliding underwater. He would appear at a spot a few feet away from Amishar, then disappear suddenly, reappearing just behind Amishar and dunking him. Amishar was getting better every day, but he still did not dare race Mizu in the water. The two challenged each other, nonetheless, for the fun of it.

The boys left the river when they were thoroughly clean and hungrier than wolves. They dusted their clothes and quickly put them back on. Then they jogged back to Mizu's house, where Mizu's mother had already prepared food for the day. She had eaten her portion before going out. There was just enough in the pot to last the two boys for one meal. Amishar was hesitant to finish up his friend's food. Mizu shrugged.

'Don't fret,' he told his friend. 'Ma will make more in the evening. We can help her if you feel bad about finishing up the food.'

'Can I cook?' Amishar asked tentatively. That was another skill which he had not managed to master yet though not for lack of enthusiasm.

'I'd think not!' answered Mizu with decision. Amishar's face fell. Then he cheered up at the prospect of meeting Misa that night. She would bring rabbits and cook them with fresh wild herbs. Delicious! Besides, he told himself, soldiers and heroes did not need to cook. There was always someone to cook for them. It bothered him, nevertheless, that his friend was quite an adept cook while he himself would probably die of starvation if he ever had to fend for himself.

After they had eaten, the two boys went to the fields. There was much to be done there. The scarecrow needed repair. Weeds were growing rampantly between furrows and needed to be pulled out by the roots. After the work in the fields was done, the leaves in the yard had to be raked. Then the plants in the yard and the kitchen garden had to be watered. Once all this was done, the boys had some horas to themselves. They decided to kill time by practicing archery and swordfighting with wooden swords. Amishar was quite skilled at both. Mizu watched in envy as Amishar hit all the targets without fail. His own arrows hit the targets as often as they went astray. However, he was as good as Amishar at sword fighting, and the two held each other even.

Back at the house, Mizu baked some bread and left it wrapped up in leaves inside the oven to keep it warm. The two boys fetched milk from the village and then sat outside on the stairs, waiting for Misa's return. A messenger had come to enquire after Amishar. He had been sent back with the fish bowl and the message that Amishar was spending the night at Mizu's. The boys were feeling tired and happy and comfortable and began to talk quietly.

'Where were you the last tempora?' Mizu enquired.

'I was at home,' Amishar replied. 'Mother wanted me to spend some time with her. She feels lonely when I spend too much time here.'

Mizu sensed the struggle in Amishar's heart. He was caught between his desire to comfort his mother and to seek alleviation from the boredom of palace life, and he was too young to know what the right thing to do was. When Misa returned later that evening, she found the two boys asleep near the stairs. They awoke when she entered and gathered around her eagerly to tell her all about their day. Misa was surprised to learn that it was Amishar's birthday too. She asked him to stay for the night though she was sure he had already decided to do so. She prepared the meal of rabbit stew, roasted potatoes and fresh buttered vegetables, which they had with the bread that Mizu had baked, and frothing glasses of milk. Afterwards, the boys went out on the porch to look at the stars and identify the constellations. Misa could hear their voices as she cleaned up. When they fell silent, she stepped out to check on them and found that they had fallen asleep again. She gently carried them inside and tucked them into bed.

Chapter 50

FATHERS AND SONS

(12 Chirshkom 5010 A.E. to 16 Chirshkom 5010 A.E.)

It was over three mondans after Amishar's ninth birthday that news of King Amiroth's return swept through the capital, jolting everyone out of the complacency into which they had settled in his absence. The entire palace became abuzz with conjectures and speculations. King Amiroth was not expected back for mondans yet; why was he returning? Was everything all right with him? Had something gone wrong? Helmed by Lord Aminor, Lord Beleston and Lord Parkiod, a frenzy of preparations ensued to welcome the king back and to address any issues that might have resulted in the early return. Everything was ready for King Amiroth by the twelfth of Chirshkom, when he entered his capital after a hiatus of almost an annus.

The entire council of ministers had gathered to receive him. The army and the ordinary people jostled behind the ministers, competing with them to welcome back their beloved king. They cheered him loudly as he entered through the city gates upon his favourite stallion, waving to the nobles, soldiers and common people alike. He looked as hale and hearty as he had at the time of his departure. Everyone heaved a sigh of relief. In their enthusiasm for King Amiroth, at first no one noticed the covered litter that followed his stallion. It was only when he dismounted and stepped up to it that everyone's eyes alighted upon it. They wondered who was in it. Had the rauz of Ghrangghirm accompanied King Amiroth to Lufurdista? Or was it some invaluable prize of the expedition? Amidst the suspense, King Amiroth leant in and said something to someone within the litter. In response, a beautiful woman stepped out of the litter and slipped her arm through his.

Everyone was stunned at the unexpected turn of events. The cheering suddenly died away. Forgetting their merrymaking at the woman's appearance, the crowd stood still, gaping. King Amiroth frowned. He had expected a more welcoming reception for Samiesna from his people. Why were they staring like idiots at him? What would Samiesna think? The thought that she might be embarrassed by his subjects' behaviour mortified him. He stood straighter, holding her hand firmly and glaring at the gathered crowd.

'This is Lady Samiesna,' he declared. 'She has accompanied me from Cordemim. I would like to extend her a warm welcome to our kingdom!'

At the king's words, the gathered citizens were startled out of their stunned state. They began to applaud and cheer in honour of Lady Samiesna. The ministers were more sober in their reception, though they all greeted her respectfully and welcomed her cordially. And no one was more welcoming than Lord Aminor, who smiled warmly at his cousin and bowed low to welcome his companion. If there was a slight exaggeration in his words of welcome, or in his bow to Samiesna, no one noticed.

Both Queen Lamella and Prince Amishar were waiting eagerly for King Amiroth's return. The queen was pale with anticipation. Amishar fidgeted constantly. Lord Aminor had convinced them to remain in the palace for their own safety. They stood ready to welcome Amiroth back home at the palace gates accompanied by Misa, Mizu and hundreds of servants, maids, guards and attendants. Suddenly Lord Aminor came riding in like his life depended on his haste. He leapt out of his saddle almost before the horse had halted. Bowing to Queen Lamella, he said urgently, 'My lady, I would very much like you to retire to your chambers.'

Surprised and upset by his sudden actions, she asked, 'Is the king all right, my lord? What is wrong? What has happened?'

Aminor did not want to explain about Samiesna in public. Judging it best to prevent the queen from seeing another woman on the king's arm, he had hurried back to the palace on the pretext of making arrangements for 'Lady Samiesna's stay'. He could not think of an excuse to make the queen return to her chambers immediately.

'The king is fine, Your Majesty,' he said, sounding far more anxious than his words merited. 'But I think that it would be more…advisable if you received him in your own chambers once he has had a little rest.'

'Did he demand this, my lord?' Lamella asked, beginning to feel confused and agitated.

Desperate, Lord Aminor looked at Misa, who had been following the exchange keenly. She saw the deep anxiety in his eyes and sensed that he was trying to shield the queen from some bad news that he wanted to avoid talking about it in public.

'My lady, I think we should do as Lord Aminor suggests,' she said in a quiet but confident tone to Queen Lamella. 'I am sure he has good reason to propose such a course of action. Since the king is fine, there is nothing to worry about. Maybe it is best if we wait for him in your chambers. He must be tired after the journey. We do not want to overwhelm him, do we?'

Lamella was still not completely convinced, but she agreed to do as Aminor had asked. She allowed herself to be led away by Misa. Lord Aminor cast her a grateful look, which she accepted with an imperceptible nod. The assembled servitors were about to disperse as well when Lord Aminor asked most of them to stay. He ordered some of them to prepare the most luxurious guestroom in the palace for a visiting dignitary and told the others to remain standing to welcome the king and his guest. Mizu heard his instructions and wondered who this dignitary was and whether she had something to do with Lord Aminor's decision to send the queen back to her chambers. He frowned as he realised that Lord Aminor had not mentioned whether the visitor was a man or a woman. Why then did he feel certain that it was a woman? Lost in his thoughts as he followed his mother towards Queen Lamella's chambers, he did not realise until it was too late that Prince Amishar had not accompanied them back.

Amishar, in fact, was hidden behind a pillar in a corridor that led to the king's chambers. When Lord Aminor had sent the others back to the queen's chambers, saying that King Amiroth would meet with them later, he had decided to disobey the instructions. He had been pining for his father for a long time; he would not be denied the joy of welcoming Amiroth home. The deep-rooted wilfulness in his nature, combined with a streak of mischievousness, impelled him to slip away unnoticed in the confusion and chaos. Now he waited quietly for the king to pass that way. When he surprised his father by appearing suddenly, the king would be overjoyed and amazed.

Soon, he could hear a hum of voices coming that way. He peered out from behind his hiding place and saw a swarm of courtiers, guards and attendants arriving. His father was at its centre, he guessed. The surprise, he realised, would not go as smoothly as he had imagined. Nevertheless, he stepped out from behind the pillar as soon as the crowd neared. No one noticed the young boy as he was almost swept away by the swarm of bodies. He had to push through the crowd to reach King Amiroth. When he finally broke through the ring of guards, ministers and attendants, Amishar saw that his father was not alone. There was someone with him. A woman. He had never seen her before. She was smiling at his father, talking to him, leaning towards him. And his father was listening with rapt attention, completely unaware of everything and everyone else around him.

Amishar did not like the woman who had her arm through his father's. Was she the guest that Lord Aminor had mentioned? Had his father postponed meeting him and Queen Lamella for her sake? Why would he do that? Amishar pushed his way right to the heart of the scrum, emerging in front of King Amiroth. Grabbing his father's arm, Amishar called out to him loudly enough for everyone to hear. The king started as if punched and came to a halt, his entourage stopping with him. Several expressions fleeted over his countenance one after the other until Samiesna gently put her other hand on his arm as well.

Glowering down at his only son, he growled, 'How dare you disturb us like this! How dare you embarrass me by showing such poor manners in front of an honoured guest and all these respectable folks? How dare you presume upon my patience and tolerance?'

Shocked, hurt and embarrassed, Amishar did not know what to say or do. Never in his worst nightmares had he imagined such a reunion with his father. He opened his mouth to say something, but pain shot through his shoulder as someone grabbed it in a vicelike grip and dragged him away from King Amiroth. Within momons, the cavalcade was on the move again, the episode forgotten. The pressure on his shoulders lessened. Amishar looked up to see the grim face of his godfather, Lord Aminor, gazing at him with sympathy. Fighting to keep from crying, he jerked his shoulder out of his cousin's grip and fled to his chamber.

He found no peace there either. His father's words continued to ring in his ears, making him want to disappear from the face of Yennthem. Then there was the matter of Lord Aminor hurting him. Everything was topsy-turvy that day. Nothing seemed real. That was it! He was having a nightmare, Amishar decided. When he awoke, everything would be all right again. He pinched himself hard on the arm, expecting the shock and pain to wake him up. All it resulted in was a purple bruise the size of a quail's egg.

He was rubbing the bruise vigorously when Lord Aminor entered his chamber. At first, Amishar would not look at him.

'I am sorry I hurt you,' Aminor said sincerely. 'I needed to stop you from saying anything more, to get you away. There was no other way. I would never hurt you willingly, I hope you know that.'

'I forgive you,' Amishar said hoarsely. He was fighting hard to control his emotions and was afraid that the tremor in his voice would give him away. He sat staring at the wall, trying to compose himself. Lord Aminor stood quietly, saying nothing. After a few minuras, when he felt more in command of himself, Amishar looked up at his godfather and asked him why his father had acted the way he had.

'He has never been angry at me before. Was what I did so very wrong?' he pleaded.

'No, Prince Amishar. It wasn't your fault,' Lord Aminor said kindly. 'But you should have listened to me and gone with your mother to her chamber, Your Highness. His Majesty must have been too startled, so he reacted the way he did. Your father is very tired from his expedition and needs to rest awhile. I'm sure he will meet you as soon as he feels rested.'

Amishar accepted Aminor's words. He needed to. Then he suddenly asked, 'Who was that lady with him, my lord? Is she the guest for whom the best guestrooms have been prepared? Will she be staying long?'

Aminor's reply was vague. 'She is Lady Samiesna. She has come from Cordemim with your father. She is his guest.'

'I don't understand why she has come or why Father was so nice to her but not to me. I don't like her,' Amishar complained.

Even though Lord Aminor felt the same way about Samiesna, he said nothing. He left Amishar feeling better and talking about finding Mizu in his mother's chambers. For once, Lord Aminor was truly grateful for the presence of the boy from across the river.

Though he was comforted by Lord Aminor's words for the time being, Amishar soon realised that his godfather had been trying to assuage his feelings. Not only did King Amiroth not come to visit him or Queen Lamella, but his life changed almost overnight. Within three days of King Amiroth's return to his capital, his son found himself bereft of the love of his father, the strength of his mother, the admiration of his attendants and the respect of his subjects. It was so sudden and shocking that Amishar could hardly believe it was happening.

Despite the incident on the day of King Amiroth's return, Amishar tried several times to talk to his father. He was rudely rebuffed every time. Even though young, Amishar began to understand that his father no longer loved him. He knew without being told that Samiesna was responsible for the change in Amiroth. He detested her with all his heart. His mother, too, changed suddenly and drastically. News of Samiesna's arrival with King Amiroth had reached her within minuras of the king's return, and it had shattered her life entirely. She was now always upset, always crying, always clinging to Amishar desperately whenever he visited her, much to his discomfort. Even those around them changed. His tutors stopped coming to teach him, and no one bothered to tell him why. The maids and attendants who had once doted on him no longer paid him any attention. Most of the nobles of the court whom he met looked embarrassed and gloomy and were curt towards him. Lord Aminor still spent time with him, but he always looked angry and distracted these days. Amishar began to feel constantly irritable and unhappy.

He spent as much time away from the palace as he could. Durnum and Mizu's house became his refuge. He hated staying in the palace, but he also hated staying away from his mother who cried even more if he did not go to visit her several times every day. It was almost as if she had become a different woman—a weak, pale shadow of the kind but principled and strong queen that she had been.

He said nothing about his mother's state to Mizu. What would his friend think when his own mother was always so strong despite not having a husband? The thought that he was annoyed at his mother for not being as strong as Misa made him feel guilty and ashamed and angry at himself. He wanted Lamella to stop being so weak and resented her for having given up so entirely, which made him feel terrible. His thoughts and feelings became a jumble of anger, guilt, resentment, shame and the desire to escape it all.

Then he noticed that the boys of the village, who had once behaved subserviently towards him, were beginning to talk back. He pointedly ignored them whenever he visited Durnum. Unable to either get rid of his anger or to take it out on those who caused it, he began to lash out at those closest to him, especially when he was more upset than usual. This made him unpopular in general and drove away the few servants who were still loyal enough to attend to him. He did not care or complain. Only Aminor and Mizu still did not react to his ill temper and tantrums.

And then he heard about his father's marriage. No one told him; the palace was buzzing with the news, and he overheard several soldiers and maids talking about it. King Amiroth was going to marry Lady Samiesna. It was scheduled the next day. Everyone was hustling excitedly to complete the arrangements. Amishar felt confused. Wasn't his father already married to his mother? How, then, could he be marrying again? He asked Lord Aminor this. His godfather replied that the king was, apparently, above the law of the land and could, obviously, do as he pleased. Amishar sensed the bitter undertone in the nobleman's words but failed to grasp its significance. All he gathered was that Lord Aminor was not as thrilled as everyone else about this marriage. This knowledge provided him a tiny ray of comfort.

On a characteristically wet day on the sixteenth of Chirshkom, King Amiroth and Lady Samiesna became husband and wife amidst great elegance and splendour. The ceremony began early in the morning with a ritual bath in milk and fragrances. Thereafter, the bride and groom were dressed in their nuptial garments and led to the wedding pavilion where the wedding rituals were completed. Due to the pelting rains outside, the pavilion had been erected inside the palace, in the throne room. The greatest lords of the country, as well as foreign dignitaries, were present for the ceremony as King Amiroth took Samiesna to be his lawfully wedded wife. They all applauded heartily. The wedding ceremony was followed by a grand banquet.

The joy was shared with the common folk of the city as well. The newly married couple stepped out onto the balcony of the king's chambers to loud cheers from those gathered below to see them. The population of Lufurdista had swelled as news of the royal wedding had spread like wildfire. King Amiroth's subjects thronged the courtyards and gardens of the palace in thousands, dressed in their best clothes and throwing rice at the bride and groom as an omen of blessing and good fortune. They had travelled to the capital to attend the wedding of their beloved King Amiroth to the beautiful Lady Samiesna. They were gathered in numbers to see this lady, rumours of whose beauty were already flying to the remotest corners of the kingdom. The newlyweds threw fistfuls of coins and gems into the crowd as a token of gratitude to deafening cheers and clamouring.

After the public appearance, the couple returned to the throne room for an audience with the most prominent citizens of Balignor. Lords of the various manors and estates were there, as were ministers and other nobles. Heads of villages from all around Lufurdista were there, and officials and courtiers of the king's court. Generals of the army were present, as well as prominent merchants, craftsmen, healers and guild masters. The wedding pavilion had been removed to free up space, but there seemed hardly enough standing room as the king led his new bride on his arm up to the double-seated throne at one end of the great hall. As the king and his newlywed queen took their seats, shouts of cheer rose from the crowd. The noise made the columns of the hall tremble and the large, canopied ceiling reverberate.

When the cheering died down, the assembled guests began to offer their gifts and congratulations to the newlyweds. As each name was announced, a resplendent dignitary stepped up to the king and his new queen. He bowed deeply, proffered his heartiest wishes and held out his gift, which was taken away and kept to one side by a servant after the king nodded his acceptance. Then the guest received a priceless gift in return, bowed again and stepped down to make way for the next well-wisher. It was late in the afternoon by the time the exchanging of gifts was complete. At the termination of the ceremony, King Amiroth addressed them, expressing his gratitude at the welcome shown by everyone towards his bride.

He remembered how shocked everyone had been when he had first returned with Samiesna. They had found it hard to believe that he could have found true love with someone as noble and as beautiful as Samiesna after having been married to Lamella for so long. It had irked him no end. But soon they had all understood their folly and had learnt to love and admire Samiesna. There were still a few who thought that he should not have married her, but King Amiroth wasn't bothered by them. He knew how to deal with dissenters. They would live to respect Samiesna or not live at all. He pushed such dark thoughts away. After all, it was his wedding day, the happiest day of his life!

After the king, it was Lady Samiesna's turn to address the gathering. There was a murmur of interest as she stood to speak. She thanked them for their acceptance and love and expressed her undying gratitude to King Amiroth for everything he had done for her. With tears in her eyes, she talked about her providential meeting with him in the wilderness. She still could not believe that one as mighty and as great as King Amiroth could find it in his heart not only to feel affection for her but to raise her to such a prominent position in his life. She blushed tenderly as the gathered assembly congratulated her and delivered eulogies in honour of her beauty and grace.

The entertainment that was meant only for the most prominent and important members of the court and the army began soon after. It was already dark outside though it was still early for twilight. Lamps and torches were lit as the guests were regaled by many talented singers, dancers, acrobats, actors, fire-eaters and other performers. Songs were sung about the king and his valour, about the new queen and her beauty. Dances were dedicated to the grace and elegance of the newlyweds. Plays depicted episodes from the life of the great king and the endearing love story of King Amiroth and Queen Samiesna. Acrobats leaping over each other through burning rings, dancers whirling fantastically with burning torches in their hands and fire-eaters blowing massive clouds of flames left the spectators spellbound. The entertainment ended with a wedding song by a well-known bard of the kingdom. As all the guests clapped loudly, King Amiroth suddenly announced, 'My lords, I agree that this bard is indeed worthy of his fame, but I have heard the song of one with far greater skill and a sweeter and richer voice.'

All turned to see what he was talking about. Before they fully understood what he meant, he stood up, Samiesna's hand in his, and stepped forward. A murmur went through the throne room. Was the king suggesting that his new bride would sing for them? It was a thing unheard of! A subtle wave of discomfort passed through the guests. They hoped that their king's new wife would either refuse or would prove to be at least moderately talented so that they would not have to lavish false praise on her. The bard quietly slipped away, sensing that his presence was no longer required. Samiesna, blushing daintily at the praise that the king had lavished on her, curtseyed to him, thanked the assembly in advance and began to sing. The first faint notes were hardly audible in the booming murmurs of the audience but, as the hall began to fall silent, her voice rose. Melodious and powerful, it wove patterns in the hearts and minds of all who listened spellbound, as their loyalty and devotion became enslaved to the woman who stood before them, singing:

> *From lands in the east—far, far away,*
> *I have come to this country to stay.*
> *And here shall I dwell forever more,*
> *For here my heart has washed ashore*
> *After floundering helpless in troubled seas*
> *For ages. Here it has found peace,*
> *It has found love, it has found home;*
> *No longer must I aimlessly roam.*
> *What wonder, what glory there is*
> *Here, and what unstinted bliss!*
> *No words can speak of what I feel,*
> *Now rescued from my dire ordeal*

By one so noble, glorious and proud

    And with the greatest merits endowed.

My Lord, My Liege, My Love, My King,

    My Hero, My Saviour, My Soul, My Being!

All that I am, all that I have,

    This moment forth is yours, my love.

Lord Aminor stood as entranced as the others, but the source of his entrancement lay elsewhere. He was, in fact, paying no attention to what was going on in the chamber where, to his chagrin, his presence had been mandated by the king. His entire attention was fixed upon someone who sat neglected at the other end of the palace. He was remembering a pale face and tearful eyes that looked dead, defeated by the despair of the truth that had devastated her life. He again thought of the proud mien of the lady who had lost first, the adoration of her husband and now, the devotion of her people, to another woman far less deserving of either. When Samiesna had first arrived in Lufurdista, Lamella had reeled under the shock but had tried to pull herself together.

When he had asked her how she was, she had quietly replied, 'I will not believe my lord capable of forgetting who I am. I am the wife of King Amiroth, it is true, but I am also the queen of Balignor. I am the daughter of Graniphor of Ashperth and the sister of Prince Feyanor, the greatest warrior and champion mankind has known for many a decadus. I am wounded, Lord Aminor, but I am not broken. I do not know what claim I still have on the love of my king, but I still retain the love of my people, do I not?'

And for him it was true, though perhaps not for most. She had his love and respect. Even if her own husband was suddenly so enchanted by another woman that he had forgotten what he owed that wonderful woman! That day she had tried to end her life. Only Aminor's timely intervention had saved her. He had reasoned with her and emphasised how important it was for her to stay alive for her son's sake. She had promised not to attempt suicide again. Only a handful in the kingdom were aware of this terrible event. Lord Aminor had entrusted Lord Parkiod with the concealment of this shameful secret. Lord Parkiod had had to bear the entire burden of ensuring the palace's and city's security since Lord Aminor had been forced to attend the wedding; he was still nowhere to be seen. Aminor assumed he was still busy with his duties. He hoped that Lamella had seen reason. Lord Beleston had agreed to remain in the vicinity of her chambers on the pretext of looking after arrangements for the wedding, the banquet and the entertainment. He would send for Aminor if anything untoward happened.

Even as Samiesna began to sing, Aminor felt a terrible rage at Amiroth's foolishness. What did he see in this woman whom he had just met a short while before that made him forget a wife as beautiful, as loving, as graceful and elegant, as kind and gentle, as noble and as incomparable as Lamella? So she could sing. So what? How could that be enough to make Amiroth forget his love for Lamella? Wrath made Lord Aminor want to box the ears of the man with whom he had grown up since childhood as brothers but who was now so distant. At one time, Amiroth had been willing to kill Aminor to win Lamella. Now he barely acknowledged her existence. How could Amiroth be so blind? Anger roused in Aminor all that was noble and fiery and proud in his blood. Anger defeated the spell that sought to freeze the blood in his veins. And though all those who heard Samiesna sing that day forever passed into her thraldom, Lord Aminor remained free.

On the morning of the wedding, Amishar went to his mother's chambers to visit her. To his surprise, Lord Aminor stopped him from at the door. Queen Lamella was unwell, he told Amishar. She was resting. She was not to be disturbed that day. He suggested that the prince should spend the day with his friend Mizu down at the village. But Amishar did not want to go to the village that day. Fortunately, Mizu himself arrived soon after. Though Amishar was grumpier than usual, Mizu said nothing. The two sat in Amishar's room, doing nothing. When Amishar asked Mizu if he would like something to eat, Mizu refused. He knew that no one would come to attend to Amishar that day, and he did not want to see his friend endure such embarrassment on his account. Things had been worsening steadily at the palace. Amishar was often neglected, which hurt the young prince's pride. He tried to pretend as if nothing had changed, but Mizu knew the truth. His mother had explained to him what had happened. She had told him to be patient with Amishar even if he was sometimes in a bad mood or ill-tempered. Mizu felt sorry for his friend. He had never known his own father, but Amishar's situation, he felt, was worse. He suggested that the two of them should go back to the village since there seemed to be nothing to do at the palace that day. Amishar agreed reluctantly.

They started on their way to the village. However, Amishar changed his mind as soon as they were outdoors. Hordes of people were rushing to attend the marriage despite the pouring rain.

'Let's go and watch the wedding,' Amishar suggested. Mizu did not want to watch the wedding. Even more, he did not want Amishar to watch the wedding. He tried to dissuade his friend. But Amishar was determined to go, so Mizu did not protest when the prince dragged him off towards the hall where the

ceremonies were being held. There was high security everywhere. Armed guards
stood at attention. The boys managed to reach no further than the main entrance
to the wing before they were stopped and gently, but firmly, turned away. Amishar
scolded the sentry, but the man would not budge. In the end, Mizu coaxed Amishar
away from there. He hoped that he could now convince Amishar to go with him
to the village. He was mistaken. The prince was determined to watch the wedding,
and nothing would stop him.

He led Mizu up an unused flight of stairs and through dusty passages and
attics. When Mizu asked him where they were going, Amishar replied, 'To watch
the wedding.' Finally, they came to a narrow room with a sloping wall. Mizu
realised that it was not really a room; it was the space behind the dome of the hall
in which King Amiroth was marrying Lady Samiesna. He wondered what they
were doing there. His question was answered when Amishar prodded aside one
of the panels on the sloping wall to reveal a crack that allowed them to look down
into the ceremony. The two boys watched intently as matters unfolded downstairs.
They stood there looking down at the gathered crowd—one impassive, the other
uncomfortable—until Mizu could endure it no longer. He grabbed Amishar's arm
and dragged his friend away.

'We have to go,' he insisted. To his surprise, Amishar protested no more. The
prince looked so pale that Mizu was worried he was about to be ill.

'Do you want to return to your chambers? You don't look too good,' he asked.

'No, I'm fine. Let's go to your home. I think I've seen enough,' Amishar rasped.

Without another word, the two friends made their way down the path that
they had taken to reach the attics. Soon they were back in the main section of
the palace. No one paid the slightest attention to them as they slipped away and
tramped down to the village in the pouring rain. They were both soaked to the
skin by the time they reached Mizu's house. Misa hurried outside to look after
them. While they were still standing on the veranda, she knelt down, rubbing
their heads dry with towels and getting them out of their wet clothes into dry
ones. She tended first to Amishar, handing her son a towel to dry himself. Mizu
did not mind. Poor Amishar could do with a little affection and care, he figured.
Misa gently passed her fingers through Amishar's hair in a motherly gesture. The
prince could no longer hold back his pain. He hugged her and sobbed into her
shoulder. She let him cry, comforting him gently. A few minuras later, he pulled
away and entered the house, not looking at either of his companions. When Mizu
was about to follow him in, Misa subtly gestured for him to let Amishar be for the
time being.

Amishar felt much better afterwards. There was steaming broth and freshly
baked bread for dinner that night. He ate the simple food with relish. Then the
three of them sat outside, the boys on either side of Misa, and looked at the stars.

She pointed to one of the constellations and said, 'That one is known as the Charioteer. It is said that long, long ago, when humans still had no kings or kingdoms, it came down from the heavens and guided a young boy to find his destiny. He was a special boy who had fallen upon hard times. He had been banished from his home and was despondent. It was then that the Charioteer came down from the sky and said to him—*follow me and you shall find your destiny*. So the boy followed the Charioteer all night. The Charioteer flew through the night sky, blazing a trail of fire in his train, and the boy followed this trail. When day came and the sun covered up the stars, he rested and waited for the night again. For nine nights he followed the heavenly Charioteer until he reached the gates of a mighty manor house where he found his destiny.'

'It's a nice story,' Mizu said. 'You haven't told it before.'

'Who was the boy? What was the destiny he found?' Amishar asked.

Misa answered, 'His destiny was to become the first ever human king. His name was...'

'Rogran!' the boys declared simultaneously.

'Yes,' Misa agreed. 'Rogran.'

'I have never heard this story about him before,' Amishar announced. He loved to hear tales of his ancient ancestors, the great kings of men. 'Tell us another one,' he requested Misa.

'About Rogran?'

'About anyone.'

'All right. Let me tell you the story of another young man who had to leave home to find his destiny. His father was a king but by marriage, not by birth.'

'What does that mean?' Amishar enquired.

'It means that he married a queen or a princess, and that's how he became king,' Mizu answered for his mother.

Misa continued her story, 'This king was a truly noble, valiant and honourable man, but there were some who did not accept him as the true ruler. They conspired to overthrow his rule. He had to give up his throne and escape from the palace to save the lives of his wife and son. For anni, he waged war against his enemies while staying hidden. But they were very strong, and he could not make much headway even though the common people accepted him as the rightful ruler and supported him as best as they could. Then, when his son was ten or eleven anni old, his wife told him that she was going to have another child. For the protection of mother and child, the king sent them to hide in a far away country. By then, his son was old enough to participate in the war. He was as valiant as his father. But he was young, and his father did not want him to risk his life.

So the king took his son to the seleighes and left him with one of the seleighe kings with whom he was friendly. There the young prince stayed for close to seven anni, learning how to fight, how to make strategies, how to get inside the enemy's head and how to defeat even the strongest of foes. He became as good at all those things as the seleighe royals were. When he turned eighteen and came of age, he returned to his kingdom to help his father. The king's position had weakened in the meantime though his enemies had not yet managed to capture him. Within six mondans of the prince's return, the enemies were on the run. Within eight mondans, the king was back on his throne. Within an annus after that, his enemies were completely thrashed. His wife, the queen, returned with a beautiful daughter. And they lived happily since then.'

The boys clapped on hearing this happy ending. 'Who was this prince?' the inevitable question was raised by Amishar.

Before Misa could reply, another voice sounded in the courtyard. 'Your uncle, Prince Feyanor,' it said in reply to Amishar's enquiry.

Misa and the boys stood up to greet Lord Aminor.

'Really?' Amishar asked Misa. She nodded.

'Are you here to collect Amishar?' she asked Aminor.

'No, I just came to check on him. I see that he is all right.'

'You need not worry about him while he is here,' Misa said earnestly. Then she turned to the boys and told them to go inside. It was time for bed. They obeyed without a murmur of protest, wishing the grownups a good night before disappearing into the house.

'I will always worry for him,' Aminor said after the boys left, not offended but making his position clear.

Misa acknowledged it with a nod. 'It is good that you care for him so much. Someone should. Especially now. How is the queen holding up?'

'Like a queen,' Aminor lied. 'She is proud and regal even in her grief.'

'That bad?' Misa said, sensing his bluff. 'I don't blame her. No one can. This isn't right!'

Aminor was taken aback at her vehemence. He had never trusted Misa, and her current behaviour was making him even more suspicious. She seemed to be taking Amiroth's betrayal of Lamella almost personally. Why would she do that? And how had she learnt so much about Prince Feyanor's early anni? He asked her directly.

'I have heard the stories,' she replied evasively.

'Where?'

'Elsewhere. Before coming here. I can't recall just when or where or from whom. If I could, I would tell you. A wanderer gets to hear many things.'

'Really? What else have you heard?'

'That Prince Feyanor of Ashperth cares deeply for his sister, that he would do anything for her sake. Are they true—these stories?'

'Why do you ask me?'

'You have spent time with him in Ashperth recently, have you not? Perhaps you have had occasion to judge whether the man lives up to the legend.'

Lord Aminor smiled. He wished he could tell her how much more awe-inspiring than his legends the man was. But, of course, he could not. Not without betraying the Order of the Lily. The thought of the order made him twinge. He had inducted Lord Parkiod and Lord Beleston into the order after thoroughly vetting that they were worthy of its secrets. The three of them were to meet that night to decide what to do in light of the recent developments. Many issues were bothering him, not least the failure of his intelligence system to inform him about Samiesna before the king's arrival in the capital with her. He was thankful that the unfortunate attempt at taking her life by Queen Lamella had incidentally saved the other two from Samiesna's spell, which he had managed to recognise for what it was. Soon after Samiesna had sung her song, he had noticed that everyone who had heard her sing seemed to have changed in some subtle way. Fantastic as it had seemed, he had come to the conclusion that the song had been a spell of some sort. Which also explained, he thought, how Samiesna had enchanted King Amiroth so completely. Only he had not fallen under Samiesna's spell. But then, he had hardly noticed the song. He had to alert the order to the danger that very night. News had already been sent about Samiesna to Ontar. Information about Samiesna's strange choice of entertainment and its effect would have to be sent. He could not linger there. He took Misa's leave, asking her to keep Amishar with her for a couple of days. Misa gladly agreed.

The boys were already in bed by then. Misa was about to enter the house when she heard them talking. She paused to listen.

'Do you miss your father?' Amishar asked Mizu.

'No, I don't even remember him. He died before I was born.'

'Maybe it is better that way,' Amishar mumbled unhappily.

Misa felt that her heart would break. She felt angry at Amiroth's betrayal of his wife and his son. How could he have done it? She felt sure that Feyanor would not take it quietly. Lamella, she knew from what Feyanor had told her, was a gentle soul. She was inevitably heartbroken. Aminor's lies had not fooled her. She hoped that Lamella would stay strong for the sake of her son. At least, Aminor really cared about the young prince. She wondered why. She knew that he had once been Lamella's suitor. Had his feelings for her lingered all these anni? It was hard to believe that one could love another so much that nothing—not even the pain of knowing that the love would never be requited—could erase that love. She had loved too. And lost. Every time. Perhaps, she mused, some were destined never to find love. She thought of Amishar and Mizu, both bereft of paternal love. What was it if not destiny? She sighed and entered the house. The boys had fallen asleep by then. She locked the door, covered the boys with a sheet, blew out the lamp and went to bed, hoping that she wouldn't dream of Feyanor, Arlem, Arslan or Leormane.

Chapter 51

A MOMENTOUS DECISION

(23 Matisal 5010 A.E. to 6 Supprom 5010 A.E.)

On the twenty-third of Matisal in the annus 5010 A.E., Witar sat by Augurk's side in the council chamber, wearing a look of defeat and dismay. The only other dharvh present was Angbruk. Even Shornhuz had been dismissed. He waited at the ready, just outside the chamber's door.

Witar was the sole survivor of the contingent that had been sent to look for the City of Stone among the reaches of the Lyudzbradh in Khwaznon. How he had managed to survive he did not know. He was grateful that his luck had held. He had seen all his companions perish one by one through illness, snakebites, animal attacks and accidents. They had got lost and had wandered hungry and directionless for days. Some had drowned while others had fallen off cliffs. Some had died of exhaustion, dehydration or starvation while some had simply disappeared without a trace—undoubtedly victims of the fearsome creatures that roamed the Lyudzbradh. Day by day, their numbers had dwindled until only Witar had been left. He had not wanted to return, but a sense of duty had compelled him to come back to Drauzern. Someone had to tell the rauz what had happened to the expedition. They had found nothing but death.

Augurk sent Witar off to rest and recover with instructions to Angbruk to 'make sure that he does not do anything stupid like killing himself.' Angbruk nodded and followed Witar discreetly, leaving the rauz in a state of meditation. Augurk knew that he would have to inform Nishtar about this. He also knew what Nishtar's response would be. He almost cursed the sumagus in his anger. He hated the hold that Nishtar had on him and wanted to break it. 'I swear that if I ever manage to find this stone city, I will tell him that we are square. I will no longer be beholden to him!' he said to himself. But how could he find the city when his expedition had been utterly destroyed? Would the results be any different if he sent another one? He was afraid that they would not. Could he just give up? That, again, was not an option that Nishtar had left him with. He feared that Nishtar would make good on his threats if he tried to quit. What was he to do? And then, just like that, he had the answer. He had found the path. One way or another, it would solve his problem.

When he told his brother about his plan, Angbruk flatly refused to support him.

'Why not? It appears to be the only solution!' Augurk insisted.

'No, you will not go. If you wish, I will go in your place. But I cannot allow you to risk your life,' said Angbruk with determination.

'But that is the only way, don't you see? I must go on an expedition myself. If I succeed in finding this city, I will have fulfilled my obligations to Nishtar. If I cannot, and I perish, I will nonetheless have paid my dues. He would not harm you or anyone else if I die trying to fulfil his commands. He would not hold you responsible for meeting my obligations.'

The brothers argued late into the night, neither willing to give in to the other. Finally, Augurk managed to convince Angbruk.

'So, will you step down as rauz?' Angbruk finally asked.

'No, not at all. I wouldn't be able to get even a single dharvh to go with me if I did!'

'Shornhuz would probably go,' suggested Angbruk.

'I'm not so sure of that,' said Augurk shrewdly. 'I don't think that his loyalty is to me personally.'

'I would go. And many of the Mermurdh too, I think.'

'You would follow me to the ends of the world, would you not?' Augurk said affectionately to his younger brother. 'As for the Mermurdh, maybe you are right. But all this talk is pointless. Do you really want me to step down as rauz before I go?'

'I want you not to go at all! But I know it is futile to argue with you. You are as bull-headed as father and grandfather,' Angbruk complained.

Angbruk was right, Augurk knew. He had hated his father and his grandfather once for being so stubborn and inflexible, yet he himself possessed those same qualities. He remembered little about his mother, but those memories were of a pleasant, sweet-tempered and loving dharvhina who would often act as a buffer between their stern father and them. Angbruk, Augurk realised, was very like her. He wondered how his life would have been if Angbruk and he had had similar temperaments. He could not help smiling at the thought.

'What are you smiling about?' asked Angbruk, surprised.

'I'm just happy that I have you for my brother,' answered Augurk. Angbruk looked at him suspiciously. Was Augurk going a little crazy under the pressure of Nishtar's constant threats, he wondered. But his elder brother looked genuinely affectionate, so he decided not.

'When are you planning to leave?' he asked.

'I want to be well-prepared before I go. Even if I begin the arrangements immediately, they will take some time. Rumours about the search for the City of Stone have already started flying throughout all the countries; we need to curb those and tell everyone the truth in a way that my absence on the expedition does not lead to panic, chaos and rebellion. There is also the matter of Khwaznon. We will have to pass through it during our search; we need to obtain permission. I don't think I can leave before Supprom. Depending on how I feel about the level of preparations, I might start off even later. I know that I will have only one chance to do this, and I do not intend to waste that chance.'

'And if the worst should happen? If…if…' Angbruk could not finish.

'If I should perish?' asked Augurk. Angbruk nodded. 'We will have to have a Zhan-ang-Razr, won't we? Would you want to try your luck in it?'

'No, I have no desire to be rauz,' said Angbruk.

'In that case,' said the rauz of Ghrangghirm, 'look after the family for me and make sure that they let Valhazar compete for the throne. As a member of my family, he has the right to do so.'

Eamilus still could not get over the surprise of his first encounter with the dharvhs. He had heard of their legendary wealth but found no indication of it in the palace. It consisted of a vast complex of plain, low chambers under the ground for private residences and confidential government offices, several large, high stone halls above ground for administrative and ceremonial purposes, and a wide terrace that looked out over a large portion of Drauzern. Eamilus's head almost touched the ceiling of the underground chambers when he stood. He would complete fourteen in two and a half mondans, but he already stood as tall as a full-grown man. He also looked much older than his anni.

Augurk had welcomed him heartily and embraced him as family on finding that he was Halifern's friend, enquiring solicitously after their mutual friend's well-being. Eamilus felt curious about the friendship between the frael and the dharvh, but was too polite to ask. Augurk had thanked him for the letter that he had brought from Halifern even though he had not shared its contents with the messenger. Eamilus felt relieved. He had fulfilled his promise to Halifern. He was free to go on his way as soon as Augurk permitted him to depart.

Eamilus was lying in bed after supper, thinking these thoughts. It was late at night. Everyone had retired to their chambers. Most lights had been extinguished. Sounds of even the cooks and servants clearing away the supper and cleaning up the kitchen had quietened down. The palace lay shrouded in a twilight of torpor.

Eamilus was beginning to drift off into sleep when there was a knock on the door of his chamber. Who could be knocking on his door so late? Surprised, he stood up quickly and almost banged his head against the ceiling. He hurriedly lit a couple of lamps that he had extinguished in anticipation of sleep and opened the door. He stared in the semi-darkness at the sturdy figure standing in the doorway. The light was too low but not for him. His extraordinary eyesight clearly picked out that his late night visitor was the rauz himself. He bowed and invited Augurk inside.

The dharvh rauz entered the chamber and closed the door behind him. He then took a chair and indicated that Eamilus, too, should sit. Eamilus obeyed and waited for him to speak. For a while, Augurk said nothing. He sat silently, his head a little bowed in deep thought. Then he seemed to come out of his reverie. He smiled and said, 'Eamilus, even at such a young age, you are as patient as you are polite. I believe that you deserve all the praise that Halifern has lavished on you in his letter to me.'

Eamilus blushed. He never felt comfortable being praised. His thoughts momentarily reverted to the good friend whom he had left behind in Numosyn, and his eyes took on a glazed look.

Augurk, not noticing the lad's embarrassment in the darkness, continued, 'He has also mentioned the circumstances under which the two of you met. And that is what I have come to talk to you about. You see, I am the one who was responsible for bringing that wretched human king into the vicinity. I beg your pardon—I have nothing against humans, only against this particular one,' he quickly added as he realised that he might have offended Eamilus. The listener nodded, understanding.

Augurk continued, 'Because Amiroth was here at my invitation, I feel partly responsible for putting Halifern in danger, and I shall do what I can to make amends. I did rush to rescue him when I learnt that a frael named Halifern had been imprisoned by King Amiroth, but I was too late. Amiroth had already departed with his contingent. To pursue him would have led to war, perhaps with Cordemim and Storsnem as well, since I would have had to pass through their lands to get to Balignor. It was not a feasible option. I had to let go of the matter, hoping that it had been a different Halifern. Fortunately, you had already saved our mutual friend by then, though I did not know it at the time. Halifern has written in detail about the entire incident in his letter. However, I do feel extremely curious about something—what were YOU doing there when you rescued Halifern? He has mentioned nothing about it.'

Eamilus was taken aback at the blunt question, but he did not hesitate to answer.

'My rauz, I was passing by and noticed Halifern imprisoned. When I realised that he was wrongly incarcerated, I could not overlook the situation.' It wasn't strictly true, but it was the best answer that Eamilus could provide.

'How did you come to suddenly discover him in the middle of such a large camp? And how was it that you managed to enter and then lave with Halifern without anyone noticing?' Augurk demanded sharply.

Eamilus answered calmly, although he was beginning to feel annoyed, 'I was curious about the camp, so I was exploring it when I spotted Halifern. As for not being detected—I used stealth.' He paused and added, 'I had heard of the dharvhs' legendary wealth and legendary hospitality. It appears that both are just that— legends!'

The moment the words left his mouth, Eamilus regretted them. To his surprise, Augurk laughed out heartily and clapped him on the back. He guffawed, 'My boy, you sure have a great deal of gumption! You sit in my house and call me poor and inhospitable without even a tremor in your voice—I like that! You are indeed special!'

Then he sobered up and said, 'Halifern has informed me that you do not like your past enquired into. He respected that, therefore, I will too. I will not pry where he did not.'

Eamilus apologised for his harsh and discourteous words. Augurk brushed it away.

'No, Eamilus, you are not far from correct. Normally, as a friend of Halifern, you would have met with a much more lavish welcome. But these are strange times, and folks often forget what is due to friends in such times.'

Eamilus could not suppress his curiosity any longer, 'Can I ask something if it does not seem too offensive, my rauz?'

'Ask, Eamilus, and I shall answer if it does not seem offensive.'

'You said that you were responsible for the presence of King Amiroth in the region. I saw their camp—it was vast! It looked like an army on its way to invade some enemy land. Was he coming to attack Ghrangghirm?'

Augurk was silent for a while. Eamilus began to wonder if he had indeed offended the rauz. Then Augurk slowly shook his head and began to speak in a sad, heavy voice, 'What you ask me pertains to something that is a festering wound for me. Listen, and judge if you will, what else I could have done.'

He told Eamilus the whole story of the search for the City of Stone, beginning with the messenger that had come from Nishtar soon after his daughter's wedding and ending with the expedition led by King Amiroth. He felt that Halifern's imprisonment at Amiroth's hands and Eamilus's rescue of him had bound the frael and the human boy to his continuing errand for Nishtar. He could not reasonably conceal the matter from the boy after what had happened. The letter from Halifern had left him feeling embarrassed, angry and sad.

'And that is how King Amiroth came to be by the Sumarin and ended up causing everyone such a lot of trouble,' Augurk finished peevishly. He briefly added about the tragic expedition led by Witar. His own plans for going in search of the City of Stone had been delayed somewhat due to inadequate preparations. He was still busy with them when Eamilus had reached him with Halifern's letter.

Eamilus suddenly began to pace the floor agitatedly. Augurk was surprised at his reaction to the story. Unknown to Augurk, Eamilus was trying to resolve a great battle raging in his heart. He wanted to return to his people to free them from the kocovuses, and this pull was very strong within him. He had learnt everything that he wanted to. It was time for him to return, he felt. His duty towards his people was calling him back. But while listening to Augurk's story, he had come to realise that the city Augurk was looking for was the same city that he had seen from Uzdal's mountain that morning when the two had met. If he led Rauz Augurk there, he could save the rauz and his dharvhs much pain and misery, even death. He felt that it was his moral duty since he had enjoyed Augurk's hospitality, because Augurk was Halifern's friend and because the rauz had trusted him with the truth. He was feeling torn between the two duties.

Finally, he stopped pacing, turned to Augurk and said, 'I know of the place you mention. And if you ask me to, I shall lead you there.'

Augurk was stunned at the boy's words. He could not believe what he was hearing. For so long now, he had been attempting to discover the whereabouts of this mysterious place and had failed. Yet now, all of a sudden, this young boy had appeared out of the blue, claiming to know how to reach it!

'Do you really know where the City of Stone is?' Augurk asked excitedly, still trying to grasp the immensity of Eamilus's revelation. 'And are you willing to lead us there?'

'Yes, I know where the City of Stone is and how to reach it,' said Eamilus. 'And I will take you there on one condition.'

Augurk suddenly reached out and embraced Eamilus. 'Friend,' he said, 'everything you say shall be done. You have my word. What is it that you wish for?'

'I wish,' said Eamilus joylessly, 'that I be allowed to leave as soon as we reach the City of Stone. There is something else that pulls upon my heart, and I have neglected it too long.'

Augurk's inner circle of advisors sat in discussion minuras after Eamilus's disclosure. Augurk was there, as was Angbruk. Shornhuz, too, was there, with his ever-present axe. Onelikh was present with his son Guzear. Durng was there too.

They listened with grave faces as Augurk told them of Eamilus's claims about Patrisha and of his decision to allow Eamilus to lead them to the stone city.

'I have called you to decide what we should do in light of these recent developments,' Augurk said after finishing his briefing.

'I do not trust this boy,' declared Onelikh. 'How can we trust him? Have we learnt nothing from our last experience with humans? I say we search on our own.'

Angbruk responded, 'There is no connection between this boy and King Amiroth. Besides, he has volunteered to guide us. Why would he do so if not out of a genuine desire to help?'

Guzear came down on the side of his father. He said, 'Just because he has volunteered to help does not mean that he can or should be allowed to. Who knows whether he is even telling the truth? Maybe he just wants to trick us into a trap of some sort. We should keep this matter within ourselves.'

Everyone turned to Durng, who was sitting quietly. No one asked for Shornhuz's opinion, and he did not volunteer one. He never did.

'What do you have to say in this matter?' Augurk asked his friend.

Durng responded in his usual halting, thoughtful manner. He said, 'We are on the verge of launching an expedition led by no less a personage than our rauz to find this City of Stone. We have no idea where to search for it or how. This boy holds out hope of a successful journey. Our rauz trusts this boy. Therefore, I will trust him too. Besides, if we judge an entire race by the behaviour of one member of it, what world of mistrust and hatred would we be condemning ourselves to?'

Durng's stand on the issue sealed the argument, and the mood in the chamber altered suddenly to one of suppressed excitement. Preparations were already underway; the new information added a dimension of certainty to the whole project and breathed new life into the preparations. Augurk declared that he would lead the expedition jointly with Eamilus. Angbruk had already been settled upon as regent in Augurk's absence; the rauz now asked Onelikh to stay behind to support Angbruk. Since Eamilus was joining the expedition, he would be able to spare his senior councillor. Guzear, who was in charge of logistics with his father, would naturally have to accompany the mission.

'How long will it take to reach there and return, do you think?' Angbruk asked.

Onelikh answered, 'Even though we now have a fixed destination, we cannot travel fast with the large retinue that we will have. If the location of the city is where this boy has suggested, we are at a distance of about a thousand miles from it, as the crow flies. The actual route will be invariably longer. Crossing the desert without using the established routes—which we must do to reduce the length of the journey—is a highly dangerous undertaking. Going will be slow. We cannot reach in less than five temporas. We must add to this time the delays that such a journey might entail on account of unexpected dangers and problems, the time we will need to explore the city and the duration of the halt there, particularly to refurbish the expedition for the return. The entire expedition cannot take any less than thirteen temporas.'

'How large a troop are you planning to take along?' Durng asked.

Guzear answered grimly, 'We are talking of crossing the Laudhern, the Great Desert. If we have too few men, we will perish; too many men and the provisions required to be carried will become a burden. We must have enough numbers to protect ourselves and yet move fast enough. Fortunately, having a known destination reduces the necessity for larger numbers on account of possible...eventualities and uncertainties leading to loss of life. But soldiers cannot be the entirety of the contingent, and we need to keep that in mind while deciding how many to take along. We must carry enough food, for game will be scarce, but even more pertinently, we must carry enough water. The desert will be blazing hot during the day and deadly cold after sundown, and we must protect ourselves. My father and I will have to redouble our efforts and bring all our experience into play to ensure that no arrangement is lacking. I suggest that we move with five hundred—three hundred soldiers, a hundred workmen and a hundred to carry provisions.'

The group dispersed at dawn, having discussed details all night. They had decided to start on the fourteenth of Zulheen, their minds heavy with anticipations and anxieties.

In the annus 5010 A.E., outomy had set in since a mondan when the festival of Eslokarar came around. Eslokarar was the festival of Lokare, the blacksmith Guardian of Fire. The mondan itself was named after him, and the eleventh of the mondan was particularly dedicated to him. Of all the mondans, Lokrin was the most important for smiths. Some began their professional annus from the first of the mondan, some spent the mondan making pilgrimages and some started new apprentices, depending on the country and region in which they lived. One thing, though, was common to smiths and their families all over Yennthem: in Lokare's honour, they lit bonfires and gifted goods made by them to their friends and neighbours. They did this at least on the day of Eslokarar. Prosperous smiths practiced this over the entire tempora starting from the eleventh. Some of the more generous ones even distributed goods to the poor and the destitute. This was supposed to bring good luck. Metalwork was a highly secretive craft requiring great skill and precision, so smiths were, as a rule, superstitious. They believed that they could flourish only by Lokare's good graces.

That evening, Rosa was out trying to find some generous smith who would give her tools or utensils for free. Temeron sat in the doorway, watching the street come alive after dusk. He was shackled, but the chain was long enough to allow him to sit just inside the door. Rosa had recently lengthened his reach; not because she was sympathetic towards his plight at being restricted to a small section of the shack but because she wanted him to clean the entire place. It was also to add to his emotional torment, Temeron suspected. He could reach the doorway of the shack, have a taste of freedom, yet never enjoy that freedom.

A charitable smith was doing the rounds of the street on which they lived. He drove a cart full of metal goods that he was distributing to the needy. When he noticed Temeron, with the usual kereighe dislike for humans, he spat on the ground in front of the boy and moved on. The smith's actions kindled Temeron's anger, and he glared at the receding cart. In the cart was a small oven to keep the smith's food warm. Temeron's eyes fell on the glowing oven, and he wished that the oven would flare up and scorch the smith. To his astonishment, no sooner had he wished for it than the oven burst into flames, setting the smith's blanket on fire. Temeron had often cursed his abusers in his heart, but never before had anything like this happened.

He sped inside, not waiting to see what happened to the smith. He was certain that he would be blamed; not because anybody would have actually suspected him but because they'd need a scapegoat. The kereighes in the street were well aware of Rosa's abhorrence for the human boy who was her slave and, knowing that he was defenceless, never missed a chance to abuse and attack him. Temeron made himself invisible in the darkness of the house for fear of pursuit. His heart was racing. He wondered whether it was a fluke that had made his wish come to life, a mere coincidence, or something more. Strange things had happened to him a few times before, but they had always been one-time incidents. There was the time when he had accidentally turned back to his kereighe form. More recently, he had overheard Rosa's thoughts. He believed that these instances were indications of his innate magical ability.

For a long time, he sat in the dark, not daring to hope. Then slowly, his heart still thumping, he crept towards the grate in which Rosa cooked their food. The wood fire had burned out some time ago though the embers still glowed. Rosa would light the fire upon returning. Hoping against hope, Temeron wished that the fire would flare up. But nothing happened. He sighed. Though he had not really expected a miracle, despair and bitterness filled his heart. And anger. He hated Rosa for causing him so much pain and anguish. He hated himself for being too weak to fight back. He hated the world for standing by and allowing such unfairness to be meted out to him. In that moment, he no longer remembered the comfort of Avita's company or the joy of his secret friend's gifts. He cursed Rosa; he cursed kereighes and humans; he cursed the stupid fire.

'You're just like the others,' he scolded the insensate embers, imagining that somewhere in Kaitshem, Lokare could hear him. 'You just want to make fun of me. You want to raise my hopes and then dash them again for your enjoyment. Else, why don't these embers flare up now? Why don't they? Flare up, I say, flare up!'

He was about to kick the dead logs when, to his amazement, the embers came to life and crackled merrily. He could not believe it! Had Lokare truly heard him and taken pity on him? Why would an all- powerful Guardian do that? Maybe Lokare had felt sorry for him and wanted to comfort him. But his brain told him otherwise. Perhaps Lokare had a hand in the miracle; his own senses told him that it was more than a chance magical incident like the others that had given him false hope before. He could feel it within himself. He remembered how he had been attracted to fire for as long as he could remember. He had been punished by Rosa for it too! He recalled how, whenever he was too tired and battered to go on, he always felt a warm glow rise inside him that gave him the strength to push on. He had begun to associate it with Avita, but now that he thought about it, he remembered feeling it even before he had met her. What if it was separate from the warmth that his connection with her brought him? What if he had an affinity for fire that was reciprocated by the element? Temeron was too young to think these thoughts consciously or coherently; half formed ideas along these lines passed like a blur through his mind. All that he felt certain of was that the fire was his friend, or could be, if he tried.

Slowly, cautiously, he put his hand into the fire. At first, the fire bit him. He pulled his hand back hastily. He tried to focus and again put his hand into the fire. It burned him again. He withdrew his hand again. Beginning to feel angry, he tried a third time, determined to succeed, not caring if he burned himself. It could not hurt worse than Rosa's tortures. This time, amazingly, the fire did not hurt him. It felt cool to his touch. He kept his hand inside the flame for a few minuras at a time, but nothing untoward happened. When he drew it back, his hand was a little dark with soot but otherwise unscathed. Encouraged by this success, he continued trying to put his hand in the fire with variable success. He began to realise that the trick worked if he was angry. Thereafter, he thought of Rosa as he tried to put his hand into the fire. It worked every time! After about a dozen successful attempts at keeping his hand inside the flame without being burned, he had another idea.

His hand was inside the flame at the time. He balled his fist and removed it from the blaze. When he opened his palm, a small ball of fire danced in his hand. Temeron's heart was racing. It was unbelievable! For a momon, he wondered if he was dreaming. No, his dreams had never been that happy and fulfilling! He was really controlling the fire! He had finally found within himself the power that would free him from his bondage and enable him to take revenge on his tormentors. Even if he never learnt magic now, he would still be able to use the power of fire to destroy his enemies. Nothing and no one could stand before the fury of fire. He would have to learn how to harness and control this power, but as he had told himself many times before, he would wait until he was ready. He had figured out that the fire responded to him only when he was angry. That would not be a problem; he had enough anger inside to burn down the whole of Yennthem. This thought gave him joy; he was strangely elated that he was so bitter inside. All the pain and anger that he had collected over his short life were now to become the source of his strength!

Mustering his anger, he hissed at the fire, 'Go out!' and the fire vanished. Not even the embers glowed. Rosa would be returning soon. It would not do for him to be caught. Temeron returned to his corner, his mind buzzing with thoughts. He would have to pay renewed attention to Rosa's magical spells, especially those that involved fire. He would have to search for fire-based spells in the spellbook that he had stolen from Rosa all that time ago. He had to learn everything he could if he was to beat her at her own game. He decided to practice harnessing fire whenever he could. For, it was the one thing that would make all his wishes come true. He *had* to escape from Rosa's clutches. He *had* to punish those who had tormented him. He *had* to discover a way to transform himself back into a kereighe. Most importantly, he *had* to find Avita. Yes, there was much to do. But he would do it all. He would be patient and persevering and would learn everything he needed to. He would bide his time until he was ready and then his retribution would be terrible. The thought of harsh vengeance gave him a greater sense of hope than anything ever before.

One morning towards the end of Patarshem, Temeron awoke to find an unusually large packet by his pillow. It was filled with several food items and a smaller packet. He immediately hid his bounty from Rosa. He had begun to suspect that his friend used magic to ensure that Rosa would never find the gifts and the food that he left for Temeron. Still, he was loath to take a risk. Once he was caught, it would all be over. Not only would the witch confiscate everything, she would ensure that he never received anything ever again. He did not want to think of the punishments he would receive. She might even move from that town, and then his friend would never be able to find him again. Worse, she might discover the hidden treasures under the floorboard, his only possessions in the world. No, it would not do to be discovered by Rosa. So he hid his gifts until he was sure that the lech was gone from the house for a substantial period of time.

He checked the food products first. All his favourites were there. They would last him for well over a mondan! Then he checked the smaller packet. It was long and hard. As he unwrapped it, he noticed writing on the wrapping. He casually glanced at it, wondering if it was one of his own notes with corrections. He started. It was a message from his benefactor. He had never written to Temeron before. The boy read the message eagerly. His secret benefactor was going to be out of town for a while, it said, and so he was leaving a larger quantity of food and a new toy for Temeron. Temeron was to consider it as his gift for the new annus, which was only ten days away. Thrilled, Temeron carefully smoothed out the paper and folded it. He put it back in his hidey-hole and ate a slice of cake before hiding everything again. His friend had not mentioned for how long he would be gone; it would be wise to preserve the food as long as possible. He then turned to the toy. It was a stick that branched into two at one end. Between the two arms was tied a strip of leather. What was it? Temeron had never seen anything like this before. What was he supposed to do with it?

He took out the message and read it again, but it said nothing about how to use the toy. He turned the page over but found no instructions. Evidently, his benefactor had assumed that he would know what to do with it. He put the note back inside the hole and began to fiddle with the toy. He pulled on the strap and let it go. It bit his hand, and he let the object fall with a sharp cry of pain. His hand was cut. He felt angry. He wanted to throw it away. He raised it to throw it out of the window, but the strap caught on something and the object was snatched out of his hand. It fell on the floor with a clatter. This gave Temeron an idea. He searched about and easily found a pebble or two in a corner. He dug those up. Then, placing one of the pebbles in the middle of the leather band, he pulled and let go. The pebble shot forward but did not go very far. Temeron eagerly snatched it up and tried again, this time pulling harder on the strap. The pebble went further this time. Temeron continued to fiddle with his new toy enthusiastically until he had figured out the best way to launch his stony missiles.

Once he had mastered the use of the sling, he began to shoot at specific objects. He took aim and let a pebble go at Rosa's cauldron. It hit the cauldron with a loud 'clang'. Temeron laughed. He took aim again and shot at Rosa's jar of lizard tails. This was a mistake. The pebble hit another jar nearby and it broke, spilling the contents over the shelf and the ground. With a yelp, Temeron ran to clean up the damage before Rosa returned. She would skin him alive if she found out that he had broken any of her jars. After he had cleaned up the mess, he desisted from playing with his new toy for a while. He had realised that he could break things using it. When he had calmed down enough after the debacle, he again began to play with the sling. This time, he took care to hit targets that could not be broken by stones. He had surprisingly good aim to begin with, and with each try, his aim improved considerably. A couple of horas later, he was overjoyed to find that he could hit anything he wanted to.

A noise from the street distracted him. He ran to his window and peered out. He was now tall enough to look out of the window on tiptoe. The street outside was milling with kereighes. They were purchasing gifts and clothes for the new annus. Temeron had never received anything on the occasion of the new annus ever before. His unknown benefactor had given him the most precious gift ever! As he watched, he noted that two boys were fighting. He knew these two boys; they were notorious bullies of the area and often fought, either with each other or with other boys. When they were not fighting, they were causing trouble for the shopkeepers. They would steal something from a shop when the shopkeeper was not watching and then make faces from a distance. Even if the shopkeeper managed to catch them, they were invariably rescued by their father, a burly kereighe who was a grocer and a money-lender. No one liked the two boys; everyone tolerated them since they did not want to antagonise the boys' father.

The two boys, as well as their father, had always been particularly cruel towards Temeron. They had spared no opportunity to wound him or insult him. The boys had kicked him, smeared his face and clothes with mud, snatched his food, torn his hair, beaten him up and even cut him with a knife. Their father had acted no better. As he saw these two bullies fighting, Temeron had an idea. This was his chance to avenge his wounds and humiliation at their hands. He dug up a large pebble from a corner, took aim and let go at the fighting boys. It unerringly hit one of them on his behind. With a cry of pain, he let go of his brother and leapt back. Temeron had, in the meantime, dug up some more pebbles. Making sure that he was not spotted, he shot again, this time hitting the other boy. The two stopped fighting and looked around, trying to spot who was hitting them and with what. They did not notice the pebbles lying on the ground along with scores of other stones and pebbles. When he was reasonably certain that they had not seen him, Temeron shot another projectile. This one hit the first boy on his forehead. It cut him, and he started bleeding. Before he could recover, Temeron hit his brother on the nose. The boy's nose broke. Hurt and bleeding, the boys let our roars of pain and rushed to their father. Temeron observed with smug satisfaction from the security of his hiding place behind the window as they tried to explain to their enraged father what had happened.

Since they had no clear idea of *what* had hit them, they could not explain very well. Their father lost his temper at being disturbed and guessed that the two had been fighting again.

'Were you fighting again?' he demanded.

'Yes, but…' began one of the boys but could not finish as his father's slap stopped him midsentence. The other tried to duck but met with an even harder slap. The grocer grabbed the two and began to propel them towards his home. Somehow, the boys managed to get out their tale between their sobs; someone had hit them with something to cause the bleeding nose and forehead, they complained. They were standing right across from Temeron's window now. He watched with his heart in his mouth. Would they point to him? Would they know? The boys did not seem clear on what had happened. The grocer asked the other shopkeepers in the area, but they had not noticed anything either. Finally, he gave up and kicked his boys home. Temeron was laughing hard by then. He clamped his hands over his mouth to remain unheard. Tears were streaming down his cheeks, and his knees felt weak with laughter. He had not had this much fun before! The sling was the best gift that his secret benefactor could have given him. He was going to put it to good use. He had already developed good aim. He would practice until his aim was impeccable. He began to form a picture in his mind: wooden pellets dipped in oil, bursting into flames at his command, whistling across to the other side of the street, setting fire to the shops and houses there and burning everything down. Oh yes! He was going to put the sling to good use!

Chapter 53

DUTY

(25 Vyiedal 5010 A.E. to 9 Samrer 5010 A.E.)

Lamella needed a new quilt. It was unbelievable that the queen of Balignor could want for something, yet it was true. Lamella and Amishar had been completely neglected since King Amiroth's second marriage. The king hardly ever saw Amishar anymore. He never visited Lamella. All her servants and ladies in waiting had been given over to Samiesna. While not exactly poor, Lamella no longer enjoyed the wealth and status that she deserved. Amiroth spent his entire time either in his duties or with his new wife. Amishar knew that his mother had given away many of her warm clothes and quilts to the poor before Amiroth's arrival, never doubting that she would have as many as she wanted. Unfortunately, she was herself sorely in need of some now. It was the last day of Vyiedal, and vernurt had dug in its roots deeply. Amishar decided to approach his cousin, Lord Aminor, for help. Aminor, like everyone else, had withdrawn himself from Amishar and Lamella. However, he was polite to Amishar whenever the two encountered each other. There was no one else whom Amishar could imagine approaching.

Amishar went searching for his godfather and found him discussing something with King Amiroth. On a whim, Amishar directly addressed his father and asked for a new quilt for his mother. To his utter shock and humiliation, instead of agreeing to his request, the king slapped him hard in front of all the guards and servants. Amiroth told him off for disturbing him with minor, unimportant matters while he was discussing important business. Aminor said nothing and did nothing, remaining impassive by his king's side. As he walked away, his face red with shame, Amishar overheard his father mentioning the purchase of jewellery for Queen Samiesna.

Though soon after that incident, warm and lavish clothes and quilts appeared in Lamella's chamber as if by magic, Amishar did not forgive his father. He wanted to believe that his father had sent the provisions for vernurt, but in his heart he knew otherwise. Yet, who else could have sent Lamella and him what they so sorely needed? He broached this mystery to his friend when Mizu came for a visit. Mizu felt sorry for his friend's plight.

'Maybe Lord Aminor sent the warm clothing,' he suggested. 'You said that he was present at the time you put the request to your father.'

'But he said nothing when father…refused,' Amishar said. He could not tell even his closest friend about the extent of his humiliation. Mizu sensed that King Amiroth's refusal had been in more than just words. He had witnessed the king's behaviour towards Amishar once or twice and had been utterly shocked. He could not believe that King Amiroth was so cruel towards his son. He remembered the awe he had felt when he had first met King Amiroth. Fatherless himself, he had become keenly aware of his loss seeing the love that the king of Balignor had had for his only son. But now that son was neglected, even disliked, and often rebuked without justification.

Mizu, like Amishar, held Samiesna responsible for Amishar and Lamella's plight. Mizu had seen this much-talked-about lady once. Mizu and Amishar had been to the new residential wing of the palace to see King Amiroth's new chambers and had seen her there. She had been sitting with King Amiroth and singing to him. Her song had seemed very beautiful to Mizu, but Amishar's face had darkened on hearing it. He had almost dragged Mizu away from the chamber without any explanation.

Amishar had started spending almost all his time with Mizu since King Amiroth's marriage to Samiesna. This did not go unnoticed by Misa, who began to worry that her son would get dragged into the painful circumstances of the royal family of Balignor. She had had other expectations from Mizu's friendship with Amishar, but those seemed doomed now. Misa decided that it was time to leave. It had been pleasant to live in Durnum; in fact, she had begun to hope that their lives were now finally settled. She had accumulated many things in their anni there, and it would not be possible to vanish as easily as they had earlier. Mizu was older now and would ask for explanations. He was also very close to Amishar, much closer than he had been with anyone in his life except her. She wasn't sure how to broach the subject to him.

One evening, around mid-Samrer, Mizu returned home from the palace to find his mother sitting in darkness. He felt concerned.

'Is everything all right?' he asked her.

'No, Mizu,' she replied, 'everything is not all right. We have to leave.'

'What! Why? What has happened? Where will we go?'

Misa put her arm around Mizu and said, 'Nothing has happened. At least, not yet. I'm sure that you know how things in the palace stand. Sooner or later, it is going to affect us. It might become dangerous for you if we stay. That is why we have to leave. Do you understand?'

'No!' shouted Mizu, as a sudden memory of a dark night and urgent packing and hasty goodbyes arose in his mind. He remembered nothing clearly except the confusion and the pain of leaving behind people he loved. And he remembered how they had constantly travelled before coming to Durnum. 'No,' he said again, this time more softly. Misa tried to explain to him again.

'I understand what you are saying, Ma,' Mizu said calmly. 'But I don't want to leave. I don't want to be moving around all the time like we used to.'

'Neither do I, my son, but we have no choice. It is for your safety that we have to do this,' Misa insisted.

'But why? Why would *my* life be in danger? I am just an ordinary village boy. Why would my life be threatened because the king has married again?'

'Because you are the prince's best friend. I am not saying that your life is threatened right now. Maybe you will live your life normally for anni to come. Maybe both you and Amishar will grow up to be fine young men. Then what? Amishar will want to be king, which is his birthright. You will obviously support him. At that moment, his enemies will become your enemies. Those who wish to harm him will want to harm you as well. Even now, some might anticipate that day and try to hurt Amishar. You might fall victim just by being with him at the time that they attack. I don't want to wait for that day before we leave Durnum. I know that you are too young to understand all this. You must trust me when I say that leaving this place behind is the best course of action!'

'No,' Mizu said again, still softly but in a tone of determination. 'I am, as you say, the prince's best friend. I am, actually, Amishar's only friend. If his life is or will be in danger, I must stand by him. If he is under threat, he needs me more than ever. I cannot leave him to face dangers and threats alone. It is my duty as his friend to be by his side at all times. No, Ma, I will not leave. If you forcibly take me away, I will run away and return here,' he added, his heart thudding hard at the strain of having to stand up to his mother. He had never imagined that he would ever defy her, but he could not accept what she was telling him.

Misa was shocked. And angry. She wanted to scold Mizu for being so obtuse and childish! 'Is he, though?' asked a small, nagging voice at the back of her head. What she was suggesting to him was inglorious, and she knew that. Was his determination to stand by his friend not evidence of his honourable nature? Was it not what was expected of one of noble blood? She was desperate to save him so that he could live long enough to reclaim his birthright, so she was willing to do anything to keep him alive. Was he not already claiming some of his birthright by displaying such a strong sense of duty? That sense of duty was as much his inheritance as was the throne of Samion. She was painfully reminded of another who had refused to leave the side of his best friend and had undoubtedly paid for it with his life.

Misa sighed and turned away so that her son would not see her tears. They were stuck in Durnum, she realised, for better or for worse, their fates inextricably intertwined with those of Lamella and Amishar. The irony of it all was not lost on her. She was suddenly reminded of one of her father's favourite sayings: 'Take heed of what you wish for lest your wish comes true.' It had always puzzled her. Now she finally understood what it meant.

Chapter 54

THE CITY OF PATARSHP

(14 Zulheen 5010 A.E. to 17 Beybasel 5010 A.E.)

Rauz Augurk's expedition seeking the hidden City of Stone set off from Drauzern on the fourteenth of Zulheen, at the peak of vernurt. It was perhaps the largest body of armed dharvhs that had sallied forth from the capital city since the war with the Blarzonians almost three aeons ago. There had been some reservations about undertaking such a venture in such cold weather, but the necessity for promptness had overruled all objections. Eamilus spent the intervening temporas enjoying Augurk's hospitality with growing impatience. He was the happiest soul in the cavalcade that emerged from the capital into the great desert that vernurt morning.

Five temporas passed uneventfully as they marched at an excruciatingly slow pace due to the size of the contingent and the harshness of the terrain and climate. They were still a good distance from the city of Orbhz, the capital of Khwaznon, at the end of that period. Because of the season, the heat was not oppressive. That was possibly the only positive aspect of their experience. Dharvhs were, as a rule, used to travelling in the desert. But they always used the established routes and pathways from one location to another. Due to reasons of expediency, this time they had been compelled to take to the roadless wilderness of the Laudhern. The terrain, the climate, the unfamiliarity of the paths they travelled and the slow march began to drain even the hardy dharvhs.

The long lines of dharvhs marched grimly along the gravelly ground of the Laudhern, trying to keep as much to the sides of the overshadowing rocky tablelands as they could. But shade was scarce, and their hands and faces were tanned and cracked by the sun although it burned with far less strength than it would in somminar. Their feet were sore with blisters. Throats and lips were parched because the available water was being rationed in the absence of a sighting of a water source for days on end. The days were bad. The nights were worse. Even thick furs were not enough to keep out the biting cold. It seemed to find the smallest gap and creep inside, grabbing the heart and turning it to ice.

In every direction, the terrain looked the same; it was easy to lose one's way. Twice the troops wandered into wrong ditches and went round retracing their steps for days before finding the right path again. Dharvhs began to die. Discontent was rife. Augurk had to worry about keeping his company from turning against him in

addition to worrying about keeping himself and his councillors alive. He wished
they had taken the established routes; the decision to travel as directly as possible,
in the end, had proven to be a bad one. They had ended up spending more time on
the road than they would have had they travelled by established routes. The best
option now was to discover the nearest established road that led towards Orbhz.

Eamilus alone seemed unaffected by the vagaries of the desert. He could
survive on a meagre supply of water as well as food for days and not tire. The sun
seemed not to affect him; at night, he never needed a blanket. He would prowl
about in the dark around the camp, on the alert for danger. It was he who found
the right paths again when the dharvhs got lost. He could not help them except
by ensuring that they kept moving in the general direction that they needed to
go in; they, unlike him, could not fly over the massive rocky hills and plateaus
that dotted the Laudhern. Their passage was limited to the sandy ground around
these obstacles and over the rocky plateaus that were low enough to be climbed.
They would have to find their own way to the Lyudzbradh, no matter how much
Eamilus might want to lead them there in the most direct line possible.

Augurk was grateful for the boy's company. The others were awed or uneasy.
Rumours about Eamilus's identity spread like wildfire through the ranks. In
the days that Eamilus had been with the dharvhs, he had begun to learn their
tongue. While he patrolled the camp at night, he heard their worried whispers and
wondered whether the expedition was doomed. On his own, he could have reached
Patrisha long ago and even taken Augurk with him. But he had to lead the large
company of dharvhs. Leading them on foot was neither easy, nor convenient, even
though they were a hardy race and trudged on despite all the hardships.

That night too Eamilus was on guard when he heard something in the
distance. Hoofbeats! A group of riders was approaching the camp. They were still
too far for the rest of the camp to hear their approach. Eamilus frowned. They
were coming from the east. Why would anyone be riding at night in the desert,
especially since dharvhs preferred to walk, and horses were a rarity among them?
He felt suspicious about the riders. There were at least a hundred, maybe more.
They were approaching fast. Under normal circumstances, they would have been no
match for Augurk's troops. However, given the speed at which they were galloping,
they seemed completely at home in the desert. The darkness, the unfamiliarity and
the surprise would act against the soldiers. If these were bandits, Eamilus figured,
even three hundred dharvh soldiers would be unable to protect the camp from
them. Eamilus rushed to raise the alarm.

The dharvhs were prepared for a horde of about a hundred, but when the
bandits arrived, they were shocked to find that their numbers were twice as many.
The horses of the bandits were large, powerful creatures, specially bred for desert
warfare and trained to move in the dark as easily as in the light. Each animal carried

two riders sitting back to back, so that when the band of marauders attacked, the dharvh soldiers were met by a number twice as large as they had anticipated. Even though surprised by an unexpectedly strong enemy, the dharvhs stood their ground. They waited until the bandits were close enough to be seen and then shot at them. Many fell, and the sudden attack upset the bandits' established tactics. However, they soon recovered and began to leverage their numbers. While half of them engaged the dharvh soldiers, the other half proceeded to loot the provisions and attack the defenceless workers and provisioners.

Seeing this, Augurk ordered a third of the soldiers to defend the unarmed segment of the expedition and assigned Durng to lead them. He kept the archers in the camp to shoot at the bandits from a distance and put Guzear in charge of them. And he led the remaining hundred and fifty-odd dharvh soldiers in an offence on the charging bandits, followed closely by Shornhuz. This manoeuvre surprised the bandits, and they reined in their onslaught momentarily. This was the break that Augurk needed. His dharvhs crashed into the hesitant bandits like a tidal wave. Before the brigands could understand what was going on, the dharvh soldiers were pushing them back. On the other side of the camp, the soldiers had successfully stopped the bandits from further plundering their reserves; the workers, inspired by Durng, aided their efforts by fighting with sticks and knives. Seeing the resistance, the plundering bandits retreated to join the others.

However, they never reached their companions. A deadly menace was waiting for them in the dark. As soon as the fight had begun, Eamilus had left the main force of the dharvhs and worked his way to the rear of the marauders. There, unseen by the main dharvh army, he began to cut down the attackers. When Augurk's forces split to protect the unarmed segment, Eamilus remained to assist the offensive of the dharvhs, still hidden. As the tide of the battle began to turn in favour of Augurk's soldiers, he noticed the other half of the band of robbers coming to join the segment that was under attack. Leaving his sword aside, he transformed into his true self and fell upon the unsuspecting bandits who had been pushed back by Durng's dharvhs. Their screams echoed in the night air and froze the blood of all who heard them as Eamilus mercilessly destroyed them, cutting through them like a knife through butter. Even the dharvh soldiers' hairs stood on end as they saw their enemies falling to the ground in droves, struck down by an unseen enemy.

By the time the encounter ended, most of the bandits lay on the cold desert floor, lifeless. The few who were lucky rode away with their lives. The dharvhs managed to capture many of the horses but as many fled. Then they patiently began to wait for dawn to assess the true impact of the nightly skirmish. They were grim despite the victory, for even in the dark, they could see that their own losses were huge. Durng was trying, helped now by all the remaining workers as well as many of the soldiers, to retrieve as much of the ration as possible, especially the water. Eamilus had quietly returned and now helped them.

The light of day brought a scene of destruction and hopelessness with it. Over fifty soldiers had died and about as many workers. Almost all the other soldiers were wounded, many seriously. The workers and the stock keepers were also injured in large numbers. But the worst was the state of the provisions. Most of the water was gone; so was the food. The bandits had not managed to take any provisions away with them, but in their attempts to do so, they had succeeded in destroying several of the carts, setting fire to quite a few and upsetting four of the carts that carried water. There was hardly enough medicine left to heal the wounded. Without enough food, water and medicine, the dharvhs would not survive even a day in the desert. The flickering sense of victory turned to utter despair.

Suddenly hoofbeats sounded again in the distance. The dharvhs prepared to defend themselves once more, this time with no hope in their hearts. They waited patiently as the riders approached, grim and dangerous. No one spoke. The very air of the desert seemed to have stilled. Slowly, the riders came into view. The soldiers gripped their weapons more firmly. Augurk stood at the head of his troops, Shornhuz and Eamilus on either side. Suddenly Eamilus frowned. He could now see the riders from the south clearly. He spoke excitedly to Augurk, 'My rauz, the approaching riders are not bandits; they are dharvhs of Khwaznon!'

Those who heard him felt suspicious of Eamilus's intentions. The riders were still too far away for anyone to clearly recognise them. Augurk, however, had read about Eamilus's abilities in Halifern's letter and was willing to believe the boy. Though he did not order his men to lower their weapons, hope surged in his heart. He continued to stare at the approaching group with anticipation. Soon, the riders were close enough for the dharvhs of Ghrangghirm to recognise the white tunics and blue and silver banners of the soldiers of Khwaznon. They rode the famous ponies of their lands and were armed for a fight. When they saw the group stranded in the middle of the desert, they halted out of surprise, but their formations remained perfect. Their leader barked some quick orders, and a few dharvhs stepped out of line. Followed by half a dozen riders, the leader galloped towards the watching dharvhs. Recognising him, Augurk ordered his soldiers to withdraw from their defensive stance.

'Stand down!' he barked. 'Eamilus was correct; the riders coming towards us are indeed dharvhs of Khwaznon.'

A loud cheer went up from the watching dharvhs. They were saved! As the dharvhs of Ghrangghirm gathered to meet the approaching party, Eamilus quietly watched the leader of the Khwaznonian dharvhs. He looked young and intelligent. He sat straight and proud on the pony's back, clearly used to riding.

Like his soldiers, he wore a white tunic, close fitting breeches of leather, a hard, leather cuirass and a leather helmet decorated with large, black feathers. He could not have been over sixty, yet there was a gravity and grace in his bearing that a human of thirty, his equivalent in maturity, would rarely have displayed. He was almost svelte, though, with a sparse beard, and his hair hung loose in numerous beaded braids. Eamilus had never seen a dharvh like this before and was impressed by the look of quiet confidence on the face of the young leader of the small band.

Augurk's voice, tinted with pride, broke into his thoughts. 'Eamilus, do you see the young dharvh leading the party?'

Eamilus nodded.

'That, my friend,' preened Augurk, 'is my son-in-law, Rauzoon Valhazar.'

After their rescue, Augurk was compelled to tell the entire truth about their expedition to Rauz Valhorz. He hid nothing except the reason for Nishtar's hold on him; anything else would have been an insult to the dharvh who had saved them from certain death and had provided them with generous hospitality. Rauz Valhorz was, naturally, angry at not having been taken into confidence from the beginning. He was not only the leader of one half of the dharvhish world but also Augurk's daughter's father-in-law. They were family. He felt that Augurk should have consulted him even before consulting his councillors. Augurk apologised profusely, acknowledging that Rauz Valhorz was correct. His entire expedition was now at Rauz Valhorz's mercy, he acknowledged.

However, whether because he felt disgruntled by the whole situation or because he did not support the purpose, Rauz Valhorz now refused to be part of it. He would provide Augurk with whatever resources he needed, he declared, but would neither advise nor discuss the matter with Augurk. Rauzoon Valhazar, on the contrary, was tremendously interested—in Nishtar, in Eamilus and in the stone city. On pain of incurring his father's wrath, he decided not just to help Augurk's expedition but to accompany it as well. He had a long discussion with Eamilus and Augurk, which none of the others from Ghrangghirm were privy to. The outcome was that the majority of the remainder of the five hundred dharvhs from Ghrangghirm were stationed in Orbhz to recuperate while a much smaller group was chosen to set off for Patrisha. The party comprised the leaders of the original expedition and Rauzoon Valhazar along with a score of soldiers from Ghrangghirm and Khwaznon. Two dharvhs of Khwaznon would accompany the group as provisioners. No workers were to be included in this party; they would first locate the city and then send for more soldiers and workers as needed.

For days, Rauzoon Valhazar kept waiting for something to arrive after all the decisions had been taken and all the plans had been formulated. Then, one night, almost two temporas since the arrival of the expedition in Orbhz, he declared that the expected mounts had arrived and that the party would set off the next day. The next morning, the mysterious mounts were revealed to be strange, ugly birds known as autruches. They were large two-legged birds that did not fly; they had long, thick legs that ended in cloven hoof-like legs with only two toes on each leg. They had small heads and long, muscular necks. Their bodies were flat, and they had stumpy wings and tails. They were covered in large, fluffy black feathers. They stood twice as tall as any dharvh and looked rather comical and unsteady.

Durng had felt sceptical about these birds' ability to carry anyone, let alone travel the desert, but the birds proved remarkably sturdy as well as fast. However, even after riding one for four days, he did not become used to the strange birds. He was not a large dharvh and was lightly built, being leaner than usual. He had surprisingly blue eyes that always looked calm and wise. But now those eyes were lined with anxiety; he was less worried about what dangers the Lyudzbradh held than about his mount that galloped across the desert in a loping gait. Durng looked up at the horizon where the looming silhouettes of the approaching Lyudzbradh darkened the skyline. A shiver ran down his spine, and even in the bright daylight, he felt a cold hand gripping his stomach. The shadow of the Lyudzbradh seemed to fall on him. He trembled visibly. Then his bird began to behave strangely. It started flapping its wings, unseating him, and sped away, making a strange hissing noise. When Durng got back on his feet, he found that most of the others had suffered a similar fate. He was starting to curse the unreliable birds when the ground began to tremble. It shook so hard that Durng found it hard to remain standing. Suddenly Eamilus yelled 'Look out!' and leapt at him.

The two crashed to the ground a few feet from where Durng had been standing. The dharvh's angry ejaculation was drowned in the collective cries of the soldiers who had been following. Durng quickly turned to where they were pointing and briefly saw a disappearing head. He could not believe his eyes! Something had dragged one of the soldiers down into the earth! The trembling of the earth stopped soon after, but no one moved. The shock had rooted them to the spot. Augurk, Shornhuz, Guzear and Valhazar slowly came to stand at Durng's side. Valhazar looked grim.

'That is the Death Worm,' he said. 'It is native to these parts. It can hear your footsteps and follow you under the ground faster than you can imagine. It will burst out of the earth and drag you down. If you are lucky, you will suffocate to death!'

'Is the danger over?' enquired Guzear.

Valhazar shook his head. 'Once the Death Worm has found your trace, it will not leave you alone until it has hunted down each and every living being it can sense.'

'How can we escape?' asked Augurk.

'You can't outrun a Death Worm,' responded Valhazar. 'It is a creature of the deepest bowels of the *dhredh*[6] and is as old as Pretvain itself. It has dark magic that will make you lose your way and wander around for as long as it wants you to. From a distance of several feet, it can spit venom that will burn you to cinder on the spot. It is faster than any dharvh or horse. The autruches are the only creatures that can outrun it. Only once has someone faced an attack from a Death Worm and lived to tell the tale.'

'Who? How?' demanded Durng. Valhazar was silent.

Eamilus asked, 'Can you summon the autruches back?'

Valhazar nodded. He took a whistle from his tunic's pocket and blew thrice on it. No one heard a sound, but soon the renegade fowls could be seen reappearing on the horizon.

Eamilus lay down with his ear to the ground and listened. Apparently satisfied with what he had heard, he stood up, brushed the dirt off his clothes and invited Valhazar and Augurk to have a word a little apart from the others. When they were out of earshot of the others, he said, 'I couldn't hear the Death Worm just now, which means that it is very deep underground and, hopefully, busy with its last prey. I have an idea—take the autruches and head straight towards the south-west. I will draw the attention of the Death Worm when it begins to surface. That will give you time to escape.'

'What will you do when it attacks you?' Valhazar asked.

'I will try to kill it,' Eamilus replied simply.

'Eamilus,' Valhazar said, 'I saw you push Durng out of the Worm's way before any of us even knew that it was upon us. I can sense that you are no ordinary human boy. But how do you propose to kill the worm?'

'With this,' Eamilus said and drew his sword. It was a double-edged sword with an ashen hilt on which leaves and flowers were embossed. For a frael, it would have been a longsword. For Eamilus, its length was just right. It shone white hot in the daylight. Augurk recognised the sword.

'Eamilus,' he said, 'I know this sword. It is a good sword and has never failed. If you can wield it well, I am willing to accept your suggestion.'

---

6 'Earth' (Eargh)

'I too have no objections to your plan, Eamilus, but *I* shall stay behind with you,' Valhazar said. 'Even with all your skill, you will not be able to slay this worm alone. Rauz Augurk, lead the party towards the mountains and wait for us there.'

Augurk was reluctant to allow his son-in-law to undertake such a risk, even though he would have done the same had he been in Valhazar's place. The young rauzoon knew more about the Worm than anyone else and was best placed to survive it, especially with Eamilus protecting him. Against his paternal instincts, Augurk agreed to the plan. A hora later, a strange sight could be seen in the middle of the Laudhern. Eamilus and Valhazar stood back to back, jumping and stamping on the ground. In the distance, the rest of the dharvhs could be seen headed on the autruches towards the terrifying silhouette of the Lyudzbradh. At their current speed, they were certain to reach there by nightfall.

'Is it coming?' Valhazar asked.

'Not yet,' Eamilus replied, tense. They continued their strange actions. Suddenly, Eamilus heard the worm stirring under the surface of the earth.

'It's coming at you!' he hissed and turned round.

Valhazar unsheathed his sword. It was a beautiful sword made of an alloy of simlin and iron, forged in the northern kingdoms of the eighes. The length of the sword was inscribed with runes that glowed in the sunlight. The hilt was of pure Simlin and contained the motif of a pair of dragons made out of grains of precious stones. Eamilus was stunned to see such a sword. He was about to draw his own sword, but Valhazar stopped him. He sheathed it half-heartedly. 'When the Worm reaches us, push me away and distract the worm,' Valhazar said. 'Take care that it continues to face you but that it does not grab you or hit you with its venom. I will strike it from behind—that is the only way a Death Worm can be killed.'

Eamilus nodded. He wondered why Valhazar had not said this when they had been formulating their plans. Had he not wanted to reveal the secret in public? Was that why he had insisted on staying behind with Eamilus—so that they had a real chance at killing the Worm? The boy could not understand why the rauzoon would try to keep such critical information secret. But he could not distrust the rauzoon, not under the circumstances. When his very life depended on Valhazar being correct. Of course, he had his own surprise to spring on Valhazar.

The ground began to tremble violently again, but Valhazar stood his ground. He could feel the land under his feet giving way, and his heart beat faster. Suddenly, he was lifted clear off the ground. Below him, the earth opened up and the terrifying Death Worm appeared, its mouth wide open, its putrid breath reeking of rotten flesh. Valhazar gagged but held on to his sword. He stared bewildered at Eamilus who was now rising fast into the air with him and emitting a strange, gurgling growl. To Valhazar's amazement, the Worm did not disappear back into the earth but continued to push upward. It appeared to be following the sound that Eamilus was emitting. When it could rise no more, the worm hovered in mid-air and spewed forth a jet of hot venom. Eamilus was too fast for the Worm, however. Before it could begin to retract into the earth, Valhazar found himself floating right behind its massive head.

'Now!' cried Eamilus, and Valhazar swung the sword with all his might. The powerful sword sliced through the mass of the red, putrid flesh of the worm's neck, and its decapitated head fell to the ground with a sickening thud, bursting into flames. The fleshy body fell and writhed awhile before becoming still. Eamilus put Valhazar down. The rauzoon of Khwaznon stared at his companion in silence for a minura while catching his breath. He wanted to confront Eamilus about deviating from the plan and for keeping secrets that bore on the outcome of the risky venture. But he had done the same, although his own secret was nowhere near as massive—or terrifying—as Eamilus's. So he said nothing about the impromptu actions of the far-more-not-so-normal-than-expected human boy. Instead he said, 'Now we must clean this sword thoroughly with sand, for the blood of the Death Worm is as poisonous as its venom.'

'How do you know so much about the Death Worm?' Eamilus asked, impressed by Valhazar's erudition about such an obscure creature.

'The only mortal to ever survive an attack by the Death Worm was my father,' Valhazar replied smugly.

Five days after arriving at the foothills of the Lyudzbradh, the leaders of the expedition reached the crevice in which Eamilus had taken shelter on the occasion of discovering Patrisha. They left the soldiers and provisioners camped at the bottom of the mountain whose name no one knew. Eamilus had reassured the party that no harm would come to them. The five dharvhs and Eamilus took shelter for the night inside a cave near the crevice. They lit a fire and sat around, discussing the various adventures they had faced on their expedition so far. The Death Worm had not been the last of them. On their way to the mountain, they had met many creatures of the dark. They had swiftly dispatched those to Zyimnhem. They felt tired and old—as if they had been battling the forces of the dark all their lives. Eamilus was the only one who sat quietly. He had led the dharvhs across the desert and through many dangers to the mountain. But would he be able to lead them into the magical valley on the other side of the mountain to Patrisha? It was over an annus ago that he had first caught a glimpse of Patrisha and, that too, very briefly. Sitting near the mouth of the cave, thinking his own thoughts, he nonetheless kept his ears open for sounds of danger outside. Inside, conversation died down. Every dharvh retired to his own thoughts.

Augurk was beginning to doze in a corner. Guzear sat polishing his knife by the fire. Durng was sitting with him, repairing his shoes. Valhazar sat in a shaded part of the cave, watching Eamilus. Shornhuz, who sat near Augurk, was unexpectedly talking. He was a massive, ugly dharvh who loomed over everyone else, intimidating by his sheer size. The impressive array of weapons that he carried on his person at all times added to his aura of danger. He was effortlessly strong and uniquely adept at using any weapon although his favourite was his axe. Usually, he was silently menacing but something—perhaps the excitement or perhaps the several wineskins full of Khwaznonian wine that he had drunk that evening after losing a bet to Guzear—had loosened his tongue that night.

'We should never have come on this expedition,' he slurred for the benefit of any who was willing to listen. 'They say that a deadly tiger roams the forests of Valdero; none who has seen it has survived.'

'Then who spread the story of the tiger?' Valhazar quipped, unwilling to take any danger too seriously and rather enjoying Shornhuz's animation.

Shornhuz gave him a withering look. He did not like Valhazar. Valhazar glared back at him fearlessly. The other three paid no attention to the two. Eamilus suddenly smelled a familiar odour on the air. He quietly rose, unnoticed by the dharvhs, and stepped out.

Valhazar suddenly noticed Eamilus's absence.

'Where is Eamilus?' he demanded aloud. Everyone was immediately alert.

'He was here just a few momons ago,' commented Durng.

'I never trusted that human boy,' Guzear grumbled. 'He isn't right; he is evil. Maybe he has gone to fetch his evil friends.'

'What if he is in danger?' suggested Valhazar.

'Let us go and look for him,' Augurk said, standing up. The others followed suit, not all of them willingly.

Before any of them could take another step, Eamilus returned. He was accompanied by a large, tanned man who wore fur-lined clothes of orange and black. The light of the fire seemed to dance in his eyes as he entered the cave. The roof of the cave was not tall enough for him to stand upright, and he had to crouch. His very bearing radiated power. The dharvhs watched him silently, wondering who he was. Eamilus was beaming. The older man had his arm around the boy's shoulder.

'Rauz Augurk, other esteemed dharvhs, let me introduce you to a friend of mine I discovered prowling outside,' Eamilus said. 'This is Uzdal, the tiger Shornhuz mentioned, the one who roams the forests of Valdero and spares none who crosses his path!'The only one who did not gasp at this announcement was Valhazar.

The next morning, Augurk stood outside Uzdal's lair expectantly, waiting for the sun to rise. After more than four anni of searching, he was about to set eyes on the elusive City of Stone. The others joined him. Uzdal and Eamilus came out of the lair and nodded to the dharvhs in greeting. The mood was silent and solemn as they all waited for the fulfilment of their long-awaited expectations. As the sun rose slowly, at first nothing was visible. Shornhuz was about to say something, but Valhazar hissed at him to silence him. He pointed into the valley that lay spread out in front of them. In the distance, a dark-coloured mass was beginning to appear out of nowhere. It slowly began to take the shape of a walled fortress city, settled in the midst of a large, sprawling plain.

'That is Patrisha, the city of stone built by Patarshp, the sculptor Guardian,' said Uzdal. The viewers stood silently, allowing the magic and the beauty of the valley at their feet to sweep over them. 'In a few momons it will disappear again. It is visible at no other time and from no other place. How will you reach it, Rauz Augurk?' Uzdal continued.

Augurk did not reply. Instead, he asked Shornhuz to hand him the longish bundle that he had brought along. He unwrapped it speedily. When the layers of cloth were removed, a bow was revealed. It was a bow the likes of which those gathered there had never seen. It was as tall as Augurk and as thick as his wrist. One end had a foot-long pointed metallic spike. Augurk looped a whip-like bowstring through the sharp end and inserted it into the earth to steady the bow. He drew the surprisingly supple bowstring with all his strength and slipped it over the upper end of the bow, creating tension strong enough to break any bow but this. Then he took an exceptionally long and thick arrow with a heavy tip and wide fletching out of the bundle and fitted it to the bow. The city was beginning to vanish as he sat behind the bow and drew the string back with both hands. The bow bent and pointed at the sky as Augurk drew the string back. When the hilt of the arrow touched his chest, he let go with a loud 'twang'. The arrow flew straight up into the air for a while. Then its heavy head compelled it to turn. It began to complete a wide arc to descend towards Patrisha. As it zoomed away, the others watched in wonder; from the arrow's thick body, other arrows were dislodging. These began to strike the earth at intervals until the original arrow, now no thicker than an ordinary one, finally struck the ground just where the gates of the stone city had been a momon before. The city had disappeared, but a trail of arrows marked the path for the discoverers to follow.

The rest of the journey was surprisingly uneventful. So much so that Durng began to wonder whether the conclusion of their expedition would turn out to be an anti-climax. He hoped that the city was real, that it wasn't an illusion caused by the angle of light among the mountains of the Lyudzbradh. He hoped that finding the city would do for Augurk all that the rauz hoped it would. He knew the risk Augurk had run in undertaking the expedition and its preceding investigations. In their relatively brief history as a nation, no dharvh rauz had ever been impeached or overthrown. If he failed, Augurk just might end up being the first one. He sighed but said nothing as they trudged down the mountain.

Durng need not have worried. At the end of a long trek down Uzdal's mountain and across a surprisingly empty plain, they found their destination. One moment they were standing in the middle of a vast, empty field. The next moment they were teetering at the edge of a sharp dip in the ground. If Shornhuz had not grabbed Augurk's collar and pulled him back, the rauz would have plummeted to his certain death. They realised that the massive deep pit was part of the illusion. It helped to conceal the city of stone from not just the nearby mountain peaks but also from the ground. There, far below their feet, stood their elusive quarry. It was much more awe-inspiring than they had imagined from their brief, distant glimpse. It rose high into the air, dark, cold and forbidding. Every inch of it radiated a sense of power and mystery; but there was also a sense of haunting danger. The party was struck silent by the menacing presence of the immense edifice. While the others remained at the lip of the pit, Augurk and Eamilus climbed down.

They stood in front of the tall gates of Patrisha. The gates were shut tight and appeared to have remained so since the beginning of time. The high walls surrounding the city were made of a smooth black stone. It was dark and shiny and flecked with spots of white. The gates were of the same material, carved out of single blocks, depicting the sixteen guardians and their emblems. The craftsmanship was elaborate, fantastic and perfect. The closed gates fitted so close together that not even a strand of hair could be passed between them. No mortal could have sculpted those megaliths.

'How shall we get in?' Augurk mused aloud. The two had walked round the city several times since their arrival but had found no entrance except the gates, which were forbiddingly shut. The city was built within a perfectly circular wall that was of even height and smoothness all over. There were no handholds or footholds in the stone of the outer wall. No ladder would have been tall enough to climb over.

'I could carry you inside,' Eamilus offered.

Augurk had by now learnt of the killing of the Death Worm from Valhazar. He showed no surprise at Eamilus's offer. He had known about Eamilus being more than an ordinary human after reading Halifern's letter, but it was the expedition and Eamilus's role in it that had proven his suspicions regarding the non-human part of the boy. He agreed to be carried inside. Eamilus put his arms around Augurk and rose into the air effortlessly. He glided over the wall and into the city. He did not descend immediately, though. He inspected with his eyes and ears and nose for any sign of danger before putting Augurk back on the ground.

'It is really a strange place,' the boy commented.

'Why do you say so?' Augurk asked. 'Do you sense some danger?'

'No, and that is what is bothering me,' answered Eamilus. 'I sense nothing—nothing at all! Neither life nor death, not the tiniest insect or grass or even dust!'

And it was true. For, there was nothing but black stone to be seen. The streets within the walls were made of the same black stone as the walls, as was everything else. The city was huge but completely deserted. No sign of life stirred among the wide roads or the vast palaces. The fountains were dry and the pools were empty. The hearths were barren and the furnaces were cold. It was clear that no one had ever lived there. And yet not a speck of dust was visible on any surface. It was as if the entire city was frozen in time, waiting for something. That was the only palpable sensation that the city bore: the sense of expectancy, of patient anticipation.

The two walked through the city until they reached the central courtyard. Here they finally discovered something more than vacant spaces. But what they discovered was far more terrifying than the emptiness of the deserted city that stood surrounding them. For, standing in the huge courtyard were rows of soldiers—about twenty thousand of them—but all made of stone. The same black, shiny stone that the rest of the city was made of. They carried weapons of stone and bore expressions of anger and ferocity on their terrible features of stone. Their stone eyes glinted with palpable fury. Even in the middle of the day, a cold shadow seemed to pass overhead, and Augurk shivered. He looked at his companion and was shocked to find the imperturbable Eamilus looking anxious.

'We should leave now,' Eamilus said, his voice edgy. Augurk nodded mutely. Eamilus flew him back across the city and over the wall. As they touched the ground outside the towering gates, the warmth of the sun seemed to return. The two companions stood silently in the shadow of the City of Stone, wondering what it really was.

'What shall we do now?' Augurk murmured.

'I have to leave, my rauz,' Eamilus gently reminded him.

'Can nothing persuade you to stay?' Augurk asked. He had grown fond of this unusual human over the past few mondans and was loath to see him leave.

'I would have stayed to see you return safely to your kingdom, but now that I have met Rauzoon Valhazar and Uzdal has agreed to help you, I need worry no more about your safety. Do not ask me to stay, for I will not.'

'Then I must bid you farewell and hope to meet you again someday,' sighed Augurk.

'Thank you, Rauz Augurk,' Eamilus answered. 'But what shall you do now that you have fulfilled Nishtar's commission and discovered the City of Patarshp?'

'To that question, my friend,' said Augurk, 'I have no answer.'

Chapter 55

THE SHORT STRAW

Four mondans had passed since Eamilus's departure. Halifern had felt rather lonely after the boy had left, but he had gradually become used to the solitude. He had taken up the profession of a teacher, much to his parents' chagrin. Every day, he taught young fraelish boys and girls to read and write, in which they had very little interest, and to fight, in which they had a great deal. This invariably reminded him of Eamilus although, unlike his students, the young homanim had been as interested in books as in arms. One evening, Halifern was returning home when a sibilant sound alerted him to the presence of another being in the vicinity. He looked this way and that but saw no one. The sound came again; this time he was able to locate its origin. An unusually tall, peculiarly dressed frael sat on one of the lowermost branches of a tree. This frael wore the clothes of a human beggar and looked completely dishevelled but cheerful. Halifern made a sign and the frael nodded, disappearing into the thick foliage. By the time Halifern reached his home tree, the oddly dressed frael was waiting for him at its base. Without a word, Halifern joined him, and the two vanished among the upper branches where Halifern had his treehouse.

'What news do you have?' he asked the frael.

'The news is not good,' the other replied. He informed his friend of all that he had learnt.

Halifern's face became grave.

'You have done well, Woroned. Is Waroned going to join us soon?'

Woroned nodded acknowledgement. As the two made their way up Halifern's tree, Woroned casually asked, 'What is this I have been hearing about you having brought a kocovus home as a pet and training it to fetch arrows that you shoot?'

Halifern smiled wanly. '*He's* gone now. He left four mondans ago. Four mondans and three days ago, to be exact.'

'You mean it is true?' Woroned asked incredulously. Halifern just smiled mischievously, feeling more cheerful at the return of his friends than he had in a long time. Woroned shook his head. He could not understand Halifern. He was so different from other fraels!

'Is it really true?' Woroned persisted.

'No smoke without fire, what?' teased Halifern.

Woroned sighed and gave up. Halifern could be pretty tight-lipped if he wanted to. They talked of other matters while they waited for Waroned. He arrived soon, looking like a prosperous human merchant. The twins teased each other about their disguises for a while before Waroned delivered his news. It was essentially a corroboration of what Woroned had said, which he did not fail to point out.

'Well, you would have been the one to deliver the stale news if I hadn't had to travel further!' declared Waroned petulantly.

'And did *I* tell you to roam about so far and wide, selling your *wondrous wares* at extortionate rates?' commented Woroned.

'At least I don't have to beg for a living,' retorted Waroned, evidently miffed at his brother's comments.

Sensing that the bickering would continue forever if not stopped, Halifern intervened.

'Have you eaten?' he asked them.

'No,' they answered together.

'Then let us first eat and refresh ourselves. After that, we can discuss other matters.'

This idea appealed to the twins. They left for their own quarters above Halifern's, still bandying words about this and that. Halifern set the table in the meantime. The twins soon reappeared, looking as frael-like as ever. They seemed to have called a truce as they told Halifern stories about the human kingdoms. They had been travelling extensively under their respective disguises and had gathered a lot of information. Halifern listened, fascinated. He wished he could see the human cities and towns, eat their strange but delicious food, ride horses and visit libraries and museums. His life seemed terribly limited compared to the experiences of Waroned and Woroned.

'Now you must tell us about your pet kocovus,' Woroned demanded after dinner.

'He had a kocovus for a pet?' asked Waroned, astonished.

'Indeed he had,' responded Woroned as if he knew all about it.

'No, I had not,' stated Halifern. 'He was a human, though a very unusual one. He was, actually, a homanim.'

'And you suspect that he was part kocovus?' asked Waroned shrewdly.

Halifern shrugged. 'No smoke without fire,' commented Woroned, recalling Halifern's words.

'Who was he, really?' asked Waroned.

'It's a long story,' said Halifern. 'And, incidentally, it ties up with the news that the two of you have brought to me about King Amiroth and Balignor.' He told them about his stay in the forest with Loyohen, Erofone and Siltare, his misadventures with the mertkhezin and King Amiroth, his rescue by Eamilus, Eamilus's stay at Numosyn and Eamilus's departure.

'So, that's why the king cancelled his expedition to Ghrangghirm and returned to Balignor in a huff!' declared Woroned after Halifern finished his tale. 'He must have thought that the dharvhs had rescued you.'

'Perhaps,' agreed Halifern, wondering why he hadn't thought of that before.

'And where did your rescuer go?' asked Woroned.

'He went East.'

'East? That's rather vague, isn't it?' said Woroned.

Halifern nodded. 'I think he was deliberately vague. He wanted to hide his identity; from the first, he had been rather evasive about who he was and where he was from. I never pushed him to tell me—it would have been unfair on someone to whom I owed my life. But I'll never be at peace until I know for sure.'

'Why?' asked Woroned.

'First, because I want to make sure that he is all right, though I have a feeling that I needn't worry. Second, I have a feeling that he isn't ordinary, and I'm not referring to his abilities alone. I think the world will hear more of him in future. I'd like to keep track of him. At the very least, I'd like to know who he was.'

'I understand,' said Woroned. 'So, which of the two of us are you going to send to the Shadow Lands?'

Halifern started. He had, indeed, been thinking of this though he had been wondering how to broach the matter.

'You know, Eamilus isn't the only reason I want someone in the East. The situation there seems to be worsening by the day from what little I have managed to learn. If that trouble spills over to this side of the Lyudzbradh, we will all be in danger. The mertkhezin is an excellent example. I have no idea why she has snared King Amiroth, but I am willing to wager that her intentions are deadly. We need to know more if we want to protect ourselves. Unfortunately, the Council will never agree to send someone to keep an eye on things in the Shadow Lands.'

'I want to go,' declared Waroned. 'Apparently, Woroned has the west covered. Therefore, I would be more useful in the east.'

'No!' said Woroned. 'It should be my reward for having done a better job than you.'

The brothers continued to bicker about who should go to spy for Halifern in the Shadow Lands as he looked on amazed. To anybody, it would have been a death sentence; to the twins, it was an adventure. And the other fraels had cast *these two* out! The short-sightedness of his race struck Halifern anew. A nation that shuns its heroes instead of honouring them is doomed to spend eternity in fear and weakness. Halifern sighed, wondering if the fraels would ever realise this.

'We'll draw lots,' said Halifern, to settle the matter. Both Waroned and Woroned agreed. Halifern held out two fingers. Waroned gripped the middle finger first and Woroned chose the index finger by default.

'Woroned goes to the east,' declared Halifern. The chosen frael let out a whoop of victory while Waroned moaned with disappointment. Woroned was performing a victory jig when his brother jumped him, and the two went tumbling into Halifern's furniture. As the two brothers fought and Halifern tried to separate them, all three rolled around on the floor for a while. When Halifern finally managed to pull the twins apart, Woroned had a bruised cheek, Waroned had a black eye, and Halifern had a cut lip. They had managed to smash a flowerpot and overturn some chairs, scattering books and parchments everywhere. Fortunately, none of the furniture was damaged. The twins helped Halifern put everything back, glowering at each other all the while. Soon, however, they were back to their cheerful selves.

'I sent Eamilus to Augurk with a letter,' Halifern explained to Woroned while the twins sat nursing their injuries some time later. 'You might want to start your search there. Or you might look at Mayndoda and Haalzona. I'm feeling bad about sending you to the Shadow Lands. How are you going to cross the Lyudzbradh? It is going to be too dangerous. Perhaps I should drop the idea!'

'Are you crazy?' exclaimed Woroned. 'Of course, you are!' he answered his own question.

'He wouldn't be sending *you* to the Shadow Lands if he wasn't,' quipped Waroned.

'I'm glad to go,' insisted Woroned, paying no heed to his brother's jibe. 'I am not afraid of the Lyudzbradh. Besides, I've always been curious about the East. I'll get some homing pigeons so that I don't have to cross the mountain range too often, if that makes you feel better. Don't worry about me, I can look after myself.'

Halifern sighed and thanked his friend, hoping that he was doing the right thing. Waroned mumbled something about 'rigging,' but the other two ignored him.

Chapter 56

ORAM'S INVESTIGATIONS

Oram stood outside the Captain's cabin in the dark of night. He was waiting for Beben to go on his rounds around the decks one last time before turning in for the night. Beben navigated his ship all by himself using his powers to do the work usually done by a full crew. Therefore, he was left with little to spend on laying complicated spying fields, alarms and booby traps. Oram had taken advantage of that; the few traps and warning systems that had been installed by Beben had been easily overcome by him. Beben was the last of his quarries among the sumagi, and though he was not optimistic, Oram wanted to complete the work to his own satisfaction.

Oram had started looking into the movements of his colleagues soon after his failed attempt to restore Sumaho's memory. When he had informed the Librarian about what he had found, Sumaho had been crushed. For a day or two, he had remained depressed but had gradually resumed work in his precious library. Oram had left soon after, placing several layers of protective measures around Sumaho. Sumaho's promise to contact him every day, and at any time if he needed help, had had to be enough assurance that the Librarian would be safe.

Investigating the other sumagi had been an uncomfortable experience for Oram. They were the sumagi; suspecting one of them of the attack on Sumaho and the library was unthinkable. The knowledge that if none of *them* was responsible, then the perpetrator was an extremely powerful magus who was unknown to them inspired Oram to be thorough in his scrutiny. Such a thing would be far, far worse than discovering a traitor in their midst!

As the leaders of the magi world, they were expected to be above reproach. They were also expected to be aware of what was happening in Maghem. Yet, he realised, they had been far more interested in other matters for far too long. They had left Maghem to its own devices for far too long. And they had become involved in secrets and plots of which the magi of Maghem had no conception. Conversely, things could be going on in Maghem of which the sumagi were completely unaware. If Nishtar knew anything, he wasn't talking. A conspiracy against the sumagi was not unimaginable, especially if powerful magi had risen there in recent times who chafed under the regulations of absentee authority figures. They might very well be working in secret to establish a new order in Maghem. A blow like that could topple not only the sumagi's authority or the rules they had laid down to guide life in Maghem but the very balance between Maghem and the other hems.

Investigating into Mesmen's whereabouts had been impossible, so Oram had concentrated his efforts on the other four. Using whatever little Sumaho remembered, Oram had managed to establish a rough timeline for when the Librarian had been attacked. All he had had to do then was to uncover whether Nishtar, Alanor, Vellila and Beben had alibis for that time. It had been easier said than done. Making enquiries about such powerful magi without being discovered was next to impossible. Yet Oram had had no choice. He had resorted to disguises and subterfuge to talk to those with whom his fellow sumagi were constantly or intermittently in contact. He had begun by looking into Nishtar. This was not because he did not like Nishtar but because Nishtar was ostensibly the most powerful of the four sumagi whom he was investigating. He was also the most invested in the prophecy. His behaviour had been stranger than ever since the pursuit of the prophecy had possessed him. Though Oram could think of no motive why Nishtar would wish to harm his one-time protégé, he could not excuse Nishtar on those grounds alone.

Finding out Nishtar's whereabouts had proven easier than expected. Nishtar had taken on students as usual, and all accounts had placed him at his school at the time Sumaho was attacked. Though Nishtar was powerful enough to fool his students by creating an illusion of his presence while he was actually somewhere else, Nishtar was too dedicated to his profession to play such tricks on his students. The day Nishtar stopped holding his vocation sacrosanct was the day that all established order would collapse, Oram believed. Therefore, he had been inclined to believe that Nishtar had not been in Maghem when Sumaho was attacked and, therefore, could not have been the perpetrator. He could not be absolutely certain, but where Nishtar was concerned, no one could ever be. He was happy to be as certain as it was possible based on his enquiries.

Oram had then turned his efforts at discovering Alanor's whereabouts at the time of the attack on Sumaho. He had anticipated, and rightly so, that it would be extremely difficult to investigate the movements of one who was constantly on the road and was well-known by the nickname of the Traveller. After travelling far and wide and talking to hundreds of magi, dharvhs and humans, Oram had managed to discover that Alanor had been in Yennthem almost all this time. Unlike Nishtar, Alanor had no clear alibi, but he had been nowhere near any of the portals through which he could have travelled to Maghem to attack Sumaho and then return unseen. Oram had also discovered, quite accidentally, that Alanor was working with Nishtar on the prophecy. He had been travelling extensively in the west, Oram found, though after the attack on Sumaho. He had also made several trips between Drauzern and Nishtar's school. These trips to the human and dharvh kingdoms, Oram surmised, were probably in connection with the prophecy.

What Oram did not understand was why Nishtar and Alanor were carrying on their enquiries secretly. Did they not trust the others? A strange sense of doom passed over Oram at the realisation that Nishtar and Alanor too believed that there was one among them who could not be trusted.

His third quarry had been Vellila. Oram's enquiries had revealed that she had remained in Vittor throughout the time. In fact, on the day that Sumaho had been attacked, she had been advising King Dorstoph on certain matters pertaining to the queen's health. Having concluded his enquiry into Vellila, Oram had turned his attention to Beben.

He had expected to find Beben's famous ship easily but had not. In fact, for a while it had seemed that Beben, too, had disappeared like his mentor, Mesmen. Just when he had begun to wonder whether Beben too had been attacked and whether he should try another transposition of his soul to discover the Navigator's whereabouts, Oram had learnt where Beben was anchored. To his surprise, Beben was anchored in the shallows off the coast of one of the remote uninhabited islands in the far east of Maghem. No one ever travelled there unless it was for reasons that required complete isolation. There was nothing of any interest among those islands except a rumoured portal to Kaitshem that, like every portal to Kaitshem from every other hem, had been closed ages ago. Why would Beben be there? Beben, though he liked to live on his ship rather than on land, was not anti-social. He *had* become very withdrawn since Mesmen's disappearance, and Oram could sympathise with him. Beben was different from most magi in that he had been born a dharvh and was, therefore, short and stout and not charismatic to look at. Not only that, he was also slightly deformed; he was lame in his left leg, and his face was a little lop-sided. His infirmities had added to his lack of self-worth until his discovery of Mesmen's location had shot him into prominence. And all his life, he had been devoted to Mesmen. Her departure without informing him where she was going or why had cut him deep. He had been famous for discovering Mesmen's location at an earlier time when she had purportedly vanished, and his failure to find her this time had instilled a deep sense of failure and shame in his heart despite everyone's efforts to convince him otherwise. He had taken Mesmen's continued absence too personally.

Oram felt sorry for Beben as he stood outside the captain's cabin. With only two days of vernurt left, the weather had turned balmy in most places. Here, upon the open ocean, the climate was lovely. A soothing breeze blew seaward from the island; the rustle of coconut and palm trees swaying in the wind came upon it. The thump of waves gently lapping against the ship sounded relaxing. Yet Oram could not relax. He had never attempted anything so daring! He had visited Nishtar's school but only when the latter had been absent. When he had visited Vellila, she had been present, but Oram had pretended to be there on a friendly visit. Vellila had accepted it as such since she and Oram were on friendly terms. The youngest of the sumagi had not suspected the true purport of his visit. The trip to Beben's ship was a different matter. He had not informed Beben that he was coming to visit, and they were not cordial enough for him to drop in unannounced. So, if he was caught snooping around, he had no excuse.

Finally, Beben exited the cabin and started on his rounds. Oram knew that he had only a few minuras to examine the cabin before Beben returned. As soon as the sounds of the senior magus's footsteps died away, Oram slipped into the cabin and began his search. He had already searched the rest of the ship but had found nothing suspicious. The cabin, he found, had a parlour with two other rooms attached to it. One was a bathroom; a quick peek inside told him that there was nothing to find there. The other was a bedroom. It contained a bunk bed, a cupboard and a stool that also served as a bedside table. Oram quickly checked the cupboard, but it held nothing besides Beben's clothes. Under the bunk was a locked chest. It wasn't hard for Oram to pick the lock. The chest, he found, was filled with strange articles: jars of sand, bones of animals, fantastically shaped colourful shells, precious stones, bottles of muddy water, dried seaweed, beeswax, rope made of human hair, glass globules and prisms, vials of foul smelling stuff, cured paws of various animals, animal horns and hooves both whole and powdered, teeth and claws of carnivores, roots and seeds of different kinds, a skull, strange diagrams and formulae, and scores of bric-a-brac that he had not enough time to go through.

Oram was feeling rather nauseated. He put the chest back where it had been, locking it again, and returned to the parlour. What was Beben up to? If he hadn't known better, he would have concluded that Beben was leaning towards the dark arts. But Beben was a sumagus and would neither need nor want to do so. Then what was he doing with all those weird articles in that chest? Perhaps he had a secret habit of hoarding odd things, and that chest was where he stored them. After all, he must have come across more unusual things in his life than the other land-bound sumagi had. Sometimes people see what their fears and suspicions let them see, he told himself. A searcher full of suspicion would probably find articles in *Oram's cottage* that indicated a leaning towards black magic. Oram was trying to convince himself, but a seed of doubt had been sown in his mind. A feeling of leadenness was settling at the pit of his stomach. All he wanted to do at that moment was to leave the ship and return home. However, he still had the parlour left to search and hardly a couple of minuras in which to do so.

A quick look told him that the parlour was designed as an office for Beben. On two sides of it were large windows that overlooked the waters. Between the windows was a desk on which stood a spyglass, a telescope, a sextant, a compass and several navigational tools. There were navigational charts spread out upon the desk next to these instruments. A thick book sitting crookedly to one side looked like the ship's log. An armchair stood next to the desk. It was moved back now, an indication that Beben did not intend to be gone long. Oram hurriedly looked at the rest of the room. On the walls were some trophies of large fish and other strange oceanic creatures, shelves that held bottled ships, more charts, some books, talismans, other bric-a-brac, and surprisingly, a collection of walking sticks with ornate hilts. A safe was set into one of the walls, and Oram was tempted to look inside. But he had no time. He decided to check the ship's log instead.

He flipped back to the date on which Sumaho had been attacked. The log showed that Beben had been miles away from the headquarters. Oram closed the log. It was almost time for Beben to return. Did he dare open the safe? The temptation was too strong. The safe was locked, but it was not protected too heavily. It took Oram less than half a minura to unlock it. Just as he turned the handle and pulled open the heavy door of the safe, he heard Beben's footsteps coming down the passage leading to the cabin. The Navigator was returning! Oram had no time to check the safe! Quickly closing it shut and relocking it, Oram slipped out, the darkness and his own disguise concealing him from Beben, who was only about twenty feet away. Oram pulled the door to, hoping that he had left everything as he had found it.

He was both happy and disappointed that he hadn't found anything to connect Beben to Sumaho's disappeared memory. Happy because in his heart of hearts, he had wanted none of the sumagi to be proven guilty; disappointed because it meant that the perpetrator was either Mesmen, who was nowhere to be found, or someone else who was extremely powerful but remained unknown to the sumagi. Who knew what the perpetrator's agenda was? In a way, it was a relief to think that the enemy was not one of them. Such an enemy could be faced by the sumagi together. That none of the sumagi had attacked Sumaho should have brought Oram comfort. Yet Oram felt a strange uneasiness.

Beben might not have attacked Sumaho, but he was definitely up to something. Oram had smelled something odd inside the safe, something that had made his stomach churn with fear. The fear had been completely involuntary. Fear was not something that Oram usually subscribed to. He had not had a chance to find the source of that sensation. Had it been something that triggered fear or had it triggered a memory or thought that was the source of fear? Oram wished he could have had time to locate the source. Then he would have known. He also remembered vaguely that one of the navigational charts had looked decidedly strange; it had looked like no land that was known to him and had lines criss-crossing all over it. Oram had not been able to investigate it due to the paucity of time. The inspection of Beben's lair had raised far more questions than it had answered. At the moment, however, Oram's goal was to get off the ship. He waited until Beben had returned to his cabin and had sat back at his desk. Then, swiftly but silently, the Shepherd left the way he had come, melting into the darkness of the night.

Avator was sharpening swords in his smithy when Lekker came running in to inform him that Igrag had sent for him. An annus had passed since the episode with Avita; in all this time, the older lad had avoided him, though never daring to be outrightly rude. Avator knew that Lekker held him and Avita responsible for his plight and hated them for it. It had taken him temporas to recover from the lashing and mondans to get well enough to feel like his former self again. Avator did not feel sorry for him. Lekker had deserved what he had got. Avator closed up the smithy and accompanied Lekker back to Igrag's tent. He noticed that all the scouts and important members of the gang, including Feerdhen, Frengdan, Qually and Lamissur, had been summoned. Evidently, some important mission was underway.

As soon as the last few attendees entered the tent, Igrag began to speak. There was suppressed excitement and urgency in his voice. 'We have received information that a very wealthy caravan is passing through the desert. I have been told that there are litters bearing the royal insignia. Do you understand what this means? It is an opportunity not only to earn good loot but also to gain a rich ransom if we bring the travellers to our camp as guests.'

The word 'guests' brought on a bout of laughter. Avator did not understand what was going on. Were they planning to kidnap kereighes now? And if they brought anyone to the camp, wouldn't they learn of its location? The camp would be compromised. Unless. Unless the plan was that they should never return to tell anyone about it. He felt a little sick. He had not expected such deliberate cruelty from Igrag. But he knew in his heart that it had been naive of him. How well did he know the outlaw captain? Wasn't he imposing his own ideals on a kereighe who was far from ideal? He said nothing as Igrag outlined the plan and assigned responsibilities. The caravan was heavily guarded, and they needed every member to join in the mission. Even the scouts had a bigger role to play this time. Their task was to take charge of the travellers in the litters while the rest of the gang engaged the guards and disarmed the travellers on foot or on horse. The scouts were strictly instructed to refrain from harming the wealthy prisoners. If anyone travelling in the litters fought back, the scouts were to disarm and render him unconscious. On no account were the travellers to be killed or injured.

The plan proceeded like clockwork. The younger lads scouted out the caravan, and the outlaws attacked it from three directions, causing confusion among the guards and splitting them up. In the ensuing panic, another, smaller, group quickly attacked the remaining travellers and disarmed them. Most of them were unarmed servants and aides; the few who had weapons quickly surrendered. Before the guards could realise what was happening, the scouts surrounded the two litters that had been travelling at the centre of the caravan. No one stood up to them. When the guards saw the litters taken, they too gave up.

One of the scouts ordered the kereighes travelling in the two litters to step outside. An elderly eighee emerged from the first litter. Holding her hostage at swordpoint, the scout who had given the order asked her to move away from the litter. Evidently terrified, she did as she was told. No one had emerged from the second litter yet. Assuming that some other elderly kereighee was crouched inside, trembling with fear, Avator pulled aside the coverings of the second litter. He almost gasped with shock upon seeing the second passenger—a young kereighee, about his own age, perhaps an annus or two older, sat inside. And she was beautiful! Not pretty like Avita but truly, classically beautiful with long, dark hair, a pale complexion, sharp features, deep red lips and large black eyes. Those eyes held the most abject terror in them. Her aura, which was a beautiful slate colour, was flickering wildly in response to her agitation. Before Avator could react, some of the other scouts looked inside. A couple of them whistled loudly on seeing the passenger.

'I wonder who this is,' one of them said, standing right in front of her and ignoring the terrified girl.

'Hopefully someone rich,' said another and they burst into laughter. They demanded for her to step outside and threatened to 'ruin her pretty face' if she didn't comply immediately, even though they were not supposed to hurt the travellers in the litters. Still huddled, she disembarked with a grace that made even her captors' breaths catch for a momon. Then they leered obscenely at her as she went to join her elderly companion.

Avator felt disgusted with them. He wanted to kick them. But he stood quietly to one side, saying nothing. He continued to stare at the eighee. Who *was* she? Her clothes reminded Avator of a life that was so far in his past that it seemed like a dream. She definitely belonged to a wealthy family, perhaps even a noble one. Despite being terrorised, she had neither screamed nor tried to run, obviously realising that either would be futile. She looked mutely from one of her captors to another even as they talked about her standing right there. Her eyes met Avator's, and he felt a deep shame rising within him for the first time since he had joined the outlaws. He felt that he could not be party to whatever they had in mind for her. Something buried within him began to stir; he felt an intense desire to help her, to save her. But what could he do? He looked away, unable to face the helpless appeal in her eyes. His gaze fell upon some horses wandering riderless nearby. An idea slowly began to grow in his mind.

He suggested to one of the scouts that they should capture the horses as well. The horses were beautiful, powerful animals. The temptation to own one proved too much for the scouts. Leaving four of the scouts, including Avator, to guard the two prisoners, they chased after the steeds. Igrag and the others had crushed the guards in the meantime and had joined the remaining members of the gang surrounding the caravan. Igrag, too, was surprised to see the young kereighee but said nothing. He addressed the other prisoner.

'Who are you and where are you going?' he demanded.

'Please let us go!' the elderly kereighee begged. 'We will give you all our wealth. Just let us go!'

'You will give me all your wealth in any case,' Igrag sneered. 'But if you do not answer my question, I *will* let you go. Right in the middle of this vast desert, without food or water. Would you like that?'

'No, no!' she pleaded, paling. Avator noticed that the younger kereighee too had paled upon hearing Igrag's threat, but she remained quiet. He could not help admiring her restraint. The older eighee broke down and began to cry. The younger one tried to comfort her. Then she turned to Igrag and said, 'I am the daughter of a noble at the court of King Kerzen. This is my chaperone. We are going to White Mountain to meet with my brother who studies there with the magus Nishtar.'

In spite of the danger and fear, she spoke calmly, not allowing her panic to affect her tone. It took great discipline to achieve that, Avator thought with admiration. It required a certain high level of breeding. She was, he suspected, not from any ordinary noble's family. The name of the magus with whom her brother was purportedly studying also seemed familiar. Where had he heard it before? Oh yes! The magus who had given Avita the dreamcatcher. He had suggested that Avator should go and study with this teacher. Avator hoped that the mention of her family's connection with a magus would impress the outlaws enough to keep them from harming her. Of course, he could not be sure. He stared at the scene unfolding before him with mounting tension, unable to do anything and unable to turn away.

'Thank you for the information,' Igrag said with mocking, elaborate courtesy. 'Now, if you will be kind enough to accompany me and my kereighes back to our humble camp, we will be able to provide you with the hospitality that those of your exalted position deserve.'

The sarcasm was obvious even to the prisoners. Some of the outlaws laughed aloud. The older kereighee whimpered, and the younger one's eyes grew rounder and more terrified. But they had no choice. They were ordered to mount a couple of the horses. Then they were blindfolded and led away by Igrag and a group of the outlaws. The rest stayed behind to take care of the loot and the guards who had been defeated or had surrendered. As he rode away, Igrag gestured for Avator to join him. The young lad gladly obeyed. He grabbed the first horse he could find and mounted it. The horse wasn't particularly pleased to have a new rider, but it was a minura's work for Avator to befriend it. He was glad to be part of the group escorting the prisoners; he did not want to lose sight of the beautiful young kereighee who had looked at him with such pleading eyes. He wanted to know what was happening so that he could help her if the opportunity arose.

The prisoners were blindfolded so that they would not know the path that they were following. When they reached the camp, Igrag said, 'Mordeph, take them to your tent and secure them. If they escape, I will hold *you* responsible.'

Avator was puzzled about the choice of his tent as the prisoner's holding but immediately realised that it was because of Avita, the only eighee in the entire camp. That was why Igrag had asked him to join in escorting the prisoners. Avator and a few of the others led the two kereighees to Avator's tent. The two kereighees were left inside with their hands and feet bound and with orders to Avita and Forsith to keep an eye on them. The prisoners were to be given food and water and all other basic facilities, but they were not to be left free or alone. This suited Avator fine though neither Forsith nor Avita was happy about it. They had no choice but to obey Igrag, they knew, but they were unhappy about the situation. Avita felt really sorry for the prisoners and asked Avator if she could loosen their bonds so that they would be more comfortable. Avator told her that it was in everyone's best interests to adhere to Igrag's orders strictly. Then he exited the tent and returned to his smithy. He needed to think.

He began to hone the idea that the caravan's horses had given him. It was a dangerous one, but there was a slim chance that it might work. He remembered how Miehaf, his master at Nersefan's smithy, had encouraged him to think of an escape plan for himself and his family that had involved horses. While not the same, his plan too involved horses. After a while, he left the smithy and went to the stables. He went straight to Habsolm's stall. The cross-eyed gelding was pleased to see his master.

'Hello, boss! How go things with you? Did you bring me an apple?' he asked cheerfully.

'You are growing fatter every day on apples,' Avator commented with mock disgust and then proceeded to feed one to him.

The horse happily chomped on the apple as he told Avator all the news that he had gathered. The other members of the gang had returned a while ago, along with the new horses, which had been housed in the stables.

'What do you know about the new arrivals?' Avator asked Habsolm quietly.

'Those hoity-toity ponies? They claim to be from the royal stables,' Habsolm said in an injured tone. 'They think they are the cat's whiskers!'

'They obviously know nothing about how superior you really are,' Avator said soothingly. 'What else did they say?'

'They said that if the tough guys—I presume they meant the outlaws—harmed even a hair of the princess's head, they would be ground to dust...'

'Whoa!' Avator interrupted. 'The princess? Did they say *the princess*? Really?'

'Yes, why?' asked Habsolm. 'I thought you would know.'

'No, she said she was the daughter of a noble of the court. That was clever of her.'

'How?'

'Can you imagine how great an opportunity it would be for the outlaws if they could hold the safety of the princess over the king's head? How much power it would give them? They could ask for almost anything they wanted.'

'I'd whistle if I could,' Habsolm said. 'But wouldn't the entire army be looking for them? I mean, the hoity-toity ponies are right about one thing—the outlaws will be ground to dust if the princess comes to harm.'

'Yes,' said Avator thoughtfully. 'And anyone who helps her will be greatly rewarded.'

'What are you thinking?' Habsolm asked. 'I do not like that look on your face.'

Avator grinned. 'Have I told you what a most amazing, spectacular and wonderful horse you are, Habsolm?'

'I know flattery when I hear it,' said Habsolm suspiciously. 'What do you want me to do?'

Avator told him what he wanted him to do. Habsolm wasn't happy about it, but he agreed to do it. A hora later, Avator entered his tent, looking worried and dishevelled. He found Avita sitting close to the two prisoners—who were looking calmer now—and obviously chatting with them. They shut up as soon as he entered. He wondered what Avita had been saying. Nothing that would jeopardise their safety, he hoped. Avita was a kind and generous child, but kindness and generosity could be misplaced qualities in an outlaw camp.

Ignoring the prisoners, Avator said to his sister, 'Habsolm is missing. I have searched everywhere for him inside the camp, but he is nowhere to be found. I think we might have to go outside to look for him. Go and get permission from Igrag. I will search inside the camp one more time, and then join you at his tent.'

Avita, who was fond of the horse, felt worried and immediately sped off to ask Igrag if she could go in search of Habsolm. Avator too left immediately. Forsith wasn't in, so he asked one of the other outlaws to stand guard over the prisoners. Avita found Igrag discussing something with Feerdhen when she reached his tent. He asked her to wait outside while he finished the discussion. Feerdhen left soon after, not even looking at Avita standing there. Igrag called for her to enter. Her face was drawn, and she looked upset.

'Is everything all right, Menithyl?' Igrag asked. He had a soft spot for this shy, pretty little girl who had been dealt such an unfair blow by fate.

'Habsolm is missing,' she said to him. 'And I want to look for him.'

Igrag frowned. Habsolm, he knew, was Mordeph's horse that also pulled the cart. How could a horse be missing? And why was Menithyl asking his permission to look for it?

'Can you explain what has happened?' he asked. 'And where is your brother?'

'He is looking for Habsolm inside the camp. He has already looked once but has not found him.'

This clarified things a little for Igrag. The girl was asking permission to *go outside the camp* to look for the horse. That was not a problem, but he could not, obviously, allow her to go by herself.

'Where is Eronsom?'

'I don't know. I was alone in the tent when Mordeph told me about Habsolm. Eronsom went out when the new horses arrived.'

Igrag remembered now. He had instructed Eronsom to have a look at the new arrivals. He sent one of the outlaws walking outside to find and fetch the horse-wizard. In the meantime, he asked Menithyl to sit down and tried to calm her, assuring her that she could go looking for her horse as soon as Eronsom arrived.

Forsith and Avator arrived almost simultaneously, the former having no idea of what was going on.

'Did you find the horse?' Igrag asked Avator.

'No, but I found someone who saw Habsolm bolting out of the camp about half a hora ago. I found his tracks going south,' answered the unkempt and panting boy.

'What is going on?' Forsith asked, puzzled. Avita told him.

'She came to me to ask permission to go in search of the horse. I have no objection, but she is too young to go wandering alone in the desert. Eronsom, go with her. You are a horse-wizard and you might be able to find the horse more easily.'

'One of the scouts should go with them,' Avator added unexpectedly. 'It is about to get dark, and neither of them is familiar with the territory outside the camp.'

Igrag looked at him suspiciously. 'I suppose you want to be the one to accompany them?' he asked.

'No, I'd rather stay here and guard the prisoners. Send someone else with them,' Avator said matter-of-factly.

Avator's answer took Igrag aback. The boy continued to surprise him when he least expected it. In the end, he sent one of the other scouts with Avita and Forsith to search for Habsolm. Avator returned to the tent alone. The outlaw who had been guarding the prisoners was glad to be relieved. The marauders were getting ready for a celebration in the face of their recent success, and he wanted to be there. Avator often avoided these celebrations where everyone got drunk and wild. Today, he did not even need an excuse; he had the job of guarding the prisoners. The celebrations continued late into the night. Around midnight, when the jubilation was beginning to wind down, and drunken outlaws were beginning to fall asleep, Avator approached Igrag.

Igrag, who was a little less drunk than the others, and still had his wits about him, was surprised to see the lad.

'Are the prisoners secure?' he asked immediately.

'Yes, they are,' Avator said. 'I stationed someone in the tent before leaving. But I had to come. My uncle and my sister have not returned yet. I am worried about them.'

'What? They should have been back a long time ago!' Igrag said.

'That is what worries me. I wish someone could go search of them,' Avator pleaded.

Igrag stared at him, but there was no guile in the boy's eyes. He was genuinely concerned for his family. Igrag was about to order one of the outlaws to go in search of the missing members of Avator's family but stopped short. Each and every one of them was hopelessly drunk. There was not one outlaw whom he could send and expect a fruitful conclusion to the episode.

'I don't think that I can send anyone tonight,' he said apologetically.

Mordeph looked pale and anxious. Igrag felt sorry for the boy. He knew how worried he was about his sister at all times. If they had got lost, or been captured, it would be a terrible blow for the lad.

'If you want, you can go to look for them,' he said generously. He knew that Mordeph was clever enough to find his way around even at night while avoiding capture.

'But what about the prisoners? Who will guard them?' asked Avator, looking torn between two equally important things in his life.

'I will assign someone, don't worry. You go and find your family.'

'May I take one of the horses? It would be faster. And if…if…something has happened…'

'Say no more. Take any horse you want from the stable.' Igrag gestured munificently.

Avator thanked Igrag profusely and left. He went to the stables and took the sturdiest of the new horses. He asked the horse if it could find the guards who had been accompanying the caravan if any of them were still alive. If they weren't, could it find its way to Esvilar? The horse confirmed that it could. It had been trained for battle and could find the remaining soldiers of the guard if it had to. Or travel to Esvilar, where more soldiers were stationed. Avator took this horse and proceeded to leave the camp. Before he left, he returned to his tent, ostensibly to make sure that the prisoners were still secure. He had not spoken a word to them since the morning. He found one of the least drunken outlaws on guard duty. And even that outlaw was too drunk to remain steady on his feet. Avator gave him instructions regarding the prisoners' security and comfort. The outlaw grunted to indicate that he had understood. He did not notice that Avator left a mug of liquor in the tent until well after the lad had gone. He drank it up greedily. What he did not know was that it had been laced with a soporific. Forsith used it on horses who needed amputations. Even if the drink hadn't been tampered with, the outlaw on guard duty would have been asleep soon. But Avator was not taking any chances.

Many of the outlaws saw him trotting out of the camp on horseback in search of his family. Not one saw him return on foot a hora later. They were all lost in a drunken stupor. Those who weren't unconscious were hardly alert enough. The few who were on guard duty along the boundaries of the camp were still reasonably alert, but Avator knew the camp well enough to avoid them. When he reached his tent, he found the outlaw on guard duty fast asleep, his snores filling the tent. The prisoners were completely alert, whether due to their terror or the sleeping guard's snores was hard to tell. He placed a finger on his lips to indicate that they should remain silent. They nodded in understanding. He took a knife off the sleeping guard's belt and cut through the prisoners' ropes. Then, with their help, he dragged the unconscious eighe closer to where they had been sitting and got rid of all signs of his conspiracy. Anyone looking in the tent would think that the guard had fallen asleep too close to the prisoners because of being drunk, and they had managed to free themselves with his knife.

Avator then led the two kereighees out the same way that he had entered the camp. The young kereighee followed him easily, but the elderly one stumbled and bungled and whimpered and sniffled despite Avator's repeated admonitions to keep quiet. A few times, they came close to being caught. However, they managed to avoid capture due to Avator's quick thinking. Finally, they were outside the camp. Avator led them through the dark desert to where he had stationed the horse that he had taken earlier from the stables, all the while erasing signs of their passage behind him. He did such a thorough job that none could have followed their tracks but the very best of trackers, and there were no trackers of such high calibre at the camp. When he reached the horse, he mounted it and told it to throw him off. The horse obeyed without question. Avator fell on the hard sand, bruised and winded. His companions cried out in alarm. It took him a few momons to stand up and catch his breath. He gestured for them to stay quiet. Then he checked himself for injuries. They were bad enough to convince anyone of his accident but not bad enough to be debilitating. He stroked the horse and said, 'Good job, boy!' The horse neighed happily in response.

Then, turning to his companions, Avator said, 'There isn't much time. You must hurry. Mount this horse and let him take you where he will. He can find the remainder of your guard, if any are alive. Or he will take you to the nearest town, which is Esvilar. It is in the north-east, on the coast. The lord of Esvilar—or whoever is in charge at his manor—will give you sanctuary. You must trust your horse to do what is right, and he will protect you. I cannot do any more for you than this. You are on your own henceforth.'

He was about to leave when the princess said, 'Wait!'

Avator turned around, wondering what she wanted to say.

'Thank you for saving us,' she said gratefully. 'I don't know how to repay your debt. But, perhaps, you will take this as a token of my gratitude?'

She took a medallion on a chain from inside her clothing; she had somehow managed to hide it from the outlaws. It was made of pure gold and bore an engraving of a conch shell, the symbol of the royal house of Emense. The workmanship was masterful. It was obviously very valuable.

'This was my grandmother's,' the princess said. 'I hid it when we were attacked. I'd like you to have it.'

'I just did what anyone else in my position would have done,' Avator protested. 'I cannot take such a priceless heirloom from you.'

The princess gave him a strange look like he was joking.

'There were many kereighes in the outlaw camp and all of them were in the same position as you. Yet none of them came to our aid,' she said. 'In fact, they're the reason we need aid. I don't understand why you say that anyone in your position would have done what you did since it is obviously not true. But I am truly grateful, and I would be really happy if you took this,' she insisted.

Avator took the offered gift. 'Thank you,' he said. 'I wish I could make sure that you reached a place of safety, but I cannot and I am sorry for that. I can only wish you good luck and pray that you find safety soon.'

'Thank you, Mordeph,' said the princess, mounting the horse along with her chaperone. She had heard the outlaws address him by that name and had used it, thinking that it would please him.

'My name, my real name, is Avator,' the boy suddenly said. He had not planned on telling his name to the prisoners, but he had been reminded of who he truly was after meeting the princess. For a brief moment, he wanted to be Avator, prince of Lyisl, who stood apart in the crowd of kereighes that the princess had just compare him to, rather than Mordeph, outlaw scout in Igrag's gang. He could not tell her the whole truth, but he could tell her his real name, at least. It was that impulse that made him tell the princess his real name.

'Thank you, Avator,' she said, nodding her head in acknowledgement of his confidence before galloping away.

Avator sighed and set off to find Habsolm. He knew where the horse would be. Exactly where Avator had told him to be. The plan had been for Habsolm to create a meandering track before finally hiding in a canyon to the south of the camp. There were many caves there, and it would take anyone searching for the horse horas to locate him, especially if the horse remained quietly hidden. Avator hoped that he had hidden in the right cave. He also hoped that Forsith and Avita were all right and that they had found the canyon if not the horse. He jogged there as fast as he could. To his utmost relief, he met with them on the way. The scout had managed to track the horse quite well, Forsith told him, although the confusing tracks had delayed them greatly. Avita had become tired and was now riding Habsolm. Avator whispered words of praise into Habsolm's ears on the pretext of checking on his sister. Upon reaching the camp, he first secured Habsolm in the stables and then returned to their tent. The guard was still fast asleep. Avator raised the alarm that the prisoners had escaped.

Within minuras, everyone was up and assembling groggily to check what the matter was. It was close to dawn though it was still very dark. Igrag, who was in a foul mood after being woken up from deep sleep, demanded to know what was going on.

'The prisoners are gone!' declared Avator, looking and sounding shocked and worried. 'I returned just now from the desert and found them missing.'

'What!' thundered Igrag. 'How is it possible?'

He sent for the outlaw who had been on guard duty. He was still not completely awake and had no idea of what had happened. He remembered Avator checking in on him before leaving to find his sister. That was the last thing that he remembered. Igrag rushed to Avator's tent where Avita and Forsith were sitting. They showed Igrag the ropes that had been cut through. The knife that had been used was found under the ropes and was identified as belonging to the guard who had, by then, confessed to falling asleep. Igrag was furious and sent out scouts in every direction to search for the escapees. While everyone scattered to search, Avator went to Igrag's tent. The captain was still terribly angry and was lambasting the outlaw who had been remiss as a guard. Avator waited for Igrag to notice him. As soon as the outlaw captain looked his way, Avator apologised.

'What are you apologising for? You didn't let the prisoners escape, did you?' Igrag snapped.

'No, I lost the horse. It threw me off and ran away,' Avator said.

Igrag had already noticed Avator's injuries. He nodded curtly and dismissed the lad. He had an incompetent guard to punish. Avator returned to his tent, tense at the thought that if the escapees were captured, they might give him up. Igrag was in a bad mood the whole day, and anyone who ran afoul of him got an earful at the very least. Avator made sure to stay out of the captain's way. When evening came and all the scouts returned without news of the escaped prisoners, Avator breathed easy again. He hoped that they had reached safety. He wished he could have done more, but he knew that he couldn't have.

He had been jumpy all day, talking to no one and trying to avoid even his family. None of the other outlaws sensed anything amiss in Avator's behaviour since they were all on edge after the prisoners' escape. Forsith, however, felt suspicious and cornered Avator as soon as he returned from work that evening. Avita wasn't home, Avator noticed. He wondered why. She was usually home by dark.

'I sent her out,' Forsith said, when Avator asked about his sister.

'Why?'

'Because I wanted to talk to you alone.'

Avator sighed. He could guess what this was about but he asked anyway.

'This is about what you have become and what you are up to,' Forsith answered in a hushed tone. They had made it a habit to talk in low voices since they never got the opportunity to talk outside the camp, and there was always a chance that one of the outlaws would overhear them and learn their true identity. Even when they fought, and it was often those days, they spoke in whispers.

'What do you think I have become? What do you think I am up to?' Avator demanded.

'Why are you playing games with these bandits? Don't you know that they are dangerous?' scolded Forsith.

Avator replied coolly, 'I am not playing games. I know what I am doing.'

'Do you? Really?'

'Forsith, earlier you were worried that I had forgotten my true goal in life. You will be glad to know that what I did yesterday was a step towards that.'

'How?'

'I will need an army to achieve my desired end, won't I?'

'And do you intend to employ these outlaws as the first of your soldiers?"

'No, I don't, though that idea isn't without merit. Actually, I took the first step of the simplest way to acquire an army.'

'And what, pray,' demanded Forsith, sounding exasperated, 'is the simplest way to acquire an army?'

'The simplest way to acquire an army,' Avator said nonchalantly, 'is to inherit it.'

He explained to Forsith who the prisoners had been and why he had helped them to escape, concealing the fact that he had felt sorry for them. He did not enjoy making decisions based on emotions and was loath to accept their role in his actions. Even to Forsith, he pretended to be inured to feelings. He outlined his entire plan to Forsith, who listened with mounting incredulity.

'How can you expect to *inherit* Emense's army?' Forsith finally said. 'The kingdom of Emense already has a legitimate heir.'

'He will have to be convinced to abdicate in my favour then, won't he?'

'And why would he do that?'

'A reason must be found—there is always something. No one is without weakness.'

'What is yours? What would *you* give up a throne for?' Forsith challenged him.

Avator thought about his weakness. He bit his lip. He wished he had no weaknesses, but he knew that there was one thing that would have made him give up a throne if he had one.

Aloud he said, 'That is not important and preferably forgotten.'

'And what if the prince of Emense refuses to, as you so eloquently put it, *abdicate in your favour*? What will you do then?'

'There's always death, isn't there?' Avator said coolly.

Forsith was struck dumb. He could think of no answer.

Avita was twenty-eight days short of ten anni when she had the strangest nightmare she had ever had. The dreamcatcher had reduced the incidence of nightmares drastically. It had also given her the ability to stop the ones that did plague her. But this one was entirely different from any nightmare she had ever had. It did not start as a nightmare, though.

In her dream, she found herself sitting by a river in full spate. It had been raining just a short while ago. A light breeze was blowing inland from the river. The air still smelled of wet earth. She drew a deep breath. The waters of the river were clear despite the rain. They were a beautiful green, like a cat's eyes. Or someone else's eyes. Whose? She could not remember. Why could she not remember? Wasn't it someone she knew very well? She sighed and looked at the river. Schools of fish swam just below the surface. Flowers were bobbing upon its tumultuous waters, whirling as they were pulled under by currents and popping back up further downstream. She felt melancholy and tired. She wanted to immerse herself in the cold waters of the river and float away upon its currents. But she couldn't. She was waiting for something. Someone. A boat. Yes, that was it. A boat that would come floating down the river. Someone would arrive by boat, and she was waiting there to meet him. Him? Or her? She could not be sure.

'There you are!' said a voice behind her.

She turned. A tall seleighee was standing a few feet away. She was very fair and was exquisitely beautiful. She had reddish blonde hair and dark green eyes, a heart-shaped face and red lips. It was a face to die for. To kill for. She began to walk towards Avita. The cat-like grace with which she walked was almost mesmerising. She wore a warrior's garments. At her slim waist was a long sword with a hilt shaped like a dragon breathing fire. Her golden aura blazed with power. Who was this radiant seleighee? Avita had never seen her before, yet she felt like she had known her for a long, long time.

'I am not sure, but I think I know you,' Avita said to her.

'Yes, you do know me,' the warrior eighee answered, coming closer.

'Are you the one I am waiting for here on the riverbank?'

'I don't know about that. But I have definitely been waiting for *you*,' she replied. A chill went down Avita's spine. The beautiful seleighee was close to her now. She did not feel comfortable at all. In fact, she suddenly felt afraid. The cool, fragrant breeze suddenly felt cold. Avita shivered. The turbulent waters suddenly looked menacing.

'Why have you been waiting for me?' Avita asked, taking a step back. The ground was muddy and slippery. She balanced herself with difficulty.

'Don't you know?' the eighee asked with a smile. The smile was entrancing, but it looked cold and threatening to Avita.

The eighee was very near now, almost in front of her. Avita tried to move further back, but the slippery mud prevented her retreat. The sky grew dark and gloomy. Avita suddenly remembered that she could control her dreams and tried to change the dream. She could not! She tried to wake up. She could not do that either! She had no control over this dream. The eighee was upon Avita now. She drew the long sword from her belt and aimed it at Avita.

'You can't escape!' she declared and attacked.

Avita screamed and ducked. Her foot slipped, and she fell in the mud. Slipping and sliding, she crawled to the river, pursued by the seleighee bent on killing her. She had barely reached the river when her assailant caught up with her. The warrior swung her sword at Avita's neck, but Avita dived underwater just in the nick of time. The blow missed her. The assailant waded into the waters, roaring with anger, as Avita tried to swim to the opposite bank. The currents dragged her down as Avita swam with all her might. As she reached the other bank, she pulled herself onto dry ground and looked back. To her horror, her assailant had followed close on her heels and was almost at the shore now. Without waiting to see if she was going to continue the pursuit, Avita ran. But she was tired, and her assailant was strong. Soon she was upon Avita again, her sharp sword at the ready. Avita stumbled and fell. Her assailant stood over her and lifted the sword to strike the fatal blow. Avita raised her arms to cover her face and screamed with terror.

Suddenly the earth began to quake violently. The ground shook so hard that the seleighee warrior couldn't remain standing. She lost her balance and fell. The waters of the river undulated in massive waves. Crevices appeared in the ground, swallowing up trees and rocks. Avita tried to stand up. It wasn't easy. She managed to get on all fours and crawl away from the disaster as fast as her arms and legs could carry her. She heard a bloodcurdling scream and turned to find that the earth had swallowed her assailant. She felt no pity for the beautiful eighee who had been trying to kill her only moments before. Suddenly the earth opened up in front of her and she fell too, screaming just as loudly as her attacker had. As she fell down the dark, endless pit, she had a feeling that this had happened before; had she dreamt of falling down an endless pit before or had she actually fallen? Before she could remember, she heard voices calling her name loudly and felt a hand on her shoulder shaking her hard.

Avita woke up with a jolt. She was drenched. At first she thought that it was from her swim in the river. Then she realised that it was sweat. She remembered that it had all been a nightmare. Or had it? She realised that the ground was actually shaking. Forsith sat at her bedside, calling her and jogging her shoulder to wake her.

'It's an earthquake, Avita,' Forsith was saying. 'We need to go out.'

Still groggy and under the influence of her weird dream, Avita managed to stand up. She stumbled outside the tent, half-dragged by Forsith. Avator met them at the mouth of the tent. Outside, all the residents of the camp were coming out of their tents. The earthquake did not last long, though. It stopped within momons of Avita and Forsith coming out of the tent. It hadn't been very violent either. The outlaws stood outside and chatted about their experiences with earthquakes while waiting to see if there would be any aftershocks. When half a hora passed and nothing further happened, everyone went back to sleep. Only Avita could not sleep. She lay awake thinking about her nightmare. Had she dreamt of an earthquake because an earthquake had already been in progress in the real world? Or...

She knew that it was an absurd thought and tried to put it from her mind. But it was a long time before she could fall asleep again. This time, mercifully, she had no dreams.

(14 Patarshem 5010 A.E. to 23 Kawitor 5011 A.E.)

It was the height of somminar and, for temporas, the heat had been rising. It was unusually hot even for somminar. Only thirteen days remained to the new annus, but no one was in a celebratory mood. Everything seemed to have been desiccated by the heat. Plants and trees wilted, animals panted and people felt tired and listless. Nobody was spared the fury of the unprecedented weather; neither beggars who died of heat by the roadside, nor Queen Samiesna who spent the days in a state of semi-consciousness despite being towelled down with chilly water every few minuras by her maids. She was with child, and her condition disturbed the chief healer who was in attendance throughout the day and slept in a chamber in the palace at night. He had been doing everything he could for four days now, yet Samiesna's condition seemed to resist any attempts at revival.

Suddenly a cool breeze began to blow from the east. At first, all were so relieved that they did not notice the direction from which the breeze blew. Nor did they notice the dark clouds that came on the wind, growing stronger with every passing moment. Soon, the sky was covered in menacing black clouds, the sun disappeared and it grew as dark as night. The breeze soon burgeoned into a gale, uprooting trees and tearing away thatched roofs. Thunder roared and streaks of lightning lit up the sky from end to end. Suddenly, with a loud crack, lightning struck the topmost tower of the palace, splitting its iron spire down the middle. And with that came the hailstorm. Balls of ice as large as apples rained down from the skies, driving men and animals before them. Plants were crushed and limbs were broken. Lightning continued to strike repeatedly. Trees and houses burst into flames. When the hailstorm ceased, heavy rain took its place. The torrential downpour lashed doors and windows, which trembled before its fury.

In the midst of this mayhem, Queen Samiesna came to. The healer rushed to check on her and found her strangely refreshed despite her condition.

'Quick!' she ordered him. 'Get ready a large bath of warm, saline water.'

Before the healer could ask why, a convulsion ran through Queen Samiesna and she screamed. She was going into labour! The healer barked clipped orders to the maids and attendants to make sure that everything was in readiness. He sent word to King Amiroth and busied himself with arranging things. He worried that it was going to be a painful, protracted delivery, and he was reminded of Queen

Lamella. The screams of Queen Samiesna and her flaring temper were, however, shockingly in contrast to the other queen's patient forbearance of her troubles. Samiesna threatened to have his head if he did not follow her instructions to the letter. Caught between a rock and a hard place, the healer decided to obey Samiesna.

The situation seemed vaguely familiar to King Amiroth. He was pacing in front of his wife's birthing chamber, his aides and attendants standing at a respectful distance. He wondered whether he had dreamt of this the night before, or at some other time, but he could not recall. It had a strange, dreamlike quality of being real without really happening. He could hear muffled screams and other noises from within the chamber, but the healer had assured him that everything was fine. He could see the terrified looks on the faces of all present, and he wondered what they were afraid of. He vaguely wondered why Lord Aminor was not there. An unreasonable fear gripped his heart—his son would be born dead and his wife would die too! He rushed forward like a madman and was about to fall upon the door of the chamber when a calming thought came to him—someone was coming to save them, an old woman, a maga. She would save them both. But she wanted him to remember something. He shook his head. No, that was not true. That was not *about to* happen; that had *already* happened. That had happened at Amishar's birth. And with that memory, for the first time in an annus, he thought about his first wife and son.

His thoughts were disturbed by the sudden hush that fell upon the birthing chamber. At first, he could not understand why everything had suddenly gone quiet. Then he realised—Queen Samiesna was no longer screaming or moaning. He raised his hand to bang on the door when he heard splashing noises followed by a loud, angry cry. It was the cry of a newborn baby! Relief flooded him, and he stepped back from the door. Within moments, the Healer opened the door and stepped out, beaming. He held a wriggly bundle in his arms.

Holding out the bundle towards the king of Balignor, the healer said, 'My liege, behold your son. He is born healthy and with great force in his lungs. May he live long!'

As he said these words, a shadow fell across his face. It went unnoticed by King Amiroth whose attention was fully absorbed by the ruddy boy wrapped in soft swaddling cloth. The healer was disturbed by what he had seen of the baby's birth. He remained standing outside the chamber, unwilling to step back inside the chamber where he had seen such strange things. His work inside was over. He stood in the corridor, respectfully waiting to be dismissed so that he could return home.

Inside, King Amiroth joined his beautiful wife on the bed, still holding the precious bundle to his chest.

'He is *so* beautiful,' he murmured. Queen Samiesna smiled at him.

'He is your son, my lord,' she responded, laying her head on his shoulder.

'Thank you for giving me this most wonderful gift, my lady,' he said, handing her the baby and taking her face in his hands. 'I promise you that I shall forever cherish him over all that I have.' Samiesna smiled warmly at his words.

'I think he should be called Samaranth,' she suggested.

'Samaranth! That is a powerful name! A name fit for a king's son,' Amiroth said approvingly. He called out for an attendant. One entered the chamber, half fearful.

'Have it declared throughout the land that Queen Samiesna has borne me a son worthy of the house of Elsidar. And have Queen Lamella informed as well,' he ordered.

The attendant was departing when King Amiroth stopped him.

'Wait, I shall inform Queen Lamella myself. You can go and do the rest.'

When the attendant had departed, the king turned to his second wife and said, 'I shall go and inform Queen Lamella of this joyous news. Do not fret, my dear, I shall soon be back at your side.' He beamed with the anticipation of sharing his joy with his first queen and his elder son.

'You are too naive, my lord,' Samiesna said with a sigh.

'What do you mean, my lady?'

'King Amiroth, you have the purest of hearts and the most innocent of minds. Therefore, you believe others as incapable of malice as you are. Not all are as full of generosity and kindness as you,' she said with another sigh and turned her face away.

King Amiroth's face darkened. 'Tell me what you mean by these words, Samiesna,' he demanded.

Standing outside the chamber, the healer heard the exchange. It shook him from head to toe. Not waiting any longer to be dismissed, he rushed as fast as his feet could carry him to Queen Lamella's chamber. He tried his best to remain unobtrusive as he passed through the corridors of the palace to where Queen Lamella and Amishar lived. When he was announced, the queen gave him immediate attendance.

'What brings you here, sir?' she asked him once he was seated and momentarily calm.

'Bad tidings, my queen,' he answered darkly. He shot a glance all round, as if trying to make sure that they would not be overheard. Queen Lamella understood the urgency of the gesture and ordered her only attendant to leave. Declaring that she needed to be examined in private by the healer, she invited him into her inner chamber. She then closed the door and led the healer to a cleverly concealed secret enclosure on one side of her room.

'Tell me fully what has caused you such agitation,' she demanded of the healer. He trembled visibly as he recalled the conversation that he had overheard. He swallowed hard and began to tell Lamella of all that he had witnessed that night.

'Queen Samiesna ordered for a bath of warm, saline water when she went into labour. When it was ready, she stepped into it much against my advice and protestations. What happened next is something I have never witnessed in my life; she gave birth to her child in the water.'

'What do you mean?' exclaimed Lamella.

'Just what I say, my queen. She was submerged in the bath while we stood all round, wondering what was happening. She would not let us near. Suddenly she trembled all over. I tried to rush to her aid, but she shouted at me to stay back. Then she went completely under the water for a long time. All of us present in the chamber were terrified that she might have drowned, but none of us had the courage to approach the bath. Then all of a sudden, she emerged holding the baby in her arms. It was a beautiful baby, to be sure, and wonderfully healthy, but how it was born underwater I cannot say. I have never in my life seen anything like it!' The healer paused, unsure of how Lamella was going to react to this news.

'Please continue,' Lamella said softly.

The healer continued to tell her how Samiesna had threatened all witnesses to keep quiet on pain of death. He repeated, as closely as he could, the exchange between King Amiroth and Queen Samiesna following the king's introduction to his newborn son.

'It ended with him promising that you and Prince Amishar are never to go near the mother and child. I believe this will be formally conveyed to you soon enough. She also managed to convince him that her life and her son's life would be endangered if Prince Amishar ever became king.' Here the healer stopped. He could not bring himself to utter the terrible promise that the king of Balignor had made to the mother of his newborn son.

'What did King Amiroth say?' Queen Lamella asked, knowing the answer in her heart but wanting to hear it said.

The healer whimpered, 'He promised her that Samaranth, her son, will be his heir, and will become king after him.'

Lamella was silent when she heard these words. She closed her eyes and sat without uttering a word. Minuras passed as the two figures remained where they were in the tiny chamber. Finally, the queen opened her eyes and stood up. The healer stood up too, but she indicated to him to remain seated.

'Wait here,' she ordered, moving towards the chamber door. In her voice was a determination and authority that the healer had never heard before.

When she returned after a hora, she carried in her hands a heavy bag and a letter sealed with her personal emblem.

'Take these,' she said to the healer. 'You have lost your son for me and Amishar; I will not have you lose your life for us too. I know you are alone in the world now. Therefore, I propose a course of action which shall prove to be fruitful for both of us. This bag contains enough coins of silver and copper to enable you to safely and expeditiously make the journey I ask you to undertake. This letter is for my brother, Prince Feyanor of Ashperth. You will depart immediately and journey to Ontar. You will give this letter to my brother. Take care that it does not fall into the hands of anyone else. He will know what to do once he reads it. Be assured that your loyalty will not remain unrewarded. You have risked your life to help me; I shall forever be grateful to you.'

Amishar's first instinct on learning of his baby brother's birth was to rush to see him. After a very long time, he felt excited about something. He imagined having someone to play with, someone who would look up to him; he wanted to teach his brother everything he knew; he would fight all the bullies who bothered his kid brother. However, before he could leave his chambers, he was summoned by his mother. He skipped over to her chamber, but his excitement died the moment he saw Lamella. She looked as pale as if she had seen a ghost.

'What is it, Mother?' Amishar asked, rushing to take her hand. 'Are you feeling ill?'

'There is news about your...about your father. He has had another son,' Lamella announced in a voice laden with pain and uncertainty.

'Yes, I heard,' said Amishar, wondering why she was upset at the news. 'Is everything all right with him?'

Lamella cast him a sharp look that made Amishar flinch. His mother continued in a cold voice, 'Yes, everything is all right with him. But we have been forbidden from ever going near him or his mother. I wanted to tell you before you landed yourself in trouble through your exuberant joy at becoming a big brother.'

Lamella's sharp tone hurt Amishar more than his father's prohibition. His heart plummeted as much as it had soared just a few minuras ago. He returned to his chamber, crushed.

The next day, he went to meet Mizu and gave him the news. Mizu was cleaning the stables and listened as he worked. Proclamations had been made in all the towns and villages of Balignor and Durnum, being the nearest to the capital, had been the first to receive news of the birth of Prince Samaranth. Misa had heard the news in the village, and Mizu had heard from her of the birth of the second prince of Balignor. Amishar's news came as no surprise to him. What did surprise him was the king's prohibition. Why would King Amiroth forbid Amishar from going near his brother? It was bizarre! More bizarre than anything else that had happened since the king's return from the expedition to the dharvh lands. He could not help remembering his mother's grim expression at the time of giving him the news about Amishar's younger brother.

'Why would King Amiroth stop you from going near your brother?' he asked aloud, unable to stay quiet at the injustice.

'I guess, I can't blame him,' Amishar concluded bitterly.

'Blame your brother? Of course not! He is a baby.'

'No, I meant my father. I can't blame him for forbidding me from going near the baby.'

'Why?' asked Mizu, surprised. If anyone was to blame, he felt, it was King Amiroth.

'It's the curse of Rogran. He's afraid of it.'

'What's the curse of Rogran?' Mizu asked.

'It's a curse that runs in our family,' explained Amishar. 'Because of this curse, brothers tend to end up killing brothers. I guess Father is afraid that I might harm Samaranth because of the curse. That's why he does not want me to go near him.'

As a rule, Mizu never said a word to Amishar regarding his family's situation to avoid causing his friend pain and humiliation. But the news that King Amiroth had forbidden Amishar from seeing his little brother for fear of a curse felt too cruel to him. 'I don't believe that just because there is a curse, you will inevitably hurt your brother. I can't imagine you wanting to harm the baby,' Mizu said vehemently before he could stop himself.

'This curse is too strong,' Amishar said mournfully. 'It might make me harm Samaranth whether I want to or not. Faced with such a forceful compulsion, one doesn't have a choice.'

'You *always* have a choice! Always have had—all your life.' The words escaped Mizu unbidden.

Amishar looked at him in surprise. He had never heard Mizu speak like this, especially since the words seemed somehow disconnected to what they had been talking about. Mizu was himself surprised. He did not know where those heated words had come from or what he had meant by them. It was almost as if someone else had spoken using his voice! He hastily apologised, saying that he did not know what had suddenly overcome him.

'It doesn't matter,' Amishar said with a shrug. 'Besides, I probably wouldn't have liked the baby anyway. I bet he's ugly and ill-tempered and that everyone will hate him!'

Mizu said nothing in reply, partly unsure of how to comfort Amishar and partly still shaken by the uncharacteristic and incongruous words he had uttered.

On the day of his tenth birthday, Mizu had a visitor unexpectedly early in the morning. Although he had expected Amishar to visit him that day, he had not expected the prince so soon after sunrise. The two friends wished each other a happy birthday and then went down to the river to fish. Misa allowed him to skip his chores since it was his birthday and Amishar looked like he could do with Mizu's company. She wished Amishar and blessed him before the two boys were left to their devices. As they sat upon the riverbank, Amishar was unusually quiet though Mizu was in a cheerful mood.

'What's wrong?' he asked Amishar, though he suspected it had to do with the prince's parents.

'Nothing,' replied Amishar at first. Then, in an unprecedented burst of self-revelation, he said, 'I wish mother would not cry all the time! I wouldn't dislike staying in the palace so much then.'

'You can't blame her,' Mizu responded sympathetically. 'She has been treated so unfairly. Now she has no one except you.'

Amishar nodded. 'I wish Father had never gone on that stupid expedition, that he had never married Samiesna, that Samaranth had never been born,' he said morosely. 'I never wanted a brother.'

'But you have one now, whether you like it or not,' said Mizu. Then, to change the subject he said, 'I have a gift for you. It's at the house. Let's go.'

But Amishar was in no mood to go anywhere. He liked the quiet at the riverside. He took a knife from his belt. It was one of the pair that his uncle had given him. He offered it to Mizu.

'Here, this is your gift. It's a hunting knife. My uncle Feyanor gave it to me when he visited. It's one of a pair. I want you to have it. That way, we will both think about each other always.'

'It's beautiful!' Mizu said, taking it into his hands. He had never seen anything so beautiful except his mother's swords. 'It must be priceless! I can't take it.'

He tried to return it, but Amishar would not hear of it. 'Of course you can take it! Haven't I told you before, whatever is mine is yours?'

'Yes, you have, but this must be so valuable!'

'So what? You are my best friend. In fact, you are closer to me than even my own brother! You can take this without feeling bad.'

Mizu was speechless. He suddenly hugged Amishar fervently. 'Thank you so very much,' he declared with feeling. 'Now you must come and see your gift.' He almost dragged Amishar back to the house. He carefully withdrew something long and narrow wrapped up in layers of cloth from under the bed and handed it to Amishar.

'What is it?' asked Amishar.

'Open it and see,' responded Mizu.

Amishar carefully unwrapped the gift. It was a long bow of ash wood; it was taller than him and had been carefully polished. He tried lifting it. It was strong but bendy at the same time. It was a little heavy, though. In time, as he grew older, it would be perfect for him.

'It's wonderful!' he declared. 'Thank you so, so much!'

'I made it myself,' Mizu said shyly.

It was Amishar's turn to be speechless with gratitude. He knew how busy Mizu was as the only help to his mother. Yet he had found time to learn the craft of making bows and had made one for him. He could not recall the last time someone had taken such pains to do something for him.

'You are dearer to me than any brother,' he said to Mizu. 'We could have been brothers. We should have been brothers!'

'Yes, we could,' Mizu agreed, still overwhelmed by the priceless gift that Amishar had given him.

'Then let us be brothers!' Amishar said, leaping up excitedly. 'Then I won't feel bad about having a brother that I don't like. Because I'll also have a brother that I like.'

'But how can we *become* brothers?' asked Mizu, puzzled.

'We'll make a blood pact,' announced Amishar. He had heard of blood pacts in his teachers' stories and had always been curious about them. He had hoped that he could make one someday; they had held such powerful bonds in the tales. 'Do you know what a blood pact is?'

'Yes,' said Mizu, nodding, unsure how he knew about blood pacts; he was certain that his mother had never told him about them. He had the strange feeling that he had had this same conversation before. He could not recall very well when or with whom. Or maybe he had dreamt it. He had such strange dreams sometimes! He suddenly did not feel at all inclined to make a blood pact. It would end badly, he felt sure. Yet he could not refuse Amishar, having once agreed to enter into the pact. He hoped that the feeling in his heart was a false warning.

The boys wrote on a piece of parchment: 'Mizu and Amishar are not just friends but also brothers from this day forth.' Then they cut their fingers, collecting the blood in a single bowl. Both boys then signed the parchment with the mingled blood, Amishar enthusiastically and Mizu with misgivings, and put the date below. Then they buried it under the tree from which Amishar had fallen into the river on the day that the two boys had first met.

'It is done!' announced Amishar, satisfied. 'We are now brothers!'

'Yes,' agreed Mizu, the sense of doom now stronger over him than before. 'We are now brothers!'

Chapter 60

POSTERITY

(1 Ach 5010 A.E.)

The first day of the Ach, the Yestirach, was the day of Remembrance. Everyone remembered the annus gone by, their ancestors and kin and friends, the people who had come into and gone from their lives, and all the good and the bad that had happened to them. Two old men stood just beyond the dharvhish camp outside Patrisha, remembering the message that had brought them there. The two stood in the dark shadows of trees as they watched the dharvhish soldiers lighting torches and cooking fires, setting up watches and patrols, cleaning their gear, feeding the strange birds that accompanied them or just mulling about, chatting. Though both of them were tall, one was lean while the other was broad. They watched quietly for a while. Then the lean one spoke. He had a stern countenance, intense eyes and a white beard lining his firm jawline. He radiated authority.

'Thank you for coming, Alanor,' he said. 'I wasn't sure that you would want to.'

'Are you joking? I wouldn't have missed this opportunity at any cost!' replied Alanor.

Alanor had been in Ghrangghirm when Nishtar had turned up at his camp on the second of Patarshem, looking excited beyond words. He had informed Alanor that Augurk had found Patrisha over two mondans ago and that he was going there. When asked why he had not told Alanor earlier, Nishtar had answered that it was too important a piece of news to be conveyed by any medium except in person, and he had not been able to leave earlier due to his commitment towards his students. He had now sent them off on their annual task and had immediately travelled to find Alanor. Alanor had been annoyed at being kept in the dark for so long after all that he had done to help Nishtar and had wondered why the other sumagus now wanted to take him along. But his curiosity about the fabled city had been too strong to keep him away.

The two had travelled as fast as possible and had reached Patrisha on Yestirach afternoon. Nishtar had seemed restive all the way, perhaps at having to travel like an ordinary mortal for a change. Alanor sometimes envied Nishtar his ability to travel using the portals between Yennthem and Maghem in a way that no one else could, which allowed the erstwhile leader of the sumagi to traverse thousands of miles in a matter of days. Alanor was known as the Traveller because of his ability to travel long distances in shorter than normal durations. But he still travelled on foot,

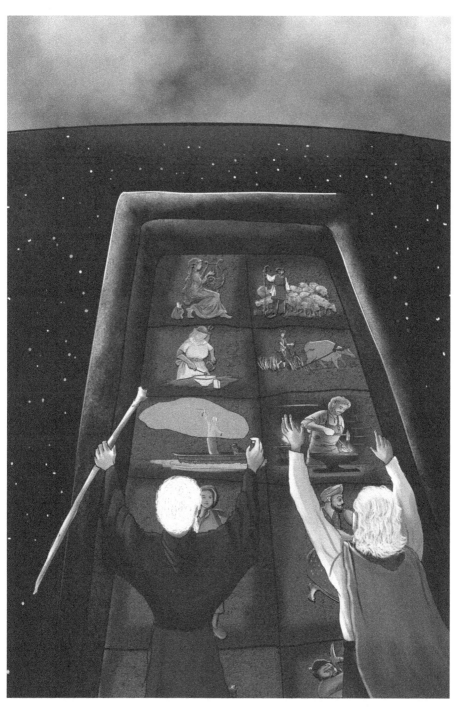

Both Alanor and Nishtar tried their best, using the utmost of their abilities, singly and in concert, but the gates of the City of Stone remained shut, mocking their efforts.

like most mortals. He had not managed to utilise his powers as a magus to enhance the speed of his travelling as Nishtar had. So, they had travelled at Alanor's pace, and this had secretly irked Nishtar though he had not complained aloud.

The two waited until it was dark enough to avoid being noticed by the dharvhs in the vicinity. Then they spread an illusion over themselves to make themselves look like dharvhs. It was not very difficult to enter the dharvh camp in this disguise. Whenever they encountered any guards, they befuddled the soldier slightly into thinking that the two had every right to be there. They passed through the camp and on towards the city of stone that loomed large just beyond. Taking care not to be seen, the two sumagi walked around the walled city while Nishtar informed Alanor of what Augurk had written about it. Nishtar had assumed that Augurk had been exaggerating when he had claimed that it was impossible to enter the city. He now found it to be the truth. Both Alanor and Nishtar tried their best, using the utmost of their abilities, singly and in concert, but the gates of the City of Stone remained shut, mocking their efforts. They had no choice but to give up. Nishtar stood frowning.

'It's no use. We can't open these gates, and there is no other point of entry,' Alanor remarked, sitting down. He was feeling exhausted.

'Yes, exactly,' mumbled Nishtar thoughtfully. 'Then how did the rauz know?'

'What?' asked Alanor from the ground. 'What did the rauz know?'

'Augurk told me that the city is completely empty except for several thousand scary looking soldiers of stone. If he could not enter, how did he know? And if he did not know, why would he tell me so? He wouldn't dare to lie to me about this. Therefore, he *did* enter the city, and he *did* see those soldiers for himself. The question is how did he do it?'

'Why don't you ask him? He's in the camp, close at hand. It will be interesting to hear everything from the horse's mouth, won't it?' asked Alanor, knowing the answer, the real answer. Nishtar liked to tell, not to ask. He liked to be seen as one who had all the answers. Asking Augurk how he had entered the city would violate both these tenets of Nishtar's life. Alanor was beginning to feel a little tired of Nishtar's strange ways. Nishtar's silence over the discovery of Patrisha still rankled. As did his indirect ways of dealing with the rauz. Nishtar could have, Alanor thought, dealt with the whole matter much more reasonably, agreeably and helpfully, not putting Augurk and the dharvhs through so much pain and trouble.

'So what do we do now?' he asked when Nishtar did not reply to his previous question.

'We go into the camp in disguise, chat up the soldiers and find out more,' Nishtar replied.

They returned to the camp disguised as dharvh soldiers of Ghrangghirm and joined a group of four who were sitting around a cooking fire, roasting wild fowl. The sumagi fuddled the soldiers' minds just enough to make them unsuspicious of two complete strangers. The soldiers invited the newcomers to join in their meal. Alanor and Nishtar readily agreed.

They talked about life at the camp for a while. Then Nishtar guided the conversation towards the expedition for the stone city.

'What odd creatures those birds are!' he declared, pointing towards the autruches.

'Yes, we saw these in Orbhz for the first time in our lives,' said one of the dharvhs, a fellow with a bald pate. 'Rauzoon Valhazar procured them from somewhere. The rauz and the first group that came here travelled on these birds.'

'Yes, we did,' affirmed another one of the group, a dharvh with a red beard. He then launched into a narration of their adventures on the way to the city. Both sumagi found much of interest in the tale, especially the actions of Rauzoon Valhazar and the strange human boy who had accompanied them.

Nishtar knew who they were talking about, but Alanor did not. He asked questions about this boy. When their companions cast them odd looks, he further befuddled their minds to make them think that they had just travelled down from Drauzern with messages from Angbruk, so they had no idea about what had happened on the expedition. This caused the soldiers to launch into more details, right from the beginning of the expedition till their rescue by Valhazar.

'Where did this *human* come to Ghrangghirm from?' Alanor asked. 'Did he come with the king from the west?' Alanor had been rather disappointed when Augurk had chosen Amiroth to lead the expedition but had been utterly taken aback when the king of Balignor had voided his agreement and returned home midway. He had spent the last annus in the western kingdoms, trying to discover what had happened. What he had uncovered had disturbed him greatly. He had decided to shift his focus to the dharvh kingdoms to take his mind off the sinister turn of events that had befallen Balignor. He had heard some of the rumours surrounding the expedition to Patrisha that the soldiers now confirmed. Of course, most of the tales had changed in the telling; some were enhanced, some diminished and others completely altered beyond recognition. When he had heard about the mysterious human boy who could perform amazing feats, he had chalked it up to embellishment. Now his interest was rekindled.

'No, he did not come with the human king from the west. I don't know where he came from. He just turned up one night,' replied Bald Pate.

'But why did Rauz Augurk trust him enough to bring him along, especially after he had already been betrayed by a human once?' said Alanor, pretending to be musing aloud.

'Because he was the only one who knew this place,' said Red Beard, giving his dim-witted companion a disdainful look.

'He sure was a strange one,' said a third dharvh from the group, one with a yellow cap. 'He hardly ever talked to anyone except the rauz and, later, Rauzoon Valhazar. And he never grew tired. And he could fight like ten dharvhs.' His tone made it seem like an accusation rather than a compliment.

'That can't be true!' declared Nishtar.

'Yes, it is true!' Red Beard insisted. 'And he helped Rauzoon Valhazar kill the Death Worm.'

'Some of the soldiers have been saying that he could fly,' said Yellow Cap, looking at Red Beard warily, 'though I don't believe it. No human can fly!'

'I'd swear by my beard that he could fly!' roared Red Beard, making a fist and turning as read as his beard at the insinuation that he was a liar.

'Calm down, both of you,' interjected Bald Pate. 'I have heard from several dharvhs that he could fly and that he needed neither food nor water, that he was swifter than a sandstorm and stronger than a dragon,' he continued, not happy at being sidelined by his two companions. He insisted that their fourth companion could support his claim, but when the assembled group looked towards this fourth dharvh, a soldier with a beaked nose, they found that he had already fallen asleep.

Alanor and Nishtar ate with the four dharvhs. Beaked Nose awoke just in time to eat. While they ate, the discussion continued. Alanor noticed that Nishtar was suddenly showing a great deal of interest in the things that the human boy had done or purportedly done, although he had shown little interest at first. He said nothing, though. Later on, they again sneaked out of the camp, having learnt all that there was to learn from the four soldiers. Nishtar was deep in thought, so Alanor walked by his side silently. They returned to the firmly closed gates of Patrisha. Nishtar stood staring at them, as if trying to open them through sheer will power. Then a smile spread upon his lips.

'I know how Augurk entered the city,' he declared.

'How?' asked Alanor.

'Before I tell you that, you must tell me what you know about Amiroth's betrayal and how you know about it.'

Alanor, though not happy to be treated so patronisingly, kept calm. He told Nishtar what he had been doing for the past annus. However, he said nothing about how he had hoped for Feyanor to be chosen to lead the expedition.

'Your turn now,' Alanor said to Nishtar when he had finished. 'How did Augurk enter the city?'

'It was the human boy who led him here. He could fly. And he was strong enough to lift Augurk. He must have carried the rauz inside the city,' Nishtar answered.

'Do you believe the fantastic stories that the soldiers are telling?' Alanor asked, surprised.

'Yes,' Nishtar answered without explanation.

Alanor was about to ask his companion why he believed those tales when several ideas fell into place in his mind all at once and formed a complete picture that explained Nishtar's unusual behaviour that night regarding the mysterious human boy who had brought Augurk to Patrisha.

'Why are you so interested in that boy?' Alanor asked, knowing the answer but testing Nishtar.

'Because I know about him and his abilities. Have known for some time,' Nishtar answered without looking at Alanor.

'Who is he?' Alanor demanded.

'A student of mine,' Nishtar answered evasively.

'The one that you kept hidden in your cave?'

Nishtar did not reply.

'Who is he?' Alanor asked again.

'I told you, he is a student of mine,' snapped Nishtar, clearly unwilling to discuss the matter further.

But Alanor was not intimidated. If half the stories that he had heard from the dharvhs about the boy were true, then he was dangerous to say the least. No one seemed to know anything about his identity at the same time as acknowledging that he was lethal. That Nishtar knew about him and wanted to protect his identity made Alanor more anxious.

'That's not what I asked,' Alanor retorted, 'and you know that. What is his identity? Where is he from? How does he have such unique abilities? Why are you protecting him?'

Nishtar glared at Alanor. For a moment, Alanor thought that Nishtar was going to attack him. He wondered who would emerge victorious if the two of them fought. They had both been warriors and were powerful sumagi; it was hard to say what the outcome would be. But he held Nishtar's gaze, and Nishtar sighed and gave in.

'That boy,' he said, 'is Eamilus. He is everything that the stories say. He is stronger, faster and hardier and has far acuter senses than any mortal in Yennthem.

He can fly, and he is highly intelligent. He has very sharp instincts and an equally courageous heart. He is noble and kind, stubborn and ferocious in equal measure. He is also only half-human. He has mastered the ability to control the non-human side of him—I taught him that. However, since leaving me, he seems to have acquired many more skills, including how to fight. You are right in worrying; he is probably the most dangerous being alive in Yennthem today.'

'What is the non-human side of him?' Alanor asked, a cold suspicion rising in his heart.

'Kocovus,' answered Nishtar, pain evident in his eyes and his voice. He looked suddenly like a tired old man clinging desperately to his failing memories.

'Why do you protect him if you know how dangerous he is?' demanded Alanor, feeling sorry for Nishtar but suspecting that the mystery went deeper than what Nishtar had revealed so far. No mere student could have such a hold upon a sumagus like Nishtar, he was certain.

'I protect him because he is the last hope of the East,' said Nishtar, overcoming his moment of weakness and recovering his proud mien. 'The forces of Vynobhem have overwhelmed the Shadow Lands. The rest of Yennthem pays no heed to it, unaware and uncaring. They think that they are safe from the vynobnie who have infested eastern Elthrusia because the Lyudzbradh stands between it and the rest of the world. They believe that it is a barrier that will stop the vynobnie from spilling over. They have no idea how foolish their belief is. The vynobnie will invariably cross the Lyudzbradh and make inroads into the west sooner or later. And from there, they will spread to every part of Yennthem. King Amiroth's story is a wonderful example of their new incursive tactics. The vynobnie have always wanted to conquer Yennthem. When the final attack comes, I suspect that it will come from the East, where the vynobnie, the servants of Zavak, already have a stronghold. If there is anyone who can delay the inevitable, if not prevent it, then it is this boy Eamilus!'

Alanor was quiet. He had known that the vynobnie had been spreading their reign in the East but had had no idea how serious the threat was.

'He is also,' Nishtar added in a voice leaden with uncharacteristic sadness, 'the elder son of King Eamarilus of Haalzona, and possibly the last of the House of Maheschom.'

Alanor finally understood Nishtar's odd attitude towards Eamilus. He felt sorry for Nishtar. Trying to lighten the mood, he commented, 'And I thought that *my* descendants were a pain in the neck!'

But Nishtar did not respond. He continued to gaze at the stony gates of Patrisha, as silent and forbidding as the city that had defeated their efforts to enter. It stood high and cold, mocking them in the bright moonlight. Alanor fell quiet too. They stood there side by side, thinking of all those who had come after them and were gone from this earth for diuras now. They remembered how it had felt to lose their near and dear ones—their children, their grandchildren, their great-grandchildren—until those that remained could hardly trace their lineages to them and yet could exert a strange pull upon their affections quite unexpectedly. Posterity, Alanor thought with a sigh, was a blessing and a curse.

ASTORETH AND ZAVAK
(4 A.N.)

Zavak stood in front of the low mud building that was an anomaly in Vynobhem, whose residents hardly bothered to construct any dwellings. They preferred to live in nature as they could, eating what and when they could and following no rules save their instincts and the desires of their hearts. There were as many races of vynobnie that were intelligent as there were of vynobnie who were hardly better than animals. Then there were the true monsters. None of them bothered with any vestige of civilised life; they were impossible to organise or discipline. Sometimes, they lived and functioned as a group with a nominal leader whose authority lasted only as long as he could prove himself stronger than the others. No one had ever imagined that it was possible to make these vynobnie work together as an army. That was why no one had ever considered them as a real threat. Yes, they were dangerous and they were strong, but they were also solitary monsters that could be brought down without too much effort. That had been the popular, and accurate, opinion of vynobnie.

But Zavak had changed all that. He had come to Vynobhem with a mission that he was on the verge of completing. He had systematically brought each of the scores of races of creatures and beings in Vynobhem under his control using wile, reward, magic or brute force as necessary. He had overcome their resistance and had beaten them again and again until they had been compelled to accept him not only as greater than any vynobin but also as their master. He had forced them to relinquish their established lifestyles and had forged them together as an army. They now answered to his call and were ready to march into battle at a signal from him. It had taken great sacrifices, even converting himself into something akin to an undead creature, a monster. He had known what his ambition would entail when he had set upon the task of becoming the ruler of all Vynobhem. A task that was now complete except for one last obstacle. There was one last vynobin that stood in his way—the one who was nominally the lord of the hem, the one who lived in the building in front of him.

He smiled as he thought about his enemy. He was a unique being: there were no others of his race on Vynobhem or elsewhere. He could look like any creature he wanted to. He could fight with weapons or through the use of powerful sorcery, for he was a master at both. He was a creature of light and energy, a being whose core was made up of the life force of his victims. He fed not on their flesh or their blood but on the very consciousness that made them exist. None knew where or how or when he had come into existence. He had always been and, if the vynobnie were to be believed, always would. He was undefeatable. No weapon existed, it was said, that could wound him, for he was not flesh and blood. He was a pillar of light that could reach out and melt one's flesh from one's bones in an instant. He was a tower of force that could suck one's soul out of one's body with a click of his fingers. He could vapourise his enemies into the tiniest of particles of dust. Even the most dangerous vynobin was terrified of him.

But Zavak was not. There was no one in existence that terrified him. This opponent would be infinitely more difficult to conquer than any other he had ever faced, but Zavak knew what to do. He stood in front of the dwelling that was called Red House, perhaps because of the colour of the clay of which it was built, and issued a challenge.

'*I am Zavak, and I declare myself the new Lord of Vynobhem. If you have any morsel of self-respect, you will come out and fight me. Or, you could crawl out and accept me as your master, and maybe, just maybe, I will spare your life!*'

No response came from within and Zavak wondered what the being inside was up to. He was cunning beyond words, Zavak knew. The longer he tarried, the greater would be the opportunity for his enemy to prepare himself. Without waiting any longer, Zavak attacked. He broke down the door of the hut with a kick. He would not enter the tenement; who knew what booby traps were waiting to rip him apart! He would force his enemy to meet him outside on open ground. Almost immediately, a blast of light came from within and knocked him on his back. Any other mortal would have been turned to ashes immediately, but Zavak merely grimaced. He stood up, brushed the soot off his clothes and returned to the task of destroying Red House.

At a sign from him, several hrenks picked up boulders the size of elephants and threw them at Red House. It was sturdily built and not merely of clay and wood as it appeared to be; magic ran in every beam and rafter of the house. The blows that would have crushed the sturdiest of buildings to dust merely dented and scratched Red House. The hrenks continued to batter the house with boulders and massive iron maces while Zavak stood patiently by. Suddenly a bolt of light emerged out of a hole that one of the hrenks had managed to make in the roof and hit him. He bawled and, dropping the boulder he was carrying, attacked the house with his bare hands. As soon as he touched the house, he burst into flames and was turned to ashes in no time at all. Seeing this, the other hrenks drew back, hesitating. Zavak stepped forward and touched the wall of the mud house.

Immediately, flames enveloped Zavak. But he did not burn. He stood there, surrounded by flames, looking as comfortable as a crab on a sea-beach. The fire burned fiercely but did not affect him. When it had almost burned out, Zavak turned it onto the house. Red House was now under attack from the very fire that had protected it before. The walls flared up and the roof burst into cinders in a matter of minuras. In no more than a quarter of a hora, the entire Red House had been razed. Zavak laughed loudly as the hrenks cheered mutedly. They were scared of their master but also of the being that dwelt within Red House. He was sure to be angry now. There was no saying what he would do.

As the smoke cleared, a figure was visible among the mounds of ashes. He was tall and looked just like Zavak. However, fire blazed from his eyes, his nostrils and his mouth as he roared at Zavak in anger. The one-time prince of Effine stood his ground, unafraid. He drew Zyimmiron and waited for his adversary to pounce. When the erstwhile resident of Red House attacked, it was with a ferocity and passion that Zavak could not have imagined. Though he managed to foil his assailant, Zavak began to fall back under the tempestuous attack. The energy being seemed to have gone insane with rage and sorrow. He attacked Zavak with multiple weapons at once, holding them in multiple hands that emerged from his sides. Zavak was hard put to fight all his arms at once. Had Zyimmiron been an ordinary sword, Zavak would have succumbed to the attack within momons. The hrenks stood by, unable to distinguish between the two and so unable to come to Zavak's aid.

The two fought for long minuras, and gradually Zavak began to gain. He used his powers to bend his opponent's weapons to his will. Realising that his own weapons were going to turn on him, the energy being discarded them and focussed on using his innate power of light and fire to destroy Zavak. This was exactly what Zavak had been hoping for. As soon as the Lord of Red House dispensed with his weapons, Zavak grabbed him in his arms. The being tried to free himself, but there was no way out of the vice-like grip of the master magus. He tried to incinerate Zavak, but Zavak was stronger and bent his fire back upon him. He screamed in agony as Zavak slowly crushed him and burned him at the same time.

'Surrender and I will spare you!' declared Zavak. 'Or continue to struggle and give me the great pleasure of destroying you.'

For a while more, the being continued to struggle, hoping against hope that he could prevail over his opponent, but it was not to be. On the verge of destruction, he gasped, 'I surrender! Spare me!'

But Zavak would not let go of him so easily.

'Accept that I am your master from this day forth and that you shall do my bidding.'

'I accept that you are my master, and I will do whatever you say,' he gasped again, now beginning to flicker like a dying lamp.

'Then,' ordered Zavak, 'relinquish all your life force, retaining only enough to keep you alive.'

The being agreed unhappily. He had no choice. It was either that or annihilation. He had no idea how Zavak knew so much about him or how he had learnt the secrets to overcoming him, but he knew that he was defeated. He knew that he would have to do as Zavak demanded. Zavak whistled and a glass ball floated out of his pocket. It was small, the size of an egg. Zavak loosened his hold on the being just enough to allow him to touch the floating ball. Instantly, electricity seemed to flow through the being and into the ball, making it glow as bright as the sun. His life force continued to pour into the magical sphere until he diminished and remained a mere shadow of his former self. He still looked like Zavak, though, since the loss of his energy had made it impossible for him to transform into any other form.

'Good,' said Zavak, releasing his prisoner and taking charge of the magical ball. The being who had been full of fire slumped upon the ground, a weak, pathetic figure.

'Now you have bound yourself to me by your own word,' continued Zavak, 'and must do as I say.'

'What do you want me to do?' the defeated being asked.

'I'd like to hear a little more humility in your voice to begin with,' Zavak remarked, his voice dripping with hostility.

'What would you like me to do, Master?' the being corrected himself. It took every ounce of his strength to accept such humiliation. He was defeated, but he did not have to like it. His heart burned with the desire to destroy the mortal that had dared to challenge his might.

'I would like you to build a palace worthy of the new Lord of Vynobhem—me! It will be a palace unlike any in existence. It will be in a bubble between Yennthem and Vynobhem so that both are equally accessible to me. I quite like the name that you had given your little hovel—Red House. Only, my palace will be vast and impenetrable. It will be called Red Hall! And it will be impossible to overcome its defences.'

As Zavak elaborated on his plans for Red Hall, the being on the ground listened with eyes widening in surprise. He had not expected the mortal to show such intelligence. Perhaps he had underestimated this yennt who had at one time been an eighe.

'I will do as you order,' he answered when Zavak had finished detailing his plans. 'But I do not have enough power to accomplish it. I am too weak.'

'Do not take me for an imbecile,' Zavak said coldly. 'I know exactly what you are capable of. Besides, I will keep an eye on you at all times. If you think of bypassing my authority to steal the life force of any being or creature, you shall have to answer to me. Do I make myself clear?'

'Yes,' the being agreed, his hopes of fooling Zavak into releasing his power dashed.

'Yes, what?' demanded Zavak coldly.

'Yes, Master,' the being acceded.

'That is much better. Now, you will get to work immediately. My hrenks will aid you and also guard you. Unlike you, they are not treacherous backstabbers. If you hurt any of them, I will forget that I have spared your life and that you can be of some service to me.'

'I will obey,' the being said, already planning in his mind how to overthrow Zavak.

'And just in case you are planning to turn the tables on me,' said Zavak with a knowing smile, 'I shall make sure that you can't.'

He took the glowing ball of energy from the air where it was still floating and pulled Zyimmiron out of its sheath. He passed the glass ball along the length of the sword, and some of the energy from the ball seeped into it. Zyimmiron glowed for a while before *regaining its original look. But the power of the magical being had passed into it. It was now capable of killing him.*

'That should take care of your immediate intentions of rebellion,' Zavak declared. 'Now do as you are told and remember that I can read even your mind.'

Zavak turned and left the diminished energy being with the hrenks who hauled him up to his feet and stood around him to ensure that he would not try to escape. One of them brought magical shackles and chained him up. He did not protest. He knew that he had been completely beaten for the present. None of the ideas he had of regaining his power and position would be of any avail. He would have to find other means to regain his freedom and his power, but that would have to wait. For now, Zavak was going to keep a keen eye on him, so he would have to be the obedient servant. But he would bide his time. He would gain his freedom and take back his power even if he had to wait thousands of anni to do it! In the meantime, he would build Red Hall, the palace of Zavak's dreams, for that was a challenge he would enjoy even though he would be building it for one he hated with every fragment of his being.

APPENDICES

TRANSLATIONS OF POEMS AND
SONGS INTO VOLEGAN

TRANSLATION OF DASTORV'S RENDITION OF
'THE MARCH OF THE DHARVHS' FROM EARGH (CHAPTER 12)

A foe since ages old,
A foe mighty and bold,
A foe vile to behold,
Had raised its brazen head,
Blinded by its pride.
This we could not abide!
Their uppishness to quell,
To Blarzonia did ride
The army of Gharzel.

Terrible was the fight,
Yet we proved our might
And with strength did smite
The brazen enemy dead!
Though great was the ire,
And scorching the fire
Of dragons large and fell,
They too could not abide
The army of Gharzel.

When the battle was won,
The enemy was undone,
The journey home was begun
Across the Lyudzbradh dread.
Through forests dark and thick,
In sport and in frolic,
Marched on through hill and dell,
Though tired and homesick,
The army of Gharzel.

They never reached their goal,
Came back home not one soul;
The Lyudzbradh swallowed whole
The dharvhs, by Gharzel led.
No seer ever divined;
No magus could find
With the strongest spell
That great force of dharvhkind
The army of Gharzel.

Translation of
'The Song of Kiel' from Eargh (Chapter 24)

I ask you, Oh all powerful Kiel,
Master of Death, Lord of Zyimnhem,
Why do you stand forever at my door
Knocking, knocking, knocking?
Are there not enough houses in the village?
Are there not enough souls in Zyimnhem?
Why do you come round to my doorstep
Tapping, tapping, tapping?

Have I done ought to incur your wrath?
Have others paid the price of my mistakes?
Why do you take my dear ones from me
Laughing, laughing, laughing?
Do not stand there so dark and dreadful,
A shadow across my courtyard blocking the sun.
I have paid in full measures of pain, my heart
Breaking, breaking, breaking.
Kiel, Lord of Death, Master of Zyimnhem,
Go away and plague my hearth no more.
Do not come again and again to my door
Knocking, knocking, knocking.

TRANSLATION OF FAREWELL SONG SUNG BY HALIFERN FROM HENTAR (CHAPTER 46)

When the rusty, brown leaves of outomy are gone,
When the chill wind of vernurt rattles my door,
When arid memories constrict my throat and voice
And yet moist remembrance clouds over my eyes,
When I look around through mundane habit
But fail to find the habitual faces ranged there,
When the myriad burdens of life become so heavy
That I wish I had not to carry them thus alone—
Then, my dear friend, I shall cast back my mind
To now, when yet you are here by my side,
To now, when I find you where I look to find,
To now, when time still has not altered us,
To now, when life still is not changed utterly,
To now, when still you are my dear friend.

A TO Z GLOSSARY OF THE CITY OF PATARSHP

A.E.	Short for Astoretherats, the calendar period followed on Yennthem starting from the day after Astoreth's demise
A.N.	Short for Astorethnytarni, the calendar period followed on Yennthem until the day of Astoreth's demise
Abluvel	Capital of Qeezsh
Abyu	True tiger; believed to be created by Vyidie, only one exists in each generation and is wiser, stronger and more sentient than most mortals
Ach	The last tempora of the annus, an interregnum meant to facilitate the transition between the passing annus and the new one
Aeon	A period of a hundred anni
Akhetash	An equesar, second son-in-law of Lord Xanther, co-founder and first chief-of-chiefs of the tribal state of Qeezsh, husband of Porillyn
Alanor Ushwah	Ancient human king, son of King Rogran and one of the sumagi
Alchemy	An ancient science aimed at understanding, controlling and purifying matter
Allaren	Late queen of Ashperth, wife of King Graniphor
Aminor	Maternal cousin of King Amiroth, master-of-the-horse and spy-master of Balignor, member of the Order of the Lily
Amiroth	King of Balignor, husband of Queen Lamella and Queen Samiesna
Amishar	Eldest prince of Balignor, son of King Amiroth and Queen Lamella
Angbruk	Brother of Rauz Augurk, councillor and military leader of Ghrangghirm

Annus	A unit of time, equivalent to a year, consisting of 16 mondans and the Ach; plural form 'anni'
Aravel Mountains	A mountain range located in central Elthrusia
Ardumel	A draconian leader, eldest son-in-law of Lord Xanther, husband of Mesthona
Arghyll	Blue, intense fire that leaves no residue, uses arghyll powder as fuel
Arghyll powder	Powder that can cause intense, blue fire that leaves no residue
Arlem	King of Samion, husband of Queen Melicie
Arrow, the	One of the signs of the Yennthian zodiac
Arslan	Prince of Samion, brother of King Arlem
Ashperth	An island country in north-western Elthrusia, ruled by humans
Astoreth	Legendary ancient hero of the eighes, king of Effine, son of King Barhusa and twin brother of Zavak
Atmut	A town in Balignor
Augurk	Rauz of Ghrangghirm, husband of Rauzina Marizha
Aura	The physical manifestation of eighes' spiritual force that wraps around them as a glow and changes according to their physical and mental state
Autruche	A strange looking flightless bird found in the Laudhern that can run very fast and can carry dharvhs
Avator	Rightful king of Lyisl, elder son of King Rannzen and Queen Iramina
Avita	Daughter of Lord Sanfion and Lady Rosa, being raised as Avator's sister
Aymur	A young man working as a spy for Lord Aminor
Azluren	Capital of Rosarfin
Balance, the	One of the signs of the Yennthian zodiac
Bald Pate	A soldier at Augurk's camp near Patrisha
Balignor	A country in western Elthrusia, ruled by humans
Barhamos	First king of Wyurr, son of Bezashy (II)
Barhusa	Ancient eighe king of Effine, father of Astoreth, Zavak and Moristol
Baruzdal	Elder half-brother of Uzdal Lyudz

Bay of Seluvinia	Bay between the two northern arms of the coast of Ashperth
Bear, the	One of the signs of the Yennthian zodiac
Beben Hoth	An accomplished navigator, one of the sumagi
Beleston	Prime minister of Balignor
Belisha	Wife of Lord Nankent, mother of Nishtar Arvarles
Bewonin	Daughter of Eroven
Beybasel	The thirteenth mondan of the annus consisting of 25 days, named after the guardian Beybasyi
Bezashy	Youngest daughter of Lord Xanther
Bezashy (II)	Daughter of Seolaston and Liravya
Blarzonia	A country in north-eastern Elthrusia, once ruled by Blarzonians, now devastated and barren
Blarzonians	A race of less civilised humans who overthrew the draconians as the rulers of Blarzonia and later fought severe wars with the dharvhs that led to the destruction of their country
Blood pact	A pact signed by two parties in their bloods mixed together; believed to have power to bind the two parties to the agreement magically
Blurz	An uncannily lucky spy of Rauz Augurk sent to discover the whereabouts of Patrisha in Khwaznon
Bolsana	A village in the Aravel Mountains in Cordemim
Brotherhood of the Secret Watchers	A secret society with the purpose of watching and warning Elthrusian nations against vynobnie attacks
Bull, the	One of the signs of the Yennthian zodiac
Carahan	First cousin of Lord Sanfion, keeper-of-the-keys and spy-master of Lyisl
Castillon	A human leader of the settlers of Illafanka, third son-in-law of Lord Xanther and husband of Dionyse
Charioteer, the	A constellation associated with Rogran
Chensey	A river in western Elthrusia that originates in the Wenymod Mountains and is a tributary of the Helawel
Chirshkom	The fourth mondan of the annus, consisting of 20 days, named after the guardian Chirshk
Chisel, the	One of the signs of the Yennthian zodiac

City of Stone	Another name for Patrisha
Colbenos	Town nearest to Bolsana
Compass, the	One of the signs of the Yennthian zodiac
Conatin	First king of Blarzonia, Son of Merayan
Cordemim	A country in western and central Elthrusia, ruled by humans
Cornen Pass	A pass in the Lyudzbradh where the borders of Ghrangghirm, Khwaznon, Qeezsh and Wyurr meet
Council of the Wise, the	Governing body of Maghem comprising all the sumagi
Cup, the	One of the signs of the Yennthian zodiac
Dar	A form of respectful address for a dharvh male
Dastorv	A cousin of Rauz Valhorz, known for his story-telling skills
Death Worm	An ancient creature that dwells deep within the earth and hunts desert travellers; has excellent hearing, dark magic and venomous spit and blood
Decadus	A period of ten anni
Demilor Forest	Forest in the west of Ashperth
Demosnart	The Guardian Yodiri's sword
Dermizh	Late rauz of Ghrangghirm, predecessor of Rauz Augurk
Dharvh	A race of human-like mortals who are short and stocky, live partially underground, are excellent warriors, miners and craftmakers, and control the mining and sale of Simlin
Dharvhina	A female dharvh
Dharvhish councillors	Incumbent and retired senior officials of the administration or the army, an advisory and ceremonial position with only few councillors actually perform functional roles
Dionyse	Third daughter of Lord Xanther, wife of Castillon
Dirsfer	A vocation. It was the vocation of Astoreth but has been lost to Yennthem for a long time
Diura	A period of a thousand anni
Dominion	An independent state with its own name and territory (term used in ancient times)

Domvaer	Son of Maheschom and Ealyse
Dormap	A general of Ashperth
Dorstoph	King of Cordemim, husband of Queen Anarneya
Draconian	An ancient race of humans that lived in and ruled Blarzonia before the Blarzonians, known to consort with dragons
Dragon	A mythical creature with a large and reptilian body, wings and the ability to breathe fire; the mount of Sachi
Drauzern	Capital of Ghrangghirm and primary colony of the Shawurth veradh of the dharvhs
Dreamcatcher	A magical device that allows greater control over dreams
Durng	Councillor of Ghrangghirm, close friend of Rauz Augurk
Durnum	A village across the river Quazisha from Lufurdista
Eaginna	Only daughter of Nishtar Arvarles, first wife of Lord Xanther
Ealyse	Fifth daughter of Lord Xanther, wife of Maheschom and first queen of Haalzona
Eamarilus	King of Haalzona, son of King Somarlus and husband of Queen Lilluana and Queen Moilyne
Eamilus	Elder prince of Haalzona, son of King Eamarilus and Queen Lilluana
Eargh	Language spoken by the dharvhs
Earilus	Younger prince of Haalzona, son of King Eamarilus and Queen Moilyne
Effine	An ancient eighe kingdom
Eighe	A race of human-like mortals who are very tall, clean limbed and graceful with highly acute senses and an aura around them that is a reflection of their spiritual energy
Eighee	A female eighe
Eighon	Language spoken by the seleighes and kereighes
Eileen	Princess of Ashperth, wife of Prince Feyanor
Elders	Heads of the Leading Families of fraels
Ellahas	An Elder of Harwillen living in Numosyn
Elsidar	Ancient human king, younger son of King Gimash and ancestor of King Amiroth
Elthrusia	The largest continent in Yennthem

Emense	A country in northern Elthrusia, ruled by kereighes
Emera	Wife of Nishtar Arvarles and later ruler of Ettarant
Engbom	A town in Emense
Equesar	A race of beings with the head, arms and torso of a human and the body and legs of a horse, known for their vast knowledge, archery skills and mastery of stargazing
Erofone	A friend of Prince Halifern, coming of age in the same mondan as him, goes with him to live in the forest during the last leg of the coming of age rituals
Eronsom	Forsith's pseudonym at the outlaw camp
Eroven	Son of Castillon and Dionyse
Ersafin	A forest in northern Elthrusia growing around the Ersa river
Eshoinh	The season of rains in the yennthian calendar, follows somminar
Eskielar	Festival of Kiel, held on the eleventh day of Kielom
Eslokarar	Festival of Lokare, held on the eleventh day of Lokrin
Esvilar	City in northern Emense
Etroval	Primary colony of the Mermurdh veradh of the dharvhs
Ettarant	A dominion in Blarzonia in ancient times, not far from White Mountain
Fambert	A man living in Bolsana village
Fassinth	Capital of Samion
Feerdhen	A deputy of Igrag
Felicia	Queen of Rosarfin, wife of King Melson
Felicim	Prince of Rosarfin, second son of King Melson and Queen Felicia
Felisa	Princess of Rosarfin, younger daughter of King Melson and Queen Felicia
Felissom	Prince of Rosarfin, youngest son of King Melson and Queen Felicia
Feyanor	Prince of Ashperth, son of King Graniphor and Queen Allaren
Flying Fish, the	One of the signs of the Yennthian zodiac
Fongun	Originally, one of the suitors of Rauzditr Meizha, later worked for Rauz Augurk during the search for Patrisha

Forsith	Aide of King Rannzen, later guardian of Avator and Avita
Frael	A race of human-like mortals who are short, slender and agile with high speed and stamina, and who have an intimate relationship with Nature
Fraelina	A female frael
Frengdan	A deputy of Igrag
Fruschya	A neighbour of Prince Halifern coming of age in the same mondan as him, one of twin sisters
Furnace, the	One of the signs of the Yennthian zodiac
Fwelhyn	Extremely beautiful fraelina, neighbour of Halifern coming of age in the same mondan as him
Fylhun	The legendary sword of Astoreth
Gamberra	Language spoken by the humans of eastern Elthrusia
Gharzel	Ancient general of dharvhs who led the army against the Blarzonians
Ghost	A spirit of a dead mortal that has not left for Zyimnhem
Ghrangghirm	A country in central-eastern Elthrusia, ruled by dharvhs
Ghrimben	A type of vynobin; a grotesque, filthy, cunning and ruthless creatures with long teeth and claws, nimble limbs, a strong sense of smell and an insatiable appetite
Ghruk	Originally, one of the suitors of Rauzditr Meizha, later worked for Rauz Augurk during the search for Patrisha
Gimash	Ancient human king, son of King Alanor
Graniphor	King of Ashperth, husband of (late) Queen Allaren
Great Desert of Laudhern, the	Desert in central Elthrusia that covers almost all of the dharvhish territories as well as a large portion of Emense
Guardians	Personified entities representing the forces of all Creation
Guzear the bear-clawed	Councillor and military leader of Ghrangghirm
Haalzona	A country in eastern Elthrusia, ruled by humans
Habsolm	A comical, cross-eyed gelding bought by Avator
Halifern	A prince of one of the Leading Families of Harwillen, lives in Numosyn
Hanmer	King of Storsnem, brother of Queen Anarneya
Harwillen	A country in southern Elthrusia, ruled by fraels

Helawel	A river in central Elthrusia that originates in the Aravel mountains
Hems	Different planes of existence that are geographically and temporally parallel, with each inhabited by a different kind of being - guardians, magi, mortals, vynobnie and spirits
Hentar	The language spoken by fraels
Herenna	Founder and first mistress-queen of the hive federation of Mirhisd, daughter of Sehira
Hervoz	Originally, one of the suitors of Rauzditr Meizha, later worked for Rauz Augurk during the search for Patrisha
Holexar	Prime minister of Samion, later King of Samion
Homanim	An individual who is half-human and half some other animal or creature
Hora	A unit of time equivalent to an hour
Horse farms	A place where horses who can no longer work are sent to live out the rest of their lives in comfort
Horse-wizard	Kereighes who have an extraordinary connection with horses and who can talk to, tame and heal any horse
Hravisht-envar	A contest to determine the five most deserving suitors for a dharvhish bride
Hrenk	A type of vynobin; a massive creature with tremendous strength and low intelligence that loves destruction and feeds on mortals
Hummold	A hill-town in north-western Cordemim, near its border with Storsnem
Hydra, the	One of the signs of the Yennthian zodiac
Idhaghloz mountain	A dormant volcano in the Lyudzbradh Mountains
Idhaghloz village	A village at the base of the Idhaghloz mountain
Igrag	Leader of one of the bands of outlaws plaguing the desert of Emense
Illafanka	A country in eastern Elthrusia, once ruled by humans, now dominated by mertkhezi
Ingash	Draconian healer and friend of Lord Nankent, later advisor of Nishtar Arvarles and Lady Emera
Inner Circle	Another name for Augurk's Special Advisory Council

Iramina	Queen of Lyisl, wife of King Rannzen
Ishenar	First king of Illafanka, son of Bewonin
Ixluatach	The last day of the Ach, and the day of Celebration
Jumradam	Agriculture minister of Balignor
Kaidiu	The first day of a tempora
Kaitshem	The hem or sphere in which the kaitsyas or guardians live
Kaitsyas	Another name for the Guardians
Kawiti	Guardian of Immortality
Kawitor	The first mondan of the annus, consisting of 25 days, named after the guardian Kawiti
Kereighe	A section of eighes with dark hair and eyes
Kereighee	A female kereighe
Kerzen	King of Emense
Khayper	Short form of khayperogh zoursfer
Khayperogh Zoursfer	'Possessor of black blood' - A monster that dwells underground and travels through subterranean passages. It has greyish green scaly skin and no eyes but a keen sense of hearing and smell. It eats the flesh of mortals and preys upon those who venture underground
Khwaznon	A country in central-eastern Elthrusia, ruled by dharvhs
Kiel	Guardian of Death
Kielom	The tenth mondan of the annus, consisting of 20 days, named after the guardian Kiel
Kinqur	Capital of Emense
Kocovus	A type of vynobin; a terrifying, flesh-eating creature that can disguise itself as human
Kocovusa	A female kocovus
Korshernon	A general of Ashperth
Krovad	An ancient human kingdom founded by King Simhurd
Lamella	Queen of Balignor, wife of King Amiroth
Lamissur	An outlaw in Igrag's gang, uncle of Lekker
Laroosa	Young boy living in Durnum village
Laudhern	See 'Great Desert of Laudhern'
Lech	A witch who practises black magic
Lekker	A scout in Igrag's gang, nephew of Lamissur

Lembar	A garrison city in Emense, close to the capital
Leormane	Chief of Bolsana village
Lianma	A town in Emense
Librarian, the	Another name for Sumaho Menshir
Lilluana	Queen of Haalzona, wife of King Eamarilus and a kocovusa
Limossen	King of Lyisl, formerly commander-in-chief
Liravya	Eighth daughter of Lord Xanther, wife of Seolaston
Lokare	Guardian of the element Fire
Lokrin	The sixth mondan of the annus, consisting of 20 days, named after the guardian Lokare
Lord of Esvilar	Lord of the city of Esvilar and its attached grounds, tough opponent of outlaws and courtier of King Kerzen
Lord of Red House, the	Energy and light being who was the nominal lord of Vynobhem before Zavak and lived in the Red House
Loyohen	A friend of Prince Halifern, coming of age in the same mondan as him, goes with him to live in the forest during the last leg of the coming of age rituals
Lufurdista	Capital of Balignor
Lyisl	A country in northern Elthrusia, ruled by kereighes
Lyre, the	One of the signs of the Yennthian zodiac
Lyudzbradh	A mountain range located in eastern Elthrusia
Madal	The third mondan of the annus, consisting of 25 days, named after the guardian Madu
Madu	Guardian of the element Air
Maga	One of the magi (female)
Maghem	The hem or sphere in which the magi live
Magi	Beings with an innate ability to manipulate minds and matter
Magic mirror	A special kind of mirror used by magi that allows them to communicate with each other
Magus	One of the magi (male)
Magus on coast of Talsear Ocean	Magus well known for using his powers to help mortals who gave Avita the dreamcatcher
Maheschom	First king of Haalzona, husband of Ealyse and fifth son-in-law of Lord Xanther

Maldufa	A tribal leader of the Ufharn Hills
Manor House	Originally, the house of a manor-lord; in later ages, the stronghold of any lord's territory
Manor-lord	Originally, the ruler of a dominion; in later ages, a lord with his own lands
Marizha	Rauzina of Ghrangghirm, wife of Rauz Augurk
Marsil	Human name of Serilla, Melicie/Misa's mare, an Istamora
Master Healer	Chief of King Amiroth's healers
Matisal	The fifth mondan of the annus, consisting of 25 days, named after the guardian Matisa
Mayndoda	A country in eastern Elthrusia, once ruled by humans, now dominated by kocovuses
Meizha	Rauzditr of Ghrangghirm, daughter of Rauz Augurk and Rauzina Marizha and wife of Rauzoon Valhazar
Melicie	Dethroned queen of Samion
Melissen	Prince of Rosarfin, eldest son of King Melson and Queen Felicia
Melson	King of Rosarfin, husband of Queen Felicia
Menithyl	Avita's pseudonym while staying at the outlaw camp
Merayan	Son of Ardumel and Mesthona
Mermurdh	One of the veradhen of the dharvhs
Merosh	A river in northern Elthrusia
Mertis	A type of ancient magical flower
Mertkhezin	A type of vynobin; a creature that lives in swamps and lures its prey into the bog by befuddling it with singing and has the ability to take on a beautiful human form
Mesmen Orao	Renowned and miraculous healer, originally leader of the sumagi, later disappeared without a trace and forbade the other sumagi from searching for her
Mesthona	Eldest daughter of Lord Xanther, wife of Ardumel
Miehaf	Master-smith working in Nersefan's secret smithy
Minura	A unit of time equivalent to a minute
Mirhisd	A country in eastern Elthrusia, once ruled by phrixes, now wild lands
Misa	Human name of Queen Melicie
Missus Kulter	Landlady of The Hollow Oak inn in Penin

Mizu	Human name of Prince Arizumel, son of Queen Melicie
Molinee	A woman living in Bolsana village
Momon	A unit of time, equivalent to a second
Mondan	A unit of time consisting of 20 or 25 days (4 or 5 temporas)
Monkey King, the	A children's story about a monkey who had many adventures and finally became a king
Mordeph	Avator's pseudonym while staying at the outlaw camp
Moristol	Ancient prince of Effine, youngest son of King Barhusa
Naetel	Port at the mouth of the Quazisha River, in Balignor
Nankent	Manor-lord of Ettarant, husband of Lady Belisha and father of Nishtar Arvarles
Navigator, the	Another name for Beben Hoth
Nersefan	Youngest brother of Queen Iramina
Nishtar Arvarles	Yennthem's most famous teacher, one of the sumagi
Niwuik	Guardian of Time
Niwukir	The fourteenth mondan of the annus, consisting of 20 days, named after the guardian Niwuik
Noroman Range	Mountain range in the north-east of Elthrusia
Norowichh Forest	Forest in central Elthrusia
Numosyn	The most prominent of the Cities of Harwillen
Obetulfer	A shadow-maker, a ghost with the power to create and manipulate shadows, to spread panic, chaos and confusion, and to possess people and take over their minds
Okker	A young shepherd neighbour of Oram
Ollivyra	Fourth daughter of Lord Xanther, wife of Thybald
Olveron	First king of Waurlen, son of Thybald and Ollivyra
Onelikh	Councillor of Ghrangghirm, elder of the Shawurth veradh of the dharvhs
Onnish	Elderly councillor of Ghrangghirm
Ontar	Capital of Ashperth
Opeltra	Capital of Haalzona
Oram Ashar	A dedicated shepherd, one of the sumagi
Orbhz	Capital of Khwaznon and primary colony of the Bremd veradh of the dharvhs

Order of the Lily, the	A secret organisation dedicated to the protection and welfare of mankind in the West
Orobis Nemsha	Author of books of children's stories including 'The Monkey King and Other Stories'.
Outomy	The dry, moderate season in the yennthian calendar, equivalent to autumn, follows eshoinh
Parkiod	Commander-in-chief of Balignor
Parned	A general of Ashperth
Patarshem	The sixteenth mondan of the annus, consisting of 20 days, named after the guardian Patarshp
Patarshp	Guardian of Creation
Patrisha	City built by Patarshp to house obsidian soldiers given by Yodiri to Astoreth
Peacock, the	One of the signs of the Yennthian zodiac
Pegasus	A mythical horse with wings, also known as a Rayainmora
Penin	A town in Emense
Phoenix, the	One of the signs of the Yennthian zodiac
Phrix	A race of very small mortals with sharp pointy ears, pug noses and bluish-grey skin who live in hives in caves or forest groves and are known for their skill at thievery
Phushketh	One of the veradhen of the dharvhs
Porillyn	Second daughter of Lord Xanther, co-founder of tribal state of Qeezsh and wife of Akhetash
Portal	A magical gateway between different hems or spheres
Pretvain	The Universe; it consists of all five hems together
Prophecy of Kawiti	Prophecy by the Guardian Kawiti regarding the rebirth of Astoreth and Zavak
Qeezsh	A country in eastern Elthrusia, once ruled by equesars, now wild lands
Qually	Senior member of Igrag's gang
Quazisha	A river in western Elthrusia that originates in Lake Lomvar
Rabedhi	Seventh daughter of Lord Xanther, wife of Trakurth
Ram, the	One of the signs of the Yennthian zodiac
Ranhenh	A phrix, sixth son-in-law of Lord Xanther
Rannzen	Late king of Lyisl, husband of Queen Iramina

Rauberk	Spy and messenger of Augurk who was sent to scout King Amiroth's suitability for the expedition to find Patrisha
Rauz	Dharvh epithet for king
Rauzditr	Dharvh epithet for princess
Rauzina	Dharvh epithet for queen
Rauzoon	Dharvh epithet for prince
Rayainmora	A mythical horse with wings, also known as a Pegasus
Rebirth Ritual	An extremely difficult and dangerous magical ritual to bind and heighten one's powers
Red Beard	A soldier at Augurk's camp near Patrisha
Red Hall	The seat of the Lord of Vynobhem
Red House	Originally, the dwelling of a powerful energy being in Vynobhem; later, the site of Red Hall
Reklan	The second mondan of the annus, consisting of 20 days, named after the guardian Rekal
Revash	Son of Akhetash and Porillyn
Rogran	Ancient human king, founder of first human kingdom in the west
Rohyllar	An Elder of Harwillen living in Numosyn, also a member of the Committee of Harwillen, father of Halifern
Rohzun	Brother of Queen Lilluana, a kocovus
Ronean	Nephew of Maldufa, his tribe's chief after his uncle's death
Rosa	Wife of Lord Sanfion, a lech and imprisoner and torturer of Temeron
Rosarfin	A country in northern Elthrusia, ruled by seleighes
Rovinon	An Elder of Harwillen living in Numosyn
Runes	Special symbols that can represent both letters and ideas. They are believed to instil strength, endurance, magic or other qualities in articles on which they are inscribed, and are typically used by smiths and other craftmakers to mark their work
Sachi	Guardian of Feelings
Sachir	The seventh mondan of the annus, consisting of 25 days, named after the guardian Sachi

Samar	Guardian of Wisdom
Samaranth	Younger prince of Balignor, son of King Amiroth and Queen Samiesna
Samiesna	Queen of Balignor, second wife of King Amiroth
Samion	A country in northern Elthrusia, ruled by seleighes
Samrer	The twelfth mondan of the annus, consisting of 20 days, named after the guardian Samar
Sanfion	Courtier in King Rannzen's court, husband of Lady Rosa
Sehira	Queen of a phrix hive, daughter of Ranhenh and Syliatta
Seleighe	A section of eighes with light, fair hair and light eyes
Seleighee	A female seleighe
Senteyon	A neighbour of Prince Halifern coming of age in the same mondan as him
Seolaston	A mercenary from Wyurr, eighth son-in-law of Lord Xanther and husband of Liravya
Sepwin	Capital of Lyisl
Shadow Lands	Collective name for the eight countries of eastern Elthrusia that are cut off from the rest of the mainland by the Lyudzbradh Mountains and are invested by vynobnie
Shepherd, the	Another name for Oram Ashar
Shield, the	One of the signs of the Yennthian zodiac
Shornhuz	Personal bodyguard of Rauz Augurk, one of the suitors of Rauzditr Meizha
Shroog	Originally, one of the suitors of Rauzditr Meizha, later worked for Rauz Augurk during the search for Patrisha
Siltare	A friend of Prince Halifern, coming of age in the same mondan as him, goes with him to live in the forest during the last leg of the coming of age rituals
Simhurd	Ancient human king, elder son of King Felador who opened the City of Stone
Simlin	Extremely rare spun gold whose secret is known only to the dharvhs; its ores are found in mines in the Lyudzbradh Mountains
Somarlus	Late king of Haalzona known as the Terror of the East
Somminar	The season of warmth in the yennthian calendar, equivalent to spring and/or summer, follows vernurt

Song of Kiel	A chant written on doorways on Eskielar that supposedly wards of Kiel's gaze for that day
Sorceress, the	Another name for Vellila Regat
Soul transposition	Transferring of one's soul into another living being, a difficult and dangerous process
Soytaren Mountain	A mountain mentioned in an ancient text discovered by Sumaho temporarily
Special Advisory Council	Augurk's closest and most valuable advisors and councillors: Angbruk, Onelikh, Guzear and Durng
Spheres	Different planes of existence that are geographically and temporally parallel, with each inhabited by a different kind of being - guardians, magi, mortals, vynobnie and spirits (also called hems)
Storsnem	A country in western Elthrusia, ruled by humans
Sumaga	One of the sumagi (female)
Sumagi	Magi who have acquired the secret of immortality
Sumagus	One of the sumagi (male)
Sumaho Menshir	Caretaker of greatest library in existence, one of the sumagi
Sumarin	A river in central and southern Elthrusia
Supparo	Guardian of Thought
Supprom	The eighth mondan of the annus, consisting of 20 days, named after the guardian Supparo
Syliatta	Sixth daughter of Lord Xanther, wife of Ranhenh, queen of his hive
Talking cat, the	A magical cat that taught Mizu to ride a horse
Talsear Ocean	The ocean in the north of Yennthem
Temeron	Prince of Lyisl, younger son of King Rannzen and Queen Iramina
Tempora	A unit of time equivalent to a period of 5 days
Temtema	A city in southern Emense
The Dancing Clowns	An inn in Lufurdista
Thief, the	A notorious thief plaguing the city where Temeron was living
Three witches, the	Three old witches who teach magic to Lady Rosa and induct her in their coven

Thybald	A human leader of the settlers of Illafanka, fourth son-in-law of Lord Xanther and husband of Ollivyra
Timror	A magus living in Yennthem, an alchemist and Eamilus's teacher
Torimach	Fourth day of the Ach, the day of Grieving
Trabedh	First king of Mayndoda, son of Trakurth and Rabedhi
Tracker	An individual with special powers to track other individuals across vast distances accurately even without obvious, noticeable traces
Tracking Crystals	Perfectly carved crystals of quartz magically connected to the essence of an individual and to each other used for tracking. They indicate the distance of the object of search through a growing or lessening degree of brilliance. When one crystal detects the quarry, it alerts the other crystals automatically
Trade of Blossoms	A ritual of Ashperth on Ixluatach involving the exchange of flowers
Trakurth	Seventh son-in-law of Lord Xanther, husband of Rabedhi
Traozon	A man living in Bolsana village, husband of Molinee
Travedh	One of the veradhen of the dharvhs
Traveller, the	Another name for Alanor Ushwah
Tribal State	A form of government in which tribes function as units of a single nation
Tribes of Ufharn Hills	Numerous tribes that lived in the Ufharn Hills and controlled the Hills until their conquest by Prince Feyanor
Tyzer	An adolescent boy living in Bolsana village, son of Traozon and Molinee
Ufharn Hills	Range of hills lining almost the entire northern border of Ashperth
Ulmyon	A river crossing on the border between Samion and Emense
Uposnesee	A cousin of Prince Halifern, coming of age in the same mondan as him
Ustillor	A village in Lyisl
Unicorn, the	One of the signs of the Yennthian zodiac

Uzdal Lyudz	A homanim who is part human and part tiger, the guardian of the Valdero Forest
Valdero	A forest in western Wyurr that was the home of the Abyus and is now Uzdal Lyudz's territory
Valhazar	Rauzoon of Khwaznon, son of Rauz Valhorz and Rauzina Neixara
Valhorz	Rauz of Khwaznon, husband of Rauzina Neixara
Vanderz	Brother of Rauz Valhorz, councillor and military leader of Khwaznon
Veber	Originally, one of the suitors of Rauzditr Meizha, later worked for Rauz Augurk during the search for Patrisha
Vellila Regat	A sorceress of great power, one of the sumagi
Veradh	One of fourteen clans into which dharvhish lands and population are historically divided. Even after being united into nations, they remain the basis of dharvhish social and geographical structure
Veradhen	Plural of veradh
Verberon	A man living in Bolsana village
Vernurt	The cold season in the yennthian calendar, equivalent to winter, follows outomy
Vittor	Capital of Cordemim
Volegan	Language spoken by the humans of western Elthrusia
Vrenhor	Ancient rauz of the dharvhs who united the veradhen into a single nation
Vyidie	Guardian of Birth
Vyiedal	The ninth mondan of the annus, consisting of 25 days, named after the guardian Vyidie
Vynobhem	The hem or sphere in which the vynobnie live
Vynobnie	Undead creatures and other monsters that feed on mortals
Waroned	An exceptionally tall frael ostracised for his height, one of twin brothers, secret friend and, later, spy of Prince Halifern
Waurlen	A country in eastern Elthrusia, once ruled by humans, now dominated by hrenks
Wenymod Mountains	A mountain range in south-western Elthrusia

Weryntza	Sister of Waroned and Woroned, a fraelina coming of age in the same mondan as Prince Halifern
White Mountain	A mountain at the northern tip of the Lyudzbradh Mountains, home of Nishtar Arvarles
Witar	Originally, one of the suitors of Rauzditr Meizha, later worked for Rauz Augurk during the search for Patrisha
Witch of Temtema, the	A white witch living in Temtema who gave Avita a charm to help heal her wounds faster
Wornychh	A cousin of Prince Halifern, coming of age in the same mondan as him
Woroned	An exceptionally tall frael ostracised for his height, one of twin brothers, secret friend and, later, spy of Prince Halifern
Wyrchhelim	A country in southern Elthrusia, ruled by fraels
Wyurr	A country in eastern Elthrusia, once ruled by humans, now dominated by ghrimbens
Wyzisia	A neighbour of Prince Halifern coming of age in the same mondan as him, one of twin sisters
Xanther	Legendary manor-lord whose daughters and sons-in-law or their descendants founded the eight kingdoms of eastern Elthrusia, son-in-law of Nishtar Arvarles and husband of Lady Eaginna and Lady Zarathie
Xylliot	A village in Emense
Yellow Cap	A soldier at Augurk's camp near Patrisha
Yendiu	The third day of a tempora
Yennthem	The hem or sphere in which the yennts or mortals live
Yennts	Another name for mortals
Yestirach	The first day of the Ach, the day of Remembrance
Yodiri	Guardian of Destruction
Yodirin	The fifteenth mondan of the annus, consisting of 25 days, named after the guardian Yodiri
Yomdelos	A country in central Khopish, inhabited by khrozens
Zarathie	Second wife of Lord Xanther
Zavak	Legendary evil invader of the eighes, Lord of Vynobhem, son of King Barhusa and twin brother of Astoreth

Zedrel	One of a race of large warrior women whose society is completely female-centric
Zhan-ang-Razr	A kingship tournament of dharvhs to determine the next rauz when the current rauz dies, abdicates or is impeached
Zibar	Son of the chief of Durnum village, a bully
Zillock	Chief of Durnum village
Zulheen	The eleventh mondan of the annus, consisting of 25 days, named after the guardian Zuleeha
Zyimdiu	The fifth and last day of a tempora
Zyimmiron	The legendary sword of Zavak
Zyimnhem	The hem or sphere in which the zyimn or spirits live
Zyimns	Another name for spirits or souls

THE RISE AND FALL OF THE
COUNTRIES OF EASTERN ELTHRUSIA

INTRODUCTION

It is a fact now almost forgotten that Blarzonia was the cradle of human civilisation in Yennthem. Almost a thousand anni after the fall of Astoreth and Zavak, the foundations of human civilisation took root there. It was neither a country then, nor was it called Blarzonia. At first, villages sprang up like mushrooms across the triangular land hemmed in by the Lyudzbradh on two sides and the ocean on the third. Later, villages became towns, towns grew into cities, cities expanded into large territories known as dominions. Each dominion was an independent state. Each had at its heart a manor from which the manor-lord ruled his lands—much as kings did in later anni—levying taxes, making and enforcing laws, forging alliances or going to war with neighbouring dominions and protecting their people.

In a few hundred anni, the population of the country swelled to such numbers that the land became incapable of supporting them. Wars became more frequent and brutal, and law and order began to be forgotten as the struggle for limited resources intensified. It was then that the migrations began. People migrated south and east out of Blarzonia. And while they found rich lands to the east, in the south they came upon only a vast desert that forced them to turn westward. Those who journeyed into the east, to the other side of the Lyudzbradh, retained their heritage and settled the lands they found in the same manner as their birthland had been settled. Those who travelled west left their heritage of civilised life behind, only to rediscover it generations later.

The first areas in the east to be populated were those just across the Lyudzbradh from Blarzonia. The humans flourished in this new land, but the migration did not stop. Driven by either a desire for exploration or the promise of greater prosperity, and also by the increasing numbers of migrants from the birthland, humans continued to move further east and south-east. The areas to the extreme north were the next to be brought under civilisation, followed by the lands south of the first settlements this side of the Lyudzbradh. These were followed by the north-eastern and easternmost lands. By then, only the southernmost area remained wild. But not for very long. By the early fourteenth aeon, humans had spread to every corner of the East except the remote south. That too was populated by migrating humans by the beginning of the sixth decadus of the fourteenth aeon.

BLARZONIA

Long before the humans had populated all of the East, a strange race had begun to emerge in the birthland. These mysterious folks looked, talked and acted like humans, but there was something oddly reptilian to their appearance and demeanour that was disturbing to the predominant human inhabitants. The reason behind the reptilian aspect of this race was discovered to be their association with dragons, those large and dangerous creatures whom mankind has feared since the dawn of time. The draconians—as this new race was called—however, saw dragons as wise and profound beings who were superior to mere mortals and whose association brought them great knowledge, wisdom and power. Although the draconians had existed since long, they had never been powerful enough to be noticed by the humans. But they began to grow in strength and prominence within three decadi of the beginning of the migration to the east.

One of their greatest and wisest leaders was Ardumel, who was born in 1554 A.E. He travelled to Lord Xanther's dominion when he was twenty-five anni old and succeeded in reviving Lord Xanther's eldest daughter, Mesthona. This was a turning point in the history of the draconians. They began to slowly capture areas of Blarzonia where the human manor-lords proved too weak to hold on to their lands. Under Ardumel and Mesthona, the lands were consolidated into a single, large dominion. Their son, Merayan, born in 1580 A.E., continued the expansion and consolidation of the territories of their territories. But it was Merayan's son, Conatin, who finally brought the entire land under the rule of the draconians in 1654 A.E. at the age of forty, naming the kingdom Blarzonia. By then, however, both Ardumel and Mesthona had died, and Merayan was old. Conatin was an able ruler and so were his descendants who ruled Blarzonia capably for diuras.

The draconians flourished for long anni in the harsh land with the support of the dragons, but in the forty-fourth aeon A.E., they were conquered by a race known as the Blarzonians, who were neither as wise nor as civilised as the draconians. They imprisoned the draconians and their dragons—those who were alive and had not managed to escape—and kept them as slaves. In later years, the Blarzonians entangled with the dharvhs, which led to a series of fierce wars between the two races. In the end, the dharvhs vanquished the Blarzonians and destroyed Blarzonia in the forty-eighth aeon A.E., leaving it barren and practically bereft of life. A few pockets of folks continued to struggle on, but most of these mortals soon gave up and either withered away or migrated to other areas.

Haalzona

However, Blarzonia was not the first of the kingdoms of the East to be founded. That honour belonged to Haalzona. The first of the new territories to be settled after the migration, it was good land but was plagued by kocovuses. This did not daunt the settlers who were determined to conquer the land and succeeded in pushing the vynobnie back. They established dominions and manor houses after the pattern of civilisation that they had been familiar with. There were some manor-lords among them, like Xanther, who thought far ahead of their fellow humans. They realised that the only way that humans in the East could survive in the middle of the hostile natives and vynobnie was by uniting into larger, more cohesive, dominions. And thus began the great consolidation of the territories to the east of the Lyudzbradh.

However, the tragedy that befell his daughters halted Lord Xanther's ambitions for a while. In the meantime, his rivals began to gain ascendancy. All of this changed after the marriage of his daughter Ealyse to Maheschom in 1632 A.E. Maheschom had been one of Xanther's own soldiers and had quickly risen through the ranks on sheer merit and willpower. When he married Ealyse, he was only twenty-five and close to becoming a general. His marriage not only propelled his career but also changed Lord Xanther's fortunes. Soon, he was the most powerful of the manor-lords, and most of the territory was within his control.

Maheschom and Ealyse did not have any children for many anni after their marriage and had almost given up hope when they were blessed with a son, Domvaer, in 1601 A.E. By then, Maheschom had succeeded his father-in-law as the leader of men in Haalzona and had brought a vast portion of the territory under his banner. His domain extended from the areas adjacent to Blarzonia in a south-eastern direction for thousands of miles. In 1608 A.E., Maheschom founded the kingdom of Haalzona and became the first king of the East. By the time Xanther died in 1614 A.E., Maheschom had established such a strong rule over his territories that it was to remain unshaken for diuras.

Ealyse died in 1632 A.E. and her husband a decadus later, leaving their son Domvaer king of Haalzona. Even as early as then, the vynobnie began their continuous attack on civilisation that was to become the hallmark of life in the East and was to give the area its infamous name of the Shadow Lands. The kings and queens of Haalzona ruled with strength and courage, driving back waves of vynobnie time and time again. Perhaps their greatest ruler was Somarlus, who was known as the Terror of the East. He subdued all the enemies of men and established peace in the country after diuras of constant vigilance and battles. The line of Maheschom and Ealyse ruled Haalzona until 5004 A.E. and acted as the last bastion of humankind in the East after the other kingdoms fell to the continued diuras of assault by the vynobnie. Somarlus's son, Eamarilus, was the last king of Haalzona before its fall.

WAURLEN

Waurlen was not only the second of the eastern territories to be settled but also the second kingdom to be established. However, the humans who settled there had to face a different kind of enemy to the humans who settled Haalzona. While the settlers of Haalzona were faced by hordes of kocovuses, the settlers of Waurlen faced tribes of hrenks. Hrenks were huge, mountainous vynobnie ten times as large as humans. They roughly resembled humans in appearance but only barely. Their strength was immense; they could smash a massive boulder or uproot an oak tree almost without effort. Fortunately, they were not very intelligent despite possessing a certain cruel cunning in finding and hunting prey. The humans took advantage of this and managed to overcome their enemies over time. By the time the struggle ended, only a handful of hrenks were left in Waurlen, and these fled to the mountains of the Noroman range.

The struggle to overcome the hrenks had prevented the humans of Waurlen from establishing dominions. When the threat passed, they found that they were more unified than any of the other settlements. Yet they were also less developed and weaker than the rest as a consequence of the toll that their constant battles had taken on them. It took a leader of Thybald's ability to bring prosperity back to the settlers of Waurlen. Born in 1555 A.E., he was keenly conscious of the plight of his fellow humans from an early age. By the time he revived and married Ollivyra, Lord Xanther's fourth daughter, he had already brought half of Waurlen under the rule of law. Yet it was their son, Olveron, who finally extended the reach of a central regime to the farthest corners of Waurlen and established the kingdom in 1618 A.E. Unfortunately, that was also the annus that he lost his mother. His father continued to guide and support him until his own demise in 1632 A.E. Olveron was a strong ruler, but it was a permanent struggle to keep the hrenks restricted to their mountain hideouts and to elevate the level of Waurlen's prosperity to that of its neighbours.

Waurlen was Haalzona's closest ally in the wars against vynobnie despite not being as prosperous as its southern neighbour. The residents and rulers of Waurlen were tough, hardy people who learnt from an early age that the price of peace was vigilance. Their borders were guarded on two sides by the Talsear Ocean, which allowed them to keep their alertness focused on the Noroman Mountains to guard against their ancient enemies. For diuras, this alertness served them well until the hrenks, who had been growing in numbers consistently but secretly for aeons, came down from their hiding places in hordes. The armies of Waurlen were swept away and civilisation wiped from the face of the kingdom in the brief period of a few anni. Haalzona came to its aid, but the assistance turned futile as the overwhelming forces of the hrenks crushed all resistance. By the end of the forty-ninth aeon, Waurlen lay devastated and stripped of all signs of human civilisation, a playground for hrenks and a place of terror for the handfuls of humans who remained because they had nowhere else to go.

QEEZSH

Qeezsh was the third territory to be settled by the migrants from Blarzonia. When humans arrived there, they encountered a strange race inhabiting its forests and grasslands. These were the equesars. At first, the humans took them for vynobnie but soon realised that they were mortals and the original inhabitants of the land. An equesar had the body of a horse and the upper body of a human growing out from where a horse's neck begins. They lived in nature, in tribes, and had their own language, customs, professions and laws. Contact with the humans brought them greater awareness—of themselves and of the larger world outside of their ancestral territories—and led to conflict between them and the humans, whom they saw as invaders.

These two races fought for generations, the wars growing larger, fiercer, more organised and more violent in nature, with neither the humans nor the natives gaining any clear edge. And all this while, the humans continued to build cities, cultivate fields, raise livestock, construct roads, marry and have children, and trade with neighbouring regions. Strangely enough, the equesars also began to establish colonies after their own fashion even though from the time of their origin, they had always lived in a wild state. A time came when the similarities in the lifestyles of the races and their co-dependence grew to a stage where war was more an inconvenience than an assertion of independence. Treaties were signed, and the humans settled down to coexist in harmony with the equesars within the territory that came to be known as Qeezsh. And while the age old hostilities were never entirely forgotten, they diminished into wisps of legends buried deep within the pages of history. Both humans and equesars continued to live in a state of mutual respect, with neither race claiming supremacy over the other.

These wars were almost at an end when Akhetash revived Porillyn and claimed her for his bride at the age of thirty-seven. Just over three decadi later, the two of them established the tribal state of Qeezsh. In 1669 A.E., Akhetash passed away at the age of a hundred and twenty-six, leaving the chiefdom to his only son, Revash. In human terms, he would have been eighty-four. Porillyn lived till 1678 A.E., outliving all her sisters and brothers-in-law, and witnessing the foundation of all eight kingdoms of the East. Although Revash was a strong chief-of-chiefs, and his descendants maintained the strength of Qeezsh for aeons, they were ultimately overcome by vynobnie. The vynobnie overwhelmed their cities and tore them down stone by stone. In the end, those equesars and humans who survived escaped into the forests of Qeezsh and continued to live in mixed tribes. The capital, Abluvel, was the last to fall, holding on against the tide of vynobnie until the middle of the forty-ninth aeon.

MAYNDODA

Mayndoda, south-east of Waurlen and north-east of Haalzona, was naturally one of the earliest territories to be settled. Those humans who came to Mayndoda faced the same enemy as did those who settled Haalzona. These ferocious monsters were known as kocovuses. Humans had known of kocovuses for a long time; in fact, these monsters were the staple of fairy tales to frighten children into listening to elders. But no one had known that these vynobnie had been living in the East in such vast numbers. Unlike Haalzona, Mayndoda had few leaders among its settlers, and the battle with the kocovuses dragged on for aeons. In the end, with the help of their neighbours, the settlers of Mayndoda were able to subdue their enemies. It was then, in the fifteenth aeon, that the true civilisation of Mayndoda began.

Under the influence of Haalzona, the residents of Mayndoda opted for large dominions right from the beginning. Therefore, when the work of consolidation was begun by Trakurth, seventh son-in-law of Lord Xanther, and his wife Rabedhi, they faced fewer albeit stronger rivals. It was their son, Trabedh, who founded the kingdom of Mayndoda in the annus 1632 A.E. At the age of 42, he was one of the oldest of the founders, third in age after Maheschom and Akhetash. By the time he was crowned the first king of Mayndoda, his mother was no more. His father passed away four anni later. However, Trabedh was one of the most powerful rulers in the history of the East. His legends were as famous in the East as were Rogran's in the West. The foundation that he lay in Mayndoda allowed his descendants to rule in peace for generations.

But the rulers of Mayndoda forgot that that peace was hard-earned, and that always in the East, the enemy lurked just out of sight. Mayndoda was one of the earliest kingdoms to come under assault from the vynobnie during their resurgence in the late fifth diura. It was also the first to fall under that assault. Haalzona went to its aid, but the tide of vynobnie was too strong to be held more than temporarily at bay. In the end, in an act that was seen as betrayal by the humans of Mayndoda, the armies of Haalzona returned to their country, unwilling to weaken its defences any further by throwing their men at a futile effort. They offered the humans of Mayndoda asylum in Haalzona, but few accepted the offer. Mayndoda was broken and its humans scattered into the wild by the dawn of the forty-eighth aeon.

Mirhisd

Another country where the human settlers encountered unusual native beings rather than vynobnie was Mirhisd. When the settlers arrived in Mirhisd towards the end of the second decadus of the fourteenth aeon, they were surprised to find the land thick with large, tunnelled mounds. They assumed that some kind of monster insects inhabited the land but were mistaken in this. These were hives, true, but not of insects. The natives—phrixes—lived in these hives. They were small, the tallest of them no higher than a man's waist, if that. They were thin with sharp, narrow features, except for their noses, which were short and upturned. Their skin had a bluish-grey hue, and their hair was bluish-black. Their eyes were large and dark blue, and their ears were long and pointy. For a race of such tiny beings, they were capable of leaping great heights and across long distances. They lived in hives, which were ruled by queens and were located in caves dug into the sides of hills or in forest groves.

At first, the human settlers did not consider them as threats, but they were mistaken. Although smaller and weaker, the phrixes were faster and stealthier. They avoided frontal conflict but attacked stealthily whenever they could. They laid ambushes and disappeared before the humans could realise what was happening. They were also expert thieves, and the humans often found themselves without vital weapons or food or medicines at the worst possible moment in a battle. In an attempt to fight fire with fire, they began to adopt the stealth and speed of their adversaries. Soon, they were settling into the hives they had captured from the phrixes due to the vulnerability of houses to sudden and devastating attacks. For close to two aeons, the struggle stood at an impasse. In the meantime, a common quality of both races—curiosity—drove them to trade and to explore the lives of the opposition. Soon, the advantages of trade overcame the advantages of wanting to destroy the enemy, which was beginning to seem like an impossibility in any case. By the time Ranhenh married Lord Xanther's sixth daughter, Syliatta, peace had been established between the two races, although not since long. Humans and phrixes were still tentative in their overtures of friendship towards one another. This changed when Syliatta became queen of the hive to which Ranhenh belonged. Under her efforts, human-phrix relationships improved dramatically to the extent that some hives became biracial, with both phrix and human families living side by side.

The friendship grew under the queenship of their daughter, Sehira, who was born in 1585 A.E. But it was Sehira's daughter, Herenna, who finally united all the hives under a single standard as the hive federation of Mirhisd and became the first mistress-queen of Mirhisd in 1624 A.E. By then, both Syliatta and Ranhenh were long dead. Because phrixes are shorter-lived than humans, Herenna was then the equivalent of a thirty-annus-old human even though her numerical age was twenty anni. Even so, at that time, she was the youngest founder of any of the countries in the East. Her descendants ruled the country for many more generations than did those of any of the other founding families but in anni, the federation was hardly longer lived than Qeezsh. And although, unlike the other eastern kingdoms, Mirhisd was never completely overrun by vynobnie, their federation disbanded, and the number of hives continued to reduce in number until only a handful were left towards the easternmost edges of the country by the seventh decadus of the forty-ninth aeon. Because their capital Borylend never fell to the vynobnie, they continued to resist the vynobnie long after there were no more mistress-queens in Mirhisd.

WYURR

Wyurr was almost the last territory to be settled by the humans migrating from Blarzonia. It was a wild, forested country full of terrible creatures that attacked the human settlers. These filthy, savage vynobnie were named ghrimbens by the settlers. Like most vynobnie, they were little better than wild beasts. But they had one major advantage over animals that almost put an end to the dream of human settlement in Wyurr. They were well organised and extremely cunning. They hunted in packs and killed indiscriminately, eating the flesh of fallen comrades as often as that of fallen enemies. It was their own ability to unite and fight, adapt to the forests and turn them into weapons that allowed the humans to survive and gradually overcome this threat to their very existence.

And so it was that Wyurr learnt a lesson in unity very early on that took the other countries much longer to learn. Their unity allowed them to expand their territories to a size that rivalled Haalzona's. Every citizen of Wyurr was required to train in fighting and to fight the ghrimbens when the time came. Their fierce warrior skills earned them the respect of not only the other eastern countries but that of the dharvhs beyond the Lyudzbradh and the eighes in the north as well. Soldiers of Wyurr were the most sought after as mercenaries. And a mercenary named Seolaston was the one who married Lord Xanther's eighth daughter, Liravya. He was a unique man; ruthless in battle but the most compassionate in life. He and Liravya had a daughter in 1589 A.E., and they named her after Liravya's youngest sister Bezashy who had never been brought back to life. And although the people of Wyurr had remained untied as a nation since their early days, they were formally established as a kingdom in 1641 A.E. by Barhamos, the son of Bezashy (II). He was only thirty anni old at the time, and both his maternal grandparents were alive to see him ascend the throne.

Seolaston passed at the ripe old age of ninety, and Liravya outlived him by eight anni. By then, Barhamos has established a strong reign and was beginning to ensure that the ghrimben menace would remain restricted to the forests at the foothills of the Lyudzbradh. His descendants continued to hold the ghrimbens back for aeons, and it was only the fall of the other kingdoms of the East that weakened Wyurr from all sides and allowed the ghrimbens to return in force. Even so, Wyurr was almost the last kingdom to fall, holding on to civilisation until the sixth decadus of the fiftieth aeon. Once the ghrimbens overwhelmed Wyurr, humans vanished from the country almost without a trace.

ILLAFANKA

The story of human civilisation in Illafanka is a testament to the resilience of humans as a race. This southernmost part of the East was the last to be settled, over an aeon after the settlement of Haalzona. The land was inhospitable and riddled with lakes, bogs and swamps that were home to numerous vynobnie that attacked unwary travellers and carried off sleeping children. But the most insidious of the monsters the settlers found in Illafanka were ones that were not immediately recognised as monsters. These were the mertkhezi, a race that could take the form of humans and lure them to their deaths with their singing. It is not known whether the mertkhezi could take human form before meeting the humans or, if not, how they acquired the ability afterwards. However, hundreds of people fell victim to the mertkhezi before the settlers realised that these beautiful humans who sang most melodiously were not humans at all. But by then, unknown to the rest, hundreds more had become slaves of these mysterious vynobnie though they had not been led to their deaths.

The survivors armed themselves to face their enemies by devising ways to protect them from the songs of the mertkhezi. They developed ways to navigate the wetlands without falling to the water or mud-dwelling vynobnie. And they found ways to quickly recognise and kill mertkhezi in their human as well as native forms. The survivors began to push the vynobnie back with painstaking slowness, enduring a defeat for every two victories. Their greatest danger, though, came from within, for those who had been enslaved by the mertkhezi would not hesitate to kill their own children if ordered to do so by their enslaver. For a very long time, the future of humans in Illafanka hung in the balance. It was sheer chance that helped to tilt it in their favour. For, it turned out that human flesh was not suitable for the mertkhezi's consumption. No one learnt how or why it hurt them, but mertkhezi stopped preying upon humans for food. In a way, though, it increased their hatred for the human race; they continued to turn humans against each other and to lure them into traps for other vynobnie to hunt. Yet, there was a marked change in the tide of the battle.

The mertkhezi were further pushed back by the exceptional persistence of a young man named Castillon who doggedly led the armies of the humans into the deepest parts of the territory, destroying nests of mertkhezi, burning swamps down along with their hordes of vynobnie and cleansing the land of the plague of these monsters. He was already a known name among the humans of Illafanka when he married Dionyse, Lord Xanther's third daughter. Together, they continued to clear a path for humans to thrive in the land that they had settled. The cudgel was taken up by their son, Eroven, after them, who succeeded in forcing the mertkhezi and other water-borne vynobnie to the smallest of the lakes and swamps. However, the human forces suffered a blow when he gave birth to a daughter, Bewonin, who was a gentle soul and could not lead the armies against the vynobnie. A leadership void threatened to undo all that had been achieved until Bewonin's young son, Ishenar, took up the standard. He had his grandfather Eroven's valour and his great-grandparents' relentless industry. The combination of these qualities allowed him to make the final push against the enemies of humans that toppled the mertkhezi and other vynobnie off the edge of the battlefield and into hiding. When he founded the kingdom of Illafanka in the annus 1658 A.E., he was the youngest of all the founders at twenty-seven anni of age.

He was followed by strong successors who kept the mertkhezi at bay over the aeons. However, the mertkhezi were always trying to return to power using their insidious abilities. And when the humans forgot the means that they had adopted to thwart these ancient enemies, the mertkhezi and other monsters crept back out of the lakes, bogs and swamps, where they had remained hidden for diuras, to retake the lands that had once been theirs. They were beaten back again and again but their growing strength, combined with the weakening of humans in the entire East, finally allowed them to overwhelm the humans. Yet the humans held on until into the fiftieth aeon, when almost all the countries had succumbed to vynobnie. But by the fourth decadus of the fiftieth aeon, they had no strength left and soon the humans disappeared off the face of Illafanka, either dead or enslaved or surviving like wild animals in hiding.

1223 A.E.	People start migrating out of Blarzonia
1249 A.E.	Emergence of draconians as a race
1259 A.E.	People settle later day Haalzona
1273 A.E.	People settle later day Waurlen
1287 A.E.	People settle later day Qeezsh
1301 A.E.	People settle later day Mayndoda
1318 A.E.	People settle later day Mirhisd
1330 A.E.	People settle later day Wyurr
1361 A.E.	People settle later day Illafanka
1528 A.E.	Xanther is born
1533 A.E.	Eaginna is born

1541 A.E.	Zarathie is born
1543 A.E.	Akhetash is born
1549 A.E.	Xanther and Eaginna get married
1552 A.E.	Castillon is born
1554 A.E.	Ardumel is born
1555 A.E.	Thybald is born
1558 A.E.	Maheschom is born
1559 A.E.	Mesthona is born
1560 A.E.	Porillyn is born; Seolaston is born
1561 A.E.	Dionyse is born
1562 A.E.	Ollivyra is born
1563 A.E.	Ealyse is born
1564 A.E.	Syliatta is born; Trakurth is born
1565 A.E.	Rabedhi is born
1566 A.E.	Liravya is born
1567 A.E.	Bezashy is born; Eaginna dies
1569 A.E.	Ranhenh is born
1571 A.E.	Xanther marries Zarathie
1572 A.E.	Zarathie tries to kill Xanther's daughters; appearance of magical flowers
1579 A.E.	Ardumel revives and marries Mesthona
1580 A.E.	Akhetash revives and marries Porillyn; Ardumel and Mesthona's son, Merayan, is born
1581 A.E.	Castillon revives and marries Dionyse
1582 A.E.	Thybald revives and marries Ollivyra
1583 A.E.	Maheschom revives and marries Ealyse; Castillon and Dionyse's son, Eroven, is born
1584 A.E.	Ranhenh revives and marries Syliatta; Thybald and Ollivyra's son, Olveron, is born
1585 A.E.	Trakurth revives and marries Rabedhi; Ranhenh and Syliatta's daughter, Sehira, is born
1586 A.E.	Seolaston revives and marries Liravya; Akhetash and Porillyn's son, Revash, is born
1589 A.E.	Seolaston and Liravya's daughter, Bezashy (II), is born

1590 A.E.	Trakurth and Rabedhi's son, Trabedh, is born
1601 A.E.	Maheschom and Ealyse's son, Domvaer, is born
1602 A.E.	Castillon dies
1604 A.E.	Sehira's daughter, Herenna, is born
1608 A.E.	Maheschom founds the kingdom of Haalzona; Eroven's daughter, Bewonin, is born
1611 A.E.	Bezashy (II)'s son, Barhamos, is born
1612 A.E.	Akhetash establishes the tribal state of Qeezsh
1614 A.E.	Merayan's son, Conatin, is born; Xanther dies; Syliatta dies
1618 A.E.	Olveron founds the kingdom of Waurlen; Ollivyra dies
1623 A.E.	Ranhenh dies
1624 A.E.	Herenna establishes the hive federation of Mirhisd
1627 A.E.	Ardumel dies
1629 A.E.	Rabedhi dies
1631 A.E.	Bewonin's son, Ishenar, is born
1632 A.E.	Trabedh founds the kingdom of Mayndoda; Thybald dies; Ealyse dies
1635 A.E.	Mesthona dies
1636 A.E.	Trakurth dies
1641 A.E.	Barhamos founds the kingdom of Wyurr
1642 A.E.	Maheschom dies; Domvaer becomes king of Haalzona
1645 A.E.	Dionyse dies
1650 A.E.	Seolaston dies
1654 A.E.	Conatin founds the kingdom of Blarzonia
1658 A.E.	Ishenar founds the kingdom of Illafanka; Liravya dies
1669 A.E.	Akhetash dies; Revash becomes chief-of-chiefs of Qeezsh
1678 A.E.	Porillyn dies
4337 A.E.	Draconians are overcome by the Blarzonians
4701 A.E.	Fall of the kingdom of Mayndoda
4747 A.E.	Last battle between the Blarzonians and the dharvhs; Blarzonia falls
4848 A.E.	Fall of Abluvel, the capital of Qeezsh
4869 A.E.	Fall of the hive federation of Mirhisd

4891 A.E.	Fall of the kingdom of Waurlen
4942 A.E.	Fall of the kingdom of Illafanka
4963 A.E.	Fall of the kingdom of Wyurr
5004 A.E.	Haalzona is overcome by kocovuses

In a place not far from White Mountain was the dominion of Ettarant. The manor-lord of Ettarant was Lord Nankent. He owned vast tracts of land and had tens of thousands of subjects in his dominion. He was one of the most influential of the manor-lords of Blarzonia and one of the few to possess a standing army. Ettarant was a prosperous and peaceful dominion with a bleak future. For, Lord Nankent and his wife, Lady Belisha, had no children. It was the greatest regret of their lives that despite their great love for each other and their mutual desire for many children, they had none. No healer had been able to find anything wrong with either of them physically, and their lack of heirs was a complete mystery. Despite this, they never gave up hope.

One day, a strange healer came to meet Lord Nankent and told him that he could solve Lord Nankent and Lady Belisha's childlessness in exchange for sanctuary. Several of Lord Nankent's advisors were suspicious of this strange man and warned him against giving the healer sanctuary. But Lord Nankent was more astute than his advisors and recognised that the healer was not human at all but draconian. He challenged the draconian healer with the truth, and the healer dropped his disguise to acknowledge that Lord Nankent was indeed as perceptive as he was reputed to be. His offer still stood, he said. He could help Lord Nankent and Lady Belisha have a child in exchange for sanctuary. Lord Nankent was not convinced of the healer's offer and asked him why he needed sanctuary and who from. The draconian healer, whose name was Ingash, replied that he was wanted by a neighbouring manor-lord on suspicion of theft. He further confessed that the charge was true as he had stolen a dragon's egg from the manor-lord's keep. However, he added, the manor-lord had himself obtained it wrongfully in the first place from one of the dragons of Ingash's people by killing the nesting mother.

'Won't your people protect you for returning what rightfully belongs to them?' Lord Nankent asked Ingash.

'They will, but the cost might be too high. We are not yet strong enough to face the armies of the dominions, and there are many who would stand by your neighbour if he decides to fight us. If my people show him proof that I have been exiled and that they had no hand in the theft of the egg, he will leave them alone.'

'But why should I risk war with my neighbour for your sake?' Lord Nankent demanded.

'Not for my sake,' Ingash replied with a smile. 'But for the sake of your heir. Besides, your neighbour would never dare to attack you since you are far more powerful than he is. And even if he tried to, the others would not support him against a manor-lord as well-respected as you. They would not want to get on your wrong side just to teach one thieving draconian a lesson.'

'But why are you telling me all this? And why should I believe a single word of what you say?' Lord Nankent demanded.

'I am telling you all this because you asked. Your noble nature and love of truth and justice are as well-known as your perceptiveness. If you had not asked me, I would not have told you. Since you did, I cannot lie to you and still expect to receive help from you. That would be dishonourable. We draconians are honourable people despite what most humans believe. As for proof, I think this should suffice,' he said, bringing out a strange object from his bag. It was shaped like an egg but was like no egg that Lord Nankent had ever seen. It was the colour of the blackest stone streaked with red and gold and blue. The colours swirled and moved in constantly changing patterns across the shiny surface of the egg. Lord Nankent was intrigued.

'Are you offering this precious egg to me?' he asked reverentially.

'No, my lord,' replied Ingash. 'I cannot do that. For no human has the right to own a dragon or its egg. Nor does any other mortal. Dragons are their own masters, and they have been friends and guardians to us draconians for ages, imparting their wisdom to us to raise us from the pit of worthlessness in which we once wallowed. I am showing you this egg to prove that I tell the truth. And because I trust you to keep it safe until I can return it to my people. My offer is still the same. In return for sanctuary, I will ensure that you and Lady Belisha are no longer childless.'

Lord Nankent was so impressed by Ingash and his honesty and integrity that he agreed to his terms despite the suggestions of his advisors to the contrary. He not only provided Ingash sanctuary but took him into his own household as a friend and brother, an unprecedented honour that no one could believe. This remarkable event took place at the dawn of the fifteenth aeon. By then, the strength of humans in Blarzonia was beginning to wane, and the draconians were growing in power and influence although it was yet some time before they would establish themselves as the rulers of Blarzonia. Lord Nankent was one of the rare manor-lords who were able to foresee the rise of the draconians and secured their future through friendships and alliances with them. Ingash played a significant role in the forging of these ties.

But that was not the only contribution he made to Lord Nankent's life. He kept his promise to Lord Nankent. On the first of Lokrin in the annus 1508 A.E., Lord Nankent and Lady Belisha of the house of Arvarles become ecstatic parents to a baby boy. Lord Nankent was then forty-six anni old and Lady Belisha was thirty-eight. With no hope of any other children, they lavished all their affection and care on their firstborn. The child was named Nishtar, which in Ankery, the language of the draconians, meant 'eternal strength'.

Nishtar had an ordinary, uneventful childhood. He was a prodigious child and from a very young age, he had a passion for learning. Whatever he turned his hand to, he shone at. He had read all the books in his father's library by the age of eight and could debate with the wisest of his teachers, presenting irrefutable arguments. He could calculate complicated sums inside his head faster than the fastest of mathematicians in the dominion. When he began to train as a warrior, he managed to outshine not only the other young men but also his father's greatest generals by the time he was fifteen anni old. At the age of seventeen, he finished his education, confident that he had nothing more to learn.

Two anni later, he married the daughter of a manor-lord from the far south of the country. She was a beautiful young woman named Emera, who was devoted to her husband. They had a daughter, Eaginna, in the annus 1533 A.E. By then, Nishtar had begun to assist Lord Nankent with the governance of the dominion actively. Ingash had left a couple of anni ago to return to his people as the political situation of Blarzonia was growing increasingly turbulent. Hostilities between humans and draconians were on the rise, and battle lines were getting drawn, metaphorically if not literally. It was in this kind of atmosphere that Nishtar became the manor-lord of Ettarant a mere two anni after his daughter's birth. Lord Nankent died a happy old man, leaving the responsibilities of governing Ettarant in Nishtar's able hands.

Nishtar proved as capable as his father at ensuring law and order, peace and prosperity in his dominion. He also continued his father's policy of friendship with the draconians. However, this earned him the ire of many of his neighbours, who began to make trouble for him overtly and covertly, rendering it extremely difficult for him to rule his dominion with any degree of ease. They had respected Lord Nankent's strength too much to go up against him. But Nishtar was an unproven ruler, and they felt that they could overwhelm him if they joined forces against him. When Nishtar proved more than equal to the task of rebutting their direct and indirect attacks, taking Ettarant from strength to strength in the process, they realised that he would not be an easy target. They decided to change their tactics to get rid of him.

They approached Nishtar with an offer of a peace treaty. But, they insisted, he would have to travel to a neighbouring dominion to sign the peace pact as a gesture of his own goodwill. Nishtar agreed to these terms, for peace was highly desirable if Ettarant was to flourish. Yet, Nishtar did not trust his neighbours. He suspected them of laying a trap for him. Lady Emera begged him not to go, but Nishtar could not refuse without acknowledging that he was afraid of them. Just as he was about to depart, he had an unexpected visitor. It was Ingash, the draconian healer who had been responsible for his birth. Ingash had come because he had heard that Lady Belisha was seriously ill. He was too late as she had passed away only a few days ago. Heartsore, Ingash offered his condolences to Nishtar and Lady Emera and expressed surprise that Nishtar was leaving Ettarant at such a time. Nishtar told him of the impending peace treaty with his neighbours.

Ingash asked him to delay his journey by three days although he did not provide any reason. Trusting him implicitly, Nishtar acceded to his request. For three days, Ingash remained shut up in the chamber that had been allocated to him, seeing no one and eating or drinking nothing. Strange sounds and flashes of light came from the room occasionally and had everyone on edge. At the end of the three days, he emerged with a vial of a shimmering green liquid and asked Nishtar to drink it.

'Why? What is it?' Nishtar asked, curious rather than suspicious.

'Something that will give you an advantage over your neighbours. You will know what it does at the right time,' Ingash replied.

He saw Nishtar off to the border of Ettarant, repeatedly warning him to be careful of traps and treachery and promising to look after Lady Emera and little Eaginna in his absence. With the old draconian's warnings ringing in his mind, Nishtar made his way cautiously to the site of the peace treaty. He was accompanied by the smartest of his soldiers, and they guarded him against an ambush adroitly. Nishtar and his party had an uneventful journey at the end of which Nishtar arrived more agitated than ever and wishing that he could know what his neighbours had planned.

The next morning, all of them met to discuss and finalise the treaty before signing it. Nishtar's feeling of agitation had given way to calm alertness as a result of meditating throughout the night. His soldiers had again kept watch alertly, but no attack had come. As Nishtar stared at the inscrutable face of an old manor-lord sitting next to him, he found himself wishing for the umpteenth time that he knew what the others were thinking. Suddenly he heard, 'These young fools should have ambushed him and blamed it on bandits.'

Startled, he asked his neighbour, 'Did you say something to me, my lord?'

'No, no, I did not,' the old man replied curtly. But Nishtar was certain that he had heard him say something about an ambush.

Before he could decide whether he was hallucinating, he heard another of the parties to the treaty say, 'I hope the information that he is fond of wine from the south is correct.'

Nishtar almost jumped out of his skin. He had been looking straight at the man who had spoken, but his lips had not moved at all. All of a sudden, a cacophony of conversation filled Nishtar's mind. It was as if everyone present there was speaking at once and yet, Nishtar could clearly see, only a few were actually speaking. Nishtar realised at once what was going on. He could hear what the others were thinking! He remembered Ingash's medicine that was supposed to give him an advantage over his enemies. Perhaps the medicine allowed one to hear others' thoughts! Or perhaps it granted one's wishes, for he *had* been wishing he could know what they were thinking. Either way, the medicine had indeed provided him an unprecedented advantage. By concentrating on one person at a time, he was able to block out the thoughts of the others. Systematically scanning the thoughts of all those present there, he was able to put together information about the plot against his life. Their plan was to drag the discussions on until the afternoon when the assembly would break for a sumptuous banquet. Wine from the south, that Nishtar was known to be fond of, had been fetched. This wine was to be the carrier of a tasteless but extremely potent poison whose symptoms mimicked choking. No one would know that Nishtar had been murdered. Nishtar also managed to discover who was going to add the poison and at what time.

Armed with this knowledge, he sent the captain of his soldiers to capture the servant who had been given the responsibility of poisoning Nishtar's drink. Although aware of the plot, Nishtar continued to play along to keep his enemies off their guard. As they had planned, the discussions and negotiations dragged on for horas until it was time for the banquet. Proceedings were postponed until after the meal. As they left the chamber, Nishtar saw the captain of his guards standing inconspicuously among other guards and soldiers. He gave his master an almost imperceptible nod that told Nishtar that he had succeeded in his mission. He need not have nodded, for Nishtar could hear his excited and alert thoughts as clearly as if the man had been shouting them into his ear!

The banquet was indeed sumptuous though Nishtar ate frugally, making sure not to touch anything that the others did not share. Although he had not heard anyone mention any other food item as poisoned, it did not hurt to be too careful. Finally, it was time for the 'execution,' as many of the manor-lords present there thought of it. From their demeanour, no one would have guessed that they were about to kill a man treacherously in cold blood. But their frenzied and nervous thoughts told Nishtar that they were all on edge. Soon, cups of the special wine were being passed around. Nishtar smiled and accepted a cup, as he was expected to. Suddenly, there was a commotion towards the rear of the banquet hall, and loud cries of 'Fire!' were heard. Everyone turned anxiously, ready to flee at a moment's notice. Within momons, though, the commotion was resolved. Apparently, one of the roasts had caught fire. Everyone returned to feasting and drinking with renewed zeal, especially when they saw Nishtar with a goblet in his hand.

Seeing their eyes on him, Nishtar lifted the goblet and announced, 'A toast to peace!'

'To peace!' they all murmured and lifted their goblets to their lips, as did Nishtar, with barely contained smirks. They were certain that any momon now, Nishtar would begin to choke and then die soon after.

But as they drained their own goblets, Nishtar smiled broadly at them. All eyes were on him now, no one bothering to conceal his hostility from a dying man. His smile unnerved them a little. He was reputed to be a serious man who rarely smiled, and his smile moments before his expected demise struck them with misgivings. Slowly, as they watched, Nishtar turned his goblet upside down, still smiling broadly. Not a drop of wine spilled from the overturned goblet. There had been no wine in it when Nishtar had raised it to his lips.

The faces of the assembled manor-lords grew pale as they realised that Nishtar had found them out and avoided their trap. Utterly shocked, they stood still, not sure what to do next. They had never anticipated that their carefully laid trap would fail. All of a sudden, they rushed Nishtar, their weapons drawn. Nishtar had anticipated this move even without reading their minds. It was the desperate attempt of men who had gambled everything, certain of victory, and had lost it all in a single moment. At a signal from Nishtar, his guards poured into the banquet hall. The other manor-lords called for their own guards but no guards came. The red and brown stains on the uniforms of Nishtar's soldiers told the gathering what had happened to their men. Despite being outnumbered and outskilled, they fought tooth and nail. But their fates were sealed. They fell to the swords of Nishtar's men; Nishtar did not have to lift his own sword even once. A few tried to escape, but Nishtar had planned for this contingency too. There was no escape for any of the conspirators that day.

When Nishtar returned home, he thanked Ingash profusely for saving his life by giving him the miraculous potion.

'It was not the potion that saved your life, my dear boy,' said the old draconian gravely. 'The potion merely allowed you to save your own life.'

'I don't understand,' said Nishtar, confused by Ingash's words.

'There is something that you do not know about yourself, something that your parents and I hid from you because we did not want you to leave Ettarant behind and go away to Maghem,' Ingash said sadly.

'Maghem? Why would I go to Maghem? Only magi…' Nishtar halted as the truth dawned upon him.

Ingash nodded despondently. 'Yes, you are a magus. When your abilities began to show, your parents asked me to get rid of those gifts. You were their only child and had been born to them late in their lives. They wanted you to be the ruler of Ettarant rather than a magus whom they would never see once he left to train at the beginning of his adolescence. Losing you was unbearable to them. So I helped them. But even my skill was not capable of changing who you were. The most that I was able to do was suppress those abilities. You were so young that you do not remember drinking a potion similar to the one you drank before leaving for the meeting with your neighbours. This potion reversed the effects of the previous one and allowed your talents to come forth, which allowed you to turn the tables on your enemies.'

Nishtar was furious when he heard this. All his life, he had been treated as a normal human. An extraordinary one, no doubt, but still normal. He remonstrated with Ingash for horas, accusing him and his late parents of ruining his life. The old healer said nothing. He stood quietly while the young man's anger burned itself out. When Nishtar finally calmed down, Ingash said, 'Now that you know the truth, what do you wish to do?'

Nishtar did not know what he wished to do. On the one hand, he felt a burning desire to explore his true nature, to train as a magus. If the merest blossoming of his abilities had allowed him to read people's minds to save his own life, what would the full attainment of his gifts bestow upon him? On the other hand, he had a wife and child, and also a dominion to run. If he left them behind, everything that his parents had achieved, and that he had achieved, would fall to ruins. His victory over his enemies would be futile as he would practically hand his dominion over to them. It was the most difficult decision he had ever had to make in his young life. Finally, after a great deal of cogitation and internal debate, he decided to pursue his destiny in Maghem.

So, at the age of thirty, Nishtar Arvarles put the running of his dominion in the hands of his wife, Lady Emera, and left for Maghem. Ingash not only promised to support and look after Emera and Eaginna, but also showed Nishtar how to use a portal to enter Maghem. Nishtar's first concern upon reaching Maghem was to find a suitable teacher. To his utter surprise, few were willing to teach him although many acknowledged that his innate abilities were strong. In the end, through his own efforts and by coaxing, cajoling or compelling multiple magi, Nishtar began to learn the art and craft of controlling minds and matter. He was equally brilliant at both; the level of talent that he possessed at controlling both was not only unusual but indeed rare. Soon, he was as good as any magus who had trained for decadi in established schools in Maghem. However, the unorthodox learning process that he was forced to follow meant that the completion of his training took longer than usual. By the time he became an accomplished magus in his own right, he was forty-four anni old.

On his first visit to Yennthem after the completion of his training, he learnt that his daughter had married three anni ago. She had married a powerful manorlord named Xanther from the other side of the Lyudzbradh. Ingash had died in the intervening anni, but he had trained Lady Emera well, and she was holding her own in a world where humans were losing ground to draconians slowly but surely. She begged her husband to return home, but the oaths that he had taken upon the completion of his training prevented him from doing so. He promised to return whenever he could to keep an eye on her and on Eaginna and her husband, even though he knew it was nearly impossible for magi to be permitted to travel to Yennthem with any degree of regularity.

He returned to Maghem and dedicated himself to deeper studies of an esoteric nature that few magi had the talent or inclination for. In 1559 A.E., he met Beben Hoth, a famous inhabitant of Maghem. Beben was best known for his search of Mesmen Orao, arguably the oldest and most powerful of the magi. Older than count, she was responsible for many of the norms that guided the lives of magi. More than six aeons ago, she had vanished without trace, throwing Maghem into consternation. It was Beben who had undertaken an epic journey then to rediscover her whereabouts. His determination and devotion had so impressed her that she had taken him as her disciple, the only one ever. Beben was, along with Mesmen Orao, one of the oldest and most revered magi in Maghem. When Beben met Nishtar, he was so impressed by the self-made magus's abilities that he took Nishtar for his own disciple. This immediately shot Nishtar into prominence of the kind that he had always sought whether as a mortal or as a magus.

It did not take Nishtar long to realise that his master, Beben, was no ordinary magus. In the first place, there was his age. If he had discovered Mesmen's whereabouts more than six hundred anni ago, he was at least six hundred and fifty anni old, which was impossible for any normal magus. Magi did live longer lives compared to ordinary mortals, but no one had heard of any magus living more than two aeons. Nishtar was determined to discover the secret to Beben's longevity. He did not dare ask directly for fear of angering his master, so he began to ask Beben oblique questions about his life and his work with Mesmen to glean answers that might provide a clue to the truth. Beben was happy to talk to his brilliant pupil and unwittingly provided him with information that allowed Nishtar to piece together much of what he wanted to know.

By the time Beben realised what his disciple had been up to, Nishtar already knew too much. Beben took Nishtar to meet Mesmen, hoping that she could convince him to give up his investigations. Nishtar met the legendary Mesmen

Orao for the first time in the annus 1564 A.E. However, even she could not change his mind. The only options left to Mesmen and Beben were to kill Nishtar or to make him party to their secret. The next annus, Beben succeeded in convincing Mesmen to share their secret of immortality with Nishtar when he realised that his disciple was on the verge of discovering it on his own. And so it was that Nishtar Arvarles became the third magus in existence to become a *sumagus*, which was the term that Mesmen and Beben used for themselves. At that time, no one in Maghem or Yennthem knew of the existence of the sumagi. Despite that, as a sumagus, Nishtar had power and privileges that other magi did not. He used these to strengthen his prominence and influence further by becoming one of the most powerful magi ever. The next decadus or so of his life was marked by great success as a magus and crushing losses as a man.

The first of these was the death of his daughter Eaginna. Broken-hearted at the demise of his only daughter, he travelled to her funeral, where he met his nine granddaughters and his son-in-law Xanther. Burdened by guilt at having failed his daughter despite his promise to Lady Emera, he resolved to keep an eye on his granddaughters to ensure that they could have a happy life. And he did succeed in doing so for a while. When Lord Xanther remarried, Nishtar was not happy, but he could not argue with Xanther's logic that young girls needed a mother to look after them. Great, therefore, was his shock when he heard of their deaths in 1572 A.E. He rushed to Yennthem to meet his son-in-law and investigate the truth behind his granddaughters' deaths. When he arrived, he learnt of Xanther's dream and decided that he would help Xanther find suitable bridegrooms for his daughters. But five anni later, he again faced terrible personal loss when Lady Emera died. Her passing was the final blow for a man already burdened by his failures as a husband, father and grandfather. He severed all his ties with Yennthem and returned to Maghem, where he remained for a period of several diuras without a single visit to Yennthem.

Having achieved remarkable personal success as a magus, Nishtar decided to enable young minds to do the same. Soon after returning from Yennthem, he chose the profession of teaching and became a teacher at one of the schools for young magi to develop their abilities and craft. In just over a decadus, he had managed to become the headmaster of the school, in which capacity he served for three decadi. He then left the school to become involved in the politics and governance of Maghem, which was complicated, chaotic and murky to say the least. His background as a manor-lord stood him in good stead in this work, and in 1640 A.E. he succeeded in establishing the Council of the Wise as the leading body for the governance of Maghem, with the three sumagi at its helm. By then, all of Maghem knew of the sumagi and were in no position to oppose their rule. Five anni later, Nishtar produced the Constitution that encoded all the rules and laws to guide life on Maghem and that would replace the norms that had been passed down orally for ages. Every aspect of life on Maghem was now regulated by written laws; Maghem would never be the same again.

The next annus, Nishtar returned to teaching, although he continued to remain a member of the Council of the Wise, a position that was open only to a sumagus in perpetuity. This time, however, he opened a school of his own. It was vastly different from the ones that had existed in Maghem before and soon became the school of choice for all aspiring magi youth. The school's success and its running kept Nishtar busy for several aeons, during which time he discovered and invented much that added to the body of knowledge related to magi's abilities. Late in the twenty-fourth aeon, Nishtar met an unusual old magus. He had gone to Nishtar to enrol his great-great nephew in Nishtar's school. This magus had been classically trained but had fallen in love with books at a mature age and had dedicated himself to the preservation of the written word. The old magus caught Nishtar's attention far more than the young one. The name of this unusual magus was Sumaho Menshir. Nishtar decided, soon after meeting him, to make Sumaho a sumagus. The next annus, Sumaho was made a sumagus and joined his three predecessors on the Council of the Wise.

It was close to eight aeons later that Nishtar met a seventeen-annus-old shepherd boy who showed great promise as a magus. Unfortunately, the boy was too old for institutional education. So Nishtar, reminded of his own struggles, guided this young magus to a teacher who had retired not long ago from Nishtar's own school. This shepherd boy's name was Oram Ashar, and Nishtar decided to keep an eye on his progress. Unfortunately, his many and onerous responsibilities prevented him from doing so, and the many brilliant young magi that passed through the doorways of his school made him almost forget Oram. By the time he got around to tracking him down, Oram had already returned to Yennthem to pursue a profession of his choice. This was something that was allowed to magi under the new rules that Nishtar had framed, though the permission allowed each magus to live on Yennthem for a limited period only. Therefore, great was his surprise when he met Oram again in Sumaho's company less than a decadus later. The greater surprise, though, was that Sumaho had initiated Oram into the secret of immortality. Since Oram was already a sumagus, Nishtar inducted him into the Council of the Wise as its fifth member.

Close to another seven aeons passed before Nishtar was called upon to induct the sixth member of the Council. The candidate was Alanor, called Ushwah, son of Rogran, who was being rightfully hailed as the founder of the human kingdoms of western Elthrusia. Alanor had had an unorthodox training but was no less accomplished as a magus for that. Accepting Oram's keen judgement, Nishtar revealed the secret of immortality to Alanor, making him the sixth of the sumagi.

By then, amendments had been made to the original Constitution of Maghem, led by the newer members of the Council of the Wise, whose ideas reflected their own times. One of these amendments allowed magi to settle permanently in Yennthem as long as they followed a chosen profession and restricted their use of their abilities to the practice of this profession or to activities that were aimed at helping the residents of Yennthem. No magus or maga was allowed to use his or her power for selfish gains. Nishtar was one of the first magi to take advantage of this new law even though he had himself framed the earlier restrictive one. In 4306 A.E., he returned to Yennthem to open a school for mortal boys, more than two thousand seven hundred anni after his last visit. Much had changed by then; the Yennthem he found bore little resemblance to the Yennthem he had left behind. He picked up the threads of his life and began to look for a new purpose in teaching mortal boys to be great.

Unfortunately, the lack of connection between Maghem and Yennthem for ages meant that Nishtar had to wait long and work hard to find any students at all. He succeeded in gathering only seven boys as students in the anus 4309 A.E., and began to teach these seven from the first of Kawitor the next annus. By the time these boys finished their education with him and left to find their own paths in the world in 4316 A.E., Nishtar was highly impressed with their capabilities as well as their potential to become influential figures in their chosen fields. He returned to Maghem for an annus to keep himself abreast of the developments there. When he returned to Yennthem just before the Ach in 4317 A.E., he was surprised to find that he still had managed to recruit only seven students despite the success of the previous batch. So he began to teach these seven. The next batch of boys too numbered seven. By then, Nishtar figured that there was some mystical significance to that number that he did not understand, and he decided to take no more than seven students even if he ever received more applicants. His school gained in success and fame over the anni until he was known as the best teacher in Yennthem and hordes of boys of every race came to be trained by him. Yet he did not deviate from the norm that he had established. He selected the seven best of these aspirants and taught them for seven anni, moving back to Maghem for an annus between two subsequent batches of students.

In 4444 A.E., he met an unusual young woman during a trip to Maghem. She was a maga but had also been trained in sorcery, witchcraft and necromancy at a young age. But her most extraordinary ability was revealed to Nishtar during a conversation when she suddenly pronounced a prophecy about him in the middle of talking about her training. Nishtar had no doubt that the prophecy was a genuine one even though he had never seen another prophet in all his time on Yennthem or Maghem. This young maga's name was Vellila Regat, and Nishtar foresaw greatness in her future even without possessing her rare ability to see the future. Eleven anni later, he met her again, this time in Oram's company. Oram convinced Nishtar that Vellila deserved to be a sumaga and to be on the Council of the Wise. Therefore, despite Mesmen's strident opposition, Nishtar managed to secure approval for Vellila's induction as a sumaga and into the Council.

In 4502 A.E., Nishtar's life underwent another turn when he first heard about the Prophecy of Kawiti. Born a diura and a half after Astoreth and Zavak, he had known about their stories all his life. Now he discovered something that was known to none. He tabled this information at the Council of the Wise and adjured them to delve into the matter. At this point, Mesmen confessed that she had known about their prophesied rebirth all along. She further revealed that she had been their companion when they had been alive and that her creation of the sumagi was inextricably tied to their rebirth. She would not explain further, declaring that the others would hear from her more on this issue at the right time. She also asked them not to pursue the prophecy on their own in the meantime. However, Nishtar was not so easily deterred. He continued to delve into rumours of the prophecy and of the rebirth of Astoreth and Zavak in secret, unknown to Mesmen or any of the others. There was precious little to be learnt, however, but what little he learnt enabled him to uncover a few of the omens that would accompany this crucial event. He also calculated that the two greatest figures of history and legend would be born on the first day of Kawitor in the annus 5001 A.E.

Nishtar began to bide his time, counting the anni down to the dawn of the fifty-second aeon. In the meanwhile, Mesmen was strangely silent, saying nothing about their purpose or the prophecy. Just before the end of the annus 5000 A.E., she disappeared from Maghem, though it was not discovered until later. Nishtar had been checking and rechecking his calculations for days when, on the last day of the annus, Mount Idhaghloz erupted and destroyed the village of Idhaghloz that had grown up at its feet. Nishtar had been quietly keeping track of the omens that he had discovered and this was the final omen before the birth of Astoreth and Zavak for the second time in Pretvain. Sure of this, Nishtar sent for his one-time teacher and mentor Beben to discuss what the sumagi would do next. Thus began his enduring involvement with the prophecy of Kawiti and the mysteries of the rebirth of Astoreth and Zavak.

CPSIA information can be obtained
at www.ICGtesting.com
Printed in the USA
BVHW031423070319
542042BV00002B/383/P

9 781645 464471